Dear Marco,
Happy Birthday to a dear,
fabulous friend!

♡ Kim + MB

PROPERTIES *of* THIRST

a novel

MARIANNE WIGGINS

SIMON & SCHUSTER
New York   London   Toronto   Sydney   New Delhi

Simon & Schuster
1230 Avenue of the Americas
New York, NY 10020

First Simon & Schuster hardcover edition August 2022

SIMON & SCHUSTER and colophon are registered trademarks of Simon & Schuster, Inc.

For information about special discounts for bulk purchases, please contact Simon & Schuster Special Sales at 1-866-506-1949 or business@simonandschuster.com.

The Simon & Schuster Speakers Bureau can bring authors to your live event. For more information or to book an event, contact the Simon & Schuster Speakers Bureau at 1-866-248-3049 or visit our website at www.simonspeakers.com.

Interior design by Carly Loman

Manufactured in the United States of America

10   9   8   7   6   5   4   3   2   1

Library of Congress Cataloging-in-Publication Data is available on file.

ISBN 978-1-4165-7126-1
ISBN 978-1-4165-7345-6 (ebook)

For Lara
you are my   yesterday   today   tomorrow
my compass
my horizon
the shoreline of my odyssey

And for Katie
the spark of my inspiration
the galaxy of my dreams
the streambed of this voyage

both, embodiments of love

AUTHOR'S NOTE

This is a work of fiction. I am rendering my sense of this historical time the way I remember it, and the language then was more incendiary than the language we use today. Today the language herein may be viewed as insensitive, but it is historically accurate.

—MW

PROPERTIES *of* THIRST

the first
property of thirst
is
an element of surprise

YOU CAN'T SAVE WHAT YOU DON'T LOVE.

—he knew that. Christ, he'd learned that from the cradle, in his father's house, at the knee of someone whose fierce love of money poured like baptizing water over every aspect of their lives. If you want to keep a thing alive (like this business, son) you need to *will* it. No one ever made his fortune from the milk of human kindness. *Thirst.* You have to want it, have to have the perseverance, self-reliance, stamina.

—all *that*. His father's frothings at the mouth.

—man stood sixty inches on his toes, could knock a person backwards with his pixie apoplexies, carnal heat for making money—knock a person down: his son, especially.

Hadn't called him "Punch" for nothing.

—christ he'd jump up on a table—full regalia—lifty shoes, the twill, the vest, the fob the starch the silk the onyx links and he would start to *punch* a person, *punch* a person with his finger, punch a person in the chest, digit homing heartward like a ferret on a rat: he would even treat his wife that way.

—go at Rocky's mother on the stairs or in the parlor—always with an audience—punching at her sternum telling her *how*to and what*for*, while Cas and Rocky cowered on the landing:

Fronting by example.

Christ, she'd been a stoic woman.

—but why *now*, why was he thinking of that little bastard, here, *this* morning?

If he wanted to have Punch along all he had to do was summon the little shit for christsake but what he didn't want and what he couldn't understand was how, like now, the reverse could happen, his father, gone these many years, seeming to summon *him*.

—from air.

—the dead.

How do they get away with *that*?

Well—they outnumber us, Rocky reasoned. Plus, they have a lot of time to spare.

But what had set it off—

—agents of recall (as Rocky remembered them: *scent*, of course; Ol' Faithful in the brain . . . a bristlecone, its history buried at the root, as old as God:) (No. He hadn't *smelled* his father.) (Had his father had a scent?) *Yes*. (Peppermint.) (And money.)

—*music*.

Music played with time in him—it was a function of time-telling, traveling over distance, dying, a *dys*function—but there hadn't been the sound of music yet this morning; only distant sounds:

Owl.

The train.

Maybe that was it: the distant train—but he heard a train every waking morning and his thoughts didn't always run to Punch:

Something had set this ticking:

Some *one* unnoticed thing.

He was a man of science—or so he liked to think—an educated man reasonably versed in the Shakespearean and more current theories of behavior, and stopping in his boot tracks under this familiar sky, he was certain he could dog this damn thing down. *Punch*: I'm done with you this morning. You're not going to interrupt this exercise.

To certify this little triumph, he looked up and clocked the point where the sun was climbing from behind Mount Inyo and noted out loud to the world, *December seventh*.

Thoreau had boasted (coot had been a feral boaster) that you could wake him up from a spell of several months and he'd be able to tell what time of year it was within two days from the way the plants and animals around his sainted

Pond were interacting. When Rocky had first come out here, he'd traveled with Thoreau's writing, ragged copies of his journals in his bindle. You look to other men to guide your manhood, he supposed—every man does that. Every boy, at least. It was Thoreau and Emerson, that pair of old Transcendentalists, who'd lit Rocky's fuse, articulated the arguments to force his insurrection and cannon him straight off the East Coast into this great wild desert. He'd built this ranch, he'd built his life, as acts of emulation of those two thinkers, those two men. Emerson had cooled for him with age, his aphorisms petrifying into righteous stone, but Thoreau could still ignite the last loose shredded strands that lingered from his youth. He still made visits to the books—turning to a random page to trace a line or two—although he didn't *read* them anymore, he didn't need to, having translated them into living memory, something that was *his*. Like Thoreau, he'd fashioned shelter from the ground up, listing, diligently, materials he'd used, quantities and costs. Unlike Thoreau, he had constructed a true residence, a *house*; and—crucially *unlike* Thoreau—he'd built it for a woman. Not unlike the people around Walden Pond had said about Thoreau, those who came by to speculate on Rocky's enterprise had ridden back to town to say he was an idiot. Madman. Word in Lone Pine since the earthquake had been that timber was the only safe material but Rocky had had a soft spot for Indian and Spanish masonry ever since he'd come out West and walked into his first adobe. Beams. Baked earth. Sustaining walls built eighteen inches thick. Bafflement of sounds. The sense that one's surround was earth. The fact that out here, in an adobe home, even in the driest months you could smell the rootstock in the walls:

You can smell the water.

The East, whenever its restrictive memory surfaced, made him wince. It felt like a tight shoe. His childhood there seemed a disease, a crippling limp he had had to overcome. While at Harvard, that one disastrous half-a-year, he'd gone out to Concord, out to Walden Pond (knapsack on his back) to pay homage, breathe the air, the stuff (perhaps an extant molecule or two) that Henry David had exhaled.

The place had disappointed him.

—far less than the stuff of dreams, the Pond seemed tame and manicured, a city park, a Bronx or Brooklyn arboretum, the sort of place a clutch of ladies might descend on for tea and a controlled embrace with Nature. Thoreau had made it seem masculine and raw—a *frontier*, on both the borders of the safe world and the limits of rebellion, but there it had been, a stagnant pond around which one could hike without breaking a sweat while listening to the clatter of traffic. *Scale* was disproportionate—unless Thoreau had been a midget or a superannuated child. Rocky, himself, was over six feet tall. Thoreau could not have possibly considered Walden Pond so large unless his sense of distance had been narratively diminished.

Maybe only *tiny* people walked the past. Most heroes are not giants, but the diminuendo of Rocky's expectations, there, at Walden Pond, must have primed him for the West. Nevertheless, even now Rocky carried in his pockets, in large part, what Thoreau had carried in that other place, a hundred years ago:

Thoreau	Rocky
his diary	his diary
a pencil	a pencil
a spyglass	binoculars
a magnifying glass	
a jack knife	a Bowie knife
twine	wire
	wire cutters
	water.

Thoreau had never had to carry water around the Pond—Thoreau had never had to carry water *in* (what Rocky called "walking water"):

Thoreau had *rain.*

Thoreau had water-sated vegetation: he had otters, woodchucks, turtles, muskrats, sheldrakes, herons, ospreys, loons, and other waterbirds.

Rocky had a redtail dogging him this morning, threading its hawk hunger through the sky.

He had coyote skat and cheatgrass, alkali sink, scrubs and dust. Thoreau could tell you in what week the pitcher plant would bloom or when pond larvae had been laid but Rocky doubted Henry David had ever seen the cholla flower, heard the echo of an avalanche in the Sierras, tasted cactus.

Thoreau had never tasted West-of-the-Rockies thirst.

Walden had been Thoreau's calendar but this Valley was Rocky's clock. His *water* clock. His Stonehenge. When he walked out here, when he walked out from his adobe ranch house, south, about a half a mile, to this footprint where the Owens River used to hit an underscarp of granite and veer west, across the property: at this point where it used to go off south again, where there was still a footprint of its bed, one version of the Valley's clock ticked in: from his experience (and from the earth's), he knew that on December 21, on the winter solstice, two weeks from today, the sun would strike the limit in its southern course behind the Inyos, hit the notch beyond which it could never stretch, hang there for a cosmic exclamation and then reverse itself toward summer, back across the sky. On one side of the Valley: the Sierras: *las sierras nevadas*, the snowy sawteeth (*sierra* meaning "saw" in Spanish; *nevada* meaning "snowy" from the verb *nevar*, to whiten, to cover with snow). From the south, from where he stood, he could see, ranging toward him, the snow-covered peaks of Lone Pine, McAdie, Muir, Hitchcock, Rooks, Thor, Mt. Whitney, Williamson and Russell, their blazing white arêtes blush with alpenglow even now, before the sun peaked above Mt. Inyo on the Valley's other side. He could tell you where, exactly, behind which jagged notch in the Sierras, the sun would disappear. On any given day he could tell you where the sun would rise and set. In daylight, he could tell the time (to within five minutes). He'd been taking this same morning walk for thirty-seven years and he knew how to watch the land for signs better than he knew his face. (When his wife had died he'd stripped the house of mirrors.) And yet, this land would always startle him, this land had never failed to be, for him, substantively, one big Surprise.

He never knew what might turn up.

What he was looking for this morning was something specific, but the things he *wasn't* looking for never failed to comfort or delight him. (A bear's tooth; some silver ore, a whole fish skeleton.) (The latter having been robbed, then dropped, most likely raw, by a careless baldie, scavenging.) Once, he'd found a button from a U.S. regimental uniform, Civil War. Once he'd found a coin, a Mex *cruz española* from godknowswhen, out in the middle of shit-blasted playa. Thoreau, he knew (from reading), had had these moments, too: these moments on the land, out walking, when time and history spoke to him. (One morning, Rocky remembered, Thoreau had found *red snow*. Emerson had mentioned it, that Thoreau had "found red snow" on one of his walks, but neither man explained it.) On his first walk after his wife died, Rocky had come out here, alone, from shock or grief or godknowswhat. There had been a freeze the night before—the night she died—and what small amount of moisture that was in the soil had hardened, heaved up like sugar crystals in a pie crust, and as he'd walked, there hadn't been a sound except his footfalls—just like this morning—mimicking the sound of someone wrinkling paper for a fire, someone walking through discarded news. Too early for the birds—the birds were sheltered in the foothills—too early for the quails, their silent running. The dogs hadn't been with him either—they had stayed inside with her, sensing, as dogs will, another ghost.

And then he'd found her footprint.

There it had been, plain as day.

It had taken the polio, from first to last, eight months to kill her—for the first three months, she'd walked with canes and for the last five, she hadn't walked at all.

But there it had been, the impression of her right foot, frozen in the soil, preserved, as live a thing among the gravel toss and bladdersage as a hidden nest or a fresh egg.

No doubt it was hers, her boot, its size, he'd know it anywhere—but its effect on him, the fact the land had saved this for him, the moment of its discovery on the morning of his rawest grief, brought him to his knees. He hadn't thought about her *walking*, then, for months—he'd denied himself that vision of her freedom, so to find this evidence had been too circumstantially miraculous for him, in his fragile state. He had swung around and looked back at the adobe house where her body had been laid out and asked himself if it were possible that this could be the footprint of her soul. Could it have been the very last place she had trod on earth, could it have been the place her soul departed?

For a while, he'd thought about casting it, making a reverse mold in plaster, and over the succeeding months of grief he'd built a stone circle around it to keep out the wind. No worry about rain, the Valley's average, in the shadow of the Sierras, was a sparse inch every year, at best—but he'd known that when the earth thawed and spring arrived again the footprint would decay and evidence of her would then be left unseen.

"Some circumstantial evidence," Thoreau had written, "is very strong. As when you find a trout in the milk."

He might have saved the footprint, had he truly wanted. Saving it had been well within his means but what had happened, as the months wore on, was that the meaning of it, his *imagined* meaning of it—that the ground needed to be sanctified because her sole, her soul, had lifted off from there—migrated: his imagined meaning of the place, itself, transformed. Consciously, unconsciously, he let the footprint go. At first, in the early days of desperation, he'd allowed himself to mythify the evidence, to seek solace in its mystical suggestion. Evidence of the Eternal was what his grief demanded and her footprint was the circumstantial proof of his thirst. *God* was in the landscape—that's what he'd come to depend upon out West: Something-Very-Large, alive and present—and Something-Very-Large had designed to leave her footprint, designed for him to find it on the first morning of her death.

What had happened next had been another form of miracle, a human one. He had walked out every morning to this single spot, this place he'd been preserving, to look at it and touch it. What he'd wanted most was to return to her, to bring her back or to rejoin her and the only place where he could manage that was in his solitude, his privacy, his silent thoughts. If he'd had the selfishness he would have walked into the mountains, becoming, like a monk, a kind of holy absence, a human desert, surviving on the barest trace of her. But he had two children, three-year-old twins, and his absence would have doubled their dispossession. So every morning, he had clocked the change, clocked his life and willed her back to being, watching as the footprint had faded into something else.

It was not for her to decide to leave; it was for him to keep her memory. If the memory of her was not to perish, it was for him to keep it alive.

She hadn't left.

All that life, all that complexity of thought—her way of speaking, her vocabulary, all the vital synapses, her surprise at stars, her knowledge (culinary; medical), her unique experience: all that was gone; but the noise she made on waking, her specific warmth, the way she'd take his hand at table as the meal began, the way she tasted food, the way she tasted, moist, beneath her clothes: all *that* he could remember, his memory of *that* would never fade.

Christ, even as he stood looking at it, now, the ranch was her, the house, every line and slope of it, every wall and tile he'd set in place *for her*.

Las Tres Sillas: that's what he'd named it all those years ago:

—Three Chairs.

One for meditation.

Two for conversation.

Three for company.

According to Thoreau.

He'd named the ranch in honor of his hero but he'd *built* the ranch for her.

—including the bell tower. Sainted pain in the ass to assemble (tallest adobe structure in the county) but she'd made the goddamn thing a condition of her coming West, and of *le mariage*, and so he had constructed it. Her *beffroi*, she'd called it (he'd refused to call it that): sainted *mère* had had one in the native village back in France. There were things, largely culinary, that his wife had found impossible to express, except in French (*mirepoix, garde-manger*), and there were things, largely Western, mostly topographical, that he could say only in Spanish (*barrada, ceja*). The sainted *mère* had told his wife the story of the village bell: if you traveled farther than its reach, walked far enough to where the bell's hourly tintinnabulation could no longer reach your ears, then you were lost. In foreign territory. On someone else's strange (and hostile) turf.

The bell was how you knew that you were home.

Bigger the bell, bigger the sound, bigger the quitclaim.

—this was the West, this was her future and her *mariage*, so she wanted a *big* bell.

He thought it made the place look like an institution. Rescue station. He thought it made the place look like a *mission*.

She thought it made the place a *home*.

They had rung the bell the day they'd been married. They rang it every Fourth, Thanksgiving, Christmas, New Year. Rang it at the birth of the twins.

He would ring it on his daughter's marriage, he hoped:

He would ring it on his son's.

Last time he'd rung it had been the morning after his wife had died.

On that morning, as on every morning since then that he'd made this walk, he'd turned back toward what he'd built, toward the adobe house, the people in it, and resolved to keep the memory of her alive. Keep her, daily, with him. Save the thing he loved.

Turning back, now, he watched the signature of smoke from the kitchen woodstove spill like ink across the sky, turning sharply north, *down*wind, on the prevailing current. Blue light. Deeper blue in shadows, the sense that water ruled—water in the vapor of the darting low flat purple clouds specific to this valley in the mornings, water in the blue ice on the mountains; water, water everywhere, except where he needed it. He leaned down and picked up a shin of tumbleweed and tossed it for the dogs as a signal it was time to turn back home. These dogs: not the ones that she had known—Cyrano, the last one to survive her, had died a couple years ago and now these three on the run ahead of him were the most current of the maybe twenty mixbreeds that they'd had these thirty years. They'd always kept between two and six at a time (the greater number when the kids were young): he had picked the first one up when he was out here the first time. (Uncle Tom. Hound mix.) Next couple dogs picked him: once he'd settled on the property and begun to build the house they had turned up, itinerant and hungry and, like the Mexicans, who had also come, hardworking and blood proud. He'd named the dogs after characters in fiction. Heathcliff. Puddinhead. Pickwick. (His wife had named her share too, in French: Lulu. Cousine Bette and Quasimodo.) Now his pointer (Huck), his border collie (Jane Eyre) and the manic orphaned Jack Russell that Sunny had brought home from Bishop earlier in the week (conveniently pre-named Daisy) raced around him. The Mexicans called Jane Eyre *enero* (Mex for January) and "Huck" lodged in their throats, like something full of gristle: *chuck*. Those older dogs were having none of Daisy's antics, turning on her, baring teeth, but she kept coming, pouncing on them, forepaws jabbing at their snouts, jabbing at their chests . . .

. . . and there it was: *Punch*: the connection: the little bitch had all his father's moves: her gambols had evoked his image: those combative feints: tireless, persistent.

Well that was one mystery solved.

. . . *fathers*.

. . . he should be the one to talk.

Hardly any better at it than his own had been. (At least with Stryker.) (Sunny was a different story.) (*Daughter* was a different story altogether.) Maybe there had been something in the mix from the beginning, from the time the twins were born, that had soured Stryker toward him (christ knows he, himself, had waged a private war with Punch as long as memory served), but whatever fuse had been lit, whatever friction had existed between Rocky and his son was redefined the moment his wife was dead.

She wouldn't of died if we'd of had more chairs. Stryker, at age five.

—cruel, accusative, precocious.

—almost funny in its childish logic:

Stryker squaring off against his father, showing Rocky he was no dummy: the house should have been called *Four* Chairs.

The underlying message was *I blame you*.

—that had been the road with Stryker, now, for, christ, too many years.

There was something almost chemical about it. Stryker's rancor. Even after he was old enough to understand how polio infiltrates, nothing could diminish Stryker's anger, or refocus it away from *him*.

Three years—long time to maintain a void in nature, sustain a breach of such ascetic stoniness, estrangement from a parent, but Stryker was having none of him, no proximity, no communication; nothing, since The *Incident*. Rocky hadn't said *Get out* or *I never want to see you again*, in fact he'd engineered the getaway that had kept his son from the law. Sunny had heard from Stryker, of course, she had been his conscience, his outer (inner) compass, since his birth six minutes after hers. He wrote to her—maybe even telephoned—then Sunny would pass the news to Rocky days later (maybe weeks). In that way he knew his son was still alive, still kicking dust: christsake he'd joined the *Navy* of all things, goddamn *Navy* knowing how precisely rooted, how devoted Rocky was to *land*. Who was it—Victor Hugo? Dickens? *Samuel Johnson* had written that being in the Navy was like being in prison with the added advantage that you could *drown*. Thing that galled him was not the rejection (hell he'd rejected Punch's favorite pastime—making money—too), what galled him was the fact that Stryker was so well suited to the land. He could sit a horse sideways and backwards from the time that he was two; rope, fish, trap, track, birddog, wrassle, and take down prey like he was Zeus. Rocky's own New York City childhood had not prepared him for ranch life—(His first attempt to run away from home, escape from Punch when he was six years old, had been prompted by the governess who'd pointed out the roof of "the Dakota" way across the park, inspiring the young Rocky to cross what he'd believed to be the greater part of the United States—in truth, Central Park—to go *West*.) (He'd got as far as the west side of Fifth Avenue before one of New York's finest walked him home.)

Everything he'd done he had had to *think* through, learning from books before he'd had the chance to learn from doing. There were few things, now, that daunted him (and *those* were bears and mountain lions; threat of thirst), but accomplished as he was on foot and horseback, he had never had the talent Stryker had, the natural ease and grace. The boy just *knew*—knew his footing, had an instinct for it, knew his balance, his next move. Always something reckless in that knowledge, Rocky thought, as if his son had had no need to learn how quickly things could go bad—still, Stryker's poise in the outdoors had been a constant source of pride, even when, to his unspoken skepticism, Stryker voiced his longing, in his teens, to grow up and be a cowboy movie stuntman.

Not the guy who falls in love; the guy who falls off horses.

Gets shot, falls off the stagecoach, falls, backwards, through saloon doors.

Tom Mix, America's First Cowboy, had been coming to the Valley to make his movies since the 1920s (since the Department of Water in Los Angeles had paved the roads), and it still made Rocky smile to think that the enduring image most early movie-goers had of a cowboy West had been the sight (site) of granite strewn at the foot of the Sierras in the Alabama Hills, a mile from his ranchland. Stryker had started jobbing out (the pay was good) along with other local boys each time a movie came to town, and it hadn't taken long, with his good looks, before he'd started getting speaking parts, hadn't taken long for him to change his horse, mid-dream, and start to want to be a movie star.

—hard to say if Rocky would have disowned him. (Having inherited, himself, half of Punch's wealth, Rocky didn't like to think along those lines. *Property* lines. He was of an age when *Lear* had started meaning more to him than *Hamlet*.)

Anyway, The Incident had ended it. (Though Rocky still believed, given his history with Los Angeles, that Stryker never would have gone to Hollywood.) (That would have been the final straw.)

He still believed (though he'd never confessed as much to anyone, especially to Sunny) that one day Stryker would return. And all would be forgiven.

—doesn't every father of an errant son believe in that?

Not for nothing is the legend of the prodigal son still kicking—hell, Punch had probably breathed his last, hoping Rocky would come crawling, start to see the glory in zinc mining, borax, tungsten—you name it, Punch had dug it up, extracted it from earth and made a nickel on it (tricked the nickel from the ground, himself). What captain of industry hasn't hoped to add "And Son(s)" to the family business, hasn't seen the sign, the hereditary blazon go up on the family's storehouse of his dreams?

Even Thoreau, senior, who for the larger part of his son's youth had tried to gang press him into the family enterprise (PENCIL MANUFACTURING).

Incense cedar, Rocky knew: wood preferred for making lead pencils. Durable. Good for fences, too; native to the Eastern slopes of the Sierras, life-hardened, scrappy trees whose little bell-shaped cones looked like tumbled *fleurs-de-lis*. He'd strung his fences from them, timbers shaped like pencils, "Thoreau" pencils: Western literary joke. His wife had had it in her head to come out here and run a herd of sheep (among the other things she did), reminiscent of the life the sainted mother had known back in the sainted French *village*.

—what a grand *folie* that had been:

Sheep.

They'll eat you out of house and holm.

Also: phenomenally stupid.

He'd built the fences (he'd have built the fences anyway) and the resident/ nomadic Basques on this side of the Sierras had jobbed up to roam the flock in the foothills on a summer basis. He had never wanted a lot of livestock on the land (certainly not beef): no ready market, to begin with, and herbivores were fatal to the semi-desert soil—the numbers had never added up, but he'd agreed to a starter string of a dozen ewes, and had sequestered sixteen acres for them to winter over, closing the parcel off inside the pencil fences. Back then, he'd been running eighty acres in alfalfa—now only one of the six windmills pumped, irrigation ditches drifted out of recognition with backfill of desert duff. Captured water—stream piracy. Geologists had a name for streams whose courses had been altered, headwaters interrupted, cut off or, literally, beheaded—called them *decapitated* streams.

His was decapitated land.

—stranded on all sides by *de facto* Los Angeles, its water authority having soaked up the deeds of the surrounding lands decades ago, rendering his ranch afloat, a body without access to its throat.

This land.

—he had tried to save this land for what was now the greater part of his life—tried to save it, first, when he was young, from the course he reckoned Nature had set it on:

What a young turk's cocking venture.

What he'd learned: Don't fuck with Mother Nature.

—don't *fuck* with her, don't underestimate her superior logic, don't think that you can improve upon her grander something, you are a nameless nothing in her cosmic mojo.

Second lesson: You can't save what you don't love but *loving*, simply in and of itself, is not enough to keep death out.

Only so much one man's love could do.

Surrounded by the pencil pushers. In the face of so much Punch.

Between what this place had been, once, in his dreams and in its history, and what it was now was a lifetime—*lifetimes*: his, hers; the family's. It was a losing proposition, he knew, only a matter of time before the last remaining well ran dry, what then:

He was sure that Sunny knew (how could she not?), sure Cas had suspicions, too. When they'd started losing legal recourse, started seeing nothing but postponements, stalling in the courts, Rocky had told his sister not to bring the subject up before the children, he'd put everyone on notice not to speak the words *Los Angeles* inside the house. He had told his sister he was willing to spend his half of their fortune to have their water rights restored but he'd be damned if he'd waste another evening, morning, goddamn minute talking the damn thing to death.

Once the sheep were gone (he'd turned them over to the Basques, no charge), he had let the fences go unmended and three years ago, when he'd first suspected that the wells were being robbed, he'd dug up a dozen cedar fence posts and replanted them in a straight line above what he knew to be the one remaining water dome beneath his soil; fed, underground, by springmelt from the Sierras. If the posts began to shift, he'd know the water table, too, was going down. Granted, water tables ebb and flow (with the moon, like tides), but he'd notched a high and low on every cedar post to mark the normal range. Twice a month for three years, on the mornings of the half-moons, Rocky had registered the heights to determine if the watershed was sinking and the news, so far, had provided cause to hold out hope.

Not so, this morning:

Even for the season, first week in December, when the underground supply of last year's snowmelt was the most depleted, the posts above the well had sunk two inches deeper than they'd been this time last year. Rocky checked the data (handmade, such as it was) twice: looked at the vapor rising off the Valley floor, then let his gaze lift slowly up the mountains into the warming sky. *Snow, you sonofabitch*, he breathed. His version of a Sunday prayer. The dogs were halfway to the house, beading a straight line on breakfast and by the time he joined them at the kitchen door they were raising hell from habit. He fed them from the pail of scraps Sunny had brought back from the restaurant, and while they dug in he took off his boots and entered into warmth.

Across the room Cas faced him leaning on the cool side of the stove, cup of that black foreign tea she preferred each morning in her two large hands.

Room smelled of coffee, carbon fire, fresh-baked dough.

Cas was dressed in characteristic monochrome (she favored charcoal greys), a fashion "trick" she'd picked up years ago: supposed to make her look "less large." She was his twin in every way, six-three in her stockings, and sometimes when he looked at her he saw, instead, himself.

Other times, he thought she looked like Spencer Tracy.

She took a sip of tea and asked him, "World intact?"

"Sun rises: Jesus walks."

He poured a cup of the strong coffee Sunny brewed all day.

"Cold?"

"I made it twenty-seven. Thermometer claims twenty-eight."

"How's the new Jack Russell?"

"Puppyish. Jane Eyre'll teach her a few things."

"—'the governess.'"

"How'd you sleep?"

"Sound woke me up. —around two?"

"Dogs found some rabbit fur this morning."

"A kill?"

"Looks like."

"Must have been it I heard screaming. —a coyote?"

"No—no trace. I'm guessing owl."

Cas began to finger something in the pocket of her sweater with her right hand: piece of paper, perhaps, or an envelope. He knew his sister, knew this thoughts-gone-elsewhere look, she was itching to make note of something, write a thought down, probably this thing about the rabbit, the sound, he could see her wondering how it had been made, that panicked noise, what hand in evolution had produced no rabbit language, as such—except a scream to express its terror. He knew that Cas's distracted look meant she was making a mental note to get Sunny to find her one, next time she dressed a rabbit: find Cas the bone or bones—the pipe, the cord—inside the rabbit's neck that had produced that sound.

Maybe she could use it. To make music.

Rocky tried to lift her from her reverie by asking, "What's Sunny into?" He raised the corner of a towel over a baking tray set out on the center table.

"Spatchcocks," Cas said. "And that pheasant you brought down on Friday."

He calculated servings. "We expecting guests?"

She shook her head.

"Music group ain't staying?"

"Group's playing at an Advent concert, up the road."

Rocky sent a look that asked her, *You're not playing with them?* and she sent back a look that answered, *You know how I feel about the yearly birth of Christ.*

"Cards later?" he proposed.

"Counting on it."

He topped up his coffee and moved toward the double doors that opened out to the *portales*.

"Where's the girl?"

Cas pointed: "Creamery."

He raised his hand to signal *say no more.* A couple years ago his daughter had started keeping goats and talked him into building her a free-standing north-facing hut where she could try her hand at making cheese. (The cheese was pretty tasty but he couldn't stomach going near the goddamn place because—to his nose, at least—the smell reminded him of retch.)

"You know where to find me if you need me," he said and entered the *portales*.

—favorite indoor place, even more than the kitchen or his marriage bedroom with its views of the Sierras. This is where he liked to sit, under the slanted roof, sound echoing down the long arcade, its four sides enclosing the open courtyard (*zócalo*) where he still kept a *barbacoa* for outdoor roasting. Visitors presumed this was an added space, a patio or porch, an afterthought, but the *portales* had preceded everything, its rooms on all four sides housing the first *brazos* who'd hired on with him to build the place, housing their wives and children; the first kitchen; the workshops. There would have been twenty to thirty people here (*pueblito*, a small village), infants, chickens, earthy tang of *masa, epazote, carne asada*. He had welcomed his bride here that summer night—white roses, white bouganvillea blushing pink (as if it, too, had grown flush in anticipation of the marriage bed). He'd taken her to Yosemite for the wedding and when they'd come back they'd found the Mexicans had unloaded the bride-doctor's medical equipment and whitewashed one side of the arcade (opposite the house). Above the door of what would be the entrance to her examination rooms someone had painted the words PREVENCION Y TRATAMIENTO in blue, in an arching script over the red cross—words still there, though faded. Thing about the Mexicans—well, first: they know how to throw *a party*. Second, they could take the simplest thing—a tile, say, or a display of fruit—and make it beautiful. He'd find some flourish in the house's finish, unrequired decoration that he hadn't ordered—a scroll carved in the cornice of a *viga*, recessed *oracion* sunk into a bedroom wall. No reason, just to please the eye. No function, just the joy of it. And she had got that, his wife had, from the start, which is maybe why they'd trusted her, had kept coming to her for her help. There were other docs around—hell, the City of Los Angeles had sent a mobile hospital to minister to the men who built the aqueduct—but his wife was unique not only in being the only woman physician practicing in Inyo County but as the only practicing physician to employ a *curandera*, a Mexican *partera* to work with her and to archive traditional practices, the native apothecary, superstitions about the body, the Paiute and Shoshone foods. (*Brine fly larvae*, he remembered. *Acorns. Pandora moths.* Crisis food.)

LA GENTE NO PUEDE ESTAR SANA A MENOS QUE TENGA SUFFICIENTE QUE COMER

They were going to do great things, the two of them. Back then.

All the slogans on the clinic walls had faded and he'd finally had to pad-lock the doors and windows to keep people from ransacking for drugs. He had wanted to preserve what she had started but once word of her polio had taken hold people had stopped coming even though the *curandera* stayed and tried to help. Eventually the county came and took the records (and the medi-cal supplies) and he had turned the equipment over to the health authority in Lone Pine. Now the clinic's rooms were moldering, littered with domestic stuff they couldn't part with (player piano; kites; a train set)—and standing in one room by itself under a drop cloth—like a casket—her iron lung. Stryker hadn't let him touch it for what seemed like months and when he'd finally agreed to let him move it from the dining room (where she had had a good view to the kitchen), the boy had refused to let him cart it off the property, as if the thing, itself, the apparatus, still contained her.

Things families do:

When she was still alive Stryker used to sit on the floor beneath the appara-tus, sometimes lying on his back and lifting his feet to touch the underside of the machine. They looked like whales, Rocky had thought: the two of them: mother and her calf.

—weight of water on the skin; weight of memory.

What sadness there had been had been brought in by outside forces (her infection; the destruction of this ranchland by the city in the south), but he had to confess, now, to a *dolor*, a daily sadness laying siege to him from *inside*, from what he knew to be a place in his mind, a place that he had made himself.

—yes, busy hands are happy hands, all that self-motivating *shit*, Emerso-nian outline for a useful life, a life of programmed purpose.

—*yes*, he knew how to keep his body occupied, even an amoeba could do that: this was a working ranch (struggled to be one), there was always some-thing needing fixing, something needing to be done.

But on Sundays what he liked to do was sit in the *portales* and make chairs.

—ladder-back: hand-planed.

He had a lathe (had several) both electric and hand turned, but what he'd recently been trying to achieve was something turned entirely by hand—spindles, slats, the rockers (in the case of rocking chairs); the works.

—take it back to when the world was young.

When the craft had been a man, his hands, the wood, a saw, an awl, a knife, the plane.

Like a lone voyager, what he missed most was the noise of human conversation—not just talk, he had plenty of that from his twin sister and his daughter (and the dogs), but the improvisation from a crowd, from a community, the way when you get a bunch of human beings in one place all hell was bound to break loose in one form or another on a daily basis. He missed that—the unexpectedness built into the routine, pan fires, interruptions, outbursts of opinions, laughter, singing; dance. When he sat out here, now, truth was he was sitting all alone. People dropped by but there were fewer neighbors since the water deals and most of the other ranchers had gone north. Movie people came, seemed like the place's reputation had become a kind of legend, that you couldn't make a movie in Lone Pine without riding out and visiting Three Chairs, as if he was just another eccentric codger, the place another Xanadu, some kind of Castle, like Hearst's ornamented pile or Scotty's weird stone mansion in Death Valley. He had entertained the best (and worst) of them from Fatty Arbuckle (worst) to Cary Grant (jury was still out). Bogart had showed up earlier this year—Rocky had opened the door and found him standing there, this familiar face with that familiar lisp, saying, "I'm told this is the place to come for a good meal." They were shooting something they called *High Sierra* with Bogart in the lead as Mad Dog Earle, villain on the lam who buys it in a final shootout up the Whitney Road. On his last night at the place for dinner Rocky had given him a rocking chair: the actor had almost cried. "Nicest thing anyone has ever done for me," he'd kept saying. Rocky couldn't tell if he was acting it, that was the thing with actors (screen actors, anyway): they may have made a seriously flawed life choice in picking a career but most of them (the best, anyway) knew how to please, how to assume the coloration of the person they were talking to, what to say and do to make themselves attractive, as a companion, like a well-loved dog, a man's best friend. No wonder Stryker thought he'd heard the siren's call, the boy had always sought to please all comers—except, of course, his father. But especially the women.

Movie star material:

—another bullet dodged.

Overhead the sun was hitting the cold roof tiles, loosing their foaled steam. He could hear a faint refrain from Sunny's radio inside the creamery, *o christ dee-vine*, exhausted Christmas carol urging him to fall on his knees. He turned on the shortwave in the workshop to drown the nonsense out. With the shortwave he could usually bypass the religious jukebox-of-a-Sunday—soon enough he found a frequency broadcasting opera out of San Francisco, not his favorite choice but it would tamp the Christmas noise and keep him company.

—it didn't take him long to recognize *Madama Butterfly*: what a story. A commentator whispered, *sotto voce*, a description of the action and the names of all the leads: a Russian singing Butterfly; Spaniard singing Pinkerton; libretto in Italian on a stage in California decked out to be Japan.

What a world we live in.

He liked the music, and it passed the time even though the story, like most opera plots (as well as Shakespeare's) seemed outdated. What sounded modern, though, was the emotion, and just at that part in the Second Act when Butterfly's presenting her son by Pinkerton to Sharpless (*Sharpless*, Rocky couldn't help thinking: good name for a dog)—right when Butterfly is telling (singing to) her half-breed son to tell (sing to) Sharpless that his name is Sorrow (*Il mio nome e Dolore*), there was a clatter on the roof—something running—and a roof tile hit the ground in front of him and shattered.

—*critters*.

—they insinuated themselves into the tunnels of the rounded tiles and wreaked havoc on the underlying structure.

Squirrel, likely. Pocket rats.

Have to get up there and see (actually: he welcomed the distraction). He went around the back side of the *portales* and set a ladder solid on the earth, shouldered to the eave. He shook the thing to test it, steady, before starting up. Stepping on the bottom rung he could feel it hold beneath his weight but halfway up he thought he might have set the thing too steep and as he stopped to reconsider, the music stopped and everything went silent before a voice, different from the opera commentator, started talking in a sudden way, a rush of words, that sounded, almost, like a foreign tongue. Rocky froze. He could not make out the words but he'd heard that cadence, most recently, in the reports from Britain and, longer ago, in the *Hindenburg* disaster when the newscaster had kept repeating *oh god, oh god* as if the gates of hell had opened up in front of him.

The man speaking could not control his voice and by the time Rocky had climbed down the drama had hit home:

Who in his Wright mind would use an airplane as a weapon?

—coward's option, coward thing to do, to drive a triggered fuse into a sitting target, at civilians for christsake—who in his Wright mind?

He stood at the threshold of the workshop and stared at the radio.

Hawaii, jesus. One thing for the Germans to fly bombs across the Channel but these sonsofbitches had to have been flying over open ocean for christknows how many miles, how many hours—

Pearl Harbor.

—where the hell was that? He thought of going in and getting out the map but the news kept building up and pinning him to where he stood, the growing certainty, the fact acquiring its shape. *Oh shit*, he knew: we're in it now. We've got ourselves another War.

In the house someone was running, then he heard the sound of women's voices and, Cas running with her, Sunny burst into the *portales*. Wise child, she had always been wiser than her age and Rocky could see, now, in the terror on her face that she understood the larger sadness in this news unfolding, elsewhere, in the world—until she spoke two words which made no sense to him:

Stryker. Honolulu.

—two words, to Rocky's mind, that made no sense, together, in a sentence. "Stryker. Stryker's at Pearl Harbor."

It seemed to take a while before he answered, accusingly, "But you told me he was with the fleet. In San Diego."

"I *told* you . . ." Words slowed, but her voice got higher: "Don't say I didn't *tell* you, Tops. The fleet was moved last year."

He knew that.

—he *knew* that, it had been reported on the radio—last April—Roosevelt had ordered the Pacific fleet from California to Hawaii as a warning to the Japanese but stubbornly or blindly Rocky had allowed himself to think "Pacific fleet" did not mean *Stryker*—"Pacific fleet," to Rocky's mind, was a code word, a specific cover, for all those other fathers' sons.

Not Sunny's fault—not Cas's either—he had made it near impossible for them to talk to him about his son.

Cas stepped forward, brought out the envelope she had been fingering—*hiding*—in her pocket. "This came yesterday."

She held it out to him and when he hesitated she said, "You need to have a look. He's married."

That caught Sunny by surprise.

Rocky took the letter and scanned it for a return address—there was none: only "USN, Honolulu" in Stryker's adolescent penmanship—then he opened it.

Sunny could see the letter was a single page and that a photograph was tucked inside.

Behind them, the man's voice on the radio halted, then started up again, recounting what sounded like a lesson in geography, an atlas of the Western states—Nevada, Arizona, Oklahoma, Utah—until she realized he was naming ships.

She watched her father give her brother's letter a quick read with no change in his expression. Then she saw the muscles in his face go slack as he examined the photograph. He looked up, locked eyes with Cas and held her gaze for what seemed to Sunny time enough to write a treaty. *Twins*. She felt left out: at an instant when the world, as she had known it, seemed in pieces, when she needed both her father and his twin the most.

She couldn't stop herself: "Are we under attack? Are they going to bomb us next?"

Rocky folded the letter back into the envelope and handed it to his own twin before he answered. "Put that from your mind, honey. California is too far away."

"But they got Hawaii—" She took his arm. "I don't understand what's happening."

Rocky laid his left hand, with its missing fingers, on top of hers. "You want to ride with me to town? Phones'll all be down. I'm going into Lone Pine to the Western Union."

"Everyone will be in church," Cas warned, and then Sunny took a few steps back from them and said, "Someone please explain to me what's going on—"

The last time death had felt this close inside this house she'd been three years old.

And her father had rung the bell.

"Let me go and try and find some facts about your brother," Rocky told her. "Come and ride along. Do you good to be with other people."

Sunny shook her head.

After Rocky left, Cas put her arm around her shoulder and handed her the letter. "I was going to show you this, regardless. There aren't secrets between you and me. Who knows why Stryker does the things he does. I don't know why he didn't want to tell you first."

"*I* do."

It had been because of Stryker that her fiancé had fled the county. Stryker was the reason Sunny wasn't married.

She turned the letter over in her hand, hesitating, as Rocky had, to find out what it was, exactly, Stryker had in store, this time, for them.

The first word was written large in capitals and jumped off the paper:

TWINS!

Sunny's eyes ran down the page—*great kid named Suzy—Stateside, Christmas—relatives in Sacramento*—then: "Named the 1st 1 Ralph the other Waldo, that should score some points with the ol' man (Emerson, get it??) Don't tell Sunny cuz she'll flip, me getting hitched before her! Imagine me a Dad! Times 2!!"

His handwriting hadn't changed since he was ten.

—and no she couldn't imagine him as a husband *or* a dad.

But there he was, in the photograph, a tall blond handsome Navy ensign in his starched whites leaning over the shoulder of the small woman looking up at him, her face partially obscured by a pair of aviator sunglasses, her very dark hair coiled along her forehead like a wad of cash or a fat sausage, lips pulled back in a smile. She was wearing a light-colored dress with large, darker flowers on it—big flowers, the kind they have in Hawaii—and she was wearing silk stockings in the sun (the light diffused along her calves). She had tiny feet in tall black pumps and tiny hands, although Sunny couldn't see the wedding band.

Stryker had landed in Hawaii over a year ago and Sunny had received half a dozen letters from him in that time, none mentioning the "great kid Suzy" who looked half his size, Sunny had to admit, and top-heavy, balancing in her arms two identical shapes that looked like swaddled torpedoes. Ralph and Waldo. Third in line of consecutive twins in the family—Rocky and Cas, Sunny and Stryker before them. But these two had broken the mold, Sunny thought. Unlike herself and their father, these two would be identical. No one but themselves—and not even they—would ever be able to tell them apart.

Sunny took her aunt's hand, nearly twice the size of her own. Since their mother's death Cas had been the defining woman in Sunny's and Stryker's lives, arriving to help her grief-stricken brother and sacrificing her own chance at parenthood. There was no woman Sunny loved more. No one more greatly trusted. "If something happened to Tops," Sunny said. "If you and Tops weren't living near each other, if he was living far away from you and something happened to him, if he got sick or had an accident—or died—don't you think you'd know it?"

"What do you mean?"

Cas stiffened, somewhat. Sunny felt her aunt's attention drift to the radio.

"—I mean don't you think you'd feel it, like a premonition . . ."

"Oh for christsake." Cas withdrew her hand. "What's the matter with you, button . . . ?"

"—as a *twin*, I mean."

"Where are you picking up this garbage?"

Where?—the first distinctive sound Sunny had probably ever heard in life must have been the sound of Stryker being born, the sound of Stryker screaming. Whole years had gone by when she'd believed *Where's your brother?* was her name. She'd walk into a room alone and the first thing she would hear was *Where's your brother?*, raising the alarm that Stryker had escaped again, somewhere on or off the premises, unaccompanied, unattended, *untwinned. Where's your brother?* meant *You're not doing your job: every time he gets in trouble, so do you. Every time he gets in trouble it's your fault.*

Sunny's life had been engineered by others to the service of her brother. Who could blame her for the habit of surveillance, for the guilt she experienced when she didn't know where Stryker *was?*

"I don't have the feeling Stryker is in danger. I don't have that feeling at all. I don't feel like Stryker's . . . dead."

"—oh for godsake don't be asinine—the nation's been attacked, boys are dying and you're behaving like some walk-on seer in the First Act. *Premonition* my ass. Pull yourself together. Your mother would be ashamed to hear you talk this way."

—big gun, Cas's invocation of the artillery: Sunny's *mother*. What would Sunny's *mother* have thought or done? How did Sunny measure up against her unknown mother's dreams for her?

Cas could see she'd landed a hit and instantly regretted it. She patted Sunny's hand. "Let's focus our intelligence on doing something useful. Despite what your father says I'm going to man the telephone. We must know someone who knows someone high up in the Navy. I'll make the calls. What are you going to do?"

Sunny stared at her. Everybody in the family had the same blue eyes. Different pieces of the sky.

"Cook, I guess. Start to make a lot of food."

"Always useful."

Neither of them dared to turn off Rocky's radio so they left it there, echoing in the empty *portales* as Cas went toward her *appartement*, and Sunny walked, with no real thought or plan, from habit, to the kitchen.

He used to laugh out loud in his sleep.

Until they were three years old they had shared a bedroom and some nights, after their mother died, Stryker would wake her with his laughter and she'd steal out of bed and watch him as he laughed with his eyes closed, sound asleep. Other nights, he'd bang his head. He'd bang his head against the bedboard or, during the day, pick up things—a book, a spoon, a stone—and bang with them. Very nearly all the time he had a black eye or a cut along his forehead, or his cheek was swollen underneath the watermark blemish he'd been born with. If there was anything to break within his reach he'd find it, break it. At some point he'd broken every one of his ten fingers, several of them twice. He broke both arms, a wrist, his legs, an ankle, and his collar bone. Before she put them both to bed at night Aunt Cas would stand him in front of her in his pyjamas and make him move each joint. Then she'd poke her fingers in his ribs like someone searching for a clue inside a pillow. He was particularly fond of running jumps from heights and loved to flip from Rocky's shoulders. When they were old enough to learn to ride a horse Stryker had refused to sit and learned by standing, bareback. Rocky liked to tell the story about the first time Cas had entered the house after his wife's death and Stryker looked up at her and swore, "Holy mountain of God." But of course that wasn't true; nor was it true, as Rocky also liked to say, that the only person who could even halfway wrangle Stryker was Cas. Truth was, no one could wrangle Stryker, he was one of those people, despite being a twin, born with a personality left over from some ancient pantheon, indomitable, incorrigible, intact. Sunny would have bet her soul that there had never been, in Stryker's life, the shadow of a doubt as to who he was. *Where's your brother* had never once begged *who's your brother—who-is-he?*—because, unlike Sunny, Stryker had never stood in anybody's shadow, but had grasped, unlike his twin, how to be a selfish person from the get-go. Rocky had wanted both of them to have the education of their choice—the finest education possible, as he had had—even if it meant flying in the face of his parental predilection (as he, himself, had flown in the face of Punch's and gotten himself out West, away from Harvard). Though he would have preferred to keep them in the West, he had sent Cas with them, separately, to see the East Coast colleges (Stryker disappeared in New Haven and got himself arrested). An indifferent student, Stryker had made it clear that he considered programmed education a rat's-assy waste of time and that as soon as he was eighteen, as soon as he could collect on his inheritance, what was owed to him, then he was history, sweetheart: outta here. All these things—the physical bluster, the bravado, his daredevil outbursts as well as the quiet instances, when he had been lost inside himself—she had preserved these images of him with purpose, kept the pictures vivid in her mind when he went away so he wouldn't fade, become an abstract equation in her thoughts the way her mother had. She was used to keeping him alive so how was today any different.

—except that it was.

No denying: might be the worst day in American history.

The difference in the way she thought about him after he had gone away and the way she was being made to think of him today was the difference between being active in the world and being history, and she was angry with the world—afraid of it—for forcing history to intrude on private life, for forcing history to the forefront, for making History instant.

She turned off the flame under the coffeepot and turned on the kitchen radio.

People were lining up on the streets of Washington outside the White House. Roosevelt would go to Congress in the morning, ask for power to engage in War. Resident alien Japanese and Americans of Japanese descent, over a third of the civilian population of Hawaii, were being rounded up and detained in Honolulu and elsewhere in the islands. Sunny took Stryker's letter from her apron pocket to examine it again. She tacked both it and the photograph to the message board beside the kitchen door so they'd be forced to see it every time they passed. Even though the woman's eyes were hidden by the aviator glasses there was definitely something about the shape of her face, her physical proportions, that led Sunny to suspect, on second sight, that her brother's wife was not Caucasian. Reading it again, she saw there was nothing in the letter to support that suspicion—but there was nothing in the letter, anyway, nothing concrete, not his new wife's family name, nor how they'd met, his sons' birth weights nor their size nor, even, their date of birth. Instead, the letter read like a notation of a stream of consciousness, *self-consciousness*, a jotting-down of unordered details as they'd entered Stryker's thoughts. Unjoined thoughts in unjoined cursive—not so much a page designed for someone else to read as it was a private memo Stryker had dashed off as a quick reminder to himself:

Like her mother's recipes.

Her mother's recipes had come to her through Cas, on Sunny's tenth birthday. Since an early age Sunny had been drawn to where the cooking happened, to the places on the ranch where the women gathered—and, sometimes, a man, or two—in the daily preparation of the food. Because, in the face of death, what else are you going to do, where else are you going to go after your mother has died except to the heart of the house, its nurturing center. Stryker had stayed under the iron lung, refusing to move—until Rocky had lifted him, kicking and screaming—but Sunny had gravitated to the *portales*, where the Mexican women were shaping the *masa*, where she could join in, use her tiny hands to mix the dough for the fry bread, pat *tortillas*, not even knowing how angry she was, as angry as Stryker, for being deserted, not even knowing there was a word to describe it—*death*—a word she would eventually equate with the loss of love.

You go on loving them, but the dead can't love you back.

—what persists is solitary love. Some of the women encouraged Sunny to think there was a place above, *cielo*, where her mother abided, looking down, still dispensing love. But when she'd asked her father and her aunt where her mother had gone, neither mentioned this Heaven, this place above the earth. They merely answered, "Death took her."

"Is Death bringing her back?"

"No."

"Then who's bringing her back?"

"*We* are. With our thoughts."

The concept of Return: *this is the day* she could remember believing—this is the day she'll come back *because I am thinking of her*.

Death is so easily misunderstood by a child.

She doesn't want to have to go through that again: waiting: and waiting: the diminishing hope.

There were films of her mother, home movies Rocky had made which he ran for them after she had died but the images had panicked the children (Stryker had charged at the screen; Sunny had burst into tears) so he'd kept the reels unlit until they'd both grown older. What Sunny had found comforting, from the start, had been the stories people would tell. Her mother had been an incomparable woman, not only adored but revered for her kindness, her service. Along with all the private things she'd been (lover, wife, mother), she'd been a healer: doctor: herbalist and gardener: chef, and the longer Sunny stayed in the *portales* the more people started telling her *Chica*, you have your mother's touch. The reaction to her presence turned from *Where's your brother?* to *You have your mother's gift for food: your mother would have made this soup this way: this tastes exactly like your mother's.* Stryker had been whelped a person on his own but Sunny had required something else, *a recipe*, to shape her personality, her own place in the world.

"BEAR,"

the first card in her mother's recipe box had read:

> Yellowish and rank.
> Rocky refuses to consume it (for religious reasons).

"BUTTER,"

the next one read:

> WINTER (white): best for icings
> SUMMER (yellow): eat with bread

Then:

RAINBOW HASH
Discard fish heads. (Trouts' eyes will
follow you around the room.)

The cards themselves, stained with mold and desiccated proteins, were
kept in a metal box, three by five inches long, the kind one saw in banks and
offices: clerical green, for filing data.

TRIPE
Wash hands. Can cause a rash. Treat as
poison ivy.

CAPON
Castrate the rooster.

Cas had claimed she'd found the box in the potting shed behind a row of
seed catalogs and its discovery, so long after Sunny's mother's death, when
Sunny was already collecting testimonies from people who had known her
mother, came as monumental—a moment such as Hamlet's on the parapet
with his father's ghost, Moses with the Tablets.

— until she read them.

FOOD FOR THE ILL
Slice the dove in 1/2. Lay the wings across
the patient's chest.

GAME
Old: roast, fry or broil
Young: stew, braise or jug

In the sense that a recipe should offer instructions, Sunny's mother's were
puzzles. Worse, they were betrayals—to a ten-year-old, at least, they betrayed
the promise of what Sunny hoped to have revealed to her, the promise of

some greater knowledge of her mother, her methods and her secrets. Instead of an ordered index, what Sunny found were traces of a person taking notes, a shorthand, the way some people talk out loud as a self-reminder, to jog memory, a memory in which Sunny would never find an active part until she, herself, followed her mother's shadow and began to try to cook.

EN GELÉE
Protein in liquid will always set, when cooled.

RABBIT
Same muscle structure as PORK.
Overactive hearts (tough).
Skin in one piece. Soak in vinegar and water. Ragu.

Her mother had been steeped in Anatomy and Chemistry, versed in the volatility of enzymes and the combinative properties of molecules, the properties of blood, so she had come to cooking with a surgeon's eye ("... *same muscle structure as* PORK"). What a doctor knew, and what Sunny would subsequently come to learn, is that every living thing has an inner structure, a covert reality, which must be apprehended ("*slice with the grain*").

SPATCHCOCK
(From the British: "Di*spatch* the *cock*.")
Can't be done in less than 2 incisions.

All that *life*, Sunny was now thinking: all that *experience*, the complicated web of craft that's mastered from the cradle—how to grasp a fork and spoon, how to fit a button through its buttonhole, how to tie a knot, how to cast a line into a silver lake, how to jump bareback from one stampeding stallion to another, how to charm your way into the woman's bedroom, how to survive, *mano a mano*, against an archetype of masculinity like Rocky as your father—
She'd be damned if she'd allow all that specificity that was Stryker to be ended:

33

She told herself he wasn't dead.

She floured her hands and punched the dough down in the bowl and formed it into equal loaves and laid them in their tins to rest beneath clean towels.

She told herself he was on another ship, somewhere.

She took the pheasant and the two hens from the icebox and shocked them under running water, checking with her fingers for quills. Then she laid them out and dried them.

If she had gone with Rocky into town she wouldn't have been able to keep busy, keep the thoughts, the memory, at bay. She would have had to see a lot of people, town people, people from the Valley who had known her, known Stryker, since the time that they'd been born. *Old water*, Cas called them, or *source water*: what she meant was *salt of the earth*. They would have been in shock, as she was, but without the added burden of direct involvement, the mirror of the twinned experience. Some, the ones with sons, would have started to withdraw into themselves as acts of conservation when they began to suspect the distance between Lone Pine and Pearl Harbor—personal and fatal—was shrinking, that a different kind of gravity was acting on them. She would have had to stand with them in an office on a street where Stryker had once stood, still, attentive, quiet, as if this Sunday were intended as a daylong churchgoing exercise, and she would have dreaded keeping vigil there, among them, untwinned, inactive, and alone.

The radio confirmed the *Arizona* had gone down.

Sunny took the first bird in her hands and cracked its backbone.

SPATCH COCK

If she ever wrote a cookbook of her own she would describe "spatch cock" as a form of presentation not unlike the process of deboning a joint, a leg of lamb. Deboned, the flesh is "butterflied," laid out concertina-fashion, like an expanded accordion, with "wings"—except, when dealing with a hen, the wings are real. Spatchcocking is a butchering skill that requires the removal of all the chicken's bones except the thighs and legs and wings and Sunny's mother had written on her SPATCHCOCK card that it "Can't be done in less than 2 incisions."

Sunny had taught herself how to do it in just one.

It had taken years of practice to perfect the method but she had finally taught herself a skill that had eluded her own mother, the trained surgeon, and every time she made the cut it felt like carving her initials on the bone of time:

She made a single one-inch clean incision through the neck bone just above the broken spine.

Then with one swift move she deboned it through its anus, using just her thumb and middle finger.

So imagine what will happen to the man who falls in love with her.

the second
property of thirst
is
recognition

THERE WAS NO OTHER WAY TO GET THERE, to get in and out, except by road, this two-lane hard top, and that was good, that was very good, because if any Japs thought they could escape by rail or other means—on *foot*—they'd be in for a surprise from Mother Nature wouldn't they, worse than Moses in the desert, worse than all them displaced persons from the Dust Bowl on their way to California and now that we're on the subject what's so great about *all that*? Cal-i-forn-eye-ay, my cracker jax, nothin' here but wetback country. Desert. *Ugly* desert. Where did this idea of a *pretty* desert come from? From the movie pictures . . . *Strewn*. A word his mother could have used, describing some catastrophe befallen the front yard. *Strewn* with all manner of junk, fruit pits, bits of rusted pipe, wheels off a bike, a sand-blasted blanket, somebody's bony dog. Sloppy country, Hauser recognized, his native Southern tastes rising like trapped flies off a sheen of oil: he knew junk when he saw it and this pit, this part of Cal-i-forn-eye-ay was about as junky as it gets.

Up—you gotta call it *up* when you are driving north in these United States—*up* from some sandy junction only God could sanction—*Mo Jave* the General called it while Schiff, the smart Jew, told him, no, excuse me, General, the people here pronounce the name *Mo Havy* so maybe we should try to say it that way, too, like it was something from the O.T. Mo Army Bull Shit, Hauser might have told them, if only rank allowed him. Mo *Bull*: He'd driven these two north, *up* from the junction called Mo Havy through shit pits of scenery strewn with the ugliest of cactuses, until the mountains started. That's when the Jew moved to the front.

He liked the Jew. The Jew was OK, not Army, not even in the slightest, couldn't speak in Army time, recite the Army clock. Ignorant of protocol, regs, codes, systems of parlayance, the slightest comprehension of who, precisely, was on top by virtue of the uniform. The Jew was from some high rung on the ladder in Interior and spoke to Hauser, a mere mortal from the motor pool, with the same lack of starch he used when answering the General. There was something going on between them, The General and The Jew, something Hauser liked to watch because it tickled him, the same way he enjoyed watching those movie Jews, the Marx Brothers, stick it to the rich fat lady. Schiff was sticking it, somehow, to General Macauley, though Hauser couldn't figure out how. There was something going on that he couldn't comprehend, as if he were a catfish in a river, monitoring a person cutting bait on board a boat, above. The General didn't like the Jew, that much he understood—but so far, in the three days of this miserable trip, Hauser hadn't figured out how, exactly, he knew this, except to notice that the General never turned his eyes to Schiff when he was talking to him, never turned his nose in his direction, as if he'd catch a whiff of something like the stink of nightshade in the air.

Schiff, for his part, had been fielding anti-Semitism from stiffs like Macauley from the time that he could read, so no amount of proto-military camouflage—*sir*, yes, *sir*—could put him off the scent of what was really up the General's nose. Not only was Schiff, himself, the ranking authority on their mission, but he was a civilian one. A Jew, to boot. German Jew, in the General's estimation, judging from his name. A Jerry, somewhere back there on the family tree.

Hauser was a German-sounding name as well, but the General never called the boy who drove the car anything but Private and probably never thought of Ricky—his family called him Ricky—as anything but an entity over which he, Macauley, was, by far, the ranked superior. Schiff liked the boy who drove the car. He liked this boy from Gadsden, Alabama, where he'd learned to swim and fish in a shiftless body of tea-colored water called the Coosa River. This boy who'd named their Army-issue car The Sweet Louisa the first hour he was on the job, who seemed to take apart the engine every night and blow into the units, one by one, and shine them on the rag tucked in his belt. *Grit*, he had explained to Schiff that first night, adding another syllable around the "i" and never really exercising any effort to assure the "t" was closed. He spoke Schiff's name as if it were a koan or a linguistic paradox

shelif

and it amused Schiff that the kid was a category of rube, gem-like in his transparency, a kind of kid he'd never had the chance to meet out on Chicago streets, a trusting Christian Southern boy. It amused Schiff that the kid could sense the General's bias but couldn't grasp its origin, hadn't measured Schiff the way the General had, by his sallow skin and quick dark eyes. The Jewish question had arisen not because the kid had raised it—he didn't have the skills for that—but because Schiff had let loose a *shtetl* expletive while they were talking late one night, the two of them.

Yiddish, Schiff had explained. First language of choice for cursing.

On the kid's vacated look he'd tried again.

Judische deutsch. The slang of certain kinds of Jews.

Oh this is going to be fun, he'd reckoned:

Surely there are Jews back home in Georgia where you're from.

I'm from Alabama.

Surely there are Jews back home in Alabama.

Sir, yes, sir. But only in the Bible. *Sir*.

Up to that significant exchange it had not occurred to Hauser that Jews were people in the modern world, that a Jew could walk around the same as him in pants and speak American. Up to that moment, to the extent that he had thought of them at all, he had thought of Jews the way he imagined dinosaurs, as things he'd been told existed in the distant past and roamed the earth before America or he, himself, was ever born. There were several hints, even back in Gadsden, that Jews existed to this day, but, like kangaroos and zebras, they were creatures that might be real, somewhere, but that he, himself, would never live to see. And wasn't that the Army for you. Sticking you in front of things you never thought you'd live to see.

If Hauser had to say what made Schiff different from the people he'd known in Gadsden, he'd be hard put to put it into words. Unlike the General, Schiff was talkative. But Hauser's mother's sister's daughter Cousin June could talk the ears off corn, and she was not a Jew. Cousin June could talk a blue streak about nothing, really, but Schiff made sense in everything he said, he opened windows in the conversation, asked polite but unexpected questions, and Hauser came away feeling he'd learned a thing or two even if he couldn't say, exactly, what it was. The second day into this trip he'd come to feel that he was getting smarter, that Schiff was teaching him something, and that kind of went along with his preconception, from the Bible, of what a Jew might do, if he could meet a Jew in person. Which, of course, he had. Courtesy of the U.S. Army.

I play with the idea—believe me—I play with the idea every day: *of signing up*, Schiff had mentioned on the second night.

He had come out after supper to the lot beside the hotel, where Hauser was polishing the Packard in the dark, to make conversation and observe the desert stars.

Hauser said, I reckon every man in these United States is thinking that.

And every woman, too, Schiff added.

That had stopped Hauser in his tracks. And Schiff had been quick to smile.

Fightin' ain't a woman's work, the boy had suggested.

I'm not saying put the ladies on the front lines, but there's plenty of ways to serve one's country. Look at us.

Hauser hadn't answered back. He was chomping at the bit to know what they were doing in the desert. He didn't know the details of the mission—all he knew was what the Army needed him to know, that he was the General's driver and that the General was a big hat.

You pulled a plum assignment, son, Schiff had ratified.

Sir, yes, sir. But, still.

You wonder why they didn't ship you where the action is.

Yes, sir.

Because you'd be an asset anywhere they need to put a crankshaft in the field.

Hauser had felt a blush of pride that Schiff had noticed he was good with cars.

Truth is, I didn't finish school, he'd told the older man.

That'll never stop you.

And the other thing. I'm not so good at reading.

I know.

For the second time since they'd been talking the boy had come to a stop. For years he had been faking it, fooling his teachers and employers, learning how to conjure meaning from the signs, dissemble, recognize the words by the pictures that accompanied them or by the ways that other people, readers, were responding to them. He had fooled his parents that way, fooled the people at the railroad station where he'd bought his ticket, fooled the bureaucrats along the way and even fooled, or so he'd hoped, the U.S. Army.

How'd you guess?

I saw you couldn't read a menu.

Menu? Hauser had asked.

I like watching people read their menus. Tells me something, watching people make their minds up—or not. Some people have no interest in imaginary food. They prefer the food they've tried and tasted, food they've had before. They scan their menus for the things they've been digesting from the crib. Some, like you, look around, at other people's plates. Others eat by price, enslaving gustatory pleasure to the dictates of their wallets. There's even people—couples, mostly: marrieds—who approach the menu as a recitation, an out-loud reading, as if the person they're with is still a child. Or an illiterate.

It's not like I never learned my letters, sir. Most times I can read my words. Just sometimes they get jumbled up.

How do you read a map?

There's lines, sir. The names of towns ain't as important as the lines atween 'em. Do you think the General knows?

I don't think Macauley spends a lot of time on thoughts about you, Ricky.

Do you think the Army knows?

Oh I'd bet my life on it.

So that was why they'd stuck him Stateside, a uniformed chauffeur to a General with an undisclosed assignment and a Jew from the Department of Interior. The "WRA," whatever that stood for. He thought the "W" must stand for "War." "W" was one of those letters that sometimes shifted round for him—it flipped—and looked, for all the world same as "M." He envied Schiff the way he spent his time alone inside a book, the way he always had a written page in front of him—a document, a manual—alive in two worlds at the same time, the world outside, the *real* one, and a world encoded on the page. The General, on the other hand, sat stony in the seat, staring out the window, or behind the aviator glasses that he wore to cut the glare or to disguise the fact that he was sleeping.

Would you like me to read to you while you're driving, Ricky? Schiff would patter from the back beside the General. I've got a riveting report here on animal husbandry, in particular, on chicken farming—

Quiet, the General would snap.

Right you are, General. Let's exclude all conversation, shall we? Inappropriate in time of war. Serious business. Let's outlaw things. Let's practice exclusion. Let's write our own Exclusion Act. What about a whisper? Should we whisper? What about a hum? Let me hum you something. Let me hum you "The Battle Hymn of the Republic."

Schiff was trying to be funny, Hauser knew, but it sounded like a kind of humor Hauser wasn't used to, more a kind of cruelty, a humor lacking kindred spirit, without laughter. Schiff could sometimes say things with a smile that came out sounding like they shouldn't have a smile attached, and maybe that was something else, Hauser thought, another thing, peculiar to a Jew. He had yet to see the General smile—*at all*—so it was hard to know if Schiff was using a certain tone of voice to try to get a rise out of the General or because it was Schiff's brand of humor. On his own part, sometimes when Schiff listened to his own voice, that note of sarcasm, the bloodlessness in it, made him feel ashamed. He wondered where in godsname *that* had come from. Where, what dark place in him had that kind of anger in it, that sound, non-musical, of retaliation. In the days after the 7th, after the attack, as the pictures and the film footage, the details and statistics, had started coming through, his grasp on humor had disappeared—as had everybody else's—it had seemed as if no one in the nation was ever going to laugh again. Nothing—absolutely nothing—could be funny anymore, the country had been plunged into an ice bath of seriousness: This-is-war. We're in it now. We're out for revenge. Maybe *that*—the voice of vengeance—was what he heard in his own voice when, at last, two months later, he had tried to make a joke. What was there to joke about? The jumped-up Austrian with the paintbrush mustache? That little manic freak? All you had to do was watch the newsreels to know that this insane aberration, this throw-back to the worst of human history, was as bad as any tyrant from the past and worse than anything America, in her raw youth, had ever produced, and here he was, this Nazi jackass, in the middle of the twentieth century, as modern as you could get, on the planet at the same time—simultaneous—with Schiff. What were the odds? Nebuchadnezzar, cholera, Cortés, the plague, smallpox, Genghis Khan, George the Third, Attila, Tamburlaine—Schiff had dodged those former scourges, thanks to fate. Thanks to the Diaspora. But now, the hand that fate had dealt him—the utter chancy dice-toss of his birth—had landed him in a shrinking world, on a modern planet where people *could fly*, a place already mapped and re-mapped, a smooth totality with no hard edges, no old-fashioned horizon lines beyond which dragons flourished. From Europe, his parents had washed up on a lucky shore—a place so often called the Land of Opportunity that to think otherwise became a tribal heresy. Everybody his parents knew was better off—financially, politically, defensively—than they had been in the Old World and although there were whispers, rumors, of black-guards and stragglers for whom the struggle to make good had not panned out, the majority opinion was that the story of coming-to-America was a story of *success*. Failed stories were rarely written, rarely told. Failed stories didn't fly. Not in a century like this one. Stories of the failure to succeed had moral implications—if you failed then you were lazy. Only the wanton or depraved could not succeed here, the drug-addled, the debauched, the undevout. There was *a thirst* for betterment as plain, as basic, as the thirst for water and the satisfaction of its need was as expected and assumed as rain from heaven, rain in summer, rain in Spain. If you could not *make it* here, in this land of opp, you did not deserve to call yourself American.

Then, out of nowhere, the hammer blow of the Depression: it seemed to hit the hardest not in the urban ghettos, not in the tight-knit warrens of first- and second-generation Americans in New York, Chicago, Baltimore and San Francisco, but at the people in the middle, on the plains where you might have to walk ten miles to find a neighbor—places too expansive for a safety net, places with no bread lines, no help of any kind except some lines from Scripture, from the Book of Job. Schiff had been fifteen the day in October '29 when the market crashed—old enough to understand the headlines but not to grasp the consequences. Some of the men in Schiff's Chicago neighborhood had lost their savings and some had even lost their jobs, but the community was relatively unscathed compared to others that his parents had heard about. They had been prudent in their banking—conservative, even—never trusting in the empty language and false promise of the boom. They'd put away enough to pay a little toward college, but Schiff had had to work his education off—first as a busboy, then as a waiter—through both his undergraduate years and his study in the law. He'd lived at home into his twenties—lived with his parents in the same house where he'd grown up and, until he left Chicago to go to Washington after law school, he had never been outside the state of Illinois. He hadn't been a brilliant student, but he had made important friends among the faculty, impressing his professors with his capacity to argue any side of any question—a trait, certainly Talmudic, that he'd inherited from his father and his father's father and his father's father's father before him. Most people, in their historical narratives, he believed, celebrate their victories. But Jews remembered slavery. Jews memorialized their losses. They kept past suffering alive as if it had happened yesterday, turning, with each new generation, to a tradition of both prior endurance and prior reflection on their pain. Schiff had argued in one of his early papers at the University of Chicago that if there had been but a single rebbe at the Continental Congress, the history of slavery in the United States might have been dramatically altered. Eradicated, had there but been two lone devout Jews at Liberty Hall in place of those two Yemeni from South Carolina. He brought not necessarily the best mind but an argumentative viewpoint of the law's fragility, a zealous Mosaic protectionism to observe, obey, the Bill of Rights as if it were a set of Commandments. If his parents were at all disappointed in his decision to go to Washington they disguised the minor hurt with pride in his commitment to what he called "a life of doing good." From the time, when he was still a teenager, that he'd seen those first photographs of the people who were soon to be labeled "Okies"—poor, despairing, dispossessed—he'd decided that he wanted to work so that their kind of poverty, their kind of enforced nomadic transhumance, shouldn't ever again have to happen in the country his immigrant parents had chosen to call home. Few of the expected totems stirred Schiff's patriotism—not the flag, not the singing of "The Star-Spangled Banner" before a White Sox game—but those Depression-era photos of families in their broken-down jalopies with their undernourished bodies straining through the gritty air of the Dust Bowl tore him up. They looked like ghosts upon the landscape, living ghosts out in the desert. So fucking Old Testament, he'd thought. So fucking Jewish.

In his first year at Chicago a female professor walked into one of those cattle-call required lectures and berated all the freshmen for never having read her books. You owe it to yourselves, she'd said, to know the minds of the people that you're learning from, to read the books they've written and plan your courses not on how to meet the minimum requirements or how to schedule for convenience but to put your mind into proximity to other minds that stimulate your own, spend your time in the company of teachers who will light you up, live your whole life by that dictum: to position and align yourself with men and women you admire. Choose *professors*, choose *employers*, not mere courses and mere jobs, and your lives will be a whole lot richer for it.

After that, Schiff had made a list of faculty who seemed interesting to him, from whom he wanted to learn. It started—the list—as a doodle in a notebook but it grew, over the years, into a dream map of his college expectations. In law school the list expanded to people he would want to work for and the fact, when he finally noticed it, that his father wasn't on the list came as no surprise. If there was a single patriarchal exemplar in Schiff's young life it was Justice Louis Brandeis, America's most famous Jew, the Supreme Court jurist who had halted J. P. Morgan's railroad and whose writings on freedom of expression and the right to privacy got even middling minds fizzing with the possibilities of how a free and equal society might expect to function, against greater, vested, selfish, odds.

Schiff's dream job would have been to clerk for the old man—Brandeis was eighty-one the year Schiff finished law school, and still on the high bench—but Schiff knew he didn't have the legal chops to qualify. Still, University of Chicago Law was not without its own door-opening power in Roosevelt's cabinet, and the most frequent recruiter on campus had been a man who, if not as refined in his wit and jurisprudence as Justice Brandeis, was nevertheless a free, if not radical, thinker whom Schiff would certainly leave Illinois to learn from: Secretary of the Interior Harold LeClair Ickes. Favorite son of Chicago and a former reporter for the *Herald*, Ickes had started as a Republican but jumped that plank with the crazed fervor of a born-again *converso* right about the time that socialism started leaving footprints in the foyers of the nation's ruling institutions. In Harold Ickes you had a guy—sometimes a little weird, sometimes a little too fervent (as when he wanted to set aside a big part of Alaska for European Jewish refugees)—so incorruptible he got the name in even the most tainted press of "Honest Harold." Schiff loved the man. He and ten other Chicago Law recruits had come to be known in Ickes's Department of the Interior as The Gang, young men in their mid-twenties, most unmarried, who lived and breathed New Deal reforms and would have gone to hell and back for FDR and Uncle Harold.

Beyond happy, a fifty on the happy scale of one to ten, too happy in his daily work to realize how rare this was, that this kind of physical and mental stimulation wasn't what life offered up for most men on a daily basis, too physically exhausted but mentally alive each night to start to dream because who needed dreams when you're already living one.

Starting with the Public Works Administration and then the revamped WPA, Schiff had become a civil servant—he loved the term—in a dedicated corps of government employees whose sole motivating force was to save the country—save it from the famine in the plains, from the poverty in cities, from the private vested interests, from the heresies and scandals of the 1920s, of their fathers' generations. As an administrative agent of the WPA, he had gone to places he'd never dreamed of going—into the field, traveling the back roads, working with his hands as well as with his mind, meeting his nation face-to-face. He'd overseen a program to construct a dam, another to build roads, others to put poets, authors and photographers to work archiving the country's migrant men and women, listening to their dialects and voices. He'd worked among the dispossessed and underfed, the undereducated and the IOUs, the transients and zealots, grifters, drifters, carney men and con men, goobers, rubes, and shoeless Revenuers, screw-loose do-gooders and sky-blue Sioux, and one thing he had learned about the great American *passe-partout* was that once you got outside the larger cities there were hardly any Jews.

And he'd learned something else:

—that what it meant to be American—what he'd thought it meant—was a portion of the whole, that what was *out there* was a spectacle beyond his keyhole view, that once you're truly in it, even from an airplane, as far as you can see—everything is still too vast too large too big to be a unified idea—nothing *out there* but unmitigated Nature, terrifying in its nothing-ness, in the breadth and depth of its emptiness: how the hell the whole thing came together under one defining nationality remained a miracle to him, the sort of thing that begged for a belief in a higher power, in the hand of God, *Man* could not have bound these separate parts together, *Man* could not have made it doable, the North, the South, the East, the West, the whole place should have ended up like South America, a patchwork of plutocra-cies. Open places scared him. They threatened to abduct his man-made reason to a place of logical dis-integration where constellations trotted out their ancient plots and ordinary shadows dancing on the foothills fore-told acts of natural vengeance he could not control. He liked to see Man's footprint on the landscape, count the clocking telegraph poles along the roadsides, hear a train. The world without some fingerprints all over it was a clueless puzzle for him. And—you'd think his Semitic rootstock would have overcome this prejudice—the desert, in particular, bored the pants off him. He couldn't see the point. Why would anybody in his right mind choose to live in one.

"Lotta rain in Gadsden, is there?" he'd asked Hauser, for the conversation.

Schiff had moved into the front seat after the last road stop—just opened the door and shoved in, much to Hauser's consternation, abandoning the back seat and the General as if both were unnecessary freight. Since they'd left Mojave, every time they'd passed a roadside stand hawking JERKY PISTACHIOS DRIED FRUIT HONEY Schiff had told him to turn in so he could grab a sample, and this last time when he'd come back with elk jerky he'd just switched into the front seat like the whole thing was his business. Schiff hadn't asked for permission to consume his foodstuffs in the car—maybe Schiff thought he didn't need permission as the ranking member of the mission—but it was an Army car and Hauser was in charge of it, in charge of keeping it shipshape and he didn't think anyone would fault him for proprietary feelings, especially when it came to Schiff's oranges. Schiff had started the trip with a crate of California Sunkist oranges, which he expected Hauser to maintain as part and parcel of the Packard's gear. It wasn't that Schiff was a sloppy eater—he was very neat—but regardless of how neat you are, oranges are messy. He liked the smell—good, *sunshiney*—but even though Schiff threw the peels away, the stickiness remained, some seeds remained, and Hauser had to wipe down the door handles and every other thing that Schiff touched several times each day. The General didn't sanction Schiff's intake, either, Hauser noticed, and punched the back vent open every time Schiff tore into something, sitting with his lip curled and his nose stuck in the desert air.

I wouldn't say it rains a *lot*, Hauser had answered. I'd say it rains the normal.

Through the year?

Throughout the whole year, yes sir.

Schiff pointed out the mountains rising on the left. "Because these mountains here, these Sierras, stop the rain from falling where we're headed."

Hauser kept his eyes on the road but stole a glance at him sideways.

"In fact," Schiff said, "where we're putting up for the night I'll bet you'll see the tallest mountain in these United States from your hotel window. Mount Whitney. Fourteen thousand five hundred and ninety-five feet up in the air. That'll snag those Japanese air balloons, won't it, General? Good old Mother Nature. That'll keep us safe."

Hauser saw Schiff didn't turn when he addressed Macauley, he was looking at a map spread on his knees and he spoke into his chest the way, all his life, Hauser had watched the women in his family talking to their dead.

Schiff had his finger on Mount Whitney's peak on the page as if it held a pulse.

"—Jesus, that's two miles and three-quarters high . . ."

He looked at the Sierra Nevadas and repeated the Lord's name.

"You ever see the Pacific?" he asked Hauser.

"I've never seen any ocean, sir."

"Well it's *that* way," Schiff told him, pointing left, "about a hundred eighty miles." He knew that on December 7 after the attack on Pearl the Joint Chiefs had anticipated another raid on the Pacific Coast and for five nights running there had been a defensive blackout in California along the coast from Bakersfield to San Diego. The very vastness of the inner nation, the same scope that made Schiff feel alone and edgy, was the main factor in its safety: the Japanese did not have planes equipped to cross the ocean and encroach on U.S. airspace—none of the combatants had that kind of flying power, including the U.S.—but, with the prevailing winds, from west to east, incendiary air balloons could be launched from boats in the Aleutians or in the mid-Pacific to do the trick. Japanese balloons could reach Washington State or Oregon or Santa Barbara in a day and even though the tactic had a less-than-perfect air-to-target accuracy, the threat of *any* air attack was cause enough to spark concern. And once the mind went there, once you started believing you were vulnerable, that your borders were not safe—that your homes were not— that way of thinking would lead you toward suspicion, into thinking that the enemy might even be among you in the city where you live. It hadn't taken much persuasion to convince the President that friends-of-the-enemy might be found among the Japanese in Portland, San Francisco and the Central Valley. Along the coast, you got these ranges that stalled the cool Pacific air moving east. Around Lone Pine, at the base of Mount Whitney, the annual rainfall for the last sixty years had been less than an inch. The mountains threw their fists into the sky and stopped the clouds. *Rainshadow*, it was called—an event from Mother Nature that made him nervous. How could a thing as periodic, as spatially diffuse as rain ever have a goddamn *shadow*? You had to watch

· these people out here in the open places naming natural things. They could mess you up with terminology as masked and crooked as the Army's. EXCLU-SION ZONE. The creation of the new "Exclusion Zone" was the reason he was here, Executive Order 9066, a law breachbirthed in the wake of fear that mandated an exclusionary area, a "rainshadow" across a map, where certain elements—rain, the Japanese—were prevented from existing. It hadn't taken long—three months—for the President to ban all citizens of Japanese descent from living on or near the western coast of the United States from Canada to Mexico. The problem, now, was where to relocate them. "Freedom in a box" was how one Department of the Interior lawyer had described the situation to him. ANTICIPATORY DEFENSIVE ACTION. TACTICAL DISCRETION. The rounding up of all Americans of Japanese ancestry. Which, in Schiff's off-duty opinion, meant involuntary internment. Fuck *habeas corpus*. You were now entering the rainshadow of universal Law.

"Big place, is it, your hometown?"

"Oh yes sir. Gadsden used to be the second-largest shipping center in the state, second only after Mobile."

"I thought you said you never saw an ocean—"

"Riverboats, sir."

"What's the population?"

"I know it exactly, sir, because there's a sign that says it when you enter into town. Thirty-six thousand, nine hundred. Doubled in my lifetime."

"Private, let's see—that's about 1/160th the number of people in the city I come from."

Still, compared to where they were headed—Lone Pine, pop. 1200—Gadsden was a hopping place. Numbers like these, statistics, were keeping Schiff awake at night. The 1940 Census put the total U.S. Oriental popula-tion under a single category ("Asian") so there were no exact statistics on the number of Japanese-Americans in the country, only estimates, but the accepted guess seemed to be around 130,000. This was considerably more than Siamese-Americans, but far less than Americans of Chinese descent, or, for that matter, German or Italian (both of whose ancestral nations were also the enemy). True, to round up all the Germans and Italians from places like

Chicago and New York would cause riots in some neighborhoods but we
weren't in the war because of Hitler or Mussolini, because of the Nazis or
the blackshirts; we'd been dragged into the goddamn thing by Hirohito and
his airplanes. Ten sites throughout the nation, all of them federal or munici-
pal properties (Indian reservations, state parks, deserted Army barracks) had
been co-opted for detaining Japanese-American citizens, and Schiff had been
assigned to build the main one, near the base of Mount Whitney on some
deserted land owned by the Department of Water in Los Angeles. Officially,
the U.S. Army was now listed on the deed, but in all the rush to get the program off the ground, Roosevelt had decided to keep the Army focused on
the wars abroad, not an imagined one at home, and he'd refused to hand the
"relocation" program over to the military, lodging it instead inside the Interior Department. There would be a U.S. Army presence at each "relocation"
center, but the day-to-day logistics of overseeing everything except policing
would remain civilian.

This was where Schiff's nightmares started.

They were saying maybe seven thousand for his site, pulled, mainly, from
San Francisco, Seattle, Portland, Los Angeles, the commercial fishing fleet at
San Pedro and the stoop laborers, the fruit and vegetable pickers from the Cen-
tral Valley—but the figure could go as high as ten. Ten thousand. In one box.

The suggestion had been made—he didn't know by whom (some unsigned
military linguist)—that the containment loci should be called RELOCATION
CENTERS, superseded by an Order to refer to them as CAMPS, since the concept of a "center" had been co-opted by the first-tier sites in the process,
the round-'em-up-and-sort-'em centers (the busiest of which would be at the
Santa Anita Racetrack outside Los Angeles where internees would be temporarily housed in horses' stalls). CAMP, then, became the operative word for
what Schiff would be constructing: an internment CAMP. The suggestion had
also been made to refer to individuals as INTERNEES. And always—always—
JAPANESE. Never Japanese-American.

Of the ten camps, most were under the control of the War Relocation Authority; fewer were under the Department of Justice. The Justice camps—and
Schiff noticed there was refreshing honesty applied to the description of them,

no obfuscating language—were outright prisons. Fort Missoula in Montana and Fort Lincoln in North Dakota were already up and running and were where the hardest cases had been sent, the prisoners suspected of treason or collusion with the enemy, all of them male, of Japanese descent and citizens of the United States.

Schiff's camp was called Manzanar, owing to the fact that there used to be a village there (now a ghost place) where apples had been grown (*el manzanar* means "apple orchard" in the *lingo*). At the beginning of the century someone in Los Angeles had realized that the city's future was to die of thirst, that the city's water was in short supply, so they'd sent some agents here, two hundred miles to the north, to buy up land for water rights with the cockamamie idea that they could send it by canal and aqueduct all the way back south, and Manzanar was one of those properties. When you looked at the survey maps you saw how much land had been swallowed by the sprawling city's thirst. Los Angeles had spread across the map to absorb its water rights like a sponge. As a land owner, its Department of Water had no vested interest in growing apples or maintaining an orchard, so the property known as Manzanar, although fenced off and secure from trespass, had gone to seed and was fallow and deserted the morning the Japanese attacked Pearl Harbor.

All 6000 acres of it.

Schiff had a rough idea what the property would look like—scrubby; flat and sparsely vegetated—but he was praying it would be more hospitable than the terrain they were driving through. He had only aerial photographs and the surveyor's map to work with, and he was worried. He had never built a city out of nothing before, and he knew no one who ever had.

—except, conceptually, any army.

Alexander, Caesar, Genghis Khan, George Washington—army guys know how to billet, pitch barracks, build kitchens, dig the holes they shit in.

This was something that your Army could have done without a sweat.

This was why Macauley sat there, in the back seat, oozing disapproval.

"Ask you something, sir?" Hauser said to Schiff.

"—sure, Private. Shoot."

"How come you're always asking me to stop for nuts?"

"Not just nuts. I'm looking for the perfect food. *Vox pop*. A kind of public survey. Takes my mind off bigger things." Schiff withdrew a notepad from his suit coat pocket—he seemed to have as many of these pads as he had pockets, Hauser noticed. He flipped through it 'til he found the page he wanted, then told Hauser, "I've put the question to hundreds of people—strangers, mostly—but now that you've brought the subject up, I'll put it to you." He licked the blunt nub of a pencil and pitched his voice like some important person on the radio: "Private Hauser, in your own opinion, what would you say is the perfect food?"

Since the road was straight and they were the only car in the foreseeable, Hauser took his eyes off the asphalt to look at Schiff.

"—come again?"

"What, in your opinion, is the perfect food?"

Hauser thought a sec then answered, "Peaches."

"Let me rephrase. By 'perfect' I'm not saying 'favorite.' By 'perfect' I'm suggesting 'whole,' *whole* in its integrity to nourish, to sustain life. Something you could eat if you were stuck on a deserted island. To survive. Something you could live on in the desert. Something you don't have to cook, necessarily. Like a nut. That's why I'm trying out pistachios. That's why I'm trying out the dates. Something portable. Replenishable. Something that comes in its own wrapper."

Hauser thought a second time and came up with, "Milk."

"Its 'wrapper' is a *cow*, Ricky—but I agree, it's pretty perfect as survivor food." He wrote Hauser's answer down.

"—and *honey*," Hauser added.

" 'Milk and honey'—Biblical and classic." Schiff nodded with approval.

"What do other people say?"

"Well it's a tie, so far, between an egg and a potato, though, frankly, we're not built to stomach raw potato, you eat a raw potato you can die. A lot of people answered fruit, as you did—banana, apple, *oranges*—but, let's face it, you can't live on fruit you'll shit yourself to death, excuse my French, and there's no protein—speaking of which, a couple answered 'steak *tartare*' but where the hell can you get Worcestershire on a desert island? Some people answered 'oysters,' which surprised me—although, when you read those 17th-, 18th-century English novels all those lower classes there are chowing down on oysters for their breakfasts—"

"How 'bout manna?"

"*Manna?*"

"From the Bible."

"I'm familiar with manna, Ricky, but like unicorns and elves, it exists, solely, in imagination."

"That's not true."

"Oh, I'm here to tell you that it is."

Even without looking Hauser could hear that Schiff was smiling.

"Beggin' pardon, sir, but on my mama's honor, manna is a thing I've seen with my own eyes. We had an elder come to visit at our church and he'd been on a mission to the Holy Land and Persia and he passed around this manna he had in a jar. One a' them *science* jars. An' he said it only grows in morning just like in the Bible, out there in the desert, from the morning dew. A farmer lady said she'd seen the same thing happen on dead trees. One minute there's nothin' but dead wood an' then it rains an' next you're crawlin' in mushroom fungus."

Schiff was enjoying this on equal fronts: the spectacle of blind devotion and the added zest of the surreal.

"—so you're saying 'manna' is a fungus."

"No sir, manna comes from *dew*."

"Did you taste it?"

"—oh no, sir. It was in the *jar*."

"What did it look like?"

"Kinda like . . . *salt*."

"What color was it?"

"—*yeller*."

"Okee-dokee, going in the book: 'Private Ricky Hauser. March 9, 1942. *Manna*.'"

Ricky smiled. "What did *you* put?"

"—me? Still thinking. Jury is still out. But 'manna' certainly makes history."

They drove in silence until what had seemed a distant specter, a wavering mirage above the land, failed to dissipate as they came closer, a large piss-colored dust cloud looming menacingly ahead of them beside the road like a septic goiter on the land.

"What *is* that?" (Hauser.)

"—*dust*." (Remembering those pictures of the fleeing Okies in the Bowl.)

"What's that stuff beneath it?"

Schiff was staring at the map. The "stuff" beneath it was supposed to be a lake—Owens Lake—the "stuff" beneath it was supposed to be water.

"Pull over a minute, Ricky."

Hauser brought the Packard to a stop and Schiff reached for his binoculars. Hauser kept the engine running for the heater and within seconds Schiff could see a smaller cloud-within-the-cloud heading with some speed from the dry lakeshore up the scattered reach until it hit the road. A pickup truck came toward them with its headlamps on, slowing enough as it pushed by for Schiff to read the gold and blue notation on the cab door. There were two men in it, driver staring straight ahead while the other leaned forward to eyeball them, and when they passed, Schiff saw two shotguns mounted on a rack. The truck went down the road about a hundred feet and then turned and stopped a bit behind the Packard with its headlights focused. Schiff turned and checked with Macauley, then got out and stood beside the car. The truck crept forward 'til it came beside them, then the second man leaned out the open window without smiling and said, as if it were an accusation: You boys lost? Schiff was about to answer when the back door swung wide and Macauley hauled himself into the cold without an overcoat, the four stars on his hat and collar, each, constituting an authoritative constellation. He stared the other fellow down.

Schiff lifted the binoculars to hide his smile as the truck slowly drove away. L.A. Water might be used to thinking it had all the power in these parts but in real war nothing kills like General kindness.

"Mind if I walk down there and have a look?" Schiff asked. Macauley tapped his watch—he was due to make a call to Washington at two o'clock Pacific time—and settled back inside.

Out on the salty playa by what should have been the lakeshore Schiff was assaulted by the smell.

In the range of putrid odors—bile, human vomit, rancid meat, methane and rotten fish—it was in the category of something chemical and vile, so strong it made a glassy color in his brain and he had to hold a folded hankie to his nose. This was no lakeshore like the one that he'd grown up beside— Michigan with her blue horizon and her arctic on-shore blasts. This was a lake in rigor mortis, the ground near what had been the water's edge now stiff as bone and crusted with evaporates, hoary as a potter's field with rime and lime. Across its brittle surface, half a mile away on the north "shore," he could just make out the grey skeletal remains of Keeler, a ghost town from the boom times when the lake was still alive and this entire region from Lone Pine in the north to Death Valley in the east had been littered with speculators digging for the money ores. So much silver had been found in the nineteenth century at Cerro Gordo, thirteen miles from where he stood, that they couldn't ship it fast enough by boat across this lake and legend had it miners had built their huts from silver ingots. Keeler had been so big back then it supported its own Chinatown. It had been the smelting locus, and five ferries at a time used to cross this lake hauling silver bullion one way, and charcoal for the hungry smelting furnace back the other. Now the lake was finished, the Owens River having been re-routed, hijacked by the water poachers from Los Angeles. What happens to a lake—or to any living thing—when its source of water is cut off? *Death*, Schiff knew. He didn't know how long it took a man to die of thirst but he was pretty sure it was quicker than the end that came from hunger. What was happening here, over the 110 square miles of this dry lake or whatever you could call it—"salt pan," *"playa"*—was that all that matter that had silted in the bed, all those suspension salts and ashes from the former smelter, all that runoff, fish shit and insect larvae had percolated to the surface to be lofted by the prevailing winds that tore down the mountains across this valley like a vengeance.

Macauley must have lost his patience and told Hauser to signal on the Packard's horn. Through the distance, Schiff heard one blast and then another, and after that, a scattering of clattered honks—traffic on a city street. Turning headlong to the wind, he saw where it was coming from:

The sky was being ripped apart.

—the sky was breaking into fragments, solitary bits ungluing like loose tiles from a mosaic, like a substance shedding itself piecemeal; another trick of light.

He had never seen white geese in flight before.

—didn't even know white geese existed but as they came down toward him in formation the whiteness of them picked up light, some pink, some blue, and scattered it. In migration, maybe a hundred, two hundred of them, undulating like scored music in their descent through the sky toward this other body of reflected light, this thing that had been water, once, and must still signal a soft landing.

By the time they hit the hard surface the sound was like the cacophony of a slaughterhouse.

Schiff dropped to a squat.

He was going to have to get another pair of shoes if he was going to make it here.

The city ones he was wearing were crusted with yellow muck.

He ran his finger across the dusty upper sole and tasted it. How would he describe it?

Biting. Acrid. *Maybe even evil*, if evil has a taste.

Opposite of manna.

Civilization persists at the discretion of geology.

—okay, take that wrapped tautology and insert "humanity," either as Civilization persists at the discretion of humanity or geology persists at the discretion of humanity. Either way, you catch the drift of what the modern options are out here in the West now that we can blow things up. Used to be geology was God but then came dynamite, followed by the railroads. Followed by the aqueducts. Still, the spectacle is something to write home about, so why in godsname in the midst of all this massive geologic litter would anybody give a place a name as lame as Lone Pine?

Legend was the name came from *a lone pine* found growing in a canyon.

—*oh really?* Schiff was thinking. Mount Whitney standing here, majestic— the whole Sierra Nevadas are—and the best your founding fathers could come up with is *Lone Pine?*

Big Pine's up the road.

What do you say about a town that's six blocks long and three blocks wide?

—*not much*, Schiff reasoned. Blink, you'll miss it.

Independence, the next town to the north along Route 395—the two-lane highway running the length of the Sierras from the Mojave Desert to Reno, in Nevada—would have seemed a natural choice for staging operations. It was the county seat, home to all the county offices, the jail, the court, as well as *The Inyo Register*. It had a decent if somewhat frowsty hotel and it was closer, in surface miles, to the campsite at Manzanar than to Lone Pine (six miles to the north, opposed to eight miles to the south). But Lone Pine had the advantage of a railway terminus and, let's face it, they were going to be bringing in a helluva lot of material (barbed wire, fence posts, telephone poles, timber, plywood, food, tar paper, electric circuitry, woodstoves, medical supplies) and people, all arriving from the clearing centers to the south if not by bus or car, then by enforced transport, by train. Lone Pine was used to outsiders. Hollywood movie crews; plus L.A. Water housed its motor fleet in Lone Pine—maintenance and utility vehicles, as well as surface crews—and, owing to geology's discretion, a famous pile of rocks called the Alabama Hills had become the go-to backdrop for the nation's cowboy movies. In other words, Lone Pine had survived Los Angeles. It had adapted to the invasion from the south. To men in suits. To men with projects to get done.

—and it was home to the Dow Hotel, a family-owned enterprise on Main Street next to the Catholic church, that had been servicing the needs of water engineers and film production companies (to say nothing of Fatty Arbuckle, Douglas Fairbanks, Cary Grant and Ida Lupino) for more than twenty years.

So when Schiff began communicating with the owner using his Department of the Interior credentials (not the "War Relocation Authority," not yet—that had to be kept secret), he knew he was in experienced hands. Commandeering a whole floor? No problem, been done before (for Roy Rogers, for *Gunga Din*, most recently for Bogart's *High Sierra*).

Schiff's immediate concern—and D.C.'s—was that all War Relocation Authority communications not have to go through the hotel's switchboard. To that effect, he had arranged for the Army Corps of Engineers to precede his own arrival to establish "secure" lines. The person on the Dow staff to whom Schiff talked most frequently was a woman named Phyllis. Schiff found her efficient and unflappable but she had a voice (on the telephone, at least) that sounded like Snow White's or that good witch's in *The Wizard of Oz*. Porcelain and disembodied, it was not a voice that he had ever heard from a real woman, and he had constructed an image of Phyllis in his mind. Woman his age, late twenties. Pale long hands with painted nails, red lips and doe-like eyes. Men can be like this, imagining dream women, constructing female archetypes out of circumstantial evidence sometimes.

Two L.A. Water trucks were parked in front even though it was the middle of the afternoon, and the thought struck Schiff that the crews, having to be vigilant around the clock, must work rotating shifts. No one was on the street as he, Hauser, and Macauley stepped out of the Packard. This was not the sort of place where anybody could expect some accommodating footman to rush out to greet them, but, nevertheless, any time you can get out of a car and see the sun eclipsed by a snow-embalmed Mount Whitney, *damn* if you don't get a thrill of Grand Arrival.

The lobby was, not surprisingly, rustic and overheated, dressed in shades of brown. A woman in a sweater set and wire-rimmed glasses stood behind the counter at reception. Schiff noticed her eyes enlarge when she saw the General's uniform and as soon as she voiced a syllable of welcome he recognized that he was facing Phyllis. (Fifties. Spinsterish and drawn. No breasts to mention. Long hands.)

Both the General and he had rooms with baths (the General in the back, Schiff overlooking Main Street with the mountain view) while Hauser had a single with the bathroom down the hall. Yes, the telephones had been installed and messages for Schiff and the General had come in through the switchboard. Keys; mail (a lot for Schiff; a single packet for the General). There was to be no cooking in the rooms but she'd be happy to have meals delivered from the local eateries. Front door locked at nine o'clock.

A teenage boy was dispatched from somewhere in the building to show the General to his room and Hauser carried Schiff's belongings up the stairs along with his.

Schiff lingered.

"They're both just staying for the night?" Phyllis pretended to confirm.

Schiff nodded wordlessly as if to signal *enough said.*

"I want you to know, Mr. Schiff: that business with the telephones . . ."

"It was nothing personal—"

"—we run a First Class establishment . . ."

"I'm sure you do, that's why I chose the place—"

"—I mean, the whole town: First Class. We're all dedicated to everything you need. War effort. We're committed. You can count on us."

"Thank you, Phyllis."

"We're all just—well, we're very proud our government is here to offer us protection. In a strange way—" She offered a sad smile: "—proud to be a target. Like Pearl Harbor."

Small-town gossip: impossible, at this late date, to hide the impending large (very large) governmental presence—that's why Macauley was along, for window dressing, to twinkle all his stars at county officials, to meet with bankers, merchants, preachers, mayors and the Chamber of Commerce tomorrow and engage their mutual support in welcoming ten thousand suspected enemy sympathizers into their well-meaning community.

Phyllis leaned in and in that crystal voice intoned: "Believe me, we'll all sleep better at night knowing the Department of the Interior and the U.S. Army is here to protect the aqueduct. We're grateful. Even though it's not our water, anymore. Those Japs fly in and bomb . . . it's our lives."

Having got that off her chest she felt free enough to tell him that she thought he'd sounded older on the telephone.

Schiff focused on his stack of messages and classified communiqués. No way, he was now convinced, had Phyllis steamed them open, read them.

"Tell me, Phyllis . . ." He hefted his mail and took a small step backwards. "Where do you recommend I go for the best supper?"

"Oh, Lou's. Hands down. But they don't serve on Mondays. I can let you see another menu if you want—"

"—not Lou's?"

"Lou's cook is picky. Menu changes every day."

She handed him a printed sheet from another restaurant.

"Take it with you—you can call down if you're busy and I'll get the boy to run your order over."

Civilized, Schiff thought:

Room service and a mountain view.

But then he realized the camp he was here to build would have the same view, too. How civilized was that? Pretty as a picture postcard and surrounded by barbed wire.

What got to him out here was the way, in almost every instance of human habitation, the natural world still dominated, the landscape still managed to control the plot, get in the way. Even if it was just some cowboy hanging antlers on the wall or nailing an elk head or a giant cutthroat trout in the upstairs hall to frighten the bejesus out of you. If there was one dead animal enshrined inside his room he swore he'd have the Corps in to rip it out within the hour. He unlocked the door and pushed the stuff Hauser had dropped off across the threshold. Then he stopped inside the door and stared.

Biggest bed he ever had encountered.

—not so much its *size* (he guessed it was a normal matrimonial) as it was the bed's position in the room, the way it was made up. It was pushed against the hall wall, four feet to the right of the door and it faced a set of double windows across a distance of (he reckoned) forty feet. Yes, the room was massive—it had a divan and a couple of upholstered chairs, a desk, two tables and a fireplace, but it was *the bed* that stole the show, which said a lot, because it was the unobstructed view through those windows of Mount Whitney and her sister peaks that should have been (was supposed to be) the central focus. The bed had (he counted them) six pillows; two square, four rectangular, each stuffed inside white (very white) starched linen, and he had never slept on any bed—anywhere—that offered (sported?) more than one. He had never slept—and this seemed crazy to admit—anywhere but on a single, sometimes on a rollaway or on a cot or in a bedroll, in a hammock, on the ground, or back home in the same "junior" he'd used growing up. Now here he was, first wartime job, finally with a mattress big enough to roll in and a white bedspread that looked like a restaurant tablecloth, draped with, not *lace* exactly, but some kind of homemade crochet with lots of on-purpose holes.

The irony did not escape him:

What this scene needed was a woman.

—or some taxidermy.

What it got was Hauser, with more baggage.

"You've got a lot of stuff, Mr. Schiff . . ."

"Well, I'm going to be here a long time. Not in this room, of course . . ."

"—gol-*lee* . . . !"

Hauser had engaged the view.

Then he turned around and saw the bed and said gol-*lee* again: "—some *bed*."

"Maybe you can rustle up an extra Army blanket I can throw on it?"

Hauser turned to him and smiled, conspiring: "Got your girlfriend for ya, outside."

Schiff smiled back: "Oh good, she's here. How does she look?"

"—*sweet!* Whatcha gonna call her?"

"Take her for a ride, and *you* decide."

"—you want *me* to name her—?"

"Absolutely."

Hauser left and Schiff took off his coat and turned the lights on in the room and put one suitcase on the divan. Then he heard the throaty roar of the motorcycle and, looking through the window, caught Hauser waving at him, peeling off, country grin wide underneath his goggled eyes.

Loosening his tie he shrugged his jacket off, rolled up his sleeves. He un-packed his clothes and then his books and when he found the quart of gin he poured a couple of inches in a glass and got to work organizing his charts and plans on the larger of the tables, then pushed both of them together under the street windows and moved the lamps around until he had a set-up that felt right. He tacked up an Army calendar, each day an inch square, between the windows to help him try to schedule, day-to-day, the impossible tasks ahead. Then he sorted the papers he'd picked up from Phyllis at the desk: Depart-ment messages from Washington were on top, one of which read MR. SCHIFF CHICAGO URGENT.

MR. SCHIFF CHICAGO could only mean his father and not even stopping to calculate what time it might be in Illinois, Schiff put through the request on the safe line the Army had installed. It took fifteen minutes for the service operator to connect, during which Schiff paced and shined his shoes (and even tried to sit down on the bed). First year out of Chicago he had called home—good son—once a week, every Thursday; second year, every *other* Thursday; third year, once a month, but since the war had started he'd been calling every Thursday once again. It was a pattern that his parents never altered, never call-ing him, even though he'd given them a number at Interior, for emergencies. Never, that is, until now.

Finally the callback came and he lifted the receiver to hear somebody yell-ing *hell*-o *hello*-o like an accusation.

"—Pop?"

His father's voice: "—*boitch*?"

"Yeah, Pop, it's me. Are you all right? What's this about?"

A silence stretched along the line, a distanced silence. An underwater sound.

"Do you know some Jap goes by the name Jimmy Ikeda?"

Schiff's father's manner was not assertive. He was a complacent cog, in Schiff's assessment, in an underrated industry, an industry that no one under-stood or even cared about. Cardboard. Supply clerk in a company that manu-factured cardboard boxes. At work his authority was negligible and in Schiff's parents' closed society Sam was looked on as a kind of *schlub*, a man who read the Torah but wasn't educated (unless you count coming to a country with nothing in your pockets and having to learn to speak another language an "education"), although every once in a while, at home, a certain roughness surfaced in his language, especially in conversation with his son. It had been Sam who had insisted they speak nothing but American at home so Schiff would grow up with the advantage of a fully assimilated tongue (a condition that nearly exiled Rima, Schiff's mother, and accounted for her habitual state of visible, but mute, confusion). Schiff had never asked his father how he'd learned to speak American—he assumed he'd picked it up like everybody else, out of necessity. Maybe that accounted for the rougher notes in Sam's expressions. Or maybe he just needed to sound tough around his son.

"Some 'Jap'?" Schiff repeated.

"Apparently he's Japanese."

"Yeah but . . . some '*Jap*'?"

"I read the papers. What's your point?"

(The Schiffs' first household rule: you can ask, but never answer, direct questions.)

"My point is—"

"—so she shows up. The sister. She comes knocking at the door. *My* door. In front of the neighbors. Mrs. Feldman, across the hall, saw her. Her cousin, too. Visiting from Wisconsin."

"Jimmy Ikeda's sister . . . ?"

Schiff was trying to remember what he could about Jimmy Ikeda.

"*Japanese*. How many *Japanese* does anybody know? And now, she's knocking on our door . . ."

Jimmy Ikeda: wizard kitchen kid from Schiff's days as a waiter at the Drake Hotel making his way through Law—kid with an amazing grin and knife skills on the kitchen line, one of maybe three or four hundred Japanese in the city of Chicago and the first Schiff had ever met. Always smiling. Blur of energy, talking up a storm. His work was way above the standard on the line, unasked-for radish flourishes, carrot coronet, that thing he liked to do with the tomatoes that rendered them as roses. Everybody called him the Chinaman. Where you come from, Chinaman? "California!" was his answer so *Califor-*

nia was the name Schiff gave to him. He was Schiff's age, maybe older, but in Schiff's mind he was a kid, the kid from California. In those days, "How did your family get from Japan to California?" seemed a less important question than "Why did you come from California to Chicago?" because, for Schiff, that first wave of immigration to the United States had already proven itself as a necessary weft in the fabric of the nation. *His* parents (Schiff's) had immigrated and so had the parents or grandparents of almost everyone he knew, so the *why* of that particular global flux had already been answered, was already moot and muted by the outcome: life was better here. The reason for the run from Nagasaki to Fresno was reflected in the standard of their lives: so, too, the reason for the route from Galicia to Ellis Island. What Schiff had wanted to logic out from Jimmy, back when he, Schiff, was trying to construct the story of his own trajectory, was why, once the family tree had already been uprooted, successive generations (Jimmy; him) feel the need to go and move *again*.

"If this is the Jimmy Ikeda I'm thinking of . . ."

"How many Jimmy Ikedas do you *know*?"

"I kinda knew him at the Drake."

"Well his sister says they came and got him. You know, the government. He's been picked up."

"You mean—"

"Feds and everything. Didn't even let him pack."

"—why?"

"*He's Japanese!* From the country that attacked us—?"

"No, I mean: why'd she come to *you*?"

"She came for *you*, Schmendrick."

Between them, Sam calling Schiff *schmendrick* (idiot) was an expression of endearment (as good as it got), because, as a boy, Schiff had invented a fantasy Jewish comic book hero: *Schmen* Drick, private eye.

"Apparently you told this Jimmy guy that you were going to be a big-shot lawyer. Gave him your address and everything."

It was true, he *had*. On his last day at the Drake.

"That was years ago . . ."

"You think people don't remember where they keep a lawyer's name? Better than a doctor's. People save that piece of paper."

"Where'd they send him?"

"What?"

"To what place, did the sister know?"

The sister: it was coming back to him, the reason Jimmy Ikeda had come from California to Chicago: It was the sister. Some kind of prodigy, some kind of music genius, and the Chicago Symphony had advertised auditions. She had been too young to travel by herself (no self-respecting Japanese girl traveled unchaperoned) so they had sent her older brother, Jimmy, to watch over her. When the orchestra hired her, Jimmy had to stay.

"Name of some movie guy," Sam answered. "Some movie director, I wrote it down."

Griffith Park, in Southern California: it was a detention facility, like Tuna Canyon nearby, a holding station for "alien enemies" picked up by the FBI before being transferred to the Justice Department-run prisons—most likely Fort Missoula or Lincoln—for the purpose of remanding extreme cases, people of Japanese descent (mostly fishermen from Terminal Island) who had met, for whatever reason, the Attorney General's criteria of being "dangerous to the public peace and safety of the United States because they have adhered to the aforesaid enemy government or to the principles of government thereof (and) shall be subject under the order of Attorney General to removal from the United States and may be required to depart therefrom."

The official-speak, the language used to write the directive governing the Justice camps, was harsher (it included deportation, for christsake) than that used in the general round-up fiat rushed into law by Congress and the President. *That* law (Executive Order 9066) called for a mass exclusion of all persons of Japanese descent within the exclusion zone, and posters in this "hot" zone had gone up on telephone poles and in shop windows overnight. ALL PERSONS OF JAPANESE ANCESTRY, BOTH ALIEN AND NON-ALIEN, WILL BE EVACUATED FROM THE ABOVE DESIGNATED AREA BY 12:00 NOON . . . giving residents three days to close shop, divest financial interests, sell their fishing boats, consign their crops, abandon hearth and home and report to the nearest assembly area with what they could carry, only, and the clothes on their backs. The propagandists in Justice and the War Department quickly added "for their own protection" to the argument. Not *all* the nation's Japanese descendants were being impounded: only those in the exclusion zone and many West Coast papers had picked up the call. *For their own protection.* Out of the goodness of our hearts. For their own benefit. In case someone in the neighborhood (presumably some white guy) wanted to do them harm. Wanted to wring their necks for what they'd done to us at Pearl.

Hitler marches, and we're detaining Eskimos. Eighty percent of the people rounded up in the Alaska Territory had been Aleuts, Schiff knew, who "looked like Japs." Meanwhile, in Chinatowns from San Francisco to Seattle, people, young and old, had started wearing DON'T BLAME ME I'M CHINESE buttons the day the war began. Some American rabbis, from some American bimahs, had praised the Japanese for the attack on Pearl because it pushed an apathetic U.S.A. to war against the Nazis (therefore saving Jews). There was so much weirdness on the ground in the United States about the Japanese, Schiff had to remind himself each day of what was going on in Europe. That there were other enemies, and most of them were German.

"What am I supposed to tell your mother?" Sam was asking.

"About what?"

"About this Jap. She needs to know. If more are coming. All the talk now is the Schiffs of North Damen Avenue are thick with Japs."

"—*one*. One Jap, Pop. And she plays in the Chicago Symphony."

"So we're in the business of helping out the Japs now, you're telling me."

"Jesus, Pop. Take 'Japs' out of what you're saying and stick the other 'J' word in, tell me how that sounds."

Another baffled silence. Then:

"You comin' home this year for Pesach? It would make your mother happy."

Schiff's gaze flicked to the calendar—MARCH APRIL—and, yep, there it was, JEWISH PASSOVER with EASTER squarely situated on SUNDAY. He reached for a pad and pencil and scribbled down *jap cal*, short for Japanese calendar, then *jap hol* (Japanese holidays) and, in a separate column, *jap Churches?* There was a full moon on the 1st, April Fools' Day, and another on the 30th, once in a blue moon, a month of two full moons. (He scribbled *jap folklore?* underneath the note about the churches.)

He had not been to Chicago since he'd passed the bar, and the brutal truth was that he believed he'd only ever go back "home" again when he had to bury his parents.

"Pop, it's war. I got a job."

Another scratchy silence, then:

"Just don't do nothin' stupid."

Meaning: don't sign up. Don't kill your mother.

"Don't do nothin' that would make your mother cry. I tell everybody here you're doin' secret stuff. Most people I let them think you're workin' with your friend Brandeis for the future state of Israel. Helps make up for all the Japs you got here bangin' on the door."

Nowhere left to go from that except to bid farewell, but his father wasn't finished:

"You ever gonna tell us what you're doin', where you are? Your mother needs to know. I take it from this conversation you ain't on an island anywhere, in the Pacific."

"*Sayonara*, Pop. Give my love to Ma."

"—we're *done?*"

"—*thank you*," Schiff said, closing.

"—for *what?*"

"For coming to America."

"—what's wrong with you?"

Despite the toughness edging in again, no truer words:

"You woulda done the same."

He was awake the next morning staring out the window without sitting up in bed to watch the mountain drip in ice cream colors. Dawn came twice here, apparently, first as the rising sun behind him in the east hit the high peaks on the Sierras from under the horizon; and then, an hour later, as it actually rose above the eastern mountain range, the Inyos, above the valley.

The night had been a rough one. Once he'd laid the stuff out on the table—the site charts, blueprints, requisition lists, population lists—he'd begun to feel too small under the mass of it, too slow on the uptake, despite his diligence for making notes-to-self, too inept, too feeble. His *aide-de-camp*, a lieutenant from Quartermaster Corps, was supposed to have preceded him to Lone Pine but as of oh one hundred that a.m. when Schiff had finally called it quits and crawled into the daunting bed, Lt. Svevo had yet to show. NOTE TO SELF file complaint w/ Army in re Svevo.

His own notes ran to a dozen pages, not to mention the pages he had to read concerning Relocation Authority regulations (the question had arisen whether or not chopsticks were to be allowed, as someone had suggested that chopsticks could be categorized as weaponry but then someone else had posed the question *what the hell are knives and forks?*). It would have done him good to get outside and test the air but he was deep in requisitions when, at nineteen hundred hours, his stomach started growling and he rummaged for the menu Phyllis had offered:

FRANKS & BEANS
with mashed potatoes
MEAT LOAF
peas and mashed potatoes
LIVER & ONIONS
mashed potatoes
HAM STEAK
pineapple ring and mashed potatoes
BEEF STEW
mashed potato dumplings
CORNED BEEF HASH
with mashed potatoes
CORNED BEEF & CABBAGE
mashed potatoes
CHICKEN POT PIE
potato crust

The lower third of the page had been taken up with desserts and beverages and "quotes" about Lone Pine but in the lower right-hand corner there had been a box with what looked like a *sombrero* drawn inside with the words

SOUTH OF THE BORDER SPECIAL
"POLLO"!
rice and beans

He'd called the "POLLO" order down to Phyllis and there'd been a silence during which he'd thought he'd heard her sigh and then she'd asked, "—*are you sure?*"

"What's the matter with it?"

"It can be a little spicy."

"Spicy's fine."

"Anything else?"

"Two beers."

"I mean did you want to tell me anything else." She'd paused (as had he), then: "How do you like the room?"

"The room is great."

"I put you in the best one."

"—'preciate it. Very thoughtful of you."

"It's the 'Honeymoon.' Roy Rogers and Dale Evans stay in there."

I'll remember that when I'm trying to figure out ways to keep ten thousand people occupied inside a compound in the desert until the war is done. He'd turned on the radio to catch a news broadcast but the only station had been a local out of Bishop with a commodities report. He'd turned the volume down and scrounged around until he'd found his bag of roadside food and cracked open a handful of pistachios to go with the gin while he stood over the site map on the table. People were going to get lost, he knew. Eight hundred acres square. How were they supposed to keep track of so many people over such a distance without openly policing them? (Another memo had suggested the appointment of a Barrack's Leader in each of the 500 barracks, but Schiff was leaning toward a self-policing option with elected representatives for each block, thirty-six barracks blocks with fourteen barracks in each block.) Still, to get that kind of democratic system up and running would take time and there had to be a system *in place* at arrival or else the whole thing would be chaos or it would have to operate along the lines he didn't want: *prison*.

Supper had arrived and he'd cleared a space at the worktable and turned his chair toward the window so as not to have to eat while looking at the bed. The rice and beans had tasted great but the pieces of the "POLLO" had been stewed instead of roasted, the skin on them limp and fatty. Half a dozen flour *tortillas* had been wrapped up in a napkin so he'd skinned and shredded the chicken and had been about to assemble his first bite when he'd remembered the bottle of red chili sauce and avocados in the roadside bag and all together—shredded *pollo*, pinto beans, red sauce, avocado and *tortilla*—the stuff had tasted so damn good he'd let himself sit back and have a sip of the cold beer and lapse into that place of wordless contemplation that accompanies good food and enjoy the moment and the finer things of life.

Except he wasn't built that way.

Hauser had brought up a dirt-colored Army blanket from the Packard's trunk and Schiff interrupted his own meal to get up and strip the flourishes off the bed, cram the lacy coverlet into the bottom bureau drawer and stuff the extra pillows onto the shelf inside the closet. People were dying for fucksake. In France. In London. In the Coral Sea and Burma, the Philippines. *Darwin, Australia*, had been bombed last month the krauts were in North Africa and had taken Poland, Norway, Belgium and the Netherlands; they owned the goddamn continent of Europe the same way the Japanese owned every beach in the Pacific, three fucking months into this goddamn war and both were still indomitable, the whole thing had been one defeat for our boys after another and MacArthur was in Brisbane, of all places, with his shitted balls between his legs, we'd lost Wake Island, Guam and Singapore and we hadn't even dropped a single bomb on Tokyo and he'd be damned if he'd sit here in this giddyup hotel with its stuffed animals and let himself get happy over hot sauce and a beer and have a goddamn frilly *bedspread* laughing at him from across the room.

—*yep.*

Night had gone like that.

Step on up, folks:

Take a look at Stateside Joe.

So manly.

So important to the future of the nation in his city shoes.

It could get a little caustic, claustrophobic, in his monologues, so he was relieved when he discovered Hauser, bright and shiny, waiting by the Packard in the cold light of day.

"Sleep okay?"

"Yessir."

Schiff suspected Hauser had started banking his per diem, subsisting on soda crackers and tinned "sausages," so he didn't ask where he'd gone for supper or if he'd had his breakfast yet. Instead they got down to the business of increased turning ratios.

"You sure you want this sidecar, Mr. Schiff?"

Why was everybody asking him if he was "sure"?

"—because it throws the turning ratio way off. Just remember that with this sidecar attached your center of gravity's no longer under you."

"Why are there bricks in it?"

"You're gonna thank me for those bricks, sir. Otherwise Rita here lifts off the ground whenever she goes left."

"Rita?"

"—she picked it, sir. They always do. They always speak their name to you . . ."

What they had to do this morning was secure an airfield; what they had to do this afternoon was fill in the local dignitaries on what their federal government was about to do. At exactly oh eight hundred Macauley climbed into the Packard and the air inside became infused with aftershave and exhaled tobacco. Schiff watched the land as they headed toward the site, evidence of the California aqueduct, its chutes and channels, running parallel to the road on the west side. He had expected there to be more agriculture in the valley but the land was scrub, unkept, reverted to its natural state of desert. He'd told Hauser to drive eight miles from the Dow and then pull over to the left and cut the engine.

Manzanar.

—not what he'd expected.

The surveyors had been out and Schiff pointed to a stake with a small red flag on it marking the southeastern corner of the massive tract of land. This is it, he said.

They got out of the car and were immediately assailed by wind.

If there had ever been an apple orchard here it was damn well hidden now, maybe over there amid those cottonwoods. The ground was hardpack and sandy and Schiff had to wonder what force it would require to sink fence posts. The land was *flat*, he'd say that much for it—flat and barren. Desolate. But the element he had not anticipated from looking at the aerial photographs and the survey maps was the profound effect on human perspective of being next to the earth's shoulders. The Sierras *loomed*. They were called Nevada because they were snow-covered year-round but at this time of year, the tag end of winter, they were white from the knees up, looking less like things the earth had rendered than obstructions hurled down as grave warnings from the sky. A man felt small—a man was meant to feel the smaller being of the two, beside a mountain; you don't inhale a mountain's size by being near it as you might an ocean's: it doesn't fit inside your mind, you can't become it, you can only look at it and judge, from where you stand, how much farther away from heaven you and all your aspirations are.

It made sense to put the airfield on the other side of Route 395—it was the better approach. But the problem was, if you thought of Route 395 as the north-south line running up the valley, at this point on its spine all the land to the west of it, including Manzanar, was owned by L.A. Water, while the thirty-six square miles of it, on the other side, where they needed to build an airstrip, was the largest remaining tract of land in the entire Owens Valley that was outside L.A. Water's grasp, still deeded to a single, private, owner.

Schiff and Macauley crossed the road, Hauser trailing in the car behind them, and Macauley, acting like he knew about this stuff, held his finger up against the wind and paced off where the airstrip should go. Pleased, they got into the car and Schiff directed Hauser back onto 395 until, a hundred feet or so beyond, they encountered a dirt entrance road marked on both sides by white adobe pillars crowned with terracotta tiles. A wide wooden gate stood open. Past the gate they came to a second one—also open—under a wrought-iron arch into which was fashioned the ranch name.

"Three Chairs," Schiff read aloud (for Hauser's sake).

—then something clicked—some long-forgotten memory emerging from its blank retaining wall, and he shook his head and halfway smiled.

"—*Thoreau*: '. . . one chair for solitude' . . . no, I think Thoreau wrote, '. . . one chair for *meditation*; two chairs for conversation; *three chairs* for society.' "

They could see the ranch house in the distance, its bell tower rising like a punctuation mark. Hauser whistled, low. "Weird place to put a mansion," he observed.

"What's our strategy?" Macauley asked from the back: "—me or you?"

"—oh this is yours, sir, all the way: Big guns. Owner's name is Rockwell Rhodes: blue blood, Newport and New York. Got his money off his father, Wellington."

"—Wellington *Rhodes*?" Hauser seemed excited. "That's a railroad name back in Alabama. It's on boxcars!"

"—silver, zinc, lead, copper—*railroads*—family fortune up there with the Morgans and the Astors, then the old guy died and Rockwell and his sister . . ." (consulting the fact sheet:) ". . . *Caswell* . . . sold off all the assets and divested—"

Christ! at the hands of anybody less adroit than Hauser they'd be dead right now, the goats—*goats!*—bleating up this hidden gully where the road took a sudden dip like the solid earth had dropped away or a river had dried up and suddenly they were in this small depression on the far side of which was a figure in a red cape of all things, a blond woman with cropped hair and wide eyes and a shepherdess's staff who leapt out of the way just in time as the large black car caromed out of the gully with the big man in the back in hat and uniform.

"—should we stop?"

"—no hell you were brilliant, Hauser, christ: . . . *goats*. Who'da thought?"

Schiff searched for the woman in the side mirror and was rewarded with another glimpse of her fine figure as she stood, escapee from a fairy tale, red cape tossing in the wind, and no doubt cursing him.

The dirt road ended in a gravel circle with a (now dry) ornamental fountain at its center. A battered blue Chevy pickup was parked at its edge along with a wood-paneled Austin and a pearl-colored red-upholstered 1930s Cadillac convertible with its top tucked in.

Even before the Army car had stopped, the dogs circled, three of them, barking, sniffing, backing—one, a terrier, jumping chest-high to stare at them—and, from around the corner of the portico, the canine bruit brought the hens, a bevy of them, red and black against the hoarfrost, which started Hauser scurrying, a delighted man, an Icarus, ecstatic at the sight of feathers.

A porch had been constructed at the front—not so much a porch, in the Midwestern sense, as a narrow limbo place to pause, get your eyes accustomed to the shade and knock the dried earth off your boots. It had a terracotta roof and an aroma coming off the beams that suggested something burnt, like a charcoal, to its elemental truth. It was less a porch than a *portico*, Schiff thought (his mind working through his Latin), something older than a porch would be. All the buildings here, like the people they housed, all the building styles, had been transplanted.

Surrounding the entrance were geraniums in pots and other Western flora (mostly cacti) Schiff couldn't name although he recognized rosemary, and there was a gnarled vine twisting up the wall beside the double wooden doors.

Schiff watched Macauley mass himself into an attitude of brisk authority but before they even had the chance to knock, the door was flung back and the entrance filled by what had to be the largest woman Schiff had ever seen, if she was, in fact, a woman and not a craggy broad-shouldered man dressed up as one. Schiff saw the instant look of betrayal in the woman's eyes as she told them, "Jesus, don't you sons of bitches have better things to do than this?"

and turned around and faded back inside, leaving the door open to the hens, the dogs, the three of them.

Schiff paused on the threshold but the General barreled through, stopped, once inside, by the layout of the place, the non-standard archways right and left—an open arcade ahead with escape routes running off in all directions— but finally he faced right and negotiated the tiled steps beneath a wide arch that led down into a large double-story room dominated by a fireplace the size of a military transport on the inside wall and a field-sized gold harp in the corner.

Schiff hung back, and Hauser with him, while the dogs determined Hauser's age or health or sex or whatever dogs determine with that thorough going-over they give humans. Protocol demanded Hauser stay outside and guard the car but, what with the dogs and all, he found himself pushed in along with Schiff.

Walls of books.

Two cowhide davenports.

Rocking chair. All kinds of Indian crap and art all over.

Schiff had never been inside a private home so well appointed. For one thing, it owned *air* the way places built for religious practice do. It had ancestral presence, like a library. Like a place where people go to think. Then, too, there was definitely cooking going on, a complicated food aroma—pleasant, not straightforward; smoky, textured, like the terracotta underfoot. You could tell the art on the walls was expensive—you could tell it by the way it made you feel—a mix of paintings and black-and-white photography, all landscapes, each a picture of the American West.

Macauley positioned himself to face whomever might appear. Schiff followed his lead, facing the room's entrance hat in hand while Hauser, having lost all sense of decorum, walked around and peered at things, especially the harp, ready to stick a finger in and pluck it.

Soundlessly—(Schiff noticed flannel slippers)—a man appeared beneath the hallway arch and towered over them, not deigning to descend to the lower room. Schiff reckoned he was six-three, six-four, same height as the woman who had let them in and, like her, his hair was white, the kind of white that augers cold. His was long and gathered in a ponytail. Their eyes were identical in color (icy blue) and in their frightening self-confidence.

"Spare the ceremony, gentlemen," the man said: "You could have done this with a telegram."

Schiff looked at Macauley and only then remarked the General still had on his hat.

"Are you Rockwell Rhodes?" Macauley asked.

"—*please in godsname*: say it quick and get it over."

Macauley indicated Schiff and said, "This is Mister Schiff from the Department of Interior and I'm General Macauley, U.S. Army . . ."

The man looked at the woman and then back at Macauley.

"—but my boy was in the *Navy*."

Macauley looked at Schiff.

Schiff looked at Macauley, then back at the man.

"Sir," Schiff said. "Perhaps you're aware of President Roosevelt's Executive Order 9066 which sets out to establish an Exclusion Zone on the West Coast—"

"—what in hell do Frank's politics have to do with my son—?"

Schiff was at a loss.

"—your son?"

Rocky stared at him.

—then suddenly, cold clinging to her cape and still breathless from running, the blond woman from the road appeared, a younger version of these two, same eyes, and grasped the elders' hands and looked at them—terrified, Schiff thought.

Rocky told her, "*Army*. I don't think they're here with news."

The scene fell silent save for the panting of the dogs and a bird outside, until Rocky told the visitors, "Three months. No word. My son was at Pearl Harbor."

—*oh shit*, Schiff thought. Let the General say some decent thing and then let's all depart. Let the General say *I'm sorry for your loss* or say *The nation's in your debt* or recite a verbal homily but don't—do *not*—on penalty of death let the General bring up the Japanese.

Brave men, Macauley said and then, in a gesture bordering on the mawk-ish, made a point of taking off his hat and tucking it between his rib cage and upper arm. Then he said, "The reason that we're here, Mr. Rhodes—as Mr. Schiff started to explain—is that we've been charged with the construction of a relocation camp—"

Schiff held his breath.

"—one of several being built across the nation in an effort to protect our citizens of Japanese descent . . ."

Rocky turned blue eyes on Schiff while Macauley went on talking:

"—on the property across the road from yours, on the land that used to be the apple orchard, and the reason we're here is to obtain consent to put our airstrip on your side of highway 395."

There was a long silence.

"A 'camp,'" Rocky repeated, eyes still drilling Schiff.

". . . a *relocation* camp," Macauley emphasized.

Still, Rocky wouldn't look at him, only at Schiff.

"How is that different from a prison?"

"If the General meant to say 'a prison' I believe he would have done so, sir," Schiff said.

Rocky swung his gaze back on Macauley:

"How many?"

"—beg your pardon?"

"—how *many*?"

"—detainees?"

"*Japs.*"

Schiff winced.

"We're anticipating thousands," Macauley said.

"How many thousands?"

"—possibly as high as *ten*," Macauley told him.

Schiff watched the big man ricochet a little, from the information.

"—that will be the largest conurbation in the county," Rocky answered slowly. "Where's the water coming from?"

The General seemed not to understand the question so Rocky said, "Ten thousand people—shitting, drinking, bathing, cooking—where's the *water* coming from?"

Macauley turned to Schiff and then all eyes did, too, but it was the old man who had posed the question and Schiff knew he had to meet the accusation if he was going to get out of this with any dignity because the question Rocky posed was *the* question, the one that undermined their moral posturing, the one that shot their propaganda all to hell and begged a simple answer. It was the kind of question Rocky had been taught to ask by his father from the cradle: *Where's the money* in this enterprise, *where's the profit* and who's making it?

Schiff knew—and he could see the old man had guessed it, too—that part of the contract between the federal government and Los Angeles to use the land at Manzanar to build the camp also involved a purchase agreement between the city and the Department of the Interior to pay for the use of water that would have otherwise been theirs. Even though the water came from here. Even though the source of all that profit-making water was the Sierras with their run-off, the land beneath his feet, the land where he was standing—the Owens Valley.

Get out of my house.

—the way the old guy spoke the words—like Lear in his Final Act, measured and exhausted but still strong enough to lift Cordelia:

"Get out of my house *now*," Rocky repeated.

"About the airstrip—" Macauley tried to interject but Rocky spun around, voice rising: "—you're the goddamn U.S. Army you can do what you damn want now *get out of my house* before I throw you out myself—" He flung his left arm toward the door and Schiff saw for the first time that Rocky's hand was a lobster claw, missing both its ring and middle fingers.

Macauley jammed his hat back on and march-stepped to the door. Schiff tried to catch the caped woman's eye with an apology (she wouldn't look at him), then they were outside in the car and maybe the big door had been slammed behind them in an irate gesture and maybe someone had dared to use profanity but Schiff doubted it. The residents had too much class.

"I'll get the Corps of Engineers out here this afternoon. *Two* runways,"

Macauley threatened. So far, the General hadn't sworn. But Schiff could feel it coming; Hauser, too. They had almost reached the highway.

Fuck him, Macauley finally ordered.

Taking leave of Hauser was particularly awkward because what was he supposed to say: "—*write*"?

When you can't read, what's the point of *stay in touch*? What's the point of letters? The kid was taking the General to Independence to meet the editor of *The Inyo Register*, then to Big Pine and Bishop for more glad-handing with the Valley locals. Shift over, Schiff reckoned, the kid would get reassigned somewhere, anywhere, in a system that had never been designed to honor boys like him.

Something for you: Schiff handed him the present wrapped in plain brown paper.

—my *word*, Ricky breathed and Schiff was worried he'd get teary.

"I can't accept this, Mr. Schiff. It's too fine."

It was a Schaeffer, not even a Waterman, and Schiff had bought a half dozen of them for his tour in California, plus two dozen bottles of his favorite colored ink, purple.

"I loaded it with ink but you can change the color."

"I swear. I'll keep this 'til the day I die."

"—well just don't go making that any time too soon, Private . . ."

Then of course the hayseed had to go and hug him.

Schiff had an appointment with Rev. Leslie of the Methodists in the Rev.'s parsonage on 1st Street and (truth be told) deciding which of the Christian ministries to visit first—Episcopalian, Congregationalist, Baptist—Schiff had picked the Methodist because of his name.

Work in Washington, work for the federal government, you can't help but catch the Christian drift, the references to God, the secret handshakes, but Schiff had yet to master the distinctions among their tribes. He couldn't tell a Baptist from a First Church of Christ–er (they all looked the same to him) but the Rev. Leslie opening the parsonage door to him looked the part exactly, like a brilliant bit of casting for a Capra film.

They settled into the small front room where the Rev. had laid out tea (no biscuits) and Schiff balanced his hat on his knee and noted the knitting basket on the floor and the potted violets on the windowsill and wondered if there was a Missus Reverend somewhere on the premises or if the Methodists frowned on sexual congress among their clerics (he would never get this straight).

Rev. Leslie was tall and thin and pink and fit but the salient quality that he projected, Schiff was happy to discover, was intelligence. This is oolong, he announced as he poured. "I'm not ashamed to say I stockpiled."

Schiff inhaled the vapor and thought it smelled like asphalt.

"Now," the Rev. said. "How might I be of service to you?"

Schiff explained why he was there, told the Rev. about the camp and watched his grey eyes grow more serious as he spoke.

Gracious—that's a lot of souls.

Yes, Schiff said. "A lot of people."

"—and you'll need to keep them occupied. Idle hands . . ." The Rev.'s gaze traveled to the knitting basket and then back to Schiff.

"I'm hoping you can help me find work for them. In the community. Colleague of mine is setting up the camp in Minidoka, Idaho, and he already has commitments from the beet farmers to hire detainees for field work . . ."

"We don't grow beets in Owens Valley, Mr. Schiff. The Valley's been in dire straits ever since the city took the water. In point of fact we don't grow anything. Most people left here twenty years ago, never to return. Why should they—? L.A. Water took our farming out from under us. I'm not exaggerating when I tell you, with the kind of numbers you're expecting, my parishioners will be lining up to come to work for *you*. You'll be hiring teachers, I presume? Carpenters? I can barely imagine what you'll have to build—*churches*, for one thing. Places for them to worship. I'm not speaking solely for my parish when I say the religious community in Lone Pine doesn't have the consecrated space to accommodate so many people. I'm not talking out of church"—(quick smile)—"when I say my fellow clergy and I will be more than happy to officiate for however many congregants you can assemble but you'll have to build some bigger churches. I'm presuming most are Buddhist, anyway?"

"And Shinto. Which presents another set of problems."

"What 'problems'?"

"—well first off: I have a personal axe to grind with any religion that asks its followers to believe a human being can be God."

Rev. Leslie grinned: "—I realize that you're talking about Hirohito but I do also hope your prejudices don't mean you have an axe to grind with *Christ*."

"In Shintoism the Emperor of Japan is God—like Christ in Christianity—but at least Jesus didn't send His believers to bomb Pearl Harbor."

"Are you telling me that if you end up with, let's say, three percent of the 'detainees'—three hundred people, based on your estimate—who subscribe to Shintoism and venerate the Emperor of Japan as a deity you will refuse to let those citizens of the United States practice their religion while they're in your custody . . . ?"

"By the letter of the law—"

"Oh good, recite the Constitution for me."

"—by the letter of the law under the present Act of War and the Federal Treason Act: yes, sir. I would have to."

"—you would 'have to' abrogate the First Amendment. On which we built a nation."

"You see what I'm up against. I said I'd 'have to.' Galileo 'had to.' I didn't say 'I will.'"

"You're an attorney by training, you mentioned? What aspect of law?"

"Constitutional."

"God has a way of balancing the powers. Do you need me to help you make your case to the other members of the Lone Pine clergy?"

"I'll be all right on my own, thank you."

"I'll send you a list of my practitioners with their qualifications—musicians, for example—we should try to get you instruments for musical instruction—and, of course, I can get you all the Bibles you'll need—you know who you need to see about musical instruction: the elder Miss Rhodes. She played the stage in New York City."

"—she was an actress?"

"She played Carnegie Hall. Foremost harpist of her time. Renowned.

Toured Europe. Played for the kings of Scandinavia. Then Rocky's wife passed away and Caswell came out to California to help him raise the children." He paused. "Shame about the son," he added. "I fear it's hit the old man hard."

"I met him. He gave me the boot this morning."

"Oh, you're no one in the Valley until Rockwell Rhodes has given you the boot from Three Chairs at least once. Last time it happened to me was for the orphans of Czechoslovakia and Rocky saw me to the door and told me never to come back again until I was willing to take care of the orphans of the Owens Valley War."

"There was a war in Owens Valley?"

"*Water* war."

"—but there were . . . shootings? —no deaths?"

"—oh, there was shooting. And someone—the culprit's identity has never been proven—blew up the aqueduct four miles from here. Disrupted water service to Los Angeles for days. Coincidentally it was around the time that Rocky lost those fingers. Some people swear dynamite can do that when a man's not careful."

By six o'clock, it was dark and Schiff was back at the hotel, in a burn over the lieutenant from Q-Corps who had failed to show. He made some irate calls before walking down to the telegraph office at the train depot, where he shot off some angry words to the friendly folks at Army. Then, deciding he was talked out, he walked up Main to Lou's.

It was the kind of joint you'd want to find in a quaint village at the end of a long journey, snug and welcoming, more sophisticated than the other businesses in town, suggesting, somehow, in its details and appointments, in the choice of tableware and wall art, that there might be quiet money at the heart of its conception but that the owner had greater currency invested in good food than in showing off.

You walked in and found yourself on a raised platform, the dining room five feet below. Everyone could see who had come and who was leaving, and you had the chance to look around at all the tables before coming down, descending the worn wooden stairs into the warm and aromatic room.

There was a banked fire in the fireplace and lace curtains at the long street window. There were a dozen tables, four-tops all, and only a few were occupied, though Schiff saw that some others had recently been occupied (because their finished dinner plates were still in place). No one was bussing tables, no one serving as host or hostess, because as he surveyed the room no one came to seat him. The diners still at table were mostly men wearing the Los Angeles Department of Water uniform, though the two tables closest to the bar had mixed pairs of men and women. The bar was zinc-topped, and looked like it had come from some Wild West saloon. A leaded mirror hung behind it, large as a pool table. On the walls were framed stills from movies filmed around the area, shot in the Alabama Hills with the Sierras in the background, and various signed glossies of the stars ("Cheers," Cary Grant. "Best of Luck," John Wayne). The room was lit just right for conversation—there were candles in short glasses at each table—but the brightest light was from the kitchen, which he could see through the open door at the back.

Schiff made his way to an empty table in the corner by the fireplace. The table had a red and white checkered cloth covered by a square of butcher paper. There was a candle, a cruet of what might be olive oil, a dish of salt, a pepper grinder, a ramekin of butter and two small sealed Mason jars containing something that looked roughly like pale pink pâté or potted meat. There were no utensils and no plates. He'd brought two books to read (both about Japan) which he placed on the butcher paper and then his instincts told him to serve himself from the long table beneath the curtain of the street window on which were stacks of china (*bone* china), cloth napkins, jars of silver knives and forks (*real* silver), a basket of *baguettes*, glasses (*crystal*), and carafes of wine and water.

He chose the chair that faced the room, fireplace to his right, table with two LADW men in front of him. When he was seated the friendlier-looking of the two nodded to him and said, *Evenin'*. The other one had hooded eyes.

Before he had a chance to respond a slim blonde in blue jeans and a blue denim shirt with a long white apron around her waist and a white napkin tucked into its drawstring came briskly from the kitchen carrying a tray of coffee and cake which she efficiently delivered to the men in front of him without a word.

When she turned to face him Schiff rose to his feet as manners dictated.

—Miss *Rhodes*!

"Mister . . . Schiff."

(Said coolly; but oh did he enjoy the fact that she'd recalled his name:)

"—are you leaving?"

"No ma'am. Just arrived. —do you *work* here?"

(He couldn't see the need for it, a woman with her family money.)

Ignoring the question: "What can I get for you this evening?"

Sitting down: "Well let me see—how 'bout a *menu*?"

Motioning: *the board.*

On the wall above the platform by the entrance overlooking the entire room there was a blackboard with the menu on it. He hadn't even noticed—

> *Soupe*
>
> *Salade*
>
> *Charcuterie*
>
> Fish
>
> Game
>
> Fowl
>
> *Viandes*
>
> Pie
>
> Cake
>
> *Fromages*

He looked at her, confounded.

"It's '*the menu*,' Mr. Schiff—not the Rosetta Stone."

"Surprise me."

She gave him what he thought might be a gambling, if facetious, smile; and as she turned away he added, "—before you go . . ." He motioned to the two jars on the table. "What's all this—?

87

"*Confits*. That one's duck, the other one's smoked trout. Both local." She turned her back to him and spoke to the men at the next table. "Mr. Cooper . . . Mr. Snow: everything to your liking this evening?"

Schiff sensed the strain among them.

"My taste runs more to steak," the one she had addressed as "Snow" told her. "How come I never see your father eating at this place?"

"My father likes to choose his company."

"Well you let him know we're thinkin' of him. How's that *fiancé* of yours?"

Schiff's eyes flashed to her hands where they were clasped behind her back and, sure enough, there it was, the ring.

—a *band* and not a stone, and on the proper hand.

She went back to the kitchen and Snow sat picking at his teeth. The other of the two, the one named Cooper, said to Schiff: "Up here for the fishin'?"

"Not me, no, sir."

"*—elk?*"

Schiff briefly entertained the thought of telling these two strangers the truth—after all, the official announcement would be on the front page of *The Inyo Register* on Friday and if any people had gotten advance word of the internment camp it would have been these LADW men, hell they might have seen the blueprints already, might have even worked on all the conduits and switchbacks, the pipes and ditches necessary to get water to ten thousand people. But war was war: posters everywhere warning that loose lips sink ships (horrible reminder of that December day at Pearl). If fear was not exactly the mood of the nation (thirst for revenge was more exact), it was still a careless notion to pretend that the attacks were over, that Pearl Harbor was a one-off and the enemy would not come back for a second round so CAUTION was the byword for each citizen—especially a government employee—BE CAREFUL WHAT YOU SAY. Say NOTHING. And say it in a way that sounds believable.

"I don't hunt," Schiff said.

"Couldn't help but notice how you know the young Miss Rhodes," Snow said.

Schiff stuck a knife in one of the jars of *confit* and spread a gob of it on bread. Crammed it in his mouth so he wouldn't have to answer.

(—what the hell was this?—was this the *best thing* he had ever tasted?)

"I bet I seen you by the lake the other day," Snow went on. "I bet that fella that I saw out there wuz you."

The only thing that could improve upon the taste filling Schiff's mouth might have been a slug of strong red wine, so he swallowed some.

"Didn't catch what it was you said you *do*," Snow ventured.

"I'm with the government," Schiff decided to admit. "Department of the Interior."

Snow rose to his feet. "You in cahoots with Rhodes? What the hell is that son of a bitch up to now—?" Snow looked at his fellow worker. "We shoulda stopped that bastard twenty years ago—!" He pulled himself together and stalked out.

Dinner *and* a show:

Schiff was having a great time.

—plus he got to stare at the fair Miss Rhodes.

"Excuse my buddy Snow: long story. Bad blood," the man still at the table said. He wiped his hand on the napkin on his thigh and extended it to Schiff. "Cooper," he proclaimed. "*Deuce Coop*. People call me that because I'm Junior. 'Deuce,' ya know? 'Trip' when you're the son of Deuce. —get it?"

Schiff shook his hand and told him, *Schiff*.

"You stayin' out at Three Chairs—?"

"No. I'm at the Dow."

"—same as me an' Snow."

Cooper wiped his lips and stood.

"—alrighty, then: I reckon we'll be seein' ya."

Schiff figured by the time the fair Miss Rhodes had served his dinner Deuce Coop would have gotten the lowdown about his mission, who he was, from Phyllis. Not that her version of the gossip would be accurate (it hadn't been, last night) but—who could say?—by now the whole town might have heard one of the many versions of the truth.

—*duck rillettes*: not pâté, exactly; earthy, not too fatty, and he thought he could detect an undertaste of . . . cognac? In the other jar, a paler pink: *rillettes* of smoked trout. Alone, a kind of feral satisfaction: but on bread? with wine? You could feel it melting in your chest.

Schiff's relationship with *fine* food had only started when he began working at the Drake (he had always had a relationship with "food"—plain food—if that's what you could call what emerged from Rima's kitchen) (and to call it that was kind). Maybe it was the discovery of fresh ingredients (maybe it was the discovery of *cream*) but he had come to recognize that he had a heightened sensitivity to taste, that he could "see" a broth, a gravy—any substance—"see" it in his mouth, detect its layers and its orchestration, and this was an aspect of his manhood that seemed unmanly: *women* cooked, *women* cared about the way food looked and how it tasted; men ate beef. American Men ate because of appetite. American Men ate to produce big muscles; Great Thoughts; sperm. His interest in what came out of the kitchen at the Drake had caught the attention of, first, the sous-chefs ("—*taste* this, kid"), then the chef, and finally the mâitre d', and when they saw how he could talk about the food to customers it hadn't taken long for him to go from bussing tables to being next in line behind the mâitre d' himself, and the Head Waiter, both of whom were decades older and had formal training and had come from France. (And for both of whom culinary service was A Life Profession.)

Schiff didn't want to do it for a living (he barely cooked), but he couldn't escape the fact that he was more appreciative, more skilled (better endowed?) at tasting food than most men, and he had come to think of this as a kind of curse because it made eating, on the road, at work, a challenge to his senses. At home his father had put up with Rima's cooking (again: if he could call it that)—all his life he'd watched his father shovel stuff into his mouth as if he didn't notice what it was. As if he couldn't tell the difference between something that had the potential to be a transcendent experience and what was merely *there*.

Show me what you eat and I'll tell you who you are Schiff had determined.

I'll tell you how you reason;

I'll tell you how you love.

The fair Miss Rhodes had *not* come back, instead the first course had arrived at the hands of a squat Indian-looking woman in straw slippers under a calico skirt, with eyes made out of coal.

Shark hoot, she said and slammed a plate of cold sliced meat (with salad) down in front of him.

The salad was the kind of lettuce Schiff had heard people refer to as "butter" and it tasted peppery and light under a tangy buttermilk dressing. But the meat—alarmingly crimson, paper thin, and larded through with veins of fat—looked suspiciously like ham.

And Schiff, for ancient reasons, eschewed ham.

Excuse me, he called after the Indian. What kind of meat is this?

Shark hoot, she repeated. Schiff glanced reflexively at the blackboard for a clue.

Pig? he asked.

"No pig."

She placed her hands on top of her head and spread her fingers (which made her look a little crazed).

He cut off a morsel of the meat and nibbled: cured in salt; then smoked. Not sweet. In fact a gamy balance to the bright note of the salad.

He cleaned the plate.

She came back and set a steaming bowl in front of him and pronounced it *Fish*. It smelled, delicately, of "fish," that was for sure, but also of tarragon and butter. Several puffy egg-shaped dumplings floated in a cream sauce topped with a tiny mound of bright orange roe. *Quenelles*. He tasted one. *Trout quenelles*. Who the hell was taking the time to make *trout quenelles* in *Lone Pine*, California, for christsake. He remembered seeing the fish chef at the Drake pound out the flesh, shaping the damn things back and forth and back and forth between two serving spoons (imagine the rare intensity it takes to have to do that) and he remembered "*quenelles of pike*" being the one fish dish he always had to push on customers—*sell*—and he remembered how they went for three bucks a plate even way back then, more expensive than a steak. Whoever this guy Lou was who was running this establishment was wasted in a town like this. Even on those sometimes-annual occasions when the movie people were in town, how many covers could he depend upon?—twenty a night? And how was he getting these ingredients? There were national caps on foodstuffs since the war had started—Schiff was dealing with those problems, himself, having to find a way to feed so many people three times a day at Manzanar: Where was this guy getting all this food?—and how much was this dinner going to cost him? Last night's (plus the beers and a tip to the delivery boy) had run a flat buck but here he was knocking back a second glass of wine without a clue about the cost.

A bullish-looking man with a shiny bald head came from the kitchen to put another log on the fire and Schiff smiled at him, with no response. The man picked up empty plates from around the room and placed them on the bar, went back into the kitchen and returned to Schiff's table with a third (and unexpected) course.

"Are you Lou?"

"I am Vasco."

"Are you the chef?"

". . . *Vasco*."

Schiff was left to appreciate the plate before him—three small, exquisite lamb chops stacked into a teepee on a bright green (parsley?) sauce, surrounding a mound of roasted carrots and parsnips next to two pieces of rustic toast on which sat two entire open heads of charred garlic inside of which each individual clove had turned to jam.

After a few minutes he realized he'd been so intent on eating that he hadn't noticed when the other diners had left, nor how long he'd been sitting all alone.

He sat back and allowed the pleasure of the meal to take effect and in that moment didn't care how much it cost. His college debts were paid, he had no siblings so no nieces or nephews to cater to (no girlfriends, either), he had free room and board for the foreseeable (as soon as he could finish building it) and he was neither vain nor prone to vices (other than eating well) (and buying far too many books than he had time to read). The two he'd brought to dinner were still untouched so, while waiting for the check—or coffee and dessert—he opened the one on top (an English-Japanese phrasebook translated from a 19th-century Dutch-Japanese original).

The question had arisen, in the preliminary organizational discussions, whether or not they (the War Authority) should allow Japanese to be spoken in the camps. It was presumed, since most of the detainees had come from California and were almost all citizens of the United States, that most would speak American, but—it had been suggested—there would be a group, predominantly older, who—if they spoke American at all—spoke pidgin, spoke in broken syllables; and couldn't read a word of Yank or Christ's own English. Schiff had maintained that outlawing Japanese would be impossible to enforce. What are we going to do, install police at night inside the barracks, listen in on what they say when they're alone in bed?

For a man in his position as Administrator he thought it would be politic (and courteous) to have at his disposal a couple of commonplaces, so he'd made a list of words and phrases:

> Hello.
> Thank you.
> There is snow on the mountain.
> What is the name of this in Japanese?
> May I offer you a stick of gum?

According to the Japanese-into Dutch-into English phrasebook there didn't seem to be a single greeting translatable to "hello," but rather a series of greetings, depending on the time of day, and, of these, Schiff thought "Good morning" would probably be most useful. It was pronounced *ohayo gozaimasu.*

Even without two glasses of wine Schiff was going to have trouble remembering this unless he could come up with a catchy mnemonic (a method that had saved his ass in law school).

> Oh, hey—Oh, go say "ma," Sue.

—what story could he make up to go with that?
—*oh, hey* (that part was easy:)

oh, go say "ma," Sue.

Schiff repeated *oh, hey—oh, go say "ma," Sue* until it started to sound natural (throwing in a little gesture, no small thanks to the wine).

"Thank you," he told himself: *domo arigato.*

> *Doe mo ah ree gah toe*

Dough, Moe. 'Arry, got toe?

It was clear the people in the kitchen had forgotten he was out there so he cleared the plates from his and other tables and moved them to the bar, all the while repeating thank you and good morning in what he hoped sounded like real Japanese. There was a double sink behind the bar so he took off his jacket and rolled up his sleeves. There was laughter from the kitchen and someone turned on a radio. Schiff organized the dinnerware for washing—starting with *whatever touches lips* (*glasses*, first; next, the silver; last, the plates). He noticed for the first time that the silver flatware was engraved—an "R" entwined with a "W"—and he wondered . . . "Ralph Waldo—"? —"Walter Raleigh"—? Then Miss Rhodes came out wiping her hands on the napkin at the waistband of her apron. She seemed surprised to see him.

"You know it's a myth, Mr. Schiff. —that business about washing dishes when you can't pay the bill."

He noticed that she was sizing up his dishwashing procedure.

"I'd be happy to pay the bill, Miss Rhodes—if anybody had been here to pay it to."

"That's why we have the honesty jar."

She motioned with a tilt of her head toward the prominent jar at the end of the bar.

Schiff reached for a cloth to dry his hands.

"—or if anyone had bothered to tell me what I owe."

She cut behind him to the end of the bar and twisted the jar so he could see the sign on its front.

SEVENTY-FIVE CENTS ALL MAINS

TWO BITS EVERYTHING ELSE

Oh, Schiff said. *Domo arigato.*

He put on his jacket and dug in his pocket and counted out the money and put it in the jar.

They were facing each other over the bar.

"Good meal. Exceptional."

"Glad you enjoyed it." (No smile.)

"Is Lou around?"

He noticed a change in her eyes. Backpedaling, he added, "I know I might have got off to an awkward start this morning—"

"—yep."

He started walking backwards toward his table to collect his coat and books: "—and I apologize for what might have seemed an indelicate intrusion on your family in your time of grief . . ." (He knocked into a couple chairs:) "—and I regret my and the General's, um, insistence on bringing up what must have been a sensitive subject to your father—"

"The Water Company."

(He'd meant the Japanese:) "—oh, sure." (He'd reached his coat, and fumbled with the books:) "—but I've spent the day with local clergy and I've been assured of the community's support, so please give me a second chance to state my case."

(He was standing at the bar again.)

"Sure," she said. (Still indifferent.)

"—if you could introduce me to the owner I'd be grateful for the chance to speak to him." (He couldn't penetrate her look. No clue what was going on in those blue eyes.) "—or if not to Lou himself then to the chef?—whoever here might give me some advice about contracting with your local produce growers . . . dairies . . ."

"Sure," she said again. "I can answer that."

Schiff withdrew one of his notebooks and a pen from his inside coat pocket. "Okay—" he started, flipping through the pages.

"—but if that number you quoted this morning is real . . . ten thousand?"

Schiff said it was.

"—then you're going to have to import all your food, or grow it yourself."

Schiff said, "—but what grows here?—what does the soil support?"

"Presuming I have water?—just about anything: grains, legumes, most vegetables . . ."

"—what *can't* I grow?"

"Probably not rice. Too cold for olives, avocados. That lettuce that you ate came out of a cold frame, but it's small scale. I 'candle' it throughout the winter—"

"I couldn't place the meat."

"Bambi."

"—you fed me *fawn*?"

"Venison."

The bald man and the Indian woman came from the kitchen carrying their suppers and she asked the bald man something in a language Schiff had never heard and then they had a brief exchange.

"This is Vasco," she told Schiff.

"—we've met."

"—and this is Pie," she said of the Indian. "Vasco came here from Basque country—Basques settled both sides of the Sierras, ran sheep for railroadmen—and I asked him where you can get good lamb—"

"—whoa, lamb's not in the budget."

"Don't discount goat. Vas will tell you who you need to call in Bakersfield . . ."

Schiff stopped writing.

" 'Swiss steak,' " she said. "*Cabrio*."

"—what do you mean, 'Swiss steak'?"

"That's what it's made of. Army tried to requisition mine, but mine are dairy."

Schiff was struck by an idea.

"—cheese?"

"—and milk. Goat butter."

"What do goats eat?"

"Anything, if you're not careful."

"Any cattle in this valley?"

"North of Bishop. But the Army has already been there."

"Do you think you can arrange a sit-down some time soon for me and my Quartermaster guy and you and Lou so I can pick your brains?"

(Again, that absent look:) "I'll try."

". . . tomorrow night?"

"You're coming back tomorrow night?"

Backing out, keeping eye contact all the way: "You wouldn't know what Lou's got on the menu?"

"Never know . . . Lou's handwriting . . . I never got a legible instruction from Lou in my entire life."

She knew damn well tomorrow was the wild boar sausage cassoulet. She had the navy beans already soaking.

"—where did you learn to wash dishes, Mr. Schiff?"

He pantomimed a man who's got a train to catch.

—sorry, lady, in a rush. Gotta get some icy mountain air.

—because, frankly?

Where did you learn to be so blond.

STOOP LABOR—how's that for a job description.

Strawberries, tomatoes, melons, lettuce, spinach, cotton, rice: you need a labor force for picking you can put out in the sun without rebellion thirteen hours every day, working down the line so close to the earth the pickers breathe in spores and dirt, exhale pollen or dried blood. Schiff had seen these fields of folded bodies, people of both sexes doubled down with labor, picking through the Southern cotton and he'd seen them out in Texas, too, harnessed to their burdens, heat so palpable it ripples like pond water when a man moves through it. Heat so thick it thwarts your movement. Brakes the heart.

He had watched the Negro crews tumble out the backs of trucks in darkness, unseen, navigating by pale cotton, galaxy of sharp-cut stars, and even he, an urban cynic, had been caught up in the mythic lyricism of pure in-touch-with-Nature agricultural work. Until the sun came up. Until the sky bleached white with heat on the bent backs and the ground became a griddle off of which the heat bled through your feet and up your pant leg to your crotch. Every part of you with pores leached liquid. Simply standing in those fields and taking notes for Interior, Schiff had soaked his shirt by nine o'clock. He'd sweated from places on his body he never thought could sweat. And even though this was years ago, now, he could remember that by noon he'd smelled of things he'd eaten and by dusk he'd smelled of death. Chest high on the field another layer in the solid stack of heat—the reek of human labor—all but knocked him out.

Nothing pretty about picking, once you moved in close, focused on the faces and the narrow shoulders, ropy bottoms, ropy arms and legs, ropy bodies; vacant eyes. Schiff had never visited the Central Valley in California—his work for the Interior had not brought him West until it sent him out here, to Manzanar—but he'd read reports. He'd read, for example, that ¼ of all table food produced in the U.S. came from this part of California. All the raisins (every one). An area approximately the size of England (15 million acres), this California valley yielded 90% of the nation's plums, 60% of its grapes and almonds, 40% of its potatoes, peaches, cantaloupes, a fourth of its carrots, tomatoes and cotton, and if you totaled up the agricultural yield in the U.S. state-by-state this single four-hundred-and-fifty-mile-long valley in California, only a few hundred miles from where he was standing, would rank fourth after the whole state of Iowa, the whole state of Illinois, and all of goddamn Texas.

Schiff remembered talk among the agro-boys, the owners of those Southern cotton fields, about how sweet their lives would be if only some bright sprat of industry might invent a way to take the human factor out of cotton. If we can get a man across an ocean in an airplane why can't we make a thing to pick our cotton. Take the humans out of it the way the threshers took the humans out of wheat. With cheap gasoline and diesel you could pick a whole field clean with one machine in less time than it took a hundred Negroes, then you could rent it out around the county never hafta give it bed an' board an' field tawlets nor face the curse of idleness. You could run your profits up and make more hay if only you could make the human labor disappear, replaced with a tool whose only needs were fossil fuel and casual maintenance.

CHEAP LABOR: in the race to lower costs, to keep profits up and the price of goods down for the good of the whole nation, nothing beats replacing human beings with machines except when finding fuel to feed the beast becomes too costly. If you were big enough—if you were putting out enough to feed a lot of people, as was Sunkist, for example, or Dole or ConAgra—the government would see you got enough of that black gold to keep your tractors running; but if you were a mid-size farmer or a private grower of, say, nonessential produce like asparagus or roses, since Pearl Harbor your access to fuel had been rationed—cut—and to bring your crop to market you were forced back to square one, Old Testament: cheap labor.

What Schiff was hearing—what the whole Department of the Interior was hearing from the California growers—was a primary response of gratitude for rounding up "the yellow enemy" throughout the state, followed by the immediate secondary complaint: Why can't you build your prisons closer to the crops? Where the hell are we supposed to go to find stoop labor?

To Mexico, apparently.

Within a week of Executive Order 9066 mandating the involuntary incarceration of all Japanese-Americans from the coastal Exclusion Zone, the state of California launched its *los braceros* program, an aggressive recruitment, from Mexico, of "the strong-armed," a corps of seasonal migrant workers to replace what had been a permanent workforce of resident citizens of Japanese descent.

Like water in a healthy well, Schiff had written to his bosses back in Washington: the more you take off from the top, the more comes up from the bottom.

California had a history with Spanish-Mexican stoop labor, starting with the Native Indian populations, followed by the first wave of Native Mexicans enslaved by the Spanish conquistadors and Catholic missionaries; followed by the Chinese left over from indenture to the mining companies and the railroads; followed by the Japanese themselves, coming at the end of the 19th-century from Hawaii; followed by East Indians at the turn of the century; followed by Filipinos and Armenians and then, with the Depression, all the Okies, Texies, Arkies, cheap white frosting on the rainbow cake.

These last were perhaps the saddest, Schiff thought—because most of them arrived expecting privileges of race, but finding in the whites of Sacramento and the Central Valley who had "pioneered" a century before a brand of class discrimination distinctive to the state: coming west by Model T was clearly trashier than coming West by Conestoga wagon. Even the Donners had a better pedigree in California than the Dusters.

The debate in California, about pickers, was about the kind of work a born American should never have to do. An American should never have to pick for other people. *Real* Americans were unfit for it (i.e., better suited for higher jobs, work that didn't break their backs, work that didn't make them *stoop*). Put the Chinese out there, on the bottom row of grapes, on the drying flats for raisins, they were built to do it, it was borne on them, squatting, it was part of God's design, the same as putting darkies under the hot sun in the cotton fields, otherwise why make the black man black the brown man brown the yellow man so low-to-the-ground, compact and nimble fingered. This was social Darwinism, at ground level: What the hell else were these people going to do? It was God's plan. Otherwise God would have made them tall, blue-eyed and sensitive to sun. And brought them into being wearing jackboots, speaking German.

If the Army had sent him back-up like they said they were going to do, if the U.S. Army had been half as efficient as its German counterpart, the guy from Quartermaster Corps would have been here yesterday and Schiff wouldn't have to spend the whole day on the telephone and typing requisition forms and trying, unsuccessfully, to buy a ton of rice.

He thought the rice would be a humanizing touch but as the day wore on and he'd grown punch-drunk with the inefficiency and doublespeak of wartime requisitioning, he'd begun to see the rice idea as stigma. Why did he think people of Japanese descent might like rice better for christsake (potatoes were 1/10 the cost), why did he think people of Japanese descent would even *need* it in their diet? It was a *starch* like yams or bread and its only arguable advantage seemed to be that it was dry and cheap to ship and he could stockpile a supply (if only he could get some) 'til the end of the war or until hell froze over, whichever happened first.

Here's how crazy things were out there on the food chain (why he needed that Quartermaster guy): California had the second-largest rice-producing area in the United States (after South Carolina; ahead of Minnesota) but the population for which he wished to purchase rice in bulk was the same population from which the stoop labor rice harvesters had historically derived, so the people for whom he wanted to buy rice were being denied rice at the source because their government prevented them from picking it, themselves.

Time was running out—in less than thirty days he would have ten thousand mouths to feed and so, late in the day, out of frustration, he'd ordered half a ton of raisins for delivery in three weeks (cheap; in-state; portable; nutritious; and, ethnically, non-Japanese). The American Red Cross had been supplying troops on duty overseas with "goodwill packs"—food parcels—and Schiff had asked Interior to send him one so he could try to replicate it for distribution to internees upon arrival to the camp. They had sent a list, instead. (So far, the ARC had refused to aid the camps:)

AMERICAN RED CROSS OVERSEAS FOOD PARCEL
CONTENTS FOR TROOPS ON ACTIVE DUTY

1 lb. Raisins or prunes
(Seemed a lot, Schiff thought, but he had yet to learn about inductees'
and internees'—constipation.)

6 oz. Liver pâté
(By which, he guessed, the Red Cross meant canned liverwurst.)

4 oz. Coffee

12 oz. Corned beef

8 oz. Sugar

1 lb. Powdered milk

1 lb. Oleo

8 oz. Crackers

4 oz. Liquid orange concentrate

8 oz. Processed cheese

8 oz. Canned salmon

chocolate bars

cigarettes

soap

Schiff tacked the list to the wall and stared at it.

76 oz. of stuff—nearly 5 lbs.—not counting the packaging, the chocolate, cigarettes and soap: a lot to carry but a lot to barter, too, in places where there hadn't been real coffee, real liverwurst, for years. Places where, it had been rumored, people were eating shoes.

He had authority to requisition straight from manufacturers and growers but Agriculture's first priority was to feed the troops and there was already grumbling from both sides of the aisle in Congress about spending Federal bucks on what one blessed idiot from Oklahoma had called government-funded "hotels for Japs." There had been articles in California papers about rationed dairy products going rancid in the sun outside the temporary holding centers, owing to the fact that Asians were disgusted by the smell of milk (and butter; but, especially, cheese). One editorialist from Los Angeles had written, "These Orientals would rather chomp raw fish than take a taste of apple pie so why are we booting our best produce off to all these plush environs in which the Japs are lazing, one of which even has a racetrack?"

Not every newspaper report had been that inane (it *was* a racetrack, stupid—people were detained in stalls constructed to house horses) but the lack of sympathy—even a starched resistance—toward Schiff if he so much as alluded to *why* he needed three tons of crushed tomatoes took him by surprise. This was not the prejudice that he was used to: Jews might pick your pocket and Jews might run the banks and Jews might practice usury but no Jew, ever, had aimed a gun at the United States, and why the hell were we—Americans—picking up the Japs and giving them protection and housing them at our expense and *feeding* them on top of everything while everybody else was being rationed? He could hear resentment in suppliers' voices and, when he finally called it quits and for the second night in a row went across the street to Lou's for an early supper—he could see it on some people's faces.

"Well your secret's out," Deuce Coop mentioned without pity. "People ain't too happy."

"No," Schiff agreed. " 'People' ain't."

When he'd walked in the couples at the tables near the bar had turned to look at him and he'd read cool distance in their stares. Even Phyllis behind the desk at the Dow, formerly so accommodating, had turned her back on him. (Perhaps someone had told her about the lace bedspread inside the bottom drawer.)

"Ever met one?"

Coop had already finished eating and was nursing a black coffee. He pulled his chair to Schiff's table and asked again: "Ever seen a Jap up close?"

"Yes, I have." Schiff looked around the room for Sunny, poured himself some wine from a carafe: "I had the privilege of working with a Japanese-American back in Chicago."

"Me an' Snow wuz talkin' 'bout it all this afternoon. Snow's from up around Colusa where they grow the rice, north 'a Yuba City, Marysville, they got a lot 'a Chinee livin' up there an' Snow said his family tol' him that first week after the Pearl Harbor, folks around Colusa started throwin' things at Chinee houses, Chinee places 'a business, rocks an' things, sometimes puttin' torches to their storefronts or their yards, thinkin' Japs and Chinee are the same—so the Chinee started wearing signs around their necks an' puttin' signs in windows sayin' 'We Chin*ee*' . . ." He did a crude impersonation and laughed. "I could always tell 'em apart—we had a lot of them where I come from. Know how you can tell 'em? *By their hats.* We got some recent Armenians moved in back home, an' Armenians, especially, they got these Charlie Chaplin bowler hats all round on top. Round bowler hats—you gotch yer Mexicans in these *sombreros* biggern a tractor wheel, the Filipinos in their half-brim felt fedoras but the Chinee and the Jap, they wear two different kinda head gear, Chinee in the *pointy* hats and Japs in their bandanas. That's how you can tell 'em. Well . . . I gotta get th' lead out. Night shift."

He stood up and Schiff noticed Snow in his Water Department gear waiting at the door.

"You know, Mr. Cooper," Schiff said, detaining him, "you never told me what you *do*."

"We're on patrol."

"At night?"

"Especially at night."

"For what?"

"Sabotage. Wild animals. Right now the chief culprit would be balloons."
Schiff let the image take effect.

"Incendiaries," Coop went on. "Launched from Jap boats workin' the
Pacific. One a' them explodes into the water line we got a main disruption."

Schiff sat very still and contemplated everything in front of him.

"But they'd have to come over the Sierras."

"That's why they're balloons."

"Well presuming they could even do that—"

"—oh they can."

"What could you do if you ever spotted one?"

"Shoot it."

Schiff stared at him.

"It seems to me they might be fairly high."

"We'd track it down. An' then we'd shoot the payload. 'Splodes out there,
above the foothills, can't do no body harm. It's open country."

"Are you that good a shot, Mr. Cooper?"

"Snow is." The two Water men exchanged a sign. "You should watch him
shoot. Boy came up in those fields around Colusa, rice shooter. Dropped back
from school age ten, been looking down a rifle all his life."

"—'rice shooter'?"

"Geese an' such. Down the flyway. Turns out best places to grow rice is the
same best places birds in them migrations loveta feed. Boy, do they love rice!
Growers useta pay Colusa boys just to shoot—give them guns, buy the ammo,
let the boys keep every bird they could bring down. Hell, Snow bought himself
a piece 'a land on what he earned when he was only seventeen. Man can shoot
the eye out'ern a blind mouse at eight hunnert feet."

He wished Schiff goodnight and joined Snow at the door and as they were
leaving two more men arrived and Sunny appeared from the kitchen for the
first time since Schiff's arrival, bearing plates of food. This was, what, the

fourth time he'd seen her—in the road surrounded by the goats, in her father's house when she made that breathless entrance; again, here, last night—and on each occasion, although beautiful and graceful, she'd seemed tense, self-protective, wary as prey. As he watched her now he saw that, yes, faced with Snow and Cooper, her body seemed rigid, and she responded to both the Water men (and possibly Schiff, himself) as if they posed a threat. But once the two left she greeted the newcomers with a previously unseen warmth, hugging one of them, and even (what a gift it was) smiling. You could print what he knew about her on a postage stamp: she was easy on the eye (*very* easy); she came from money but, unlike the monied girls he'd seen at the Drake or shopping with their mothers along Michigan and State, Sunny wore no affectations—no lipstick, no false scent (that he could notice), nothing from the catalog of practiced privileged gestures. She didn't even wear a dress. Yes, she had acted cold toward him and maybe just a little haughty but why not. She seemed intelligent—and healthy—and underneath the denim and the apron enough raw energy was on display to signal physical activity was something she was good at and she definitely seemed to know her way around if not a closet then, at least, a well-stocked kitchen pantry.

He liked his women to know food.

"You're back."

"As promised. What should I be ordering tonight?"

"There's a venison shepherd pie—but you had that venison *carpaccio* last night—there's roast chicken—but you should try the *cassoulet*. Work intensive. Very rare. First time we're serving it this winter."

Schiff faced an empty page:

"I don't know what '*cassoulet*' means: —what is it?"

(Not a smile, exactly, but her eyes got playful:)

"Casserole, of sorts . . . in the French tradition. Usually with goose, mutton and pork—white beans—but I make mine with native duck and wild boar sausage."

You make yours, he thought he had repeated. Instead—it took a couple turns for the penny to drop through all his cogs—he said, "There is no guy called 'Lou' back there in the kitchen, is there?"

"Oh there's a 'Lou.' "

"But he's not back there now."

She shook her head.

"*You're* the chef," he clocked. (He should have clocked it earlier. He should have *known*.)

"Listen, nothing off the stove tonight is *à la minute* so I could sit out here, if that's okay with you, and we can have our conversation while you're eating."

Is "okay" a word in heaven? He *had* put on a better shirt than the one that he'd been working in and he *had* put on the jacket to the suit (it seemed ridiculous to try to dress the cowboy part or look like he was anybody other than the guy who'd come to town from Washington) but he hadn't put his inner charmer in the game since the brief affair that had ended badly on that pull-out bed in Georgetown. Now he knew, from experience, that any chance he had would come not from playing Romeo (that guy was a joke) but from a stronger self—his inner Yiddish comedian.

Self-deprecation: up against *goy* women, it was money in his pocket—when done right. The key was not to make yourself look chicken or too cowardly—this was not the century for non-heroic Jews.

He started off telling her about working tables at the Drake Hotel to put himself through law school. He recounted his history of learning how to eat, how he'd learned that there was something better than his mother's dreadful cooking, that there was *joy* in the experience of cooking and in eating outside Rima's kitchen. He made his youthful experiences, his youthful journey-to-be-him, sound picaresque, triumphant, human and . . . sadly funny. He turned his life into a string of pearls, a caravan of Chaucer tales, bread-and-butter cup-and-saucer parables to win her over, entertain her, even at his own expense because once he started on this *shtick*—once she started smiling—a switch was thrown, he couldn't stop himself, he couldn't keep from acting like he hadn't toiled his youth away pursuing law or spent the day today in mindless tedium or that outside the dark was pulling in and all red-blooded males in the United States, including him, went to bed each night afraid they wouldn't make it into 1943 alive.

New normal, everywhere: busting out a laugh where none existed. Gallows humor. All the better with a drink, or two, and a full belly. All the better with a pretty local girl.

An hour, maybe two, had passed—all the other customers were gone and they were sitting by themselves inside the warm consoling room.

"So who's this?" he finally got around to asking, pointing to the band of silver on her ring finger, left hand.

She twisted it, as if unlocking something in her.

My guy, she said with pride.

"Congratulations."

He expected more—a name—but nothing was forthcoming.

"Where does this 'guy' reside?"

"I'm not at liberty to say."

"You're joking."

"No."

"Is he a spy?"

"—absolutely, how'd you guess: he's a spy and I want everyone I meet to know."

"Is he working for the government?"

"—that would be *you*."

"Is he 'wanted' by the government?"

" 'Wanted,' yes. By me. —but how 'bout you? Any future Mrs. Schiff?"

"Married to my work. —or, at least, 'engaged.' "

He told her how he'd spent the day, this time sticking to the facts.

"Sounds like you need coffee—"

"—no it's getting late, I'll stick to wine, I didn't sleep so great last night. Sound of my own heartbeat kept me awake."

Perhaps the humor had exhausted him; perhaps the food, the day's frustration, the red wine. He ran his hand, uncharacteristically, the length of his whole face, as if to wipe a mask, and said, "I'm pretty sure I'm in over my head."

Everybody is, she told him.

"—*you*'re not. Your father isn't."

"My father . . . lost his son."

"I'm sorry, that was thoughtless."

"What's the worst thing that could happen?"

"Now you're really joking, right?"

She let him know she wasn't.

"—oh let's see: cholera, typhoid . . . hepatitis. Mutiny. A riot. Fire. I could fuck it up so bad they starve to death. One person dies inside this camp, my name goes in the history books with Aaron Burr, John Wilkes Booth and Torquemada—"

"—so your worry is your reputation."

"—no. —no. —*no*. (And this he meant:) "My worry is the Constitution."

Now she laughed.

"My worry is," he tried to counter, "doing right by all these people."

"Tops says my mother used to say the most common thing a doctor can get wrong is to treat the sick like children. They've already been through god-knows-what and I'll bet you bucks to brass they have as much experience as you in self-determination. Think of them as partners in the exercise, not wards. Out of ten thousand people you know damn well a lot of them already know how to put out fires—"

"Most of them left jobs in agriculture . . ."

"—well, there you go."

"It's getting it all built in time . . . it's the first couple days—the *first* day— keeps me up at night. Housing them. Feeding them the first night."

"You got yourself a hundred ladies, easy, in Lone Pine, alone, who'd gladly take an extra dime to put up sandwiches. Pre-made. Like they do for soldiers. Food parcels."

"But these aren't soldiers."

She threw him a sharp look. "Times are hard. You could pay them."

"We tried that, or something like it—food parcels from the Red Cross. No go. You know what they put in those things?"

He recited from the list for her.

"Nothing real," she said.

"Coffee's real. And I'm guessing the raisins. And the soap. It would be redundant to make artificial soap and raisins." He brightened. "Here's a question for you . . ." He reached inside his jacket for his notebook.

What would you say is the perfect food?

"I don't understand."

"Okay, too broad. Let me rephrase: *As it exists in nature* what would you consider the most perfect food? Not necessarily something that tastes great but something you could survive on if you had to. Something you don't have to cook. *As it exists in nature*," he repeated. He was a little drunk.

She watched him rifle through the notebook 'til he found a certain page.

"What's the deal, why are you asking?"

"It's my favorite question."

"But what's with the notebook?"

"I ask a lot of people. I write down their answers."

She leaned across the table and unwrapped a cube of sugar. "This isn't bad . . . but sugar isn't found this way in nature and I'm not sure you could survive on it . . . Some kind of seed, I guess. Or some kind of nut. Seeds or grains or fruits or nuts. What's the answer?"

"There is no 'answer.' "

"Then what's the point?"

"Other people's answers. It's a *survey* . . ."

"Walnuts. No. Pistachios." She wagged a finger at him. "No. Avocados. Definitely avocados."

"Okay. Avocados. Going in the book—"

He poised his pen above the page and watched, to his amusement, something light up in her—an engagement, like a person realizing halfway through a sermon that she just has to dance. She reached out and stopped his hand.

A jolt went through him.

"I see what you're doing," she said. "A *trick question.* First you tell a person 'perfect' then you throw us off by saying 'taste' is not a factor—'taste' is negligible—but how can food be 'perfect' without 'taste'? All that gets us is 'orange concentrate' and powdered eggs."

She'd taken her hand off his but the sense of it remained.

"I'm going to tell you my own 'perfect' food. True story."

She leaned back; Schiff put down the pen.

"I guess you know about Grand-dad."

"—Wellington Rhodes."

"—land baron, major villain in the writings of John Muir."

"I don't know who John Muir is."

"—how is that possible?" (Schiff scribbled "JOHN MEWER" in his note-book.)

"—suffice to say among Grand-dad's deeds at his death were a thousand timber acres up in the Sierras on Lone Pine Lake along the tree line. You know mountains?"

"Basically, since Moses—with the exception of Mount Sinai—I come from a long line of people at sea level."

"—you get up there, at a certain point (*tree line*) there's just ice and granite but down where Grand-dad had the land along the lake there were—there *are*—lodgepole and Jeffrey pines around a meadow growing on a granite flat—plenty fishing in the lake—and if you think the way my father does, like Henry Thoreau, a 'perfect' place to build a cabin. Two days, horseback, to get up there. Where he took my mother after they were married, inside a tent— and after she died, that second summer when my brother and I were five, he took us back. Ballsy thing to do—a father all alone, two little kids, think of all that could go wrong. We loved it. We went for two whole months so Tops could start the cabin—went up, three of us on horseback—my brother and myself on ponies—two mules with supplies. Every fourteen days two more mules with fresh supplies would make the trip. Tops taught us how to swim, to fish—how to trace the constellations in the dark, identify birdsong . . . two kids without a mother, I think Tops knew from instinct what 'the great outdoors' would give to us. How much we needed its embrace . . . Anyway: this one episode is family legend—I don't actually remember it. You've met my Aunt Cas, right?—imposing presence. You meet her now, she's rusticated, but when she first arrived here she had that New York voice—she'd been a debutante—and me, every time I read a Henry James or Edith Wharton novel I hear every word in Cas's voice. Family legend is, Tops had me and my

brother set up in the kitchen to pack dozens of raw eggs for our camping trip.
—This part I *do* remember: he'd got these baskets made by the Shoshone—
elongated baskets the French call *paniers a pain*—and me and Stryker had to
put the raw eggs in them packed in fresh hay. Apparently Cas came in and
said . . ." She mustered up a Cas impersonation: " 'Rocky. What. In God's
name. Are. These children *doing?*' Legend has it when he told her she said,
'God. Sake brother. If you need. To transport eggs up. Mountains. Pack some
chickens.' . . . so we did. There's bears up there—foxes and raccoons—so
fresh food is always . . . perishable. But that first night, when we were finally at
the lake, Tops brought out a box in which he'd packed a dozen eggs and before
we got into our bedrolls he told Stryker and me to dig small holes around the
circle of the fire inside the perimeter of rocks and place an egg inside each
hole and cover it with ash and bury it . . . I remember, that first night, I was
scared. I had never been so far from home—there were sounds I wasn't used
to—nights are cold up there, even in the summer—and I remember waking a
couple times not knowing where I was and being afraid we'd lose Tops, too,
the way we'd lost our mother and how we'd have to live there in the woods
like wolves and how Stryker would be just brilliant at it and I'd be terrible,
and then seeing Tops sitting in his bedroll next to me beside the fire, sitting
there staring at the embers . . . and knowing he was there and I could fall
asleep. I remember waking up—it wasn't dark—to the smell of fatback and
fresh coffee . . . everything tastes—smells—better in the open air, especially in
morning at ten thousand feet. Stryker was already up—already up and doing
what he does the best, being best at everything, and I remember waking with
the feeling that the night before had been a dream and that now, I was caught
between those bad dreams I had had and cold reality. And Tops said, 'Hey,
Sunny: look what I found here—' and he led me to the fire and he brushed
the soil away to show a buried egg. He reached down and unearthed it and
told me, 'Hold out your hands.' I can still remember how warm it felt against
my palms. He pulled the shell away and told me, 'Taste.' " Schiff watched her
face transform with memory: "—that first bite—you know what eggshells
do, they're permeable, you put eggs in salt water they end up tasting of the
salt, you put eggs in the earth around a fire you're going to get the taste of

soil and ash—the earthiness—inside the egg inside the whites in that first bite and then you taste the yolk, still warm, just barely cooked, a sweet warm custard down your throat . . . My whole life: I. Have never. Tasted anything. As perfect as that egg."

Schiff sat watching her until she told him, "Go ahead and write that down."

Sunny Rhodes, he wrote. Then, next to her name: EGG.

Afterward, he stopped in the empty street, looked up. What a tiny life he had lived. Could he name constellations? Could he recognize birdsong? He thought maybe, theoretically, he could build a fire, but the only times he'd eaten anything outside had been hot dogs on street corners and sandwiches on benches and some abortive outings on the lakeshore with his parents and those few occasions when a girl might mastermind a picnic in Lincoln Park because what college male is going to turn down a date that starts with spreading out a blanket on the ground. When she'd finished her story about the egg, he'd fled, because as long as he was talking he was keeping up the pretense of attracting her to him but as soon as he stopped talking, started listening, there was no distraction from the fact that, between the two of them, the "attractive" one was her. Idiocy, on his part. Poison. Get your wits about you, Schiff. The girl's *engaged*—and second: this is just another case of me trying to be like the other boys who drank on weeknights, never studied for the bar exam, of not keeping to the task at hand.

Coming from the cold into the overheated lobby of the Dow he was aware of the electrical device behind reception searing the oxygen on broiling coils: the room smelled like burnt carpet and charred metal and something slightly musty that he traced to Phyllis's grey clothing.

"Your brother's here."

"My 'brother'?"

"Lookin' for you."

"What makes you think I have a brother?"

"He looks like you."

Her fingers gripped Christ on the chain under her collar.

"*Acts* like you."

"'Acts like me.' —how?"

"You know. *Busy.*"

There was a thin edge, here, between having fun with her and prodding at her prejudice with a sharp stick.

"What does this person look like?"

"Pale."

"You think I'm 'pale'?"

"Skinny."

"I'm not skinny."

She thought a second. "Frank Sinatra."

The door opened and closed behind him—rush of resuscitating air. A man pulled in behind him and said, "These people are so hayseed they think every Jew they see must be a Dago." Schiff turned and the man saluted. Sharp. His uniform, his leather jacket, hat, the whole gestalt, real sharp. "Lieutenant Jay Svevo, Quartermaster Corps. Reporting for duty."

"Where have you been?"

"New York."

"Not your post, Lieutenant."

"Pressing need."

"Absent without leave—"

"I decided to get married."

Oooh, that's nice, Phyllis—long fingers still playing at the cross—couldn't help from cooing.

Schiff and Svevo looked at her, then at one another.

"What should we call two Jews in a California hicktown?" Svevo posed.

Serious business, Schiff entertained.

A ghetto, Svevo said.

It's a pleasure to be here in the Sierra Negev.

He was a joker, this Svevo. What Schiff's father would have called a *me-shugganah*, a *dreykop*. Fast talking, faster thinking, always ready with a comeback or a (mostly inappropriate) joke, but—as Schiff learned almost at once—he was outstanding at his job. Maybe the Army had a patent on producing Fixers—maybe Brooklyn had—but wherever he had acquired his skills, he was among the best procurers the Quartermaster Corps had ever . . . well, *obtained*. Within hours of arriving in Lone Pine, Jay had taken over the remaining rooms on Schiff's floor at the Dow—staying up all night—to establish his own beachhead with four typewriters, a telex, two hot plates, a small icebox and five more telephones, one of which was always ringing. Each had yards of extra line so Jay could walk around while he was talking, walk one phone to an adjoining room so he could talk on two or sometimes three phone lines at once, receivers tucked into his neck or looped over his shoulder so he could use his hands while he was talking. If he had to wait to get some warehouse on the line in Pennsylvania or some supplier in Detroit he'd walk across the hall to Schiff and start to tell him, "You can't really think of Mickey Rooney without coming up with Judy Garland, can you, but you can think of Judy Garland without coming up with Mickey Rooney, why is that? I'll tell you why:" and then the person he was waiting for would come back on the line and Jay would walk back down the hall and disappear, only to come back again, minutes later, phones in both his hands, to say, "Man is the only species on earth known to put out fires with his urine. Or to vomit into his own hat. Or helmet, as the case may be. Or to get his pubes caught in a zipper." Then the guy talking in his ear would say something and Jay would shout into the mouthpiece, "No *this* week! Not *next* week! Are you from Montana? I swear, where do these people come from, don't they know how to do *business*? I bet half these guys have never seen a naked woman, have never been off the farm, never crossed a street . . ." his voice fading down the hall only to return again with, "Nothing in the world matters as much as you and your woman, that's all I'm gonna say. Not friendship not valor nor religion, not Dolph Camilli in the ninth, not Coca-Cola, not pie, not Lucky Strikes, not the Articles of the Constitution, not FDR, not General Motors, not Ford, not Judy Garland—"

Even on that first hectic night, in those first hours, Schiff had had to wonder what the hell the deal was with Jay and Judy Garland.

"You sleepy?—you need to go to bed?—'cause I think we should discuss our progress on this stuff so far. You need some joe? I'm gonna make some. Real joe. Italian kind. Fucking Mussolini, man. I'll tellya—"

He may have kept Schiff waiting but Jay had done his homework in advance, breaking down the camp project into categories—STRUCTURAL SUPPLIES, CONSTRUCTION, LABOR, CIVILIAN STAFF, EDUCATION, FOOD, SAFETY, RECREATION. Jay's list was much the same as Schiff's but whereas Schiff's organizational pattern was haphazard (scribbled notes thumbtacked to the wall) Jay's looked like a blueprint for a stupa built from hierarchical logic. He had managed to procure (for starters) two fire trucks, an ambulance, two X-ray machines (1 chest, 1 dental), 200 coal stoves, hospital beds, searchlights, blankets, school desks, mattresses, syringes, aspirin, light bulbs, refrigerator units, washing machines and toilet paper—plus delivery contracts for diesel, coal, flour, powdered eggs, canned milk, dry cereal, frozen chicken, frozen peas, potatoes and canned ham. Under the category LABOR he had already determined from the relocation rolls for the processing center at the Santa Anita racetrack that enough doctors, nurses and dentists would be interned at Manzanar to limit the number of Army Med Corps needed to be transferred, but in the category of EDUCATION Schiff needed to consult with the State of California about whether or not interned former teachers were still certified.

"We're looking at around eight hundred kids so we need to get them sorted out, enrolled. Especially the older boys. I love the ladies as much as anyone, even as a brand-new married man, but girls don't start the revolutions. Where you from?"

"Chicago."

"—so you know streets. What we don't want is gangs of young men forming, young men staring at barbed wire with nothing but frustration in their pockets. Keep them busy. Keep them occupied. Recipe for peace and harmony, and I'm not just talking marriage. The big picture: what I'm talking, here, is Life, in general. Life with a capital 'F.' "

Any time things went temporarily wrong or there was yet another situation normal, all-fucked-up, Jay would shrug, say Well that's Life with a capital "F."

You'd be forgiven, thinking maybe Army's favorite "F" word might be *flag*, but that would only prove you were naive, at best, or that you'd never listened, up close, to the way the enlisted really spoke. Country boys don't swear like city people but once the favorite "F" word gets a foothold there's no end in sight. Something deeply satisfying in its fricative, forced utterance. Fuck this. Fuck that. Among the nation's raw recruits the "F"s were epidemic, a verbal flag for boys fresh off the farm, an off-color word which, when flown, made as much of a political statement as the nation's other proliferating flying colors:

After Pearl you couldn't take a piss without seeing stars and stripes.

—after the attack FLAGS had sprouted everywhere—flags on buildings, flags in yards, flag pins on lapels; you'd see cars coming down the road, flags flying on their hoods like an emissary from a small country was coming. People draped them on their houses. Walk down Main and every mom-and-pop place had one in the window. Couldn't step into a grocery store without saluting. Couldn't buy a quart of milk without Old Glory. Schiff, himself, from his stint in Washington, working at Interior, was used to seeing flags in many places—flags standing at the ends of lonely corridors, flags behind reception desks in lobbies, flags in the corners by the windows at Department meetings—these had been the everyday, the desultory flags that he remembered from the classroom, indoor flags, domesticated ones, like pets, that never roamed the wild, nor flew, nor trumpeted, nor cried out in desperation, not the brazen flags that flew anew, the ones that had a full-blown message to deliver, not merely a whispered cue.

Schiff had never fallen prey to self-advertising patriotism—Jews in Holland, all autonomous Jews in German-occupied territories had been made to advertise themselves since Hitler with distinguishing emblems on their clothing and every time Schiff spotted a co-worker at Interior with another flag pin in his lapel he wondered what message he was signaling.

Night of Jay's arrival they had spread the site map out across the "matrimonial" (the desk and table, even when combined, had not been large enough, Jay said, for either one of them to see the whole "big picture"), and they had stood on either side and used Jay's cue sticks (he always traveled with a set in case a chance to play a game of pool arose) to "walk" their way around the barracks blocks, commit the layout to their memories, imagine—re-imagine—

lines of sight for the surveillance and the ways they could control pedestrian traffic flow.

Messes, laundries, toilets—routes to these destinations would be the most traveled and needed to be in view at all times by the eight watchtowers. Jay reconfigured placement of the school and of the prospective "places of worship" to farther corners of the compound and suggested moving all offices and Army housing closer to the highway so visitors would never have to travel to the real heart of the internment camp. Jay penciled in a square for a commissary— something Schiff had overlooked—where internees could purchase household and personal hygiene products, and they set aside areas within the barbed-wire perimeter for playing fields, a chicken pen, pig farm and market gardens.

Schiff couldn't go to bed until they'd rolled the site map up but even after midnight Svevo kept walking his cue stick back and forth between the barracks, down the fire breaks.

"What are we forgetting?"

"—I'm foggy, Lieutenant. It's late. I'm tired. —trees?"

"Fuck trees."

"Places to sit down?"

It had not occurred to either one of them that people of all ages might need places to sit down outside mess halls or the toilets . . . or just plain *outside*.

"Wooden benches," Jay suggested. He made running dashes on the blueprint, "—here. —and here. —and here. —and maybe along here. Where's the airport?"

"Off the page, down there. On private land across the road."

"We've done the paperwork?"

"I already filed it—eminent domain."

"Put the perimeter in place to start," Jay said, talking, it seemed, to himself while he traced the straight line that was one side of the compound, along the public highway, Route 395. "—then build up this area, the barracks along here, the Administration and police buildings, all the stuff that fronts the road. Let's get this entrance here, this main gate, let's put a guardhouse here, built out of stone . . ." He stared at their creation, then let out a snort:

"—fuck me stupid if we didn't both forget the cherry . . . !"

Half an inch behind the guardhouse on the "main road," a distance that would translate to a couple dozen yards, Svevo drew a little circle on the map and filled it in to look like this

•

then he smiled across at Schiff: "Now it's finished."

"What the hell—?"

"—think about it . . . First thing that hits you, that you have to see as you come in . . ."

Schiff stared at the lonely dot.

"—come on, come on . . . —starts with a capital 'F'?" Jay prompted.

Oh sure, Schiff thought. "Life," with a capital—

Now we're cookin', it's official:

Manzanar had got her ("F" for) *fla*gpole.

Another tic of Jay's: always talking about "film."

—never called them movies like an ordinary person—never called them moving pictures as Schiff's parents did—no, Jay (opting for another "F" word) talked about the "film" he'd seen.

Not just with Judy Garland, Jay had an ongoing (one-way) correspondence with myriad "film" personalities, the majority of whom Schiff had never heard of.

For instance, Jay might walk into his room while he was on the telephone and ask him, "Whadja thinka *Kane*? Whata genius, huh? Changed my life, I swear. Went to see it, that first day. Orson, man. What a fucking genius."

The only Orson Schiff had ever heard of was some guy who used to be on radio.

"All-time favorite film," Jay would say so Schiff would take his clue and tell him, "I don't go to movies much."

"*Citizen Kane?* What is *wrong* with you? You don't go to *movies?* How do you *learn?* You don't go to movies in this country, man, you don't learn how to *be*, how to wear a suit or *walk* or kiss a girl or talk to cops—"

"Who are you in civilian life, Svevo?"

"—who *am* I?"

"What did you do? Before December 7th."

"It's in my file. Didn't you read my file? I would have read my file."

"—classified: Army. I'm Interior, remember?"

"But there's ways of finding out. You got no people skills, my friend. Me, I asked around about you and even if I hadn't I woulda got you pegged. First-hand evidence, I woulda said you are a guy who lives inside his head too much. You overthink. Definitely would have known you for Joe College. Thinker not a doer. Idealist. On the plus side you're the kind of person who if I had to choose somebody after Jimmy Stewart, I'd send you to Washington. I'd vote for you. I'm just not sure I'd hire you to get me outta jail."

In this case Schiff actually knew who Jimmy Stewart was, he knew Jimmy Stewart was an actor who had gone to Washington as "Mr. Smith." He didn't know how the Army worked, but he suspected this new instant Army put in place since Pearl operated more from expediency than Old Boy connections and was starting to advance men to officer status by shortcuts the old guard would have never dreamed of. Schiff had wondered how Jay had gone from raw recruit to a lieutenant in less than three months—not that he was undeserving—but in Schiff's experience swift advancement (to the *Law Review*, or the best assignments in Interior) hadn't always had to do with merit: often it had to do with who you knew, which lit Schiff's fuse because he had gotten to where he was the hard way, *solo.*

In town—starting at the Dow—he could see people were surprised that he was so young, that someone in his late twenties had been given a position with authority but the fact was, in terms of moving up the ladder in his career, this job was a stall. Of all the things he could have been doing in the effort against Hitler and Mussolini and Hirohito, administrating relocated internees wasn't vital to the nation's victory. He was, in the crudest terms, a jumped-up prison warden, and he knew it. Worse: most days he couldn't make himself believe the Executive Order excluding Japanese-Americans from general society would stand up in court.

Schiff was certain his ambivalence was showing in the details, but it didn't help to have Jay telling him to find a fix and find it quick before he fucked up bad enough to lose the job. Besides, other people were involved.

Ten thousand of them.

You need to learn to game the system, Jay insisted.

"Take me: I enlist. No fucking way do I do combat. First thing? I find out which ones are the non-combative units. Next I teach myself to type. I bring myself to the attention of the CO—"

"What *did* you do before the war—?"

"I worked for Uncle Sam. No kidding. Beryl has an Uncle Sam. Beryl's the bride." It would have been impossible for Schiff not to know who Beryl was because the first thing Jay unpacked in his room at the Dow was a traveling altar to the Mrs. Svevo. Plus he packed about a hundred pictures of her in his wallet. And made little kisses every time he took them out.

"So you and Beryl knew each other—"

"From the neighborhood."

"—but decided *last week* to get married."

"I'm here, ten-week rotation. At your service, thank you very much—after which I ship to some place in England called East Anglia and they boot me up to Captain. Game the system."

"You already know you're shipping out to England in two months?"

"Better odds to marry first. This way Beryl gets the Captain's pension if I catch a sizzler. Plus I get home leave, again, before I ship. Gotta play the favored odds."

"So this Uncle Sam of Beryl's—"

"Biggest bookie in the Borough. I'm the leg man. Manage the pool halls. I enlist, I go to this CO, I tell him any book that's made in camp I'm going to be the first to know it. Same with graft, black market. Boost me up the ladder and I promise to rat out all profiteering."

"So you're a gambler."

"—'*gentleman*' gambler. More Rhett Butler than Ashley Wilkes. —how did you *think* I made my living?"

"I don't know, you get things done. You know where to find things. I thought maybe you managed a department store."

"Well, that's just insulting."

On Jay's second day two WACS turned up at his bidding (both named Janet) to start in on the administrative load (a file needed to be kept on each internee; a paper trail, in triplicate, needed to attach itself to each administrative action), and three subalterns from Quartermaster Corps arrived to carry out Jay's orders. Phyllis climbed the stairs that afternoon to assert that she could smell something funny up there—"There is to be no brewing coffee and *no cooking* in the rooms!"—and Schiff's education in "people skills" increased by watching Jay square off against her. Seven people making progress by inches actually turned out to be a system and by the end of Jay's third day Schiff had started to see something taking shape. Jay and he didn't socialize with "the kids," they holed up in Schiff's room at night while the others hit Main Street for a bite to eat.

"Let me ask you something," Jay entertained one night. "If you were me. What would you say if Beryl says she's going to try to get pregnant next time I'm back on leave." Before Schiff had the chance to answer (thank god) Jay said, "Odds are good. I checked the calendar. Odds on conception, even. Odds on me dying on the ground in England, pretty much the same. I just got off the telephone with her. She's saying, 'If I'm pregnant and you die'—"

Someone had crept up on them and was standing, squarely, on the threshold of the open door.

Jay nearly jumped a foot into the air. "Jesus fucking *shit*—!"

It was the Indian Schiff had seen at Lou's—but it was Jay's *first* Indian and she scared him half to death, the silent sum of her, four foot eight right side up and sideways. She wore straw sandals, which was shocking, first of all because it was freezing outside and second because her feet in every aspect from her toenails to her heels were hide-bound and hideous. She was wearing layers of contrasting skirts topped by a butcher's apron which, from the look of it, lived up to its possessive adjective. Under it there was a calico shirt over which she sported a moldering suede vest. Her hands were liverish and chafed, but the single most remarkable detail of her appearance, in Jay's eyes, was the little bowler hat with an elastic chinstrap, rounder than a porkpie, with a higher crown, miniaturized, as if it had been tailored for a monkey, perched high on her head like a slapstick punctuation mark.

Schiff took a step toward her and with some miracle of memory recalled her name:

"Hello, Pie."

"She say, 'Come,'" she told him. "*Now*."

"'*She*'?" Jay said out loud.

Oh boy, this was reminding him of that scene when Scarlett sends Prissy to get Rhett at Belle Watling's to help Miss Melanie (not that his and Schiff's quarters at the Dow could be confused with the upstairs rooms at Belle's). He loved when incidents in life played out like scenes in films, when the seemingly spontaneous minutiae of everybody's everyday migrated unscripted across the borders of the unrehearsed onto staged territory, onto the pages of his cinematic memories. This one was playing out to be The Hero Summoned.

Schiff was halfway out the door:

"If you need me for anything I'll be across the street."

Jay watched the Hero disappear. "'*She*'?" he called after him. "Who the hell is '*she*'—? And why would I need you for anything?"

Along the street in front of Lou's there were more parked cars than usual—*dream cars*, slotted parallel, all of them in shades that Schiff associated with the seaside—aqua, sky blue, dune—shining, in this underpopulated place, like pebbles in the moonlight, eggs deposited on sand.

California plates. Three of them with soft tops.

He could hear the tide of conversations, inside, even from the street.

He could smell perfume.

He took the restaurant steps two at a time—and at first, inside, thought he'd been transported back to the Drake: a weekday night, a certain kind of louche and low familiarity among the paying clients.

There was a crowd of people in the dining room, *loud*, all standing the way that people stand while waiting to get *into* something, for a star to show, an act to open.

No one turned to notice him.

A pale vagueness hung above them, thin stream of cigarette smoke through which he tried to see back to the kitchen (Pie was already there, her back turned toward the room; Sunny, wrapped in focused thought, was carving something on the block). In the middle of the room Vasco was clearing space for all the center tables to be pushed together, banquet style, and behind the zinc bar a fellow with improbably orange hair was holding forth with a cocktail shaker while two other men leaned against the bar and turned their profiles to each other. Only four "regulars," two tables of two L.A. Department of Water men, were there, against the wall—sidelined, like extras, from the spotlight.

From the kitchen Sunny looked up, saw Schiff and put her palms together in a prayerful gesture, then made a Christian four-point sign, the cross, athwart her upper body. *My Savior.*

He moved into the room and nudged past cigarettes and furs to get to her. Wisps of conversations entrained after him.

Lubitsch, he *should talk*

> *All I'm saying, darling, is back East they'd still be hawking rags and knives from donkey carts*

> Oviatt's. Cary *sent me*

> *Why is it everywhere I*
> *turn I see*
> *Hungarians?*

As Schiff edged through the room, Vasco sent him a primal message with his eyes while he set the table:

Thank god you're here, Sunny told him when he reached her.

What's going on, who *are* these people?

Seventeen of them, didn't call ahead—

You can tell them there's no service without prior notice—

"No, I know the guy—the one behind the bar?—orange hair? We have a kind of History . . . but besides: I want to see if I can do it. Get this kind of service out."

Something in her eyes told Schiff she didn't want to argue.

"I've done seventeen before, just not all at once."

She handed Schiff an apron and he tied it on.

"You and Vas take front of house and Pie and I will hold the line."

She took Schiff through the menu and realized she hadn't prepped a fish course, and Schiff watched her stop and think about it . . . she had on hand a store of her own smoked trout . . . she had pre-boiled potatoes: she could make a hash.

He touched her arm to slow her down.

"Sunny: seriously—don't make yourself insane, just give 'em what you've got. They're passing through, they probably expect a burger—"

"Like I said. There's History."

She sent a knowing glance out to the orange-haired man.

"That's Bobby Kaye. A director. Lone Pine knows him, he's got a reputation, he's brought a lot of money into town. He's on his way to Reno with this bunch to make some kind of booster for the troops. He stopped here for a reason."

"Because he's eaten here before—"

"Because last time he came to Lone Pine . . . my brother killed his elephant."

Getting them to sit down was a circus and Schiff could see there seemed to be a pecking order governing the way they moved, limiting their choices, who needed to sit where, who needed to sit first (and last), who needed the best light, who needed the corner spot nearest to the bar, to the bathroom, until finally a clear leader emerged, the *director*, the orange-haired one, who took control and placed them on their marks like players in a drama, Darling you sit here by him and Doll you go over there and Sweetie you go down beside the guy I'm saying wouldn't hurt to be your boyfriend.

Vasco had laid the table from Sunny's eclectic collection of inherited Rhodes china, and Schiff was serving the bread, *rillettes* and *tapenade:*

What's this?
Taste it it's an olive spread
Why's it black?
Like I said it's olives
All olives I know are green

> *How come the plates don't match?*
> *Darling, turn yours over: just as I thought, it's bone, Bavarian:*
> *mine's Spode: and good god it's real silver*

> *Huxley wrote it*
> *No it was that other one that Graham Greene*
> *Don't be an idiot:* Pride and Prejudice: Huxley

> *Two point seven mill, one-hundred-thirty-three-*
> *day schedule*

> *Well of course they can't use London so*
> *they're subbing with Vancouver*

> *Who's Van Coover?*

Schiff stood slightly behind the orange-haired man at the head of the table and waited for a lull in conversation. In law school it hadn't taken him too long to figure out he didn't have the stuff for oral arguments. He had a voice, a nice one, and good diction, he had practiced rounding out his vowels so he didn't have the flattened Midwest accent, that brass Chi-*cegg*-o dissonance that sounded like a tin piano: he had a pleasing voice, at its best in private situations, not on display, but—and this was what had kept him from the trial arena—what he didn't have was courtroom presence, what he didn't have was *stance*. He'd seen those big guys, born performers for the court's arena, turning toward the jury from the waist, keeping all the power in their hands which they controlled, like knives, before their chests. He didn't have that lighthouse sweep, that magic beam of X-ray vision—(his professors warned him about his "tender eyes")—he didn't have the spatial aptitude to find the one most perfect spot and stand there and deliver. He'd turned his back on the students pretending to be judge and jury in the moot court exercises, he'd waved his hands and interrupted his own and other people's arguments. He was okay on the page but in the courtroom exercises, not so good. More like Leslie Howard than Clark Gable. More Ashley than Rhett, as Jay would say. And here he was, in front of all these hungry types from Hollywood, trying for attention. He raised his hand:

"Hello . . . good evening . . ."

He gestured down the table—needlessly—then pulled his hands into his chest, self-consciously.

"Some of you have been here before—"

He gestured—needlessly, again—toward the orange-haired man, then toward the chalkboard menu on display, then put his arms down by his sides, where they didn't stay for long:

"—but for those of you who are dining at Lou's for the first time let me tell you how things work. The board is *there* . . ." (Gesturing again; then interrupting his own train of thought:) "*Wartime*, yes . . . *rationing* . . . so I should explain that all ingredients are local, the chef grows all the vegetables herself, the game and fish are caught and cured right here, the poultry and lamb raised on the chef's own ranch right down the road . . ."

Oh christ we're back in the Dark Ages

Basil darling tell us how they ate in Sherwood Forest

Schiff looked at their faces. Lesson Number One: *convince the jury*, even when one member of it, he now saw, appeared to be Sherlock Holmes without the deerstalker and another, he was pretty sure, was the unctuous foreign guy from *The Maltese Falcon*. And, now that he looked at her more closely, there was the chance that the woman halfway down one side at the center of the table (the centerpiece), still wearing her fur and a pair of outsized sunglasses to hide the bandages, might be someone famous, somebody Svevo would assassinate him for later, for not having had the chance to meet.

He turned to the presumed host, the orange-haired man (Schiff couldn't remember his name) and said, "You know about the pricing, right?" (The orange-haired man looked somewhere else.)

"Okay, '*Soup*' . . . tonight we have three of them, the first is *soupe a l'oeuf provencale* . . ." (No one winced at his pronunciation:) ". . . that's a garlic soup with a poached egg . . . the second is a roasted beet—a *borscht*—served hot . . . the third, a cinnamon-scented rabbit consommé."

He paused to let them mull that over. (Their faces were expressionless.)

" '*Salad.*' There's only one tonight, that's the Candlelight Salad, a *mélange* of baby lettuce leaves the chef grows in a cold frame this time of year—" (Gesturing:) "Interesting story . . . you'll appreciate this: Chef lights candles in her cold frames at night in winter so the baby lettuce plants stay warm—"

> *Bobby, he's auditioning for us*
> *Sweetie, are you looking for a job?*
> *Are you an actor?*
> *He's pitching to us—let him, let him*

The norm was for little-or-no speech from the waiter, he'd learned that at the Drake, he knew that better than they did, he'd earned his education by being a *dumb* waiter—in the hotel dining room it had been the *sommelier* who might preach, or the maître d', or, for the special few, the chef might swan out in his *toque* to chew the fat about ingredients. But the whole point of Lou's was that the menu changed from one day to the next: How else to explain it but by talking? But because they were in show business, Schiff intuited, this crowd believed that everybody else was, too. *Fine*, he thought: if entertainment value was the only value they were seeking he could let them have it:

"At the top of the entrée list tonight we have 'Game' and that's a rabbit baked in tarragon mustard, garlic and cream, served over mountain grits. In the 'Fish' category we have a smoked Sierra lake trout hash, topped with griddled quail eggs. The 'Poultry' tonight is the chef's version of fried chicken. There are two '*Viande*' selections: a beef carpaccio served with basil oil and green tomato marmalade; the second is Sierra thyme-encrusted roasted grass-fed lamb."

He turned to the woman on the orange-haired man's left and debated whether he should call her "Miss" or "Ma'am" but before he could address her she complained she didn't have a menu. Then she asked if there were any "specials."

> *Does your fork have an 'R' on it?*
> *An 'R' and 'W.' 'Will Rogers,' maybe.*
> *Oh, pooks, I know Will Rogers and Will Rogers eats with his hands*

Ladies first, always give the ladies preference, always take their orders first, always bring their plates in first (with a restrained but sacrificial flourish calibrated to impress not so much the *ma'ams*, themselves, as the misters with the bankrolls). *And for you, Miss? What will the* lady *have this evening?* Schiff made his way down the table:

> *So I say to him I say, 'Who do you think you* are? *Whom* is kidding *whom?'*
> *Could not have said it better, Joan . . . even if you tried—*

Ladies?

Schiff had reached the center of the table where the actress in the fur coat and the sunglasses was engaged in conversation with the woman facing her across the table.

She turned her famous face to Schiff and said, Here's what I want: I want a cup of chicken broth, then I want a wedge you know the wedge they serve at the Brown Derby. Then I want a baked potato s-a-n-s the buttah.

She has to watch her figure, the woman facing her told Schiff.

She's a writer, the first woman said, "so she doesn't have to worry about lookin' good."

"She's an actress so she doesn't have to think. I'll have the garlic soup, a salad and the lamb. Brain food, Joan."

"No wonder you're unknown."

> *No, I have it from the grip who watched it happen, 'stead of*
> *normal credits, credits like we know, at the end he gets the cast*
> *to say to camera, 'Hello, I'm Joseph Cotton and I played' . . . you*
> *know, whatever Joseph Cotton played—*
> > —himself
> > > *That is* so *theatrical*
> > > > *And then and then, get this, he turns to*
> > > > *camera and he says, 'I wrote and directed*
> > > > *the picture. My name is Orson Welles'*
> > > > > *—what an asshole*
> > > > > *me me me me* me

The last woman at the end of the table was younger than the others and sat as if posing for a portrait, her chin and eyes lowered in an attitude of coy submission contrasting with her almost-white blond hair and pink angora pin-up sweater. Schiff was forced to lean in to hear her whisper that she wanted some tomato soup, the, you know, creamy kind, and a grilled cheese sandwich with the crusts cut off. She didn't look him in the eye but he could sense the fragrance of her exhalation when she spoke: bubble gum. Across from her were two men, intent on watching her, one of them the guy from *The Maltese Falcon*; the other wearing a beret and a sporty ascot and tweed jacket, sitting noticeably apart, his head down while he seemed to try to transfer the blonde's essence to his artist's sketchpad. When Schiff asked them, *Gentlemen?* they both looked up and Schiff felt his heart catch in his chest.

HOW   TO   SPOT   A   JAP

The scare-mongering by the press inside the Exclusion Zone, even from the high-toned papers, from the *San Francisco Chronicle*, *The Sacramento Bee*, the *Los Angeles Times* and *Herald*, had been monitored by the Departments of War and the Interior, even manipulated, in the weeks leading up to the Executive Order: *round 'em up* had been the unified cry in editorials: *kick 'em out* and send 'em packing back to where they came from, because you cannot be a Jap and an *American* at once, it is a case of either-or, you're one of *us* or you are one of *them*.

Every American of Japanese descent had been subject to derision in the press, to suspicion by the government, but not *all* Japanese-American citizens were being transferred, forcibly, to relocation centers—only those residing in the Exclusion, or Pacific, Zone, in California, Oregon, Washington and southern Arizona. Japanese-American citizens living in the interior (of which there were fewer than several scattered thousand) were not required to give up their businesses and homes, nor were the Japanese-American citizens on the East Coast. But citizens of Japanese descent everywhere in the forty-eight were objects of a latent racial hatred. Schiff remembered the article in *Life* magazine:

HOW   TO   TELL   JAPS   FROM   THE   CHINESE

The Jap is "earthy" (lemon) sallow; the Chinaman is "parchment" (tan).

The Jap will have a less pronounced epicanthal fold (rounder eyes than the Chinaman).

The Jap may have some facial hair; the Chinaman a longer, narrow face.

Look for buckteeth in the Jap, and "rosy" cheeks; the Chinaman will never blush.

Since Pearl, what the government was looking for were signs of enemy activity or infiltration, suspect behavior. The hatred that arose that morning in December was something you could see on people's faces, in their jaws and eyes and fists, and you could hear it in their whispers, in their speech. If the man sitting in front of Schiff at this table right now was Japanese, or, let's say, even an American of Japanese descent, he was breaking federal law by sitting here in California, and Schiff, in his capacity as a public servant and, particularly, as the Chief Administrator of a relocation camp, was duty-bound to apprehend him. But all Schiff did was stare.

My religion, the man was telling him, *prohibits me from eating certain foods.*

His English was impeccable, colored by, if anything, a highbrow New York accent, Schiff perceived.

In particular, the flesh of animals.

"Tak, my friend—" The actor from *The Maltese Falcon* laid his hand on the other's sleeve: "Would it offend your piety to watch me gorge myself on roasted lamb?"

"I would not presume to force my values on my neighbors."

"—*good*: the lamb," the actor ordered. He touched the other's arm again: "Would it offend your Buddhist heart to have to watch me eat it pink?"

"Peter," the man replied: "you must abide by your conscience."

"—*good*," the actor answered. (To Schiff:) "*Lamb*. And make it *rare*."

"A plate of vegetables, perhaps?" Schiff suggested to the Japanese.

But no butter, he was told.

The man turned the page in his sketchbook and Schiff rounded the end of the table, ostensibly making his way up the other side to finish taking orders, but also wanting to look at what the man was drawing.

Oh, he said: "Is that a comic strip?"

A *storyboard*.

On Schiff's look: "Each frame is a camera shot, you see? A different scene. For the film we're making."

Schiff stared at the man's handiwork, then looked around the room, not at the assembled guests, especially, but for the details a spy might notice: if you can draw a face then you can draw a blueprint. You can draw a map.

The good thing about Lou's décor was that it looked more like a French country bistro—rustic, apolitical, Schiff imagined (except for Vasco's photograph over the flattop of Generalissimo Franco with a knife stuck in his eye)—than what you might expect at your local Main Street place in Lone Pine. And the good thing about Lone Pine was that there was nothing here, as

Schiff was learning, of any interest to the world in general, nor to anyone at all, especially an enemy combatant.

Except water.

All the water that the fifth largest city in the United States needs to survive.

A shadow passed through Schiff as he stood there with the pencil poised above the order pad.

We are bringing 10,000 political detainees inside spitting distance to the California Aqueduct, to the only source of water for Los Angeles.

Fuck *me*, he thought.

—what genius thought of *this*?

A million gallons every day—how much poison would it take to contaminate that amount of water (and what toxic substance would be needed)? What safeguards were in place to guarantee the safety of the transport system—spillways, pipes, canals, containment dams—and also the safety of the stuff itself, its purity, its potability?

What if toxicity were not in play, what if safeguarding the product and its transport wasn't necessary to the safety of the city, what if somebody just canceled the delivery, blew the whole thing up, picked a juncture on the several-hundred-mile pipe-and-spillway system where the oversight was lax or weak, and dynamited it? What would happen if the tap were suddenly turned off, if the city of Los Angeles suddenly went dry? He remembered that someone—Sunny's father?—had tried to blow up the aqueduct already. Water wars and all those little fights, but now there was a real war on. How much water did the system have in storage—how long would Los Angeles survive? He knew, from the planning documents for the internment camp, that the average adult working human under moderate conditions needs to consume four to eight ounces of water per day to prevent dehydration—double that amount in a hot, dry climate such as the high desert or Southern California. Bathing, cooking, flushing, laundering—all of that was extra. Growing plants and vegetables—extra. Watering the lawn and putting fires out—extra. Of all the potential rationed items—milk, flour, sugar, butter, coffee, beef, pork, rubber, silk, gasoline—nothing was as crucial to survival as the thing most people took for granted, used for free, or squandered by the glass and gallon every day.

Air and water, that's where they will hit us first. This wartime danger suddenly took on new meaning. Strategic strangleholds: cut off the breath, the victim suffocates; cut off the access to their water, everybody dies of thirst.

In the kitchen, Schiff read the orders off to Sunny.

"—*seven garlics*, four *borscht*, three consommés, twelve salads. No takers on the hash. 2 rabbit, 3 beef, 5 lamb—2 pink, 3 done—4 hens. What's the chef's position tonight on off-menu ordering?"

Sunny answered with a look he'd never seen.

"Tomato soup—?"

"How many?"

"One."

She nodded curtly.

"—grilled cheese?"

She stared at him.

"—no crusts."

She said something to Pie in Spanish at the flattop, then cursed under her breath: "What is *wrong* with people?"

"—also: one vegetarian. No butter."

"I know what 'vegetarian' means."

"—also: any iceberg lettuce?"

"See *this*—?"

It was a knife.

One of the English actors—Schiff had seen him in a movie playing the lover scorned—wandered from the dining room to ask for more crushed ice.

Schiff and Vasco got the soup course plated and topped the glasses up and served the salads. Schiff was able to pass off the rabbit consommé as chicken broth to the actress with the sunglasses and the facial bandages, but when he placed the Candlelight Salad greens in front of her she said, *This isn't what I asked for.*

"It's *green*, for christsake, Joan, it's gotta be less fattening than all the gin you consume."

"It's *vodka*, darling, and vodka isn't fattening unless it's got vermouth."

"—and Chamberlain was right about Herr Hitler."

"Oh can't we just for once not mention *Hitler* at the dinner table he's so *hoy pal-oy*—"

"Stick to *scripted* writing, bubbie: you can't handle the ad-lib."

On his way back to the kitchen Schiff was waylaid by the orange-haired host: *What's your story, fella?*

"—'story'?"

"New in town? What are you doin' here? I know everybody in this place and I've never seen you. You're not another goddamn brother of Sunny's, areya?"

"You know Sunny—?"

"We go back. Almost to the time of Hannibal." He laughed at a private joke. "How come you're not in uniform?"

Why aren't *you*? Schiff wanted to reply.

"True you wanna be an actor?"

"Oh no. God no."

The man with the orange hair made a sweeping gesture around the table and said, "But everybody wants to be in pictures."

Not me, sir.

"Then tell us what you want to do in life . . ."

Schiff tried to back away. Something not too nice was threatening to happen.

"Come on, kid. Tell us what you want to be if you could crawl away from this hick town."

Something we can ridicule was the clear suggestion.

Schiff looked at him and said, "I'd put myself through college. Go to law school, be a lawyer and work for the United States government in the Department of the Interior."

—a comedian!

—kid's got a certain quality

Bobby give the kid a job

No one sees you when you're waiting tables, that was something he'd learned long ago. But this crowd, this "movie" crowd, had blinders on, as far as he could tell, specific to the lights and artifice of its own world. *I got contacts*, the man with the orange hair announced and handed Schiff his card. Four words were printed on it—BOBBY KAYE, ENTREPRENEUR. HOLLYWOOD.

Schiff and Vasco cleared the soup and brought the mains, accompanied by sides—roasted carrots, roasted beets, creamed spinach, black beans, white beans in oil and garlic, *frites* the French way (fried in duck fat), biscuits, *aioli*, *salsa verde*, corn *tortillas*. It was a lot of plates, a lot of carrying, a lot of coming and going from the table to the kitchen, and it took a while for Schiff to notice he could hear his breathing, that the conversation had all but ceased.

> *—did you try this?*
> > *—mine's delicious*
> > > *—taste it with the sauce*
> > > > *This lamb is better than the lamb at—*

Sound of people eating.

You're a hit, Schiff whispered to the chef.

The blond hair at her nape was dark with perspiration and pasted to the flesh behind her ears but when she turned to look at him there was a play of satisfaction on her lips.

The crowd got loud again as the plates were cleared (the alcohol was kicking in). Dessert was served family style—Lompoc lemon pie, Crater Lake Volcano chocolate cake, gingered orange peel, Pacific-salted caramels, spiced *pepita* brittle—and Vasco was pouring coffee while Schiff finished totaling the bill, and just as he had handed it to Bobby Kaye a telephone began to ring. The damndest thing: he didn't even know the restaurant had a telephone. He answered it. A voice asked, "—*chief?*"

He could barely hear above the crowd.

"*Svevo?*"

"We need your signature."

"—how did you get this number?"

"Don't insult me."

"—kinda busy, can't you forge it?"

"—no can do, boss, I got two by-the-number types from Griffith Park and Tuna Canyon Detention with work-release forms, they got 'MP' on their helmets and they need to prove you are who you say you are."

Schiff looked around the room. "Okay," he said. "I'll be right over."

He took the apron off and left it on the bar and braved the cold again, down Main Street to the Dow.

Jay and two MPs were waiting in the lobby. One look at them (the MPs) and Schiff could sum up how large a part humor was about to play in these proceedings (zero). They were tough-looking specimens within a tough-looking breed—*Army* cops, which is to say cop *cubed*, Army to a higher power, the *nth* degree of military regimen, law enforcement coupled to a shoulder rifle and a truncheon. They had driven up from Los Angeles (four hours) for the express purpose of implementing the release of one hundred men (*100 prisoners*) into Schiff's less rigorous authority for what seemed to them (or so their faces seemed to say) something like a picnic at the beach. This was not a Justice camp that Schiff was running, after all. What Schiff wanted was to use one hundred of these men (with the War Relocation Authority's approval) for indentured labor—he needed it *quick* and so this work-release arrangement was initiated. Men of Japanese ancestry already behind barbed wire for suspected treason would be let out to build camps to contain more Japs. No wonder the MPs couldn't crack a smile.

Plus they had to get his signature and drive four hours back.

In the dark.

"I appreciate you gentlemen coming all the way up here for this," Schiff said.

Their eyes told him: It's our fucking job.

Miraculously (or not, now that Schiff was getting used to Svevo's ministrations), Jay had brought Schiff's suit jacket from the upstairs rooms and Schiff slipped it on, trusting its fit would not only lend the needed guise of authority but also dispel the fog of garlic and tobacco that he carried from Lou's. The question *How did you ever manage without me?* flickered across Jay's eyes as

Schiff subtly ascertained his billfold was secure inside the breast pocket. His civil service identification card was there.

"Are you Mr. Schiff?"

"I am."

"May I ask you to verify that for me, sir?"

Schiff opened his billfold to the card's photograph which caught him looking drowsy and slightly criminal but served to prove to strangers who he was.

The MP handed him a clipboard with a form attached.

"If I can ask you to initial here and here and sign here, sir?"

Schiff held up a hand: it could drive subalterns crazy, especially in times like this, but he would never sign off on a document without having read it first, each word. The requisition had four copies and he read each one, making certain they were all the same. "Is there a detailed manifest attached to this?"

"They gave me a list," Jay told him.

"Is there a Jimmy Ikeda on it?"

"There are two Jimmy Ikedas on it."

Schiff nodded.

"Do you gentlemen require any food or a place to rest?"

No, sir, he was told.

"And what time can we expect delivery?"

"Fifteen hundred tomorrow, sir."

Schiff nodded again.

The four of them stepped outside and the shorter MP, the one who wasn't driving, asked, "Sir, where, exactly, *is* the camp?"

"Eight miles north."

A quick look passed between the MPs: "We drove up there. There's nothing there. Not even a fence."

Schiff and Jay stared at them, stone-faced—*oh ye of little faith!*—and stepped into the street to watch them speed away.

Buddy, we just ordered up two hundred souls denied their right of *habeas corpus* who have every reason to despise us and we've got no secure place to keep them.

Yep.

No place even to house them.

Tents will be here at the crack of dawn.

Nor anything to feed them.

Convoys being loaded as we speak. Tinned meat and powdered eggs. Plus a thousand CARE packages. Courtesy Red Cross.

—you *didn't* . . . !

I *did*. Plus eighteen hundred rolls of toilet paper.

Schiff noticed people coming out of Lou's, assembling around the cars. "I gotta go," he said, and handed Jay his suit jacket. "Have you eaten? Come up to the restaurant for a bite . . ."

"I gotta check on personnel . . . Jeez what's goin' on up there, look at those fur coats . . ."

Schiff sprinted back to Lou's and pressed through the crowd and helped them find their coats. He put the apron on and herded them a little so they'd leave the bar. He stepped back as the last one closed the door.

Sunny came out, hands on her hips.

"You did it," he told her.

"—feel like I've been up and down Mount Whitney, legs are killing me . . ."

They sat in adjacent chairs and Sunny swung her feet into his lap, that easy way she had in every moment with her body. Her shoes were ridiculous—he was used to quirky footwear on the average kitchen crew, everything from *sabots* to *mukmiks*—but Sunny's were like clown wear, a pair of big-toed rubber boots carved down to form a heel-less mule.

"Give us a rub," she pleaded. ". . . *pleeeeze?*"

He put his hands behind her calves. Her jeans were thin with age, and he felt her muscles, tight and steely, as he tried to knead them. *Hard* woman, he recognized. He moved his hands upward to behind her knees and then with a jolt imagined moving them higher.

"No one ate my hash," she pretended to complain.

—*yet*, he said.

"—really, are you starving? I'll get us some."

She slid her feet back off his knees.

"I'll do it, let me do it," he said, rising.

"—no, you get wine," she told him. "What else do you feel like having?"

". . . that *carpaccio* looked great. You could see right through it . . . how'd you slice it?"

But Sunny was already thinking of something else.

"Can you come to Three Chairs for dinner?" she asked Schiff.

He was moving toward the bar but he halted at the table's head:

"Dinner?"

"Saturday night."

He was about to answer when he saw something, a piece of paper, and looked at the empty table one more time.

"Sunny—?" He picked up the paper. "Did he pay you?"

She came back into view.

"Ask Vas if there was money on the table—"

Sunny said something to Vasco in his language (Schiff understood when she said *dollarrou*) and then she shook her head and Schiff went to the honesty jar and stared inside: two dollar bills, a dime, two bits . . . sonofa*bitch*!

He was in the middle of the empty street when Jay came up behind him:

"*Que pasa?*"

Sonsofbitches stiffed us . . . !

"Us"—? Jay was wondering.

They stared together down a darkness punctuated only by the neon bar sign at the northern end of town.

"How much they stiff 'us' for?"

"A hundred nineteen dollars."

Jay whistled. "Heading north?"

"Tahoe . . . Reno . . . I don't know, someplace up there."

"I got MPs I can call in Bishop. There's a tungsten plant up there. For some reason you and I will never fathom tungsten . . . at this hour, gets more coverage than the President . . ."

"You can do that?"

"I'm the U.S. Army, brother. I do anything I want."

Sunny came out from the restaurant and Jay pulled his shoulders back. He glanced at Schiff. *Okay,* he recognized. Plot thickens.

"—are they *gone?*" she said.

Schiff nodded.

Jay cleared his throat.

"This is Lieutenant Svevo, Sunny—Quartermaster Corps. Jay, this is Sunny Rhodes. She runs Lou's, best restaurant for miles around."

Sunny offered her hand and he collapsed a little through his thighs (nothing anyone could see) in response to its brusque strength but what really made him take a second look was the roughness of her skin. Here was one of the most arresting women he had ever seen (no makeup and still the eyes the skin the short-cropped hair the *look* were fall-down—"film"—stunning) but she had the hands (the *hand*) of a gorilla.

He noticed Schiff was looking at her like a puppy with a brand-new master and he had seen this wet-eyed look a hundred times before, patented by star-struck goofies (Bolger, Rooney, *Jimmy Stewart*) who fall for girls who always end up going off to live with Cary Grant.

"Jay says we can call MPs in Bishop. We can stop them," Schiff explained. "You just have to say the word."

Her *hero!* Jay was thinking—so it took him by surprise when, cold as Agnes Moorehead in *Kane*, Sunny answered *no*.

He watched her lay a hand on Schiff's forearm. *No*, she said again. "Just let them go."

Schiff laid his hand on top of hers, looked her in the eyes and asked, Are you certain?

Yes, she answered.

Jay watched him pat her hand again and move his face a little closer to hers. *Is this about the elephant?*

Hell *yes* Jay saw (even if Schiff couldn't): this was *all* about the big thing in the room, all about the big one, grey beast, massive thing, lust love romance— this was *the elephant* all right: Capital *ph*.

"Know what's funny? I'm just saying: the word *shiksa* could be Japanese. Could be the name of a Japanese pet or something . . . little *shiksa* dog."

"Six o'clock in the morning, Jay. Too early for your crap."

"We say o six hundred hours in the Army, Schiff."

"—o-six fucking degrees."

They were standing by the Army car on Main Street in front of the Dow waiting for the convoy with the wire and fence posts: enough timber, Jay contended, to lay a fucking boardwalk between here and Independence. Someone had made a fortune on the purchase order—that "someone" being the Department of Water of the City of Los Angeles. They had won the contract for timber (there had been no other bidders), as well as for sewage tanks and power lines and water pipes and, by Jay's reckoning, they had soaked the War Relocation Authority for double the real cost. "People making money off this war, man. We should send them to Germany. Speaking of Aryans, how come you never told me about Blondie—?"

"Tell me again why we're in the middle of the street instead of waiting where it's warm inside?"

"I don't like the way the lobby smells. Besides it's pretty out here. Stars still out. Snow-covered mountaintops. What's her story, is she single? Have you asked her out?"

Jay had found some Army boots for Schiff for the field work at the camp and they were chafing him around the ankles and he could feel the biting cold, already, through their soles.

"Can't we wait in the car and run the heater?"

"—bitch sinking poles today in frozen ground, glad all I have to do is push the paper. I was talking to the guy who's going to do my job at Poston—you know the camp planned for Arizona?"

"—I know all the sites, Jay. I was there when they unfolded the map."

"The site is on a fucking Indian reservation."

"They put all the camps on federal or municipal-held ground. Anti-profiteering."

"—yeah well they didn't count on the City of Los Angeles . . .—anyway this guy going to Poston says they got pre-fab barracks but aside from that they can't get lumber. They gotta make their own adobe bricks. Can you imagine? How do you make adobe bricks in winter, I mean—don't you need hot sun? 'Nother strange thing 'bout those Arizona camps, they've been ordered to grow *marigolds*. What the fuck is *that*? How does *that* help the war effort?"

"They use them in the powdered eggs. For coloring."

"No kidding. —how do you know that?"

"Like you say, I read too much."

"I take it back."

"Apology accepted."

"How are those boots?"

"I shoulda worn thicker socks."

A pair of headlights shone in the thinning dark—a truck—and they saw it was a solo, hauling north.

"So if you don't want to tell me about Blondie at least tell me about this Ikeda kid I had to pledge my first son to get down here."

"Was it difficult?"

"'Difficult' is for amateurs."

"I worked with him. Back in Chicago—he was a nice kid on the kitchen line. Chicago isn't even in the Exclusion Zone."

"File says they picked him up on suspicion of 'treasonous acts.' —*if*, in fact, this 'Jimmy Ikeda' is your guy . . ."

Schiff turned suddenly serious.

"—talk about 'suspicious.' Saw one last night."

"'One' what?"

"Japanese."

"In Lone Pine? That *is* funny. —just walking around?—what was he doing?"

"Ordering his supper."

"—you mean there was a guy in Blondie's place last night, a Japanese-American? Did you make a citizen's arrest?"

"Why would I do that?"

"—oh hell I don't know . . . because it's the law and you're a lawyer?"

"Like I said—he was ordering his supper."

"—oh you are really gonna hafta get your head in this. What if he had been a Nazi?"

"He wasn't a Nazi."

"—but what if he *had* been?"

"He was a Buddhist. Ordering his supper. Vegetarian."

"—*Hitler*'s a vegetarian!" Jay looked at his watch. "You had a legal obligation to detain the guy.—or at least ask some *serious* questions. You're in charge of the camp. Am I gonna hafta come behind you every night make sure you've locked the gate? If your head's not in this, Schiff, take my advice and take another job."

"Don't think I haven't thought about it. Joining up."

"—*are you crazy?*"

"Don't think I wouldn't like a shot at Hitler."

"—*mishpokhe*: they use boys like me and you for candles. It would kill your mother."

Schiff let out a snort which blossomed from his nose in vapor.

"Something my father could finally thank Hitler for."

Another set of headlights showed, too low to be a truck.

"She asked me on a date. I think."

Jay stopped mid-draw on a Camel and asked him, "How are you not still a virgin—? *Man*'s supposed to ask the *woman*."

"I was supposed to ask *her* out?—to *where*, exactly? There's nothing to do here but go out to eat and she already cooks at the only place in town worth going to." He let out another vaporous breath and said, "She asked me to come for dinner."

"When?"

"Last night. When we were closing."

"—no I mean *for* when?"

"Tomorrow night."

"Oh you gotta go with something."

"—yeah I know."

"—flowers, something."

"Tell me where I'm going to find flowers in this town in winter—"

Jay flicked the Camel to the street and smiled at him.

Schiff's parents had always told him, if invited, bring a little something.

Don't go empty-handed—it's an insult—and even though both his parents had washed up empty-handed on these shores (*un*invited) neither saw the irony in telling him, Don't knock without a token, little something in your hand. Home-cooked something *on a china dish*, "dish" being the key agent in the exercise because, like an echo, it had to find its way back, insuring future repeats. *She hasn't sent the dish back yet* was a thing no woman wanted to be said about her. About the dish (the plate) itself: it had to be "from over there," preferably from Poland, Russia or Bavaria; it had to be singular or prized and older than this century, have legible credentials, *the china mark*, still on it. Rivka's dish, Zeporah's dish, the dish belonging to the cantor's cousin's husband's mother: these were the guest dishes that came into the house and were revered, washed separately from other dishes, in different water (guest dish water), dried and wrapped, as something holy, waiting out a ritual. The *kreplach* dish, the *latke* dish, the "visiting" one—the dish iconography of the Jewish woman's kitchen made stepping in there hell (you never knew what you could touch). And if the kitchen was a place of such unbridled fear, imagine the other rooms. The memory—even now—of going out to other people's houses for a meal made Schiff feel like one of those rubes who had showed up at the Drake from Peoria afraid he'd brought his country manners to the table, terrified to choose a fork.

"I can get you flowers," Jay said, rising to the challenge. "Wha'dya want? Orchids? Orchids say, 'I'm classy.' "

"Orchids say *Hawaii* and her brother died at Pearl."

"—roses, then?"

"I'll think about it."

"Funny thing about women and flowers: I knew I'd fall in love with Beryl when she told me violets were her favorite. You can always tell about a woman from what flowers are her favorite."

And from her perfect food, Schiff thought.

A row of headlights—unmistakably the convoy—approached from the south and Jay touched him on the shoulder, said, "That's us." Schiff started the car and Jay stepped into the middle of the street and waved the truck to follow, then he got in and told Schiff, "Well . . . let's go make history," as Schiff headed through the silent town toward Manzanar.

IT HAD ALWAYS BEEN A NASTY LAKE, sulfuric, stinking like a lesion, brackish, yellow, good for nothing other than the incubation of mosquitoes, salt flies and the harlotting illusion—although seen from the heights of the Inyos the lake must have seemed a gift to westward-trending humans, it must have looked like gold, as lovely as a promised land (which, let's face it, can never really hold any *promise* without Water). Even now, when Rocky looked down on it from his standpoint on the Whitney trail in the Sierras—distant, ringed in white—he tasted water. But now there was another something in the distance, too—a ghost, transparent, grainy, like a faded photograph or an X-ray of a shadow in the lung: above the lake was a cloud of dust.

Rocky could remember the first day he'd seen it:

One big fucking cloud.

If he'd been living in the age of the Old Testament he would have chalked it up to God, to a brush with what William James called a "personal religious experience."

And the thing about it was that it was *moving*, stiffly, like a thing just born, gaining poise and learning—how to put this—*life*.

For a crazy moment he had even thought that It had eyes.

If It speaks, he remembered thinking, I might have to start a Church.

When, in the 20s, the bastards had drained the river of pure snowmelt that fed the lake, what had been left was a brackish muck that had reached a point of no return and—*hey presto*: lift-off. Earth flew.

They hadn't called their crime of engineering *drainage*; they'd called it "channeling," they'd called it "re-distributing," sometimes they'd called it "conveyance." (Rocky called it: *theft*.) Goddamn Bill Mulholland, biggest son-of-a-bitch ditch-digger who ever crawled out of the Irish Sea and goddamn the City he worked for and its spawn its thirsty ilk its rotted soul its bloated gullet, fuck 'em, fuck 'em all.

He could remember that first morning of The Dust as if it had been yesterday:

—the way The Thing had lifted off the surface, shredding after a few minutes in the wind, becoming nothing.

Only to return, next day.

And the next.

A daily winnowing—not of earth; of *lake*—a daily winnowing of what had once been water, although *sour* water, and was now a sour crust the chaff of which was like a bitter powdered sand polluting their air.

Down in the city, at the butt end of the pipe, they had named a road after Mulholland—*road to hell*, he hoped—and there were *swimming pools* on private properties and *fountains* in the public buildings. Inside every man he guessed there was a point at which the trigger springs, the point at which he guns the itching finger, and for him, that point was reached when anybody said the words *Los Angeles*.

The first time with the young attorney things had not gone well, Rocky hadn't liked him much even though he liked him somewhat better than the General, but now Sunny was telling him the fella wasn't half bad, that he seemed decent in a half-assed way, so he'd given her the nod to go ahead and ask the fella over to the house and he'd grill up some steaks and they could talk about the chances of Rocky getting all those Japanese, if they developed symptoms, to sign on with an *amicus curiae*.

He was in the *portales* getting the potatoes on the fire when the dogs put up a ruckus. Rocky opened the door before Schiff had parked the motorcycle and he watched him take the goggles off and navigate among the dogs. Even from a distance he towered above Schiff and as Schiff approached the older man loomed even larger, partly from his size but also, by no small measure, from his captive source of energy. *Intelligence*—Schiff could feel the assay of his host's experience, his mind, the older man searching for Schiff's assets, weighing him for value.

"Mr. Rhodes—"

"Come on in."

Up close there was an aroma coming off his clothes and skin as if he had been tending kindling and he held a cut glass tumbler of what Schiff thought might be scotch or bourbon.

"Get rid of your coat so we can get you started on the liquid sustenance . . ."

Rocky watched Schiff shrug the stiff fabric from his shoulders then he took the coat and placed it on a peg in the bell tower, which served as a vestibule, left of entrance.

"Oh, but—"

Schiff remembered that he'd put a gift for Sunny in the pocket of his coat and reached for it.

"For the hostess."

Seemed to make no sense to Rocky.

"Kindly of you," Rocky said and started to rip the wrapping open with his free hand (the one missing the two fingers) and Schiff, in a momentary seizure of a kind of panic, took the present back.

(He'd settled, after all the talk with Svevo about flowers, on a book already in his hotel room—a cookbook—a guide to Japanese culinary practices which he knew Sunny could appreciate but which might seem insensitive to the father of a son killed at Pearl Harbor.)

". . . it's a cookbook," Schiff explained. "For Sunny," he added.

"Well, all right," Rocky acknowledged, "we'll leave it in the kitchen where she'll find it." He led the way.

His back, Schiff noticed, was straight and broad and the queue of white hair at his neck was bound in (this was shocking) wine-colored satin. The hall floor was tiled, Spanish style, in burnished terracotta squares; the white adobe walls partitioned by dark wood and works of art.

"This is a beautiful home—" Schiff started to admire.

Rocky turned and told him: Built it all, my own two hands. He raised his mangled claw to illustrate. Ground up, he added. Every inch. Just like you, over there across the road, with your Utopia.

Schiff locked his gaze:

"Are we going to fight about the camp?"

"Prob'ly. Let's find you that liquid courage first."

They were halted in the hallway in front of a painting of a Western landscape—blue mountains in the distance, sun-soaked foreground, purple sunset; and there was something about the orientation or the shadows, something coming from the sky onto the land that looked familiar. Yep that's the place, his host confirmed: "The view from over there" (he pointed long, beyond the walls). "Maynard Dixon. Interesting fella. Giant hatsize. You probably know his wife's photography . . ." (turning to the facing wall:) "Dorothea. There's a German for you. Breaks the mold. You probably know these pictures from her time with Frank's New Deal Works Program . . ."

Schiff turned to see a photograph of a woman with a distant desperate stare, gaunt jaw resting in her hand, unkempt children hanging on her.

"I'm not a . . . connoisseur of art," Schiff remarked.

He saw the little muscles around Rocky's eyes adjust to a new vision of him.

"But you read," Rocky said.

He gestured to the gift Schiff clutched.

Again, that readjustment in the old man's focus:

"Who's your favorite character in Shakespeare?"

"—'favorite'?"

"One that pushes blood through you."

Schiff was at a loss, he knew some people read Shakespeare—actually sat down and *read out* all the parts—but he wasn't one of them, although he'd had to read the three most commonly taught in college (*Hamlet, Romeo and Juliet, Lear*). The only Shakespeare play he'd witnessed on the stage had been *The Merchant of Venice* in a university production because the student he was dating had a minor part and he wanted to get laid.

"I'm not well-versed enough in Shakespeare to answer that," he answered.

"Take a stab."

"Based on the three plays I've read . . . Cordelia."

This got a smile (eyes only, not the mouth).

"I was forced back by that little jumped-up Nazi into *Richard* Three last night, looking for some insight into character. Read a piece in *The New Repub-*

lic says this Adolf was a painter in his youth: so there's your art appreciation—
or as you call it, *connoisseur*ship—"

Schiff could hear voices down the hall coming from what he supposed
might be the kitchen and he hoped he'd find Sunny there to help him out of
this.

Rocky started down the hall again, talking with his back to Schiff.

"—antic diabolism. You take Richard: compound of charm and terror.
They say Hitler has the charm in person—I don't see it, he's a clown to me—
my father would have laughed him from his office and you have to wonder
what Emerson would have to say about the little shit."

On Schiff's left the wall opened to a courtyard lit by lanterns where a black
horizontal barrel-shaped contraption was spewing smoke.

"—Evian in '38. Thirty-two countries, including us, had the chance to
censure him for all his refugees, on 'human rights,' and we let the bastard get
away with it. Fucking Chamberlain, excuse my French—"

Rocky strode into the kitchen, and Schiff stopped on the threshold to take
the whole thing in.

It seemed bigger than the hotel kitchen at the Drake.

"Chamberlain was not the modern man we needed," Rocky went on,
"—reality outstripped him—he was coming at the little monster from a previous century's perspective, hell his mental world could not contain a character
like Hitler—he obviously also had not read his Shakespeare—you can't fight
the Bard on character, what's your poison, what can I get for you to drink?"

"This is some kitchen."

"Well there's a story to it . . . What are you having?"

On one of the large tables there were two bottles of French wine, one
of which had been decanted into crystal, next to two wineglasses. Beside
them there were two small white plates, each filled with green ovals in bright
contrast to the porcelain—a dish of tiny green olives and a plate of shelled
pistachios.

"I'm drinking my own *calvados*—" Rocky said, "—hard cider I made from
the apple trees that used to grow there on your Manzanar—but I've got a
pretty well-stocked bar, so anything you want . . ."

"I'll have a beer."

"—one *cerveza*, comin' up."

There were two iceboxes, Schiff noticed—there seemed to be *two* of everything—those two wineglasses, those two plates, two stoves, two long tables, two stone double sinks, two flattops, two butcher's blocks, two fireplaces. Copperware hung from iron racks over the stoves, and pans and bowls stood at the ready on the shelves above the tile work counters. Rocky quartered a small lime with neat strokes then took a bottle from an icebox, opened it, and plugged a lime wedge with his thumb into the bottle neck, handed it to Schiff and raised his drink: "Two chairs," he toasted. (Schiff heard it as, "To chairs!" until Rocky added:) "To conversation—!"

Schiff tried to suck some suds past the citrus while he wondered where Sunny was and why the wineglasses on the table were only "two."

Rocky signaled Schiff to sit and pushed the white dish of olives at him as he grabbed a handful of pistachios.

"Sorry it's not daylight or I'd walk you 'round the outside so you can see the kitchen's out of scale. Double the size I drew it, throws the profile of the building out of balance when you look at it from out there"—he pointed—"but I make no bones about the fact I built this out of love—took me two years start to finish—I was building it to lure my future bride out here, and it's the kitchen that Lou wanted." He looked around him. "Lot of eating's come through here."

For Schiff, the penny was about to drop:

"—'*Lou*,'" he repeated.

"Sunny's and Stryker's mother . . . Stryker is my other child."

"I'm sorry, Mr. Rhodes—"

"*Rocky*. Everybody calls me Rocky."

"—so the restaurant . . . '*Lou's*' . . ."

"—Sunny's place in town, yeah . . ."

"—it's named for Sunny's mother?"

(Why didn't she just *say* that, he was wondering . . .)

"Both those women, boy, I'll tell you, cooking's in their blood—I read 'Self-Reliance' in my days at school but what Emerson can't teach you, living by yourself on horseback will. I had to teach myself to be a dab hand with a cut of beef, a pot of beans, but Lou brought magic the way she cooked—talk about your art appreciation—my god the meals we've had here—and Sunny, well she picked it up like it was natural to her and then went off from there . . ."

"Where *is* Sunny?"

Rocky cocked his head: "At Lou's. Saturday's the big night."

Schiff hoped he hid his disappointment.

"I thought maybe after that big crowd the other night she'd take a night for herself—"

Rocky studied him.

"You're referring to the asshole Bobby Kaye and his traveling circus . . . That's a story that requires more drink for the telling. Come on, let me take you on the two-bit tour and then we'll sit down to some chow and talk of kings and solve the problems of this too-flawed world . . ."

Rocky led him back into the hall, pausing at a farther archway to tell Schiff, "This is Cas's wing back here—a late addition—"

Schiff gestured to a photograph framed in wood on the wall—

"The President?"

"We spent our summers with the family."

"We?"

"My sister and myself."

Rocky pushed through into the *portales.* He showed Schiff the workshops, some of which had been converted to guest rooms (the place was as big as a hotel in size, Schiff thought), then they stopped in Rocky's woodshop (which smelled of applewood and sawdust) to look at his chairs and Rocky showed Schiff through Lou's old *clinica*, telling him about the work his wife had done among the resident Indian and Mexican populations. Schiff was struck by the reverence that modulated Rocky's voice when he spoke about his wife—and about his children and his sister—but he noticed that the stories seemed to circle back to when both Lou and Stryker had been living. When Rocky spoke of Stryker, he always ended before the war, as if Stryker's narrative, for his father, was a tale of past events and what had happened at Pearl Harbor was, merely, its coda.

Rocky grilled thick steaks and Schiff took off his suit coat and assisted laying service at the table in the dining room. Sunny had left a *sauce béarnaise* and they brought it, the steaks, the roast potatoes and the red wine—lit the candles—and sat down to their repast in a room that looked to Schiff (who had never been to Europe) like a throwback to Ferdinand and Isabella. The table was carved of darkened wood, so were the elaborate chairs, and on top of the sideboard, which ran the whole length of one wall, was an ancient uniform edition of the collected works of William Shakespeare, Bard.

"What brought you out here in the first place—to this particular valley?" Schiff asked.

"Well I'll tell you," Rocky said—and then proceeded to relate the story of his wanting to live differently than his father had done ("All the *Henry* plays—") but being conflicted by his father's shadow ("*Hamlet*") and his own inheritance. Punch (Schiff surmised this was the family name for Rocky's father) had let Rocky leave school early and kept him on a stipend on the condition that, if Rocky insisted on traveling West, he perform as field agent and report back on Wellington Rhodes properties—the land and mineral holdings—as he made his way across the map. Rocky told Schiff he had just spent three weeks in Death Valley at his father's borax mines when he'd come across the Panamint and Inyo mountains on horseback to the Cerro Gordo lead and zinc lode, and he decided to make camp that night beside Owens Lake. "Back before they came here, the water people from the city to the south—this was thirty years ago—spring of 1912. First thing that happened was—that very night—there was a moonbow in the sky as I was sitting beside the fire."

"I don't know what a 'moonbow' is," Schiff admitted.

"It's a rainbow, except cast by the light of the moon."

"—at night?—all the colors?"

"Scares the life right out of you. And I was young, you know—what choice had I but to take it as a sign. Next morning—remember this is a long time ago, before the Great War—before the modern age—I went down to the water's edge and I happened to turn north and look up at the sky and all of a sudden I saw this thing like the whole blue sky breaking into pieces."

He sat silently a moment.

"It was the snow geese coming in—hundreds of them, thousands—from up north—white wings taking on blue light—waves and waves of them, swooping down on Owens Lake—"

"—I *saw* them . . . !—just the other day . . . I didn't know what kind of geese they were but I saw a couple hundred of them try to land . . ."

"Then I guess you saw them *crash*."

Rocky took a sip of wine:

"—they keep coming. Back then I took those two phenomena as something in the cosmos sending me a message—as if Earth exists to auger personal Fate—I thought *divine intervention*—I thought what a remarkable sight—the Sierra Nevadas, plentiful water, beautiful lake . . . You go out there now to Owens Lake this time of year in the midst of their migration—it's too painful. Ghost in their memory, some code written in their blood they keep coming back—or maybe the mineral surface looks like water up there in the sky. They keep coming down like they are going to land on water—you know those big goose feet—breaking their legs when they hit crusted salt. I guess if you were out there then you must have seen 'the cloud.'"

Schiff nodded.

"That's the whole lake going up in air. That ochre dust?—that's all that's left of Owens Lake. And that dust—? —son, this valley is a suction tube you can't hardly stand sometimes the wind comes blasting from the north or south or roaring down the east face of those mountains."

What Schiff hadn't given any notice to at the far end of the sideboard was a stack of what he now recognized as legal files toward which Rocky gestured.

"I've been in a holy war against the sonsabitches thirty years—lost my wedding finger and my wedding band: I can't win, on most fronts. Teddy Roosevelt decided that way back when he handed out his Executive privilege to the city to the south—'*Needs of the many outweigh the needs of the few*'—and fucked us Owens Valley farmers front and back, excuse my French. I can't beat 'em, I know that—I've spent the greater part of my half of my father's fortune trying to. But *this case*—" He pointed to the stack of files again: "I think I have a shot."

The key, he went on, was dust mitigation.

Schiff knew what "mitigation" meant—it meant "moderation." Every post-Depression corporate lawyer had lost his milk teeth on the finer points of debt restructuring and although corporate law had never been his field of expertise Schiff had heard the words a thousand times—*debt mitigation*—and knew that "to mitigate" was to make a situation less severe (from the Latin *mitis*, meaning "soft").

But *dust* mitigation?

That was the term Rocky's lawyers had come up with in this latest case against the Department of Water in Los Angeles—"mitigation" because people were getting sick breathing the air polluted by the dust that blew off the drained lake and Rocky's latest case was after the city to the south to pay up.

"Sunny said she thought you could be sympathetic to my cause—so that's why I had her ask you here."

Schiff's heart sank. *He* had asked him here. Not Sunny.

"Old Doc Bridges here in Lone Pine—nice man, bit outdated: no one you'd want to have to visit for brain surgery—he's deposed. He's had a lot of people coming in with breathing problems since the water from the lake was drained. And Doc Skogerson in Independence has testified—neither one could hold a candle in their know-how to my Lou—but the problem's in the proof. The other side contends there's the absence of a baseline—no medical index of the incidence of geriatric emphysema or pediatric asthma going back to before the bastards started stealing. So we can't prove that those disorders have arisen *solely* from the water being lifted from the resident environment or even that they have increased significantly. But *you* . . ." He leaned toward Schiff: "—*you* got 10,000 possible new case studies coming in."

All Rocky wanted Schiff to do was to agree to have the internees—especially the children and the elderly—examined by the camp's doctors at the outset of their confinement on the valley floor for breathing problems and irritations to their eyes and throats.

"I pray as much as any man this war is over sooner than later but if we're in it for a course of years then we're going to have these individuals as our neighbors for quite some time—and if, during their confinement, they start to develop problems with their eyes and throats, their lungs, then we get a baseline that can be backed up with real data. Will you help me do that—?"

"I hope you're not suggesting that you *want* these individuals to develop symptoms—"

"—*god no.*—god . . . *no.*"

Schiff could see he'd struck a blow to the man's honor and wondered which play of Shakespeare's covered *that*.

"My own wife . . ." He paused. "I wouldn't wish disease of any kind on anyone. Especially not the lungs." He paused again, his focus moving to an empty space against the farthest wall. "She died right over there," he said and Schiff was shocked, afraid to turn his head and look. "We put the iron lung in here, in the midst of where we ate, close to the kitchen, at the center of our family life. Stryker used to sleep beneath—you could hear the bellows echo through the house forcing air into her lungs. Night she died she turned her head to me and barely whispered, '—*drowning*.' And I knew that it was over. Fluid fills the lungs, that's how it kills—You drown in your own fluid." He had started to tap out a gradual rhythm on the table; a dirge. "Don't think I don't lie awake at night picturing the way Stryker must have died—the likelihood that he was in the water when the planes came in, that he drowned. Don't think that I don't think about those two deaths, I do. The similarities. They haunt me. Death by drowning."

Schiff was mortified. No one in his experience—certainly no one in his family—had ever dared to speak their private thoughts so openly, and on the face of it Schiff might have thought the man was drunk except that there was nothing maudlin in his manner, nothing bathetic or sentimental, simply *bare*, a man soliloquizing on his tragedy.

"'Too much water hast thou, poor Ophelia/And therefore I forbid my tears . . .' *Hamlet*," Rocky told him: "Act Four, Scene Seven. Spoken by Laertes when he learns his sister's dead. '. . . *Too much water hast thou* . . .'" He stopped his finger drumming, placed his palm down on the table. "—tried to teach my children everything they will face in life has been faced before, by others, that it wasn't only *Christ* who'd died for them but the heroes of those former literatures—Prometheus and Hector—and then, much later, Ophelia and your Cordelia." He paused to interpret Schiff's unblinking silence. "You must think I am a madman in my castle."

"—*yes*. I do."

"Well then," Rocky told him. "There's a real chance I could warm to you."

It was after midnight when Rocky walked him to the door:

"Are you all right on that motorcycle—? —free to hole up here the night. Standing invitation."

Schiff, like any self-deluding drunk, walked purposefully to the bike—*hello, Rita Hayworth, honey*—and slid the goggles somewhat crookedly over his eyes. Rocky stood in the open door to safeguard his departure and Schiff braved a farewell wave (*whoopsie!*) and managed to keep Rita upright until the first turn in the dirt road where he could be assured that he was out of Rocky's sight and then he cut sweet Rita's engine, tore the goggles off his head and rocked the motorcycle back onto its stand. He extinguished the headlamp and sat there in cold silence underneath a canopy of bright stars.

Even had he known where to look for constellations—even had he known their names—the overpatterned sky was teeming with too many points of light to find a logical geometry. Once his eyes adjusted to the dark, he could discern in the distance, to the north, the ghostly snow-capped peaks of the Sierras and, now and then, between him and the horizon, a fluttering within the dark, quick black wings against black foreground; the night as quiet as a boneyard, until, on listening, a rustling habitat emerged—wind through winter scrub, a skittering, a rasp, an owl, a howl, a twig snap—and then, subtly audible, a noise beneath, a distant hum, a motor idling, a cough, a shout, a laugh, the clang of metal like the clanging of iron rigging on a boat: the camp.

They were still a skeleton crew—the internees from Griffith Park and Tuna Canyon Detention, as well as the MPs, and some men from the Army Corps of Engineers—but you could hear them, even in the dead of night. Schiff turned the headlamp on and walked the motorcycle down the dirt road to the highway and went across to where two empty troop transports had been pulled up across the "gate" to secure the entrance and where he found two MPs in front of the perimeter of the newly built barbed-wire fence with their service rifles focused on him:

"—oh, Mr. Schiff, sir.—had you in my sights for fifteen minutes, lucky thing I didn't shoot you. Thought someone was trespassing out there where the airfield's gonna be . . ."

Schiff looked along the line of fence posts and glanced up at the guard tower where there was another rifle aimed at him.

"You comin' in, sir?"

Schiff nodded, and the MP jotted something on a clipboard. "Lieutenant Svevo has you in the first tent to the left, sir."

"Which tent is Lieutenant Svevo's?"

"I believe Lieutenant Svevo shares your quarters, sir. But the lieutenant is off-base."

"—'off-base'?—where?"

"He didn't say, sir. But he said he'd only be an hour. And that was forty minutes ago, sir."

"He didn't say where he was going?"

"No, sir."

"But he's the ranking officer. You're supposed to know where the ranking officer is at any given moment."

"—yessir."

They had gotten the fence up in record time—they had the tents and the cots deployed and the mess tent fitted out and provisioned, but even in the half-light of the propane lanterns Schiff could see how temporary it looked, how fragile.

He wheeled Rita to the designated tent—Svevo had nailed a hand-painted sign CAMP ADMINISTRATOR outside—and went in through the closed flaps to see that Jay had ordered up two cots and a coal stove which, thankfully, was generating heat. Until the telephones were in and the electric power up, Schiff would conduct camp business from the Dow, but he didn't feel like traveling back in his condition so he picked up a pillow from the foot of the nearest cot and began to make himself at home. Then, once more, he heard the clanging sound—regular and metallic—like a sound you'd hear lakeside, down where the boats were kept. There were other sounds—men's voices, the wind in the tent sheets—but this one sound, repetitive and inexplicable, drew him from the shelter of the tent back into the open compound.

And there it was—he didn't know how he had missed it: eighty, maybe a hundred feet high, nothing flying as of yet but how the hell had they gotten the fucking *flagpole* up so soon—?

Headlights hit him as he stood gaping and a Jeep pulled up and Jay jumped out and said, "—*hey*. How was your date?—didn't think I'd see you here tonight, hopin' you'd get lucky . . ." One look at Schiff supplied an answer. "—*ouch*. What happened?"

"The date was with her *father* . . . Where the hell have you been in the middle of the night?"

"I had to drive to Independence."

"—at midnight? What for?"

"I had to go to the post office."

"—why?"

Jay reached inside his jacket and pulled out a bunched-up flag.

"You stole a flag. From Federal property."

"I 'requisitioned' it. We're 'Federal property,' too—I mean you order one of these things you'd think they'd send *a flag* along—Come on, let's get this baby up, do you know how to do this?" He started to unfurl the flag but it blew back over his head, covering his face. Schiff reached for the rope on the flagpole and began to pull the tackle down while Jay wrestled with Old Glory. "There should be two grommets on the side that has the stars," Schiff said.

"—listen to you: 'grommets' . . ."

"—you got it down, Jay, you should know how to get it *up* . . ."

"—I *cut* it down . . ."

"—here let me do this . . ." Schiff took the flag from him ("—don't let it touch the ground—" "—don't be so prissy—") and, somehow, they got it attached without debasing it and Schiff hauled it, flapping like a banshee, to the top and tied it off.

It went like crazy up there, in the wind.

"Well," Jay said: "I guess we are official. Should we salute, or something?"

Or *something*, Schiff agreed.

All that night and all the next day—and all through the following weeks and years—that whipping noise, that *cracking* sound, the sound of that flag flying in relentless wind, was the sound that would dominate the camp—more than all the sirens, more than all the mess hall sirens, curfew sirens, air raid drills and fire drills—the noise, at night, the noise all day, of that flag battling the wind is what would keep them all awake. Some people said it was the sound of a cracked whip, some people said it sounded like doors slamming— but for Schiff that first night as he tried to get some rest all he heard was the persistent sound outside of a noise reminding him of distant shooting.

Shots heard 'round the world.

the third
property of thirst
is
memory

THERE HAD BEEN TWO GODS (OVERLORDS) IN HIS MOTHER'S KITCHEN, Schiff told Sunny: Overcook and Oversalt.

This—not only this—had made her laugh.

"The Overcook and Oversalt are daily gods—hard workers, seven days a week, never slag off, never take vacation, at your table breakfast lunch—and, here, they shine: the evening nosh, by which I mean the meal you eat at sundown, five o'clock, sometimes earlier, in winter. Which means that They and Ma have been up since daybreak, boiling. Overcook can take a cabbage or a carrot and reduce it to a liquid state. I never knew a leaf of cabbage was not a see-through object until I graduated college. Never knew that 'rare' or 'raw' were words that could describe food, remember seeing beans and onions in their natural states on the carts of a street vendor and wondering, *What are those? What is this exotic delicacy?* Everything was cooked beyond a fork- or tooth-requirement. Celery? Liquid. Beets? Like aspic. Onions? Jam. Meats? Ever grey, including liver—or, in the case of chicken, cooked beyond white: cooked to Death. Never pink. And never, never, never brown."

"—but, still: you learned what 'aspic' is."

"From working at the Drake Hotel. Oversalt, by the way? Sometimes a god identified only by its absence—like a vengeful Yahweh playing hide-and-seek. Sometimes you'd get a plate that seemed to cry out in the desert *O, Salt!* Why hast thou deserted me? *Egg salad*—right where Oversalt was needed—not a grain in sight. *Knaidlach*? Never salted. *Matzo brei*? The same. *Overcooked*; but never salted. Whatever she could do to ruin something, Ma had the culinary genius to accomplish it."

"—what's a . . . *k-naidlach*?"

Another of those moments, not uncommon, that distanced her from him.

"A ball of dough, like a dumpling—made from crushed up matzos."

On her look (capable of leaping a great distance in a single bound):

"Matzos are the unleavened 'bread' Jews carried into exile—no time to let the dough rise—*flat*bread. Dried, they're like a tasteless cracker. No, that's not true: they taste like roasted flour. Desperately in need of salt. When Pop sometimes complained a dish was oversalted, Ma would answer, 'From my tears.' Every time he tasted her matzo balls he said, 'Over this, you couldn't cry enough?'"

"Used to be . . . salt was a measure of wealth. People at kings' banquets would be seated 'below the salt' according to their status, so being oversalted was a sign that you were—"

"Believe me, honey, we weren't rich."

"All the same: I envy you the memory."

"The memory of awful cooking—?"

"—of a *mother's* cooking."

She hadn't meant to play the pity card and quickly covered it:

"Philosophically the big question for cooks is whether their job—'cook'-ing—is to ennoble natural flavors—to showcase the 'thing'-ness of a stalk of celery—or a matzo, say—or to invent a tasteful way to disguise food that's 'gone off' or has 'no flavor.' Hence, French sauces . . ."

"—the French god 'Oversauce' . . ."

"—and the saucy French word *nappe*, which means 'cover' with sauce. Same word for 'sheet'; same word for *nap*kin."

Until that moment the portrait he'd been painting of her in his mind had been of a kind of Nordic goddess, perfect in her pale blond beauty, privileged, though rusticated, wealthy—very wealthy—but provincial. She had grown up in a valley where the public school—all the grades—numbered fewer than sixty students, and she kept goats. Her hands were as rough as a working man's. She seemed well-read and witty but, as far as he could see, the scope of her existence had played out between two California mountain ranges in a narrow place not known for its sophistication.

"How do you know . . . *French*?" he asked.

"*Ma mere etait une francaise.*"

"—'*Lou.*' Short for 'Louise'?"

"Short for 'Louisiana.'"

" 'French' French?—or Cajun French?"

"French French." She smiled at him. "How did it *smell*? Your mother's kitchen. When she was cooking."

The question prompted different thoughts and she could read, by watching him, that some of them were pleasant.

"I'd come home from school . . . and I could smell the meat. I guess the *fat* of it—is that what causes the aroma? Carrots. Onions. The aromas of it. Always better than the taste."

"*Sense memory,*" she said. "Cooks try to lard each plate with it. But most times it's out of one's control because each person's sense memory is different. My brother's, for example. You know that aroma of hot wax you get when you blow out a candle? Every time he caught a whiff of it, Stryker would say, 'Smells like birthday cake.' And my aunt—whenever I bring dill into the house she thinks she's back in Scandinavia."

"What do you remember?"

"About what?"

"About the way your mother cooked."

Her mother's death was none of this stranger's business and she was not willing to admit to him she had no memory of her mother as a person, to say nothing of her mother as a taste or smell. Her mother on a plate. Her mother-in-the-kitchen. Sometimes she thought she could remember the metallic hum of the iron lung and the so-called memory of it inspired a metallic taste, a nickel on her tongue. After Cas had turned over her mother's "box of recipes" (box of cryptic cards) Sunny (at a period in life when she and Stryker had discovered murder mysteries and were reading them in secret) had set out to "interview" the witnesses, depose the people who could testify about her mother, reconstruct if not her person then the way she cooked. "Well you know," she'd been told on more than one occasion, "she used to come around here, too, with her notepad. Take down family recipes. She even interviewed the Indians. She was writing her own book."

There's no evidence of that, Sunny had taught herself to answer. No evidence at all.

"Well it must be *some*where 'cause I seen her write it down myself."

"Was Maman writing a book when she died?" Sunny had finally asked Cas.

"I don't think so, button. I wouldn't know. Ask your father."

So one night at dinner: "Tops, where's the book Maman was writing when she died?"

There *is* no book. There *was* no book. There *is* no way to replicate her cooking. All of that is gone. Put to ground, along with her.

Sense memory:
—something that's been buried; coffined.

It had been clear, from early on, that Sunny had her mother's instincts, her mother's touch for food, but how much of that had been inherited (Stryker had none of it) and how much had been manufactured out of Sunny's need to fashion her own self into "her mother's daughter"?

Her father had enshrined her mother's little clinic, her doctor's office at the far end of the *portales*, but her mother's kitchen had, of necessity, been kept in a much less sacred way. Her specialty pans and cookbooks receded slowly, glacially, as daily needs dictated. Who was going to need the copper *bain-marie*? the *chinoise*? The volumes (in their original French) of *La Bonne Cuisine de Mme. E. Saint-Ange* or *La Physiologie du gout*?

TELL ME WHAT YOU EAT AND I WILL TELL YOU WHO YOU ARE

She knew her mother had believed this—she had heard from many people, including the Paiutes and Shoshones, about her interest in Native American Indian foods—but she would have never guessed that the catchy slogan had been originated by an 18th-century Frenchman with the un-catchy name of Jean Anthelme Brillat-Savarin, whose book, along with scores of others, she had found pushed back on a wide shelf in the kitchen.

Hidden to make room for Rocky's fishing lures and things that he and Stryker brought in daily from the outside: birds' nests, feathers, stones, dead insects. The needs of daily life after her mother's death had replaced the need for cookbooks and her mother's volumes (some in English, most in French) had been preserved *in situ*, but concealed, both in distance and in time, by the detritus of the present. Still, there they were, as Lou had left them, the last person to have touched them, and Sunny's thrill in opening each one was as great, surreal, and unexpected as traveling, backwards, into time. Inside, there were stains on pages (some had blossomed, mossy, thriving on the sugars in the paper like hothouse penicilla), page notes in her mother's ink (all in a bold, distinctive hand), pressed stems and leaves and—most thrilling—pages of thin blue paper on which her mother had written what appeared, on first inspection, to be completed recipes (but, once translated, never were).

POUR PREPARER LA VINAIGRETTE, *MELANGEZ*

la moutarde et la vinaigre jusqu'a
l'obtention d'une sauce onctuese.
Ajoutez l'huile d'olive petit a petit
et assaisonnez de sel et de poivre

TRUFFES
Hachez les truffes.
Chauffez la graisse d'oie dans la cocotte
et addez les truffes

For a girl of ten, translation from French to English was only the beginning of the problem—first she had to make her way through the penmanship (*d'une* or *dure*? *oui* or *oie*?) and this she did by writing out each word, along with its variations, and looking up the meanings in the French/English dictionary she'd found in her father's library (then looking up the meanings of the English words in the larger, more difficult to understand *Oxford*). *Unctuous*? (She as-siduously wrote out, "*Having the quality or characteristics of oil or ointment; greasy.*") *Truffle*? ("*Any of various edible, fleshy, subterranean fungi, chiefly of the genus* TUBER.") "Subterranean"? *Fungi*?

After a morning going back and forth among the words and meanings (after she'd finished her other chores) she might end up with this:

EEL *(PREPARATION DE L'ANGUILLE)*
To kill an eel, seize it with a cloth
And bang its head violently against a hard surface.
To skin it, put a noose around the base
of its head and hang it up.
Slit the skin in a circle just beneath the noose.

Pull off the skin, working from the
head toward the tail.
Cut off the head, discard the fins
and draw out the flesh.

Grill and slice.

"Have you ever seen an eel, Cas?"

"Oh yes: I've eaten them. In Scandinavia. Smoked the way Rocky smokes our trout. Except the eel is black and shiny."

"—any good?"

"On rye with lemon, and a healthy slug of *aquavit*: not bad. Better than eating SHOE."

Aquavit, she'd written down: "*(Particular to Norway.) A potent brew of carraway and potatoes, spiced with anise, fennel and coriander.*" (Even in En-glish, the only food-word she recognized in that description was "potatoes.")

After a month of daily application, Sunny had "translated" (she used the word loosely, but with pride) her mother's notes on how to sauté truffles and prepare a vinaigrette (although she still had to ascertain proportions or to what use a "vinaigrette" might be applied), but she then had to learn to cook a food that anyone might want to *eat*.

Boil *until all the goodness in the pan* has been
absorbed into the stock

What did this *mean*? Was "the goodness in the pan" something to be *seen*? What did it look like? How was she to know when it had been "absorbed"?

Laissez froider.

Servez aussitot.

She had no ear for French—if her mother had ever spoken to them in French, Sunny had been too young to remember—and each word she'd learned to say "in translation" she said in her own straightforward English way. *Pain perdu*: "pane per doo." It had been the first thing she'd taught herself to cook. (If you didn't count coffee, fried egg sandwiches and bacon.)

Damn good French toast, Rocky had rewarded her.

No, Tops, it's pane per doo.

(This had brought her aunt and father to near tears of laughter:)

"—where did you learn *that*?"

"From Maman's cookbook *Lee Kway Zine*."

"Oh god, Rock: there's an American in Lou's French kitchen!"

Sunny's French would always betray the auto-didact, but worse than that— at the start, at least—her way of learning marooned her in the imperative:

faites cuire
faites bouiller
faites chauffer la graisse
faites fondre la buerre

There is no "I" in French *recettes*. *You* chop, *you* mince, *you* boil; the *I* does not exist. "I" do not chop, "I" do not boil—first person singular is, in general, absent from instruction, so should one depend on cookbooks as a gateway to a foreign language, one is going to find oneself without, first, a pronoun and, second, a conjugated verb.

Furthermore, "you make" is always "*vous faites*": nowhere in French cook-books can you find the *tu* of true intimacy, so Sunny's French to a Francophone always bore the formalism of a chef, a *chef-d'oeuvre*, of instruction. Not until she happened on the volumes of Escoffier and Brillat-Savarin (which she had been avoiding, owing to their seeming difficulty) did she discover her first culinary *je* (which she pronounced "gee") and those singular appearances made her feel, at once, as if their tutoring was personal. (Not even in her mother's notes had she encountered the long sought-after "gee," and when she first saw its letters she had no idea what they meant.) How comforting (for a young girl, at least) to find *a personality* on those pages—even if it wasn't, at first, the personality she'd been seeking—how calming and companionable: here's what *I* believe, here's what *I*'ve experienced, *I*'ve learned this, this is a gift from *me*. There he was, August Escoffier, speaking to her from the 19th century, addressing her directly; there he was, Brillat-Savarin, enumerating senses from the start

la vue	sight
le son	hearing
l'arome	smell
le gout	taste
le toucher	touch

knowing *she* could share them, knowing *anyone* could share them, *humanizing* the whole culinary endeavor.

> ". . . and lastly (*et enfin*), the sense of
> *le desir*,
> which *brings the two sexes together*
> and whose aim is the reproduction of the species."

Her mother had underlined the words "*reunis les deux sexes*" in purple ink, next to which, in the right-hand margin, she had written "*exacte*" followed by an exclamation mark ("*!*").

Sunny remembered that she hadn't known then, nor would she know for quite some time, what the words meant (neither the French nor their English translation) but she'd recognized, even then, that she was staring at a secret, at a moment in her mother's life when she'd been moved enough by something on the page to print her own assent of it, her seal of approval. She had no way of knowing how old her mother might have been when she'd left the exclamation mark, but there it was, in black and white (well, *purple*) as fresh as if her mother had just set it down. This was a *direct contact* to the way her mother thought and even though Sunny hadn't understood (could not have understood, at ten) what *le desir* imparted, she had guessed, rightly, that whatever this meant, in any language, it embodied something fundamental (*exacte!*) to the way her mother had lived and cooked. She had been too young to join the dots and guess that *sex*, in Brillat-Savarin's (and her sainted mother's) opinion, was subliminal to cooking, but she had been raised, so far, in a household where the kitchen was the largest, most frequented room, where the shadow line between the outdoors and in-, between all life and humans, was architecturally and philosophically blurred, and where the distance between food sources and their consumption was never more than several miles and candlelight, cloth napkins and conversation were *de rigueur* (the daily prayer) at every supper.

Sunny, herself, starched and ironed the napkins.

Stryker lit the candles ("Smells like birthday!").

In the end she'd learned that if you know *how* a person eats (not *what*) you can safely guess at who that person *is*.

She and Tops and Cas and Stryker, and all the other people captive to the household, had created their own patterns. Some meals were more formal than others, some ways of eating were dictated by the weather, all were dependent on the season. Tops liked to take his breakfast in the kitchen, standing up. Lou had kept a small glass bowl of water on the sill to catch the sunlight and refract it in a prism, and he maintained the tradition, eating before the scattered, broken light. Her rainbow—Newton's rainbow. And he used that rainbow as a bridge to cross over to her. He never buttered toast, but wiped it through the bacon fat. Thought tomatoes were the perfect breakfast fruit because they went so well with sausage meat and tasted salty. He wouldn't tolerate a "product" with the name of Kellogg's in his house. He liked the taste of winter milk the best. He liked *calvados* with brussels sprouts. Liked the taste of *calvados* with chocolate.

(Liked *calvados*, period.)

Cas drank double-strength black coffee with peels of lemon through the day (even after supper). She had grown up conscious of her height and weight and had tried every diet that had been the rage (the bran purge of Kellogg's). She was the first (and only) person Sunny knew who regularly ate flowers. She had a gentle touch in the kitchen, preferring lighter meats, and had once confessed to Sunny that if she hadn't taken up the harp as a profession she would have liked to have become a *confiseuse*, a candy-maker, in some place like Denmark. She cultivated pansies and violets for the purpose of glazing them with sugar. She was the only member of the family who didn't like to sit a horse and would set out in the fall, on foot, with a tall walking stick, to forage mushrooms. It was she who had persuaded Rocky that a Grand Tour of Europe was in order for his rowdy children the year the twins turned thirteen so they would have the opportunity to experience art and a way of life that didn't necessarily depend on weather: so they could learn to *eat*. Tops and Stryker had gone off to England and Scotland to hunt and fish. Cas had accompanied Sunny to Paris, and it was during those two months that Sunny first encountered things she'd previously believed existed only in books (ocean liners, elevators—*eels!*—taxis, *chefs*). She'd never seen a battery of men in action, a trained *corps* of individuals dedicated to the execution and performance of *a meal* before. Back home, at Three Chairs, for as long as she remembered, there'd been extra women in the kitchen, Indian and Mexican women who cleaned the meat and vegetables and managed pots and baked the bread and did what Cas instructed them to do; and Tops had always had his right-hand men (Vasco, in particular) to help with dressing game and with the smokehouse and the firepits, but Sunny had never seen *a chef*, a person like a preacher or a priest with his own type of uniform and hat, a person with that aura of authority whose skilled and sacred business was to be personally conversant, if not with God, then with food. At Sunny's urging Cas had persuaded not only the captains of their ships but also the *concierges* and *maîtres d'hôtel* on land to let the young (blond) *americaine* (a student of your culture) step inside, stand there with her wide eyes, gloved hands and little notebook and experience a kitchen.

Sunny's own sense memories:

Eating her first oyster.

The abundance in the markets: iodized air above the fish on ice: musk of sheep's milk cheeses.

Caviar.

In New York, before they'd gotten on the boat to cross the ocean, she remembered stopping at the curb (the smell of hot dogs), grabbing Cas's arm and needing to sit down because right there, in a single city block, had been more people than she'd ever seen in her life. Nothing, 'til then, had prepared her for the numbers—not her education, not the cookbooks (which were never populated), not the mystery novels, not the movies, none of the lessons, sermons, shelves of books could have prepared her for the fact that there were more people in the world than she could dream of and that the numbers—one million, two million, even *ten thousand*—meant nothing *to one's senses* until you stood among them, saw them, smelled them, each a repository of involuntary memory—unique, explicit, irreplaceable.

Schiff had estimated there would be "ten thousand" but the mind resists that number: the mind transforms that number to a cipher with no face. Yet here they were, busloads of them, silent and confused, transported only with the things they carried in their arms and pasteboard luggage; their memories. She supposed that when she'd thought about this day, what they would look like on arrival, she'd imagined them as *poor*—and now she was ashamed of this—she certainly had never thought of them as middle-class (or better), but here they were, wearing their best shoes, their "good" dresses, coats and hats.

Most were wearing layered clothing, sweaters, jackets underneath their coats to save the space inside their suitcases—too few wore footwear suitable to the terrain and many of the women wore what furs they had (fox; some muskrat) and feathered hats. That they were unprepared was a statement of such moral equivalency that within the first hour she had worked herself into a state of silent outrage: worse than the internees' unpreparedness was the government's: the *State* was unprepared for this, the Facility was unprepared; the authority that had issued the Order for detention was unprepared. Detention, as a theory, was hard enough to rationalize for citizens who had not committed any crime, but the nuts and bolts of that argument, the retaining walls of it, looked shoddy, even more disgraceful. There was sporadic water from the standpipes. The women's toilets were without partitions inside, and they overlooked the women's showers. Rats were seen beneath the mess halls. Rats commuted between messes. There was nowhere to sit. Pocket mice were at the tuff around the doors. Many of the barracks had no glass yet; most windows were cladded against wind with only paper. Dust—by-product of depleted soil—blew everywhere until some enlisted genius had the inspiration to hose down the Intake area to puke-colored mud. Rocky had refused the call for local residents to turn out along the road and on the street in Lone Pine to "welcome" the arrivals ("*Never*," he had said) but Sunny and Vasco had arrived with the pickup loaded with tangerines and oranges. Church ladies from Lone Pine and Independence dispensed weak Lipton tea in waxed paper cups and handed out brochures advising of Christ's mercy, and the family from the hardware store was already taking orders for washboards, enamel basins, pitchers and pisspots. With their manila camp identification tags tied to their coat buttons, the arrivees looked like merchandise themselves—discounted and reduced in value—especially the children, on whom the five-inch tags looked so much larger, by proportion. The church ladies had provided lollipops, the cheap cherry-flavored fructose of which had turned their lips a shocking red, adding to the disturbing illusion that they might be life-sized dolls. When Schiff had said "ten thousand" Sunny had not foreseen so many of them as children. Nor had she foreseen the elderly, the infirm, all the women, wives and mothers, women who had maintained homes, cared for families, shopped for groceries; *cooked.* Now they stood in their best shoes in the mud with dazed looks of displacement as if, in their distraction, they'd failed to bring along the thing they loved the most. Some of the men, she noted, tried an awkward air of nonchalance, as if this were just an inconvenience—some teenagers even laughed—but the women's eyes glanced off the men in uniform, glanced off the barracks and the guns and focused inward, faces shuttered. Next to her, in Basque, Vasco breathed an expletive and when she turned to him he wouldn't meet her eyes. Svevo passed and he, too, looked away as if preoccupied. A man was loitering around the tailgate of the truck where she and Vasco were unloading oranges and when she held a crate out to him, he pointed to the brightly colored sticker on the crate and told her, "This is me."

Printed on the sticker on the crate was the word SUNRISE. There was a picture of an orange. Rays of sunlight emanated from the orange against a bleached-out sky. It looked a little (if you thought about it) like a land of rising sun. Like the flag of you-know-where. Japan.

"My orchard," the man said.

He touched his index finger to the image of the orange.

"You were a picker?"

Too late, she heard she'd used past tense.

"I grow for them." (He used the present.) "The co-op. I own an orchard."

"Well then," she said. She meant to turn this thing around. "*You* should be the one to pass these out." She pushed the box on him and watched a flicker of a smile.

"I'd like to keep the crate," he told her.

She guessed he'd use the thing for furniture; she'd seen it done before.

Or else he'd keep it as a trophy. A sense memory.

She motioned to the empties on the truck. "Take all you want."

The man took four—enough to make a table—and walked away from her along the fire break between the barracks. All he could carry. Or else, she thought, he would have taken more.

A woman with two children in her charge came up and asked for directions. She held the piece of paper everyone was given at the Intake, a drawing ("map") with numbered rectangles set against an empty field, arrayed parallel or at right angles to each other on a perfect grid. Sunny recognized the smaller rectangles as barracks, the slightly larger ones as messes (one large mess for every pocket eight, or grid, of barracks). Sunny hadn't been inside a barrack yet (each one housing eight to twelve) but Schiff had asked her to "give some thoughts" on how the messes were shaping up. From what she had observed Hell was making time on Earth.

If you want to live a codified existence, join the Army.

If you have to get your daily bread from military messes you're going to eat some powdered eggs.

The woman couldn't find the place where she had been assigned to eat. Her children were hungry and she wanted to be at the head of the line, even though they'd told her the mess would not open until five o'clock. Sunny led the woman and her children to the building and was surprised to see a line already forming, as if a fear had taken hold in their displacement that food, like luck, was going to run out on them.

Svevo had told her that "If there's going to be a mutiny here—and there will be—it will happen over food," and she had thought he was being reckless, making light of conditions, until he'd added, "*Watch*: first industry to happen here will be black market. Guarantee."

"—in *food*?"

"Well, maybe hooch. Not too sure Japs drink."

"But there's food—I mean: *enough*, right?"

"Three full squares a day."

"So where's the need for a black market?"

"Oh baby girl: ain't you ever had a *craving*?"

Schiff's plan had been to staff the kitchen with internees who had experience, once they had arrived (extra eighteen dollars every month), but for the first week meals (like camp policing) were under the control of Army, as per Army protocol and followed classic Army standards: dinner = "meat" + two veg. Schiff had asked Svevo to tell the Army cooks to lay on something "special" for the first meal and Sunny knew that evening's "special" would mean soup. She could smell it as she passed out tangerines and oranges, canned soup warming in a cauldron, institutionalized aroma mingling with the smell of boiled potatoes. She knew the soup had come from Campbell's; she'd watched the vats go by on a truck. Canned soup; pre-sliced white bread (Schiff had said Japan is one of the few cultures in the world that has no "bread" equivalency, only rice); pre-portioned pats of butter (a true "special" in times of rationing) (even though, as with bread, the culture had no history of milk or butter); canned corn; mashed potatoes; pre-formed meat patties (another "special") in reconstituted gravy; coffee, iced tea, water, milk, an apple, tapioca. Tomorrow morning (*every* morning) there would be coffee; toast with butter and grape jelly; powdered eggs and corn flakes. *Lines*; more lines. You needed to get dressed to go to the latrine. You needed to put on your shoes. You needed to fight off the cold before your coffee, with your bladder full, get dressed in the near dark of the drafty bunkspace and get outside before lines formed for the toilets. Then you had to hurry to the line for breakfast. Stand in line for lunch. Line up for the requisition forms. Line up for physical exams. Line to send your (censored) letter. Line to get your (censored) mail. Dinner line. Shower line. Line to see the doctor. Line to get your children registered for school. By late spring the most frequently reported ailment among internees would be constipation. Second: melancholia. Third: contact dermatitis (censored), rashes on the skin. Even on the first day the lines, the inefficiency of transportation of the multitude, of moving thousands, verifying all their names and dates of birth, processing identities, enumerating their possessions, examining the things they carried, examining their coats and bags for weapons and other contraband, looking in their mouths, inside their hatbands, through their billfolds, having to address the older ones through translators—all this was taking too much time and backing up the line. People had been standing in the cold for hours and by late afternoon only half of the transported had been processed, the Intake area was overrun, she watched as she made her way along the main defile leading toward the entrance. *Not right*—the words formed in her mind, rekindling the outrage: *this is wrong.* She stopped to take in the whole picture, Rocky's land, her family land, in the middle foreground, snow-capped Inyos in the background, human chaos crowding up the front. They had not been here long enough—their genetic footprint had only arrived onshore a century ago—to have started to fill out, shoot up from the change in diet, from the corn and meat and milk and eggs. They were still distinguished by diminished stature when you saw them in the lines your brain worked hard to compensate perspective—especially out here on such a scale—they looked so very tiny. Were they standing very far away, these smaller people? Like toy cattle in the distance? The watchtowers around them loomed and MPs with rifles pushed through the crowd, mythic giants. You could spot Caucasians, in or out of uniform, head and shoulders taller in the crowd. Even the church ladies, sitting down, measured up superior in height to the average non-Caucasian and there was something very *not right* about the way this looked, the way this was playing out. When the water thieves, the L.A. bastards, hit the Valley—when they'd invaded here—Rocky hadn't folded like the others; he'd stood up to them (according to his legend) and waged a brand of Native war. Perhaps the memory of that was why he'd stayed away today—you have to pick your battles, and this one wasn't his. The Japs had killed his son. Three months since the day and though they had no proof that he was dead they had to face the fact that Stryker wasn't coming back. But these people crowded in behind the barbed wire, these aliens imported to her neighborhood, were Californians, every one American, and this—this cattle call—was a far more egregious act than when the other bastards, the real ones, had come to town to steal the only thing on Earth that makes life possible. What the hell had any of these people done to deserve this kind of treatment from their government? What had the children done, what residual threat to the fabric of our democracy did all these children pose?

Schiff was coming toward her, she recognized his rapid way of moving, he had torn himself from where he'd stood between the MPs, surveying the crowd. He wore a hat as he had done the first time he'd arrived at Three Chairs, but now the brim was pulled down in front against the wind, obscuring his eyes and he was walking very fast in his black coat, someone making a quick getaway from a crime. He was barreling in her direction, head down, and she was thinking *you son of a bitch*, you didn't write the Order but a man has got to take a stand in life, the way her father had, a man has got to tap his inner best, say fuck this when he sees injustice, not take the devil's pay and be a party to it. Roast in hell, that's what she'd tell him (someone had to and she had a vicious sanctimony strict as any church lady's when the situation called for it).

He didn't see her coming at him 'til he almost ran her down and when he raised his head what she faced completely caught her off her guard because his eyes were momentarily vacant, as if his soul were somewhere else. He reached out and grabbed her forearm with both hands, a man about to fall, and, reflexively, as she laid her hand on top of his, she watched the muscles of his face collapse, his eyes grow soft with grief and her outrage, like a stolen river, seemed to drain into a distant sea.

the liquid should appear to shudder (frissoner);

gently introduce the egg

the fourth property
of thirst
is
desire

SUNNY'S LOVE STORY PALED, she knew, in comparison to the epic of her parents, but as far as love stories go (as per Shakespeare) hers was more than just a welterweight:

Hers got its tonnage from the elephant.

It seemed ludicrous at times—and that was Stryker's influence at work in her, Stryker's manic impulse to play life/love/everything for laughs: Countless misadventures—impossible to list—all the broken windows, broken promises, broken bones, scrapes with every figure of authority, bailouts, betrayed damsels pounding on the windowpanes at night—Stryker had the ground for misbehavior sown with wild oats before she'd even dawned to her own puberty, forcing her into the role of being the good twin, a well-behaved good sister, the one who didn't bring the roof down or the sheriff out or make the other members of the family pick up all the pieces of her wreckage.

Or steal the vintage Cadillac.

Or highjack the elephant.

Not for her the old role of romantic heroine and those torments on the Yorkshire moors, wild men racing through the pelting rain—not for her the pain of dissolute impassioned love: hers was the role of prig, forced on her to balance out the role (WARNING! DANGER!) Stryker always played. Which is not to say that what she felt wasn't a real Romantic love (even though it played out tame compared to any passing "love" of Stryker's), and she had hoped that in the four years since she'd seen her brother on the night the elephant was killed (the night of "The Incident," as Rocky still called it), Stryker's flamboyance might have waned.

He had joined the Navy, an act so anti-Stryker in its acquiescence that she'd thought, at first, he'd lost his mind. He'd gone to sea, apparently obeyed his orders and washed up in a hotbed of good times, Honolulu, with a sterling service record and (!) a wife (and kids).

But even a reconstituted Stryker was still Stryker, skating on thin ice, breezing through the checkpoints and the roadblocks of adulthood on his charm, effecting his clean getaway without a rearview mirror, with no residual evidence that he'd had a moment's caution or a thought about the wreckage he'd left behind.

Collateral to the catastrophe of his death was exactly that—what he'd left behind—his wife and his two babies: *"Suzy"*: *"Ralph"* and *"Waldo"*: All of Rocky's inquiries to the Navy about "Suzy" had come up with only shadow information—a marriage certificate (her birth name listed as SUZUKI KOMOKO; place of birth, HAWAII; age, 19; profession, TYPIST) but nothing as to where she was now, nor even if she and Stryker's sons had survived that day at Pearl. The fact that he had grandsons he had never seen or met moved Rocky to a depth of quiet anguish and it fueled Sunny's own frustration with all the other stupid tricks Stryker had pulled to ruin things, most notably, her love story.

More collateral: Sunny's love story—her future—not just Stryker's: *hers*: her *love story*, the story she had told herself for years about how she would grow up and start a restaurant and live here in the Valley on the ranch her father had built and marry her childhood friend, the only boy she'd ever loved.

They had grown up in this windswept valley and though they'd never gamboled on the novelistic Brontë moors, they'd shared one another's histories: He could finish Sunny's thoughts. He could say the things she meant to say before she said them and up until the night he'd had to leave she'd thought her future had been bound to him. And the fact that the promise had been broken was her brother's fault.

People who aren't twinned can't fathom the complexity of having come to life with a built-in Shadow. Her feelings about Stryker had been complex from birth—a doubling act—and although any anger she might feel toward him had always been redeemed by love, now that he was most certainly dead, whenever she engaged an angry thought the guilt made her feel like she'd been punched.

Same, too, if she ever thought of other men—other, that is, than the one she loved—in a certain way.

Which she almost never did.

Except those few times when a member of a crew from Hollywood, a stuntman, say, or one of those young grips in jeans, would stop by Lou's in the company of those would-be starlets who, like preying birds, knew how to fix their gaze and use their talons. Then she'd think about what it might be like to get into a car with one of those strange boys and let him tune in music on the radio and steer with one stiff arm while the other grazed her shoulder or her hair. She was old enough to want a man for something other than just dancing and she missed being with a man, missed the muscles there beneath his shirt, the peppery smell of perspiration (like marigolds), his bass and throaty laughter. She was not a virgin but she was innocent, in practice, of most of the things she'd read that women do to please or attract—or keep—a man. Pictures of her mother showed she'd shaped her lips with color, shaped her eyebrows, worn earrings and high heels, but since her mother's death, Sunny's guide to womanhood had been Cas and, well: what was there to say: shapeless shifts and sturdy shoes. A career in scaring men. Lifetime occupation with a solitary large stringed instrument too outsized to carry in a pocket or to strum in bed. Glass of gin and a thick book every night.

There had never been a feminizing force or source in Sunny's life except what she could observe in women in the world outside her family, or in movies or in novels or in cookbooks. Cookbook reading, especially, had heightened her awareness of the sensual properties of color, scent, arrangement; the dressing of the plate and how to play up lesser assets, how to dress old mutton as new lamb; how to trick the eye with sauces. How to slaughter.

As a poet might proclaim she's good on paper, Sunny had directed her seductive efforts to the table by learning to be good on plate before she'd fully realized food is sexual—*not always*: sometimes food is life-or-death with nothing sexual about it—but the cookbooks she was reading had not been written for the starving masses—(what cookbook ever is?)—but rather for a class of individuals with both time and money on their hands: *This is how the wealthy eat*—you, too, can learn to eat this way: *this is the standard that the wealthy set*; you, too, can *meat* this standard.

She kept her mother's French cookbooks and the ones that she'd collected on her own on the recessed shelves above the oiled ash butcher's block in the kitchen but she read them only at night, in bed, a habit she'd developed in her youth when she was stumbling through her self-taught French. She'd stay awake at night like someone committed to the study of religious texts, transposing recipes in French onto the left-hand pages of her notebook, translating them, with effort, into English on the right. It was here that she'd discovered her mother's margin notes, those exclamation marks in purple ink, those exuberant *exacte!*s that made her feel a living *rapport* with her. The pleasure of her mother's company, the intimate discoveries, became a source of trust and comfort, which had carried over, through the years, to reading *all* cookbooks in bed.

The first ones she'd tried to read had been in a language she couldn't understand and that was what learning about sex was like, wasn't it? Reading what you've never read before, in a different language. Trying hard to understand.

Herbs against melancholy: she would come across such phrases—*Salts of evaporated love*—and her body would react the way it had when she was reading girls' adventure stories or, later, the bodice rippers Stryker lifted from the pharmacy in Lone Pine. Food and sex: they were incorporated for her—like a broth—the one ingredient submitting to, and losing itself within, the other. Where were hungry souls more vulnerable, at the table or in bed? How better to learn the fundamental mysteries of life than to learn the names of plants, the sources of proteins, the chemistry involved in fire and emulsion? As with cooking, what she'd learned of sex was that it's witchcraft: secret, potent, personal; indifferent, in its execution, should you fail to execute with love.

As challenging as the foreign words had been at first in her mother's French cookbooks, she'd felt lucky that the foods in those French markets and larders were familiar to her, ingredients and things she recognized. Bread (bread pans), beef, chicken, butter (butter churns), wine—even olive oil and artichokes—were not only staple items for California cooks, they were grown or produced within the state. Early Spanish, French, Italian immigrants had found the climate similar to parts of Spain and France and Italy and planted fields of garlic, olives, lemons, grapes, tomatoes, *courgettes*, oregano and onions. Reading the French cookbooks required less imagination for her than, say, reading Lewis Carroll or *The Wizard of Oz*—she had never encountered a hare in a bow tie or one that ran perpetually late but she could look up *un lapin* in the dictionary and find out it meant "rabbit" and she could figure out from the instructions how to quarter it and stew it. She knew what *poulet* ("chicken") was even if the French breeds were not the same as California's, and she could duplicate French cuts of *porc* and *boeuf* and lamb on the animals she had at hand in California from the cookbook diagrams. Where it all went south for her was when the recipes called for ingredients she'd never heard of—not exotic spices, they were readily at hand among the Native population or from the Mexican *curadoras*—but *fish*. Not "trout," of course—she was familiar with those—but when it came to creatures from that unknown realm, the ocean, Sunny had no clue.

What was *turbot*?—how did *that* translate? Her only knowledge of aquatic creatures was of the ones her family pulled from lakes in the Sierras: the freshwater ones; the redsides, cutthroats, bullheads, rainbows. She could determine how old a trout was, what stage of life it had been in, by the colors of its scales. But what was "halibut"?—what was a "flatfish"? How were you supposed to eat a "scallop"? *Bar, loup, merlu, lotte de mer*—what were these, what did they look like, how was she supposed to summon up their taste, what the color of their flesh was, did they have straw bones like speckled dace or were their bones like glass or thorns? French or English, Sunny couldn't tell a *huitre* (oyster) from an *homard* (lobster), a scallop from a *langoustine*, a monkfish from a pike, because she'd never seen one.

FOREIGN FOODS: what housewife in America didn't know the taste of cinnamon?—vanilla?—black pepper, coffee, chocolate, nutmeg, tea? The introduction of "exotic" flavors from the East to enliven and delight—or, more honestly and crudely, to mask disgusting food, perfume its rot—had so improved medieval European life that by the time the enterprising ships had breached the shores of North America on their misbegotten quests for spices, European palates had been educated to appreciate surprise and sweetness beyond the groats and rendered boar fats of their grandparents, and by the time Williamsburg and Boston had been planted in Virginia and Massachusetts, kitchen gardens were already seeded with purslane, ginger, thyme, chives, rosemary and pungent small hot peppers. Strong black China tea had become so primal a public need that a foundling nation had been ready to wage war against a tax on it.

It had taken Sunny years after her mother's death to appreciate the inheritance of those French cookbooks—their precise and armored wisdom, their bloodied and adult Life Lessons—but even as a toddler she had benefited from the kitchen garden that her mother had left behind, playing among its magic scents, among its stalks and leaves, and before she could even walk or form a sentence she had breathed in her mother's "native" kitchen vocabulary—wild dill, wild fennel, *yerba santa*, *yerba buena*, *epazote*, pepper-root and Mormon tea and California coffee, miner's lettuce. Among these California "natives" Lou had planted her "exotics"—saffron crocus, clove and cumin, purple onion, eggplant, garlic—so successfully that Sunny hadn't stopped to question their provenance, assuming that everything in her mother's garden had taken root as a gift from God and not from a mail-order catalog. Her mother had brought to Lone Pine her French legacy of *culinaire* sophistication, but her level of culinary worldliness was not exceptional among Lone Pine's other ladies whose Scandinavian and Teutonic family trees had birthed "exotic" specialties—*ginger*snaps, pickled herrings, sauerkrauts—more foreign than the "native" Californian fare of maize, acorns, calabash and roasted squirrel. Transplanted immigrants had arrived with more seeds in their pockets than coins: seeds are light to carry, on foot or in a covered wagon, and they spring from devout history, weighing nothing, same as dreams.

What Lou had brought to Lone Pine, though, that was exceptional was, first, her French and English (from England) cookbooks and, second, her medical training insofar as it informed the recipes she practiced, the notes she left about them on her handwritten "recipe" cards, and the seeds and herbs she chose to cultivate. From those cookbooks Sunny guessed the world might be a bigger place than her mother's garden and the desert and the mountains she could see. She had known about large cities—especially hellhole Los Angeles, which Tops raged about—and she'd known there were whole countries where her own language wasn't understood. But you grow up in rainshadow under mountains puncturing the clouds before any rain can fall on you, you can't be blamed for never learning about fish. You can't be blamed for dreaming about water.

By her eleventh birthday she had struggled through *Tome Une* of Carême's *L'Art de la Cuisine Francaise*, which was all about *potages* (simple: *soups*: stuff she knew), but then came *Tome Deux* (Two) which started with

TRAITE DES GROSSES PIECES DE POISSONS.

"*Treatise on Big Pieces of Fish*," she'd translated into her notebook in an adolescent way.

(What a little *prig* I was, she now considered.)

TURBOT A L'ANGLAISE

"Turbot The Way The English Cook It," she'd written down (with the priggish margin note *Find out what a "turbot" is*.) (Followed by an even more priggish margin note: TURBOT: EUROPEAN FLATFISH.)

{french}	{english}
NOUS DEVONS D'ABORD CHOISIR CE POISSON TRES	"First, we must CHOOSE (our) fish
BLANC DANS TOUTE SA DIMENSION, SIGNE CERTAIN	. . . very white in all dimension . . .
DE SA FAICHEUR; BIEN EPAIS ("THICK"), FERME AU	. . . a sign that it is fresh,
TOUCHER, ET SURTOUT OBSERVER QUE LA SURFACE	TOUCH and OBSERVE its surface . . .
SOIT COUVERTE ("COVERED") D'UNE GRAIN ("TEXTURE")	
SAILLENT ("OUTSTANDING"?) ET ARRONDI ("PLUMP"),	
CE QUI ATTESTE QU'IL EST GRAS ("FAT") ET DELICAT.	. . . fat and delicate."

"*Nous devons d'abord* CHOISIR ("choose") *ce poisson*":
. . . which means what? We're not *catching* it—?
We're *choosing* it,
in other words:
We're going to a place where fish are *chosen*, bought and sold.

—what kind of place was *that*, she'd wondered.

—a *fish* market?

Paris wasn't even on the ocean, so how did the "ocean" fish get there to be "chosen"?

Were they alive,

or dead?

(Not "dead," she'd supposed: otherwise Carême would not have instructed how to judge their freshness.)

What would such a market look like? Open air or covered?

What aroma would it render, how would it smell?

(Later, from experience, she would learn the scent of a really good clean fish market is PEPTONE (Fr: *le peptone*), a converted protein compound obtained through enzymatic HYDROLYSIS (the process of life dissolving into water). It smells like salt.

Actually, it smells like snow-washed granite. It smells, an ocean liner chef would later tell her, like an iceberg melting.

—*oysters:*

how could she have imagined what an oyster was—the shock of brine on the tongue—from its mere description or, even more impossible, from Carême's drawing of one? They looked like stones, like things you'd kick over on the hardtack. Moreover, in every one of her mother's French cookbooks, every time *les huitres* were mentioned there was the dominant *l'avis* that the preferred *methode* of consuming them was *raw* and as far as that was concerned all she could think was *blech*. She'd watched Rocky filet fresh-caught trout and steal a raw taste in the process and she'd swallowed a raw egg on a dare from Stryker and sampled Cas's favorite beef *tartare* but the idea of downing raw mollusks (whatever *they* were) remained outside her ken—like sex—and when she'd scoured her mother's notes for further explication the only card mentioning OYSTER had this written on it, in her mother's distinctive purple ink:

—PROTEIN

—CALCIUM

—IRON

and then on the bottom, in darker, fresher, ink:

> SALT balances thunder and silence on the surface of a steak.
> SALT is lightning in the BLOOD.
> Salt is the only ROCK we eat.

—whatever *that* was supposed to mean.

In a century (the 17th) when Native Americans subsisted on acorns and raw leaves, the King of France had supped on "mirrored eggs addressed with truffles and shaved gold." So Sunny had learned to trust the French, but still. She'd found a tin of "smoked" oysters at the IGA in Bishop but when she'd prised the cover with the key what she found inside reeked of saddle oil and looked like puppy turds and even Stryker, on a dare, wouldn't go near one and Cas later confirmed to her that the smoked specimens were nothing like the "divine jelly" of the live ones, in the flesh.

Except getting to "the flesh," apparently, even if you lived near an ocean, involved a specific *knife* and a good deal of manipulation (the instructions for which had been written at length in the cookbooks and seemed to involve a more-than-average degree of danger to the chef). (Can you call a chef a "chef," she'd wondered, when all she does is "open" something?)

At eleven she'd more or less taken over the preparation of the evening meals from Pie and the other local women who'd run the household at Three Chairs but "fish" remained a small part of their diet. She read at night about the history of "exotic" foods—difficult food, food that needed specific knives and special preparation, food with thorns (artichokes, pineapples), food with vice-grip shells (cashews), and she'd had adventurous daydreams conjuring their moments of discovery. The very improbability of there being some-thing tender and delicious inside these thorny things—or inside mollusks or crustaceans—defied logic and had made her wonder how humans ever thought to try to eat them. Unless somebody with experienced culinary knowledge led you to one what do you really think you'd do the first half dozen times you came across an artichoke or a lobster or an oyster in your wild?—not *eat* it, that's for sure. Even as a child, Sunny had figured whether you're a human or a reptile, there must be a desperate place in hunger when *let's crack it open* might become your only option for survival. But if desperate hunger, alone, had been the motive for learning how to eat oysters, they would have dropped from necessity, like acorns, as soon as people started breeding stock and killing lambs. *Oyster pavement* was a term, she'd learned, that described not only the bottoms of the marine beds where oysters bred but also the surface of whole lanes in Rome and Paris, Boston and New York, where people had consumed so many cheap and plentiful bivalves every day that the shells had been ground up to pave their ancient streets and build their ancient temples (churches, too). For a creature with no head or spine, awash in its own transparent blood, the oyster had survived as not only a modern luxury but also historical *food*. So oysters, then, had been at the top of Sunny's list—she'd kept a list—of food things, food*stuffs* she needed to learn about, to taste and to "discover." (There had been another list too—she was such a little *twerp*—of non-food "things" she'd needed to "discover," the *ham* knife, for example, *oyster* knife, *tournet* for rendering potatoes into spheres, that knife for dealing with raw chestnuts, those forceps-things for clasping snails . . .)

oysters
    belons
    bouzigues
    gravettes
clams
    razors
mussels
    green
winkles
    blecch
lobster

O the *lobster.*

("The small pointed head bears long antennae and its abdomen is in seven sections terminating in a fan-shaped tail.")

Like a *peacock's?* she had wondered.

Fortunately there'd been pictures in the encyclopedia. And in *Alice's Adventures in Wonderland.*

Which is whom she'd felt she was, while reading.

Sacrificez l'homard.

SACRIFICE THE LOBSTER all the recipes commanded her (as if the little monster were a pagan martyr). *Always* buy the lobster *live, never* buy the lobster who displays signs of mating warfare or has a lost appendage. Bring (preferably *sea-*) water to a rapid boil. SACRIFICE THE LOBSTER by plunging it headfirst into the boiling water and holding it down with a wooden spoon (there was probably a specific wooden lobster spoon for *that*) for at least two minutes. The lobster should die within fifteen seconds. At which point it will turn *bright red.*

Curiouser and curiouser she remembers having thought. "Will you walk a little faster, said a whiting to a snail," Alice observes in "The Lobster Quadrille" (which sounded to Sunny as if it should be *food*), "there's a porpoise right behind us, and he's treading on my tail—

> *Will you, won't you, will you, won't you, will you join the dance*
> *Will you, won't you, will you, won't you, won't you join the dance?"*

Sunny had liked reading the *Alice* books because from the first mention of ORANGE MARMALADE right through DRINK ME and EAT ME and the tea party (that tea party!) the story is a cautionary fairy tale about the things a girl

should/and/should not

EAT.

"I hear"—(actually she'd *read*)—"there are places you can go that sell live *fish*," she remembers having said to Cas. (—she'd been ten, eleven?)

"—*fish*mongers, of course. We had them in New York. Never went myself—*Cook* went. There was a fish market, too, down on Fulton docks."

What would *that* be like, Sunny had wondered.

Paris had one, she knew from reading Lou's cookbooks, although how were ocean fish delivered there, two hundred, *three* hundred years ago to please Louis XIV at his royal groaning board at Versailles? What was that— two days, *three* days after they'd been caught? She knew from experience what a trout looked like—*smelled* like—after only several hours in the sun. Protein *rots*, it stinks to hell, a testament to everything that happens after the spirit leaves the body. No one would ever eat a rotted fish on purpose (well actually, she'd learned later: some cultures *do*) so how do ocean fish arrive *alive* at inland markets (such as Paris) and how do those markets *smell*?

They come on *ice* (if they're not already salted, to preserve them . . .)

Tons and tons and tons of mounted *ice* she was to discover, the ice—its component oxygen—keeping them alive and—she would learn this later— giving off that "fish market" smell, plus the PEPTONE.

"Do we have a 'fishmonger'—or a 'fish market'—here, in California?" she remembers asking Cas.

"—*many*. There's a thousand miles of ocean coast—"

"Where's the nearest one?"

"San Francisco, I should think. Or Los Angeles."

CAN YOU TAKE ME THERE?

—*that* question, *that* request had formed (in Stryker's subsequent accusations) the basis of The Most Awful Christmas when they'd been twelve.

He'd had every reason to believe, waking up that Christmas morning, that when he ran into the Great Room in his pyjamas he'd discover one or both things he'd asked for waiting for him beneath the tree:

    1. a pet wolf
    2. a motorcycle

Instead what he and Sunny found when they'd run into the room had been Cas and Tops already hard into the *calv* and *aquavit* with coffee, sitting, waiting, and an envelope for each.

Stryker tore his open—because when you're Stryker, you can believe there is a wolf inside an envelope. There hadn't been. Instead there'd been a single sheet of paper holding two words:

ENGLAND/SCOTLAND

Sunny's sheet had PARIS written on it.

I need to talk to *Santa*, Stryker had lobbied.

They'd been handed, each, *another* envelope, this one containing boat tickets and itineraries.

Worst Most Awful Christmas *ever*.

This is your fault, Stryker had told Sunny. With your *fish*.

"We'll be going," Tops had announced, "Cas with Sunny, me with Stryker, for eight weeks—May, June—separate boats—separate countries— to *Europe*—!"

(Dead air.)

"Plenty things to learn about, plenty of adventures . . ."

(Dead, *dead* air.)

. . . until Stryker had asked if Hace could come along. (Hace being their best friend.)

"No."

So . . . just me and *you*?

"Yes."

What are we going to *do* there just the two of us?

"*Fish*, for one thing—"

(I HATE YOU TO HELL Stryker had whispered at her.)

"—jump horses, English style: *box* . . . Let me remind you these are the countries that invented *dragons* so there's archery—longbows—*sword fighting* . . . castles . . . forts . . ."

"—cannons?"

"Yes."

Shoot me from a cannon, then, Stryker had said.

Rocky had the foresight to hire a Pinkerton man to stand guard over

Stryker at night on their Atlantic crossing so he (Stryker) wouldn't jump ship into god-knows-what-infested waters just for fun and so he (Rocky) could catch some much-needed sleep but for the rest of the time he (R.) had been able to keep his son's daredevil impulses reined in short of harm. They (S. & R.) had flown across the country to New York (TWA three-stop service) while Sunny and Cas had caught the trans-continental train from Truckee, a seven-hour drive north from Lone Pine above Lake Tahoe, for which they'd started before dawn in order to meet the Silver Chief that afternoon. It had been Cas's idea to buy Sunny's traveling wardrobe in New York so for that first part of their journey they'd traveled relatively light (Cas's trunks were waiting in Manhattan) and when the train pulled into Truckee (an unscheduled stop; they'd been the only people boarding) a passenger car with the logo WELLING-TON RHODES had stopped right in front of them and three porters in wine-red livery and a man dressed like a *chef* (he *was* the chef, Sunny later learned) and the engineer, himself, had descended to welcome them aboard and shake Cas's hand. Stryker was already at the Waldorf in Manhattan by that time and had written his first letter to Sunny

I think we might be *rich* (he'd written)

but Sunny hadn't thought it was *that* unusual to have an entire train car to oneself nor for the train's engineer to hurry down the platform just to shake your hand. What she *had* noticed, though, was Cas acting in a way she'd never seen before—for one thing she'd looked *bigger*, out in the world; and for another she seemed to be dispensing money, secretly, through those many handshakes in which everyone on the receiving end had gone on pretending that he hadn't noticed.

Their porter—one of the first people of color Sunny had ever seen (there were no black people in Owens Valley, only Indians and Mexicans)—had been a gentleman of middle age called Lucius James who seemed amused at every-thing Sunny said. Sunny had heard Cas ask the chef if all the "details" had been arranged and once they'd been situated in their car (two adjoining bed-rooms and a parlor) and the train had started to move, Mr. James had asked

Cas where they'd like to take their supper—"In the dining car, ma'am, or in your parlor?"—and Cas had asked, How many cars distant were "the goods"?

Three.

And the dining car's adjacent to them?

Yes, ma'am.

"Then we'll dine in the dining car this evening, Mr. James, thank you. A *discreet* table, we don't want to put on a big show."

She'd drawn Mr. James aside and whispered something and there had been more of that coded handshaking and then Sunny had unpacked her few belongings and gone to sit beside the great parlor window and watch the American landscape unfurl. Mr. James had given her a rail map: three thousand miles to New York City: three days. (It had taken Rocky and Stryker a tenth of that.) The rest of Stryker's letter #1 (he'd numbered them) had read:

Definitely going to learn to be an airplane pilot!!

It was only at six o'clock when they'd repaired to the dining car, walking through two other passenger cars to get there, that Sunny realized all the cars along the train were definitely not like their own.

A table had been laid for them in the dining car, adjacent to the galley but separated from the other diners by a half-glassed partition, and Mr. James had changed into a short white jacket and was smiling; ready. He'd seated Sunny in the banquette facing down the dining car and had handed Cas a starched white butcher's apron, which she'd donned with what Sunny could only call "gusto."

Close your eyes, she'd told Sunny. When she said, Now open them, the chef had crowded in with a cart covered in shaved ice on top of which were forty/fifty grey *rocks* and *stones* of varying sizes. Surrounded by lemons. And what appeared to be wet grass.

Voilà! Cas had said. (Mr. James had poured her a flute of champagne.) *Smell*, she'd told Sunny, handing her one of the larger stones: your first *oyster*.

Cas had got to shucking, showing off her prowess with an oyster knife— her manly hands—and had done three of the larger ones when she'd realized, subtly, she was stealing the chef's thunder and *somewhat* demurely (though she'd never had it in her to be "demure") relinquished both the knife and apron and pressed in, across from Sunny, at the table.

The chef's name was Chef Daniel (Sunny had written this in her notebook next to a tracing of the first oyster shell): "Harvested only last night," Chef Daniel had told them. "Delivered this morning from Washington State. These are the Olympics . . ." (the larger ones) ". . . and these smaller ones, the *Kumos*."

That *iceberg* smell (not that Sunny had ever smelled an iceberg): that inside-the-icebox aroma. Cold and metallic both, at once.

This is *definitely* better than anything Stryker is doing, Sunny had thought.

Ate my first oyster, she'd noted dutifully, describing the experience and all the accoutrements (*mignonette* sauce vs. horseradish vs. a plain squeeze of lemon vs. two grinds of white peppercorns from the peppermill vs. splashed Tabasco).

Ate my first lobster.

The lobster, served by Chef Daniel simply boiled with little pots of perfectly drawn butter, had come by this very train from Maine the day before. "I've seen people bring them West in suitcases," Mr. James had told them.

So much to document!

She was going to need more notebooks—Cas had promised to buy her ones from Sennelier on the Quai Voltaire in Paris—but decent stock could be obtained in New York City, too, and until then her little Mead copybooks from the general store in Lone Pine would have to do. She'd brought three of them along. All three were filled by the time they reached Chicago.

Drawings (of food), menus, l o n g descriptions of the meals and ingredients, of the galley kitchen, interviews with fellow passengers about their "native" foods, sampling from the trackside emporia at train stations where they stopped, interviews with porters (*Southern* cooking) . . . what a little twerp she'd been. *Definitely.*

Their second day at lunch (crossing Colorado) she'd asked Mr. James where the water in the glass he'd poured for her had come from. Since there was no source of water on the train.

"This water here—? From the water tank in Denver I suppose. Where we loaded up."

Drank my first Rocky Mountain water.

Slightly mineral.

First night out (Nevada) Mr. James had turned their beds down and she and Cas had changed into their nightclothes and she had written in her notebook for a while and then turned out her light and called goodnight to Cas.

She'd had no direct line of sight into Cas's stateroom from her pillow through the open door and although the light fanned across the floor and the lower reaches of her bedclothes, it hadn't been that which had kept her from sleeping but the feeling of a lurking something—not a *nightmare* but the tightness in your chest that tips you off that one is coming.

She'd stared hard into the night, then got up, feeling the train's movement through her legs like walking on water, and walked to the open door that separated their compartments.

Hello, button, Cas had said.

She'd been propped up, reading, against her pillows inside a cone of light: "Bad oyster?"

There were "bad" oysters—?

Curiouser and curiouser . . .

No, Sunny had signaled.

"Too much excitement?"

Again, *No.*

"Come. Sit." Cas had patted at her sheet. "Talk to your Aunt Cas."

Going into Cas's bedrooms (her *appartement*) at Three Chairs was like going to another country. You left the rustic Southwestern ambiance of the *portales* and entered a cultured realm of complicated *rugs* and shelves of books and oil paintings in gilt frames and tables flounced in brocades, flowers—always flowers—in diamond-cut lead-crystal vases.

Much of that practiced effect—the spirit of it—had been transported to the stateroom on this train via careful orchestration, via (Sunny realized) *atmosphere* . . . and aroma . . . and lots of little *things*. A potted candle in a glass jar was burning on the bedside console (letters painted on the glass read SKOG, which Sunny would later learn was Swedish for FOREST) and the comfy cozy littered space around Cas *had* smelled like a pine forest . . . plus there were Cas's leather jewelry boxes, a framed photograph, the silver ice bucket and squat tumbler of her frigid midnight gin.

Cas herself had been swathed in a silk bed jacket which seemed to melt around her in the candlelight.

You can trust your old Aunt Cas you know, she'd said: I'm all you've got these next two months.

Sunny had tried to put her feeling into words and finally told Cas, If I fall asleep right now, I don't know where I'm going to be when I wake up.

Hm. Well now: does Earth not turn?

Yes.

—then, really, even when you wake up in your own bed back at Three Chairs you're not in the same place, *are* you?

But the *outside* hasn't changed.

Well what can I say, button: you'll be the same inside your skin.

Nice try, but Sunny hadn't found the comfort she'd been seeking and sought to change the subject.

"Who's *that*?" she'd asked, focusing on the photograph inside a silver frame next to Cas's berth.

Cas had passed it to her.

"—you know who this is, poppet, you see her painting on the wall each time you come inside my room: she's my mother. 'Cassandra Roque.' I was named after her. We both were—Cassandra/Cas: Roque/Rocky . . . the -'well' at the ends of both our names came from 'Wellington,' our father . . ."

". . . I didn't think you *had* a mother."

"She was a beauty, wasn't she? I got none of *that* . . . She died when I was just your age."

"—from polio?"

"Not everybody dies from polio, button."

"What did she die from then?"

"*Gravity.* Fell down the long stairs. Ask your father and he'll tell you she was *pushed*."

She'd replaced the portrait on the bedside shelf, retrieving a handsome leather portfolio from among her many altar artifacts: "Before I left New York for Scandinavia—you know I toured there, with my harp, for two years—I had this made . . ." She unwound a velvet ribbon and allowed the portfolio to fall open: ". . . because I suspected, and I was dead right to have done so, that at some point in those lonely winters in an unfamiliar setting, I would feel a tiny little bit uncertain about where I was, much as you might feel right now. So I made up this collection . . . and I kept it with me, always, to allay those fears on all those nights . . ."

Inside the portfolio—no bigger than Sunny's notebooks—was a handful of loose photographs:

"You know who *this* handsome chap is don't you?"

—a taller older version of Stryker, hauling on a line in a sailboat:

"—Tops?"

"—yes that's Rocky in his skiff in the harbor in Newport. We were still at private school . . .—*this* . . ." (a picture of a snow-covered park seen from a height) ". . . was the view from my bedroom window in the house where we grew up: that's Central Park, which you shall see with your own eyes in a few days . . . and—*ah*—this is what we're looking for . . ."

Picture of a radiant young woman, dark-haired, laughing from within the white lace frame of her wedding veil:

Maman, Sunny had recognized.

"—very *best* of women, loved her as a sister from the moment we met. This was on their wedding day—which they weren't going to commemorate with photographs until I organized that Mr. Ansel Adams who was in the wedding party—strange man, always had his camera with him, *long*-suffering wife—and we were all up at the Ahwahnee in Yosemite and I said, We have to have some evidence of this, Someone take a goddamn photograph, and so he did. Isn't she a gorgeous creature? *God* she had amazing skin, always wore a sunhat I wonder where those *pearls* have gone we need to get your father to allow us to go through her jewelry now you're starting to be old enough— she was this tiny little thing I was afraid I would break her or your *father* would . . . and she was vury vury *franch* her accent would have slayed you, kept us all in stitches: mind you we had had a French mother, too, but ours was

French-Canadian and nothing like your mother *god*—that woman had such style in everything could sit a horse could *fish* could cure the plague deliver babies *cook* godknows like a magician tell a joke and sing a song, she had a little prayer she used to say at night—this might help you, button—she said she got it from Tolstoy but I've had a dip inside his books and I can't find it:

'*Dieu*, let me sleep in *calme* tonight
but rise up in the morning like new bread.'

"The picture's yours to keep of course—I should have propped it beside your bed the moment we entrained—we'll go shopping for a frame once we're in Manhattan . . ."

"I want a frame like yours."

"—*this*? This I got at Tiffany & Co. not sure they make them anymore—in any case: *we'll find out* together won't we? Do you need me to tuck you back in? . . . Otherwise my light will be on quite a while I'm only halfway through this gin and well stuck in the middle of this novel by our trusted guide to *Les Halles*, Emile Zola."

THE RIGHT BOOKS AT THE RIGHT TIME—that had been one of Cas's lessons to her:

—not the most useful or sustaining information she might be looking for, as a young girl desperately searching for a mother.

> CHOOSE A STURDY WALKING SHOE.
>
> RULES FOR STRAINED BUT NECESSARY SOCIAL CONVERSATIONS
> Ask what they're *reading*
> Ask where they plan to *travel*
> Find something to compliment them on and *state* it. *Early.*

"You are named after a great Southern river, Mr. James," she'd commented (early).

"Yes, ma'am. And a great grandfather, too," he'd let her know.

"To say nothing of *a king*! And a *Bible*!"

It seemed to Sunny now, all these years later, that the Paris trip had been the turning point in her childhood resistance to her aunt as "mother"—Cas was *not* her mother, she could never be her mother and with a different sort of woman to advise her, a regular sort of Lone Pine woman—or her *real* mother—Sunny, herself, would have been a different woman. But Cas was who she had, then and now, and how many of those hypothetical other mothers—even her own beloved one—could have taught her about the mon-eyed handshakes or the ramrod demeanor the aplomb the unfussy bravado the non-flirtatious confidence with men or—this had happened only several months ago at the restaurant—barged through the back door in the middle of the dinner service and announced: "I finally found that goddamn prayer in Tolstoy don't go looking for it: it's worse than I remembered," and then stormed the hell back out again.

LORD JESUS CHRIST HAVE MERCY AND SAVE ME!
LET ME LIE DOWN LIKE A STONE, O GOD, AND
RISE UP LIKE NEW BREAD

Lunch of oyster stew, cold lobster salad (2nd-day leftovers).

Ate fried catfish!

Passenger from Wyoming says no oyster from the briny deep can stand up to eating one good "*prairie* oyster."

(Cas says never speak to the Wyoming man again.)

Ate *clams casino.*

Ate shrimp cocktail! (Chicago.)

Ate fried "calamari" (squid. frozen).

Ate *smoked salmon* (with cream cheese).

Ate pickled herring.

On the last morning she'd woken to a view of factories and warehouses, backyards with strings of laundry, junk and vines and skinny women, skit-tish dogs and threatening children—then there'd been the drama of the disembarking, the mammoth enclosed space of Pennsylvania Station the clamor and reverberations thick as a miasma, more *noise* than she had ever heard people everywhere all hurrying and all determined all *important*, and she had taken hold of Cas's hand because the whole thing had been like that panic that you have of drowning when you just start to learn to swim.

As they'd neared the platform's end Cas spotted something that had stopped her dead and said Well knock me over with a feather: *"—Declan!"*

A portly gent of some considerable age dressed in a polished livery moved toward them, grinning ear to ear.

"What a sight for sore eyes—" Cas had gushed, "I was going to hail a taxi.—How did you know we'd be arriving?"

"I'm under strictest orders, Miss." Leaning down to Sunny: "Miss Rhodes, this is for you . . ." An envelope bearing the gold and crimson Waldorf-Astoria stamp and Stryker's inimitable scratch, LETTER #2.

Declan had been the Rhodes chauffeur and when Rocky and Cas had sold off the assets and divided the estate they had given him a severance bundle plus the stately 1919 Pierce Arrow to which he'd ushered them, parked outside the station.

"Lord she doesn't look a single moment worse for wear," Cas had told him, appraising the car.

"—nor, Miss, dare I say, do *you* . . ."

Sunny had never heard English spoken in an accent such as his (*Irish*, Cas told her later) (Charm the rings right off your fingers so *beware*)—she'd been speechless as the two old acquaintances had gabbed—as much by the strange lilt to Declan's speech as by the size and height and numbers of the buildings and the noise (*more* noise) and all the traffic and the people in the streets.

"I'll have no argument hereabouts: *lunch* has been arranged by young master Rhodes."

You could tell Stryker to do something and count on him doing the opposite but there had been something in their parting for so long for the first time in their lives that had frightened both of them a little (even Stryker) and he'd promised with fresh spit in his handshake that he'd write letters to her. Every day. About *food*, which he'd thought would make her happy (and, for once, he had been right).

At his best he was an indifferent eater but she'd pledged him to transcribe menus ("I'll just steal them") or have Tops describe what *he* was eating. So the fact that he'd arranged a lunch on their arrival to New York (after he'd already departed) had been—(dare she say)—a *charming* act of givingness from her (mostly) selfish brother.

They'd driven not even five minutes when Declan pulled to the curb before a royally appointed building with stone lions perched in front which she'd thought must be the Supreme Court. When Cas had explained it was the "Main" Public Library—("There's more than *one*?")—the process that had started when they'd left Lone Pine on the drive to Truckee (which was still, at least, in California), that the world she'd known for all her life was not THE WORLD but only one among the many . . . this process began to test the measure of her previous experience. Yes there had always been grandeur and expansiveness around her, she could look up and see *the highest point in the United States* each morning of her life but . . . hell: you could stack the whole square footage of the stores on Main Street in Lone Pine into any one of these tall buildings. This could either make you want to chuck your small-town life for good or make you want to jump a stagecoach back to Dodge.

Stryker had designed *un repas* for them streetside, no reservations needed, under an umbrella, three cents each. No seats, just condiments.

Ate a New York City hot dog!

"Your classic bun—they're always *steamed*, that keeps them fresh—will be the *top*- and not the *side*-loader," Declan had enlightened her. "You've got your *kosher* that's without the casing—the Hebrew National; the Nathan's out on Coney Island—you've got your *casing* dog that's toothie that has the extra crunch when you bite in. And then you've got the '*withs*' . . ."

> MUSTARD
>
> KETCHUP
>
> SLICED DILL PICKLE

RAW ONIONS

SAUTÉED ONIONS

GREEN RELISH

SAUERKRAUT

SAUTÉED POTATOES

CHILI CON CARNE

CHOPPED TOMATO

SAUTÉED ITALIAN PEPPERS

CELERY SALT

People had been standing on the sidewalk or sitting on the library steps, eating. Outside. No plates.

"—now *this* is 'New York,'" Cas told her. She'd already ordered up a "fully loaded" and was struggling to contain it in her hand while Sunny had struggled, equally, to make up her mind.

She asked to taste both the green relish (looked suspiciously too *green*, she'd thought) and the sautéed peppers before she could commit—finally settling on MUSTARD and SAUTÉED ONIONS.

"—your brother, now," Declan had confided to her, "was not the onion man. I myself eschew the wrath of mustard for, like Hamlet's ghost, she comes back to stalk me on the night."

He'd taken them the short distance uptown to the St. Regis and had forborne with dignity Cas's pronouncement that they really didn't need him for the week, that most of their destinations were within walking distance. She knew he lived in Queens but also that he lived to drive the P-A around the city so she told him she would count on him to take them to the boat. Sunny had watched in vain for the magic handshake but saw no coin exchanged between the two of them other than sincere affection.

The "New York Cas" had proved to be yet another version of the Lone Pine Cas or the Wellington Rhodes private train car Cas: the New York Cas, it seemed to Sunny, had been in her *element*. She'd started wearing *hats*; she'd started wearing shoes with lifty heels as if she hadn't cared how tall they'd made her as if one couldn't be *too* tall, even when one was a woman, in New York.

—and *christ* how they had hiked.

They hiked through the *Park* they hiked to the *museums* they hiked to Tiffany's, Bonwit's and Saks, Cas setting the pace with her capacious strides—woman-on-a-mission—so that Sunny had to scurry like a minion to keep up. At Bonwit's she'd been measured for three lightweight velvet coats—one in a color the showroom woman had called "heliotrope," the second one in "moss"; the third in plain *black*—which were to become her uniform for going anywhere and everywhere in Paris. She'd been outfitted in *shoes*, in *sundresses* and skirts with those annoying shoulder straps; blouses, white gloves, hats for visiting churches, hats for strolling, *straw* hats, *dinner* dresses and *toile* underwear ("Most *breathable*," said Cas). Declan had recounted that Stryker's favorite New York sight had been the Museum of Natural History, where he'd seen a reconstructed dinosaur and a Blue Whale but when Sunny asked to go there Cas had told her *A Whale is not a fish* and hiked her to the Metropolitan instead where the statues were all boring and the Egyptians never seemed to *eat* but where there had been paintings—*many* paintings—of tables set with *food*.

"Showing off their wealth," Cas explained. The Dutch merchant who had commissioned this oil owned bragging rights to that particular *ham*. And all his cutlery. But when we get to Paris you'll see other paintings, other ways of painting food, especially Cezanne's fruit: sometimes an apple or three apples or a pear, an empty cup, a bunch of grapes were all the artist *had* in his possession.

Looked at what Cas calls Dutch "masters" who only painted things that cost a lot.

Ate at an "oyster bar"! which Cas says is just like a Bar except there's oysters!

Cas's regimen had consisted of militant a.m. shopping followed by a large lunch at one of New York's finest restaurants (Sunny kept the menus)—*Ate caviar!*—followed by an afternoon of viewing Masters in museums followed by a hike to sightsee (the Hudson and East Rivers, Cloisters and cathedrals, downtown "neighborhoods") followed by an early supper from room service. Breakfast, too, had been taken *en suite* with the morning papers and with

Cas's running commentary on the news and what was playing in the concert halls. They're doing *Winterreise* at Carnegie tonight, she'd mention or They're doing Orff, and Sunny had to ask what those things were.

Concerts, button.

I like concerts.

You like the Lone Pine marching band.

We should go.

I would not subject you to my eclectic tastes . . . besides, they start at eight.

Well *you* can go and I can stay here, I'll be safe.

Never.

I'm old enough.

Never.

Why not?

What Sunny had not known at that early point of understanding was what Cas had found when she'd arrived at Three Chairs after Sunny's mother's death: Rocky in a state of psychic disarray. Rocky in the depths of loss. Rocky in the throes of depression. Worse than Rhett—Rhett Butler, button—in the Mitchell novel where Rhett holes up in that room with Bonnie's corpse and sweet Melanie has to go in there and reconstruct his personality.

I was my brother's Melanie from *Gone with the Wind* for godsake finding him unshaven unresponsive to the needs of his own children and—lord knows—relentlessly petitioned by those local women those spinsters and grass widows with their casseroles and marital designs as soon as they heard he was "available" they'd drive out to Three Chairs from as far away as *Bishop* for godsake to offer up their fried chicken and miserable lamb stews I had to beat them off I had to make myself for*mid*able and scare them all away while combating my brother's spectral demons and I swore then and I have never once relented, I swore then that I'd do everything within my power to protect him from another loss. If any unforeseen thing should befall you or your brother on my watch I know firsthand the devastation it would bring upon my brother and I would never find a way to absolve myself of it . . . So, *no*: I won't be going out at night and leaving you alone in this hotel.

That evening when they'd returned from another hike a Steinway had been delivered to their suite of rooms. If Mohammed cannot go to the mountain, Cas had said (Sunny hadn't known who this "Mohammed" was), then move the goddamn mountain.

That night they had entertained the first of that week's *en suite* concerts— Cas had sent a note to her former harp instructor who had invited others, all old acquaintances from Cas's musical career—and they had come to the suite with their cellos and violins and thirsts for champagne and appetites for caviar and Sunny had thought at first that they'd been from a single large Italian family called *Maestro* and what she'd learned was, first, that caviar existed in an array of colors (*orange!* and *gold!*) and, second, that there were people who inhabited ecstatic lives in making music and, third, that there was a version of her aunt she had never seen before, a Cas who laughed a lot and had a great time around men and looked radiant and beautiful.

Is he your "boyfriend"?

What are you talking about?

Maestro.

Women can be friends with men without there being romance, button. Despite what we read in English novels.

But you could marry him and then have children of your own.

I *have* children of my own.

Not really.

Don't make me want to spank you, button. Both of us would cry.

On their fourth day Cas had hiked her unexpectedly to a place called Murray Hill where they'd stopped at a residence of red brick in a row of other houses made out of stone the color of old mud.

Cas had rung the bell.

Whose house is this? Sunny had wanted to know.

Mine, Cas had told her.

The day before on the hike back from the Metropolitan Museum down Fifth Avenue Cas had pointed out the house where she and Rocky had grown up and pointed to the windows on the third floor that had been their separate bedrooms and Sunny had said it looked more like their current hotel than a house where children once lived—and so did the one in Murray Hill, the one that Sunny had subsequently learned had been her grandmother Cassandra Roque's dowry (whatever *that* was) that Cas had inherited and still owned, as income property.

A gaunt man dressed like the men who brought room service to them at the St. Regis had opened the door and immediately closed his eyes and laid his long fingers to his chest where she'd supposed his heart might have been and taken a dramatic inhalation. Opening his eyes again he'd breathed out *"Fraulein."* Cas had turned to Sunny and said Regen, May I present my niece, and "Regen" had snapped his heels together and bowed from his shoulders and said *"Fraulein"* again and it had occurred to Sunny that everybody Cas knew in New York City either spoke in a foreign accent or spoke a foreign language altogether and, figuring it was this man's native way to say Hello she had been about to bow and say *"Fraulein"* back to him when Cas had pushed her through the door and she'd found herself before two curved marble stairways in a "foyer" (she had learned the word) the size of their local bank in Lone Pine.

Marble stairs were non-existent back home and a *double* staircase was unheard of so while Cas had gabbed away with "Regen" in the gaunt man's language Sunny gawked but then remembered her grandmother had met her death falling down some stairs and had wondered, morbidly, as kids will do, if these had been the ones to kill her.

Regen, it turned out, had been the head butler in the "big" house on Fifth and had translated into service here along with "Cook" after the house on Fifth had been sold.

Cas and Regen had continued to gab away in what Sunny later learned was "German," Cas sometimes slipping into English as they'd moved into a room where tea had been laid accompanied by the smallest sandwiches Sunny had ever seen (they'd looked like they'd been made for dolls) and yummy cookies with "cloudberry" jam. The tea service had been ornate very shiny and had a Dutch Master been around, Sunny had concluded, he'd have painted it.

"Cook," whose name was Kuch, apparently, but who was also the *cook*, had been summoned to a place called Yonkers to *sie Mutter*, according to Regen, but had prepared the sandwiches (filled with *cucumber*, of all things;

with butter and dill and transparent layers of smoked salmon) and had baked the cookies because she knew they were Cas's favorites and had been heartbroken (*Herzeleid*) at the prospect of having not been there to greet the Frauleins. The family renting the house, Regen had related, were very clean, *ordentlich*, very generous. As with Declan Sunny had noticed Cas's manner with him was familiar and affectionate and had not included special handshakes.

"Regen, one last matter—"

"—*ach, ja?*"

"We want to go to the fish market—"

"We use Russ, Fraulein, on First."

"—no, the *Fulton* fish market. In your opinion, would it be seemly for *zwei Frauen-Personen* to fetch up there on their own?"

Long fingers to the chest, again. A panicked look: "You need *der richtige Mann*, Fraulein, it's very dangerous down there, *ist nicht einfach*, you need a manly man, a *Mensch* . . ."

Cas had looked at Sunny and Sunny had looked at Cas and both had the same thought at the same time:

Declan.

—who'd turned up at the St. Regis the next morning in the pre-dawn dark with thermoses of strong black coffee and a flask of Bushmills and several pairs of green galoshes which he kept referring to as "Wellies." He'd been dressed not in his chauffeur's uniform but in a "fisherman's" sweater ("I'm *Irish*, after all") and work pants and Sunny had thought he'd looked twenty years younger in his casual attire. They'd headed downtown through the deserted streets and Cas had asked if the Pierce Arrow would be safe parked in that rough neighborhood and Declan had told her not to worry, "There'll be a Paddy on the job who'll keep an eye on her . . . there's *Paddys* everywhere in our New York."

Sunny had collected eighteen menus by that time and in addition to her three Mead notebooks from Lone Pine and an extra notepad Cas had packed in her purse, had halfway filled a new one from Tiffany & Co. with her field notes:

Beef is always the same color when you cook it no matter what the breed and so is chicken but cooked fish are different colors— Some are

white (halibut, sole, cod) and some are pink and some are dark like
bluefish. I don't understand this.

Passing an art supply store on West 57th Street she'd begged Cas to let her
buy a set of colored pencils and so was equipped at every meal to note the *ex-*
acte color of the fish she had been served, and on entering the imposing market she'd had at the ready her notebook and all her colored pencils in a book
bag on her shoulder the same way she'd prepared for the museums and the
Empire State Building and Radio City Music Hall and Central Park, but what
she hadn't been prepared for were the crass harsh cries of commerce and the
raucous tumult of male voices and, then, the raw smell of *ice* and *sea* and all
the *fish* their goddamn little faces and their *eyes*, enormous, still and focused.

Porgies, grouper, swordfish, widemouths, eel and shad.

Never look a monkfish in the face!

Are you all right, lass? Declan had asked and she'd tried to answer Yes.

He'd dropped on his haunches to look at her and told her, "You don't *look*
all right."

For some reason she'd taken hold of Declan's hand when he'd stood up
and told him, "I didn't know . . . there'd be . . . so much."

She'd been, then, only eight days out of Lone Pine.

"Ah, yes," he'd said: "There is a lot to Life . . . and you have yet to see the
ocean!"

Where she'd been ferried to next.

Wait until you see the ocean! [Stryker: LETTER #4]
I'm definitely sailing around the world alone some day!

All that blue stuff, all the *blue* around the different-colored continents on
maps—she'd never really focused on how much there was, of water, on Earth.
She'd been on a boat before, on their wooden boat, she'd been *on water* be-

fore out on their lake in the Sierras but to compare their little *put-put* to the *Normandie* was like comparing canned tuna to the real thing: a crime against imagination. For one thing, the *Normandie* dwarfed the human figure, it was as large as a small town, you could fit the whole of Lone Pine into its lower deck and still have room to run the road right out of town to Independence. Their set-up on board—their "staterooms"—followed what was by then the familiar pattern of two bedrooms connected by a central "parlor" where Cas had immediately instituted a series of special handshakes with men in white uniforms (and white shoes!) but most especially with one she'd called The Purser whose title apparently derived from the fact that he was in charge of the ship's money—its *purse*—and not because he pursed his lips, which he had done (and which Sunny hadn't liked about him). He was the man who decided who sat where at dinner, who had been allocated which stateroom, who would get to meet the Captain and whose luggage would be off-loaded first in France.

PROTOCOLS OF SOCIAL HIERARCHY, Cas called the tactics of survival in the ship's environment: "We're now captive," she had said, "for the next ten days and that little pissant is in charge of meting out all the elements of our desired comfort."

How much did you give him? Sunny had by then wised up enough to ask.

The amount had shocked her.

Hell yes, she had noted in her letter to her brother (using newfound grown-up language): We *are* rich.

What had occasioned the Purse-onal visit to their staterooms even before they'd sailed (Sunny had *definitely* wanted to be out on deck for *that*) was an invitation in a fancy envelope to dine at the Captain's Table that night. Cas had accepted the envelope and at that moment *voilà*, Sunny had noticed, slipped the folded hundred-dollar bills into The Purser's palm.

"But this is addressed only to 'Mlle. C. Rhodes,'" Cas had noted. "Where is the invitation for 'Mlle. S. Rhodes'?"

Panic in The Purser: *beaucoup des excusez-mois, mais* (looking all around). *Qui est la deuxieme mademoiselle?*

"My niece."

Sunny had noticed that, although proficient in French, Cas had chosen to address the man in English so she (Sunny) understood him when he answered in the dictated *langue* of choice, "But she is *a child*. We do not feed children in the First Class eight o'clock *repas*. She is scheduled with the other children to be served at six."

You watch; you learn.

How to use a fish knife? watch and learn. How to make the handshake? how to ingratiate yourself through charm? how to STARE a pissant toady *down*?

Sunny would never have what Cas had—a superior education in a world-class city and its advantages in understanding different kinds of *people*—but she would have one singular advantage: she'd have the thing itself: she'd have *Cas*.

Cas had made eight trans-Atlantic crossings—four round-trip journeys—so she knew the clues, she had the puzzle solved. "What they will try to do to us, button, over the course of ten days, is they will try to feed us into a stupor so we can't complain they will ply us with so many opportunities to gorge ourselves we cannot move we cannot turn a corner without encountering a *buffet* or ascend a stair without someone there to greet us at the top with a *sorbet*. Here's what we will do: we will take our morning coffee in our room we won't go traipsing upstairs to the first chowline of the day, we will avoid the *omelettes* and arrays of *brioches* and *croissants*: we will *hike*. We will amuse ourselves on deck in the *plein air*, we will *exercise*—perhaps we will often forgo lunch, that's up to you, you need your calories, but we will at all costs avoid the second chowline of the day in the Dining Room and focus all our hunger on the formal supper: a concentrated program of selective dining finishing with an extravaganza fit for an experienced *gourmande*."

These nightly suppers could be tedious, she'd explained, they seat you at the same table each night with the same people and by the third you know the names of all their children, grandchildren and pets and what their tells are in the *après*-dinner poker and you want to throw yourself into the frigid North Atlantic, but we'll muster on for the sake of your culinary education and we'll make an adventure of it, you and I, with tales to tell back home about the characters we met on our fabled odyssey. And when we tire of the pretense and the dressing-up each night we can always eat a humble pie together in our stately rooms.

Once they were under sail the first day had blown by, what with the excitement of being outside on the deck for the horn-blowing and seeing the tall buildings slide away (*No one ever told me New York City is an island!*) and putting on the life vests for the safety training and breathing the sea air and remarking that the Statue of Liberty looked a lot like Cas and then, finally, putting out beyond the harbor and its tugs.

Why do people dress up in the first place; what's the point of it? Cas had probably spent a small part of her fortune on clothes Sunny would never wear in Lone Pine and would most likely outgrow within the year. Stop varnishing, Cas had warned her but if *this* was what they had to do each night for the so-called privilege of having dinner in the Dining Room, Sunny was all-in for the idea of eating humble pie in her pyjamas and watching stars collect among the beads of water on their porthole windows.

—but once they got there, *wow*:

So this was what "First Class" was all about—chandeliers and monogrammed white linen, plates with the ship's portrait on them, encircled in real gold, Baccarat and Sèvres and Limoges and Cartier and Hermès and champagne, all French. *Hell* yes. Bring on the vittles.

The Captain's Table had been positioned in the center of the room where everyone could see it, a long affair with twelve seats on each side, gold-embossed vellum name cards designating places and Cas had found herself seated *en face le Capitaine* at the center . . . while Sunny had been stuck in, as if an afterthought, at the very end.

This won't do Cas complained but Sunny had told her she'd be fine—it was an adventure!—and had let a starchy waiter seat her and pour her water, which she'd wondered where it had come from, and had opened her too-small-for-everything evening clutch and lined up all her colored pencils. For the first few minutes she'd been alone—the two seats across from her empty as well as the one beside hers—but a man and a woman had been ushered in across from her and the woman had been seated by the maître d' but the man had stood there staring at Sunny and then said (actually he'd shouted) *Godammit Dotty* (whoever "Dotty" was) *I haven't paid twenty thousand dollars to sit here and* babysit *all night* and the Captain's Table had gone silent

215

and the surrounding tables had gone silent and then a very very blond (her hair was practically *white*) woman in a form-fitting emerald-colored strapless taffeta fishtail gown three places down from Sunny had stood up and marched around and slapped him.

Things had moved quite quickly after that.

Sunny had noticed Cas had gotten to her feet but the maître d' and several waiters had swarmed the scene and the man seated across from the blond woman had stood up and grabbed her by the wrist and dragged her out and then, after the maitre d' had ushered "Dotty" and her husband to other seats, a man in an impressive uniform—all white and gold—had sat down across from Sunny and withdrawn a flat leather wallet from somewhere inside his jacket and had shown her a picture of a pretty girl who looked to be about Sunny's age.

Ma fille, he'd said.

And then immediately translating himself: My daughter.

Elle est très belle, Sunny had said, making a point of speaking French.

"She wants to be a nurse when she grows up."

"Why not a doctor?"

The man had smiled genuinely at that and introduced himself as M. Brouillard, First Mate, and Sunny had introduced herself as Sunny, First-Time-at-Sea, and had surprised herself declaring (another First) not "I want" but "I'm going" to be a chef when I grow up.

Then no doubt you'd like to see the galley, he had said.

Suavely—there was no other word to describe the way he acted—*suavely* he'd procured Cas's bemused permission to accompany her niece to the ship's "kitchens" and led Sunny across the room to a decorative screen which shielded diners from the drama of the dinner service, through two bronze-faced swinging doors into a hot and hidden world, the crucible from which emanated every morsel on every plate on board.

It was the *size* of all these places—this and the Fulton fish market and *Les Halles*, in Paris, yet to come, that most humbled her, the sheer *numbers* of people rapt in the daily manufacture, wrapped up in all the things we eat. She'd just been hiked through Saint Patrick's Cathedral in New York City but you could put a choir *and* an organ, sixty-seven stained glass windows and a thousand *covenants* into that hallowed space and never equal the *soul* of any working kitchen, the amount of human energy that rises like a common spirit, floats, ignites, transforms and blesses life.

"What do you notice is the same about the people here?" M. Brouillard had asked her.

They're all dressed in white.

"What else—?"

She hadn't understood what he'd been getting at until he'd pointed it out to her   Everyone   at   work   in   here   is   male.

"That's because females are bad luck on boats, *n'est-ce pas?*" she argued.

Non:

"That's because in France, *peut-être* everywhere, women *cook at home* but it's up to men, alone, to cook for money and to wear the *toques*, the *hats*."

Women cook at home—she'd written that *all caps* across two pages in the notebook: *Men wear the hats.*

No one was telling Stryker (the WORLD was not informing him) that men can't sail around the globe alone, that men can't pilot airplanes or be shot from cannons or be President or *Capitaine* or lead a risky expedition across this very ocean and have two continents named after you (*Americus* Vespucci).

There were women who owned restaurants—there had to be—but looking back on her experiences in the restaurants in New York—and on the train— she'd realized women hadn't figured in that landscape, had been not so much erased (they'd never been there in the first place) as rendered immaterial. In Paris, it would be the same—*women* in the daily markets with their baskets and their net bags full of onions but *men* at the door in restaurants, serving at table, in the kitchens. Women were the *cooks*; and men, the *chefs*. Women reigned at home; men, in the workplace. Women cooked the family meals; the men made history and money.

NEVER TRUST A MAN WHO DOESN'T COOK, Cas had once said, apropos of nothing in particular—or perhaps apropos of yet another stunning serving-up of Rocky's grillwork—and Sunny had written *that* down, too.

—and look at *Cas*, for heaven's sake, a woman who could strangle a brood hen in the backyard and strip it of its feathers with her bare hands but could not finesse a sauce if her life depended on it: *she* lived like a man, doing what she wanted, when she wanted, *if* she wanted to.

"Do you think it's because you're rich that you are the way you are?" Sunny had asked next morning while they hiked the deck.

"How 'am' I?"

"You know. Bossy."

" 'Confident,' you mean."

"—no, I mean 'bossy.' "

They had already hiked around the whole ship twice and Cas had gone for an hour's swim starting at 06.00 in the indoor pool and Sunny had yet to start her French lesson (09.00–11.00) nor her tennis (11.30–13.00), when, passing by the First Class Lounge, they encountered the platinum-haired woman in the emerald fishtail gown looking no worse for wear than she had the previous night except for the fact that she was carrying her shoes and sporting a gentleman's white dinner jacket over her bare shoulders.

Well *hey*! she'd said. Look who's here!

Cas had halted in her hiking tracks.

"Good morning," Sunny had said and the woman asked, And what's *your* name, honey? And Sunny had told her and the woman had said Well I guess your mommy and daddy sure had been countin' on a *boy*!

"It's with a 'u' . . . not an 'o,' " Sunny had explained, pointing toward *le soleil* itself.

"Oh you're an *adjective*! Glad to meetya. I'm two nouns: Rosemary Dust."

They'd shaken hands and Sunny had presented her to "my Aunt Cas."

" 'Aunt,' " the woman had repeated, checking out Cas—who had yet to speak—top to bottom. "I'm working my own narrative here . . . adopted?"

"—no she's really my aunt."

"You're not her sex slave, areya?"

You could have heard the whales *tsk* at the bottom of the ocean.

"What if she were?" Cas had finally spoken.

"Well then I'd have to slap you, too," Rosemary Dust had said, at which, to Sunny's surprise, both women had laughed.

A waiter bearing a tray of little covered cups—*demitasses* with lids, Sunny had observed—had suddenly appeared out of nowhere asking everyone on deck, "*Bouillon?*"

"What are you selling, honey?" Rosemary had asked him.

Beef tea, Cas had explained.

"—beef . . . *tea?*" Rosemary had taken a cup and looked inside and said, "—well I know *beef* and I know *tea* and there's just no excuse for puttin' them together . . ."

"*C'est très restorant*," the waiter said.

Honey this ain't no "restaurant" . . .

"He means it's 'restoring' . . . It will get you through the morning," Sunny had volunteered. (Such a little twerpy twerp.)

"Well give me *two* . . ." Rosemary had said. After which she'd said, "Y'all are jokin' on me, shit, it's *soup!*"

"Where's your husband?" Cas had asked.

"—*Frank?* Frank's not my 'husband'; he just picked me up to sit in on his poker games. He's still at work in there"—nodding toward the Lounge— "selling shit to Germans."

As a rule Cas was stiff-backed when it came to *language*, limiting her own off-color declarations to damns, as needed, and *god*damns, as required, and Rosemary as a type—not that Sunny had ever seen her "type"—would normally have been the "type" of person Cas would have stared down or discountenanced, but: "Why did you strike that man last night? It was very bold of you," she asked.

"—*him?* He'd been getting on my nerves all afternoon making slurs at me—*and* Frank, by association—so when he started in on cutie here I'd just had enough . . . well, plus I'd had about a gallon of that stuff they call 'sham' *pain* . . ."

"Do you play *tennis*, Miss Dust?" Sunny had been surprised to hear Cas ask.

"Honey I'll play any game that depends on a racket . . . and some balls."

"Sunny has her lesson at eleven-thirty. You should join her."

Looking all around: "What time is it *now?*"

"Eight-thirty."

Musing: "Well I suppose I could still be awake 'til then."

"We'll meet you here."

Looking around again: "—and where is '*here*' . . . ?"

Sunny had drawn a map for her, and all through her French lesson (with the pinched and awful Mlle. Pinot who looked like a dogfish) she had been distracted by the pretty-much-odds-on certainty that Rosemary would never show but there she'd been, on time, with her white hair all slicked back and wearing a tennis costume equally as white, which she must have just purchased in the ship's "sport" shop because the price tags were still on.

Rosemary was a "sport" herself—a professional card shark—a "confidence" woman, Cas had called her (which Sunny had taken to mean that, as a woman, Rosemary was full of CONFIDENCE). She had become their Third Wheel on the ocean crossing—the squeaky one, as Cas called her—the Fourth and suavest one being Henri, M. Brouillard, First Mate, who had shown up at their stateroom door that second day with a purloined copy of the *Normandie*'s FOOD PROVISION MANIFEST, a "book" more elucidating, more exciting, than any Sunny had ever read (eight *hundred* lobsters, six hundred *pounds* of shrimp, two *thousand* oysters . . .). Following the first night's *affaire* in the Dining Room, Cas had ordered the Purseperson to secure a private table for them—table for *four*—and every night that he was not on duty Henri joined Sunny and Cas and Rosemary for supper there and they'd become fast friends, Sunny hoping through the week to catch some spark of romance between the sailor and the card shark which never ignited, alas, owing to the fact that the sailor had *a cook* at home to whom he was happily wed and Rosemary had no interest whatsoever *zero* in any man who had settled for fixed wages regardless of how handsome.

Later, looking back through the notebooks she'd kept in Paris, Sunny would notice that they read as lists of food. Not really peopled. A mention here or there of the *concierge* at the Lutetia, a colorful though unnamed personage at market hawking cheeses or *fraises de bois* but no one else like Declan or Rosemary or M. Brouillard. For all the fish she'd sampled, fish she'd eaten, fish she'd seen in markets, there were equally-as-long lists of increasingly bizarre and ornate dishes Cas had ordered in her campaign to tempt Sunny to try (at least *taste*) something other than goddamn *poissons* while they were in the culinary capital of the world: Cas had taken to ordering the most complicated entrées to lure Sunny into one small bite—"*Potée aux queues et oreilles de cochon* . . . that sounds good" (no, it didn't), which turned up looking like the thing it was, Boiled Pigs' Tails and Ears served with a pot of extra-*fort* mustard and a saucer of coarse salt and a jar of sour gherkins with roasted garlic to be smeared across grilled rustic bread.

Épigramme d'agneau—("What do you suppose *that* is, button?").

Théâtre du canard.

If I live in Lone Pine all my life, Sunny argued, this could be my one big chance to eat these fish so I'm doing it.

"You're not going to live in Lone Pine all your life."

"You don't know that."

"You don't know it either. No one knows where she'll end up."

They had stayed on the Rive Gauche—Cas had been adamant about choosing a hotel on that side of the river—and one morning early in their stay as they started toward the little islands in the Seine, Sunny had been struck by a sense of *déjà vu* and had asked, Do you think Maman was ever here, in Paris?

"I know for a fact she was—she took her baccalaureate at the Sorbonne."

"Do you think . . . do you think she ever walked on *this* street?"

"—*this* one? Can't testify to that but I can take you to a street she *must* have walked . . ."

They had hiked to the École des Médicins and sat in the café *en face* and Sunny had let her imagination transform young women on their way to classes into visions of her mother.

"She wasn't from here, though," Cas had volunteered, "I remember that she told me *Parisiennes* intimidated her at first."

"Where was she from, then?"

"—don't test me, button . . . some village in the east, *cheese* village—*fromage*—I'd know it if I saw it on a map . . . She talked about the caves there where Grandmère and she had put up cheeses to acquire *mold* and how the mold had fascinated her as a curative . . . led her to want to be a healer . . . Plus her father had died in the Great War from *gangrene* of all things . . . *death* mold . . . and her mother had been left a widow in the backwards cheesy village with its damp and moldy caves—one can but imagine. Anyway, the Mère picked herself up and remarried—you know your *maman* was an only child—enterprising Mère marries *up* hitches her *étoile* to some provincial scion of a plantation family—their money was in coffee if I remember—and off she goes with him to *Indochine . . .*"

"I don't know where that is."

"You do, button, you've seen it on the map it's that place to the right of India just under China. Anyway, Lou by that time—she was probably your age or slightly older when the Mère goes swanning off with husband *deux* to French colonial Southeast Asia so your mother—an adolescent!—says *non, merci* and stays put in said cheesy village with Grandmère—what the hell was that village called I know it wasn't *Roquefort* but it was another *bleu*, story short she comes to Paris for her *bacc*—she had this idea even then that *food is medicine*—you got her started on the subject of food-as-medicine—and she was never far from it let me tell you—and she was like a little engine that *would.* I remember her talking—on her wedding day while we were dining!— about the transfer of energy in matter, that food is *alive* in our bodies . . . She'd started out, I think, more a nutritionist than a physician and pursued the medical degree to legitimize her philosophies. Spent half a year on Corsica taking histories from madwomen there the *sage femmes* the *obstetriques* writing down their herbal remedies and she told me she'd been about to spend a year on Martinique—that's a French *département*, button, an island on our side of the world—when one of her *professeurs* asked her to accompany him to North America to research healing remedies among the Plains Indians. He was attached to the University of Chicago and *c'était ça.* There you have it . . . *Gex!*—that was her village's name!: *Gex*: you hear it once you don't forget it. We should ask at the next cheesemonger for a *bleu de Gex . . .*"

"Or we can go there, ourselves. Instead."

Cas had never considered champagne a beverage to be sipped with food— "It's more like water"—and would therefore drink it through the day as a refreshment and had been doing so when Sunny had put forth the unforeseen proposal of visiting the place where her mother had been born and had set the glass back down and said Of course. "I should have thought of that myself."

"Not because I want to find a cousin there or anything . . ."

"One never knows . . . though I suspect the Grandmère must be long dead . . ."

" . . . *her grandmère.*"

"*Her grandmère.*"

"What happened to *mine?*"

"*Your grandmère*: dead in Indochina."

"—from polio?"

"From malaria . . . ('jungle fever,' button) . . . which was another malady your mother was convinced could be prevented via herbs . . ."

"Did Tops meet Maman on an Indian reservation?"

"He met her in Chicago—saw her from a train. She was standing on a platform and he was on his way from California back to New York City—probably the very same train we were on—he was coming back east because Punch, our father, had just died and, as you know, the train halts in Chicago and he looked out the window and saw your mother and disembarked and ran across the tracks or whatever route he needed to have taken and ran up to her—you know your father's height and your mother stood five-one, five-two at her best length—he loomed over her to introduce himself and she said something in the way of *Fichez le camp*—stop *bozering* me—and he persisted in explaining he had seen her from the train and had to meet her—he must have seemed to her a veritable crazy person—and she made a tiny little fist with her tiny little hand and *hit* him—*hard*, she told me—right there, right against his sternum on that bone. 'Now look what you've done . . . you've broken my *reest* . . . !' (or some such, she exclaimed, and your father said): 'Don't be so dramatic, I'm sure it isn't broken . . .' '*I'm a docteur,*' she told him, 'I know when a bone ees . . .' Fainted. To hear your father tell it, 'She fell into my arms,' but who knows: he lifts her up and transports her from the station in a taxi, 'Take us to the nearest hospital . . .' which turns out not to be *her* hospital so when she comes to—still in his arms—there's a great carry-on about re-routing and then telling him to go away again and him following her all the way through to the orthopedic surgeon so her wrist bone can be set and staying with her as a cast is made all the while telling her about himself what a sincere and honest lad he is etcetera etcetera and how he'd like to stay in Chicago to get to know her but duty calls him to New York for his father's funeral—which he had already missed, by the way—and that he'll make a point of coming back to see her after he puts his father to rest in order to take her on a proper date so she can get to know him better if she'll let him. Quite the charmer. And he does: he goes back. He'd learned her name, of course, from the hospital records and he'd learned her address and he makes a goddamn nuisance of himself sending flowers to her from New York sending singing telegrams and whatnot—absolute buffoon— until she agrees to meet him for *lunch*. In the commissary. Where she works. Surrounded by her co-workers with surgical training and methods of *dispatch*. Your father tells her about a place he's found called 'Owens Valley' where he plans to build a ranch and shows her drawings that he's made of his dream house and tells her he will build a clinic for her there that there are tribal lands nearby, Shoshone, promises her the sky. If she will only marry him. Well, she says, '*Peut-être*, I *might*,' but she would need a *kitchen* and dictates a floor plan and her detailed particulars. Took Rocky two whole years to build it but you know that. Wrote her every single day."

"I would like to read those letters—ones *she* wrote, I mean."

"There are none. I lie. She wrote him *once*. Well into the second year."

"She didn't write to him?"

"—*once*."

"—in *two* years?"

"She'd given him her word—that's the way she put it. 'I'd given him my pledge: *ça suffit*.' Sufficient."

"Do you know what she . . . what that one letter was about?"

"She wanted a bell tower. As part of the house. With a French bell inside."

"I always thought the tower had been Tops's idea . . ."

"Nope."

"—why did she want it?"

"Because in the village where she grew up—*Gex*—there were churches with their local bells, each bell a slightly different pitch than all the others, and she said she would know when she had wandered too far from her home when she could no longer hear her village bell . . ."

I need to hear that bell, Sunny had said.

It was in the 18th century (1700s) she had entered in her notebook (pissant know-it-all) that the handwritten menu (*carte*) had been introduced to diners. Before that French people ate what they were served and had to try to figure out what they were eating.

Like *life*, she now reminds herself.

By the time she'd made that entry in her notebook she'd collected over fifty *cartes* (seventy-three to be *exacte*) from New York City through Paris— Bofinger, Drouant, Lapérouse, Prunier, the Ritz, Café de la Paix, Brasserie Lorraine—as well as vintage ones she'd scavenged with Cas's help from the *antiquailleurs* and bookstall vendors on the *quais* along the Seine. Stryker had sent *zero* descriptions of food from London except to say that people there ate beans on toast. For breakfast. And that there was a vegetable at dinner called "mushy" peas. Eaten by adults. She had the sense from what he'd written that he (Stryker) was not as thrilled as she was to be abroad:

SCOTLAND MIGHT BE A NICE PLACE TO VISIT IF YOU COULD

UNDERSTAND WHAT THEY WERE SAYING (LETTER #9)

Rocky's long (*long!*) letters to Cas—*christ* it will take all morning to read this, button, and we have so many things to do!—had hinted at the challenges of traveling round the clock (on a boat, on the ocean) with a live cannon. Rocky had gone to Europe for the first time with Cas and their mother when he'd been Stryker's age and had loathed the pretenses of First Class dining and all the dressings-up-for-such-and-such artifice/occasion and had burned his former formalwear (the cutaway and the tuxedos and the cummerbunds) in the fireplace on Fifth Avenue the week of Punch's funeral and pledged he'd never wear such shit—ever—in his life again (he got married in a buckskin jacket) so when it came to dinner on the Cunard Line he opted out, investing neither in the fantasy nor in formal clothes for him and Stryker, which meant that for the ten nights of their trans-Atlantic crossing he (Rocky) had to discover alternative evening entertainments for his restless son which, by dint of limited resources, meant *cards*. "We settled in the Library that evening," he'd written to Cas, "to pursue a game of chess—for which the boy had not a jot of patience—and how was I to know it was the very place these god-damn dowagers flock to play their games and drink their gins? Now he is their mascot—*lucky charm*—and given his cunning and native instincts I had no doubt that by the time we docked in Southampton he'd become their bank and hold significant mortgages on all of them, which, in fact, he did." Younger women on the ship had also flocked to him, Rocky had written, turning up at night to ask if he could accompany them to tour the deck and escort them to dances in the Lounge.

Don't know what to make of it, he'd written:

GRAVITATES TOWARD WOMEN.

What Sunny had noticed in her brother's letters was a diminution in their frequency and detail:

DON'T EVER COME HERE

he'd written (LETTER #10).

THERE ARE PEOPLE EATING OATMEAL STEWED IN SHEEP INTESTINES

WET WET WET WET WET WET WET WET (LETTER #11)

The engaging summer weather in Paris, by contrast, had been so perfectly delightful it seemed not to exist—one never had to worry about foreshadow-ing clouds, protective gear or chills, the weather was too exquisite, even in the cool of evening an earthly glory to behold: not too hot and not too cold: extension of one's body: joy.

The *concierge* at the Lutetia with whom Cas had exchanged yet another bonus handshake displayed undisguised superiority at the prospect of arrang-ing their rail travel and accommodations in Gex—"... *mais, Madame* (they all called Cas MADAME) *êtes-vous absolument certain?*" He had not been happy and had it not been for the handshake (or maybe even in spite of it) he would have demoted them in his esteem to provincial rubes because Gex was in the Jura, a district that to the majority of Frenchmen, Sunny had learned, was the back of the backwoods, in the *mountains*, for godsake, and a mere twelve kilometers from Geneva on the French side of the Lake where there was little-or-no Parisian culture and—far worse—almost in Switzerland, bland zone of clocks and yodelers. Nevertheless the journey had been arranged and Cas and Sunny, sporting gabardine and knapsacks, had fetched up on a Saturday morning at the Gare de Lyon in time for a civilized coffee in Le Train Bleu before boarding the First Class car for Bellegarde and thence to Gex. Saturday was market day in Gex and the plan had been to arrive before closing and buy the famous cheese—lunch locally and listen to the bells—stay the night at a nearby château—listen to the bells again on Sunday morning and return to Paris.

All had gone according to the plan for the first five hours—until they were deep into the heart of France where the first suggestion of the Mont Blanc Massif to the east began to rise when it had started, mildly at first, to drizzle then to shower then to rain to pound down and clap with thunder and shock with lightning and deluge. It was coming down in veritable planes in Bellegarde—*sheets*—and they had to run to catch the two-car coaler (the rails out there had yet to be electrified) with water rushing through the paving gutters (they hadn't thought to bring umbrellas or even a raincoat), every stable and unstable surface weighted, dripping with an overflow rain bouncing *up* in pellets round as marbles, rain carried on the sweeping wind *sideways*, rain arriving in three dimensions and all at once Sunny had leapt away from Cas, off the train platform in Gex where her mother had been born, and ran for the first—or second—time in her entire life into a liquid wild, a liquid world.

It never rained in Lone Pine, the talons of the Sierra capturing all moisture from the sky, from the evaporated Pacific, and hoarding it above the peak, and Sunny had grown up watching only promises. The pretty mounting cumuli above Mount Whitney massing like meringue but then withholding, water was only ever delivered from the slopes as grounded streams—but Gex rain had come from heaven holy cleansing and transformative unlike anything Sunny had ever felt: rain for the first time on her body *rain* as miraculous and mysterious as ice must seem to a Colombian living in the jungle on the Amazon *rain* the second of the three necessities for life *rain* the first baptismal *rain* the nurturing embrace *rain* the food provider *rain* the mother.

What she hadn't known because she could not know was that as she thrust her face up toward the sky to drink, Cas, standing beneath the roof of the provincial station, had experienced a vivid shock as visceral as lightning in the realization that Sunny, acting for this once as Stryker *always* acted, had put herself at fatal risk the kind of risk that kills you sets your hair on fire sends you feverish to bed and then to God. *George Washington*, Cas's long-gone Swiss nanny had always said when it had stormed in Newport or in New York City, George Washington had *died* from catching cold outside riding on his horse in rain you'll catch your death if you don't stay inside you'll die—and a wave of panic had immobilized her, a wave of understanding, *really* understanding, how her own brother must feel every time his son ran or jumped or took a flying leap or put his hand into the lion's mouth or lit a match or picked up a knife or went outside unaccompanied in the dark to watch the stars . . . and here was Sunny dear sweet girl, amenable and non-complaining, trustworthy, polite, resilient—a good girl, a good *good* girl—acting like a crazy person and Cas remembered an East Indian woman she had met somewhere sometime explaining a monsoon to her, the monsoon season in Bombay, and how as a grown-up person you start out thinking every year that you will try to cross this street while trying to stay very very dry but within a minute of the weather coming you end up going out and stopping traffic and just standing there, surrendering, to this insistent cleansing dominating power. She'd put the knapsacks down for their safekeeping, taken off her hat and shoes and gabardine jacket and marched straight out, lifting Sunny by both hands and twirling her around, feet off the ground, fast as she could. What the French had thought had no doubt been no different from what your average American might have made of this—reaction being human, not national—a few called *brava!* but most stood mute, perplexed, especially when Cas had realized it would soon go two o'clock and asked the stunned observers for directions to the nearest bell tower (*s'il vous plaît, mes copains, ou est le* BEFFROI *le plus prochain?*).

The streets had been deserted, windows shuttered to the storm, the market *place* a barren lot, but for Cas and Sunny, who had placed themselves in front of the town hall in the pouring rain and, following directions, stared up at the belfry atop the strangely Tyrolean-looking redbrick building waiting to be impressed or (more to the point) emotionally transported by its profound and resonating sonic gothic ecclesiastical *bong* for which they had traveled all these many kilometers and gotten very very very wet. And at exactly 13.59.59 hrs. *et* secs. a tiny wrought-iron man slid out from the clockface and made a little turn and lifted up his tiny woodsman's axe and struck with Swiss precision at a tiny bell *ting/ting* and slid back inside the clock where to Sunny's mind he no doubt existed on tiny bits of chocolate and fondue. *Ting/ting?* She'd turned to Cas and they both burst out laughing and within the hour Cas had had them in a change of clothes in a hired *camion* that reeked of cheese back to Bellegarde through the still-pouring where she'd secured a *wagon-lit* on that evening's night train from Geneva back to Paris.

All of that, all the wildness of it and the downpour—the aroma of wet granite paving stones, wet plane trees wet gabardine—Sunny had reduced to a single entry in her notebook:

Went to Gex. It rained.

—as if consuming her first lobster or first oyster had been a far more exciting milestone in her life and more deserving of an exclamation point.

The Paris notebooks, as Sunny would come to think of the journey's diaries collectively, lived on the far end of the lower shelf above the kneading table in the kitchen where the cookbooks were amassed along with all the menus she'd collected and her mother's recipe cards and she rarely referred back to them once she'd returned to Lone Pine because whenever she did they made her sad. Not sad in the way of missing someone or some distant thing or place that you can never re-create but sad because of all the gaps, because of how little evidence they contained of her emotional life. Sad the way her mother's notecards made her feel—not because of what was written on them, but because of what had been left out.

One card read:

ON THE VIRTUES OF HOT SOUP

—in its entirety.

Another:

PROPERTIES OF THIRST

She likened reading through her mother's cards to reading an anthology of silences, the lost history of a soul . . . and on the few occasions she'd gone searching for her younger self in those Paris notebooks she'd come up with as little authentication of personality as she'd found in Lou's recipes. Neither of them were diarists. Both tended to jot half-thoughts in code. Where Lou came most alive to Sunny was in the margin exclamation points, exuberant *exacte!*s—made in her trademark purple ink—to this day Sunny was still uncovering them in the foxed and faded pages of Lou's culinary library.

ah c'est le sel ici q'ouvrit le goût
IT'S THE SALT HERE THAT UNLOCKS THE FLAVOR

Who was I, back then? Sunny would be forced to ask herself whenever she tried to make a narrative of her own notebooks. What had I been feeling? What did I think about the world?

There was no mention in the Paris notebooks for example—she'd gone looking for it—of what was for Sunny the most important thing that had occurred during those weeks: she knew for certain it had happened after Gex but when she tried to find the day, the place, it was nowhere to be found on those pages. Not even an allusion to this one significant event that had arisen out of nothing in particular, an afternoon of refulgent limestone-and-river light when she and Cas had stopped along a curb to wait for traffic and Cas had taken a full breath and announced in passing, "I could have been quite happy here . . . *I could have had a life,*" and then guided Sunny through the intersection to wherever they'd been going never noticing the tears in Sunny's eyes. Sunny had never thought—she had never *really* thought—about alternative lives for her Aunt Cas—no child thinks that way—but through that day and into that night she'd thought about who Cas might have been, the lives she might have lived had she not made the decision to help her brother raise his children. Sunny had taken Cas's words not as proof she was *un*happy—no one would ever think that of Cas—but that there might be many happinesses in a single life, many possibilities, some explored and others not and that the life one chose to live, if one were fortunate enough to choose, was but one of many. Not that Sunny at the age of thirteen had fathomed all of this but her shadow instincts, her adolescent ones, had intuited the existential questions, at least, if not their answers and before she'd climbed into bed that night and turned out the light in her room in the Lutetia she'd padded into the salon in her bare feet and the prissy little nightgown Cas had selected for her from Bergdorf Goodman . . . into the salon where Cas sat writing letters in her own prissy nightgown at the reproduction Louis Quatorze *écritoire* and Cas had looked up and remarked, "Turning in, button?" and Sunny had nodded *yes* and strode right up and said goodnight and kissed her on her cheek.

They had never been a kissing family—*death* having been the obstacle that they'd had to overcome—they clapped each other on the back in stalwart ways of showing cheer and offered affirmations of a job well done but theirs had never been a vocabulary of spontaneous bursts of physical affection and they never kissed. Not ever. Nor threw their arms around each other. Nor complained nor cried, they just got on with things under Cas's and Rocky's tutelage and unimpeachable firm examples.

Next night: same thing.

Sunny had found Cas wrapped up in bed reading, Scandinavian forest candle burning, gin to hand, and had gone in and had kissed her goodnight and that had been their ritual, with Cas eventually landing her own benison on Sunny's forehead without saying a word about it, but Sunny couldn't find the calendar *day* this had happened, the calendar *night* that this had taken place. Certainly it didn't change the fact that it had happened but now every day that passed with no word from Pearl Harbor seemed further proof that every scrap of evidence of one's history needed to be hoarded, needed to be dusted for fingerprints, case re-opened to maintain one's innocence against the overwhelming testimony that everyone we love and everything we are and everything we might have been are doomed to vanish without trace. What did it matter now that she had eaten *sole a la meuniere* on the sixth of June, 1933, and *moules-frites* for the first of many times ("*My favorite!*") when it had been the height of the Depression in the United States and Adolf Hitler had wrested the title of Chancellor from the multitude in Germany? She had eaten sea bream, sand dabs, hake, dogfish and John Dory. Monkfish, mackerel, *langoustes*, winkles, cod. But never made an entry about Declan or Rosemary Dust or M. Brouillard or the three strange boys she'd encountered shipboard on the Atlantic crossing home aboard the *France* who dressed in old men's black frock coats and wore black broad-brimmed hats and had long ringlets of black hair dangling in front of their ears from their hatbrims and wouldn't speak to her directly because she was a girl. Going over on the *Normandie* to France there had been at most a dozen children not counting babies but coming back there had been more than a hundred, enough to justify organized entertainment and instruction, and Cas had signed her up for a Celestial Navigation class at night outside on the bridge where she'd been the only girl with two other boys, both Austrian, plus the three strange ones in the black coats. When it had been ascertained that she was an American the tallest of the three in black coats had asked one of the Austrians to determine Of what *Statt*? *California*, Sunny had answered. I am to ask you There is gold everywhere on *der* ground?

Yes.

For the picking up from ground?

For 'picking,' with a *pick*, sure. But most of it's been 'picked' already.

And there are Indians?

Oh yes.

And they live naked?

Oh those are Jews, *dear*, Cas had told her, no need to think them queer they're merely different in the way that they perceive the Universe.

She had made no entries about people on the train from New York back to California, of the fires burning in the fields along the tracks, the makeshift tents, the men with bindles watching with enlarged eyes, hungry eyes, at crossings. If they'd been there on her trip east she hadn't noticed but although she saw them everywhere along the tracks on the journey home she'd never noted their existence. *Ate "she" crabs shell-and-all! Catfish!* Salmon cheeks. Ate a lobster roll! Ate *"Novy"*! *Escabeche*! Lobster Thermidor (why bother?). Lobster Newburg! HANGTOWN FRY. Picked at lump crabmeat with my fingers. Ate a *"po'boy."* Something called *"lutefisk"* (not really fish). *Crawdaddies* (ditto).

That was where the notebooks stopped—on *crawdaddies*, ditto—"ditto" being the final word, no mention of her arrival back in Truckee jumping from the train and seeing Rocky there—no Stryker—feeling so happy to be home believing Stryker must have been playing hide-and-seek with her then hearing Rocky say: He's in quarantine. The chicken pox.

—*pox* is never a good word in any language—Cas used it as a curse word: Is he going to *die*? she'd asked.

No kissing, still no kissing:

He'll be fine, Rocky had told her.

But her brother had NOT been "fine" when she'd seen him through the windowpane of his bedroom standing on a chair so he could see out to where she and Hace had pulled up their own chairs outside so they could talk to him through glass: he'd been painted all over in a pink liquid, his eyes red his hands wrapped and padded like decorative cushions so he couldn't scratch himself, his lips swollen. Underneath the pink paint were the pox. Hundreds of them.

On the car ride back from Truckee Cas had sat up front with Rocky and they'd gabbed non-stop with Sunny leaning in from the back seat to keep her arms around her father's neck which for once he hadn't seemed to mind. Rocky had met ALBERT EINSTEIN (Sunny didn't know who "Albert Einstein" was) on the Cunard Line's *Southampton* during the trip home, their staterooms had shared a private balcony—and he was all lit up about it and then he and Cas had started gabbing about politics and why so many Jews and Austrians were getting clear of Germany and all the other things Sunny didn't need to understand because she'd been *so* glad to be back in the familiar where the eye could finally rest—in France and in New York you're always *looking* 'cause you don't know what comes next, she'd tried to explain to Hace, who'd come running out the front door carrying two bunches of flowers, one for Cas and one for Sunny, when he'd heard their car arrive. Cas and Rocky could go inside Stryker's room because they'd already had the pox but Hace and Sunny had to wait outside the closed door where they sat on the cold stone floor of the *portales* and carried on a conversation with The Quarantine through the oak door with blankets shoved up under it so Stryker's pox could not get out. If she had been a true diarist she would have entered rich emotive passages about those days. She would have written, too, years earlier when it had happened, how she and Stryker had first met Hace when Rocky had taken them to Manzanar to buy apples from Señor Mendoza and there had been a kid there, their age, old Mendoza's grandson who spoke pretty good *ingles*, Stryker had told him, for a Mex, and Jesús had punched him, not for the last time, though Stryker—*always*—punched him back and always won. Jesús's parents had left him with old Mendoza so he could be in school while they'd gone to work the picking fields in the Central Valley and from the day they'd met—except for the trip to Europe and until The Incident—it had been the three of them the Three Musketeers of Three Chairs palling around making mayhem getting into trouble, Sunny always the third wheel on an otherwise dynamic duo— the *girl*—and she could keep up on the horses and on foot and keep up in the running and the jumping and the climbing but she couldn't wrestle and she could not keep up—she just couldn't—with the devotion Jesús always had to Stryker, his devotion to her brother over her. Plus she spent so much time on her own in the kitchen cooking trying to translate goddamn French in all those cookbooks. When they'd left for Europe the primary pair within their triad had been Jesús and Stryker, but by the time Stryker had been liberated from Quarantine it had become Jesús and Sunny, thanks to the pox. Which, had she been a true diarist, would have filled pages and pages—pages about how she and Hace had found new common ground and had started to appreciate each other more had started to like each other and have so much in common that even Stryker, once he was let loose, had observed that the two of them should just get married and had performed a mock ceremony complete with matching rings courtesy of a couple Cracker Jack boxes he'd lifted from the IGA in Lone Pine.

Stryker had *seemed* fine with the new dynamic among the three of them, but he'd soon moved out of the main house to live alone in the *casita*. Even with his withdrawal there remained remnants of the brotherhood between him and Hace, the original male bond that Sunny knew Hace would always answer if it ever came to *choosing* between her and her brother, if it ever came to life-or-death. *Everyone* chose Stryker over her, everyone *liked* Stryker better he was the twin that people warmed to the more attractive one the more social and outgoing and flamboyant one. The twin who knew exactly what to say or do to charm, the one with pitch-perfect grace notes in conversation the one with the *bon mot* the perfect gift . . . Sunny had brought him a French knife she'd found at E. Dehillerin in Paris that had all kinds of jimmies in it—screwdriver, Allen wrench, awl, scissors, corkscrew—and he had loved it and it had been a thoughtful choice but what he'd sought out for her from a stationer's in Edinburgh had *soul*: a fountain pen and six jars of ink—the same magenta—*purple*—as their mother's.

The gift had been meant to be enabling, she knew—Stryker could tease and taunt but he was never cruel—yet moved as she'd been by his thoughtfulness, she'd found the gift too loaded with meaning, the act of writing in her mother's color too daunting, too bold a move, and although she'd filled the pen and tried to break in the nib practicing her signature, she'd never written more than that and kept the fountain pen and the jars of ink in her bureau drawer to look at and sometimes to touch.

Until he'd written to her when he'd joined the Navy.

—she'd taken up the pen then to write to him and told herself *I own this*: I can own this.

When he'd shipped to Honolulu, she'd known he'd see that ink—their mother's ink—on the blue airmail envelopes before he'd even opened them, and she'd wanted the sight of that expressive ink to telegraph their memories and signal *Home*.

She had his letters from that time, the ones he'd written following The Incident, from San Diego first and then from Pearl—but one night a month ago she'd gone into a panic searching through her room for the letters/postcards he'd posted on his trip to Europe—she was certain she had kept them but she

235

couldn't find them in the ordinary places—she'd torn her room apart, alarming Cas who'd finally counseled *Calme, du calme, cherie*: Have you checked the notebooks? And there they'd been. Tucked inside the well-placed flaps for saving scraps of paper on the inside of every hardbound cover of the Paris notebooks . . .

Talk about falling down your rabbit hole:

—fish and fish and *more* fish; fish fish fish.

She'd carried the notebooks from the kitchen to her bedroom, to her bedside table and tried to read them at night but there was really only so much *I ate* [FILL IN NAME OF FISH/BIVALVE/MOLLUSK/FISH EGG/CRUSTACEAN]*!* that one can bear to read even if one is the Author of the [FISH]-tale. Cas had given her a subscription to a new magazine called *Gourmet* and there were those to read in bed as well as the new novels Tops had pressed on her (James M. Cain and Pearl S. Buck and Virginia Woolf no middle initial) and the cookbook Schiff had left for her when he'd come to dinner—*Fundamental Techniques of Classic Japanese Cooking*—as if anyone as steeped in French *cuisine* as she was would have any interest in how the Japanese cooked their food. Except we were at war with them and they had killed her brother and there were 10,000 of them living half a mile away from her across the road and that same brother had married one of them and had two half-Japanese sons. So her feelings about the Japanese in general were pretty complicated and her feelings about "classic" Japanese cooking were zero. Schiff's book sat unopened beside her bed under the Paris notebooks for about a week.

If she were to start a diary today—and she should, she thought, considering the times . . . (she still had four pristine Sennelier notebooks left over from Paris in their tissue wrappers, and plenty of *ink*)—her first sentence would probably be "*I read cookbooks in bed.*" At night. To fall asleep. To help me dream.

—not *every* night. She didn't fall asleep to cookbooks *every* night; some nights, the working nights, she'd barely make it up the back stairs to her boardinghouse-style room above Lou's overlooking Main Street in Lone Pine, too exhausted to turn down the counterpane—sometimes, on nights the restaurant wasn't open, she'd stay at Three Chairs in the kitchen making *fonds*, and while Cas and Rocky massacred each other through brutal rounds of cards at the long table under the aromas of her simmering stocks, she'd chop and dice and purify with egg white and, toward midnight, strain the holy liquids through *chinoises* from her prized 40 litre stockpots into gallon jars . . . Some nights she stood before a stove some nights she was on her feet some nights she was on her knees in the garden under torchlight: other nights she read, *re*-read cookbooks. And searched for previously undiscovered notes left by her mother in that vibrant hand which still seemed alive and so expressive in that historic purple *ink*.

> HUMBLE with broth.
> ELEVATE with melted butter.
> DISTINGUISH with salt.

She'd been re-reading one of those books very late one night a week before The Incident when she'd heard footsteps in the *portales* and the terrier ("Hester Prynne") at the foot of her bed had stood up and growled and then wagged her tail at Stryker in the doorway.

Hey, he'd said.

—hey, she'd answered.

Saw your light on, he'd said.

Doors were always open up and down the *portales* (except for Cas's) so the dogs could wander through and had it not been for the self-same dogs all the Rhodeses (except for Cas) could have been murdered in their beds by now or robbed or godknows studied in their sleep by extraterrestrials.

> When you arrive in a kitchen,
> set a pot of water to boil.
> You'll use it for something.

Left you some supper on the table, she'd told him.

He could not be trusted in the kitchen, he fried bacon in butter. Glazed his meats in root beer. Smothered everything with chilies.

Saw it. Thanks, he'd said.

He hadn't even touched it, she'd already known as she'd studied him for signs that he was sober.

He'd walked in.

Lay down on his back across the foot of her bed next to Hester Prynne.

Tobacco on him, as usual. And something else.

Ask you a question? he'd said.

—*shoot*, she'd answered.

He'd started to play with the dog, instead, snaking his hand under Sunny's blanket like a mole or something in the earth to drive Hester Prynne crazy.

". . . how do you know," he'd started. ". . . when you're making something: How do you know when it's *done*?"

—when it's "done"?

He'd rolled over, propped his head up, stared:

When you're cooking something. How do you know it's finished?

Depends on what it is.

What are you *after*, Stryker? she'd been thinking: What did you come in here for?

They almost never came to one another's rooms.

Say "a meal."

—a whole "meal"?

I don't care. Not a "meal," then . . . Say a "cake" . . . I'm just looking for advice, here . . .

For baking *a cake*? she remembers having thought. OK, cowboy:

"With a cake . . . or a biscuit . . . any cakey thing, you stick the point of a sharp knife an inch or so into the center. Comes out coated in batter, needs more cooking. Comes out clean *it's done*."

—a *knife* . . .

Not the answer he'd been hoping for:

"Let's say . . . a 'steak,' then."

He'd cooked steak a hundred times when they were camping but she'd gone along with what-the-hell his game had been and told him: Make a fist.

He'd made one.

"*This*," she'd told him, jabbing at the flat top of his hand, "is what a piece of *bien cuit—well-done—*beef feels like if you jab it. *This—*" she pinched the flesh around his fisted thumb, "is what *medium* well-done—*à point—*feels like and *this,*" she pinched the tender flesh beneath his fisted pinkie in two places, "are the '*saignant*' and '*au bleu*'; '*medium*' rare and '*rare.*'"

He'd studied her like there was something else he'd wanted her to tell him or something else he'd wanted to say.

"Well that's just gorgeous, Sis . . . Thanks a magnum."

He'd stood up.

"Sharp knife or a clenched fist. That's some great advice. I'll remember that."

And he'd left, without goodnight.

My god: *He was saying he was leaving*, she now realized. Too late: He was trying to explain to me that he was *done* . . . Done with all of this, the way we live here, his life in Owens Valley, done with the Sierras and Main Street in Lone Pine, done with Three Chairs . . . *done* with all of us.

> YOU KNOW IT'S DONE when it's reduced to half
> when it turns red
> when the surface shivers
> when it holds a peak
> when you knock on it and it sounds hollow
> when it turns brown
> when you can stand a spoon in it
> when it reaches blood temperature
> when the liquid from the thigh, when pricked, runs golden
> when the liquid from the thigh, when pricked, is no longer pink
> when it springs back to your touch
> when the shells open
> when a knife stuck in its heart feels soft
> when the shells "yawn"
> when it coats the spoon
> when it thickens

when the oil on top forms a reflective surface

when you can see your face in it

WHEN IT FLOATS.

"*Japan is an island nation*," she discovered herself reading now, "its land surrounded on all sides by tides. The sea has always fed its inhabitants. No part of its land lies more than 80 miles from an ocean, lake or sea. Its language is awash in references to water . . ."

She turned a page.

WASTE NOT A SINGLE GRAIN OF RICE, she read.

THE ONLY SIDE EFFECTS OF FOOD SHOULD BE HEALTH AND LONGER LIFE.

"The Japanese are *polite* to food," she kept on reading: "These are the FIVE METHODS of Japanese Cooking:

> Boiling
> Grilling
> Steaming
> Frying
> RAW."

Next to this statement, in the left-hand margin of the left-hand page, someone had posed the question *No baking?* And written APPEARS TO BE NO OVENS! in purple ink.

Across the top of the facing page that same someone, in that same ink, had scrawled,

> *Appears to be a culture without* bread
> *Culinary culture based on* FISH!

—what the *hell*?

She flipped back to the frontispiece, which she'd overlooked when she'd picked the book up from her bedside table.

There was an inscription there.

"*March, 1942,*" it read:

> *For Sunny,*
> *with gratitude—*
> *This used book*
> *for you to put to better use—*
> *Schiff*

In purple ink.

She got out of bed and went to the bureau and took out the pen, shook it, licked the nib to moisten it and filled the barrel with the purple ink Stryker had bought for her and then went back to bed and drew a straight line across the page beneath Schiff's name and watched it float for several seconds on the surface of the paper until it etched itself into that property of thirst and sank and eventually hardened and dried, resolving into its true color.

Knock me over with a feather, as Cas would state:

Stick a fork in this:

It's done:

The three inks, her mother's, Schiff's, her own, appeared to have been drawn from the same source, from the same well: *identical.*

Exacte!

ROSEMARY DUST

Cleaning rosemary leaves from fresh branches is tedious
because the oily needles don't submit to pressure from
one's thumb. Peri-dry the branches, if you can, by
hanging them upside-down until the needles dry. What you're
hoping for is 1 c. needles from which the moistures
(water, oil) have evaporated, but don't let the needles
turn to brown.

Put your dried but still-green needles in a *molcajete* and
grind to a fine powder.

Rosemary used whole can be overpowering and powdering
it this way provides a subtle substitute.

Use on lamb or pork.
Or add to salt, oil and lemon as a marinade for fish.
Sprinkle into soup for woody flavor.

Mixed with equal parts of suet in the wild, the resulting
paste can temporarily cauterize a wound.

I owe the inspiration for this recipe to a woman I met in 1933
on the S.S. *Normandie.*
Her name was Rosemary Dust.

BLUE MOONS:

—just his fucking luck to draw two fulls in a single month; APRIL 1942 *two* full moons the first falling on the night of Intake the other four weeks later—no wonder he couldn't sleep—he never slept during a full moon.

Better blues than blacks, Svevo had argued when he'd bellyached: two *new* moons in a single month: month of two *black* nights.

—maybe that would have helped. If there hadn't been a goddamn moon. If the whole disaster had played out in a partial light from the watchtowers, so the internees couldn't see the wire fences in the foreground, couldn't see the barrenness surrounding them, beyond.

He had never failed at anything—well, with women, but not at anything the smart boys do. He had been the kid who'd come, like many of his generation, out of the city tenements into the Big Time. He'd gone from smart bar mitzvah boy to undergrad to a law degree to Washington, D.C. in a series of successes, and the mess he'd made the first day on this job was maybe another reason he was wide awake. Once, back in Chicago, some old guy in the building across the street had been dragged out by the cops one morning and Schiff had watched him from the window as he'd yelled from the middle of the street *at least I'll get some peace in prison!* "Prison," Schiff had thought, must be some place actually desirable—solitary; quiet; peace-full.

Not like this: you-and-me and the uninterrupted sounds of each-and-every one of our nightmares.

So it's come to this, he kept turning over in his mind: he had always thought his parents were the springboard from which his success would catapult but now when he compared his trajectory to theirs, when he tried to uphold his previous belief that no one on his family tree had gone as far as he had, he had to stop and reckon with this current mess. They had leapt from the *shtetl* to Chicago. That originating wave of immigrants: try all you want, as a first-generation American, you couldn't out-distance them, you couldn't out-run them, their generation had gone farther, longer, on less pay, less food and while you're at it Mister Smartypants, on nothing but that *shtetl* education.

How his father ever got a wife remained a mystery to Schiff but how he got to the United States was a lesson repeated countless times:

His father got here empty-handed.

—not a penny to his name. You hear the plot retold across America, how the founding father had arrived with nothing in his pockets, how the founding mother had arrived with nothing but an heirloom pearl sewn in her dress. What the hell else was there to carry? A bit of tatted lace, two inches wide, not even silk, from someone's (his great-grandmother's) dress. A miniature Torah. Black soil in a folded packet. Fairy dust and rainbow water.

When his father arrived in the United States (by boat, in steerage) he could have brought along a trunk (if he'd owned possessions in the first place), he could have paid to ship the furniture as the Rothschilds had done, all restrictions on his holdings dictated by poverty, not law. There seemed to be no limit to what you could export/import, but if you were going to be a ward of the United States at one of its internment camps you had to come (you *had* to come) only with the things that you could carry.

No pets.

No swords.

No banners with Japanese writing.

No "art" with Japanese writing.

No books in Japanese.

Nothing printed in any language other than English.

No photographs of Hirohito.

No pictures of any emperor.

No cloth with Japanese writing.

No bandanas with Japanese writing.

No bandanas.

No round objects used as ritual weapons.

Cameras were allowed, but only a Caucasian could press the shutter.

—what's *this*?

[LET THE RECORD SHOW a blackened object, not that big, but deep,
   rectangular, pitted, sooty, heavy as all shit.]
Hibachi.
In English?
A grill.
Its purpose?
. . . grilling.
So there'd have to be like, what . . . a *fire*?
Charcoal.
But you'd hafta light it.
Yes.
Impounded. Next—?

—what's *this*?
[LET THE RECORD SHOW an object of teakwood or mahogany,
   folding, four feet high. Looks like a screen, but with open spaces,
   like a ladder.]
Kimono monohoshi.
—English?
For hanging kimono. Very old. Family treasure.
Bud, I got no problem with it but I have to put down what it is. So
   let's start again.
Kimono monohoshi.

—what's *this*?
Rice fan.
Come again?
Implement for fanning rice.
Lady now I've heard it all . . . *next*?

What kind of tree is this?
[LET THE RECORD SHOW a potted plant.]
Sakura.

—in English?

Weeping cherry tree.

Whoja think you are, *George Washington?*

How long's he been here?

[LET THE RECORD SHOW THE SUBJECT IS REFUSING TO SPEAK
ENGLISH.]

My grandfather has lived in California thirty years.

And you expect me to believe he doesn't speak the lingo?—*Mr. Schiff?*

"What's the problem, Corporal?"

"Old guy here says he doesn't speak the language. Plus all his docs are
Japanese."

"Sir, you're translating for this gentleman?"

"Yessir."

"What is your relationship to him?"

"He's my grandfather."

"May I see your documents, please?"

[LET THE RECORD SHOW THE 2ND SUBJECT IS A U.S. CITIZEN.]

"Sir, how did your grandfather come through the process this far with
no acceptable documentation?"

"This is his birth certificate . . ."

"—in Japanese. I need to see his residency papers."

"He didn't bring them."

"—he didn't *bring* them."

"He had them but he didn't bring them."

"—*bringing* them was not optional: *bringing* them was mandatory."

The lines had backed up from the start of the Intake, some moving at a
rate of five registrations/three inspections every hour. Svevo had press-ganged
Army Corps of Engineers into service—press-ganged the female (Caucasian)
secretaries—had even sat at a makeshift desk himself to keep things moving
but the process had gone on well past the planned mess call into the night.
Schiff had tried to process families with young children first—and also fam-

ilies with the aged and/or infirm—but even in the face of his best intentions children were still standing, unfed and unhoused, under the full moon, when he'd ordered the searchlights turned on, drawing attention to the watchtowers and the men in uniforms, with guns, positioned there. He'd been counting heads down one of the lines when a little girl asked her mother why there were men *up there* and he'd heard her mother answer Don't be silly—they're *up there* to feed The Rabbit in the Moon tonight. *Can I feed him, too?* the little girl had asked and Schiff had borne a coded look—another one—masked in obedience, from the mother, rebuking him.

RABBIT IN THE MOON.

Japs are strange in many ways, Svevo maintained, not in the least because they see A RABBIT there, on the surface—a whole fucking *rabbit!*—every time they look at a full moon instead of what *we* see which is the face of our own white old guy *MAN* IN THE MOON.

—what the *fuck*:

—how can you see a *rabbit* there?

Svevo went so far as to postulate (and Schiff admonished him for this) that THE RABBIT in the moon had to be an optical illusion that arose from looking at the sky through slanted eyes.

Schiff's week was shaping up like that: slanted views on everything: prejudice from unexpected places: prejudice in every corner of the job: racism at work all the day long. Even from the very best of the good guys.

Schiff couldn't sleep. He hadn't slept—maybe an hour, two—the last three days. He'd put his head down on the pillow, hear them whispering. Hear the wind tear up the flag outside. Hear an argument in strangled tones. Hear the convoys going by along the road. Hear a muffled cry.

Svevo was still convinced a revolt was in their future, that no full-blooded Americans would submit themselves and that the revolution would ignite in the black market fed by the disparity of privileges, not so much from hunger as from a steady diet of captivity, boredom and its bitter harvest, rage.

It'll spark in idle groups of the young unmarried men, Svevo predicted. Like he'd seen all this before.

The preventative course, then, was to break the bachelors up at night, break the bachelors up by having only one or two in every family barrack but the numbers were too stacked, the odds weren't in Schiff's favor, there were too many young unmarried males and Schiff had to house most of them together and the best thing he could do to keep them from plotting revenge or organizing mutiny was to police them, to quarter them in barracks under the watchtowers, house them where the sentries could eyeball them all night long.

He had to find them things to do. "Constructive daily routines," his orders read. Because idleness is incendiary.

Thoughts of what they might be plotting among themselves at night, their open anger, kept him awake in his bachelor barrack, plagued by the same night terror every captor shares through History: If "they" could get their act together—and "they" would—they'd turn the tables, trade on the fact that "they" outnumbered *us*.

Listen to the noise they made at night the farts the infants crying exhaled breath the phlegm in someone's throat a dream an exclamation foreign shout the female protest:

Who the hell could sleep through all this even on a guilt-free conscience. Even on a halfway decent mattress.

Military transports back and forth between Los Angeles and Bishop, roaring from the tungsten mines, rendering the road a sounding board, trucks barreling outside with loads of ore and produce, slaughter beef and oranges: then rolling over on his other side, he could hear the sounds of people trekking to latrines outside his window, toilets flushing, mess crews waking up.

He tried to measure the few beats of silence, never got past *one*. Not once. Every night: he never got to *two*.

—*so what*, he thought: there were people living through this war on nothing but adrenaline—and some on *fear*—his two or three hours of interrupted sleep were his own softass luxury and he was up those first few mornings in the camp, shaved and showered, unfed, dressed in a suit and tie and his grey fedora, prowling the perimeter for godknows what, a sign of forgiveness, before the sun ascended in the east above the mountains.

He liked to walk.

The pacing gave him solace.

He laced himself into the Army boots Svevo had requisitioned, tediously securing his rolled-up pant cuffs with two bands, then stepped out into the fenced-in garrison with its watchtowers beneath the too-big sky and played for a moment with the idea that he was that stand-up guy in the white hat (John Wayne) in charge of some isolated fort in some Western. Because goddammit: that's where he *was*. In a goddamn western desert. In the goddamn West. Which made him feel unreal, when he looked at all the land surrounding him. Not in Chicago anymore. Now appearing in a kind of movie—but in the movies he was thinking of, the *wild, wild* threat always came from outside the stockade, while his was coming from within. *Congratulations, Mister Smartypants: you've built yourself a* ghetto. For FDR. For Roosevelt. For your government. For all the civic statutes that you cherish. PROTECTIVE CUSTODY. All this for their own protection. If they weren't here—sequestered and protected—christ knows what their fates could be. Mood since Pearl was nasty in the heartland. Listen to the radio, Father Coughlin calling for their deportations. Even Walter Winchell. *Drop them off on some godforsaken island out in the Pacific.* Runem outta town. Feedem to the sharks. Don't belong here. Fuck 'em. They're not one of Us.

He liked the desert air.

—the way, near dawn, it woke him when he took it in his lungs. The way it startled him. The way it scared him shitless. Stars he should have known the names of semaphored their coded dots-and-dashes and a non-blinking planet—Venus?—glared at him: *I'm a fixed Eternal in mythology, I'm a lasting thing and you're a minor happening upon earth's surface.*

Gotta love what being Jewish in America this century has done for you. Gotta love that inner voice.

The kids' name for him was "Uncle."

—started weeks ago when these fresh Army boys arrived: Army-speak is flat and fast and pungent, who knows why they "Uncle"'d him or why it stuck, probably because he was in charge, like "Uncle" Sam (despite the fact he had, at best, a mere five years on most of them).

He checked in at the Main Gate each morning before walking the perimeter and the MP there would radio "*Uncle*'s coming," or "*Uncle*'s on the prowl," or "*Uncle, Uncle*" so the boys in the watchtowers wouldn't focus their ammo on him as he paced off his ritual in the pre-dawn dark.

But yesterday he thought he'd heard the MP at the gate radio ahead Here comes Uncle *Abe.*

"They're calling me 'Uncle *Abe,*'" he'd told Svevo.

So what?

Because I'm Jewish? *Abraham?*

—because you're *from Chicago.* Get a road map. Illinois. "Land o' Lincoln," princess: *Abe.*

So this morning when the MP at the gate radioed the towers Here comes Uncle Abe, Schiff asked him Why do all of you call me that?

"Sorry, sir."

No need to apologize.

Won't happen again, sir.

You can sorry me all you want, Staff Sergeant, I'm just curious as to *why.*

Same as "Ike," I guess. Or "Monty," sir.

Those are those generals' *names.*

Yes, sir.

"Abe" is not my name.

It's not?

Schiff held up his ID for him to read.

Well, that's a mouthful.

Biblical.

I'll say. What did they call you in school?

They called me Schiff.

Actually in school they'd called him something else he'd rather not remember.

The sergeant took to the radio again: Look sharp, boys. Uncle *Schiff* is on the way.

The story of his name was family legend and even he would have doubted its veracity had it not revolved around his mother, who was wonky in a lot of things—especially the kitchen and her practice of religion—but she never lied. Schiff used to think she wasn't smart enough to lie but he'd come to appreciate that she had a kind of peasant genius that had saved their lives on more than one occasion, so she wasn't stupid. Just a little crazy in the *keppie* sometimes. All the *meshuga* stuff with made-up rituals, wrapping her hand in linen before touching "modern" things (the telephone, the fridge), never going through a front door where a back door could be had, speaking to God in public places. But lying? She didn't own the art, it wasn't in her heart. She'd never been a joy to look at but she had the finest hands, dexterous long fingers that turned out precision stitches valued by the *schneiders* in the neighborhood: she was a brilliant buttonholer: she took in piecework to augment Schiff's father's income and her stitches never frayed. Twice a month she'd *schlep* to the North Side to collect supplies from the *schmatta* factory and on one of those trips, shortly after she'd discovered her first (and only) pregnancy, she came out of the back door of the supplier to a landing overlooking the back alley and there was the entire North Side Gang, Bugs Moran, Hymie Weiss (who was a Catholic Pole born Henryk Earl Wojciechowski; not Jewish, despite his alias), Dean O'Banion—the famous "Little Hellions" with their pants wide open and their *schlongs* between their mitts, the *gonifs*, "pishing" all together in a row against the redbrick wall, their uncircumcised *pipis* leering up at her (Schiff's own adolescent elaboration); and she'd fainted. Legend held she'd somehow collapsed diva-ishly, slipping feet-first on her back down the steps into the alley where she'd woken to an array of coins and paper money and her skirt wet in spots. The *mamzers* had shaken off their *schmucky* onto her skirt and then lavished her with *shekels*—their debasing money not only touching on her body and her clothes but on her womb and on the child she carried.

Maybe that was when she'd started going crazy because she'd become convinced (legend had it) that the only way to free her unborn child from the curse she had encountered was to seek the counsel of a *reb* and do exactly what he prescribed—the *reb* in this case being not their normal rabbi but a half-cracked mystic Rima had heard about from someone who knew someone who knew someone from her village back home. This *reb*—"I looked at him with only one good eye," Schiff's father always said—told the expectant couple that the only way to ward off the curse of the *goyim* "pishing" on her was to name the child prophetically, not genealogically. Give the child the same name as a Jewish hero or a prophet. Protect the child with a name directly from the Torah. We would have named you—by Hebrew tradition—for your mother's father, Nachim, in honor of your *zeyde*, if it wasn't for that *reb*, his father had confided. "*Still?* as names go, we coulda done a whole lot worst."

—which was true: there were lists of *worst*-sounding names in O.T. genealogies—Bilshan, Mispar, Bigval, Zattu, Azgad, Immer, Akkub, Hagab—Schiff had, at least, been spared those. But the name with which they'd titled him had been no easy thing to bear as a young boy in Chicago—he'd rather have been called "Alphonse" he remembers having wished after Rima erected a pagan altar of newspaper clippings in the front room in memory of Al Capone who had attempted to gun down all of her assailants in a shooting spree that became known as the St. Valentine's Day Massacre. Al Capone's gang murdered five members of Rima's despised North Side Gang. *Alphonse understood,* Schiff grew up hearing his mother say. She hadn't picked up any of the *goyim*'s money—hadn't even touched it—and through Schiff's youth she wouldn't let him pick up pennies, nickels, dimes on sidewalks. Don't pick that up you don't know where it's been, don't touch it. Lucky penny? No such thing in Rima's world. O the fortunes he'd allowed to pass him by. To this day he never picked up anything he hadn't earned. Always looked askance at anything Chance or Fortune dropped in front of him. To walk with his mother to the greengrocer's—walk with her *anywhere*—entailed tolerating the expiating rhythms beating in her head, walk, walk, *pray!*, walk, walk, *recite!*, walk, *touch your forehead!*, walk don't look at him don't *look* at any strangers don't *eat* that you can't *go* there *look away* don't pick that up don't *touch* that if you touch it touch your forehead right away . . .

He realized with a start that as he walked along the fence he compulsively touched it every other step. Well isn't that just rinky dink: I've turned into my *mother.* He wondered how long he'd been doing it and if any of the tower boys had noticed. Of course they had. He imagined they were laughing out their asses at him every time he passed.

This fucking fence:

—he had never wanted to put it up, hadn't supported the idea in the first place, especially making it barbed wire, taking it so high. When they'd been building it, here in the northwest corner, farthest from the road, a young male deer had jumped over, foraging for apple mast and become trapped inside. Panicked, the deer had tried again to vault the fence only to ensnare himself and bleed out. The Army boys took pictures of themselves beside the hanging carcass until Schiff shut their circus down. A boy from South Dakota asked if he could keep the antlers; another asked if he could keep the meat. The blood, attracting crows for days, was still here on the barbs, only now the women hung their washing there, their laundry out to dry, which made the whole back stretch look like a flight experiment, like a long line of kites that could go airborne at any gust. Somebody's shirt had flown off to the other side. Somebody's underwear. On any given day there was a littering of trash stuck in the wire thorns along the ground. Toilet paper. Candy wrappers. Cigar bands. A paper swan. (Don't *touch* it!)

—must be fifteen, twenty folds in this thing, Schiff thought, bending to retrieve it: he'd read about this craft the Japanese do, making animals from paper, folding it. He couldn't swear to it but he'd bet this thing could *float* the folds were that tight. Security demanded that the Army take a look at this to make certain nothing had been written on the inside and then folded up, and he knew the boys up in the watchtowers were all over him so he placed it nonchalantly in his pocket. Some kid's missing toy. Some heartbroken lover's artifact.

The sun, still down, was casting alpenglow along the peaks—an otherworldly orange—and as he came down the long western side he could sense the movements in the barracks, the tense start of another captive day.

As the sky lightened, plumes of smoke from the coal stoves in each unit became visible snaking sideways to the contours of the valley their pitchy scent mixing with the rotted apple mast and stagnant water in the irrigation ditches to an aromatic cocktail he was starting to identify as "Manzanar": you couldn't smell the humans, yet. That specific smell would arise with warmer weather, right about the time it grew too hot to sleep indoors and the cesspools had all reached the point of saturation.

The southwest corner of the enclosure was its least guarded spot—there was no watchtower here and it housed the motor pool and fuel storage tanks, the firehouse and machinist shops as well as the back gate to the service road where all deliveries entered. Walking the perimeter three days ago, Schiff had intended to cut this corner and head off diagonally through the barracks area back toward the Main Gate and his office. Then he'd noticed "The Hats," a group of seven male adults standing by the fence smoking cigarettes. The curfew had just lifted yet all seven were already dressed—notably, wearing individual distinguished headgear: a fisherman's cap, a leather moto helmet, a beret, a fedora, a tarboosh, porkpie, bowler—so he'd adjusted his route to pass more closely by them, curious about what they were doing there. As he'd passed, they all stepped back to give him wider berth and when he'd said Good Morning they'd stopped smoking and simply stared. Same thing yesterday—same men, same hats, same clothing, same routine—so when he spotted them today, same seven of them, he determined he would stop and chat. They seemed nonplussed: not rude but not forthcoming either.

You gentlemen are out early every morning, he observed.

He hadn't meant to sound censorious but the conversation stopped.

He fingered the folded swan in his suit pocket and thought of taking it out and asking them if it had any meaning but then he thought better of it. The valley clouds, he'd noticed this morning and yesterday, were unusual, torpedo-shaped, about a hundred feet long and moving swiftly south to north like a school of predatory fish on a hunting mission, low, low to the ground.

Some clouds, huh? he said. Never saw the likes of *those* before.

The Professor was just saying, the Porkpie said.

"*Lenticular*," the tarboosh (the "Professor") said. "Specific to deep valleys. Fast-moving. I've been here before to photograph them for my class at Stanford. Meteorology."

Schiff, Schiff said and put his hand out: he went around the circle introducing himself (and committing everybody's name to memory). "Meteorology was everybody's favorite science class where I went to school," he said.

"And where was that?" the Professor (MURUMOTO SHOZO) asked.

University of Chicago.

O there's weather *there*, MURUMOTO said. "Lake effect."

"—*cigarette?*" the Porkpie (MAMURA HITOSHI) offered.

Thank you, I don't smoke, Schiff said.

They seemed to all inhale their weeds in unison:

—there had been a long debate via telex and telephone among the camp heads and the tall brass in Washington on MATCHES, whether or not MATCHES and CIGARETTE LIGHTERS should be classified as potential WEAPONS of destruction (all the camps were made of WOOD) and, thus, prohibited, until someone at Interior no doubt pulling on his umpteenth Camel or Lucky Strike that day decided FUCK THIS. People gotta smoke. People gotta have a way to stay awake and socialize. People gotta have a way to *think*. And what was *tobacco*, anyway, if not American . . .

"Well, my door is open," Schiff said, referring to the "open door" hours in his office every morning: "If there's anything you gents need to talk about—"

Are you married, Mister Schiff? (KEN OHARA: *beret*.)

Not yet.

They studied him: he noticed all seven of them wore wedding bands:

—and he became suddenly aware of how *young* he was, compared to them, one of whom (he would discover later that day, looking up their names in the registration documents) was a lawyer in private practice—*fedora*—one of whom was a branch manager for Bank of America—*bowler*—one of whom owned an orchard—*moto helmet*—one of whom was a professor, a fisherman, an accountant, a car salesman.

"The way the curfew is set up right now," the one called TANAKA TETSUKO said: "Sunset to sunrise . . ."

Yes? Schiff said.

They looked around at one another wondering which would speak.

(It was OHARA:)

Sunset to sunrise . . . he finally repeated: "Long time in closed quarters with one's *wife*."

I see, Schiff said.

They hoped he did.

They all blew smoke his way.

"And with summer coming," (this was TANAKA speaking:) "sunset will come later, anyway."

"Yes, of course," Schiff said. He was about to ask what exactly do you need a later curfew *for*? but remembered how his father loved the summer evenings on the stoop, outside, away from Rima, playing cards or chess or sitting by himself, buried in his reading, in his thinking, in his *solitude*, anywhere the house could hide him, him *alone*.

What were they *saying* to each other, all these married couples, through the nights. Four, five, six couples per barrack nothing separating them from the other couples but a blanket for a wall. If they'd had worries in their marriages before—what couple did not?—what graver worries did they have now? How were they explaining their new quarters to their children? How many of their kids could actually believe the men up in the watchtowers with rifles and binoculars had been magically put there to feed lettuce to the goddamn RABBIT?

He needed to deliver *jobs* to fill the idle hours. And they needed one more hour—a simple extra hour—in the day to try to be the persons they had been before being sent here. To try to be alone. To smoke their cigarettes. To watch their matches burn down to nothing, wisps of smoke.

The whole place had shaken itself awake and the noise increased by increments—a shouted greeting, shouted warning, baby's cry; a song, a motor. Morning mess was from 0700 to 0830 and people were lining up to shower, lining up at the latrines, carrying their pisspots and their soaps—kids running in the firebreaks between the barracks where the women shook out bedclothes and the bachelors stood around and flipped their coins to try to look like they were busy.

Lunch was 1130 to 1300.

Supper 1700 to 1830.

And that was pretty much the day.

The school wasn't up and running yet but those plans were moving right along—they had teachers in the population but needed books and the curricula delivered from the State—they had the music teachers but they needed instruments; they had the phys ed teachers but they needed sports equipment. Yesterday he and Svevo had overseen setting up stations (tables) outside the Admin Buildings for JOB REGISTRATION with the intent to create a CAMP

DIRECTORY: Need a lawyer? That would be Mr. So-and-So in Barrack such-and-such. Seamstress? Miss Such-and-Such in Barrack "*x*." They had, just from yesterday's initial sampling, 16 hairdressers and 5 barbers. *Ours is not a model under which to test free enterprise*, Svevo had concluded: "You got *sixteen* hairdressers you just know *one* of them has got to stink and *one* of them—okay, maybe *two*—are going to out-'do' the rest. All the girls are gonna wanna go to *them*: those two, and not to stink-o which is how free markets work—but what *we*'re tryin' to do is distribute these jobs evenly so what we gotta do is *assign* each hairdresser to a certain group of barracks.—*dig?*"

"I went to college, Jay."

"—I mean with five barbers we can just set up the chairs and let the best man win but *sixteen* hairdressers? That's a circus for sure right there."

The first day of Schiff's "open door" *had* been a circus, with people lined up in the belief that Schiff could let them *out* . . . but the second morning had been better once the word had gotten around that *Internment is not negotiable*: DEAL WITH IT.

Like the ladies who expected baths.

Thirty of them—which was a lot of *ladies* in his office at the same time—one from each family barrack, all of them over fifty, all in need of a *hot* soak and *shower shoes* but none willing to talk to him directly, he was told by the single (younger) woman delegated to address him.

"Why are they all here if no one wants to talk?" Schiff asked (as politely as he could).

"They will talk: they will talk to *a woman*," he was told.

"Well that's interesting . . . but *futile*," he had said, "because *there is no woman with authority* to help you: I'm it."

Ultimately Betty—his secretary—had been recruited to listen to the women's tales of woe about the lack of tubs and decency within the current shower situation and the lack of privacy in the female latrines (which Betty, bless her, had been led off to inspect in person).

No one's getting *tubs*, had been Svevo's final word on the matter but they'd found four plumbers in the population who seemed to understand the problem and were willing to "deal" with it.

So that had been, at least, *one* bullet dodged.

"Open door" hours were 0900 to 1100 and when you've got ten thousand people to administer it's not enough time every day to hear that many pleas. Svevo had let him know he thought the hours were a laff. For one thing (Jay said) it turned the Admin Buildings into Greyhound stations and for another it made them all look bad. Made them look like idiots, he said. Like a cabinet of French bureaucrats. But Schiff believed in it as good public relations plus, without it, he knew he'd *never* sleep.

Betty, I'm going to draft an Order amending curfew hours and you'll run off copies to post on all the buildings. Has Jimmy Ikeda shown up yet?

No, sir.

He'd sent for Jimmy, his old work acquaintance from the Drake, the day after Intake and kept trying to find the time to track him down, but so far he'd failed to do that.

Maybe he doesn't want to see you, Svevo goaded him.

Who wouldn't want to see *me*? I'm the Head Guy.

Maybe he doesn't know that. Maybe he forgot your name. What *is* your name?—want me to send an MP out to find him?

No . . . I want *you* to find him.

That had been yesterday; and still no Jimmy.

Instead he had the Inyo County rep from Pillsbury. He had the rep from P&G (Proctor and Gamble) pitching CRISCO at him. (What *was* that? what was a "hydrogenated 'non-piggy' *lard*"?) He had Kraft Foods and Oscar Mayer—he had sales reps from Phillip Morris, Bristol Myers; Bayer. He had the rep from Coca-Cola telling him that two refrigerated units of Coca-Cola dispensers would make the "campers" (the Coke guy had called them that) happy, wouldn't cost the camp a cent (he forgot the *refrigeration* cost, Schiff had noticed) and Coke would give the camp back half a cent on every bottle sold. *No*, Schiff had told him. They're gonna want their Coke, the guy had said. They *need* their Coke. Schiff understood that what these reps saw when they looked at the camp was one big potential market—*As the largest "city" in Inyo County*, they would all start and Schiff would show them his palm upright and tell them STOP and call out, *Svevo!* to show them to the door. How the reps had heard about his "open door" he didn't know (he guessed they'd gotten the word from Lone Pine merchants) so although entrance to his inner sanctum (the Pope will see you now) was on a 1st-come, 1st-served basis he'd told Betty to send the reps to Svevo who knew best how to (yes) *deal* with them:

—goddamn PROFITEERS: trying to make money during WAR.

He'd had the print shop make a poster for his office wall of Roosevelt's "Four Freedoms," which people faced (and he had to face) when they walked in:

> FREEDOM of Speech.
>
> FREEDOM of Worship.
>
> FREEDOM from Want.
>
> FREEDOM from Fear.

Well that's a fucking laff, Svevo had said: WHOM ARE YE KIDDING?

On his desk this morning there was the usual paper pile, and he placed the swan on top of it.

They're rationing shoes, he noticed in a flyer from the Office of Price Administration: my country has begun to ration *shoes*.

—in addition to rubber tires (those had been the first things rationed), steel, nylon, sugar, *red meat*, butter, tin, wool, cotton, soap. Coffee. Gasoline. The Office of Price etc. (the OPA) was asking (requiring) him to put up posters in the camp that read:

AMERICAN MEAT IS FIGHTING FOOD!

—to encourage *what*, exactly, he was wondering, when two Shinto priests in pearl-colored robes and tall black *hats* appeared, silently, before him, his morning's first "open door" guests. Accompanied by their lawyer.

"Dr. Takei," he greeted her.

"Student Schiff," she formally acknowledged.

Schiff knew from Intake that the priests had taken a vow of silence in protest of "protective custody" so he bowed toward them and they bowed back, and sat.

Georgina Takei, Doctor of Law, was by all measure a solid jurist but by his own personal measure a kind of living embodiment of what one could be when one put her actions where her conscience was because she was here at Manzanar of her own volition—she could walk out any day, as a resident of Illinois, outside the Exclusion Zone. He had never had a class with her at Chicago—her seminars were always over-enrolled—but her lectures on Ethics were legends and even while he was still in Illinois it had been rumored she was slated for judgeship. She had never married, Schiff knew—she'd grown up in San Francisco, where her father was a hotshot journalist covering "Asian" issues and had been such an all-out fan of his adopted country he'd named his only daughter after George Washington. Now she was a resident of Barrack 38 and partook of showers with the ladies who desired tubs. She was here in solidarity with her fellow victims of injustice (her words) not only to bring her own lawsuit against Frank Roosevelt's "illegal incarceration" (her words) of Japanese-Americans but to file other briefs—twelve, in all—in U.S. courts against the legality of his Executive Order 9066 and subsequent unconstitutional measures targeted against Japanese-Americans, including those who practiced Shintoism as an act of faith.

"I trust you've read the brief," she said.

"I have," Schiff answered.

This was the dance they had to do:

At issue was the Oath of Allegiance the government (Schiff's government, her government; our government) required each internee to sign pledging to uphold the flag of the United States and all that it stood for and to renounce all prior allegiances to Japan including allegiance to its Emperor and the belief in his divinity as well as in his divine right to rule on earth. It was a fucking piece of work, this Oath, in Schiff's opinion—badly conceived, badly written, overlong in its multiple dependent clauses, fuzzy, wuzzy, just plain *wrong*—but Washington had handed it along to all the camps (*more* paperwork), which meant that part of what made Intake such hell was having to explain to the elderly, especially, what exactly they were renouncing when they signed it. *If* they signed it. If they *didn't* sign, Schiff was required to notify Interior of their presumed "treason" and then those individuals would be transferred to more secure camps operated by the Department of Justice (which were, in practice, *prisons*).

As best as Schiff could understand, *Shintoism*, in its veneration of the indigenous Spirit (*gods-in-trees* and *god-in-rocks* and all that crap) was the closest Japan, as a communal people, had come to the true gen, as Hemingway would call it: the real thing. The country had no invention-of-itself from the ground up, it had stolen every totem that defined it—its alphabet, its language, *Buddhism*—from either China or Korea. Except, of course, its topography. Its *land*. Its deep forests, perilous seacoasts, isolated peninsulae, limestone caves, inland seas, wind-tossed moss-felted heights, *volcanos* . . . and the native gods that lived there. Shintos believed the spirit of their place was *in* the place, that *streams* were sacred, that each river was the home to many gods, that there were *air* gods soil gods night gods and mountain gods and that each God had a name and that each Name was but one part of a whole that made Japan *Japan*.

Not so very different than Greek or Norse mythology:

Not so very different than the Sioux Nation's Great Spirit.

—been there, done that, in world history, but if there were a current cult in Utah dedicated to the Church of Zeus would he call that a "religion"? More to the point, would he defend it, first as a citizen and second as an attorney under Frank Roosevelt's second Freedom, Freedom of Worship?

Absolutely.

But in Japan what had started as a Big Tent became a rationale for noninclusive politics. To be a Shinto was to elevate all matter specifically Japanese—*not* foreign—to believe that the spirit that arose from Japan's soil and Japan's water was God-given and that that Spirit was most perfectly manifested in the human person of Japan's Emperor. And here's where it got tricky: *England* has a Divine-right King (and England was our *ally*) and the Catholics have their Divine-right Pope: but what the recent crop of militantly jumped-up Japanese had done, as best as Schiff could figure, was to take control of a previously fairy dust cult religion and turn it into a state-sponsored manifesto for the Emperor to rule the world. Because He is the human embodiment of their Shinto gods.

Georgina's argument was a watertight defense of the second freedom—Freedom of Worship—defending the constitutionally endowed rights of American Shinto-believers *not* to sign the Oath owing to the fact that it would go against their faith, their belief in the divinity of Emperor Hirohito. It was an elegant argument, both logical and sound. And she had presented it to Schiff in the hope that he'd join with an *amicus* brief of his own. And lose his job.

"It's beautifully written," he told her, the praise sounding flat even to his own ears because, legitimately, he wasn't old or wise enough to condescend to her: "But you won't win."

"I know. Not on this round. But I will win, eventually. You won't join with me, though, will you."

"No."

"I thought not."

She leaned forward to touch the folded swan with her fingertip and exchanged a smile with the Shinto priests:

"*Origami*," she said.

"I don't know what that means," Schiff said.

"It means '*origami*,'" she explained. "—*de facto*: 'folding paper.' It's a prized art. This is a lovely crane."

"—it's a 'crane'?" Schiff had never seen a crane. "I thought it was a swan."

"A cultural miscalculation . . ."

One of the Shinto priests had reached into the cloth bag he carried and extracted a square of bright blue enameled paper which he smoothed on his lap before making a first fold, at which the other priest nodded, as if he'd understood a code, and then took the paper into his own lap and made a *second* fold.

—from which the first Shinto priest seemed to derive a lot of pleasure and took the blue square back and made a *third* fold: all jolly stuff—like kids—Schiff noted. Back and forth and back and forth they went; folding.

"Because you're afraid to lose your job?" Georgina asked Schiff, taking up the subject.

"No. Because I think somewhere along the line what was once the innocent heart of this 'religion' was appropriated for military purposes."

"Well, you're entitled to your opinion," she deviled him, pointing to the poster of "Four Freedoms."

"You don't have to do this, Dr. Takei," he tried to argue with her, knowing that if she didn't sign the Oath she—and the two playful innocents before him—would end up in a high-security prison somewhere, most likely in Montana.

"On the contrary: *I have to do this.* This would kill my father, all this—he's dead; but this would kill him all over again." She made one last try for his cooperation before leaving: "May I ask how many internees refused to sign?"

"You know I can't tell you that."

She nodded.

—and even as she did, Schiff slid six prepared pages toward her on which were listed those internees who had refused to sign the Oath, along with each one's barrack location, one hundred and twenty-one souls. It was the same list he was going to have to send to Washington later in the day and each person on it was going to need a lawyer—a good one—and there was nobody better suited to that task than the woman in front of him.

Thank you, she mouthed, restoring a needed luster to what he was beginning to think of as his tarnished conscience.

The original *origami* square, having been folded into a much smaller quadrangle, was now between the palms of one of the Shinto priests who raised it to his lips the way Schiff had watched kids in rural places bring a blade of green grass between their palms to make a mouth harp. He watched the Shinto blow into a crucial narrow gap in the folded square—a single *puff*—and then, through the miracle of human breath *inflate* the thing into a shape resembling a blue globe with corners: not a perfect globe—not a perfect *world*—but a balanced one, nonetheless. The priest handed it to Schiff, and bowed.

They left.

Situated beside the paper crane on his desk, the little "world" looked all out of proportion:

Then Svevo trotted in:

"I still love you, sweetie," he announced, "but you're into me for this. *Big time.*"

Behind him trailed a rail-thin member of the mess crew carrying a mixed aroma of bacon grease and hash browns—jumpy kid in a soiled apron, short-sleeved shirt and a skullcap with the suspicious eyes and involuntary tics of a street junkie. *I ain't rattin' on nobody*, this creature volunteered to him: You can put those tubes in me again I ain't got nothin' new to say.

"*Jimmy Ikeda*," Svevo prompted.

Not possible, Schiff was thinking.

—and on his part, this "Jimmy" didn't seem to recognize Schiff, either.

"It's Schiff," Schiff said: "From the Drake."

Still nothing. Lot of twitching.

"We used to work together," Schiff reminded him.

I'm not ratting, he was told.

Schiff stood up, thinking maybe that would help identify him but the kid just stared, pulling off his skullcap and scratching at his head, which had been shaved.

He must have lost at least twenty pounds since the last time Schiff had seen him. And he had been a skinny kid in the first place.

"Sit down, won't you, Jimmy? Can I offer you refreshment? A glass of milk?"

Svevo looked at him as if he (Schiff) had gone a little crazy.

"Your sister went to see my father—she had my old address. Asked if I could help . . ."

"That's bullshit . . ."

Schiff stepped around the desk; the boy backed up.

The kid was staring hard at Schiff—still twitchy—but starting to fill in the pieces to his puzzle.

"She went to find our dad. He's at Fort Lincoln," he said.

"Sit down, sit down, won't you, Jimmy? Let's just talk. I want to help . . ."

Something had happened to the kid—something had spooked him—either that or he was artificially fucked up.

"—why's *he* got to be here?"

Jimmy obviously had a beef with Svevo. Or with Svevo's uniform.

"He's here because he's my friend. Like you once were . . ."

"We were never 'friends' . . . We were *never* friends."

He sat down. Scratched his head.

"What happened to your hair?" Schiff asked.

"What do you *think* happened? *Lice*," he said. "For starters." His legs kept jumping.

Schiff sat on the corner of his desk.

(*Suave*, Svevo thought.)

"You were the best line cook I ever saw," Schiff said. "Why'd they pick you up?"

"You tell *me*."

"I'd like to . . . but honestly, I don't know. Doesn't make any sense to me, on the surface of it. Why're the Feds interested in a hotel line cook? Someone do you in?"

"I wasn't on the line no more. They moved me up—after you were gone. Got myself a jacket. Good tips. Room Service. Then they moved me out to be in front. *Bellboy*."

"Money in that," Schiff said. "That's great."

Both the kid's legs were shaking like it was bitter cold.

"What's so great about it, man? What a fucking joke . . . I mean . . . the only reason I was there was to look after my kid sister . . . That's the only fucking reason I was even fucking there in the fucking first place . . . And what fucking good was I—? Couldn't even fucking take care of my sister . . ."

Jimmy gave a kind of jerk—his whole body jerked, his arms jerked up, his hands gripped his shoulders, his knees jerked up toward his chest, his feet left the ground and he broke down and cried. Right in front of them. Kid just got inside himself and cried.

It was hard to watch. But it was something both Schiff and Svevo realized intuitively that they had to do. Finally Schiff patted Jimmy on the shoulder. And the kid calmed down.

"I can pick up the phone right now, Jimmy, and call Bismarck . . . I can get you transferred out to Fort Lincoln so you can at least be with your father . . ."

"—no, that's the last . . . my father . . . my father doesn't wanna *see* me . . . No. Just put me in a uniform, man. There's rumors there's a guy out east, some general, man, putting a bunch of boys like me together. Fighting unit. All Japanese. You wanna 'help' me? Help me join up. I need it, man. For my honor. I got something I need to prove."

Schiff glanced at Svevo who indicated When pigs fly; but Stranger things have happened.

There *were* rumors—even Schiff had heard them—of a corps of young Japanese-American males being recruited from the camps—but so far Schiff hadn't seen the paper on it.

And he hoped to hell, if the plan *was* legitimate, it indeed had these boys' dignity as its founding principle. And that whoever was in charge of such things would have the wisdom and the grace to dispatch such a unit against Hitler, in Europe, and not into the Pacific, against Japan.

"—before we move in that direction, Jimmy, let's get you to go with Lieutenant Svevo, here, over to the Infimary and have you checked out and get you back to fighting trim, okay? We'll get you checked out and then Lieutenant Svevo will hook you up with a Recruitment Officer, how does that sound?"

You sooooo owe me, buddy, Svevo whispered, going out.

Schiff spent the next hour at his desk, fielding requests, seeing people, holding up the honor of his "open door" philosophy and then, toward 1100, Betty ushered in a Caucasian with the whispered cue to Schiff, "He says he's *not* a sales rep," and handed him a business card.

Schiff took one look at it

BOBBY KAYE
entrepreneur
Hollywood

and thought Oh goody.

Here was Bobby Kaye, in person, shiny suit, black silk shirt and cloud of cologne, running off his mouth, as usual:

Here's what I see here's what *I* see *here's* what I think this place can use: *Movies*. I'll donate the reels no charge I'll donate whatever it takes: projector. Screens. —tell you why:

I *like* these people, see a future for them, want to come in with a small crew, keep it small use their faces for the close-ups come in here and THEY'RE A VILLAGE! it's RURAL JAPAN! and—I don't know how this happens but we'll work it out A U.S. AIRMAN HAS EVACUATED dumped his plane he's shot down—maybe Gary Cooper, maybe John Garfield maybe Jimmy Stewart— Gable, even—shot down over this JAPANESE HILL VILLAGE I'm telling you there's *work* here *paying* work for all of them their authentic Asian faces—

"You don't remember me, do you?" Schiff asked.

He watched Kaye's eyes narrow and the weaselly mind behind them try to calculate. Don't tell me, Don't tell me: Kaye shook a scolding finger toward Schiff's face:

You auditioned for me right? Tried out for a part? Face is coming back to me . . .

"I waited on you."

—what?

"I was your waiter. Here. In Lone Pine."

So you *are* an actor!—we can make this work—find you a little part TWO AIRMEN! one dies! but you get a little scene—*death scene!*—up front . . .

"—*Betty!* I need two MPs in here—!"

Svevo was the first one to his rescue—"You all right, buddy?"—followed by two big policemen.

"Escort Mr. Kaye out to the road, please, gentlemen: he's to speak to no one on the way if he opens his mouth again in front of you hit him with any- thing you've got and tell The Gate this fella is A Suspect if he ever tries to get in here again Shoot him."

The dust hadn't even settled when Svevo said, "Feeling our Old Testament this morning, are we?"

"Not funny, Jay."

"No one's twisting your arm to make you see these people. Though I have to say: scoring points. Huge success. Crowds are lining up outside just to touch your hem."

As if on cue, Betty led in the last supplicants, two civic matrons of the stringent ilk—Mrs. Engroff and Mrs. Aukamp—dressed almost to caricature, powerfully buttoned up against the devil, sin and immigrants—each mirroring the other's mental whalebone—each with a little *hat* and badge, advertising their position on the Rationing Board and their importance to the nation's Ration-al survival. They brought enough righteous indignation to the room, Schiff thought, to spawn a miracle.

"What can I do for you two ladies this fine morning?"

"We're here officially," Mrs. Engroff told him.

"Oh good. So are we."

He gestured, though without an introduction, toward Svevo, who was still posted beside him, on his feet, thinking If an ironic tree falls in a non-ironic forest are any little bunnies killed?

"It's about the rationing," Mrs. Engroff said.

"A thankless job for which both you ladies should be lauded."

Mrs. Engroff had come to Schiff's attention when he first got here and had started reading every column, every advert, every *word* in local papers to better understand the natives. He remembered her columns on RATIONING in the weekly *Inyo Register*, the first of which—now a classic in his mind—had been titled "War Cake Whiperoo" and the most recent of which (yesterday's) had been devoted to SUET MOLD and A MESS OF PEAS A LA EVAPORATED MILK MODE D'IOWA. And HINDOO POWDERED EGGS.

Mrs. Aukamp, it was now returning to him, had also made the paper with an article on raising snails. For supper. "A tough bite," she had reckoned, but worth the trouble (after you had harvested them from your lawn, starved them, fed them cornmeal and starved them again; washed them, cooked them with a passel full of charcoal in boiling water, sauced them and broiled them in the oven).

"It's about the butter truck."

"The 'butter truck,'" Schiff repeated.

"That sat here all day in the noonday sun."

"It might have been an ice cream truck," Mrs. Aukamp amended. "Reports vary."

"Anyway it was *dairy*," Mrs. Engroff testified. "Which I don't need to tell you comes under 'rationed foods.' Happened on your property right here, last week. And what we're told—whichever: butter or ice cream—it was parked the whole day while everything inside melted. Gone to waste."

Schiff could read on both faces the thrust of their argument: *While brave boys overseas are eating beans and mud. And the English, starving.*

"And another thing," Mrs. Engroff said. The fingers of her right hand fluttered to her badge. "This is Inyo County. And—as such—we are honor bound to follow Federal guidelines for the rationing of food. In wartime. What we don't understand—and I'll speak plain—what we don't understand, as townspeople, is why we loyal citizens have to make these sacrifices while all the 'other' people living within our county limits get to have bacon every morning for their breakfast with real butter and real eggs and meat, again, at lunch and dinner. It's not fair."

Svevo watched Schiff's profile.

Boom, he thought.

Well, Schiff said. He took his time:

"First, let me respond by saying that whoever your sources are—and I'll find out and deal with them—*whom*ever your sources are, they are correct in their report about the bacon. And the eggs. And the butter. And the meat. But you see that guardhouse out there? That checkpoint you had to go through with the MPs? That signifies a Federal perimeter—basically, an Army base. Containing—against their wills—ten thousand American citizens. You want to 'speak plainly' about sacrifice? About what they've 'given up'? They've given up their homes. They've given up their neighborhoods. They've given up their pets. Forget 'gas rationing'—they've given up their *cars*, they're denied the freedom to travel, the freedom to congregate after dark, the freedom to earn a living, pursue a college education, even to own a bank account or communicate in writing with their relatives without a censor reading every word. So, yes, ma'am, if Frank Roosevelt tells me I can go ahead and offer these citizens three strips of bacon every morning and some true-blue scrambled eggs, you betcha. Along with hamburger twice a week. And the occasional lamb chop. That should answer your complaint about what's 'fair' or not. About the 'butter truck'? Lieutenant Svevo—? —any insight on the 'waste' complaint here?"

"Yes, sir . . ."

Turning to the ladies:

"Again, your 'intel' is correct—that would have been the delivery we took on Monday from Bishop of twelve thousand frozen ice cream Dixie cups. In three flavors."

"—that 'Neapolitan' kind?" Schiff asked.

"The same."

"—my favorite."

Rub it in.

"As it happened," Svevo continued, "after we'd off-loaded the ice cream to our freezer, Harvey—that's the driver's name—Harvey mentioned something might be funny with the coolant system—turns out he was right, it was a problem with a broken fan belt—so we took it over to the motor pool, which as you know, sir, is located over there behind the fire station—"

"Where you can't see it from the road," Schiff mentioned.

"Where you can't see it from the road . . ."

"—which means whoever has reported these things to you," Schiff told the women, "isn't someone who was casually driving by on the highway but someone on the inside, most likely someone we've hired from the local population. Betty—!"

Schiff's secretary appeared.

"Betty, if you'd be so kind, please, get me that list of local people we've hired—" He turned to Svevo. "How many jobs did we put on offer in the county?"

"Forty-eight."

"Forty-eight," Schiff repeated. "And what was the employment status of those forty-eight before they came to work at Manzanar?"

"They were unemployed, sir."

"And by employing these forty-eight people—which, really, doesn't sound like much—just to put this in perspective: after the Los Angeles Department of Water, which is the Number One employer in the county, where does that put us?"

"Second, sir. Number Two. We're the second-largest employer in the county—ahead of the county, itself, which employs thirty-five people . . . three sheriffs, twelve teachers, whatnot."

(They could take this on the road, Svevo was thinking. They could be an *Act*.)

Betty made a quick return, handing Schiff a sheet of paper.

"—thank you, Betty.—oh look: it's alphabetized: how convenient." He looked back at his audience. "I think both you ladies know how hard I've worked—meeting privately and in groups with your civic and religious leaders, as well as merchants and individual families—to assure that we could get this done, put this mandate in place according to the President's desires without rancor, suspicion, or prejudice. And with the added benefit to the community of forty-eight new jobs, forty-eight previously unemployed local people who now have the distinction of working for the War Relocation Authority, a Federal agency, and all the prestige and honor and—let's not forget—strict limitations that go with it, limitations such as the Federal Treason and War Secrets Act"—(he was making this up)—"which prohibits civilian employees from sharing information obtained in the course of government employment. But, well, human nature is what it is—we work hard all day, we come home, we're tired, we want to have a good meal and relax and talk about our day. 'Loose lips sink ships'—absolutely; but 'loose lips' also break the law so what I'm going to do is read down this list and you're going to tell me which person or persons on it have been spreading rumors about what goes on inside this camp. Under punishment of Federal Law."

(Svevo kicked Schiff's leg, but it didn't stop him:)

" 'Althea Addams. 62. Independence. Retired librarian.' "

"She's our 'book lady,' " Svevo reminded him.

". . . but is she 'our gal'?"

The two women in their impassivity seemed to signal "no."

" 'Harold Attwater. 56. Lone Pine. Retired county auditor.' "

"One of mine," Svevo said. "I hired him. He keeps the books."

Again, the women, frozen, signaled "no."

"—oh look at this: 'Donald Aukamp, Jr. 19. Lone Pine.' . . ."

"He's the stock boy in the commissary," Svevo prompted.

"—'19'? Why isn't he enlisted?"

"—kid had polio . . . You've seen him . . ."

Schiff looked at Mrs. Aukamp.

"Relative of yours?"

She took her time before she answered, "—he's my son."

"Alrighty, then . . . Well. Do I need to read through all these other names?"

Obviously not.

"Well such is life," Schiff said. "It's funny, isn't it? Lieutenant Svevo and I were just talking about this the other night . . ." (Svevo nodded: loyal puppet.) "—here you are with, I mean, I'm guessing 'Aukamp' might be German— maybe Flemish, maybe Dutch, who am I to question?—'Engroff': there's another German name—'*Schiff*': German, definitely—not my father's real name but the one given to him by the Immigration Officer on Ellis Island—and Lieutenant *Svevo*, here: Eye-talian—we were just saying the other night what if Frank Roosevelt—God forbid this should ever happen—but what if President Roosevelt wakes up tomorrow and says to himself My God we're not only at war with the Japanese, we're at war with Hitler, too! and Mussolini! with Germany and Italy so let's round up all the folks with German names with German ancestry and relatives in Germany and put them in internment camps like we did the Japanese-Americans and while we're at it let's round up all Italians, too—I mean, Lieutenant Svevo and I, on the basis of our names or our ancestry would definitely be in an internment camp, and you, too, Mrs. Aukamp, and your son (unless the name *is* Dutch) and you, too, Mrs. Engroff, and millions—I mean *millions*—of your fellow German-Americans would be put into captivity, whole cities would lose half their populations—well, Lone Pine definitely would, I've been out to the cemetery, and as you know, half the souls interred out there are first-generation *Germans*—there would be nobody left! except American tribal Indians, of course . . . and the English, and the French . . . and Spanish . . . it would be like it was when America was colonies—"

"—and the Negroes," Svevo said.

"Right."

"—and Poles."

"Okay."

"And Greeks."

"I think I've made my—"

"And the Scandinavians."

Schiff placed both palms flat on his desktop and pushed himself into a stand:

"—praise heaven that's not what our President is thinking . . . yet." He moved around his desk and started herding them. "—thank you both for taking time out of your valuable work to share your thoughts and your concerns . . ."

He had them at the door:

"—so *you*," he said to Mrs. Aukamp, "will have a talk with your son . . . and *I* will have a talk with him and if he fails to understand what I say to him, or if he fails to comply with Federal regulations, I'll terminate his employment." He smiled.

"Making friends left and right," Svevo assessed once they were alone again.

"Go talk to this kid," Schiff told him. "He'll respect the uniform."

"Unlike your sad grey suit."

"What happened with Ikeda?"

"Chances are the kid can't pass the physical . . ."

"So the rumor's true?—about a Japanese unit?"

Svevo shrugged.

Schiff sat back down at his desk.

Still, Svevo hung around.

"I need to ask," he started: "What're we doing about Friday?"

Schiff thought maybe he was joking:

"An eternal question," he said. But his sarcasm fell flat.

"It's Pesach," Svevo said. "—*Passover*."

"I know what 'Pesach' means, Jay. I just don't know why we're talking about it."

"We're 'talking about it' because I think we should celebrate."

Schiff stared at him.

"—*why?*"

"Because it's my favorite Jewish holiday."

"—you have a 'favorite' Jewish holiday?"

"—don't *you?*"

"No."

"—but if you did wouldn't it be Passover?"

"*No.*"

Unbidden memories—"relatives" of questionable provenance, cheek-pinchers, aunts who reeked of *schmaltz*, bald men trailing hints of pickled herring—threatened to darken his mood.

"You *do* remember we're the only two Jews for a gazillion miles?"

"Which is why we need to do it. Especially *here* . . . in this place. This *year.*"

"Have you had *a stroke?*"

—but Svevo wouldn't joke.

"Where the hell are you gonna find a whatzit . . ."

". . . matzo?"

". . . *Haggadah.*"

"I got one. We're *doing* this . . ."

"Don't we have to have more of us, a *minyan* or something—?"

"I'll handle it—just agree you'll *be* there. Friday's our only day to do it . . ."

A commotion erupted outside Schiff's office and Sunny blew in like weather, followed doggedly by Betty spouting no you can't you can't just, *no*—

Schiff rose abruptly, holding up his hand to calm the scene, saying, "It's all right, I know her," in a way that Betty suspected had hidden meaning even as she backed, obediently, out.

"You march in," he turned to Sunny, "that's what you do, like you own the joint?"

Sweet, Svevo told himself. This should be fun.

"Two words: *street food*," Sunny announced.

"What do you know about 'street food'?" Schiff said.

"I know a lot about *street food.*"

"From where, the two blocks of Main Street in Lone Pine?"

"I've been to cities."

"Oh, yeah? Which ones?"

Svevo sent Schiff a look that begged, Man what are you *doing*?

"New York," Sunny said. "And Paris."

"Paris, *France?*"

Sunny turned and said, "Hello, Lieutenant Svevo: nice to see you again."

"And *you*, Miss Rhodes," Jay answered.

"*This* one," she said, nodding in Schiff's direction but not looking at him, "was invited to our house for dinner a while back."

"I recall the night distinctly," Svevo said.

"And he brought a gift."

"*Suave.*"

"A cookbook."

"Apt."

"—*used.*"

"—oops."

"—that he'd *written* in."

Jay turned to Schiff and asked, "What's the *matter* with you?"

"It was out of print. A classic."

"—so you had to *write* in it?"

"I didn't mind the writing, really," Sunny said, finally looking back at Schiff: "It was interesting and I'm sorry it's taken me this long to thank you but I only just got around to reading it last night and that's what gave me the idea: these women need to cook."

"—what 'women'?"

"—*these* women . . . All these women here, these people need the food they're used to, food that *means* something to them . . ."

"Are you suggesting 'these people' aren't being fed?"

"I'm not suggesting that at all—"

"—or that bacon and eggs in the morning and Campbell's soup for lunch doesn't 'mean' something to them?"

"Can you *listen*—?"

Svevo pretended to cough so he could hide his smile behind his hand.

"—I'm trying to say something *important*—"

"—by insulting me?"

"—*how* have I insulted you? I'm not even talking about *you*, I'm talking about un-regimenting what these people *eat*—"

"—'these people' . . ."

"—reintroducing some delight into their lives, encounters with uninstitutionalized food . . ."

"There's a commissary, Sunny, if they need to buy a candy bar."

"—that's exactly what I'm saying: not 'if' they need but 'when' they need . . . when they need a bowl of Mother's homemade soup, when a family wants to eat their grandma's recipe for yams . . ."

"—'yams'?"

"—roasted yams are big 'street' items in Japan . . . don't get distracted by the 'yams' . . . rice, then, rice the way you're used to eating it at home—I did the math—there's probably three thousand married women here—"

"Three thousand one hundred and seventy-two," Svevo quoted.

"Say we set up a general kitchen in an empty barrack where thirty women can cook a family meal every day—"

"—whoa whoa whoa," Schiff said.

"—their families could have a home-cooked meal and then we could do pushcarts—"

"—'we' who? Who's 'we'?"

"You asked me for ideas."

"—about nutrition. About a better gravy. Tasty biscuits . . ."

"Now who's being insulting—?"

"You can't just barge onto Federal property and act as if you own the place—"

"—you asked me . . ."

"—and anyway: even if I thought your idea of a cooking school—"

"—a communal kitchen . . ."

"—had wheels—which it sorta does . . . I don't have the money in my budget."

". . . I do."

Stopped 'em:

—two talky guys, both struck all of a sudden dumb by one woman's bald admission.

You would think Cas's experiences with society beaux had proved that men liked women with a private income but not these two apparently because they both took on expressions of affronted masculinity as if she'd just reached down and twisted something private. Suddenly each of them decided to stand up straight and try to look like he was taller.

"How is this a problem?" Sunny asked.

Schiff's mind raced through the already existing list of corporate partners at the War Relocation Authority—General Mills, Chase & Sanborn, P&G, Pet Milk, Pillsbury . . . not to mention the biggest cat, Los Angeles Water Department, on whose very ground his two feet stood—but he sidestepped Sunny's question by saying, "There are no empty barracks."

"Yes there are," Svevo said: "Two."

Even Sunny could see the murder in Schiff's eyes when he answered, "Those are 'extra' barracks, Jay. You know that."

"Oh right. 'Extra' for what?"

"For . . . expansion."

"So not for pets, then."

He was getting back at him for the Jimmy Ikeda thing, Schiff knew. Or because Schiff hadn't jumped for joy at the idea of celebrating Passover.

"Would you like to show her one of them?" Schiff asked, pointedly.

"Wouldn't *you*—?" Svevo answered. Point and match.

"I have things to do."

"—and I *don't*—?"

"*Boys*," Sunny reminded them: "I grew up with a brother so I get it: tell me where these barracks are, I'll take a look myself . . ."

"They're locked. Lieutenant Svevo will be thrilled to let you into one, won't you, Jay?"

"Thrilled," Jay said: "My Jeep's outside." ♪

"—after which," Schiff told her, "you can write up a formal plan."

"Don't try to scare me, Mister Schiff: I know how to write . . ."

Blind Christ, Svevo was thinking: go audition for a Frank Capra film, already, you two. Romantic escapade.

"Why don't *you* go drive her all around?" he asked Schiff when she'd gone to wait for him outside: "I thought you're keen on her . . ."

"Who told you *that*?"

"You're killing me right here, my buddy . . ."

"Besides: you're a married man and all . . . You can ask her stuff. About the 'boyfriend' . . ."

"*Nine* Passovers we could have—*ten*, make it a *minyan*—and you could never pay me back the things you're owing me on this day alone . . ."

The barrack was on the remote west side of camp and as Jay cut through the motor pool and past the fuel tanks soldiers saluted loosely, calling Dodge! Hey, *Dodge*! leading Sunny to ask, What's with the nickname?

"I'm from Brooklyn. We have a little business back there, maybe you've heard of them, called the Brooklyn Dodgers?"

"Who hasn't heard of Pee Wee Reese and Ebbets Field? Red Barber? Johnny Allen? Dixie Walker?"

"Listen to *you*, Blondie—!"

"Even in Lone Pine we have radios, Lieutenant. That World Series—my brother wouldn't leave the *house*, he hung on every word Red Barber said . . ."

"—can't be so bad, this brother of yours, if he's a Dodgers man . . ."

Shadow flickered on her face and he remembered Schiff had told him something about Pearl, something about the brother and he instinctively reached out to touch her—but then didn't—and recovered with I'm sorry.

"That's okay . . . It's . . . it's kinda nice to hear somebody talk about him as if he's still alive."

"Must be rotten for your parents . . ."

Yet another flicker.

Shit, Svevo almost said.

Two for two, he thought, in Red Barber's lingo.

Sunny changed the subject:

"This used to be apples," she explained: "All this . . ."

They pulled up to a solitary barrack fifty yards from the wire perimeter. The land around it had been bulldozed and showed no sign of life despite the season but there was the faintest hint of apple blossoms from the few remaining trees.

Svevo rifled through his keys and made what sounded even to him stupid small talk about the steps taken to safeguard against kids loitering but then they both saw the padlock had been broken, the door ajar, and right inside the entrance, on the floor, a little midden of smoked butts and empty beer bottles. And a candle. Just for, you know, Svevo thought, *atmosphere.*

Geez, he said.

He flicked a switch, four bare bulbs cast a dim light into the corners.

"It's *big*," she said. "Bigger than it looks from outside."

"Try sticking six families in: gets small real quick."

She walked to the far end and back: she could imagine two flattops, a stove; work counters:

"—water?" she needed to know.

"Two exterior standpipes—but hell this is L.A. Water land and they can run Niagara through here if you need it . . . propane's easy to attach, that's what we've hooked up to the messes . . ."

He could see her mind at work, then suddenly she was at the door and back outside. "What about all this land right here—what could we do with this?"

"What do you need to do?"

"—picnic tables.—*fireplaces*."

"Like a city *park*? where families grill hot dogs—?—surefire no-no from our fire warden, sweetheart, whole place is made of wood . . ."

To his surprise she sat on the raised platform to the door. *We're sitting*—? he asked himself and joined her at a polite distance.

So tell me, he began: "Who's this?" He pointed to the ring on the fourth finger of her left hand.

"—*this?*" she said, and touched it. "This is my guy."

"Uh-*huh*. And where is 'he'?"

"—*right here*, actually.—in this land."

—he's *dead?* Jay wondered.

"—this is where he lived . . . in a house right over there . . ." (she pointed) ". . . with his grandfather." She was off in her own remembered past, which was fine with him—not only for the facts he could collect for Schiff . . . but because he liked this kid.

"—like I said, before Los Angeles came north and bought up all the land, all this—*all* of this—*Manzanar*—was one big orchard worked by Señor Mendoza who ran an apple stand out by the road—well it was more than that: it was a kind of *bodega*, he called it: the only place between Lone Pine and Independence where you could buy milk or gum or a pack of smokes . . . fresh *tortillas*: *masa*. Rocky—that's my father—bought apples from him in the fall—Tops makes his own *calvados*—but he made a point of coming here with me and Stryker at least once a week for stuff we didn't need to 'honor the enterprise.' So anyway one day we stop by and there's this kid, Mendoza's grandson: *Hace*."

"That's not a name."

"—short for Hey-*soos* . . ."

"—still ain't a name . . ."

She made a fist and clocked him on his shoulder: "—*snob*.—it's Spanish for 'Jesus' . . ."

Svevo nearly choked:

—the *shiksa*'s "guy" was called "*Jesus*"—?

Schiff was gonna have a coronary.

"Childhood sweethearts . . . I get it." He held up his left hand showing off his own wedding band: "They know everything about us." Her band, though, he'd noticed, looked like something someone had knocked out of a Cracker Jack box. "Don't mind me saying this but yours looks a little temporary."

"—yeah, well: we were only thirteen."

"—*illegal*, in most states."

"Stryker married us. One day in the dining room. The dogs were witnesses."

She realized she hadn't talked this much to a stranger in years—not counting Schiff.

—and the lieutenant was right about one thing: all the people she loved had known her all her life . . . or almost all her life. At least since before she was a grown-up.

"So when do you and He go permanent?"

"We *are* permanent."

"You know what I mean."

She'd never told the story outside family and even in the family The Incident was hardly ever mentioned and, then, only in the barest terms.

Should she open up to strangers? Who does that? *Okay*, she decided: let's see what a *stranger* makes of this:

"Old Mendoza never owned this land, he was tenant to a local codge named Eddy who sold it to the Water boys who let him stay, provisionally, to grow his apples . . . *Abuelo*—Granddad—dies and Hace takes over for a while—he was still a kid—until the Water boys decide the best use for this property is to transport water south so they turf him out and he comes to live with us."

"Where were Hace's parents?"

"Central Valley. Pickers by the season . . . *anyway*, the summer after high school Tops lets me into some of my inheritance and I opened Lou's. Bought the building. Tops had to sign because I was a minor—"

"—how old?"

"Eighteen."

"Impressive."

"Stryker had been on Tops's wrong side all year—Tops wanted to see him at Stanford or someplace and Stryker was having none of *that*—just hanging around until he could get quits of us—"

"—for what?—for *where*?"

"Acting; Hollywood. Which drove Tops red. And Hace had won a place at UC Davis for an Ag degree—Tops was gonna help with his expenses— meanwhile, that summer, a movie comes to town so there are jobs. *Hannibal*—"

"—never saw it."

"—never *made* . . . This guy Bobby Kaye—"

"—I just met the *putz* this morning!"

"—he's the guy who left Lou's that night we met, he didn't pay . . . anyway Hannibal, turns out, was a real person—something about him and the Romans and his crossing the Alps with elephants—Tops knows the story—Bobby Kaye decides to make a movie up here owing to the fact that we have mountains that he thinks look like authentic Roman mountains."

"—*Alps.*"

"—brings his own *elephants*. *Three* of them. He's so cheap this guy, what he plans to do is keep using the same three elephants in rotation—film them in a line and then *stop camera*—go back, film the same three elephants in different gear etcetera etcetera."

"I would have done that," Svevo reasoned.

"Stryker gets a part as a Roman soldier—he got a lot of lines—and Hace is hired as the elephant *mahoot* because he's so good with animals." On Jay's look: "—it's a *word*, Lieutenant: it means the guy who trains the elephants."

"—because this Kaye guy is too cheap to get a 'real' *mahoot* . . ."

"—*exacte.*"

I would *not* have done that, Svevo told himself.

"Kaye was bringing along the career of this *ingenue*, I forget her name, who went off and got herself doped up after this—and he was so jealous of anybody getting near her he had her quarantined between takes up in Independence in the Indie Hotel instead of down here at the Dow where the crew could ogle her . . . *catnip* for my brother. I mean she was pretty and all that but the fact she was Off Limits made her irresistible. Anyway . . . we're a family of utilitarian cars—pickup trucks . . . Cas—she's my aunt—drives her Woody— but this same Eddy who sold this land to the Water boys had bought himself some kinda grandee classic Cadillac convertible—never drove it anywhere except down Main Street for the Fourth Parade. After he died, his widow kept it locked up in a garage from which my brother gets the grand idea to jack it one night to impress the Princess up in Independence. Has this great date with her, does whatever Stryker did with women—there was drink involved—and he's driving back to Lone Pine in the wee hours of the night when he lands the Caddy in one of the Water boys' wide roadside ditches. Stuck. Can't get out. So pretend you're Stryker now: What would you have done?"

Took Svevo two seconds to say, I'd go get my best friend the *mahoot* and one of those damned elephants.

"—*see?* You're just like him!"

"We're cut from the same cloth."

"Stryker walks the half mile to the barn where Hace is living with the elephants . . . thing you gotta know about the two of them, Hace would go anywhere—ends of the earth—for Stryker. They were *brothers*. So they take some ropes and one of the elephants—the biggest one, the male—and they traipse back to the ditch in pitch-dark and lasso up the Cadillac to Jumbo and haul it out. *Spectacular*: signature Stryker. As they're dozing back to Lone Pine, Stryker in the Caddy going real slow next to Hace and Jumbo, who shows up, on patrol—lights, guns—*Water boys*. This next part I've only ever heard from Hace—and his memory of that night is pretty sketchy: two Water boys in their vehicle—you've seen how they drive around all over here like a private army—two guys, *Snow*, the first one, with the dead eyes? he's still around—"

"I've seen him, the creepy one."

"—other guy, his partner back then—McCloud. Hace says they came down from the north, from behind, shining their searchlights, shouting *Trespassers!* and *Halt!* and Hace swears he couldn't keep the elephant in tow the thing just went *mammoth* on him swung around and reared up and Snow got off his best shot, then kept shooting, caught Hace in the leg—not the bone but that artery that's there—Snow's a crack shot—everyone around here knows he used to ride rodeos—hits Jumbo, brings him down . . . and I mean *down* right on top of both him and McCloud, their vehicle, whole thing."

"Holy shit."

"Killed McCloud."

"—holy *shit* . . . !"

"Stryker didn't know that—he couldn't have known that at the time—all he knew was that Hace was down and bleeding bad . . ."

"—it's like a fountain, I saw a guy bleed out once on the street in Brooklyn from a stab wound in the thigh . . ."

"—so he pulls Hace into the Caddy and hauls him to Three Chairs to try to save his life."

She paused and drew a breath:

"Here's what you have to know about my father: back in the 20s he tried to blow up the Aqueduct, went out one night to the Alabama Gates right down the road here with homemade bombs and tried to blow it up. Did some damage—nothing big. Since then—all through the 30s up 'til now—

he's fought them in the courts for what they've done to this valley. I don't even know the total, maybe *fifteen* different lawsuits against L.A. He won't even come to Lou's because I serve the Water boys who bunk at the Dow. He doesn't hold it against me—I think he respects me for it—but he won't even give his own daughter his custom, won't set foot in Lou's. It's a blood feud for him; primal . . . Here's what *I* remember of that night: house starts to come alive. I wake up because I hear Cas moving, get up, go outside, there's Stryker getting yelled at by our father—he was *livid*—things were happening *very* fast—Stryker had at least the sense to cinch his belt high on Hace's thigh but Hace was unconscious . . . we had to carry him to Cas's Woody . . . and then the next thing I knew they were gone, the two of them. Ferried away by Cas who believe me can drive like a bat outta hell . . . all the way to Escondido where she had an old friend from the music business—an *impresario*—who had a mansion on the shore where they could hide.

"McCloud is dead—the elephant is dead—Snow is taken to L.A. unconscious—and when the sheriff shows up in the morning asking if we know where Hace could be, Tops lies. No problem for Stryker of course because there's nothing to tie him to the scene, but a man's been killed by an animal Hace was in charge of. Thing goes to court—turns out Bobby Kaye never took insurance on the elephant so the owner's suing him. So he sues Hace. Meanwhile, Snow wakes up and fingers Hace as having been there plus remembers seeing Stryker, so Hace, *in absentia*, despite Tops's best lawyers, receives a bench warrant for manslaughter. Stryker hitchhikes down to San Diego that same week and joins the Navy. And Cas's friend takes Hace by boat, once he can walk, back home to Mexico. Where he takes on a new identity in his mother's name."

"—so he's not called 'Jesus' anymore?"

She doesn't laugh.

"Why didn't you go with him that night?"

"I *should* have: don't think I don't beat myself up for that . . . never crossed my mind I wouldn't see them again—"

"—but you *do* see him?"

"—not enough.—he and I can't even write letters . . . Lone Pine's such a small town sheriff has our postmistress watching all my mail . . . *upside* of all of this," she gestured over Manzanar, "is now our California growers are deprived of pickers—all the labor from the Japanese community is locked up so big farms in the Central Valley have been bringing up migrant labor from down in Mex flooding the border with *braceros* and Hace has come back across unnoticed. And he's *pissed off*: About day-work conditions. Politicized. Wants to *unionize*."

Sirens blasted for the second seating at lunch mess and an attendant movement flooded between barracks like a tide. Half a dozen kids honed in on Svevo's Jeep as if it were dessert chanting Dodger! Coke! *Ice cream!*

(Sunny noticed that the draw was an ice chest in the back of Svevo's Jeep:)

"I used to hand out Cokes until I found out they were selling them," Jay explained: "—now I give them ice cream that they have to eat before it melts . . ."

Kids pressed in on him:

"—*okay*," he said: "Only if you finished all your lunches . . . what did you *eat*?"

Bologna sandwich.

"—*can* peach. Chocolate milk. Raisins."

"—nothing *hot*?" Sunny prompted.

Tomato soup.

"—nothing *green*?"

Cold slaw, one of them said.

Sunny stood and said I'm gonna hike back, Jay—thanks for everything.

—*hey*, he answered: favor? "I'm looking for some bitter herbs."

"You gonna poison someone, Jay?"

"—*Passover* . . . Friday night."

No rise from her.

Jewish holiday: "I'm missing some ingredients . . . well actually I'm missing the whole meal . . ."

Well I've got a garden and *I cook*: "Come up to the house tomorrow morning and pick out what you need . . ."

Early, she stressed. 0730, they agreed. He asked again if she wanted a ride back to the Main Gate but even he could tell as she strode off that she and the landscape were bound up in some remembered conversation.

There must have been a hundred—*two* hundred, *three*—trees in this one corner of the orchard when she'd been growing up . . . reduced to twenty, thirty now, most having been plowed up by the Water boys when they took ownership, not having wanted to take on any extra tasks—cultivating, growing—other than the collection of Sierra runoff, the free harvesting of H_2O. Still, the trees remaining were resplendent in bridal-veil blossoms and a faint green-apple aroma. Sunny snipped a star-shaped flower and put it on her tongue. A middle-aged woman accompanying an older one under the protection of a parasol approached on what appeared to be a postprandial stroll and the younger one asked Sunny, What kind of trees are these?

"Apple."

—ah. *Ringo*, the younger told the older: "*Ringo no ki* . . . apple trees." To Sunny: "We were hoping they were cherry. Cherry blossom. *Sakura*. Like in Japan."

"Nope. Just apple," Sunny said. ". . . like in the Garden of Eden."

The woman looked surprised:

"Ha. You're funny."

Then they both laughed the way only exiled people do.

The camp in front of her opened out to its repetitive grid of barrack after barrack: 14 to a block; 36 blocks, 504 barracks in the pattern. She passed an ironing room and a laundry; a men's latrine and a women's shower outside of which rubber shower shoes were neatly placed. A man was raking sand; another man was laying "paving" stones around his "yard." Gardening is being human in the face of despair, she remembered having read somewhere. Or maybe Cas had quoted it. People had planted out their plots; collected soil in empty cans they'd salvaged from the mess hall middens. As she turned the corner at a firebreak a blue ball bounced down the stairs and rolled in front of her. She picked it up and turned to face a kid—a baby, really—on all fours on the barrack floor inside an open door on which was hung a handmade sign, THE CHILDREN'S VILLAGE.

Sunny had climbed inside and passed the ball back to the baby when a woman with her back to her, working in a corner, said, "Come on in they've all been fed I just have to change these last two diapers but see if you can get our Mister 'M' to stop his bawling, willya—?"

Sunny looked around:

—at least a dozen babies in those single-baby *bassinets* (or whatever they were called)—some older babies sitting up in playpens, some in larger cribs . . . and one red-faced tiny tyrant—the aforementioned "Mister 'M'"?—squalling in his basket and kicking like a bee-stung mule.—*hey there*, Sunny told him. She'd lifted maybe two or three live babies in her life: "—I had a brother just like you, angry with the world from Day One . . ." She picked the bundle up, careful of its tiny head: "—would *not* shut up cried and screamed and carried on until know what? our father built a *rocking chair* yes indeed and then he built him a *rocking horse* . . ." She rocked the infant back and forth: "—and he started *rocking* just like this and know what? He stopped his crying . . . just like *you* . . ."

She looked into the face of the woman who had spoken when she'd come in, now standing in front of her cradling another baby.

"—*sorry*," the woman said: "I wasn't looking when you came in, I thought you were one of us girls."

"—I *am* a girl."

"But not one of *us*. You're Caucasian." Then more kindly: "—you're the 'orange lady,' aren't you? Handing out oranges first day . . ."

"—yep that's me." She smiled to drive the humor home: "Utilitarian 'Caucasian' . . .—always glad to be of service . . ." Then she put out a hand and introduced herself: *Sunny*.

"—Rose Ito."

They shook hands; went back to rocking.

"What is this place?—some kinda nursery?" Sunny asked.

"This is the orphanage."

She knew what an "orphanage" was, but:

"—how can that be?"

"We were an orphanage—functioning Catholic orphanage—in San Francisco and then the Order came down . . . and now we're here. Without the priests. Only all of us who are, you know . . . not Caucasian."

Sunny looked around, again, noticing what she hadn't seen before: all the infants had full shocks of dark black hair.

"—but these are *babies* . . . That's not *right*."

Rose let out a laugh: "Thank you for the confirmation . . ."

"How many *are* there?"

"Thirty-four."

"—and you're in charge of *all* of them?"

"—there's another nurse—Yuko—she's got the older ones at lunch right now . . . and most of the time we're thick with *mama-sans* . . . sometimes it feels like all the women in the camp are in here all at once—believe me, these are the best-hugged children on the reservation . . ."

Mister "M" had taken hold of Sunny's finger and was staring up at her.

"He *likes* you," Rose said.

"He just needed some attention."

"—no: he especially likes *you*." Then: "You don't see it, do you?"

"See what?"

"—how he's fifty-fifty."

Sunny didn't understand.

"—mixed race," Rose emphasized. "—you can't *see* it, now I've told you?"

Sunny was embarrassed.

—all babies looked the same to her.

And all *Japanese* babies . . .

"His *hair*," Rose alerted her. "—look at his *eyes* . . ."

Still:

Sunny couldn't see a difference. "What's his name?" she asked.

"We don't know. We call him Mister 'M'—he's not one of ours from San Francisco, he came in from the processing center at Santa Anita—when they took him in, all the data they had was a big letter 'M' printed on top of one hand and the bottom of one foot—their guess was to distinguish he was 'Male.' Mister 'M' . . . We're just waiting for his mom or dad to notify us . . ."

"—but how can . . .—how did . . ."

"People die. Parents get sick. Some parents got sent to Justice camps, splitting up the families . . . all the clearinghouses . . . Santa Anita and others: *zoos,* you should have seen it . . . it's a miracle more children did not get lost . . ."

"What can I do—? I want to help . . ."

She had another look around and noticed for the first time a battery of electric bottle warmers and two refrigerators:

"Do you need food?—what are you feeding them?"

"The mess crew have been great— We're fine with what goes *in,* it's what comes *out* that's giving us the nightmares!—wanna help? Help us wash these diapers . . . ! I'm on my feet 18 hours every day . . ."

No flush toilets in the barracks, Sunny knew. Only in the shared latrines; and there was only one of those, one for each sex, for every 14 barracks. How these women were managing all these dirty diapers, she could only imagine:

What they needed was a place to *sit down:*

"I'm gonna smuggle something in for you—no, better yet: Do you know Lieutenant Svevo?"

"—everybody knows the 'Dodge.' "

"I'm gonna make sure he delivers these personally tomorrow morning . . ."

"What are they?"

Not toilets, alas.

—three hand-carved rocking chairs.

Sunny passed the afternoon in prep at Lou's for the supper crowd—if she could still call it that: her numbers were down, though the Water boys, in some twisted justice, continued to be loyal and even though the War had imposed its inherent economic restrictions on eating out, a few locals still came in now and then to take advantage of her genius skills with egg-diminished batters, and the long-haul truckers on Route 395 had passed the word among themselves that Lou's was the place to stop for decent vittles. Not the "crowd" she dreamed of in her restaurant fantasies—her entrepreneurial ones—she was feeding people who wouldn't know a *sauce soubise* if they were swimming in it, but they said Thank you, Miss, on leaving and seemed to have their moods inflated, along with their bellies. She was basically giving food away to them—

not covering her costs, not making salary, pulling weekly from her inheritance which was large enough, let's face it, to go on for the foreseeable but if she was going to be in the business of *giving* food away, there were other ways of doing it and needier people to whom it might be given.

She was going to close Lou's for the duration of the War—not yet; and not completely—she was going to let Vasco run a backdoor dispensary for breakfasts and pre-made lunchboxes for the Water boys and Lone Pine work crews, and she was going to start to *can* and *jar* and *brand* her sauces and her cheeses and her butters and try to make (at least a minimal) income that way to offset the losses.

Every once in a while on late nights such as this one, driving home (*goddamn* Svevo and his early visit the next morning, by the way, it was one of the only reasons she was driving back to Three Chairs late at night and not staying in her room in Lone Pine above Lou's), she'd work herself into a state—something about *driving* did this—of self-rationalization where she had to tell herself Good for *you*, Sunny, you're out here, trying to make a living, *did your father ever do that*? No.

A sore spot for her:

—though she loved him none the less for it.

Lights were out in the Great Room—Tops was probably reading in his study—and she headed for the kitchen and the shelves of cookbooks:

"Passover"—quite the hunt through Christian French, Christian English, Protestant American cookbook standards: you have to go back to the 18th century and those food writers prodded by Thomas Jefferson to be more inclusionary, write down the lesser-mainstream *receipts*, the lesser-known *recettes* (from which—both *receipt* and *recette*, which mean "money received"—the modern word "recipe" derives) . . . already—even way back then—proving cooks were looking for the vig and praying to get paid for all their effort.

"**PASSOVER**: Fixed to the Paschal full moon, an annual celebration by those of Jewish persuasion, commemorating their Mosaic story of escape from slavery, out of Egypt, to a Promised Land and upholding many traditions associated with the event (unleavened bread; bitter

herbs, representing Misery; and salty water, representing Tears). An
Empty Chair is left for the PROPHET ELIAHU, as well as an unsipped
cup of wine poured for those not in attendance (THE DEAD). The meal
is called THE SEDER and is accompanied by chinaware especially
designed for it. During the meal the story of the Exodus is retold
and Four Questions are asked. Among the traditional foods are
roasted hard-boiled eggs dipped in salt water, parsley dipped in
salt water, *maror* (bitter herbs), *matzos*, and *charoset* (a fruit-and-nut
chutney)."

The whole thing sounded more like a punishment than a meal though she
liked the idea of the Empty Chair and had to wonder what the Four Questions
were.

A light was still on in Cas's *appartement* and Sunny found her sitting up
in bed, per habit, book and gin to hand.

"Hello, button, how fares the thriving metropolis of Lone Pine *ce soir?*"

Sunny stretched out on the bed:

"What do you know about Passover?"

"—*bloody.*—*bloody* hour. Dreadful time to be Egyptian.—*plagues . . . ten*
of them, including—if my memory of my youthful churchgoing serves—boils
and frogs. God at his most inventive."

"—when did *you* ever go to church?"

"—with my mother, as a whelpling. Only chance to be with her. Every
Sunday.—loved it . . . Anyway I *do* remember all Egyptian water turned
to blood, that's *one* passage from the Book of Exodus your father loves to
quote . . ."

"But what do you know about Passover *food?*"

"Only slightly less disgusting than the plagues. As far as delicacy goes.
Entirely inedible. Why the interest—*Mr. Schiff?*"

"—someone you don't know."

"I know everyone."

"Lieutenant Svevo."

"*I* know Lieutenant Svevo.

"How do *you* know Lieutenant Svevo?"

"He's behind our poker games."

"You're not taking these poor farm boys for everything they earn are you?"

"—play for matches. Gambling is frowned upon in Uncle Sam's armed service. I'd presumed Svevo was run-of-the-mill Italian Papist."

"—apparently not. He asked me for help with food for the . . . Seder." (She pronounced it *cedar*.) "He's arriving early a.m."

"I'll be sure to dress."

"You always do. No one has ever seen you naked, Cas."

Off-script: Sunny must have something on her mind: Cas waited.

"I met an interesting woman today," Sunny finally ventured.

Voilà, Cas concluded. Prematurely.

"She runs the orphanage. There's an orphanage over there. Actual orphans . . ."

Hard to tell what her niece was thinking.

"That's just *wrong*," Sunny said.

"No argument from me," Cas said. And still waited.

One presumes what one is being told in moments such as this are the important things but Cas knew better.

"I'm going to close Lou's."

. . . *et voilà*.

"—not entirely, not tomorrow; but soon."

"Ah," Cas said.

"—can't afford it. Town can't support the kind of restaurant I want to run. Especially, wartime."

"I understand," Cas said. "But, dear, you need to *cook*."

"I know."

"—you won't be 'you' without it."

"You're just repeating what I tell myself."

Alrighty then.

What else?

She watched Sunny rub her eyes. *Here it comes*, she thought.

"I don't think . . . I think Tops acts like he believes that Stryker isn't dead," Sunny said.

Didn't see *that* coming:

"I don't agree," Cas said.

"He hasn't *mourned*."

"—believe me, button, you don't want to see your father *mourn*: I speak from experience. I think he learned—we all learned—a lesson about *that*."

"—but he doesn't . . . he hasn't . . . said anything. *Done* something. I think he needs A Ritual. I think we need to create A Ritual for him."

"—*ah*," Cas repeated. Pieces fitting:

"Like the Jews do with their Empty Chair," Sunny said, "—or like Pie and Tia Lupe do, rinsing Maman's grave in water."

"Pie and Tia Lupe did not *invent* their ritual: a 'ritual' is handed down: it does not arise from air . . . like Venus . . . who, excuse me, rose full-blown from the sea."

"Pie and Tia Lupe didn't *start* the water ritual?"

"—god *no*, button—people have been cleansing graves for centuries . . . *dark* ages; before Christ."

"I thought they started doing it because, you know: the *polio* . . ."

"—they 'started' doing it because their grandmothers had taught them how."

"So they didn't make it up."

"They didn't make it up."

"I liked it better when I thought they made it up."

"Well that's a problem with 'a ritual': it can die on you. Believe what you need to keep the thing alive."

"—but if I said something to Tops about . . . I don't know: a *memorial*—"

"—*no*."

"—or us sitting down and talking—"

"No. He needs to do it on his own."

"—have *you* done it?"

"—yes. —have *you*?"

"Not really."

"—then whom is our conversation actually *about*?"

Sunny stared awhile at the blank ceiling:

". . . you're all right with Stryker being dead?" she finally said.

"Absolutely *not*."

"—but you believe it."

"—from the first: just *knew*. I absolutely knew."

"—not the same for me: I still can't understand it. What its 'story' is, if Stryker's dying *is* 'a story' . . . Still can't grasp the *plot*. Or any meaning . . ."

Sunny fell silent. When she looked at Cas again she was surprised:

"—are you *blushing*?"

"No.—well *peut-être*: a tad."

It had taken Sunny years to certify that what appeared to be a rash from time to time in the middle of Cas's forehead was, in fact, her manifestation of embarrassment—not a rosy full-face flush in the manner of most people but a culminating *dot* that bled out above her nose like a drop of red wine spilled on a white carpet.

"—why are you *blushing*?"

"Won't say."

"—well you have to, now."

"I'll incriminate myself.—besides, it's not appropriate to the line of our discussion."

"—*Cas!*"

"—all right, all right: keep in mind this started about Exodus . . . which you should read by the way to answer all your questions about Passover . . ."

"You're *varnishing* . . ."

"—all right: You remember that night last summer when Humphrey Bogart came to supper?—that movie they were making up here . . ."

"*High Sierra*."

"—and he brought John Huston with him . . ."

She blushed again:

"I've never said this . . . I'm completely gaga over that man."

"—*Cas!*"

"—put me in front of that man and like *raclette* I'm born to *melt* . . ."

"—*Humphrey Bogart?*"

"*Huston*, for godsake. What a *charmer* . . . *oozes* sex. I don't know if you noticed it at supper but I couldn't speak. Couldn't *drink*, Humphrey kept saying You're nursing that gin like it's *acid*, sweetheart, but I was *para-lyzed* he had a para-lyzing effect on me, that man. Anyway they gabbed all night—I think you'd gone off to bed—they went on gabbing, *actors*, talked about themselves about the other actors that they knew about the movie 'business' and at one point John—I'll call him 'John'—was leading us along about what constitutes good drama, makes 'good story,' and he said There are only *two* plots in literature/drama/*whatever*—TWO—and I'll tell you what they are: NUMBER ONE: *Someone disappears . . .*"

Stryker, Sunny thought.

". . . NUMBER TWO: *A stranger comes to town.*"

Schiff.

Ten *thousand* strangers.

Well, Cas said:

"I looked into my drink and I downed it in one gulp—*Dutch courage*—and I said, 'Mister Huston, if you're looking for a paradigm to plot'—I used the word *paradigm*—I said, 'You need look no further than *the Bible.*'

"Well that shut them up:

"—for one thing I hadn't breathed a word all night and then when I did I came out sounding like Cotton Mather . . . I said, 'As far as Plot goes you can't better the first two books of the Old Testament: First one—Genesis: YOU'RE BORN. Second—Exodus: YOU LEAVE.'

"*Well*—

"They all went quiet. Then John—I thrill to call him that—*John* rolls back in his chair and lets loose that Irish laugh of his the one where he shows all his teeth and you can hear it all the way to Independence then he leans in close and clasps my hand—I nearly died—and he says, 'You're born/You leave: *honey* . . .' He was the first and only person to have called me 'honey'—he says, 'You're born/You leave' . . . *honey*: that's not a Plot . . . that's an *obituary.*'"

She smiled to herself, remembering of that night, Sunny thought, the man's *touch* more than anything.

"So, yes," Cas said, "go read Exodus: it will teach you all you need to know about *Passover . . .*"

Sunny stood and took the few steps toward her aunt and leaned in to her cheek and kissed her. "*Ritual,* old woman," she said: "Get used to it."

"—I never will."

Sunny started to depart, then, at the door, turned:

"Do we even *have* a Bible?"

Cas gestured: "Dining room. Credenza. Next to the *Collected Shakespeare.*"

"Have we ever *used* it?"

"Let me think . . ." Grandstanding, Sunny could see: "—*oh.*—good heavens.—*yes:* I'm surprised you don't remember . . . Stryker made you pledge your love on it the day he 'married' you and Hace in that little ceremony . . ."

You're born/You leave, Sunny recited in her mind.

. . . but somewhere, in the middle of all that, the boy will kiss you for the first time.

All of Svevo's girls were regular Army—highly skilled; razor sharp—and Schiff had been the uncomplaining beneficiary of their efficiency from the beginning, but when they finally moved from the Dow Hotel into camp offices he'd wanted his gateway presence—his "face"—to be civilian so he and Svevo and all of Svevo's girls had put the word out in the community and at the eleventh hour Betty had fetched up, under-trained and over-looked, and though her potential had gone unexplored through her brief professional life she made it clear from the start that should they decide to hire her—and she hoped they would—there was A Condition: she had to have her Friday nights. Unconditionally. She had to leave every Friday no later than four-thirty.

Other bosses might have asked her why; Schiff hadn't.

—he might have, if her work had fallen off or if any reason for her termination had developed, but it hadn't, and for the first few Fridays she'd announced her departure at four-thirty from behind a neat, cleared desk and turned up half an hour early each Monday so tonight when he saw her parked there in her thin cloth coat and her little hat holding her purse in front of her like a life buoy he had to ask Why are you still here?—it's five o'clock.

"I'm not allowed to leave until I get you to the party at five-thirty *sharp*. In this clean shirt." She pointed.

He looked.

There was a pressed shirt on a hanger on the door between them.

"This isn't my shirt," he remarked.

"It came from some swank store in Chicago. I had to iron it. It's a *party* shirt. You're supposed to wear it to Lieutenant Svevo's *party*."

"—what 'party'?"

"—his *Jewish* party. He's been working on it all day. And I'm not allowed to leave until I get you there. In the shirt."

"Betty, Lieutenant Svevo doesn't make the rules around here, *I* do."

So you *think*.

She wouldn't leave—she just wouldn't—until he'd changed his shirt and water-tamed his hair and water-shined his shoes and brushed his suit and washed his face and then she *still* wouldn't leave until the tent Svevo had set up for the Passover dinner was in sight and then she ran through the Main Gate to a black late-30s Olds parked across the road, waiting for her, and jumped in as Schiff watched it roar off, north, at speed.

Falling in with him, from the camp, toward the Passover tent, was a family of three he recognized from Intake, though he couldn't remember their names: a Japanese-American male, mid-30s, who had a guitar slung across his back; his Caucasian wife, who was here voluntarily; their eight-or-nine-year-old mixed-race daughter.

Schiff remembered them because the wife was Jewish.

She smiled in greeting, and her name came back to him:

"Esther," he said.

"*Passover!*—in a place like this!" She tried to act as if coming to a U.S. Army tent for the Seder was a normal thing to do, these days. "This is my husband, Kenji . . . and our daughter, Rachel."

"That's some dress you're wearing, Rachel," Schiff noted.

It was pink. And it was flouncy.

"It's my *afikomen* dress," the child said. "Lieutenant Svevo bought it for me. I'm going to find the *afikomen*. I'm the *afikomen* girl . . ."

Svevo had sprung for a superior tent (Schiff was not going to ask the four money questions—*how? where? who? how much?*—on a night when there were Four Other Questions to be asked and answered)—a *raised* tent with a wooden floor and formal porch on which he stood decked out in chocolate-brown full Army dress jacket, radiating his best Eisenhower (if Eisenhower could ever be Italian. Or Jewish).

"Did you hide the *afikomen*?" Rachel asked.

"I did."

"Is it going to be hard to find?"

"You told me not to make it easy—"

"—it was too easy last year, Mommy hid it in a napkin right there on the table . . ."

"—well it ain't on the table this year I'll tell you that much . . ."

"—but I'll be able to find it?"

"Go have a look—you're a smart kid, I bet you'll see through my tricks in no time . . ."

Schiff held back from entering; Jay told him, Nice shirt.

Schiff could see a group inside the tent—Caswell Rhodes, the Rev. Leslie—standing, talking, and he felt, all of a sudden, ill at ease. Past Seders had not prepared him to play the role of an adult—he hadn't been to one in years—and what he remembered, chiefly, of the yearly ritual was "Uncle" Marty grating horseradish out the kitchen window so the women wouldn't faint and himself (Schiff) being the beloved youngest *afikomen*-seeking child for six glorious years until his dreaded cousin David deposed him. That was it.

"—if you're counting on me," he started to tell Jay:

"I'm not counting on you."

"—to even try to read in Hebrew . . ."

"—got this, buddy. All you have to do is thank me later."

Two long tables had been set up in the "room"—one laden with food, running the width of the back "wall"; the other, perpendicular to the first, running down the center, laid with pre-designated place settings, lit candles and sprays of wildflowers. Although both were draped in what his practiced restaurant eye could identify as quality white linen, Schiff also noticed that the Seder table had been purposefully set with run-of-the-mill mess "china" and "silver" and all the chairs were Army issue.

Except the one that would stay empty: that was a hand-carved rocking chair. Made by Rocky, Schiff recognized.

The whole front half of the tent was where the guests had congregated, plied with beverages by "waiters" (Army NCOs) Svevo had no doubt—Schiff was afraid to ask—handsomely *paid*. Along with Caswell Rhodes and the Parson, whom Schiff had run into several times since his first visit to the parsonage, there was another Christian poo-bah—Congregationalist?—whom he'd met before but whose name escaped him—*Dunst*, Preacher Dunst—and a couple, the Oelbaums—*Jews!*—Svevo had unearthed in Bishop who'd driven down for the occasion and had brought a clarinet (his) and an accordion (hers) for entertainment and a Persian couple, the Yentobs, from Olancha, twenty-odd miles to the south, who, Schiff discovered, operated the same fruit-and-nut roadside stand from which he'd stopped to buy pistachios when he'd first been driven up here by Hauser with Macauley all those (few) weeks ago . . .

What a small world, he heard himself declaiming.

What an asshole I sound like, he knew.

Mr. Yentob (Omar) had brought a bottle of date syrup from his own dates (a meager gift, he insisted) and handed it to Schiff (he pronounced the name *chef*), who, rather than holding it looked for somewhere to place it on the long *buffet* table where he finally noticed, first, Jimmy Ikeda dressed like a proper food server in a starched chef's jacket and a cloth napkin covering his shaved head and, second, the full panoply of gustatory opportunities on offer, each, in contrast to the spartan table setting, ornately and professionally plated in regulation domed hotel pans and covered chafing dishes with discrete Sterno flames to warm them—just like Sunday lunches in the old days back in the Drake dining room.

"Jimmy," he had to ask (the kid seemed to have recovered his old self): "—did *you* do all this?"

"Hey no—*boss lady* brought it in. Knows her stuff, though. *Real* good."

Sunny.

—which he would have figured out himself because each hotel pan had a folded freestanding handwritten label in purple ink (the same color he used!): *matzo ball soup   stuffed grape leaves   cucumber salad with dill and nasturtiums   pot-roasted brisket with knishes   roast chicken with honey, grapes and rose petals   peas with chive blossoms   fried artichokes with white carrot blossoms   pistachio pilaf   potato kugel   beetroot salad with caraway and mint   candied citrus peel   matzo-meal almond cake with espresso glacé*

The plate of *charoset* even listed ingredients:

Grated MANZANAR APPLES

Crushed OLANCHA WALNUTS

OLANCHA ORANGE BLOSSOM HONEY

Cinnamon

THREE CHAIRS CALVADOS

First thing you do, Svevo had told him their first day on the job together: find out who the experts are.

—then let them do the work for you.

How Svevo had talked Sunny into doing all this had been a matter of his showing up—this is what she liked to do, this is what she *did* and she was genius at it—all he'd had to do was put the dice in play: he'd driven over, as rehearsed between them, at 0730 and the first thing that hit him were the dogs and he was not a dog person—what self-respecting person from Brooklyn ever *is?*—and then the second thing, once inside: dark haunt of European coffee. The place was a fucking mansion, he'd had no idea, and once she'd led him through the dog rut to the kitchen and sat him down to an espresso he'd almost completely forgotten there was another world, at war, somewhere. He'd brought along six boxes of the matzos. Blondie had sat across from him with a goddamn little notebook and started grilling him about the Seder meal—what were the requirements, what did he remember, what were his *sense* memories, his favorite dishes . . . and they'd made a list of the traditions—the *charoset*, etc.—and at one point she'd asked about the matzos, Where did *these* come from, and he'd said, "Brooklyn—well actually Queens," and she'd torn a box open and broken a corner off and tasted one and said You're kidding me.

It tastes like . . .

—chalk?

Cardboard.

She'd got him talking about *joy* for fucksake what had made him happy about the Seder meal when he'd been a kid and he'd started talking about brisket about the *soup* the chicken soup and how the *knaidlach* shouldn't sink like stones but *float* and how you couldn't have a risen dough or anything that *rises* because the Jews were in a hurry to kick Egypt that night—that's what the *un*leavened matzos represented—so she couldn't make the *knaidlach* for the soup with yeast and the key was—his mama's recipe: you mix the matzo meal with carbonated water, makes them float. And they shouldn't be the size of testicles for godsake—excuse his French—you got some women in the neighborhood made their *knaidlachs* size of baseballs while the key was: *delicacy*: small and bouncy. Along with the brisket there could be maybe a chicken. Potato something. Cakes made with grains other than flour. Beets. Beets were always big. Cucumbers. Blondie had made him *pain perdu* and hand-squeezed navel orange juice and the old woman, the card shark, had wandered in and Blondie had started asking which china service she should use from their collection of china services (!) that would be the most appropriate and the old gal had wagged a finger and said, *Not.* We're at *war*: you're *not* catering to the goddamn King of England. That's when Jay had asked them both to come and Blondie had said No she had to work and the old dame had said Yes. Then the old guy had come in from the outside with more of their *goy* dogs and asked what wines he planned to serve.

Jay had stayed 'til almost 0930—had to load some rocking chairs into the Jeep to deliver to Rose Ito at the orphanage and then he'd driven off with no clear certainty but his blind trust in her that Blondie would deliver anything—all this—in less than thirty-six hours:

He tapped an Army spoon against an Army glass summoning everyone to the table and, as prearranged, the Oelbaums launched into "*Shabbat Shalom*" which sounded almost authentically *klezmer* and then, with everybody seated, he deftly led the group through the *Hagaddah*, excerpts of which he'd had mimeographed. Jay's Hebrew was differently inflected from that of Schiff's parents—Jay's family was Sephardim; Schiff's Ashkenazi—but even so, the ancient sound wound through him to a latent nerve and he felt, involuntarily, a pulse of inexplicable emotion and sat very very still in an effort to contain it. The bitter herbs were sampled and explained; the *charoset* was tasted; the Four Questions were asked—and answered—the *afikomen* successfully discovered by Rachel under the cushion on the seat of the rocking chair kept empty for Eliahu (which meant that had the Prophet actually dropped in he would have *sat* on it . . .); the matzo-ball soup was ladled out and even though he was sitting next to her and she was being very nice to him and very chatty, Schiff could answer only "yes" or "no" or "I agree" to every comment Esther made to him. Jay led them through the more difficult parts of the oral tradition and then they ate with gusto and then he called on Cas to recite a reading of her choosing—he'd asked her to prepare something secular but appropriate to the celebration of survival and of absent loved ones, absent friends—and Cas handed a book to Rev. Leslie, saying, "This will sound best in a man's voice, Reverend, if you will: for our friends in England and in France . . ." and Rev. Leslie stood, and read.

Schiff didn't know which play of Shakespeare's it was from but he recognized that it was Shakespeare—there was no disputing that—it was the one that has the king (whichever) telling his men, "We few, we happy few, we band of brothers," that History will not forget them for the way they fought that day to save their nation . . . and no one spoke when Rev. Leslie finished except Rev. Leslie himself, who said, "Play something for us, Kenji," and Esther's husband took up his guitar and told them, ". . . as you said about Shakespeare, Miss Rhodes, that those words sound truer in a man's voice, I like the sound of this one in a woman's . . ."

He looked at Esther as he played the bridge and she said, "I see what you're doing here, okay: I can do this," and she let him elaborate the intro and then delivered (maternal; raw . . .):

I dreamed
I saw
Joe Hill
Last night,

Alive
as you
and me.

Says I,
"But Joe,
you're ten years
dead . . ."

"I never died,"
said he.

I never died, said he.

Esther's voice had roots: no top notes. Only burial. Earth, only.

"The Copper Bosses killed you, Joe.
They shot you, Joe," says I.

"Takes more than guns to kill a man."
Says Joe: "I didn't die."
Says Joe, I didn't die.

Kenji kissed his wife and swung his arm into a barrage of upbeat chords, then sang:

This land is *your* land
This land is *my* land

From California,
To the New York island,
From the redwood forest
To the Gulf Stream waters
This land was made for you and me.

Rachel was clapping in rhythm and, Woody Guthrie–style, her father leaned toward her and half-spoke, half-sang, the next verse:

As I went walking, I saw a sign there
And on the sign it said *Noooooo Trespassing*
But on the other side IT DIDN'T SAY NOTHING!
That side was meant for you and me . . .
This land is *your* land. This land is *my* land

They ate dessert.

—and Schiff heard Esther tell Cas (since the news was out): "Your niece is a brilliant cook . . ."

"—she *is*."

"I wish *I* could cook."

"—*I* wish you could cook," Kenji joked.

"—well everyone has something she wishes she could do—and *can't*," Cas said. "For me it's dancing . . . size of me . . . my poor brother had to accompany me to all my balls. I do find some approximation to the dance in water, though . . . the feeling of *flight*."

"Are you a proficient swimmer, Miss Rhodes?" (The Rev. L.)

"—with these arms? They should weaponize me, my dear man, send me to Hawaii, I can out-propel a U.S. destroyer . . . when, really, all I wish to do is tango."

Did you say *tango*? Incredibly, it seemed to Cas, the Persian, Omar, had stood up (though his paper *nappe* was still tucked in): "Do you want to *tango*?"

Yes I "want" to, but . . .

We tango. (He proffered a hand to his wife:) We are the *best* at tango. He turned to the Oelbaums and asked Do you play *tango*?

Of course they did.

He said a few words to them about how many bars and then before anyone could grasp what was happening the Oelbaums had broken into that tango music you used to hear in the streets of Paris, that music from the solitary corner entertainer or—more authentically—from behind the beaded curtains of the smoky bars . . . suddenly the Oelbaums were launched into *"La Cumparista"* and the Yentobs into what had now become the "dance floor" of the tent, he clasping her too close it seemed to Cas until she leaned back from her hips, stared at an enigmatic spot on the tip of her toe and raised her shoe up to her buttocks *This is thrilling!* Cas exclaimed and off they went. The thing went on until Mrs. Yentob died from love (it seemed to Cas), swooning backwards in her husband's menacing erotic clutch and going limp for all to see as he sustained her weight the way one lugs a mattress to one's bed: *O bravo!* Cas said.

Goys, Svevo marveled to himself (although even he had been knocked sideways by it all): ask them to your party and they make a spectacle in ways you never even knew existed.

He was barely able to explain the meaning of the toast

L'shanah haba'ah b'Yerushalayim!

before they were all on their feet, handsy with each other in that stiff-armed Christian way, saying *goodnight!* like they were off to bed (except for Cas who gripped his shoulders and told him, "Effervescent evening!") and then everyone was gone except for him and Jimmy Ikeda and the boys and Schiff, who'd barely said a word all night.

Svevo told the boys to dig in before they broke the service down, and he grabbed two glasses and a bottle of Rocky's wine and joined Schiff where he sat, looking at the camp, on the tent's porch. Under Schiff's extended curfew the camp was still alive with movement, noises of contained humanity.

"Really nice," Schiff told him. "—really, *really* nice . . ."

"—I think we oughta mandate *tango* into every *Haggadah* . . ."

"That was the best Seder I've ever had," Schiff elaborated.

Jay thought he sounded tipsy.

"I'm a little blotto myself on this wine, I'd love to get a bottle of Rocky's *dago rosso* to my ol' *papa* in Brooklyn his Italian liver would explode . . ."

"—you call him 'Rocky' now?"

"We've been to the wine 'vault' together. Which an ordinary human being would call a 'wine cellar' but he calls a '*vault*.' Who the hell other than a bank manager or the Pope's architect ever uses 'vault' in daily conversation? So I've been to the wine 'vault.' Have you ever been to the wine 'vault'?"

"No."

"So I get to call him 'Rocky.' "

"Great party, Jay. Memorable. *Thank you.*"

"Thank Blondie: she did the whole thing: that *charoset*? that was the first *charoset* I could ever *eat*. Made by a *goy*. Go figure. She's a keeper."

"She's a 'keeper' kept by someone else."

"—not so sure on that front: trust me—I think there's something bogus about 'Boyfriend.' "

"You wouldn't lie to me?"

"I wouldn't lie to you. She had the chance to be with him and she didn't take it. I'm just sayin' . . . I think there's room for you to make a move . . ."

Schiff fell silent.

—listened to the flagpole rigging echo through the air.

"—ask you something?"

"Shoot."

Schiff took his time:

"What does Betty have to do every Friday that she has to leave at four-thirty?"

"Who's Betty?"

"*Betty. My* Betty."

"You really want to know?—it won't make you happy . . . She has to leave at four-thirty to get up to Reno by twenty-three hundred 'cause she's the star act at a club in the midnight show. Torch songs. Bills herself 'Lava Girl' . . ."

"You're lying."

"—she has to leave at four-thirty every Friday 'cause she has a guy, married, salesman, who passes by here every Friday on his way home for the week to Bishop so they can squeeze in two hours of heavy love."

Schiff stared at him.

"—she has to leave here every Friday at four-thirty because her mother's in a charity home in Independence and if she doesn't get there by five o'clock they won't let her take the old broad home with her for the weekend to brush her hair and feed her."

Schiff stared out across the roofs of all the barracks.

"It's a guy, isn't it?" he finally said.

"It's always 'a guy,'" Svevo confirmed. "*Always.*"

They let another moment pass.

"Okay, buddy," Svevo said: "—you need me to walk you home?"

"No, I'm okay."

Still, he didn't move.

"Okay: I'm gonna go call Beryl . . ."

"—but it's . . . almost eleven o'clock in New York . . ."

"She waits up." He stood. "What are *you* gonna do?"

"I'm gonna join up."

"Oh for fucksake *why?*"

"Because of *Hitler.*" He smiled at Jay: "It's always 'a guy' . . ."

"Don't do this, brother—you're too smart for this you're a lawyer for christsake not some street guinea like me you belong *Stateside* on a desk in Washington writing policy or making up some shit to put through Congress not serving as cannon fodder for some jackass Allied general in the Old World . . ."

"—gotta do it."

"Don't do it."

"Gotta."

"Wine talking. You've been weird all night. Let me walk you home."

"I'm okay."

"You're *not* okay."

"Go call Beryl. Tell her Schiff says Happy Passover. . . . or whatever we're supposed to say."

" 'Next year in Jerusalem.'—that's what we're supposed to say."

"—next year in *Berlin*."

"—you're not going to Berlin, my brother."

"—next year in *Tokyo*."

"—don't make fun of this night."

"I'm not, I'm not . . . All I'm saying is . . . if we could go around the world tonight, whole world . . . ask people *all* the people everywhere—China, India, Paris, Egypt . . . '*Where do you want to be next year?*' do you know what I bet half the people in those places would all say—?"

"No."

"—well *I* know. *I* know, buddy. They *wouldn't* answer 'Next year in Jerusalem,' that's for sure. They'd say the same thing *I* would say . . . 'I want to be . . .' "

Anywhere but here.

THE OLDEST BUILDING ON THE PROPERTY was one that everybody called the *casita*, a former prospector's rubble standing alone by a dry streambed, which pre-dated Rocky's arrival, he'd figured, by at least half a century. It had fallen into itself but the stone foundation was solid and, with a second adobe room added as larder, it had sheltered him well that first year while he'd planned his future. Back then the stream had run in the winter; a hand pump by the door had worked in the heat. Nothing electric, of course—water and fire, tile roof, a stone floor and four plaster walls the only amenities. He'd sunk the eyes for the hammock ten inches deep into the walls (he'd had to, at his size) and added more height to the roof so he wouldn't feel cramped but most nights, at first, he had still slept on his bedroll under the stars next to the sound of the trickling water. He'd already fallen in love, both with Lou and this land, and he'd spent the first months on his own, thinking and scheming of how he could shape them—two different loves—into one. His father had died the previous spring, falling down on a Manhattan street, like a beggar, his heart having given up on

its compounding interest. Because of his clothes and his manicured nails people had stopped to assist him and maybe Punch's last moment, Rocky had still
let himself fantasize (though he'd known better), had been one of grace and
(this was a long shot:) gratitude. Who starts out as a child—starts out in life—
thinking Death will end up our Best Teacher? Right up there with Love, Rocky
had learned. He'd wished someone had told him: he'd wished he'd read more
about Death when he'd been younger. Punch's death had made the front pages
in all six of the Manhattan papers but it had taken three days for the news to
reach Rocky out West (less than an hour, by telegram, to reach the head of the
mining concern at Cerro Gordo, followed by a seventy-two-hour three-horse
manhunt across the valley). Four days then, by rail, to New York City. Cas had
always maintained Rocky would have succeeded in missing the funeral entirely
if she hadn't had the foresight, early on, to put Punch on ice—but even then,
Rocky arrived too late. Neither he nor Cas had foreseen what their father's
death would mean to them—how it would change their lives—primarily because Punch had never told them how much money he'd acquired, he'd only
talked about its acquisition, the excitements of dealing, getting, having, own-
ing, winning. They were his only heirs. There had been gobs of cash. Articles
in all six papers had touted Rocky as one of New York's most eligible bachelors and Cas as the city's 11th-most-desirable (read, "wealthy") marriageable
female (read, "milch cow"), descriptions both had found alarming, especially
Cas who, like her brother, had cultivated from the loveless desert of her parents'
marriage a rabid thirst for romance and romantic love and now felt disobliged
to trust any man who, given her less-than-comely physical appearance, might
have dared to take an interest in her. Easy for Rocky, who was in search of
some hermetic life out West anyway, but what was she to do? Someone had to
run the family business if they were going to keep it and Rocky had made it
clear that he was finished with the East Coast, finished with New York. They
had fought like hummingbirds, the two of them, speed of words replacing
skirring flight, until, with the help of several footmen, buckaroos, and lawyers,
they'd divested Wellington Rhodes of every piece of mineral-bearing property
and rolling stock and chamber pot Punch had acquired and then walked away
from everything their father had once owned for a sum that would have killed

him, into their separate futures. Cas had taken off for Scandinavia where she'd believed t-a-l-l men resided in hopes of finding one who had never heard of her inheritance who might fall in love with her for qualities yet to be appreciated and sweep her off her outsized feet. Of all the properties they'd come into possession of, they'd kept only two, one for each of them, as the places where they would live. Cas had chosen the brownstone in Murray Hill that had been in her mother's dowry; Rocky the land in Owens Valley, California. They'd sold the house on Fifth Avenue and the house in Newport and gone their separate ways, writing to each other weekly but never really speaking of the life they'd left behind nor visiting the ground in which their parents were interred, two feet apart, beneath the family mausoleum. Cas had kept their mother's jewelry, giving half to Rocky's bride after he married. Punch had hoarded jewelry of his own—sometimes wearing something only once—and his miniature bespoke brocades and vests had hung like a rack of elfin clothing for an elaborate opera in his mirrored dressing room. Rocky couldn't stand the sight of all of it and had told Cas to let the mortuary people choose the final wardrobe. His father's shoes, with their emboldened heels, had depressed him. His father's rings. His foppish kidskin gloves which served no purpose but to add another layer between Punch and everything he touched. From a man who'd had so much, so many things, you would have thought that something would have spoken to his son, some talisman to have and hold, to guide him on his way, which he could keep, which might remind him of his heritage and bind him through his history. The things we keep are meant to triumph over things we've lost but as Rocky had looked at all his father's junk nothing stopped his leaving empty-handed, a fitting balance, on the cosmic scale of things, to all the money he'd inherited. The fact that he was living off his father's money, still, was never lost on him, even when he tried to seek atonement through his "independence"— Three Chairs, as a working ranch, had not made a profit in a decade. As a rancher he was all fraud: he put in the muscle but he never had to suffer the indignity of failing when the bottom line collapsed. He had known that was the gift he'd walked away with at his father's death, and that this gift—his birthright to material wealth—had been the other major player in his life even if he'd been "disowning" it in his self-righteous rebellion: he'd always suspected that no matter what he did Punch would never disinherit him—his father had "acquired" him at birth—so that nothing Rocky could ever do, short of disinheriting himself, would ever really make him independent of his father's wealth.

Back in the *casita*, following Punch's demise, when he was living all alone here after three weeks in New York and another eight in the Windy City, wooing Lou, to make this deeded land his own—his dream had been to sever his dependence on his father's money, to build a modest house, a modest life and shape a marriage and a family with the woman he loved. That first winter all he'd done was work on the *casita* rebuilding its walls, adding the second room to the original foundation. Word had spread and now and then a Mexican itinerant or two had shown up to help with the heavy lifting but on the whole it had been just him, a horse, a mule, the dogs, hard work. He'd kept a log of where the sun came up, its rising times and settings, and plotted its shifting monthly arcs across his topo map so he could judge how to situate his future dwelling. He'd paced its outline on the ground, changing its dimensions twenty, thirty times and when the roof had finally been raised on the *portales* he'd moved into a room there to be next to the building crew but still stole away to the *casita* now and then for privacy and dreaming. The little place had endured, even after Three Chairs was built, as a refuge for married workers or a place to put up the odd (very odd) visiting vaquero but once the stream had been rechanneled by the bastards from Los Angeles and the little well had dried, the *casita* had become less comfortable for human habitation and although they'd kept it clean and (somewhat) furnished it had sat abandoned until one night at supper after they had all come back from Europe Stryker, then thirteen, stood and announced, "Starting from tomorrow I'm going to go live in the *casita*."

Sunny had cooked her signature fried chicken, the first non-French dish she'd mastered other than pancakes, and Rocky had taken advantage of the meal to put his drumstick down and then to lick each finger and then wipe his napkin around his lips before he'd answered, "Take two dogs. Close them in with you at night. Take Huck and Pip." On hearing his name, Pip, the border collie, had raised his head and pricked his ears.

"You know the well is dry."

"Yessir."

"So's the stream. There'll be no water. You'll have to take your baths down here."

"I know it, sir."

"Don't think this lets you out of supper."

"I would never think it, sir."

Every night: Rocky's rule—unless you're off-ranch, up on the Sierras, in a different town or state, you showed up at six o'clock for family supper. Rocky had been fairly sure the supper rule would break his son's resolve to spend each night a quarter of a mile away in the *casita* but Stryker had proven his determination, setting off each night with his schoolbooks and the two dogs after supper and showing up like clockwork for a shower and his breakfast every morning. Cas had voiced concerns about his safety but Rocky knew from his own experience that there was nothing wild out there that could do him harm; still he got into the habit, in the beginning, of walking out each night before retiring to spy on Stryker from a distance but he gave it up when Stryker started driving and it had become obvious to everyone, even to his father, that the boy had somehow grown out of his boyhood and become a young, still-in-progress man.

Then Cas had worried he'd have liquor out there or loose women or un-suspecting girls or some combination of the three or he'd set the place on fire with the cigarettes he'd started smoking, but still Rocky had held out in support of his son's semi-independence and, besides, by then it had been too late to voice objection. From that first evening at supper, onward, Stryker had lived in the *casita* five years: still living there the night he'd left, that goddamn business with The Incident. And in all those years, plus the years that Stryker had been gone, Rocky had never trespassed on his territory, on Stryker's state of independence. He'd never gone to look at what his son had established for himself inside the building, never felt the need to check on him while he was still alive, nor the need to seek his shadow after he'd been forced to leave. 'Til now. And what it was about this day that made this morning different he could not begin to say, surprised as the dogs had been when they'd heard him command, *this way*: let's go see what's going on in the *casita*.

Hardpan had solidified around it, worthless goddamn California caliche rutching up like chiseled paving stones, calcium carbonate creating the mosaic that spelled *thirst* to any living thing: dry earth had choked the stone foundation in its stranglehold and the little house was tilting like a boat in wind but the adobe showed no fissures and the roof seemed sound. The streambed was now all but invisible except for a slight depression to the trained eye and when he tried the handle on the pump beside the door it let out a metallic sigh and a ghostly puff of yellow dust from its corroded spout. A dead Joshua tree had collapsed into itself like a broken scarecrow but a barrel cactus by the door was thriving and the beavertail beside it was in bloom with waxy yellow flowers and cigar-shaped shoots. The wooden shutter on the little window had been bolted from the inside and Rocky was surprised to find a padlock had been added to the latch. About as effective and prohibitive out here as a PRIVATE PROPERTY or NO TRESPASSING sign, he had it broken off its hinges with a shim of manzanita and his pocketknife before the dogs had finished peeing. Door creaked, the dogs rushed in, there was a flurry of some unseen business from the rodents across the floor but on the whole the place was not the worse for sitting idle for so long and once he got the windows open and the daylight in he was stopped in his tracks by the clear force of Stryker's personality.

The hammock had been sheaved. Pushed into that corner was a single metal hospital bed from Lou's old *clinica* (christ knows when Stryker had hauled it out here: Maybe when he started having sex).

On the floor beside the bed were two pairs of boots, toes to wall, and as she sniffed at them a ridge of hair on Jane Eyre's back stood up and a low sound started in her throat which mounted to a whine and Rocky met her look and patted her: "I know, girl: I feel it too."

There were shelves made out of reclaimed wood along one wall where Stryker had kept his books—*White Fang*, Jack London; shorts by Hemingway; Steinbeck's best two novels; *Stunt Riding and Barrel Racing*; *How to Act for Motion Pictures*; *The Lives of Stars*; biographies of Douglas Fairbanks, Errol Flynn, Meriwether Lewis, Gary Cooper. There was an unvarnished writing desk and chair beneath the window and atop the desk there were an inkwell and pen, a notebook, a tin bait box and a collection of found things arranged by size. Everything was neat and ordered—even in the hearth the ashes had been cleared and new logs laid (just as he had taught both his children) to welcome oneself home at night after a day's work.

Inside the tin bait box: hand-tied flies, transparent thread, a collection of bright feathers. (He must have sat in this chair, Rocky thought, fashioning his lures with knots.)

In the notebook: a page where he had practiced with his new pen: practiced signing *Stryker Rhodes. Stryker Rhodes, Esquire. Stryker Rhodes, Actor.*

A page titled *Horses' Names*:

SPIKE

PROSPERO

AGRIPPA

Page titled *Places*:

UTAH

YUCATÁN

TAHITI

On a peg beside the window there was an old lead mirror and beneath it, on a plank of wood balanced on two nails, a shaving cup, a shaving brush, the shaving soap, a straight-edge razor dulled by air. Rocky picked up the razor and ran his thumb along the dull blade that had touched his son's face.

He looked around and put the razor down.

Even in the added room, the "larder," the practice of organization was on display: everything was neat, as if someone of a Spartan or a military or a perfectionist's demeanor had ordered it, not the person that he'd known his son to be—wild, impulsive, physically immune to caution.

At the foot of the metal bed one of Stryker's saddles lay atop the foot locker he'd used on their Atlantic crossing and Rocky touched the horn before sitting, warily, on the mattress's edge, afraid to leave his imprint.

On the bedside table: the lantern and an ashtray. A water glass and a decanter, signatures of dry evaporates, ghost writing, etched into their sides. Framed photograph of Lou, radiant and happy in a straw hat and bright sun. Another photograph, unframed, which Sunny must have taken on the lake one summer that showed Rocky kneeling next to Stryker when the boy was nine or ten, Rocky holding up the giant cutthroat trout Stryker had just caught, the goddamn fish the length of the bare-chested boy whose adult teeth, that summer, had been too big for his still childish face, his grin too big for this world.

He tucked the picture in the pocket of his shirt and stood up—the dogs, anticipating, already at the door. He latched the wooden shutters from the inside and, once outside, found a heavy stone to roll against the door, thinking as he did it how fucking Biblical the gesture was, that whole thing about Christ's body disappearing from its stone-locked grave only to be met again, re-animated, elsewhere. *If only*, he told himself. If only our metaphors made better sense the first twelve hundred times we heard them.

The dogs were on the run now, toward the kitchen, sensing a clear shot at breakfast, and Rocky noticed for the first time how Jane Eyre was skewing her hindside to ease some kind of pressure on her hip: bitch was thirteen by his count, much of that time spent in full trot and he hoped he wasn't seeing a first sign of something sinister or fatal, though he suspected that he was: he hated putting down his animals (was this morning going to go that way, one goddamn funeral leading to another?). *Christ.*

The dogs had pulled up short beside the back doorway ahead of him, backing with their ears up, doing that low sideways dance they did whenever they were up against uncertainty, and he was wondering if they had cornered a rattlesnake when the first peal of unanticipated laughter reached him.

People—sounded like a pack of girls—were laughing in his house. In his kitchen, from the sound of it. Having a high old time.

Jane Eyre shot him a look for a second time this morning that begged, *What's happening?*

It had been a long time since there'd been the sound of laughter in the house, and Rocky realized now in the sudden shock of it that the evidence of daily laughter, daily joy, was the thing he missed most about his son.

Fifteen faces turned to him, fifteen pairs of eyes locked onto him as he stood inside the door. The women looked vaguely identical as if an alpha-Oriental *femme* had replicated thirteen times at various stages in her life and stature— younger, older, stooped. He stood at least a foot above the youngest (tallest) of them and they regarded him as a giant come alive from myth until, at the farthest corner by the stove, Sunny raised her voice and told them Ladies, let me introduce my father to you, this is Mister Rhodes.

At once their heads bobbed, there was a kind of seismic repetitious bowing and repeated whispers like successive wavelets in a sheltered cove, until Sunny added, "Tops, these are the lady chefs," and the assembled women straightened up and looked at him expectantly except for one, an assimilated Asian in her thirties who was sending him the evil eye.

Rocky touched the front of his Stetson and acknowledged, "Ladies," then under pressure from the evil eye took the Stetson off and stood turning it in front of him close to his body. "What are we making here this morning?"

"*Dashi*," Sunny told him and, again, there was the communal bobbing of the heads. "Want to taste it?"

Rocky didn't know what "dashi" was and stayed away in general from foods whose names he couldn't understand, plus the kitchen, he had noticed as he'd entered, smelled suspicious and a little bit like fish and, frankly, all he really wanted was to satisfy his hankering for strong black joe.

"Thank you, no—but you can tell me about it."

Dashi, she said (as much for his benefit as to resume the classroom atmosphere he'd interrupted) is a mainstay of Japanese cuisine—the foundation, like a stock or a *bouillon*—of soups and sauces, based on dried fish, and the women were showing one another their versions.

"I'll leave you to it," Rocky said. "Pleasure meeting you." He took a step backwards and the women, too, backed away in unison like iron filings from a non-attractive pole.

Normally he'd take his cup of joe through to the *portales* and find something to putter with among the workshops until lunchtime after which he'd go outside again and face the chores. But without his normal cup of coffee he wandered idly not in the direction of the workshops but down the hall into the Great Room. He rarely sat here anymore. They used to throw a lot of parties back when Lou had been alive, but this room, which had once held so many people and such a lot of noise, was dominated now by an outsized harp and felt oversized, itself, too big for the family's current number, echoing each solitary sound, each breath, into the rafters as a cruel rebuke. The room had held their Christmas trees and Christmas morning rituals; it had been where Lou and he had sat at night to read in front of the walk-through fireplace and where, after his wife's death, Rocky had tied two ponies up for the twins on their fifth birthday. Now the hearth was cold for weeks on end, the only ritual was Cas sitting down to practice at the stringed harp in her sweaters and those half gloves with the fingertips exposed, next to that electric fire which she wheeled in for the purpose. Mail accumulated here. Either he or Cas would go to Lone Pine to collect it and the stuff they didn't read at once (magazines and county notices) found its way into the stone font which used to be a Spanish mission trough, at the bottom of the two tiled steps, inside the entrance arch. Last week's *The Nation* was still here along with copies of *The New Yorker* and *The New Republic*. He took the weeklies to a favored leather chair and had a seat. But he didn't read. An hour, maybe more, slipped past. Before he knew it ladies were parading down the hall, unaware that he could hear and see them, Sunny herding, then a series of goodbyes and *sayonaras* as she watched them from the threshold climb into the flatbed of the pickup, Vasco at the wheel, each one clutching a gallon jar of her own *dashi* like some stolen water from a pilgrimage, a purloined elixir, proof of where she'd been.

Behind her in the open doorway, Rocky brought his arms around his daughter's shoulders, tugged her in and scared the bejesus out of Sunny. Proud of you, he told her.

She'd jumped at his embrace but this admission was an equal jolt—Tops had never been a toucher; he would reach that hand out when he talked to you, that lobster hand, even when he talked to men, it was part of his persuasiveness, but it would never connect and he would rarely hug, if ever (she could not remember the last time) and he had never, to her memory, expressed a sense of pride or admitted being "proud" of either her or Stryker.

This was not the same as never having said he loved them—he was good at that (*had* been good at that) and regular in its expression up until their getting old enough and tall enough and fast enough to offer resistance and embarrassment—but he had never been the kind of parent who could bandy "pride" as either incentive or straight compliment. "Pride" was something that you couldn't "earn" from Rocky: he'd meant to let them know his pride in them was "given." But now he realized maybe he had failed to get the message through.

Turning 'round within his arms to look at him, Sunny scanned his face for traces of an early dip into the *calvados* but his eyes were clear (if a little sad) and his skin did not betray the brandy's blush. This is a good thing that you're doing, Rocky told her: I can see your mother's signature all over this. She had a theory that white flour and white sugar were the true white scourges of our Indians . . .

Sunny searched his face again for clues before saying, simply, *thank you*, though she knew this show of sympathy wouldn't change his mind about what was going on across the road. Rocky had made it clear he would not step within one inch of the camp. He'd watched it grow—couldn't fail to see the spectacle of it every time he drove down the dirt track from the house to the paved road. "—anything I do," she said, "is just a drop in the bucket: three thousand women used to cooking for their families every day and all I can fit in here are a dozen at a time . . ."

Rocky freed her from his arms but kept her in close focus:

"Reminds me of the way your mother used to work with Native people. If she'd lived I always thought she'd have written about those things that she believed in. Put them down on paper. Effects of eating from the local earth. Eating things that you were meant to eat . . ."

What's with the "chatty," Sunny wondered: What's going on here, Tops?

"Well, everything they're eating over there is what the Army wants to feed them," she said. "Beans and franks. Canned veg . . . what the kids think is the epitome of eating 'American' . . . *Coke*. Campbell's soup. They want to be 'American' through the food they think defines 'America.' *Lotsa* kids across the road, Tops. *Orphans*, too."

"Well, *war is always about children*," Rocky said.

They walked back to the kitchen. Rocky sat at his seat at the table, the rainbow light refracting through the glass bowl of water in the window. Sunny ground some beans to make fresh coffee.

"How's our friend from Chicago doin' on the job?"

"—could be worse."

"I liked him."

You're in a strange, strange mood this morning, Sunny almost said out loud.

"You know what I was thinking—?" Rocky posed. "How long has it been since we've been fishin'?"

"Long time."

"Why don't you and I get in some time up at the lake? . . . maybe even head up to Yosemite."

"I would like that," she said honestly.

"—next week?"

Sunny leaned against the cool lip of the stove while the coffee perked behind her. Shared her secret with her father:

"I'm going off to be with Hace around then."

"How long has it been?"

"—couple months: five. Haven't had the chance to tell him yet. About Stryker." She watched the shadow in her father's eyes. "This is going to hit him hard."

Rocky couldn't hold her gaze: "—never easy. Never. I remember how impossible it was for me, to try to find the words for you. About your mother." He finally looked at her and said, "But Hace isn't a child: he'll understand: he'll hate it but he'll understand . . . *Now listen . . .*"

This directness, this emotional directness from her father was alarming but at the same time charming her:

"I think you should go live where Hace finds work—wherever he is living now—go and be with him. I don't speak like this too often so you know I mean it. The two of you were going to end up with each other anyway and this separation is doing no one any good. As long as that bastard Snow's around looking for what in his tiny mind he thinks is justice or revenge, Hace can never show his face in Owens Valley so it's up to you to go and be with him, wherever that might be. You know as well as I do that you're wasting time around here 'til you do. I should have sent you out with him that first night but I didn't and now it's something I regret. I want you to have a happy life,

Sunny; I truly do. And if that means I see you only once or twice a year then that's a price I'll fiercely pay."

"It's not your decision, Tops."

"I know it's not but you need to know that if your heart is taking you in that direction then you have my blessing."

"My heart . . . belongs here, too."

"I know it does. But, Sunny, this place isn't going to be here too much longer. When the water's gone, she's done."

"Don't make this about *water*—"

"I'm not." She made him feel confused: he was trying to tell her he cared about her happiness, but clearly the message wasn't getting through.

And Sunny wanted to move the subject away from her:

"—same bullshit every year," she told him: "You could plant forty acres— you could build a goddamn swimming pool out there—but *no*. Rockwell Rhodes the millionaire will never *pay* for what he thinks belongs to him . . . Who says the water underneath Three Chairs is 'yours'? Who says that water isn't 'everybody's'? Plenty water for the asking, Tops—you just refuse to ask for it. God knows what Maman would be telling you if she were here today—I hope she'd say you built this place with two hands and with two hands you're destroying it."

"—don't malign your mother, Sunny . . ."

"—don't *you*. Pay for the water, Tops—everybody does, it's the price we pay for living in the modern California. Call 'em up; they deliver. If you don't, if you let this place go under on account of stubbornness, you'll destroy our family's history with your pride and it'll end up being more of a death wish than anything even *Stryker* could have done . . ."

This was not the way he had anticipated his talk with her would go. How it had gone off the rails he didn't know but he suspected it was something he'd said and the absence of any joy between them—the opposite of laughter—was not the sound he had been thirsting for.

Propelled by the aroma of fresh coffee, Cas crashed in and, observing their deadlock, told them, "Don't let me spoil the *fun* . . ."

Father/daughter held their silence:

"Was he on about the Water boys again?"

"*Yes.*"

"Give it up, Rockwell: there are more soul-shaping things to occupy your thoughts."

She poured out three cups of coffee, and sat.

Finally Rocky mentioned, "I looked in on the *casita* this morning."

"How did you get *in*?" Sunny asked him.

"—*knife*," he said and Cas reminded her, "That is not the issue, child."

"We need to find that wife of his . . . We need to find his sons."

"Hear, hear," Cas seconded: "Hire a P.I."

Rocky looked at her:

"What the hell have you been reading, Cas?"

"Dashiell Hammett. Ripping stuff."

"What I don't understand," Sunny said, "is why she—*Suzy*—why hasn't she found *us*? Unless they died together. All of them."

"—let's not be morbid, child, she could be locked in an internment camp down there like the one across the road . . ."

"—where *do* you get your information, Caswell?"

"—it comes to me from outer space as you well know, dear brother."

"—*are* there camps down there?"

"Stands to reason . . . If we rounded up the Japanese Stateside you can bet your cowboy boots we corralled them all in Honolulu the very night of the attack—"

"I'll get Schiff on it," Rocky determined.

"—why *Schiff*?" Sunny wanted to know.

"—because he's in the business. They all must know each other . . ."

"—they're not a *club*, Tops, it's not like everybody went to Princeton . . ."

"That's *exactly* what it is," he told her.

"We're not even sure we have her name right," Cas reminded them.

"—*Suzy*," Sunny insisted.

"—but 'Suzy' *what*?—are we sure about her given name . . . ?"

"Well we know the boys': Ralph and Waldo," Rocky said: "Ralph Rhodes and Waldo Rhodes."

It was the first time any of them had said the babies' names aloud.

—and Cas was the first among them with a giggle.

"Why would you name a baby 'Waldo Rhodes' in the middle of the twentieth century? Poor child . . . What was Stryker thinking?"

"What was Stryker *ever* thinking—?"

Rocky took the photograph from his shirt pocket and laid it on the table.

"He kept this next to him . . . this and the picture of your mother. Tears me up he didn't have these with him . . ."

"Look at how you're looking at him, Tops—like he was the sweetest thing you ever saw . . . No wonder this is what he wanted to wake up to every morning . . ."

Not about the fish, then, that grin, Rocky saw. Not about the fish at all.

Cas looked through her reading glasses and asked Where was this taken?

"—up at the lake," Sunny told her: "I took that picture . . . we'd been fishing . . ."

. . . so *that's* why Tops wants to go back.

Impulsively she took her father's hand:

"—*I* remember when this was, the Summer of the Big Teeth," Cas said: "Look at his skinny legs—*god* he grew into such a handsome young man I forgot all about those audacious spurts of unannexed *growth*—what in godsname happened to his hair—?"

"He'd started cutting it himself that summer," Rocky reminded her.

"—*oh* the scamp was always dangerous with scissors, remember how he got into my closet and cut up my recital dresses for a kite?"

"—a *parachute* . . ."

"—*that*, too—most expensive flying apparatuses ever seen from our backyard!—*oh* that boy did have it in for me . . ."

"—he did not, he *loved* you, Cas . . ."

"—not at first. Not when I first arrived—he was mad at me, remember? He wanted his mother back. He was having no part of yours truly—don't forget he locked that skunk inside my room . . ."

"He never confessed to that, Cas—"

"—*oh* and I suppose the skunk reached up with its little paw and turned the doorknob to *mon appartement*. Those were my *recital dresses*, Rockwell. Two of them were Jean Patous all the way from Paris.—*oh* he knew where to strike, that Stryker. I used to wait in fear for him to try to take a target run against the harp."

"—he *did*."

"—*no!*"

Part of it was mock outrage but part was honest shock, Rocky could detect, which added to his sense of fun.

"He was going to oil the strings with motor oil. So your fingers would slide off," Sunny told her.

"What stopped him?"

"I told him only angels can own harps—that angels loan them out to humans that they like and if he oiled the strings the angel that had loaned it to you would be mad at him . . . and I guess I might have let him think the angel that had let you use it might have been someone he knew . . ."

"God, child, you tormented that innocent with your creative lies—"

"Beg to differ. He's the one who—"

"—telling him ice cream is frozen moonlight."

"—*that* was all pure Stryker . . ."

"—that he could improve in mathematics if he ate a lemon every morning." Sunny smiled:

"—well that was worth it just to watch his face while he was chewing them."

"—and remember how he'd drag in every living creature?"

" 'Lizard Land.' A nickel got you in to see 'Stryker's Magic and Colossal Zoo' . . ."

"—that nest of baby owls?"

"—*oh* don't make me relive it, brother, I thought I'd *die*— . . . I still can't figure how that mother owl got into the dining room . . ."

"She came down through the bell tower . . ."

"—*christ* straight after him while we sat there eating supper—"

"—eating *bird*, too, if I remember—"

"—biggest goddamn bird I've ever seen, talons, eyes and goddamn wings—"

323

"I never saw a human move so fast my god the boy was underneath the table and out the room before the rest of us could figure what was going on then *boom* he's back with those two baby owlets on his outstretched palm to satisfy the demon—reflexes like steel. Fearless in the face of animals."

"—they trusted him."

"They did."

"—remember he was going to train that horse to count?"

"—somebody told him if he was going to make a name for himself in Westerns then he had to—"

"Cary Grant."

"—what?"

"—it was Cary Grant who told him that. When they were making *Gunga Din*, and Stryker was an extra."

"—that he had a better chance at fame with a trick pony. With a horse that had a circus act."

"—I remember that. Whatever happened to that project?"

Rocky couldn't keep from laughing:

"Stryker couldn't get the horse to eat the lemons."

Borne by laughter, borne and born again—the first sound we hear at birth is screaming, no one, no *body*'s born with laughter on her lips, Rocky thought. Why not? *Laugh* me into being—Life should start that way, why not enter into Life with the infectious sound of laughter ringing in your ears as if to say You're gonna love this, bust a gut, this is gonna crack you up you're gonna laugh until you die.

Stryker had had the best laugh they'd ever heard—laughed while sleeping—laughed with his entire body which enriched the sound, that sound which when you heard it shot clear through you like a witch's spell. You could hear it and no matter where you were (outside, asleep, rapt in your own thoughts), it would take you over and before you knew it you were laughing, too. No one could laugh like Stryker—no one could do his impromptu Celebration Dance. Your own puny laugh would join his and then, like someone throwing kerosene on fire, the whole sight and sound exploded into the air and you would end up, gasping, on the plane of simple joy.

Darest we not neglect the Celebration Dance . . .

—oh lord the Celebration Dance!

—where *that* came from . . .

—the child was born with it . . .

—then how come *I* don't have a Celebration Dance?

—you have other *éclats*, button.

A seafaring friend had once told Rocky that when Stryker laughed it sounded like a colony of seals, and now as Cas's laughter issued forth Sunny heard the echo of her brother's laughter fill the hanging pots and strike the tinkling ladles. Cas was getting started on the time Stryker tried to build that tightrope and then as if no one was going to notice—using just her thumb— she reached over and wiped a tear from Rocky's face.

One of Lou's recipe cards, Sunny remembered, had said, only

PROTEINS

Tears of human sadness contain 20% more protein than tears of human joy

. . . which she now announced out loud.

Cas and Rocky looked at her in silence.

Then they all laughed like a bunch of raucous seals.

Laughter, like the perfect pastry crust, she thought she'd tell them later, is so much sweeter for the added salt.

It was perceptible, this planetary shift, the lengthening days, equating tilt: this week, alone, he'd noticed dawn's palette lightening earlier each morning, shadows thinning more quickly at the edge of darkness, away from green spring, toward summer's yellow. The boys up in the towers, too, had changed, their interest in his every movement shifting toward an almost-boredom, the repetition of his habit growing thin in their narrow range of excitements. *Schiff*, again. Schiff on the perimeter. The guy's a robot. Every morning. *What a surprise.*

Another thing that marked the march of time: the work these people did to make things grow: their goddamn gardens—*everywhere*—like a slap against the tyranny of imprisonment *ha ha* Mister Roosevelt you misguided ass you can't kill my spirit here's a *pea shoot* as my weapon *stand back* from this hibiscus.

Out here every morning: things were calmer, routine was setting in and he was sleeping better, getting used to . . . whatever-the-hell this was: his job.

—his life.

This morning: more *summer*-like; less ghost-cold from the mountains: less *nip*, more *dew*; a sense that things were heating up . . .

What he had begun to do to break his habit of touching barbs along the fence with every other step was he had started swinging his arms—less compulsion; more exercise. He'd started *breathing* . . . focusing less on what was underfoot, more on the mountaintops. More on the crowns of snow above the tree line . . . more sky, less earth. More blue, less brown.

—kept trying to convince his inner know-it-all that his was a job well done: no more surprises. He was on top of things; and this was all okay . . .

He was back there in that northwest corner which was his favorite stretch— the most peaceful—when he first heard the plane's low growl—so low, in fact, it took a while to grow on him—and then he saw it, overhead, coming up the valley toward the north, low over the camp, swinging 'round to east to counter the prevailing wind before turning wide and west again for landing.

From its profile: Army transport.

Except there was no scheduled flight this morning.

—which meant . . . either a surprise inspection or some unexpected snafu, and he started to walk fast, *real* fast, back toward the Main Gate, the Admin Buildings and his office. He could hear the Douglas drop its wheels, he could hear it land and then the low purr of its taxi on the airfield that they'd built across the road on Rocky's property and he started to jog the last hundred yards—no Betty, yet; too early—only Svevo standing sentry by Schiff's desk, full dress, cap in place, coat over his arm, crammed duffel by the door.

"Sorry, buddy," Jay announced. "They just gave me an hour's notice."

Schiff was panting from the jog—good thing, because it gave him cover for his speechlessness.

Jay wasn't due to go for three more weeks.

But here it was: the Army: Situation Normal:

All fucked up.

"I'll walk you over," Schiff said.

He extracted a sealed letter from his top desk drawer and tucked it in his pocket.

He still had the stupid bands around his cuffs above those stupid boots but he didn't give a flying fuck.

They strode together toward the gate.

Word had gotten out and passed among the boys and all the MPs had come out, some bare-chested from their beds, to stand salute.

Nobody spoke.

—except Svevo, who kept running his mouth, "—you'll be fine, place runs on its own now, the Janets know everything I've left them a bible and my little black book but do me a large and stand them all to drinks tonight they're gonna need a couple stiff ones and a cry I didn't have a chance to say goodbye . . ."

The two-engine had swung around, props still going and a groundsman ran out to hoist Svevo aboard. Schiff handed him the letter.

"For Beryl," he told Jay: "She needs to know the kind of man she married."

"Should I read it first?"

"—just the parts about your love affair with Judy Garland . . ."

They did a version of a man embrace—other men were watching—had a final look at one another through eyes filling with tears then Jay cut a dashing figure toward the plane, turned and shot a final hand salute into the air before he disappeared.

Sunny had been coasting down the road in neutral when she spotted first the plane, then their quick embrace, then Jay racing toward the plane—and she shoved the truck into first and gunned across the dust. The plane taxied to the eastern end and pirouetted before revving her two engines.

—pilot must have seen her then, god knows what he was thinking as she barreled over the tumbleweed until she hit the tarmac and jumped out of the truck *the crazy broad* what was she doing, calisthenics? Jay could hear him on the radio to the ground crew and he crossed the body of the plane to have a gander from the window and there she was running right beside the barreling machine running like a goddamn kid waving both her arms and shouting what he guessed was some big Blondie *shiksa* bon voyage:

Keeper, this one.

Schiff will fuck it up, Svevo was pretty sure but the woman had the stuff. He waved back and smiled at her. He wasn't sure that she had seen him but then, as he roared by, Sunny hurled herself into the ground and executed a wide cartwheel.

Chutzpah:

KEEP HER.

the fifth property
of thirst
is
the thwarting of desire

THE HOUSE WAS ALWAYS OCCUPIED—that's what she remembered thinking from the start—even when Hers Truly was the only one at home. Thing about these too-big houses—all the ones she'd known had felt abandoned: the house on Fifth deserted, underheated, even in the summer—and the summer house in Newport plagued by such deplorable acoustics it had always sounded like ghosts were rushing up the stairs. Maybe because her brother had constructed this one himself—*from the inside*, as he liked to say—or maybe because he and his bride had lived in it with so much love . . . either way, she'd liked it from the start and it offered great comfort. You would think a house this size would get too cavernous at night but even with the multitude of doors and open porches she felt safe all hours, even in the middle waking hours before dawn when she was most alone. She routinely felt another's presence—and, most commonly, there was someone stirring, somewhere, Rocky or her niece or nephew or one of Rocky's sidemen or the sonorous *señoras* who came to wax the floors and sort the laundry. When Rocky was indoors the radio was going and when Sunny was at home there was something doing in the kitchen, so even though, across the greater part of every day, Cas rarely saw the people that she lived with, she was, to her mind, for most of her waking hours, *accompanied*. She read, campaigned for the war effort, wrote letters, met with other ladies of her age for cards: and for an hour every other day at least, she sat down in the Great Room and submitted her body and her soul to music.

This is what you need to know about harp music: it's harmonic: the periodic waves of its individual strings exist through time for longer than a violin's or cello's—therefore the sound of any one plucked string overlays another, like a layer cake: an effect which drives the dogs berserk.

Or Rocky's dogs, at least.

No matter where they were if they were in or near the house, once Cas began to play, the dogs began to howl so she timed her music exercise to Rocky's morning walks, knowing he would keep the bitches with him, out of earshot.

Decades in, her hands were now more instruments of memory than mothers of invention and she usually had started, from rote, with some old chestnut from Debussy to loosen up but lately she'd been working on a suite of pieces she called *Scandinavia*, a series reminiscent of her past. These she worked through without taking notes, never writing down the chord progressions but allowing the music to build as improvisation: as jazz: as new sensation. She was even—this was radical for harpists—noodling around, sometimes, with atonal effects—disharmony—and trying to transcribe current hits from the big bands (all brass), especially Glenn Miller's compulsive opus "In the Mood," trying to translate his Swing to string. There were parts that were pure harp (that octave bridge) but the Swing sound was based on clean sharp transformations, unanticipated accent—and on syncopation—and a harp, let's face it, is an instrument built for rendering effects of fogs and fairy tales and watery emotions. Still, she was having fun with it, remembering ways to hit precise staccatos and she couldn't help it if she hummed out loud and tapped her foot and closed her eyes and lost herself, for once, to a music grounded in the present day, linked, through rhythm, to the meter and the matter of reality, the sound of automobiles and tanks and anxious heartbeats, marching boots and pounding—

Without the dogs to send up warning, the arrival of a stranger at the door was left to hard knocks and repeated banging and by the time Cas realized and got herself across the room into the entrance hall the voice outside the door was shouting Mr. Rhodes! it's Hetty Gunderson and we've got Sunny—!

Her fist was clenched, mid-air, to knock again—even though the door was kept unlocked—but then Cas opened the door and looked past Hetty to her husband Wendell standing behind her holding Sunny like a sack of grain slung across his arms. The woman gripped Cas's arm and said, ". . . she ain't dead. She's breathin' but she ain't in no good shape. Her mare brought her in, our boy is lookin' after it.—she ain't come 'round since we found her. Doc's outta town. We didn't know what else t' do . . ."

The Gundersons were longtime locals, breeding quarterhorses on the foothills, and though she didn't know them but for random passings at town events she got them in and down the central hall of the *portales* to Sunny's room and helped Wen lay out Sunny on the bed, mindful of her neck and spine.

She had blood and scratches on her forehead and a deep gash that ran crimson down the right side of her face. Her eyes were closed and she was barely breathing; her hands were bare and torn up, fingers blue.

Wen was one man who was Cas's size and he had a quiet gentle suasive manner he'd acquired from the horses but she needed him to be *a forceful messenger* right now, a firebrand, so she gave him orders in a tone that brooked no compromise:

"Wen, you need to drive like hell to the camp across the road: at the gate ask for *Schiff*, 'Mr. Schiff,' he's the main man there—don't take *no* for an answer. Say his name for me—"

"*Schiff*," Wen said.

"—don't take 'no' for an answer," she repeated. "Tell him everything that's happened, tell him Sunny's life is in the balance and he has to send his doctor and an ambulance—you understand?"

Wen went tearing off and Cas pointed Hetty to her own suite of rooms next door and told her to bring every pillow and woolen blanket she could find. It was clear that in addition to her head wound Sunny must have spent a long time exposed to the mountain temperatures so Cas refrained from taking off her boots but started layering her into warmth, all the while telling Sunny *There's my girl, you're home now safe and sound, we'll get you warm.* She and Hetty built levees of fortifying warmth tucking in the insulating layers, watching for a sign of life beneath her papery skin. Hetty, breathing on her fingers, began to hymn.

"Keep at it, Hetty: I'm going to fetch her father," Cas expounded.

Mornings such as this one—clear sky, dissipating chill, late spring—Rocky could be anywhere for miles, his inner thoughts determining direction and she knew even on wheels or horseback she'd be damned to catch him.

—but she knew what could:

They had never rung the bell in all the years she'd lived here, although when Stryker had been his wildest Rocky had rigged the bell rope to an iron ring twelve feet off the ground so Stryker couldn't reach it—the bell weighed half a ton, it would take two strong-armed men to move it and all the times when he was growing up Stryker had tried to throw his weight into the job, the bell had refused to budge and he'd hung there like a fly on sticky paper.

Cas looked up at the grey doves high in the tower bundling on the cast-iron instrument above her:

Say this for calloused fingers, you can fuck with rope.

On *three*, she told herself.

If anyone could make this baby loose its music *she* could.

—and she rang that thing like it was proclaiming everybody's lasting entry into heaven.

If he had to second-guess the problem in the harem it would be that Scarlett O'Hara had out-bitched the other girls—whatever we're supposed to call it when the top dog wrests control and dominates the pack: *alpha*, he presumed. She was the *alpha* dog despite her youth.

All this mad love on her part—that wasn't new; she'd become obsessed with him from the day Stryker had brought her home . . . *boom* she took one look (one sniff?) at Rocky: deal was done: fate sealed: the whole thing had been *cute* she'd been a real cute pup but now she had some weight on her, some claws: taller than Jane Eyre by half a foot the other ladies in the pack knew to *hold back* when she was out here sportin' with her man and when he tried to steal some private play with, say, Daisy Buchanan or Lily Bart, Miss Scarlett would look at him with doleful shaming eyes that preached him Don't do this to me: you *promised* . . .

She was a funny little pooch, Miss Scarlett was, sleek and earnest in her moves, and she could set a covey or a lone bird at three hundred feet like no pointer he'd ever seen but she was crazy-in-the-head with her possession of him (like the other Scarlett for her Ashley Wilkes) and it was time, Rocky reckoned, that he hauled her up to Bishop to Doc Lake to neuter her or breed her out.

And every time she looked at him these days she made him feel she knew what he was thinking.

So he worked her hard: she was not so much the "fetch" dog Daisy Buchanan was but she could outstretch Daisy on the run and always won even though the "game" was an unfair use of Rocky's arm (it wasn't really work that accomplished anything) and he paid a price for it at night and in the sobering realization that he grew sore—and tired—before the dogs did.

Of course it was the dogs who heard it first, stopped in their tracks and turned back toward the house, ears like masts against the wind:

The ringing of the bell.

—he didn't recognize the sound when he first heard it, had never heard the bell from a distance, only standing under it in all its blood-pounding arterial thunder, so once he recognized it for what it was his first involuntary thought was My god we've killed Hitler My god the war must be at an end but then his reasoning kicked in and he told himself No we haven't even landed in France or Italy . . .

Oh christ the Japanese have landed

or

Some shitbrass from the Navy has fetched up with Stryker's remains

or

Stryker's wife has fetched up at the door with both grandsons

He broke into a run his upper body heavy on his hips at every stride—*christ*! when had he become so old?—dogs tearing up the dust in front of him except for Scarlett, lapping at his heels with dedicated caution:

—had to stop to catch his breath, a sudden wave of nausea disabling him:

I'm okay, girl . . . (he told the dog).

(She did not believe him.)

He couldn't tell for certain if the bell had stopped, the ringing in his ears took up its alarm and despite his best efforts it seemed to take forever to get to the kitchen door

—where he had the sense to leave the dogs behind as he burst into a scene that was *so normal*—fragrant empty kitchen—that it seemed obscenely incongruous with the reality he had conjured, until he blew into the *portales* and encountered all at once his sister, two men in white coats bearing an ambulance stretcher, *Schiff*, another man in a white coat, and two women in white all rushing toward what he knew was Sunny's room.

Sunny, Cas confirmed: "Thank god you're here . . . !"

—and then, for a reason he would have liked to take up with Albert Einstein somewhere in the future, TIME as he had come to know it went pear-shaped and s l o w e d down.

Still, Rocky took command:

Sunny had been laid out, he'd immediately seen, but *she wasn't dead* otherwise all these people wouldn't be here so he swung around and filled the doorway with his body and put his palm flat along the doctor's sternum and told him This is my child in here and I don't know you.

"Dr. Toru Arakawa," the man answered calmly. "Head of Internal Medicine, St. John's Hospital—"

—*don't say Los Angeles*, Schiff had warned him—

"—Santa Monica. And this is Dr. Annie Oe, third-year resident, St. John's, and our surgical nurse Miss Memoto."

Rocky stepped back, allowing them to pass. "I'm Mr. Rhodes, this is my daughter Sunny—"

"—'*Sony*'?" the female resident clarified (she was taking it all down on a chart pinned to a clipboard).

Rocky started to spell it out for her but his voice broke as they moved over Sunny's body and Dr. Arakawa started speaking softly to the women in the kind of code Lou would have understood—temp, *b.p.*, *pulse*, pupils, prep that wound, Annie, I'll need a facial thread to close—

"How long has she been unconscious, Mr. Rhodes?"

Cas stepped in: "—at least an hour."

"Can you describe the accident for me?"

—they couldn't, no one could.

Rocky drew Cas back into the doorway to ask What the hell happened and she told him all she knew.

I rang the bell she said and then broke down.

He drew her head against his shoulder and said Yes you did, sister . . . *you did*: good job.

Back in the room they had determined Sunny was hypothermic and asked if Rocky could raise the temperature so he built the logs up in the fireplace but when he knelt to light the match his hand was shaking so dramatically Cas had to do it for him.

"She would never come off the mountain in the dark," he said out loud: "She knows better, she would never do it . . ."

The Gundersons had told him she had tied herself into the saddle, roped herself onto the horse.

"Makes no sense," Rocky tried to fathom: "No one was with her—?"

This seemed to confuse the issue:

"—*should there have been?*" Schiff asked and Rocky shot him a loaded look. Rocky and Cas were the only people who knew Sunny had gone to meet Hace somewhere in the Sierras—and Rocky wanted to keep it that way.

The women had begun to cut away Sunny's clothes so Arakawa could examine her and Rocky stepped back into the *portales*. Only then did he register what Schiff had done, that Schiff had rushed the medics to the scene.

"You're asking me to trust this guy—?"

"—my god he's the head of a department at a teaching hospital in a major city . . ."

Rocky laid his deformed hand on Schiff's shoulder:

"—something must have happened to make her come down from that mountain in the dark . . . if those Water boys are part of this I'll kill 'em I swear to god . . ."

The doc stepped out to order a saline set-up from the ambulance attendants and told Rocky there didn't appear to be any other wounds and he was going to close the one over the eye—it would leave a scar, she was lucky that whatever had hit her hadn't been a centimeter lower or it would have cut the cornea—but he didn't like that she was still unconscious and he advised that she be transferred to a hospital for X-rays—especially the cranium at point of impact and the spine which he was very worried about.

Rocky didn't like that he kept saying "the" instead of "her": *the* cranium, *the* spine: "I'm sure your own local Dr. Bridges would recommend the same," Arakawa added.

"—oh the hell with Doc Bridges he hasn't cracked a medical journal since Bayer started making aspirin . . . Don't you have an X-ray machine over there, yourselves, across the road?"

Arakawa's eyes shifted to Schiff and back again:

"The camp is not a hospital, Mr. Rhodes. If she were my daughter I would want her transferred as soon as possible to the nearest facility equipped to care for her."

"Which is where—?"

Don't say Los Angeles, Schiff hoped:

"I would have to say . . . *San Francisco*—because I'm not acquainted with the care facilities in California outside major cities . . ."

Rocky paced. In the aftermath of Lou's death a rumor had circulated through Lone Pine (started by Doc Bridges he'd assumed)—that Lou's death could have been prevented, that polio did not have to be a killer—look at all the people who survived with *limps* look (much later) at Frank Roosevelt! The Doc had had an axe to grind with Lou showing up and "stealing" his patients—but the rumor had earned legs and stood: Rocky Rhodes had kept his wife at home in an iron lung instead of getting her to a proper hospital to save her life.

This was not the truth:

—but it had a nugget of truth in it, most rumors do:

Rocky had been then and was still convinced that Three Chairs held healing properties for all members of his family, that it was, *as a place*, a property of well-being, a property of life and health.

"She *stays*," he said.

"I cannot agree."

"She stays," Rocky repeated, "for the time being. If she's not conscious by tomorrow—"

"Why bargain with your daughter's life?" Arakawa asked, his gaze traveling for the first time to the former clinic's shuttered façade at the end of the *portales*:

"—was this a *hospice*, Mr. Rhodes?"

"—*clinica*. My deceased wife's."

Something seemed to shift in Arakawa's eyes: Schiff watched as a window opened.

"Look if you had to break it down," Schiff said, "enumerating minimums— what are we looking for in a 'care facility'? I've got a staff of people who can check with places between here and Frisco—" He took a pad and pencil from his pocket and began to take dictation:

"—first priority," Arakawa said: "cranial X-ray . . ."

"—so you're telling me there *is* no X-ray machine across the road?" Rocky broke in.

"—there's a chest X-ray: *Vertical*."

"Well what about—Doc Lake has a unit he hauls out to barns to X-ray broken legs . . . He's our vet. Cows and horses."

"Where is he?" Arakawa asked.

"Ten miles up the road in Independence."

"*Call* him."

Miss Memoto opened Sunny's bedroom door and announced, "She's awake."

As far as response reflexes, Schiff observed, Doc was way out front, getting in ahead of Rocky to where Cas was holding Sunny's hand, cooing at her like a mother dove while Doc whispered Keep her talking, ask her questions—*facts facts facts*—

"—*button . . . such* a scare, poppet, but now you're back in your own room and we need to ask some—" Cas's fingers had stopped on Sunny's left hand where she'd been kneading her skin to restart her warmth: there, suddenly, on the fourth finger, Cas felt the absence of the ring and she pressed the empty spot and locked eyes with her niece and breathed O *honey*, not *you*, too . . . Sunny's eyes filled with tears and complicated anger: "—*he married someone else!*" she managed to articulate before succumbing once more to her crying.

Arakawa had taken a position at her other side and introduced himself and laid out the situation in the simplest terms before asking if she was feeling any pain. Schiff watched Sunny swing her head toward him and let out the betrayed mewl of a kitten who's just tested fire for the first time and then she started kicking at the blankets and swatting at the nurse and jacking up and trying to reclaim her turf, shouting at all and sundry: Go away! leave me *alone*!

—so much for that spinal injury, Schiff thought.

Legitimately he couldn't leave any of the internees on their own but he had stretched the legitimacy of his duties so far, already, he had no argument with his conscience in returning to camp with everyone from the ambulance crew except Dr. Arakawa.

"He'll stay the night," Rocky had decided.

"No 'he' won't," Arakawa had countered: "I'm not your . . . I'm not your *employee*— Aside from the fact that there are two pregnant women in their ninth months who could go into labor any minute across the road, and ten thousand other people dependent on my advice to cure their migraines and their nightmares, indigestion, constipation, chest pains, athlete's foot and contact dermatitis . . . My wife and three children are over there, behind barbed wire, and I must refuse on principle to avail myself of any conditions—even for an hour—more privileged than the ones to which they are being subjected."

Rocky cocked his head: *quite the little speech*, Schiff could tell he was thinking:

"Well hell *I'll* go spend the night behind barbed wire with your wife and kids if that will satisfy your principles," Rocky said: "—seeing as *on principle* I pledged never to set foot over there . . ."

Mutually honorable men, they appeared to congratulate each other and when Schiff left they were getting on like two peas in a pod. Rocky had told Schiff, Door's always open—come back later on tonight, Cas and I will need the company.

—which went to the heart of it, he thought: his own loneliness, since Jay had gone. Great letters—Svevo was as entertaining on the page as he was in life—but truth was, Schiff had made no other friends because he had to keep official distance. And the gilt had been peeling off this trophy-of-a-job for him almost from the day it started. Maintaining the delusion that he was "doing good"—(as Horace Mann had written, Do not even entertain the thought of dying until you have *done good* for humanity)—was eating up more effort every day and although he fantasized about "better" employment, a "better" job—even joining up—what he really longed for at the start-and-end of every day was an old acquaintance, an old friend.

—*hello, Rita*:

Rita Hayworth had been rusticating underneath a tarp behind his office and when he got back to camp he asked Betty to have the motor pool give her a shampoo and curl and, as the dinner siren blew, he kicked her into life and found the old friend he'd been looking for. Sunny's outburst, "He married someone else!" hadn't really registered until he turned north at the Gate and hit the open road into the wide valley that had defined the boundaries of her life.

—and loves.

He remembered a guy at law school from somewhere up in Maine who was just brilliant, beat out every comer for the clerkships and *Law Review*, who'd decided on graduation, to return to Maine and practice whatever they do up there (teeny-tiny *maine-ly* domestic law) and one of the professors had warned him Oh christ *no* don't go back you'll end up marrying your cleaning lady, which is exactly what had happened. *Proximity* . . . you fall in love with whom you see and what you've got and sometimes that's a Capulet and other times Clark Gable on a silver screen. We feed our loves because we have to. We feed our loves with what's available.

—seemed a logical extension of the (joy) ride to take ol' Rita up the dirt road to Three Chairs.—why not? he'd been invited . . .

—and the door *was* open. *Dogs* came at him—Pip—or whatever the fuck—*Shylock* and *Ishmael*—though once they got their whiff of him as A FAMILIAR they were on their merry ways back into the secret warrens of the house.

Schiff went along the silent hall to the *portales*, turned left toward Sunny's room where, through another open door he made his presence known to Rocky, who was sitting in a rocking chair by an embering fire, reading.

"Doc sewed her up and gave her something to calm her down," he whispered. "Cas is in the kitchen."

—where Schiff found her sitting at the far end of the long oak table, all alone, staring at her open palms.

"I sent everyone home," she said: "now there's no one to make our supper. And Sunny will need something when she wakes. Can you make a chicken soup?"

"I'm Jewish."

"—yes we know that, stalwart, I sat Seder with you not that long ago—but can you make a goddamn *chicken soup?*"

What I meant to say: "It's in my history."

"—*good:* let's get started." She rose and opened one of the refrigerators, finding a chicken carcass trussed with butcher's string: "—both my brother and my niece insist one shouldn't cook the game the day it's killed—*always let it rest a day*, they say—something about the taste of blood in meat—except for *fish* of course which the soonest that it's eaten after death the better—"

She slapped the chicken on the counter, pointed toward the stockpots and the larder: "—onion, celery, carrots, parsnips—everything you need, you'll find—*turnip?*"

"—*yes* . . ." and the signature ingredient he'd learned from the *garde-manger* chef back in Chicago at the Drake: "—a green apple. Trust me, you'll taste the top notes in the broth."

Cas donned an ample apron and handed him another: "—*allons-y*," she rallied. "I'm going to kill another chicken for tomorrow: do me good, the mood I'm in."

Schiff hadn't moved.

"—*problem?*" Cas asked: What else is required?

Nothing, he assured her: "I just want to watch you kill the chicken."

—which was not a pretty sight, given the animal's recognition of what was happening to it but Cas knew what she was doing and the death was break-neck quick. She bled the chicken out with one cut to its throat and while she sat plucking it under a dusking sky she told him, "I had a Great Love once, myself. In Scandinavia, so I understand what Sunny has to go through now and I would rather sacrifice my left ventricle than see her captive to its torment and its doubt."

"I'm not sure I—"

"—he left her. The jackass. *Hace.*"

"Oh."

"—at least in my case he was an outright predator, a person with no connective tissue to my family . . . does it happen more to women than to men—? I don't know: Shakespeare writes about the *violence* in the hearts of men when heartbreak happens: Jane Austen writes about the violence women do to our own selves; self-directed suffering . . ."

Schiff wasn't sure why Cas was telling him her story—the details of how she'd met the so-called Love-of-Her-Life Karl Tomas in Oslo and how, despite her acquired reflex to distrust any man who could profess to love her and not her money, she had succumbed to his blatant charms and to the lengths he'd gone to convince her his attentions (and *in*tentions) were sincere. Schiff suspected the confession was a sort of cleansing—how many people in her past could she possibly have told?—and that the telling (or *re*telling) had the curative effect of chicken soup.

"You would think that the fact that he took me for a considerable portion of my fortune would have made it easier to revile him—but when I finally had to share the fact with Rocky he wanted to enact serious damage on Karl Tomas and I reined him in. Besides, what could we do to a professional con artist a continent and ocean away—? I didn't take the loss of all that money lightly, mind you, but it was my loss of confidence, to have been so willingly duped that hurt the most . . . confused my sense of self. *She*'ll bounce back, our button . . . it will take a while but she'll be back."

—except she did *not* "bounce back" but spent whole days in bed refusing the restorative properties of soup and/or to explain to Cas or Rocky what had transpired between Hace and her (and when she finally did it was too late for Rocky to exact revenge).

She wouldn't leave the bed (except to pee) and then she wouldn't leave the room. Schiff—developing his own routine to relieve his loneliness—started showing up at Three Chairs almost nightly, sometimes to enjoy a cowboy barbeque with Cas and Rocky, sometimes to engage in politics, always to enjoy their conversation and their banter. Some nights they weren't even in a room with him where he'd made himself at home with business or a book—Cas being out, in the odd coincidence, at a card game at the camp and Rocky on a long walk under the stars with his fictive-characters-as-dogs.

—which is what the situation was, late in the second week following her accident—when, as he was writing letters at the table in the kitchen before dark, Sunny drifted in, unkempt, barefoot in her pyjamas and an oversized man's flannel robe, black stitches punctuating her right eyebrow:

what are you doing here?

—an accusation leveled without effect:

Surprised—and pleased—to see her, all Schiff could answer was, "I was invited."

Not the same as being WANTED she let him know in no uncertain terms.

—which didn't stop him coming back.

He'd fixed it with the MPs for them to accompany Doc Arakawa to Three Chairs on Rita Hayworth (Doc riding sidecar) so he could check up on Sunny without going AWOL and Schiff was standing at his office window one afternoon when he saw Rita come roaring back through the Main Gate, Doc getting out still wearing the goggles.

—minutes later he was tapping on Schiff's open office door:

—*may* I?

Schiff stood, out of respect, staying on his feet until the doctor had sat down, the rings of the goggles having created two dust-free zones on his face which made him, from a distance, appear owlish and round-eyed.

"I've been to see your friend across the road."

Yes, Schiff acknowledged.

"—she's melancholic."

Schiff had to agree.

"—not as melancholy as most of the people I see here . . . but it has her in its throes."

"What can we do for her?"

"—well there's no such thing as a Happy Pill, though I'm sure our Army is working on it. *Amphetamines*, yes—pills to kick-start the *body* into action . . . but she's the opposite of her name right now . . . not sunny."

"—not Sunny . . ."

"—based on her history I believe she will get over it in time . . . I did a good job with the stitches . . . that will be the most minor of the scars this episode will leave on her—anyway: she's not the reason I am here. Annie Oe . . ."

"—yes?"

"—from New Jersey. Took her boards and interviewed at both Johns Hopkins and St. John's but I lobbied persuasively for her to come to California . . ." He turned from Schiff to look out the window. "And now she's here," he said. "Her medical career in ruins. There should be reparations."

"There should. But there's *not*."

"—had she gone to Baltimore to Johns Hopkins outside the Exclusion Zone she'd be walking free as Tweety Bird right now."

Schiff couldn't argue.

"—what if I were able to convince Johns Hopkins to renew their offer—? My wife had a letter from a friend who's at the Nyssa Detention Facility and they're letting internees 'out' each day, paid labor in the sugar beet fields . . ."

"—I know."

"—could you not, then, arrange for Dr. Oe to be transferred to Johns Hopkins to fill a similar labor need? Physicians across the country are being pressed into active service and domestic hospitals are thirsting for trained talent . . . I think we have a case."

His use of "we" provoked a smile:

"—second thing," Arakawa said. He paused to wipe an invisible mote from his immaculate suit sleeve: "Jin . . . my youngest . . . he's three: has begun to manifest symptoms of asthma. He's begun to wheeze."

"I'm sorry to hear that."

"—along with several of the elderly."

"I see."

"I believe it's coming from the air we have to breathe each day since we've been here."

"You've been talking to the owner of Three Chairs."

"I don't need Mr. Rhodes to point out the yellow cloud hanging over what was once Owens Lake every morning noon and night but, yes: I've been talking to him. And I'm going to make a study of the air. For which I'm certain I must obtain your permission."

Schiff was conscious of the fact that Arakawa spoke to him as if he were an irritating student but it didn't bother him—he thought maybe Doc spoke that way to everyone:

"—and I'm going to requisition cotton face masks—nose and mouth—as voluntary health precautions: it will alarm some people—those who understand, as I do, that this camp isn't *temporary* . . . that we're entrapped here until the War ends. I'll say it's for 'dust.' I won't call it 'life-threatening.' We can use discarded masks as evidence of what we're forced to breathe."

—again the "we." Not the Royal one . . . the Medical. *How are* WE *feeling this fine morning*—? *Aren't* WE *looking swell . . .*

"What do you mean when you say 'not temporary'?—the camp's not *permanent*," Schiff clarified. "—unless the *war* is permanent, which it won't be."

The doctor elegantly swept another unseen something from his sleeve:

"Rumors are rife, Mr. Schiff—the camp is a rumor mill. Nine-tenths of the people I treat ask the same thing—perhaps because they know I am a man of Science and therefore speak the Truth—'Doctor, can you confirm what everybody says, they're letting us go home next month . . .' Self-delusion is a happy pill, you see: a self-medication." He turned his gaze on Schiff: "The sadness that I see in Your Friend and in the population here springs from losing control over one's life. You have a moral obligation to announce the truth . . . Without the truth these people have no purchase, no rein on their own destinies, and the lies they need to tell themselves *just to get through every day* mask their sad realities: *face* masks. You need to tell them," he emphasized.

He smiled—falsely, Schiff thought:

"—because the pill has not been invented yet for me to medicate them."

—using the singular this time, Schiff noted: *me*, not "us." For *me* to medicate ("cure"; "handle"), as if to suggest that the power to do that might be encroaching on Schiff's control. *As of today*, Schiff reckoned—and the good doctor's estimation had rung true—maybe one-out-of-every-ten Americans here had figured out the truth that the length of their imposed internment in days/months/years was going to be determined by how long it took the U.S.A. to beat the crap out of Japan.

That meant he was here as well, and his own timeline, the term of his duty, the same as theirs. Not that he would dare compare what he thought of as his unwelcome plight to theirs but sometimes every *schnook* needs a happy pill, and Svevo had been his and *hell* even the Greek gods tucked into ambrosia on Olympus, so why shouldn't he take advantage of the wit and urbanity at Three Chairs and spend some evenings with Cas and Rocky?

When good fortune comes—*ven dos mazl kumt*:

Pull up a chair.

—so it was there, some two weeks later, that he'd gone for supper—Tia Lupe had made these Mexican concoctions with spiced beef and tomatoes and chopped lettuce and avocados dished up inside fried *tortillas* Rocky said were called *tacos* and Schiff couldn't get enough of them and the talk around the table had ranged from FDR's packing the Supreme Court to the Democrats' advantage (Cas and Rocky were in favor) to the novel Cas was reading (Daphne du Maurier) back to Rocky's broken record of frustration getting any kind of information out of Honolulu about Stryker's wife and kids. When it was time for coffee Schiff felt enough at home to volunteer to make it for them and when he entered the kitchen, much to his surprise, he discovered Sunny at the far end of the table. He hadn't seen her in weeks, only heard about her progress—or lack thereof—from her father, aunt and Dr. Arakawa.

She was dressed—or at least she wasn't still wearing the bathrobe: she had an old crewneck sweater on over her pyjamas and her hair was combed. In front of her were a basket with piles of fresh-cut herbs . . . a pair of scissors, pieces of orange peel, a head of garlic, ball of string and small squares of kitchen muslin. And a cut-glass tumbler full of water.

Sunny, he said. He stopped some distance from her: it's so good to see you.

At some point in the evening Cas had done her imitation of First Lady Mrs. Roosevelt and they'd laughed so hard it would have been impossible for Sunny not to have heard them:

I've missed you, he said.

Her immobility kept him at a distance but when she picked up the scissors and cut a length of string he felt he could move closer.

She's making *bouquets garnis*, he assessed.

People at the camp have missed you too. Rose Ito asks after you . . .

She took a sip of water from the tumbler.

You know, he said . . .

He took another slow step forward:

What happened to you isn't your fault.

—*this isn't going well*, he knew.

What I mean to say is: "I hate to see you blame yourself."

What he meant to say was, I would love you better but what came out was, "He didn't love you well enough."

"—*shut up!*"

The tumbler didn't hit him but the water did—the tumbler whizzed by his head and crashed against the tile backsplash above the sink and broke into a nova of shards that showered like falling sparks onto the zinc:

"—what the hell do you know about *love* you don't even know him—!"

The noise had brought first Cas then Rocky on the run into the room:

"—you stay out of this old woman this is none of your damn business—"

"—*Sunny*," Schiff heard Cas intone. It sounded like a threat.

"—and *you* . . ." (turning toward her father:) "—why is *he* in our house?—you *had* a son! and when that didn't work the way you wanted you got yourself *another* son . . . and now that Hace is gone you get *another* one . . . *three* chairs, Tops, not three *sons* . . ." (toward Schiff:) "—you're *not* his son, you're *not* our family I don't want to see you *get out*—"

Stop it, Rocky told her, This man saved your life—

"*I* saved my life: *I* did, nobody else did, *I* got on that horse and got away from there *I* did because *I* knew that if I stayed up there and had to listen to him tell me that he couldn't make a life with me that he'd met someone who was his *kind* that I was not his *kind* that I was a different *race* I would have lost my sense of who I am so don't stand there and try to tell me someone saved my life because *no one* saved my life except myself—"

Seemed like he held his breath the whole ride back to camp he had no memory of breathing nor of seeing anyone he knew or recognized not even as he passed the Main Gate 'til he was in his darkened barrack with the door closed and locked and his head and spine against it, but still breathing.

Well that was close, he thought.

You   can't   save   what   you   don't   love

—Rocky had said those words to him . . . not about some*one*, Schiff remembered, but about some*thing*; his land; his turf; his *earth*.

But if you love some thing, some one, some times you can't control how things turn out.

She would have been all wrong for him.

It would have been a real disaster.

Life with a capital "F."

Funny . . . Sunny thinks she saved herself?

Thank you.

Hell no:

She had just saved *him*.

the sixth property
of thirst
is
truth

THE TWO PHONE LINES FROM THE GATE WENT STRAIGHT TO, first, Schiff's office and barracks and, second, the Fire and MP dispatch. There was also an Alarm that had never been used. The Gate line sat on the left side of Schiff's desk, away from his general line, and didn't go through Betty. It had a ring, peculiar to it, that sounded like a buzzer on a quiz show on the radio or a kazoo. When he had someone of importance in his office and it rang, he was pretty sure it brought him down a peg in that person's esteem:

"Sir, I got a man out here says he knows you, mentions you by name, but won't submit to protocol."

"Why are you calling then, Sergeant?" Schiff had to ask.

"He says—these are his words, sir, not mine—he says I'm supposed to tell you before he'd step an inch inside this Gate he'd have to watch Frank Roosevelt, um, do something with an 'F' word and a castrated donkey. In a hat."

"That's treason, soldier. To talk about our President that way. I think you ought to shoot him."

The really good MPs, the singularly sharp ones, were, of course, either already in the Pacific or on their way to police our boys in training camps, so Schiff got the duller instruments. The ones with no initiative. Who might actually shoot somebody if he told them to.

"Is he about six-foot-three and missing most the fingers of his left hand?"

"Let me look . . ."

"White hair, ponytail?"

"That's the one."

"Tell him I'll be right out."

He was leaning up against the ranch truck when Schiff got outside the Gate and as he approached, Rocky hauled his long frame in a single fluid movement up over the side into the bed like he was jumping on a horse and Schiff thought *christ*: How God came to make the cowboy is just plain discourteous to Old World men.

It had been six weeks since he'd seen him.

Not that Schiff was counting.

In the truck bed Rocky unwound a drop cloth and lifted a rocking chair onto the ground and then jumped down.

"Peace offering," he said.

In a kind of Gothic ornate script carved into the top slat of the back, letters spelled out SCHIFF.

Never carved like that before. "Had to teach myself," the cowboy said.

Lawyer almost choked:

—this is the *best gift anyone* . . .

"*Comes with strings attached*," Rocky warned.

Schiff didn't care; he wanted the chair.

"Fella wrote to me couple months back, I was going to mention him to you when you were still coming to the house but I wanted to check his *bona fides*. He's asking us—Cas and me—for money and Cas has a history of bad-penny men so I needed to make sure this one was on the up-and-up. Turns out he's the real deal—cattleman over in Santa Barbara County, made his first million bottling Coca-Cola—and he's come up with a Plan"—he shoved some papers from his back pocket at Schiff—"where he and Cas and I would all contribute a substantial amount of money to establish a kind of co-operative, a limited trust or whatever the legal harness is—you would know—for the purpose of guaranteeing the properties of these internees against foreclosures. Three of us wouldn't hold paper—*they* would—we'd just belly up the cash and step back, let them run it . . . fella's called Lyndon Finn and one of his ideas is to try to get the War Relocation Authority to back these people's mortgages or rents so the banks don't move in and repossess—which they've already started doing . . . I mean, most these people, Schiff, they thought this whole round-up was going to be a month or so, that Uncle Sam would round them up and ask them a few

questions and then let them go—they didn't make far-reaching arrangements
to take care of their houses or boats or orchards or other properties . . . plus
they've been cut off from earning any kind of living wage . . . And there's people, believe me—*Anglos*—who are profiting from this, moving in on all these
properties . . . it would turn your stomach. So what Finn is proposing is that
we hire agents with some of this money to bring in these people's crops and
make sure their properties are safeguarded . . . What do you think?"

"Well I'll have to read it first . . .—but I think it's a grand idea. Noble. Very
nearly impossible to implement . . ."

"Well that's where you come in."

Rocky laid out the theoreticals, how the plan would need inside data to get
off the ground, census gathering, people who could document the fiscal risks
and the financial burden, a cadre of professional board members who could
run the goddamn thing and determine where the money needed to be spent.

THE HATS, Schiff was already thinking, they'd be ideal for this: plus the
legal genius of Professor Takei . . .

"Here's the thing," he interrupted: "I haven't exactly . . . Bull in the china
shop: you start this rolling you're going to tip off people that the camps aren't
'temporary.' "

"They don't know?"

"Not in concrete terms."

"How can they not know?"

"Nobody's told them."

"Well, you need to fess up, son."

The sound of Sunny's accusation echoed in Rocky's use of *son* and Schiff
recoiled a bit:

—but the honesty of anything arises, first, along its boundaries of resistance . . . so, yes:

"I've got some people in mind who might be interested."

"—good. Set up a meeting? You and them up at the house? Lyndon's coming."

Schiff had less hesitation about taking internees off campus than he had
about crossing Sunny's path again.

"How's *tomorrow* suit you?" Rocky asked.

"—thanks for the *advance notice* . . ."

"Well it took me longer than I reckoned to carve your name into the chair."

—are you sure you're not Jewish? Schiff was tempted to say: 'cause that was an adept deployment of the Guilt. He wanted to inquire about Sunny but asked instead, "Any word from Honolulu?"

"—it's a shambles down there, those people who survived the hit have more pressing needs to think about than finding some old geezer's missing grandkids."

"People disappear in war," Schiff said.

"People disappear in peacetime," Rocky answered. "People disappear. It's what we *do* . . ."

Both of them took a moment to stare at the barren landscape stretching from the camp before Schiff asked, "How's—?"

"—she's fine. *Jesús* wrote to me . . . about Stryker. Didn't get the letter 'til after Sunny threw her scene with you . . . You know, I'm not exonerating him but going back to Mexico was a turning point. All about *La Raza*— he wanted to tell Sunny in person, which I respect, instead of ending it from a distance . . ."

He turned his sharp blue eyes on Schiff: "—tomorrow then? Four o'clock?"

Now all Rocky had to do was rope his sister in.

To get to Cas's *appartement* he could either enter from the *portales* into the first of her three rooms—the darkest one, the one he called the Scandinivian Museum—or take his preferred route—the outside one—which is what he chose to do, going through the kitchen, through the kitchen garden, around the southeast corner of the house, past the *bocce* court where he and Cas tossed metal balls around in a game Sunny called "Bowling with Giants"— through the gate Cas never kept locked on the eastern side of the adobe facing the Inyo Mountains, up the sanded path at the center of her "English" garden overgrown with roses to the Dutch door of her bedroom. When he could hear the clack of the keys of her Royal typewriter through the open upper half of the door he knew she would be sitting in front of the mountain view, composing either one of her pithy personal letters or a politically-charged missive to one of the several newspapers and journals she barraged, like the British at Fort McHenry, with her deadly aim.

A wicker basket and a fearsome set of secateurs lay on the ground before the rose bed where she had been Anne Boleyn–ing faded blossoms (*dead*heading them).

"Jesus Clarence Christ on rubber crutches," she said from her perch at her crowded "desk" (a round table covered in damask): "You're on my land."

"Well, technically—"

"—oh here we go . . ."

"—you're on mine, twenty years rent-free, room *and* board . . ."

"I pay for mine own gin. *Et* . . . I eat less than your dogs. What do you want: you have that *look*."

"—you remember that fellow I spoke to you about who wrote to us with a plan for the folks across the road?"

"No."

"—sure you do, the fellow who's the cattle rancher over in Santa Barbara County who's also a Buddhist and you asked How can he be a cattle rancher and a Buddhist at the same time . . . ?"

"No."

She was going to answer no to every question he posed just to bother him.

"Well here's his Plan."

He handed her the pages and she slid them to the bottom of a pile of correspondence on her desk.

"You need to read it."

"In the fullness of—"

"You need to read it *now*."

"—oh god what did you do? He's turning up here isn't he?"

"For supper. Tonight. Actually he's *bringing* supper—"

She slid the Plan back out and scanned it through her reading glasses.

" 'Thirty thousand,' " she remarked.

"The three of us."

"*Ninety* thousand dollars for one hundred thousand people. That's not A Plan, Rockwell. That's an insult."

"But not all one hundred thousand in the camps own property. Some of them are children."

She removed her glasses. Dramatically.

"Finish reading it before you dismiss it out of hand."

"I don't need to finish reading it to know his figures are too low."

"—but you're willing, in principle?"

"In principle. If I'm going to give thirty thousand dollars away to a war-time charity it may as well be this but he needs to rethink the premise."

"Well you can tell him that at supper."

"I have my cards tonight."

"Mary Christmas, Caswell, sometimes I think the pyramid of your priorities balances on a tiny head—"

"What time is he arriving?"

"Five-thirty."

She slid her glasses back on and took up a red wax pencil from the stack she kept in a cloisonné box on her desk to mark up published articles which she then sent back to their authors. Go away, she told him so he went. The thinking wasn't bad—in fact the man could write—but even if they limited the effort to the ten thousand just at Manzanar across the road she didn't see how they could do it on less than . . . on a separate sheet of paper she began to factor hypotheticals before resuming her earlier task of Anne Boleyn–ing. Then she had a bath and washed her hair. Both she and Sunny kept their hair short in the fashion of the Roman emperors (the ones with hair) and honored their standing bi-monthly appointments with Monsieur Bob the Barber in Lone Pine rather than granting custom to the questionable Miss Mabel's Pompadour next door. She dressed, as was her habit, in what Sunny called her Gertrude Stein look—loose jacket with pockets, calf-length skirt—and on a whim dabbed her wrists with her favorite French perfume. Rocky was already at his *calvados* in the Great Room when she handed over her edited Plan:

"Why are you dressed up?"

"I'm not dressed up."

"You're wearing your silly *lobo* tie."

"—*bolo*. It's a *bolo* tie."

"—even sillier."

She set to making herself a gin martini which she allowed no one else ever to do, even those who styled themselves professionals.

"Should you be drinking—?"

"Jack Christ listen to yourself you sound like an old woman—"

"Well you'll be driving."

"—for a mile and a half down an untraveled road. And by the way: how *does* one spiritually reconcile cattle ranching with the Buddha?"

"He calls it 'evolving.' "

"And we're to trust this man."

"I like him. "

"I think his Plan calls for at least a quarter of a million." She raised her glass toward her brother before taking her first swallow: "Would you go for that?"

"—three ways?" She had always been the quicker at the math:

He blanched. *Eighty* thousand?

"Eighty-three thousand three hundred and thirty-three," she corrected him. "*Dollars*."

They heard the car arrive outside across sand gravel, and the dogs set up a simoom.

"He's here."

"*Patently.*"

"You answer."

"—he's not here for *me* he's here for my money . . ."

They both went.

—finding on the other side of the door a fit ecumenical man in the process of taking off his shoes who—when he uncoiled to his full height—was equally as tall as they (which no one ever was).

"—well look at us! Unless there's a circus in town we have to be the three tallest people in the county! Lyndon Finn—" He thrust a hand toward Rocky. He was wearing crimson socks.

"*Rocky*," Rocky said. They shook. "May I present my sister, Caswell . . ."

The stranger cocked his head at her and Cas took him for a hand kisser, steeling her wrist against a *baisemain*, but he merely shook it and said This West Texan takes the pleasure . . . (*he's going to call me* MA'AM, *they all do:*) "My lady," he said.

"—is that Arpege you're wearing?"

A spot of red appeared on Cas's forehead right between her eyes. On the rare occasion that she wore perfume at all she wore Lanvin's Arpege because it was the French for *arpeggio* . . . which derived from the Italian word for "harp." No one had ever noticed.

Rocky kidnapped the moment, explaining, "Cas has left me with detailed notes about the Plan but she won't be joining us this evening. She has her cards."

"Bridge with the ladies?" Lyndon asked.

"Poker with the card sharks," Cas said.

A smile danced behind his eyes, she observed, before he asked her, "What's the buy-in?"

"More than thirty thousand," she informed him with a hidden small smile all her own before pushing out the door toward her Woody in the driveway.

"Shall we see you later?" Lyndon called.

"Don't wait up," she warned, not turning.

The dogs accompanied her to the Woody and Lyndon watched her go then looked at Rocky to inquire, "—*widow*?"

"—*god* no!" he might have answered too strongly because even he was aware that his tone might have impugned his sister's attractiveness but fortunately Tia Lupe had arrived from the kitchen in her bare feet (*always*) to relieve Lyndon of his valise and bring his shoes inside and he (Lyndon) started talking to her in Mex and said something Rocky couldn't catch which had made Tia Lupe laugh when she tried to take the cooler he was carrying.

"—is that the treasure?" Rocky asked, pointing to it still in Lyndon's grip as Tia Lupe padded down the hall toward the *portales*.

"—*prime rib*," Lyndon affirmed.

"Well let's get to it, then."

Lyndon had alerted Rocky to the fact that he would be arriving with his own beef—*not just any beef*, in his words—and Rocky had passed the word to Sunny who had laid on a *buffet* to lionize (mixed metaphor) the beef, which Tia Lupe had assembled in the dining room:

"*—well this is civilized*," Lyndon (under)stated as Rocky passed a steaming rosemary-scented *nappe* to him from a domed hotel pan to refresh his hands before Lyndon decanted his prized joint from the cooler onto a carving board and began to skinny off nearly transparent *carpaccio*-style slices of the *saignant*-cooked beef which he insisted Rocky taste *au naturel* before compromising his palate with Sunny's lavish *accoutrements*.

Feinting toward his well-stocked liquor cabinet Rocky, ever the solicitous host, had to ask, What's your current "evolving" state *vis-à-vis* hooch?

"'No animal has been killed in the manufacture of wine or spirits.'"

"Excellent—So what's your poison?"

"I always like to drink what my host is drinking: that way I get to know him."

He did *not* expect three fingers of *calvados*: but it taught him something about Rocky.

Sunny had prepared

SALTS

PEPPERS

A BOUQUET OF HOMEMADE MUSTARDS (saffron, tarragon and calvados)

GARLIC CONFIT

CHARRED ONION "PETALS"

GERMAN-STYLE POTATO SALAD WITH CAPER BERRIES

RAW MUSHROOM & RADISH SALAD WITH PEA SHOOTS AND MINT VINAIGRETTE

YOUNG ASPARAGUS WITH TAPENADE SAUCE

BUTTER LETTUCES WITH BUTTERMILK DRESSING

HABAÑERO TOMATO ASPIC

The last of the BLEU DE GEX, which Cas had gotten out of France before the Occupation

and an array of homemade breads to be toasted in the *pièce de résistance* TOASTER from a 1900s Wellington Rhodes Railroad Dining Car which branded each slice with the charred, entwined monogram

WR. Growing up, Rocky used to imagine these were the initials of his hero—Ralph Waldo—and he'd slather his toast with creamery butter and fruit jam and think of "Self-Reliance."

"I used to watch WELLINGTON RHODES stock roll through my little town," Lyndon reminisced.

"And where was that?"

"Marathon, Texas. How's that beef?"

Rocky said he thought it was the best he'd ever had. Even better than the beef in Scotland.

—oh the Scots know beef . . . Let me tell you how this happened, Lyndon said: "has to do with why I came up with the Plan: Eight years ago, now, I'd arranged me a little getaway—fishing on a river up in Oregon . . ."

"—Columbia?"

"Snake."

"—fly?"

"Net."

"—steelhead?"

"Rainbow."

"—'evolving'?"

"You know how it is—staying at these lodges what you want for supper at night after standing all day ass-high in cold water is a steak. Well this thing comes out, I mean . . . You're tasting it here under these salubrious conditions but imagine beef this quality suddenly appearing at a backwoods sportsman's place nine hundred miles from Texas. Had to see the chef about it clearly there was something he had *done* so I march straight into the kitchen tell him I'll set you up boy anyplace you want if you promise to cook steak like this for paying customers, don't even have to share your secret just get out there and do it. Kid—and he *was* a kid—*line* cook, really—tells me 'I just fry 'em up, sir, it's the *beef*' . . . It had a singular fat-to-meat ratio. Kid tells me there's this little ranch—not even that—Japanese man down the road with something like two dozen head of cattle that he kills one at a time and you can bet I head straight there, next day, sun-up. Kai Tajima: fella's name. Brought the four calves over—*illegal*—into Canada from somewhere in Japan called *Kobe*.

Down to Oregon, his wife and him. Thin cows, *thin* flanks, you'd never think this was *beef* stock—*grass*-fed, nothing but green grass, and you should see the things they do, Kai and his wife Oki, they go out and *sing* to them I swear to salt get up every day and hand-feed their stock and *sing* to them and give 'em rubdowns and *mass*ages down their legs and backs, all over their flanks. Kai has this idea that Death belongs to . . . well to *God* or Buddha or *the gods* . . . that slaughter for human consumption is a thing that we should do the way the *Greeks* did it—the way that it was done in the Old Testament—as a godly thing, a sacred rite—*through God*, the way the Sioux did it when they set out to kill their buffalo. He believes a taste of fear lingers in the meat in cattle driven to their slaughter so he lays his hands on every animal he kills as he is killing it, and talks to it."

Rocky stared down at his plate.

—*goddamn* why can't some people just praise the lord, shut up and pass the gravy?

"—had the marks of *cottage* industry all over it but you and I both know there'll always be a market for high-end chew so we struck a deal, I found us a tract of twenty thousand acres north of Santa Barbara—rolling hills, sweet grass, right on the ocean—built Kai and Oki a little house there—one for me, too—and he and I entered the business, cross-breeding at first with Charolais, then Angus, 'til we got the herd up to several hundred which is all that we could handle. Two restaurants in that city you don't want me to mention, two in Chicago which was a tough market to break into owing to the stockyards—three in New York City . . . All of this before Pearl Harbor . . . And then the Order. Jesus Christ what is Frank Roosevelt *thinking*—? Naturally I told Kai and Oki I'd take care of everything . . . They were assigned to the Poston Camp . . . I drove out there with some things for them . . . *towels*, these people have no towels, no sheets, no soap . . . aside from every other thing they own . . . This camp, this Poston, it's in the middle of the Arizona desert—nothing, nothing, *no thing* for miles and miles around . . . they wouldn't let me in but I talked to people from my side of the fence . . . that's where the Plan was born . . . right there . . . you know the rest. Did my diligence, looked where all the camps are situated and came up with you. Then . . . a month ago: OPA—the ration crew—come calling at the ranch, tell me they have to 'requisition' all my stock to feed the Army. 'Well that's some very expensive chipped beef on toast you're making,' I tell them. 'Oh no,' they say: we're not paying you. We're not paying you a cent this is your civic duty . . . *and* . . . *and* . . . *and* . . . we need you to raise *more* beef. You've got twenty thousand acres here you need to put it to good *use*.

"I'll tell you, Rocky: this idea that every square inch of this earth has to be *monetized* . . ."

"—*ah*: so this is where the Buddha comes in."

"This beautifully marbled meat we're eating? Last piece of Wagyu beef to be consumed by American civilians until our war against Japan is done."

"—hear, hear."

"And as far as my twenty thousand acres? I told them: *sue* me. Slap a fine on me arrest me for sedition I don't care. Land *use*? I'm using it to look at. I'm using it for *you* to look at—go ahead, walk around—Take a breath—It's free! I'm in the Nature business *now*, I'm pasturing *Nature*! People ask what I do with twenty thousand acres—how I *use* it—I say I grow Nature."

Rocky raised his glass:

"As the sage said, 'Can't save what we don't love.' "

"—Buddha?" Lyndon queried.

No, Rocky enlightened him:

Rockwell Rhodes.

Capital night's rest, absolutely *capital*, he had to get the name from Rhodes of the firm commissioned for his mattresses: *capital*. Million bucks, no aches, feeling like a *prince* today and life is absolutely beautiful. Look at this room. Just look at these rustic touches: tasteful. "Not a First Class hotel," Rhodes had told him, "but we hope to make you comfortable."

We: *we* hope to make you comfortable. Royal? No, Finn thought: genuine. A true generosity. Real thing.

Here's what he liked to do at home, on waking:

— bendies, first: then coffee. Shave.

—but in someone else's home on someone else's schedule?

Rhodes had asked the night before what he (Finn) required for his breakfast: "—coffee?—or *Coca-Cola?*"

The long engaging night had enjoined, somewhere, Finn's bleak confession that the war was very good for him on the financial front in terms of what he held in *Coke*, how Coke had ridden into Congress on its caffeine cargo and convinced the War Department Coke was *good* for soldiers, kept them *up* awake alert, *good* for patriotism and the war effort good for folks at home goody goody good for all who drank its blah dee blah. No tax on the imported sugar thanks to Washington no gas ration for Coke delivery trucks the thing was making money hand-over-fist and he was done with it—ethically—except for getting rid of his last several hundred thousand shares of stock.

"Well," Rhodes had told him in rich confidence: "Let's do this thing and pay down all our guilt."

Guilt.

—well there's a word, Finn thought, you don't hear too often spoken in church—and not a thing he'd cop to, casually, now that he'd looked into Buddha as a Way.

But here was the problem with the folks of Buddha's Way:

None of them eat *beef.*

And *beef* was his new money-making venture now that he was done with Coke.

Balzac (French writer he'd never read): "Behind every great fortune lies a great crime." Rhodes had quoted that last night. "Well what crime is yours?" Finn had had to ask.

"—*inheritance*," Rhodes had answered: "—and my father's was *ex-traction.*"

Finn had laughed and said it sounded dental.

"He extracted from the earth for his own profit." Dead serious. No joke. "Coal, zinc, silver, nickel, boron. *Talc.* I think he mined talc to ease the rash he got from capitalism. Took the minerals, never turned them into anything. At least with what you made from bottling Coca-Cola you have your money *making* something. Coca-Cola doesn't come straight from the ground."

"But water does. You think Coca-Cola pays for the water that it uses?"

Finn had watched a penny drop.

"My little bottling plant—you think we ever paid a dime to use the local water in West Texas? And when you hold that green bottle of Coca-Cola to your lips, what percentage of the goop inside do you reckon is plain water? Free. All I had to do was twist the tap. Was that a crime? Well in a place like this, the California desert, you would think so. But the day I have to pay for water is the day I stop. No one should make money off water—*no*, sir. *That's* a crime."

Be of moral spirit.

Cultivate a Way of Gratitude.

Never subscribe to the ethic of Mulholland—that bastard from Los Angeles whose MANTRA was "Cheap water is *wasted* water."

Be One with Nature.

Be in the Moment.

Be:

Rhodes had said someone would leave a thermos of hot coffee in the "dumbwaiter" in the adobe wall beside the door and DANG if there wasn't a tray there someone had made up for him including the coffee, a grapefruit, an orange, a crisp green apple and a bowl of blackberries along with a little pot of cream, three biscuits, butter, some kind of cheese and two boiled eggs, still warm, under one of those dome affairs they serve your food with in hotels.

He had never liked the term "dumb" waiter.

Until he reasoned, just now, how the meaning could be "quiet."

Capital coffee, just the thing, rich with an illusionary thickness. Had to get the name. Find out where Rhodes got it.

The bathroom, not private, was through a door, connecting with another door that led to the exterior and shared by anyone else bunking in the *portales* but Rhodes had assured Finn he was on his own out there so he felt fine inaugurating his ablutions in full buff. He'd noticed sediment at the bottom of the toilet bowl and the amber tincture to the water from the faucet the night before, but now he looked on in dismay as a rusty fluid trickled from the bath tap and he kept it running, out of deference to Rhodes's fight to reclaim it, only until the fusty water reached a depth sufficient to sit his ass down for a moderately good soak.

Shaved; dressed.

One thing he liked about the Buddhist Way: we don't wear shoes in houses. *Capital* idea.

Traildust at the door. *Leave* it.

He carried his breakfast tray toward the kitchen in his blue and yellow Argyle socks, to discover:

No one home, apparently.

—or rather, no one visible.

There were signs of previous activity along the counters near the stove (a bowl of rising dough) and a fresh pot of coffee standing on the stovetop; he watched prismatic light dance playfully on the wall from a crystal bowl full of water left (intentionally, he imagined) on the windowsill. Rhodes had laid out the day's paperwork in tidy piles on the table but there was no one to be seen in this smooth-functioning hive as if all the actors (as if this were a stage play) had fled the set.

Still, *capital* kitchen, what a room, what details, what planning, someone who had known exactly what a kitchen ought to be had put a lot of thought into its intricate design . . . and then, of course, there was the garden, kitchen garden, herbs, bees, he could see it through the window—

DANG the Buddhists and their no-shoes he couldn't wander out in Argyles which is what he wanted very much to do—look at those nasturtiums!—he'd have to take his socks off, leave 'em at the door, wander in his bare feet into an unexpected Eden, but some woman, the first he'd tried to love, had told him no one wants to look at *men's bare feet*, so he'd always been ashamed of his but now here he was: an Adam from the ankles down, naked as a jaybird for his first four inches and this was absolutely *something* absolutely *capital* the aroma of turned earth the whadjacallit *chlorophyll* fermenting in the morning sun *by god!* Someone knew what she was doing here someone had put in a lot of time and thought and work to make a place like this a *sanctuary* really no a *nursery* a nursery of green, of life, my goodness, too early for the tomatoes but you could smell them coming smell that acid green that *life* inside these leaves and *look at this* teepees of early peas, beanpoles, a whole apartment house of glass for early lettuces starbursts of celestial borage mints and mints and mints and marigolds and—oh my—*chickens*, chickens in the corn rows chickens at his toes and morning glories arcing toward the sun the place is Eden *Eden* eggshell moon still etched against the western sky, slipped into the blue in secrecy like a fresh deposit from a brooding hen and suddenly he had the sense—exhilarating!—he was flying his heart seemed to be wanting, absolutely, to escape his corps.

But not in a bad way:

—in a way that seemed to want to take his body, his whole being, *out* and *up*; on a meringue of cloud. This was embarrassing—he wasn't wearing *shoes* and then he realized it was music—or *not*-music, a harmonic sound—coming from some deeper chamber of the house, a *sea*-sound, a sound sad water makes in ebbing a sound that he associated with the descent of angels or with that good witch in-the-bubble in *The Wizard of Oz.*

UNREQUITED—UNQUIETED

beautiful and mournful

dangerously sensual

NEEDLING the heart, embroidering on it, emblazoning it as if it were a kite attached by chords to music, to a higher meaning

diabolus in musica

the devil in the music.

You could put what he knew about music in a thimble *no* on the head of a pin he had no talent for it that much was for certain and what little knowledge he did own had come at him on the anthems and the marching music of parades and preachers telling congregations in his childhood Let Us Raise Our Voices Together Now by Turning to Hymn Number Fifty-Six.

Gongs.

—that was another thing about the Buddhist Way:

it saved you from Christ's dismal hymns but—dismal though they were—a hymn will teach you about up and down about a music that goes *up* and rises and a music that goes down (descends) though most the music he'd had to listen to in church before he voyaged toward The Way had been the sort of up down up down tedium you get from clocks the kind of music meant to *soothe* console confirm one's righteousness but *music*—oh my—there was other music (devil's music) which set out to break the rules to torment test the spirit *laud* the unexpected

lyrical

the sound of the impossible

interdeterminedly probabilistic

transposing downwards from a hairpin crescendo:

the sound of impossible love.

It was coming from behind the wall at the west end of the garden, from inside the house, and his days of vaulting walls, of vaunting them, were very much behind him

—*harp,* he suddenly realized:

that's why the music sounded slide-y, like you're sailing through the air like you're gliding over ice

on a thin hope

stringed knotwork of harmony

the not work of emotion—

Finn retraced his steps, stopping on the threshold to readorn himself with Argyle socks, then padded soundlessly, following the music, through the kitchen, down the long tiled art-filled hall Rhodes had proudly shown him the night before, pointing out the photographs, the paintings, the ceramics, all the rugs—down the long hall culminating in the elegant arched entrance to his left (his *heart's side*) in the Great Room, the Receiving Hall, the living room, at which, in the southeast corner, stood the harp and at its service, seated, head bent, eyes closed, even more monumentally captivating than when he had first encountered her, the day before:

A goddess.

Borne on her music, weightless as if in water, Finn, in his socks, slid across the room to be beside her.

Here's what you have to know about a standing harp:

once you choose it as the instrument of your expression—say, instead of a tuba or a snare drum or a triangle, each one limited in its own way—once you've reconciled its range to all the things you think you have inside you that you want or need its music to reflect, then you have to learn what you can do within its range, its spectrum, within the boundaries of *what the thing can do*, to define what *you* can do, as well.

That's what she'd learned.

Six-three:

that was her upper boundary, as a woman.

So she'd learned to sit.

And she'd taken up this *sitting* instrument and against all odds—she had *giant* hands—she'd mastered delicacy, the delicate pluck, like harvesting the tiniest of alpine flowers, and she had the reach, godknows, her arms could *fathom* in the dictionary sense, in the old-fashioned sense where *fathom* was the distance one could extend one's arms and *fathomless* meant a place beyond one's reach (as in the distance of lost love). It had been that balance of scale that alluded to a sense of beauty—she would have looked ridiculous with a flute or violin, all out of scale, no, she'd needed something large and graceful that could offset her size and her large hands, and it had not been easy, reining in her gestures, training her hands in restraint (she had snapped a lot of string, in the beginning). Her harp master, a sparrow-like Czech a quarter of her size had had to say repeatedly, *delicat   delicat   delicat   il n'ya pas la terreur dans une harpe*

THERE IS NO TERROR IN A HARP

Indeed, that had been the drawback for her, at the start, the only sounds that she could coax from it were signature *arpeggios*. Nothing terrible—no terror—is ever going on in harp-land. Everything is nice—which is to say, every chord resolves itself, every sequence seeks its resolution and discovers it, all tied up inside its musical boundary with a tidy bow, chromatically perfect. A pretty instrument, the harp, designed for pretty thoughts. "Feminine." No fundamental discord. No fury. NON FURIOSO.

—and Cas had had a lot of fury in her, in those days.

Never pretty, never the chosen one at deb balls, always the outside girl, single at social functions, towering over the young men in her plain minimalizing frocks. Dancing with her brother or her brother's (unlucky) friends.

When she'd taken up the harp she'd done so with a vengeance: to be admired and not gawked at:

To be pretty.

—and she'd practiced resolutely, pulling in her anger to a diamond hardness of proficiency and—amazingly—real talent.

When she'd gone on tour in Scandinavia (not merely on the promise of encountering tall men), she'd brought those half a dozen off-the-shoulder fishtail gowns that Stryker would later cut into pieces. She'd arrange the hems around her in pools of color (chocolate, caviar, wine, prawn, champagne and oyster) where she sat. She wore her mother's diamonds at her throat and on her fingers—nothing on her wrists to draw attention to her arms; nor on her ears, to draw attention to her face—and she'd conspired to be seated on the stage, already, as the curtain rose (if she were playing in a theater) with spotlights focused on the fire of the diamonds, or—if the concert were more private—to be seated in the dark salon as guests entered, under candlelight.

It had been theatrical—but what the hell about the "feminine" was ever *not*?

PERFORMANCE, her Czech master had insisted from the start, UN-LOCKS MEANING.

Many nights she would perform alone, but on most occasions she was joined by a vocal soloist (which is how she'd met Karl Tomas) or by someone at piano or, on one memorable occasion, by a trumpeter.

That had been in Stockholm at the beginning of her tour and they were featuring a piece by Erik Satie—of whom Cas had known next to nothing—written for, yes, *trumpet and harp*.

She had been completely captivated by the mind behind the music and had immediately sought out his other work (all devoted she discovered, sadly, to piano).

Recorded music for gramophone was still an infant business, especially in Europe, so she'd had a baby grand delivered to her hotel suite and had hired Swedish pianists, in rotation, to play through all of Satie's works for her, *Trois Gymnopédies, Sports et divertissements* and "Three Pieces in the Shape of a Pear" (*Trois Morceaux en forme de poire*), which was actually seven pieces, and among her favorites. It was said of Satie's work, even then, that he wrote in a musical language equivalent to French Impressionism—out of focus, scattered—that his compositions sometimes failed to end within defined harmonies, that they did not *resolve*, all the acrobatics of his chords (unresolved sevenths and ninths) leading to a sort of *nowhere* in the listener's mind.

The shape of unrequited love, Cas had called them, and she had fallen madly and dramatically in love with the sounds of all of them.

Of course, that had been at the same time Karl Tomas had entered her life, so the two life-changing forces were experientially, ecstatically, entwined.

He would arrive for their late suppers—always in a formal cutaway, always with some rare delicacy in hand: a nosegay of violets in the dead of winter (and in her heart it was always winter), a jar of exquisite cloudberry jam; a single blood-dark rose—and they would have their supper in the room adjacent to the pianist's (Karl Tomas always serving Cas, pouring her champagne) and then, after a shared *aquavit*, Karl Tomas and the pianist would depart, Karl Tomas rolling the dining cart out of the suite's foyer in front of him and Cas would wander back into the candlelight and pick out, with one hand, one of Satie's melodies, one long sustained note at a time, which is what you're meant to do with Satie.

All of that—the smell of juniper and snow and fruited mushrooms, the non-setting Nordic sun in June skipping like a stone on the horizon; his lips—was now very very long ago.

—but when he broke her heart he'd marked it, like a time signature at the beginning of a measure.

Silence is a difficult sound to produce between notes on a harp, because notes from a harp are designed to endure

—and *silence* was the only music that could meet the depths of heartache that she'd felt.

She couldn't get it to *resolve*—to end—but it had to end, wouldn't end; it had to.

If she hadn't had to cure her brother of his own despair after the death of his beloved wife she probably would have let the black dog take her.

—who can postulate these things . . .

As it was, he needed Cas to punch above her weight and keep the enterprise afloat—to "mother" his two toddlers—and the day she knew her fate was sealed to California, that she was here to make a lifetime of it, was the day she'd had her harp shipped out from Stockholm.

—now it was always going flat in the dry heat just as it had always sharpened in the Nordic cold.

She tried to work with it every day, to keep her fingers fluent and her hands in tune—Rosetti, Handel, Mozart, blah blah blah all the expected harp-land repertoire—but after she'd established this quiet outpost in the Great Room, undisturbed in morning solitude—and with her heart still broken—she'd begun to try to get the harp to make a "Satie" kind of music from her heartbreak, get the goddamn instrument to sing *her* song, tune it to go sad and minor, find the *terror* in it.

She'd read—long after leaving Scandinavia—that when Satie, himself, had experienced heartbreak after his great love, Suzanne Valadon, the French Impressionist, had left him he'd sat down and written a piece for piano called *Vexations* fifty-two beats long, consisting of four plangent As held, each, for thirteen beats, accompanied by his notation that *Vexations* could never be played to its fullest meaning until it was repeated—all fifty-two As—840 times.

Why he signified 840 as the number of repetitions was a mystery to her but she'd understood its relentless tedium, the *locked-in* experience of lost love, a love that kept repeating through one's soul to find its resolution—

Twenty years ago, now, maybe a bit longer, she'd returned to the harp to try to set her broken heart to music.

Every now and then—not every week, sometimes not for months—she'd try the melody again, if she were in the mood, but she had yet to finish it, to find its end, she'd never made the goddamn thing resolve because there *is* no terror in a harp—only false hope—but every time she failed to "finish" it the memory of the pain receded, just a bit, a tiny bit, and once she'd opened her eyes from having been inside the sound of it while playing, it took her a moment to get her bearings in the "real" world. But this morning, opening her eyes in that silence, now, there was a long tall drink of water of a man, standing very close to her wearing a radiant, if not outrageously beatific, smile.

No, *dear*, he said: no, *no*. Don't stop.

He collapsed to one knee (*very close to her!*) like someone kneeling on a step to tie his shoe—except he wasn't wearing shoes, he was wearing socks with yellow diamonds on them—and he said, "*Please*, dear. *Please*. Keep playing."

So she did, from the beginning.

—only, this time, with eyes open.

Another thing the Buddhist Way had going for it, in Finn's view, was how happy its believers looked.

—well he'd only met a half dozen of them but he'd never seen such a bunch of happy-looking people (although every now and then you'd see a nun with that kind of inner-holy, eyes as pure as water, skin as pure as milk), but Kai-*san*, his business partner, had hosted some of them, some Buddhist monks, last summer (*lot* of trouble with the beef stock issue, *couldn't* let them know the cattle were for slaughter . . .) and he and Finn had piled these happy guys into two cars and driven up the coast north of San Francisco where the giant redwoods are so they could see Muir Woods and when they tumbled from the cars in their orange and yellow robes, their little sandals and white socks, they ran around like kids let out of school—so *happy!*—and then one of them put his left foot on the bottom of a redwood where it met the earth and his left arm around the giant trunk as far as it could go, balancing himself there—and then he lifted up the whole right side of his body toward the sky! laughing! asking the tree's soul to run through him like lightning up into the sky.

The idea that all life flows freely that all life can be united—that there might be a unifying energy available for use and all you had to do was *plug in*—was manifestly exciting to him: made sense: *circuitry*.

—the way you try to re-ignite your tractor with a set of jumper cables.

So without thinking very much about it he reached his left hand down and circled Cas's left ankle as she played with both her hands on the harp.

Then he put his right palm flat against her nape and then—this was the unexpected part—he laid his head into her lap, closed circle.

Huh, Cas thought.
—*this has never happened.*

Rocky came in through the front door from his mail run into Lone Pine with the dogs and stopped short—so did the dogs—at what he saw.

It took a moment for the sight to register but then the word *Finally* came to his mind and lit up his eyes and Cas matched his silly grin with one of her own.

She was remembering Norse sagas, how full of *terror* Odin seemed compared to tales from farther north, tales from Finland where the organizing myth was one of a divided *egg*, wherein the known world had been split, like twins, into two separate but identical parts—the oceans being the egg whites; the earth, the yolk; the sky, the thin protective shell.

Well, she was thinking:
This may not be the Scandinavian that I've been dreaming of

—but at least it is a *Finn*.

They pulled up into the circular driveway of Three Chairs in a school bus painted Army drab, and Schiff was the first one off.

Clutching a clipboard to his chest, Finn was there to greet them, along with Cas.

Hello *hello*, Mister Tetsuko, Mister Hitoshi, Mister Momo, Mister Ohara (Schiff had phoned in advance with their names and job descriptions, and Finn seemed to have memorized them) *I'm Lyndon Finn*. They were basically Schiff's "Hats" with the addition of Mister Tanaka (insurance salesman),

Mister Komachi (lawyer), the law professor Georgina Takei and Miss Sagawa (shorthand stenographer). Welcome *welcome* go right inside there are refreshments Mister Shozo, Mister Kappa, Mister Kenji, pleasure, *pleasure* . . .

The little Schiff had been able to say about the nature of the meeting wasn't reflected in their faces as he led them through the double door beside the bell tower into the entrance hall and down, three steps, into the Great Room where Rocky stood to shake their hands and greet them all, all over again.

And then they didn't know what to do.

There was a fireplace at one end of the room as big as a garage, and at the other end a harp the size of a delivery truck: a long table on which there was a samovar of coffee and pitchers of iced tea and lemonade and cups and saucers and platters of icebox cakes and brownies.

Have some cake, please, help yourself, take a seat, please, sit, Rocky told them:

—still, they stood.

"—*Sunny?*" Schiff took the precaution to ask.

"Sent her on an errand up to Bishop—she won't be back 'til after you're all gone . . ."

They'd kept the meeting secret from her, Cas stretching the truth about needing cakes for a "bridge club fete" and Rocky elaborating on the need for her to drive to Bishop (two hours each way, there and back) late in the day to pick up somesuch from one of his attorneys (who had promised to delay her, further).

Finn rustled them all in—Have some of this lemon cake, Miss Sagawa, it's very refreshing—and got them to sit down and then—(they couldn't help but notice he had taken off his shoes)—launched into his introduction:

What a showman, Schiff admired: guy knows how to play a jury, I'd vote for him, whatever he was promoting: guy knew how to work a room.

—still, from the looks on all their faces, "the room" was not so much covertly unfriendly as it was openly suspicious.

"—get to it without a lot of fuss to put us all at ease. I'm a cattleman—not here to sell you any beef—I ran a ranch in Santa Barbara County with my business partner, Mister Kai Tajima—Kai-*san*—breeding stock never raised before in California that he brought in from Japan. Probably on the same day you all got wind of it, we were notified of Executive Order 9066 and Kai-*san* and his wife Oki had ten days to put all their belongings, their investments, and their family relics in safe-keeping and report to the processing center, in their case, in Fresno. Not blowing on my own feathers but they knew that they could trust me, that I'd look after everything they owned—and my fervent wish for all of you is that you had someone like myself you could trust. They were ordered to Parker, Arizona, to the camp out there and within the second week I drove out there to take them food and whatnot and I'll tell you, God's honest, thanks to Mister Schiff, here, your living conditions at Manzanar—onerous as they are for any free citizen—are a far sight better than that camp in Arizona. I got rawly exercised at that—I usually try to hold my temper but I went up to Washington, to the head of the War Relocation Office, to register my displeasure, there.

"It shouldn't surprise you looking at this place that Mister Rhodes and I—and his sister, Miss Caswell Rhodes—are not without some wealth and pull.

"I talked to the head man—a toady, name of Milton Eisenhower—Rocky knows his family, brother's a big bob in the Army—and there's one thing he made clear: and this is not going to come as welcome news to anybody in this room, but Mister Schiff can back me up on this:

"Your current situation is not temporary."

There was a perceptible *shift* in the attention in the room.

—*now* he has them, Schiff thought.

"I'm here—we're all here—to get down to the nitty-gritty—but before we can join forces for a remedy we need to understand the scope of this: Mister Schiff will back me up but what I learned in Washington is this entire enterprise—the administration of all ten internment camps—has been designed to last until Japan is unconditionally defeated.

"I'm going to say that to you again:

"These internment camps have been designed from the beginning—have they not, Mister Schiff?—to stay in place until the war against Japan is ended."

You could have sliced the silence with a sword.

"Like you, I listen to the radio I follow every foray our boys make in the Pacific, hang on every word and the word, let's face it, isn't good:

"We are nowhere *near* a toehold against Tojo—we are in this for the long haul, maybe two years, maybe three or four before we start to even smell the faintest whiff of Victory.

". . . so this camp, I'm telling you:

"This camp is your foreseeable.

"You're not going home any time soon."

Miss Sagawa, who, Schiff knew, had been engaged to be married to a young man now interned at Tule Lake, in Northern California, began to weep. Lyndon went to her in his stocking feet, drawing from his pocket a pristine handkerchief to wipe her tears, but she refused to take it.

The expressions on others' faces, Schiff observed, were less suspicious now, more shocked; but still not trusting.

"—*mortgages*," Finn went on: "*Crops*. How are you going to meet those payments, bring your oranges or your melons in, how are you going to keep your homes, your farms, your businesses, your boats while you're exiled from earning income or from accessing your savings? The freeze on your bank accounts—that's just outrageous—I'm going up to Sacramento next week to talk to the AG about getting those things open—Nippon Bank, I don't think there's hope there, the Feds are adamant about that—but anybody with Bank of America—Mister Tetsuko, you were a branch manager there—I think we have some rational-thinking people at Bank of America, I think we have some friends there—they've always been on the side of the California laborer—I think we can get those bank accounts open for you . . .

"But look, I've gotta tellya: more hard news:

"The communities in our cities up and down the Pacific coast—'Little Tokyos,' 'Japantowns' and even some 'Chinatowns': those are gone: they're done: emptied out: I've been there. In some cases they've been looted and picked dry but in most cases—in L.A., San Francisco—they've been vandalized—or, as in San Jose, even burned down to the ground. By American morons. I want to draw police attention to these areas or hire agents to protect them—*dear*?"

He turned to Cas:

"—*dear*?" he repeated, "might I ask you please to pass around the clipboards?"

Had Schiff heard correctly?

He shot Rocky a quick look: trace, just the glimmer of a smile, playing on his face.

"These are for your own use—pencils are included—I don't want them back—jot your thoughts down, take some notes—Miss Sagawa has already volunteered to keep a record of tonight's proceedings for your reference—are you still feeling up to that, Miss Sagawa?—yes? Alrighty then. There's some blank sheets of paper there for you to make your notes . . . but if you flip down to the bottom page . . ."

They flipped:

"—you'll see the bare bones of our proposal—a non-profit trust, governed by a Board of Trustees that you elect among yourselves—and how much the three of us are willing to put up to get this off the ground."

There was a palpable reaction; you could feel it in the room.

"Once the trust is established—outside this initial contribution—the three of us are out: except to try to raise more money to finance its operation, this baby is all yours. You'll make all the decisions on how the money's to be spent."

"What's in it for *you*?"

This came, not unexpectedly, Schiff thought, from Ohara, Mister Tough Guy, longline trawlerman from San Pedro.

"—well I'm no lawyer—not a finance expert—but both Mister Tetsuko and Professor Takei, here, can tell you there's a tax write-down for the three of us."

Schiff was studying their faces:

To a few, it seemed to him, the figure on the final page of the clipboard registered as a gift-from-God:

But to the white-collar professionals in the circle he thought he saw a judgment:

Ninety thousand dollars = NOT ENOUGH.

"As to your chances to recover income," Finn continued: "Two of the government facilities—Nyssa up in Oregon and Minidoka camp over in Idaho—are smack-dab in two places where the workforce has been depleted by the war, the Army call-up, so those sites have negotiated with the local farmers and whatnot to job out cutting sugar beets and digging potatoes. But here you all are in Owens Valley, where, thanks to the City of Los Angeles, there are no *jobs*, the only industry is *water* and its harvest is already vested in the employees of the Department Thereof. So you're looking at no income for, let's say, conservatively: two years: more realistically, three: possibly even more. Some of you have relatives on the East Coast or in the Midwest and that's a good thing—maybe they can help keep your orchards and your farms, your homes, afloat: *liquid*. Mister Schiff, here, tells me there's a plan afoot to get some kind of manufacture up and running at Manzanar that could provide you with an income—?"

"Maybe a camouflage net-making facility, like they have at Santa Anita Detention," Schiff announced.

Even he knew that sounded lighter than air.

"If we *do* have income . . ." (Kappa, a San Diego rice merchant:) "—are you saying that we have to share?"

"I'm not saying anything about the money you earn, or how you spend it. That's up to you," Finn said.

"Maybe we could follow more along the lines of Sunkist . . ." (Hitoshi, the orange grove owner:) "We kept private ownership under the association but there were certain things we pooled, to save on cost, like lowest rates on crates, on fertilizer, smudge pots . . . A *co-operative*. A lobby."

They're getting it, Schiff thought.

"How you want to run this is the conversation you need to have," Finn said. He, too, sensed that some of them were "getting" it. "I know Mister Schiff wants to say a few words before we open this to general questions . . . and more cake."

Schiff stood.

Jury persuasion in summation had never been his strongpoint, but he had sense enough to know the approach of Let's All Give a Big Hand to Lyndon Finn and the Rhodes Twins for Their Welcoming Support Tonight was not the way to go:

So he went personal,

—starting with "You all know me . . ."

"—you all know me, you know I'm breaking some rules today by, first, approaching you about this topic and, second, putting everybody on the bus . . . I've got a job to do: all right, I do it: but I'm first and foremost a human being. There are things I can and cannot do, and things I can and cannot risk. The Census. You all know the first day—what we called the Intake—yielded information I can't share with you—names, addresses, job information, assets. It was gathered by the U.S. government, and it's classified therein. But I will not stop you, in my capacity as Camp Administrator, from obtaining that info on your own—going 'round, barrack to barrack, collecting those same statistics. Who owns what—who *owes* what—you'll need this information. What I *can* give—and what I *will* offer—is private office space—desks, paper as you need it, typewriters—I can't offer telephones, you know that—"

Schiff heard the front door open and two dogs rushed in all olfactory-ecstatic and from the corner of his eye he saw Sunny looming in the entrance—so did Rocky, who rose to his feet: they were the only two she saw from her limited point of view so she swore *Jesus*, Tops, *the enemy?* here? in our *house?* By which time she had come down the three tiled steps into the Great Room and the open circle of shocked citizens who had heard the words *the enemy* as meaning "Japanese" instead of (its intended meaning), *Schiff*.

To her credit, Schiff observed, she immediately self-martyred.

Finn, acting as a human salve, glided to her in his socks and took her by the elbow (forcefully, Schiff thought) and led her to the first guest in the semi-circle (Mister Tetsuko), saying, "—well and here she is our *fourth* member, the lady who's made all these cakes: Miss Rhodes, might I present Mister Tetsuko . . ."

Tetsuko rose.

They all did.

Tetsuko shook her hand.

"—and Professor Takei—"

(Another formal handshake.)

"—Mister Hitoshi . . ."

"*I know you*," Hitoshi said: "—first day . . . 'orange' lady . . ."

"I *was* 'orange' lady—I remember—I gave you the orange crates . . ."

"My wife makes *dashi* with you."

" . . . 'Hitoshi' . . . 'Hitoshi' . . . your wife is *Mae* Hitoshi? Hers is the best! She has a secret *dashi* recipe she won't share with any of us—"

"It was her mother's recipe."

"—then she must honor it."

Around they went, bowing from their waists, hand-shaking, Finn gripping her arm.

I should wait outside, Schiff whispered to Rocky.

The elder took Schiff's wrist in that mauled lobster-claw of his and told him No . . . *you* stay, in such a decisive way that it was clear to Schiff that if anyone needed to exit present company that person was Sunny.

She felt it, too—could feel her father's disapproving glare burning her back, sense her aunt's smoldering disappointment—so she made a final sort of leave-taking bow and muttered *Very nice to have made your acquaintances*, backing out, avoiding Rocky's scowl, avoiding Cas, avoiding Schiff, encouraging the dogs to follow her—and then encouraging them to take the lead into the kitchen, straight for water.

Her realm, *her* room—she was attuned to every nuance here the way an athlete feels a muscle, this was *her* domain, her father and her aunt could occupy a temporary stance, voice an opinion, try their best at eggs and toast or coffee or a cocktail but this was *her* plot on the Earth, the where and how she lived her life; the kitchen.

Why the ruse, she wondered, why the thin excuse of a "ladies' bridge fete" and the cakes—they had never lied to her before—*had they*? This was *Schiff*, his influence . . .

Why couldn't they have said We're having people over from the camp for a meeting and we need some cake—? What were they discussing, anyway—and why wasn't she included? She, after all, more than her father or her aunt, had more involvement with the daily life across the road . . . what the hell were they up to and why had they excluded her?

Schiff.

That excuse of running up to Bishop—Vasco had been going up today to meet his brother with some sheep and what with rationing and all Sunny had just passed Rocky's chore on to him to save on gas—the whole thing made her angry.

The idea that she wasn't to be trusted.

Stung. It stung.

Schiff, again.

And what was going on in *here*?

—had they invited him for *supper*? behind her *back*?

Clearly they hadn't eaten yet:

Rocky's chili pot was on a back burner and she could determine just from the aroma it was his mess of *elk*, sticking to the bottom of the pot as usual. She turned the flame off and had a look, pungent vapor forcing her to step back.

Needs liquid, but she didn't dare to touch it:

Rocky would want to add some coffee to it or some *calvados*, or both.

Game had always figured in their domestic diet and this mess of elk, braised shoulder with green chilies, had come down in family history as Rocky's "specialty" even though the elk was no longer shot by Rocky and was delivered now already dressed by Donald Aukamp, Senior, off the back of his pickup truck. Elk is *dry*meat, muscle muscle muscle, hardly any fat at all, and Rocky's chili had evolved over Sunny's lifetime from a potent but inedibly stringy chew to an elegantly larded complex stew of garlic onions smoked paprika chilies cumin cinnamon *masa* (Rocky's own hit-or-miss discoveries) *calvados* and coffee. Never beans. ("No beans in real man's chili" could have served as Rocky's motto.) (That, and "Never pay for what, essentially, is *rain*.")

Three plates—*three*—and their service settings had been placed at the stove end of the long deal table so they were planning supper, here, the three of them, without Schiff. Or her.

Okay:

Her mind went automatically (survival tactic) to the practice that would restore her calm (restoring things, *restaurer*) to what made her happy: menu planning.

Green salad—*green*—to offset the elk:

"If you're going to make green salad, keep it *green*," she'd learned in France: no non-green elements: *no tomatoes*. (Though flowers were permitted.)

She took a basket, garden knife and shears and strode into the garden to cut lettuces, basil, parsley, spearmint, chives, nasturtiums, borage blossoms: the asparagus was finished but runt buds had sprouted in the elbows of the stalks and she nipped them and several infant (*heart*less *heart*less *heart*less) artichokes.

Elk

green salad

and . . .

Cheese soufflé, she said out loud, back in the kitchen.

The solace of the classical French kitchen is that so many of its tasks—slicing dicing stirring slurring—become, in time, functions of pure habit, automatic, the practices of which require as little thought as breathing; so that, while at work, while appearing to be rapt by action, one is but a spectator to one's own performance, thinking *thinking* about other things why one man could *agitate* her so much

agitez les blancs vigoureusement avec une pincée du sel

why, every time she saw him now she felt a rush of irritation, no, embarrassment, no, pique, *annoyance* at what he seemed to perceive about her *that* was it, the way he looked at her as if he had an inside track a privileged insight as if he'd studied all her tricks and knew that most of them were shamming postures to invent a kind of womanhood in the absence of

love breaks

instructive guidance from another woman from a living mother.

an "emulsion" *sometimes breaks*

He bothered her. Something about him now just made her *mad* the smugness no the attitude no maybe all his city-ness and his presumptive weariness, as if he knew too much and she would never be as wise or smart as he. His air of superiority, that's what it was

air captured in the egg whites increases the volume

the way he *talked*, that undertone of irony, no, sarcasm, no, laughing-at-her the way he judged her with his eyes the way there always seemed to be something going on inside those eyes something shadowy and challenging

CASSER
to break, to make discontinuous
to divide into two parts
a sauce or an egg emulsion, might "break"
an emulsion "breaks" when the two liquids fall out of equipoise
and are not equally suspended.
A sauce can "break."

So can concentration.
So can a romance.

She could hear them leaving, hear them in the foyer so now she could separate the eggs and start the *fond*, put the *béchamel* to rest, to cool. Wash the salad leaves. Salt the vinegar. Massacre the garlic.

Cas came in bearing a tray of used cups and saucers.

I know you're angry, Sunny said: so don't pretend.

Cas shoved the tray across the counter with too much vigor. Not *angry*, she said: Disappointed. She grabbed an empty tray and left the room.

Angry, Sunny knew.

Rocky came in—it was like a French farce—carrying the samovar.

"Don't start," Sunny said. "What made you think you had to lie to me?"

"Your proven behavior made me think so. You're not getting an apology from me." He focused on her actions. "Are we eating—?"

She nodded, curtly.

"I'll get some wine. How's my chili?"

"Controversial."

He left and Cas came back in with more china.

"Just get it off your chest," Sunny challenged her.

"All right. You're a brat. You act like a brat, you talk like one. You have as much common sense when it comes to social graces as a common dungheap *escargot*. I'm going to say this once then we're going to put the subject to rest: Don't take love for granted. It doesn't come that often to one's life."

She left again—it *was* a French farce—and Finn came in. *What* love? Sunny was thinking when he leaned against the kitchen counter and announced Well that was a sleigh ride through hell.

"I'm sorry, Mr. Finn," she apologized.

No no dear, not *you*, though you were a prickly distraction right when things were starting to unite—What are we making *here*?

Cheese soufflé.

The man had twinkly eyes. Fire in his ice. Very very high-class diamonds. And *all this*? he asked.

> smashed garlic
> salted vinegar
> lemon
> orange
> (*3 acids!*)
> *Moutarde*
> oil from France
> s & p
> *sucre*

Vinaigrette, Sunny said. "Emulsion."

Emulsion, he repeated. Laughing at her? No: not the way that *Schiff* would. Isn't this *capital*, he said. "I just usually slap some oil and sherry vinegar together."

She dipped a leaf into her—so far, unbroken—"emulsion."

Taste, she told him.

Damn, daughter!

The diamonds blazed.

He pointed at his throat:

"—that hits you *here!*"

He looked at her more carefully, then laid two fingers on her wrist.

"—you know that boy is keen on you," he said.

So everybody seems to need to tell me she was going to say but Rocky came back in bearing two bottles and the news, "I think you're going to like this claret, Lyndon, it's from your neck of the woods," and started to decant them. "Tetsuko took me aside, outside," he said. "Before he left."

"—me too," Lyndon told him. "What did he say to you?"

(Cas came back in, apprehending everything, as she always did:)

"He said it's not enough money."

"—yup."

"He said it's a drop in the bucket."

"—ditto."

"I asked him, 'Are you saying it's not worth it?'"

"How did he answer you?"

"He hedged."

"—tried that on me too and I'll tell you, Rockwell, at that point I was so tired and so far out of my depth I told him, Well *you* go figure out how much you need. I can't. *We* can't. *You* go run the figures and get back to us. I'll give you two days. Not like I'm saying we'll take the offer off the table but *jesus christ* . . . I gotta run up to Sacramento in two days to talk to the AG and I'm doing all I can." Running his hand across his forehead: ". . . well: that's not true . . . I'm not doing *all* I can . . ."

They sank into an existential silence.

"Let's *drink*," Cas suggested. "*Cocktail* time."

Capital idea, Lyndon said:

"What are you drinking, dear?"

Gin martini.

Let me make that for you, Lyndon said.

Sunny and Rocky froze. *No one*—no one who treasured life—was allowed to mix Cas's gin martini.

Tell me how you like it, Lyndon was saying. "Flavor profile . . . Worked my way through college tending bar.—*dry?*—*oily?* —*briny?*—with a twist of lemon?

Sunny watched Cas like a hawk.

"—*like a Norwegian fjord*," Cas announced. "In the dead of winter."

Finn rubbed his hands together: " 'Norwegian fjord. Dead of winter' . . ."

Cas caught Sunny's deadeye with her own look of cunning:

Watch and learn, she seemed to say.

Sunny began to beat the hell out of some egg whites.

Don't stop what you're doing, just point me in the direction of the gin, the ice, mortar and pestle, cocktail shaker, strainer and the glasses . . .

Sunny gestured with her head toward the full zinc bar.

"What do we do if Tetsuko comes back with a figure of, say, a million?" Rocky posed.

"He won't," Finn answered.

He stood regarding Sunny's spice shelf: took down the jar of juniper berries. And flaked salt.

"He *could*," Rocky argued. "Schiff says . . ."—(he watched Sunny stiffen at the name)—"there's close to twenty-five hundred families—even if only two-thirds *own* their houses—plus some will also own a business— What's an average mortgage payment these days on a family house—?—fifty, sixty, a hundred a month—?"

Finn studied Sunny's bundles of herbs. He chose some borage.

" 'Winter Norwegian fjord,' " he consulted with her: "—bay?—rosemary? —dill?"

Bay, she answered.

"—that's maybe twenty-five hundred families, times, let's say *eighty* dollars a month . . ."

"Not all of them own their homes," Cas reminded him.

Finn pestled a thin fingernail of white green-onion bulb with a juniper berry, the bay, coriander and . . . a surprise ingredient, Sunny thought: mustard seed.

"—that's two hundred thousand a month right there," Rocky marveled.

"That can't be right," Cas said.

She was watching Finn fill the silver cocktail shaker with the ice, the bruised essences . . . *six* totes of gin. Barely any vermouth.

He made a drama of the shaking.

"I ran into this fella once down in Del Rio," he said: "—that's a border town—Spanish fella, film maker, on his way to Mex . . . He told me the perfect way to make a gin martini was to shake the gin with abandon—he used the word 'abandon'—over ice . . . and strain . . ."

He strained the concoction into an inverted-pyramid martini glass.

"—and then grace the gin with what he called an 'exhalation' of vermouth—I'll never forget that: 'exhalation'! . . . and then hold the glass toward heaven and allow a ray of sunlight to pass through it."

He held the glass up.

". . . or *moonlight*, depending on the time of day . . .—anyway it was *Newtonian*: a ray of light passing through the *prism* of the glass . . ."

He set the glass before Cas on the table and dropped a blue borage blossom onto the surface of the liquid, with a single flake of salt.

"That's the *iceberg*," he said.

She touched the glass.

No one was breathing, Sunny noticed.

"It could be colder," Cas assessed.

"The next one will be," Finn promised.

She raised the glass and sipped.

She closed her eyes.

She made a few soft smacking noises with her lips. Something Sunny had never seen her do.

Like a cunning fish.

Fishy, Sunny thought.

Very to my liking, Cas announced, opening her eyes: *Very to my liking*, she repeated: "V-liking."

Finn lit up like a Swedish kid at Christmas, you could see the candles on his head:

O you clever woman, Sunny thought.

Cas was sending her a look:

Imperious.

O you clever woman

Sunny beat the shit out of those eggs:

—I could never do that . . .

—I *would* never do that

—if *that's* what it takes . . .

But Finn's happiness lit up the room, he leaned back and balanced on two chair legs, looking ten no *twenty* years younger.

Sunny folded one thing—the inflated egg whites—into the other, *le fond*— with the greatest care, aware of both their fragile properties.

She set the timer, said a little chef's prayer, placed the hopeful if not improbable construct in the heat and closed the oven door.

Rocky had set out an array of briny California olives—which Cas never ate, on principle ("Like chewing seawater")—but when Sunny turned from the stove she saw Cas reach for one and pop it in her mouth.

The things we do for—

"—could I do a quarter of a million?—or a half?" Finn was musing: "Well I guess I could. I guess I *could*." He rubbed his eyes. "This goddamn war," he said—then put his hand on Rocky's arm and told him, "Sorry, Rockwell: this war has cost you more than anything it can ever take from me . . . But every day—some new charity pops up I get another letter in the post the Jewish orphans, London orphans, Polish emigrés, Europeans trying to get out of Europe, all the French the *French* godknows, the *gypsies*, what's going on in Palestine, what's happening to antiquities poor Greeks, I mean Hitler's men are throwing orgies on the *Acropolis*—"

"—and on the *Champs*," Cas put in. She reached for another olive.

"There are days—and nights—I don't know what makes sense. Rich man's problem—not complaining—but I feel most days I'm way out of my depth— don't you, Rockwell?"

"—oh don't turn to me: my sister is the one with money."

True, Cas said.

She had nursed the drink. All dainty-like.

By this time on any given cocktail she would have been more lively.

Sunny watched her size up the martini glass, still half-full, and with a deep breath finally close her eyes and resolve to swallow.

"Same again—?" Finn asked.

Please, Sunny could not believe Cas said.

"*She's* the one who knew how to invest," Rocky was going on: "—me? Sank it all into this property."

"—and attorneys' fees," Cas prompted.

"Right. And lawyers," he amended.

"How much do you reckon, brother, that you've spent commanding the City of Los Angeles through our California courts?"

"I cannot tell you, sister."

"—a million?"

"Nowhere near."

"—over *twenty years?*"

"—well . . . possibly."

"With no return on your investment."

"Yes and *you* on the other hand—"

"—*I* on the other hand own *properties*. In plural."

Finn had poured another drink and she downed this one, halfway.

"Well I have to say, Rockwell," Finn said, mediating: "if this magnificent home is your only asset then god bless you: it must be worth a fortune."

"Not a penny," Rocky told him.

"—I'm looking around, this room alone!" Finn gestured. "—those enamel stoves my god you must have paid a fortune for them . . ."

"Yep: imported. Lou wanted her French kitchen, so—"

"—the slate floor?"

"French."

"—the tile work, the leaded glass, these ceiling beams?"

"Redwood."

"—it's a mansion on the lines of Hearst's and we haven't even traveled down the hall to all that stuff up front—you've got a goddamn *bell* up there where did *that* come from?"

"France."

"—the *saltillo* pavers, the *talavera* inlays on the arches, I've *been* to Mex I know *calidad exquisita* when I see it so don't try to tell me—"

"I'll tell you a funny story, Lyndon . . . you'll appreciate the cosmic irony . . . Our father, Wellington—everybody called him 'Punch'—made his first fortune in ice."

"—ice?"

"*Ice* . . . before refrigeration. Then he branched out to mining and then, as he so often put it . . ."

Rocky raised his *calv* toward Cas, who raised her gin, and they both intoned in voices meant to mimic their dead father:

I-picked-up-a-railroad!

—a standing family joke, Sunny had heard it hundreds.

"I don't know if you know it, Lyndon," Rocky expanded, "but about ten miles down the road from here at the head of Owens Lake there used to be a little silver mine . . ."

"Cerro Gordo—everybody's heard of it."

"—Punch had a piece. More important he had exclusive rights to all the zinc they pulled from the tailings—all the zinc you see in here—all these zinc counters—originated from that mine. My father and I . . . well we were cut from different stone. By the time I was halfway through my college years I was roaring to get out. I was done with the East Coast. I wanted to go off and be a cowboy, explore the West—go to Mex or South America. That was a letdown to our father, a real blow, and he had no problem expressing his disappointment. All right, he said: you go, but you'll need a stake to make a go of it because I'll cut you off. Work for me a year—I'll pay you to inspect our operations out there and report back and then after a year we'll give it a review. He thought I'd change my mind. So I came out here for a year—lived

on horseback, mostly—took the train to Denver but after that it was mostly
horse. Lotta time in Nevada, Arizona. Owens Valley was the western terminus
of what Punch owned and previous to coming here I spent three weeks on the
other side of the Panamints in what they call Death Valley filling out reports
on Punch's boron holdings there. Came across to look at Cerro Gordo then
the last property holding I was to inspect were these fifteen thousand acres
we're sitting on right now. Punch had the mineral rights sewn up but there was
no extraction going on, just a flat green valley. I took one look and fell in love.
Not the prettiest sight in our western vastness but, for me, I saw my future.
And then . . . you tell him, Cas."

"Punch died."

"—fell down dead on the street in New York City. Probably from too much
money in his veins. Anyway it took a while to find me and by the time I got
back I missed the funeral. I told this one—" (he pointed to Cas:) "—all I
wanted was this Owens Valley land: she took our mother's family's house in
Murray Hill for her own pleasure: we sold the Fifth Avenue place we'd grown
up in and divested from all the rest and split it down the middle. *This* one—"
(pointing to Cas again) "—was smart, holding on to shares . . . everybody
took a hit in the 30s—*I* certainly did—but it wasn't until a year or so into
my marriage that I finally went up to the county seat here in Independence to
register the Deed in our names, mine and Lou's. This was just around the time
those first bastards from That-Hellhole-I-Will-Not-Name started to show up
buying the land up here in secret under different private names. So I'm looking
at this Deed—Punch's original had been negotiated by his land agent out here,
before my time—and I see he had never secured—well you know this having
your land in Santa Barbara County—'first-use water rights.'"

"I know it 'well.'—*pun* there, dear," he said to Cas.

"Punch—you'd think with his experience in ice he'd have nailed down
those water rights but East Coast racketeers—mill owners, tanners, builders
of canals—never thought that way, to East Coast businessmen the water's
free so Punch had overlooked it in his deeds. Well, I said to our county clerk,
who's got the rights? He told me who—Pete Dorwart, my neighbor—and I
said Well I'll talk to Pete and have him deed them to me and he said Well he

just sold them, Rocky. *To who?* I asked him. To some fella from That Place I Will Not Name."

Rocky took a long draw on the *calv*.

"—that was the start of it."

He waved his wounded hand in front of Finn.

"How I lost my fingers in the fight."

"He tried to bomb the aqueduct," Cas said.

"—*did* bomb it," Rocky boasted.

"Lost the fingers . . . lost his wedding band."

"Ring came back, though . . . had to take the vows all over again, the two of us," Rocky said. "And that was pleasant . . . So you see: this whole thing about the property being worth a fortune? . . . ain't worth the sand it's sitting on."

"But . . ." Finn stared at him. "—this valley is *alive* with water . . . with snow melt from the Sierras. You could purchase plenty of it if you needed to . . ."

"Never."

". . . or a prospective buyer could."

"I would make non-purchasing water from That Place a condition of the sale."

"Why are you talking about *selling*?" Sunny interrupted. She heard an edge in her voice and tried to put a smile on it: "—if I didn't know that you were joking I'd be scared . . ." Despite herself she felt near tears (though those tears had been building through the afternoon's events)—and in the midst of her emotion a feeble ding occurred, the timer of the soufflé in the oven had climaxed, a forlorn and run-down sentence.

"Don't you need to take that *out*?" Lyndon asked.

This is the point, she might have started to explain, where you have to let it rest. And pray it doesn't fall.

"Here's a funny *soufflé* story," Cas engineered.

"Not *this* again—it's never funny," Rocky told her: "regardless of how many times you tell it."

He stood to pour the claret for them and Cas couldn't help but notice a distant something, some unfinished business distracting him.

"*This* one," (she told Finn, gesturing toward Sunny) "—*child*, here, and I were on our way from Paris on the French Line in the North Atlantic . . ."

"I had Einstein," Rocky interrupted.

"—*he* and Sunny's brother did indeed have *Albert Einstein* in the stateroom next to theirs—on another boat—the Cunard Line—*however* 'Child' and I had nothing but a gaggle of French-*parley*ing oceangoers and on our second morning out a bunch of the fore-mentioned gathered at the rail shouting '*souff*lait! *souff*lait!' (which is how they say 'Thar she blows!' in French) and there on the horizon were a pod of *whales* spewing straight into the air like *soufflés*—"

Not funny, Rocky said.

"Well but it was, it *was*," Cas argued. "*Eight weeks* I'd been with *child* here—no conversation that wasn't about *food*, food *this*, food *that*, *food* all day, *each* day, every day all Seven-of-Creation food *Adam* food *Eve* and finally—finally!—we chance on an actual Event in Nature something not created by a chef, a wild and wanton miracle of Life and what happens? The French appropriate it with a word that echoes *food*—"

Sunny opened the oven door—

A new aroma hit their senses:

"—*lordy*-pie," Finn marveled: will you look at that!

Sunny set the temporary masterpiece before them on the table its fragrant high hat shimmering with danger, its delicate existence a chemical chimera, a fragile twist of fickle science, built to disappear into itself. It used to be another game of chicken Stryker forced them all to play, another game of nerves, to see how long the magic held its spell to wait and wait and wait until the very last—before the whole thing fell, collapsing into nothing before their eyes. Sometimes he'd make her wait too long and she'd come close to tears—as she had just now—over all that work all that wasted energy reduced to ruin. But it still tastes the same he'd taunt. Then he'd grin with his mouth full and tell her Still tastes like my favorite sister made it . . .

Green salad, terrine of elk: *soufflé*.

Perfection.

Claret.

Everything *exactly* perfect in the world that they'd constructed.

The sunlight sparkled through the water in the bowl in the window: her mother's spectrum, Sunny remembered, rainbow disappearing like a ghost of light.

Tops, you do the honors, she told her father, passing him a ladle.

Before the truth arises.

Before this whole thing disappears.

the seventh property

of thirst

is

spontaneous combustion

TEMPERATURES COULD EDGE to triple digits in July and August but the Valley was a wind machine its motor revving in the desert to the south where languorous Mojave hot air spread like a torpid flag of an arid puppet state prime for ripping by onrushing airs of revolution: laws of *thermo*, always *active* whether in the kitchen or across the land when something *heats* it rises and expands and you can blow a heavy lid sky-high off a cast-iron pressure cooker just by failing to tamp down the flame so imagine what competing mountain torques can hurl into a simple valley:

—it was *hot* but the air was always active, you could feel it rush across your skin, sand skittering across a dune. Days were long, the cooling mountain shadows crawling from the western foothills by late afternoon when the Janets, changed into their sporty clothes, unfurled the net and stretched it taut along an east/west axis so no one on either team had the disadvantage of playing right into the sun.

Spike! (their nickname for her)—come 'n' join us! When she played she played in her standard daily uniform of rolled-up chinos and denim shirt but when *they* played they dressed in flouncy shorts and bow-tied blouses so their midriffs showed and they rolled their hair in sausage rolls like Lana Turner and wore *lipstick* for godsake and there was something decisively, aggressively *flirtatious* about it, about their moves, less competitive with one another than overtly sexual toward the happy all-male crew of off-duty pleasure-seeking volleyball aficionados gathered to observe them.

Sunny didn't like that aspect of the "sport"—being ogled—but the Janets surely did and as the summer heated up the shorts got shorter, Sunny noticed, legs got tanner and the bottoms of the blouses kept creeping up and up. She reffed, now, more than played—and they had just retired a close set and were fanning down around the Coca-Cola cooler, re-rolling their hair and running ice cubes down their necks, as way out along the farthest northwest corner of the fortified fence, a lone figure appeared running along the western boundary of the fence—male, shirtless in the heat—and first one and then another of the women perked up, looked, stood watching.

"—floats *my* boat," one Janet said.

"—every evening," Janet Second uttered. "—every *night*."

Sunny turned to see what they were staring at and he was changed, somehow—thinner but at the same time more robust more . . . masculine, even at a distance:

"Forget it, ladies," another Janet told them, "that boat has sailed. That opportunity is gone: I typed his transfer orders up myself."

"*Enlisted*—?"

"That's what he's doing out there . . . Running for his life to get in shape . . ." They laughed, appreciatively, never noticing how she (Sunny) stepped away from them, for balance, the way you inch backwards over breaking ice, the way you veer back from a precipice from fear you're going to fall because the earth you're standing on has just gaped open.

OF ALL THE GENIUS MOVES SVEVO HAD ACHIEVED in his brief tenure at Manzanar, installing the shower in Schiff's private quarters was the capstone, in Schiff's evaluation, because, first of all, no other barrack in the camp had one and, second, the pressure, thanks to the Los Angeles Department of Water, was dynamite and, third, thanks to the Army Corps of Engineers, the water from the shower head was not only like a spray of gunfire, it came out *hot*. You're gonna thank me every day for this, Svevo had said, and he'd been right. At the start and end of every day the last thing Schiff wanted was to strip down in the moldy men's and lather up with a used and forlorn lozenge of Lava soap thin as a playing card along with all the other guys (GIs). *Perks*, Svevo called these small entitlements that went along with Schiff's position: private shower, private toilet, kitchen; a window in the bedroom ceiling so he wouldn't have to see the lateral (camp) view. To call the space under the skylight a "bedroom" was a stretch because the whole barrack was really one big room, except for the closed-in shower and partitioned john. The front (and only) door faced, thankgod, toward the Main Gate, and had a porch that looked out on the highway and the eastern Inyo Mountains. The "living" area within was furnished with a bookshelf and a table and a davenport he never used, and Rocky's rocker; the "kitchen" with an icebox and a propane two-top and a window view of the Admin offices; then the back part, the "bedroom" where he slept and from where, if there had been windows in the walls, he'd have a view of all the other barracks every night and every morning. Instead, Svevo had given him a window in the roof so at night he had the stars. And the shadows from the searchlights. The new Administrator was a family man and the Corps had built him a real house with dining room and bedrooms for his kids and a bathtub for his wife and they'd dug a real "lawn" large enough to play croquet so the job had gained some perks, Schiff guessed, other than his (meager) own. The transition had been smooth enough, the new man appreciative of the precedents that Schiff had set, but wanting, as Schiff's follow-up, to put his own stamp on the camp, a stamp Schiff was quick to figure would be more conservative, politically, than Schiff's program, and blatantly more Christian. Schiff had stayed on as *aide-de-camp*, effecting seamless regime change, but now he felt the time had come to go, just go. He could feel the subtle hints coming from the new head man—and his wife—that he had pretty much exhausted every welcome.

What he had been doing, once he'd taken the decision, was to try to put his body into readiness, strengthen it the way his mind had strengthened once he'd known what he was going to do: embrace a daily discipline he thought of as pre-Training training. He was running, now, an hour and a half three times a week. Hiking with, at first, a ten-pound load and then fifteen, then thirty. Sprints. The goddamn calisthenics. Was it *personal*? It was. Did he want to *hurt* the Nazis? Did he want to *kill* them? No. Was he fueled by anger? Yes. By a "*justice*"-driven anger, a litigator's fulminating rage for RIGHT. What he wanted was to see the Nazi bastards brought to ground, humiliated and then tried before some nonexistent higher court of universal law. What he wanted to bring to it was his own brand of fight, a brand of moral outrage that he'd absorbed from Hamilton and Adams, Jefferson and Brandeis. He *did* believe, he *did*, in a more perfect civic construct than the one that Hitler was imposing over Europe—he *did* believe, he *did*, in a more perfect civic construct than those the arthritic European monarchies imposed, but at least this current King George had his own Patrick Henry in the form of Winston Churchill and Schiff could fight for that: he could; he would. Hitler, for Schiff, was less a singular anomaly, a lone maniac, rogue Devil, as the American press was trying to brand him, than a symptom, like a boil, of a subcutaneous poison in the corps of Europe, the same residual toxin that had driven people from its collieries and *shtetls*, its ghettoes and its peasantries, for centuries: driven people like his parents to *get the hell out* while they could. So hell yes this war was personal for him. That lie he told himself, if it was a lie, was central to the "why" of his commitment to join up, because if he could argue he had more at stake—*personally*—than, say, Jo-Bob Grits from Christianville, then he could ramp his nonexistent soldier self into some sort of serviceable bravery. *Not a Jewboy Army*, Svevo had warned him. If you sign on you'll find a General God on top and *goyim* all the way down. Blue-eyed shit and secret handshakes. Crucifixes. Lots of crosses. Cross symbologies. I had this guy in Basic, told me "shouldering" our rifles is an exercise designed to make us think of Jesus "shouldering" the Cross. Yeah, I told him. And didn't Jesus *die* from that?

Schiff knew he had never had that kind of "shouldering" in him, that kind of stance to take things physically, through suffering of the *oo-rah!*-kind or even of the random push-up. His was not a backyard kind of background that included vigorous horseplay or any sort of physical exercise. His entire exercise as a boy had consisted of, mainly, climbing up apartment stairs. The first-generation Jewish immigrants of his parents' acquaintance hadn't risked their lives to come to America to be robust Americans—they'd come to be *Jewish*. Their religious "exercises" had been outlawed so they came here to "exercise" an over-compensating kibbutzy slathering of the old country's prohibitions, exercising everything "traditional" but in a bigger better louder way with more moxie and more *meaning*.

Zo, *nu*: Are you "American"?

O *ja, o ja*—but from der *Oder* side!

Schiff's father's favorite joke.

Repeated and repeated.

Yet never funny, to Schiff's mind, even when he'd learned that "Oder" (a Yiddish-speaker's way of saying "other") was the name of the river that ran through Germany and Poland where his father's family had been from.

Idiomatically, his had never been an Anglo catechism, nor did he have a childhood that embraced the open air or the "taking" of "regular" exercise. Even as late as law school, at a mixer where a coed raised a glass and told him, Everybody's body is their temple, he thought when she'd said "temple" she'd been talking about *shul*.

So there was this daily "exercise," to get his body *shul*-shape which was, christknows, mind-numbingly boring. Svevo had warned him about that, too—the tedium of Basic, its ritual exhaustion. The flattening out of private (haha) thinking. Loss of personality. Pissawful food. (Though it was hard to think that he'd find Army food any worse than his own mother's.)

Svevo had been right, too, in insisting on an icebox for Schiff's private quarters—originally conceived to keep beer cold for both of them—damn thing chugged like a truck in low gear struggling up a hill at night, but when he pulled the plug on it to try to get some peace and quiet all he heard were *camp* noises, ten thousand people turning in their cots, not dreaming, so he got up and plugged the damned thing in again, no more troubled by the noise it made than by the sound of his own echoing heart.

He'd taught himself to cook, a little—scrambled eggs, melted cheese, baked potato. Twice, three times a week, he'd purloin a chop or a couple of patties from the mess crew, but his usual routine, these days, was evening run, hot shower, cold beer, something basic from the fridge, couple of hours reading, writing letters, bed.

Tonight, after the shower he'd thrown on a sleeveless undershirt and a pair of chinos now too large for him around the waist, cracked a cold one and leaned into the open icebox, hair still wet, trying to decide on what to eat, then let the door close, not deciding.

Maybe it was time to sort his books.

Fiction he'd leave here—why not? donate to the sad, but promising, camp "library." But his law books? What had he been thinking, shipping out his law books, like he might be called upon to argue torts. Now he had these goddamn *books* to deal with before he left—send them home? ship them to his parents in Chicago who would complain (his mother would) about the way they took up too much space?

Rocky?

—*Rocky*, sure.

He could entrust *law* textbooks to Rocky.

He sat down, barefoot, with his beer, behind the davenport in front of the bookshelf and started the triage—a painful word—bits of his life, like moths, like sparks, escaping from the book spines. He'd marked them up—he was a marker-upper, in the manner of a Talmud scholar, with the (pretentious) purple ink from his Waterman pen which he'd been so proud of in law school (*what* a little twerp he'd been) . . . but there he was, as he had once been, in all the hopeful energy of youth, mind released from the captivity of his parents' triviality, thirsty curiosity engaging law's eternals, encountering the possibility for the first time that he (it) might *do* something with his (its) latent abilities, achieve a career and *go* somewhere. He *liked* that boy: the way he'd thought—a mind at work to understand the threatened verities, the greater truths . . . where had *he* gone? You know how it is, you open one of those old books and another version of yourself appears. It was not uncommon for him to lose himself in reading lose awareness of the things around him nor was it uncommon, now that he was no longer the Head Guy, for people to show up at his barrack unannounced—Janets with "homemade cookies" they'd "made" for him (he doubted it) or Dr. Arakawa looking for better conversations than the ones he'd had all day—they'd give a light rap on the screen door, let themselves inside and, if he were reading, sometimes he didn't notice 'til they spoke and then they took him by complete surprise so the sense that he was not alone tonight wasn't new but the feeling that some restless presence like Hamlet's father's ghost was prowling through his living quarters got him to his feet real quick and there she *was* standing—where else?—in his kitchen, arms crossed over her breasts a look of fuming confusion on her face, spoiling for a confrontation.

—*is it true?*

If they'd glimpsed each other in the camp these last couple of months they'd pretended that they hadn't and he had not come anywhere as close to her as this in . . . a long time, and she looked *great*: When had she ever looked (to him) otherwise?

"This isn't your house, Sunny, you don't get to come barging in—"

"Just tell me *is it goddamn true?*"

"I live here, I sleep here and—you know what?—I *dream* in here so I don't want you mixing with—"

"*Have you joined up?*"

"It's none of your business what I—"

"Did you fucking join the Army?"

"What do you care if I did or didn't—?"

"I think you can do something better—"

The scar from Dr. Arakawa's stitches had left a white line through her eyebrow like a bolt of lightning.

"—something different with your life."

She wasn't taunting him, he heard . . . she seemed to be *mourning* him.

"I don't want you to die," she said.

Too quick he parried, "*Too late* . . . I've already been born," and the look on her face lost its edge and collapsed into its underlying sorrow.

Schiff, she started—and as if that lightning bolt had struck him at the source of any independent will he bucked forward and seized her in his arms and kissed her, all conscious thought erased except those registers that tasted something sweet like (yes!) homemade cookies on her lips and responded to the not unpleasurable shock that every measure his wild hands were taking of her body found pure muscle.

How long an embrace it was could be measured, itself, only in galactic time and it would have expanded like the universe itself had it not been for

Jimmy Ikeda knocking once then stepping in and standing there, grinning like a cat that had eaten a canary, holding a little parcel wrapped in butcher's paper.

"—brought you three lamb chops for your supper—didn't know you'd be entertaining: hello, boss lady."

"—hey, Jimmy . . ." He'd been her main *sous* setting up the communal take-out in the unused barrack and Jimmy handed the wrapped lamb chops to her, not Schiff, as the three of them stood there in excruciating silence.

"—okay well just wanted to swing past and tell you bye-bye," Jimmy explained. Though he was still skinnier than even Svevo, he looked more muscular than he had before. "That Recruitment guy—he's taking guys like me from camps, forming our own Asian unit, the Hitler-Killing Japanese . . . I might be shipping out—heading off to Europe . . ."

Me too, Schiff said: maybe I'll seeya over there.

Alone with him again after Jimmy left, Sunny stared.

—just so you know, she said, I was going to sleep with you, regardless.

She had wondered what she would have asked her mother, through the years, had her mother lived—she'd wondered what she would have learned from her, the little things, stupid things, how to brush her hair, or dress or how to wear a slip, or sit. She remembered now—how old had they been?—she'd once asked Stryker—must have been when they were nine or ten—what he would ask Maman if she came back to answer just one question and Stryker had said he'd ask if there were animals in Heaven. And if there were then how about fish. How did fish survive.

You're an idiot, Sunny had told him. I mean something about *life*. About *her* life.

Well what would *you* ask her.

I'd ask what her favorite food was.

Tops could tell you that.

I'd ask . . . what's the one thing she would want to do that she'd never done. That she regrets not doing.

Probably growing *old*, Stryker had said.

So not always the idiot.

Sunny had acquired a mental list:

> *why did you come to America?*
> *did you dream in French?*
> *are there things a woman shouldn't do?*
> *did you ever have to lie?*
> *what is the first thing you remember?*

but this morning she would want to ask her mother What do you need to know about a man before you fall in love with him? How do you know if he's the one you should marry?

That's what she'd been thinking when Schiff opened his eyes and smiled at her.

"I slept."

"We both did."

Sunny had told him to put a shirt on—and his shoes—and meet her outside the Main Gate where her truck was parked and when he slid in on the passenger side there had been a basket of, like, a hundred eggs and what looked like a giant jar of *schmaltz*. Sunny had explained she was delivering them to Lou's where Vasco had started a back-door breakfast service and, with the basket settled on his lap, they had fallen into what might have seemed a surreally casual conversation, as Sunny drove them into Lone Pine, except for the fact that both seemed already attenuated to a rhythm of inevitability toward what they were about to do. Sunny filled him in on the current details of Finn and Cas's love affair, and he told Sunny the news from Svevo that he and Beryl were expecting their first child. They had driven in silence the last five miles, not touching, and Schiff had succeeded in not breaking any eggs before Sunny pulled into the alley behind Lou's and led him inside where he'd been crestfallen to see the stripped-out kitchen and the chairs stacked on the tables in the closed-up dining room and then she'd led him to the stairs behind the zinc bar he'd never known existed, up, into her second-story hideaway overlooking

Main Street, kitty-corner from his old room at the Dow. The place, she'd told him later, had once been a boardinghouse—more likely a brothel, catering to the silver-mining clientele from the Cerro Gordo Mother Lode down the road—with a saloon downstairs (what she'd turned into Lou's) and half a dozen rooms on this second story, which she'd gutted, keeping the original claw-footed bathtub exposed in the center of the floor under the rafters, and a certifiable "water closet" in one corner, a sink in another and, thankfully, a large mattress positioned against the wall and done up with all the girlie things like pillows and soft sheets where he and she had been entwined the last (how many?) eleven hours.

It was, Schiff thought, if not his sudden newfound favorite place on Earth at least his favorite *room*.

—and like the best of newfound lovers he could not—and she would not—stop touching the discovered other; nor stop smiling.

He traced a finger on her eyebrow where the scar was and asked, "Why did you . . . What made you change your mind about us?"

"—whole long story?"

"In case you haven't noticed I'm not going anywhere. And I'm not in any hurry."

She smiled: "—remember I once told you Tops started taking us up to the Sierra camp when we were really young? We must have been I don't know—four or five this one summer—we couldn't swim yet—and he had us out in the little boat he keeps up there—just a simple rowboat, really, with a motor on the back—out in the middle of the lake to teach us how to fish."

"—and you couldn't swim."

"We could paddle around but . . . And he had us out there without life vests. I don't even think we *own* a life vest. Anyway Stryker's at the bow and I'm athwart—"

"—'athwart' . . ."

"—*athwart*, facing Stryker with my back to Tops who's at the stern and Stryker and I have our little rods and our lines in the water waiting to catch fish—the lake is stocked with trout by the Forestry Department up there—and out of the blue Stryker stands up and speaks to Tops over my head and asks him, '*What's down there?*' pointing into the lake and behind me Tops says, 'The bottom,' and Stryker says, 'There's a *bottom*—?' and jumps right in feet first and goes looking for it. I'm sitting there and he's got his hands over his head and I watch his body disappear and then his head and finally his fingertips. Just gone. Hole in the dark water. And then before I know it Tops dives in after him, vest and shirt and pants and shoes and everything, and he's gone too . . . another hole in the water. Couldn't have been more than four or five seconds, the whole thing, but what I remember is sitting in the middle of the boat in the middle of the lake which is pretty big and looking up at the mountains all around me and the big blue sky and thinking two of the three people I love most in the world have just disappeared and I'm completely and entirely alone all by myself on Earth. Utterly abandoned. Not knowing where to go or what to do . . . Just myself. Me and the world. And yesterday the Janets were playing volleyball and they stopped to watch you on your run along the fence and one of them told all the rest that you'd joined up and suddenly there I was all over again feeling like I was five years old in the middle of the boat in the middle of the lake under the enormous sky completely and entirely alone with no one there to tell me what to do or comfort me . . ."

He stared at her.

—during the night he had deployed the "L" word and asked her to marry him several times (*suave*, Svevo might have sized it up) but now he kept his ardor checked and simply said, "You're not alone."

"—I know. . . . Believe me I was as surprised as you . . .—anyway the only other time I had had that awful feeling Tops ends up throwing Stryker back into the boat and hauling his own wet self back in and firing up the motor and yelling at my brother, "*Next time you ask a question wait for the goddamn answer* and we spent the rest of that day in water and the next one learning how to swim and breathe . . ." As if to test her memory she took a breath and asked, "So if I hadn't shown up were you just going to go away and that was it—?"

"No."

"Liar."

"—I was going to . . . what I was doing at the time was sorting through my books to take to Rocky."

"—so you were going to tell *my father*."

"—*and* you . . . somehow. You weren't exactly offering positive reinforcement, Sunny . . ."

"How long have we got?—'til you have to—"

"—what's today?"

"—Thursday."

"—ten days."

"Are you going to go back home first, see your folks?"

"No."

"Have you *told* them?"

"—no."

"That's not good, Schiff."

"—it's a kind of family arrangement you've never seen, in your experience . . . Difficult for me to describe . . ."

"—then we should go somewhere. I've got gas rations, we should go somewhere you've never been. Give you something to remember. Have you been to the Grand Canyon? We should do something *spectacular* . . ."

"This is pretty spectacular, right here."

"I'm serious."

"Okay."

"We've got *ten days* . . ."

"Okay . . . let me think about it . . ." He closed his eyes and pretended to think about it: "Okay . . . here's how I see it . . ." He drew a map of Europe in the air. "Here's Germany, Here's Occupied France, Here's the English Channel . . . all our boys in England . . . Italy, down here. You don't have to be a genius to see that when we make our move we're going to have to come in here, on the French coast, or maybe through Belgium . . . also up through Italy from the Mediterranean . . . so I figure what I'm going to be doing once I'm there, once we make our move and I get ashore *alive*, is I'm going to be walking across France. Rain, snow, like a mailman—sleeping rough, walking through garlic fields, planning my survival. The boys who are going to excel at that? *Boy Scouts* . . . not city boys like me but the ones who can light fires in the rain and fashion mattresses from fallen branches and build shelters out of rock and corn husks—"

"They'll teach you that in Basic—"

"I'm *OT* . . ." shorthand for Officer Training which, to Schiff's ear, sounded Old Testament: "—they're not going to teach me half the things *you* could."

"You want to go camping?"

"—yes."

"—you know there are no showers there, or anything."

"—yes."

"—and that it's . . . basic."

"—yes."

"—and that no matter where we go, it will be freezing cold at night."

"It will give me something to remember when I'm trudging across France."

She had a think:

"We can drive up to Yosemite. It's beautiful there. But for the last two nights? There's a hotel, the Ahwahnee—fancy stuff—where my parents were married. Decent grub. Room service. *Hot water.* And a roof over our heads . . ."

Schiff was like an excited first-time camper the rest of that day, packing up, effecting his farewells. Betty was already gone, having not been kept as secretary under the new Administrator; so the only people he had to say goodbye to were The Hats, Dr. Arakawa and Georgina Takei. When Sunny was ready to drive from the Main Gate with his rocking chair and books loaded in the truck he asked her to pull over so he could get out for one last look and was caught off guard by the memory of Svevo hauling up the Stars and Stripes for the first time. He was almost tempted to salute, but stopped himself. This was not the place for patriotic gestures. Whatever patriotism he had in him was built on more eternal human principles than the ones that had built Manzanar.

Sunny had become a marshal in the field commandeering supplies—the tent, the tarps, the ropes, the camp stove, the coffeepot, the frying pan, the cups, the plates, the *food*—all massed by the door at Three Chairs for a dawn departure. Rocky was on his own trip in the Sierras and Cas and Finn were down in San Diego inspecting Japanese-American properties so there were notes that had to be written and instructions given for the maintenance of the dogs and goats and horses and just as the sun had disappeared, right after dark, when she was thinking about what to do for their last civilized supper for a week Schiff said Let's go right now. Let's start.

"In the dark?"

"—*yes.*"

"I don't think you understand."

"—no, leave all this stuff just take these blankets and drive out into your own backyard. I want to sleep under the stars tonight. With you. And maybe a sandwich and a couple beers . . ."

A halo of ambient light lingered in the dark above the camp, even at a distance of several miles, but aside from that the night was seamless from the ground up, with the darker more intense presence of the mountains keeping sentry in the farther scenery. Sunny had found an air mattress to throw into the bed of the truck and they hunkered under wool blankets and it didn't take too long for Schiff to start complaining he was cold.

—but very very happy.

Giddy.

—*there's* a word: where does *that* come from? "Gid-dy. Giddy-*up* . . . Tell me all the names of all this stuff."

"What stuff?"

"All these stars and stuff."

"Well that bright one that's not blinking? That's a planet. They don't wink at you."

"Which planet is it?"

"In our family we always say it's 'either *Yupiter* or *Weenus.*'"

He hugged her closer.

"Did Tops tell you any of his Albert Einstein stories?"

"Just that one about God leaving clues for Isaac Newton in the form of rainbows . . ."

"But he told you they were on the boat together, right?"

"Right."

"—staterooms next to one another with this kind of shared deck . . . a balcony . . . that had a half partition so each stateroom had some privacy but if you walked out to your railing you could see your neighbor . . . and the first morning at sea Tops, with his hair all down, walks out to the railing in his bathrobe and to his left two feet away is another white-haired gentleman in the *identical* bathrobe except this man's hair is all *boing* and he's clutching a hairbrush. Top says, *What are the odds?* and a female voice from behind the partition on the other deck says something in German and the man— *Albert Einstein*—starts to calculate. Turns out Einstein's English isn't all that great and Tops's German isn't either—although *Cas* can hold forth in whole paragraphs—and Einstein's wife, who can't show herself because she's in her nightgown, does all the translating from her little hidden place. So they do this every morning and every night the whole trip across the ocean and according to Tops Einstein never actually gets around to *using* the hairbrush and one night there's a very bright star in the North Atlantic sky just like this one above us and Tops points it out and asks Einstein what star it is. Einstein apparently understood *that* much and answered, *der Planet ist YUPITER oder WEENUS.* Stryker used to lose it every time Tops mentioned 'Weenus' he just thought it was the funniest word he'd ever heard . . . He laughed a lot, my brother. He liked to laugh. He laughed in his *sleep*. Plus he had his own Celebration Dance . . .

"Show me."

"No I can't, I can't do it."

"—yes you can."

"—no I really can't . . . First time we ever saw him do it was at the Sierra camp when Tops let him build the fire one night and Stryker kept adding logs and this thing was *huge*—a *bonfire*—we had to move our bedrolls back—and it was throwing sparks, a galaxy of sparks into the air real *fire*works and for some reason at that time of year there were these moths up there that came across the water, attracted by the fire and they started swarming through the sparks—I'm not kidding it looked like there were *thousands* of them and Stryker got so excited he broke into this *dance* . . ."

"—*show* me."

"—side-to-side . . .—right before he left home we saw a Bob Hope movie with Bing Crosby and there were *hula* dancers in it and we nearly fell out of our seats because they were dancing Stryker's Celebration Dance, except you know how the *hula* ladies make their arms go *wavy* like the ocean? Stryker used to go like *this* more of a *push, push*—"

A beam of light suddenly swept above their bodies, focused on the truck:

"—what the—?"

"—*merde!*—get dressed get dressed get dressed . . . !"

Sunny scrambled through the blankets on the truck bed and Schiff found his boxers by his feet and pulled them on—*backwards* it turned out—and got on his knees then to his feet raising both arms to shadow his eyes so he could see beyond the bright white blinding light behind which he could barely delineate the outline of a Department of Water truck that pulled to an abrupt halt several feet away. From its far side Schiff could see a man emerge and prop one arm against the hood to steady a rifle. From the nearer side another man emerged, this one in charge of the spotlight and Schiff had just enough time to recognize him as Deuce Coop—before Cooper said, "Mr. Schiff!—what are you doing out here, sir?"

He's with me, Sunny announced, standing up from the truck bed. Coop swerved the light in her direction and it was plain as day that her denim shirt which, praise the lord, had shirttails long enough to cover both her ass and her forward privates, was the only thing that she had on except, of course—and Schiff found this second thing even more surprising—the rifle she was shouldering, aimed at Cooper's partner.

"Put the gun down, Snow," she told him.

He refused and Sunny swung her own gun forty-five degrees away from him and aimed high into the desert and let go a live shot then swung back and pointed the barrel straight at Coop.

"Tell your crazy partner to put his gun down, Coop, or I'll blow out all your tires and leave you stranded here. You're on my land."

Schiff watched Cooper give the other man a coded signal and he laid his gun down as Coop told Sunny, "Eminent domain."

Sunny laughed and broke her own gun down and held it by her side and said, "Now Coop you know Mr. Schiff here is an attorney, which means he knows the actual meaning of 'eminent domain' so don't be throwing words around you don't understand."

"We're protecting the canal. There's a war."

"There *is* a war—five thousand miles away. As for the canal, it's three-quarters of a mile away and we're not doing anything to threaten it."

"How long you plannin' to be out here?"

"My whole life probably."

"You need to check with us next time—"

"I don't need to 'check' with you for anything, Coop, this is my family's property and as much as your sidekick is a deadeye shot *my* sidekick can haul your ass to court for trespassing . . ."

Schiff saw him give another coded nod to Snow and they both got back into the truck, but not before Coop asked Sunny, "When's Lou's re-opening? I miss those garlic mashed potatoes. You oughta tell Vasco to put them on the breakfast menu . . ."

Then they drove away and Schiff watched Sunny discharge the spent cartridge and slide the gun back into its case.

"—where did *that* come from?"

"We always keep one in our trucks."

"Is 'one' coming with us?"

"—*bears.*"

No one had mentioned bears:

God's honest: "You have to be the scariest woman I know."

"—really? Have you *met* my aunt—?"

Adrenaline receding, Schiff was cold again and he pulled her back down and nestled beneath the blankets.

"Do you think they've gone for reinforcements?"

"Coop's pretty reasonable. But if Snow were on his own he'd be out there in the dark with our hearts in his gunsights all night long."

"—think they knew what we were doing?"

"Snow was probably confused. Coop? Coop's a married man so I bet he had a theory . . ."

"I've never had a gun aimed at me before."

"—if it's any consolation . . . you're not alone."

"You were magnificent."

"Tops contends you're not a true American 'til you've had a gun aimed at you. By another American . . . like those ten thousand true Americans down the road."

He gazed up and wondered how large a part of the sky ten thousand stars might fill. Then he pulled her close.

"We should have done this sooner," he finally said.

She took a while before she asked, "If we had, would you still have joined up?"

"—*yes*," he answered, too quickly. "It's not an either/or: go with Sunny *versus* go to war.—it's *both*. This war is personal.—*personal*, for me. Hitler . . . I need to see him brought to trial . . . and executed."

" . . . 'tried.' "

"Absolutely—captured, first, then tried. Humiliated and debased. In front of all the world."

"—so you need to go over there to make certain Hitler dies. *You*, personally."

"I'm absolutely going over there to make certain Hitler dies. Me—*personally*—and all my boys. We true Americans. And then I'm coming back here in my righteous splendor and marrying the living daylights out of you."

What had he been *thinking*—?
What the hell had he *thought* they were going to do with him

Svevo is going to bust a gut—
Svevo is going to laugh his ass off over this one.

Kill *Hitler*?
—you want to what, kill *Hitler*?
Son step back and get in line.
We have about a hundred thousand sons of bitches just like you
waiting to do that.

You on the other hand:
You know how to write a Constitution.
Plus says here you parlay-voo their lingo.
And you *lived* with them.

If he had been the one in charge of looking through his file he would have
reached the same conclusion.

What in godsname had he been *thinking*—?

They were going to send him to Japan.

They put him on a plane for the Pacific.

the eighth property
of thirst
is
re-invention

HE COULDN'T BE PRECISE in dating the decision—sometime in his second year of war—but at some moment after landing in Hawaii, some night sitting in a bar in Honolulu, Schiff had vowed he wouldn't drink again until the war was over.

War guilt. No more alcohol for him: that would fix it: that would show that kraut maniac what one Jew could do: if there was drinking to be done then let the front lines do it. Those behind the front lines were drowning secondary fears and selfish sorrows—some, especially the newly drafted, got tanked every night.

The company of young drunk males, the way they talked about women—the way they treated them—had never been his favorite social pastime (he had always been a solitary drinker), but the symbolic gesture of sobriety made him feel marginally superior to the idiots still boozing in the *hula hula* dives along Hotel Street or dancing with the white girls at the private clubs on base.

These girls, out here in the women's services from flat Christian towns in the American Midwest: girls accustomed to humidity but not to rolling surf and palm trees: white-fleshed girls with pressed rolled hair and padded-shouldered frocks and alabaster pumps with cotton socks—girls who had convinced themselves that they had signed on out of patriotic duty, for their country, when the truth was they had signed on to invigorate themselves, to get as far away from rural flatline boredom as fast as Uncle Sam could take them. Definitely grab a guy along the way. Maybe land a husband.

These girls would come up, stand near the bar like they were waiting for a bus and start the conversation, "Crazy world, huh? Whereya from?"

You were expected to participate in this ritualistic quasi-patriotic ex-change, maybe pay for her beer and join her at a table with her girlfriends and their "catches" for another night of ethics molestation.

Maybe crowds were not his thing. Or maybe it was that since he'd gotten himself involved in a love affair so profound he had no interest in any part of life that did not touch on her. So no more standing at the bar (an existential problem, in the Law) no more drinks. Instead he limited himself to clubs on base and sat most nights at a small table ordering his food, acknowledging in grave monastic code the other solitary officers at the other solitary tables, each in his own way, like Schiff—single or not—devoutly married.

He liked this officers' joint because the food was better than at the others, the music was discreet and, unlike the other clubs around, it catered to officers of all the military services.

Plus, the émigré Hungarian prince (of course he was) who oversaw the place let Schiff put up his posters by the cloakroom and inside the bar.

On occasion, when he grew tired of eating by himself, Schiff would ask Boot and Klonis to come along. Together, the three formed one unit of a brain trust dispersed between the Pacific and back home in Washington. The Pacific divi-sion of this cadre was not unlike a school of sharks in a suite of offices on the top floor of the Judge Advocates' Building. Reporting in at Honolulu, Schiff had discovered more lawyers than he'd seen in any men's room since he'd left Wash-ington and the Interior: reedy learned men with penetrating eyes, some young, some old, some from the private sector and the universities, a couple steeped in constitutional law, a couple in international trade and Oriental culture, a couple (had to watch your back around these) steeped in Machiavelli on the prowl for sloppy thinking and raw meat. Schiff's first job, with Boot and Klonis, was to formulate "positioning" papers on the future of a defeated Japan. Papers that made pictures of that future for the top brass to consider. *Position* papers. We're like the authors of the *Kama Sutra*, Boot wisecracked. Where Uncle Sam's the big dick and Japan's the you-know. Other one. Boot had seniority, not in rank but certainly in years, and he'd left a wife and kids back home. Schiff and Klonis (George Klonis: He was first-generation Greek-American and never lost an op-portunity to let you know it, never lost an opportunity to teach a word's Greek etymology) looked up to him and it was usually Boot who had the final word. They were going to give Japan universal suffrage, that they all agreed on. (Take *that*, France, you artificial puppet of Democracy.) And freedom of expression— even Truman in his "Proposed Program for Japan" from the Potsdam meeting with Stalin and Churchill had been adamant about that. "Freedom of speech, of religion, and of thought, as well as respect for the fundamental human rights shall be established," the Statement proposed. So fire up your engines, all you boys and girls. Here come your round-eye freedoms.

One of those positioning papers had been adapted as a flyer, to be dropped on Japan by air. Across the top, three bold-faced banners:

CITIZENS OF JAPAN
WE COME IN PEACE
YOU CANNOT WIN THE WAR

The three of them had discussed it sitting at this very table. (Like Lou's, the Hungarian's was *compact*.) Schiff had argued "peace" was bullshit ("What 'peace'-ful thing has ever come out of the sky at humans?") but Boot and Klonis had argued for it.

God, for one. (This was Boot:) "God comes from the sky."

"And God is love." (Klonis.)

Not *my* God, Schiff had thought.

One night, Boot was remembering: "I had this student once, we were reading the *Maharabata* and he raises his hand and asks, 'What is Death a *metaphor* for?'"

"'*Meta*,' meaning 'change'; '*phor*,' meaning—"

"Oh for fucksake *can* it, Klonis," Boot snapped and immediately regretted it.

He knew George didn't deserve the kicking. Kid had two brothers in the fight—Mike in North Africa and Archie in the Mediterranean—and he'd just had a letter from their teenage brother Nick back home saying that their only sister, Mary, had eloped with a non-Greek. "Chances are I'll never see her again," George said. "The Old Man will disown her. This fucking war. She never would have eloped if Mike or me or Archie had been there."

"Maybe he's a nice guy," Boot put in. "Maybe he'll win the family over."

"If he's so nice what's he doing sitting on his ass Stateside?"

"Maybe he stayed because he's in love with your sister."

Schiff felt a little pinch of masculine guilt: had he, himself, been too eager to leave—would it have been more noble to stay behind for The Girl?

During the weeks in San Francisco before departing for Hawaii he had begun to sense a pattern to the work he'd been allotted, he'd started noticing the legal material assigned to him—started to intuit underlying themes: the constitutionality of fundamental rights; "constitutionality" of freedom of expression, freedom of religion; "constitutionality" of universal suffrage, the fundamental right of "constitutionalities" to maintain standing armies, "constituted" rights of citizens to (privately) bear arms. He'd been asked to write a brief on what constituted "fundamental rights" (he'd already pulled this short straw as a pre-law student); write a brief on what constituted "sovereign rights"; outline a hypothetical proposal for the future of a:

defeated

and/or destroyed

and/or occupied

JAPAN.

If he was good enough, if he played his cards right, he suspected, they were going to let him sit at the table with the big boys, sit in on the drafting of some history: they were going to let him play Ben Franklin some time in the not-too-distant future: maybe even let him play Tom Jefferson; Alexander Hamilton:

They were going to let him draft an actual Constitution.

For a Japan that hadn't happened yet, for the Japan-of-the-future that everybody in Hawaii hoped to live to gloat at: a Japan reduced to dust; humiliated; *fucked*.

PROPOSED PROGRAM FOR THE FUTURE OF JAPAN—this was why they'd kept his brains intact, prevented him from joining in the bloodthirst in Europe: he was more valuable to them (his Army) as a thinker than as a fighter and they needed him alive, and scheming.

He could end up making history—so no more drink for him.

Personal ambition in wartime should be subject to court-martial Schiff believed but he had come to see how the whole Pacific acted as a self-reflective mirror for MacArthur and even the littlest fish in his group of sharks jockeyed to ingratiate themselves with "Doug."

Immediately following the attack on Pearl, everyone in Honolulu had gotten busy blaming everybody else for what had happened. On that December Sunday morning Secretary Knox, the Secretary of the Navy, had dumped the blame in the lap of Japs covertly working in the islands—fifth-column Hawaiian Japanese. Reports had come from witnesses that Japanese cane cutters on the plantations had carved out arrows in the sugar fields to guide planes to the harbor.

Reports had come in of Jap dogs on the beaches barking military secrets ("japping") to submarines offshore.

Rumors had it Hawaiian Japanese had poisoned all the water.

Rumors flew that Roosevelt himself—the President!—had been in cahoots with Winston Churchill all along, had known well in advance what the Japanese were up to and had let them stick it to us just to force us innocents to war.

It was Churchill's fault, or it was Roosevelt's; it was the Army's fault, it was the Navy's—nothing of the magnitude of Pearl and its ensuing loss of life had ever happened to the nation, and it had to be somebody's *fault* there had to be someone, some*thing* to point the finger at, to blame, because to the average mind *God is on our side* and a catastrophe like this one doesn't come along for nothing, doesn't happen in America without a devil (or *the* Devil) being called to pay. Someone or something had to shoulder local blame for the global shame we suffered (in many patriots' minds the global shame outweighed the global pity) and it was *shame* that had the kids in every small town in the nation signing up in droves, willing to put their bodies and their futures on the line in Europe and the Pacific to expiate the national guilt of having been caught napping on a Sunday morning in December instead of at their stations of the cross inside the crucible of war.

Nine days after the attack, Admiral Husband Kimmel, commander in chief of the Pacific Fleet in Honolulu, was relieved of duty by order of the Secretary of War and, presumably, the President himself.

Simultaneously, Lieutenant General Walter Short, Army's corresponding chief commanding officer in the Hawaiian District, was summarily relieved.

Heads needed to roll—blame needed to be leveled—but to pit the head of Army against the head of Navy was a further blow to servicemen stationed at the devastated port, and when Schiff arrived the following fall morale was still struggling to boost itself off the ground and Congress was still calling for the commanders' mutual courts-martial.

The statute of limitations would expire on December 7, 1943, and already certain members in the joint houses of the legislature were proposing bills to extend the statute so that the ticking clock would not expire before one or both of them could come to trial.

To build an airtight case involved not only assembling the official transmissions and written exchanges leading up to the morning of the attack but also gathering eyewitness testimonies from anyone and everyone on the ground that Sunday, and although most people found that reliving the story in its telling provided them a modicum of psychic healing no one really had the stomach to finger their commanders outright, and the majority of servicemen resented what the smartass investigators, mostly lawyers, had been sent to do and stonewalled them, from loyalty, when they saw one coming with a notebook and a pen, including Schiff, whose luck it was to pull this shit assignment when he wasn't writing briefs about a future fairy-tale Japan that might function in the global league of nations as a constitutional democracy.

What separated Pearl from Stateside—this was where the planes had targeted the innocents, this was the hallowed ground, the bloodstained water where the bodies of the dead had been entombed, as yet unfound—you couldn't crack a joke out of plain decency and you could tell the raw recruits from how the room went silent when they tried it, you could tell they'd come from someplace else, where the war, though felt, had yet to hit the lungs and sting your eyes or make you dry heave. To have been at Pearl that Sunday morning bought you the lifetime pew, the family name engraved, and you never knew if a man or woman standing next to you was a survivor or if the man or woman you were sent to interview would open up or shut down or cry. But one thing was certain; he or she was never going to laugh about the things they had survived that day. You could smile—he'd noticed girls, especially, had started smiling—but it was as if the God from the Old Testament was back and heaven forbid *He* caught you laughing. *If I weren't in love with you, if I didn't have the two of us to dream about I'd end it all from loneliness*, he wrote to Sunny. *I'd kill myself from general lack of humor.*

Never try to catch a falling knife, she'd written back.

Kitchen wisdom.

—*the fuck?* he'd thought. What was the knife? Was *he* the knife? Was love—past love—the too-quick blade?

"Love is for *amateurs*," she'd say.

The girl could pun.

Eleven months since he'd seen her last, the excitement she elicited from him was undiminished—if anything he'd grown to want her more, to cherish those unanticipated flourishes of wit and style and tenderness of hers. To cherish *her*. Her letters were packed with local color—what was new with Cas and Lyndon, how the women of Lone Pine were leaving for paying aircraft factory jobs in Southern California, how the trout were running. She sent him spices rolled in cigarette papers twisted at the ends; she sent him a green powder she called "rosemary dust," dried chilies, Mexican oregano, fragrant dill, sundried tomatoes, *bouquets garnis* with dried orange peels. Anyone who bunked near him could tell from the aroma when another letter had arrived. She sent him dried duck *prosciutto*—duck jerky—to add to Army beans. She sent rolls of Rocky's smoked game sausages with a cautionary note on mold. She sent dried corn for popping. And flavored salt. Food from her was foreplay, a kind of distanced eroticism: she must have known or sensed the sexual charge her cooking had for him from the way he watched her do it, the way he watched her move and watched her taste, the way he watched her hands and mouth. She must have picked up on the signals whenever she got caught up in the excitement of telling him a story about discovering her mother's notes in the kitchen cookbooks and how she'd struggled to translate them from French, how she'd begun experimenting in the kitchen at an early age and growing vegetables from her mother's seeds. I need to taste imaginary meals, he'd written early in their separation. I hunger for them in my mind. I need to devour them.

Coded sex.

427

He was sure the censors used a lot of extra ink each time they read his letters, but what the hell, even if his sentences didn't get to Sunny whole, he felt better for having written them. *Miss your cooking. Miss your magic culinary touch. Miss the touching.*

She wrote to him of meals she would concoct when he got home, and there were many nights—too many—when he'd rehearse the steps, the recipes, lying awake, as a way of fighting off his body's bold desire.

Sunny-side up.

She was as sexy for him on the page as she was in the flesh.

But what he hadn't written to Sunny yet, was that even when the war ended he would not be coming home. He would be staying on. Headed for Tokyo, or what remained of it.

He felt stymied in Honolulu, as if he was not allowed to say what he was thinking, either in his letters to Sunny, or in this whole Army-Navy tug-of-War over who to blame for Pearl. *Who, Schiff thought, can fault the Navy? I'd like to tell these Navy boys I'm on their side. The only reason there's an Army presence in Hawaii is to make sure nothing happens to the Navy not the other way around. Navy wasn't sent here to secure the Army's presence for christsake as if some foreign infantry was ever going to storm the beaches of Oahu. It was Army's job to make sure the fleet was safe. The Navy people see me in my Army uniform and think I'm Army and not a thinking individual—that's what being in this Army is—even when you're not in combat you're a faceless part of a machine, another yahoo. If it weren't for loving you I'd be crazy by now. If a guy ain't nutso for enlisting all he has to do is wait and Army life will make him certifiably insane. I miss fun. Definitely miss f——*

"*—is this you?*"

Schiff looked up at the Navy emissary in the duty whites standing before his table holding, face out, one of the flyers Schiff had posted by the bar.

Do I look like I'm a young Japanese woman clutching her two infants?

Schiff could see the Hungarian maître d' looking sheepish by the bar and figured he had fingered him and, besides, what's the point of putting up WANTED posters begging for info on a missing woman if he wasn't going to own up when somebody asked if they were his. So he said yes.

"Come with me, please, sir."

"Why?"

Even though he hadn't mastered all the complicated Navy stars and bars Schiff was pretty certain he outranked this guy and by rights was owed not only a salute but some respect.

"Follow me, please."

"Where?"

"The Commander."

Commander was one reason Navy outranked Army in Schiff's view, helluva title. He'd go to sea, himself, if someone promised everything he said would be a Commandment.

"Sorry, mate. He'll have to wait. I just ordered dinner."

"No you didn't."

Schiff saw the Hungarian shoot a look at an isolated table in the rear where an older gentleman in formal travel blues was seated. The Commander. And his wife.

Schiff approached them and saluted.

Up close the ranking man had pale impassive eyes and the empty look of hardpan prairie stamped onto his face. Beneath her little hat his wife seemed grandmotherly and had put herself together in the style of Eleanor Roosevelt.

"Sit down, Captain—we don't want to pique the others' curiosities."

Schiff knew his walk to the Commander's table had prompted looks among the other officers so he followed the Commander's order and sat down across from him, next to his wife.

On her right wrist, the wrist next to him, Schiff noticed a corsage, a large Hawaiian orchid that looked incompatible with the way she'd put herself together—too bold, too vivid, too sexy—and when she saw him looking at it she moved her arm to the empty space in front of her, as if he might have improper designs on it, as if he might be a bee.

"It's our anniversary," the Commander said.

"—congratulations."

"Normally I'd call you to my office for a situation such as this but as you probably already know I'm on the 2100 tonight for Washington."

As soon as the Commander announced his name Schiff recognized it as belonging to one of the high-ranking naval officers who had been summoned to depose in person before Congress and he listened to his inner Solomon's advice: Less said the better.

"I promised Mother we would celebrate our anniversary before I left."

Schiff pressed his lips together at the use of *Mother*.

He'd been summoned, he suspected, for a dressing down—a WANTED poster picturing a Japanese in this climate was volatile and he was ready to receive the tongue-lashing and get to the local grilled *mahi-mahi* he'd been looking forward to all day.

The Commander's hat was on the table between them and from beneath it he slid, like an ace from the hole, another of Schiff's WANTED posters featuring Stryker's missing wife and their missing children.

When he'd designed it, when he'd laid it out and had it printed, Schiff had thought it minimalist and to-the-point—eye-catching, clear, concise—but seeing it laid bare in front of him against the tablecloth in candlelight, his well-meaning design looked inflammatory, his cropped reproduction of the picture of Stryker's bride that Sunny had sent from California looked as if it might be targeting an Oriental and the accompanying prose

HAVE YOU SEEN THIS WOMAN?

STATESIDE FAMILY URGENTLY SEEKS CURRENT WHEREABOUTS

stank, he now realized.

Suppose this were Amsterdam or Warsaw instead of Honolulu and the woman on the poster was a Jew, what would people think then?—what would *he* think?

"The woman is the wife of a Navy ensign, sir, one of yours, MIA since the attack on Pearl. Her name is Suzy Komoko Rhodes and she and her two children are—"

"I know her name, Captain. I know who she is."

Schiff was surprised.

"—but what I don't know is why you'd try to get away with falsely representing yourself as her 'Stateside family.'"

"I'm sorry, sir, I should have made it clear I represent the Stateside family of her husband, Ensign Rhodes. His father, Rockwell Rhodes, is a friend of mine, a prominent citizen back in California. Perhaps you recognized the family name—the ensign's grandfather started a mining company last century. His name was Wellington Rhodes."

Air escaped from the Commander's wife: "I've seen that name. I've seen that name on *boxcars*. Stryker never said. Father, did he say a word to you?"

"Suzy was a high school friend of our youngest daughter Hilly before Hilly went back to the States for college."

"Do you know her well?"

"Not 'well.' Socially. In passing."

"We held a small reception for her at the house after the wedding. Even though we didn't know her all that well."

They should come with operating instructions, Schiff thought—a *goy* manual—instructions for decoding or a decoder ring: How do you throw a party for someone but still say you don't know them "well"? Why do you call your husband "Father"?

"Not as many people as we thought would be there, were there, Father? Friends of Suzy's from the high school crowd. Airmen Stryker knew. He was starting Basic, for the Navy Air."

"So he wasn't on ship duty?"

"Not at any time we knew him."

"And Suzy's family—?"

"They were Japanese. I think she said she was an only child. Her parents came out to the islands to cut cane, so we were told."

"Maybe they could tell us where she is."

"They're dead. Something happened to them shortly after Hilly left."

"Suzy never told us what."

"And of course, it wasn't our place to inquire."

Schiff looked from one of them back to the indifferent other.

"Here's what I don't understand," he said: "How do four people, a husband and a wife and two children—a whole family—how does a whole family go missing for over a year—eighteen months—and no one bothers to ask questions—? They had family housing I found out, they had a Navy bungalow. No one seems a bit concerned. Excuse me if I sound a little agitated—I don't want to spoil your anniversary celebration but *they've been missing for eighteen months*. Why aren't people in the Navy all over this like flies on—"

"Need I remind you, Captain, how many disappeared, the numbers Navy lost December 7th—"

"—you don't need to remind me, sir, you don't need to *remind* any citizen of the United States how many Americans were lost that day—or remain missing—and like most Americans I can only imagine what anyone on the ground that morning must have gone through, the hell the two of you, as residents of Pearl, must have experienced—and I don't want to deprecate the force of the trauma but I believe you and I, sir, especially, as agents of the government in the disaster's aftermath have a duty to the dead and to their families to act knowledgably and swiftly to help them through their grief and give some answers . . ."

As Schiff spoke, two orders of shrimp cocktail arrived, pink and glistening, arrayed in sunburst patterns around pools of bloodred cocktail sauce in widebrimmed champagne glasses filled with ice.

"I'm sorry, I should go," Schiff said.

He pushed back his chair but the Commander signaled him to wait and, once the waiter had departed, told his wife to "Let the Captain in on what had happened."

"As I said, we didn't know them all that well," Mrs. Commander started (between bites), "didn't see them, really, after the wedding until the babies were born and they came by the house to show them off. Two peas in a pod, those tykes, you couldn't tell the first one from the second—We both thought Suzy looked a little pale and tired that day, didn't we, Father, she had had some kind of problem with her heart when she was little, Hilly told us, might have been the scarlet fever but it was not my place to ask. Suzy mentioned Stryker had leave coming at the end of the year and they were going to the States to see their families—Suzy has an aunt there in California somewhere and her grandmother was coming over from Japan—and I happened to mention I go over before Christmas every year to see our daughters and one thing led to another and before you knew it we said we'd try and get the same flight out so I could help her with the babies and then Stryker would fly out later and be there to help her with them on the airplane back. So that's what we did. We flew over on the same flight. I had Ralph and she had Waldo. All the way to San Francisco."

"So she flew to San Francisco December '41?"

"Yes."

"What day was that?"

"December 7th."

Schiff's nervous system made an involuntary response. Something in his chest dilated.

"It was the oh six hundred flight, wasn't it, Father, still pitch dark—you know how these flights from Honolulu to the mainland run, you either leave before daybreak or you leave last thing at night and of course we were two hours out by the time it all began to happen on the ground back here. Innocent as babes. Without a clue. If the pilots knew—and Father says they must have known—they kept the news to themselves I don't think they sent a word to the flight crew those girls were just too bright and cheerful the whole time. I hadn't stopped to think that we were flying in two separate classes but there I was up front with Ralph in First Class while Suzy was stuck way in back with Waldo. I had his papers with me for the Customs and a bag with diapers and the bottles but the little tyke slept the whole way through. They were such the little angels, both of them you couldn't tell which one was which just looking at them—even their own mother—Suzy had to write the letter 'R' on the top of Ralphie's hands and on the bottom of his feet, and a 'W' on Waldo's *and Lord only knows* what would have happened if the letters ever washed off in the bath or if there were any other kind of mix-up. Ralph just slept away there in his little basket with his little 'R' written on his little fist above the blanket."

Schiff waited while she finished off another shrimp in a single bite.

"When we landed they had us park way out on the runway at a distance from the terminal and they told the hostesses to say there was a small electrical fire in the building that they needed to contain but then the plane was boarded by a group of men with what looked like passenger manifests and they started going row by row up the aisle and the airman sitting next to me drew me in and whispered, 'Something isn't right here, something's up.' They held us on the runway quite a while and then they started taking people off, men and women both and before I had a chance to say a word to her Suzy was taken off the plane with Waldo in her arms—right by me—she gave a little wave and soon after that the engine started up again and we taxied to the terminal."

She ate another shrimp, this one with some cocktail sauce.

Well things were *strange*, she said: "You could feel it in the air—no one was saying anything at first but people knew something *strange* had happened, and then I guess people who'd heard it on the radio, heard about the attack, started bringing news into the terminal because by the time I located Hilly she was just a ball of nerves, let me tell you . . ." Another shrimp; the Commander showing just the slightest edge of impatience: "Of course our first order of duty was to find out if Father was all right . . . but what to do with little Ralphie? Fortunately Hilly has her father's clear head on her shoulders and she went around to all the Orientals waiting at the gate and said Suzy's name and finally tracked the aunt down, and the grandmother who was there with her, visiting from Japan. No English, that one. We gave her the baby."

She took a swallow of champagne.

"So that answers your questions, Captain," the Commander told Schiff.

". . . um: *no*."

"I beg your—"

"—you just handed a baby over to two strangers?"

"—*not* a stranger," the Commander answered for his wife: "—to a woman recognized as Suzy's aunt."

"Do you remember this 'aunt's' name?"

"—'Komoko,' I believe. Hilly took care of it."

"—and what happened to Suzy? and the other kid?"

"We didn't think that was any of our business . . ."

"—do you remember if Suzy had U.S. papers?"

The woman appeared sincerely helpless: "I don't see why you have to ask so many questions . . . as I said, I had my *own* problems to fret about that day . . ." She tried to pat her husband's hand but he withdrew it from her touch.

"Satisfied?" the Commander asked him. Schiff could tell that he was eager for his entrée. And maybe even for the flight a little later away from his wife. But Schiff's mind was racing: if Suzy hadn't applied for U.S. citizenship, California might have sent her and the babies back to Hawaii, given the news of the attack . . . or kept them, interned, ultimately, in a Relocation Camp . . . or, through the back channels of the neutral Swiss and Swede envoy, deported them to Japan in those early days after Pearl when such exchanges were still being made.

"I'm sorry for you both that you had to live through the terrors of that day," he said, "and I'm happy for the both of you that you survived, Commander."

Stone-faced silence.

"What happened, on the ground, after you both saw your wives off on that plane?"

"What *happened*—?"

"I mean, did you go for a cup of coffee or—"

"—he was an *ensign*, Captain. I barely knew him. We parted ways. It was barely light outside."

"Father had his dawn tee-off that Sunday. I remember you had your golf shoes in the car . . ."

"—and Ensign Rhodes: did he say where *he* was going?"

"He seemed to know I would disapprove of where he was going, but I remember he seemed to want to flaunt it. He said he was going to join a 'floating' card game. On the *Arizona*."

"That wasn't his ship."

"No."

But they both knew it had been the hardest hit.

A waiter came to clear the appetizer plates away and Schiff took his cue. He stood.

"Sir, I'd like to have a look inside their quarters if you could arrange it."

The Commander raised his chin and a naval emissary stepped forward to receive whispered instructions.

Rocky—or more specifically Schiff and Lyndon, with their camp connections—should be able to track Suzy and the boys down if they'd been detained in the United States, and this was the news Schiff was itching to telegraph to Sunny. As far as Stryker's fateful rendezvous on the *Arizona* was concerned: it was an active shrine, already, in a nation's memory.

Their dinner plates arrived. And two more glasses of champagne.

"Tomorrow?" the Commander ascertained: "Oh seven hundred. One of my chiefs will meet you there."

He didn't wait to answer Schiff's salute before he cut into his steak.

MORNINGS IN HONOLULU brought out the ghost aroma of petroleum from the damp earth, the smell of all the gallons spilled in the attack, keeping the mosquito population on the decrease at least but adding a slick rainbow to the top of every pool of sewage water, even, sometimes, a viscid sheen atop one's morning joe. When your a.m. rain stinks like a fuel depot you know you're not in paradise no matter how waxy all the flowers are, how exotic all the palms. The water burned: the surface of the water in Pearl Harbor was on fire the day of the attack and what happens when you burn petroleum that way is that it smears the atmosphere with its carbon fingerprints and there hadn't been enough new rain yet, even after all this time, to wash away the oily residue of both chemistry and fatal fact. Wet and grey and oily: he had to swipe at dew most mornings on his shaving mirror just to get his face tonsured. Water tasted like gunpowder. He had to stuff newspaper in his shoes at night to keep them dry. In contrast, when the sun came out it was blinding. Fortunately for him, the sun was well occluded behind the lead-colored clouds this morning so no need for the ubiquitous sunglasses that everybody wore (in imitation of MacArthur). There were regulations about this (there were regulations about everything) but everybody flouted them as soon as the clouds broke: "—white men, white uniforms, white buildings, white teeth," he'd written Sunny: Melville would have to write a whole new thesis here.

He wouldn't go so far as to say there was hostility between the Army boys and Navy—but egos had been bruised in the blame game and he didn't want to give his Navy liaison this morning an inch to sow the seeds of a dispute so he timed his walk to Stryker's former place of residence along the row of MOQs (Military Officers' Quarters) so he'd arrive at least ten minutes ahead of Chief Petty Officer Lincoln Abraham (whose resonant name, Schiff was deliberating, might resolve around a missing naval comma).

—but there he was grasping his clipboard close to his crisp uniform even earlier than Schiff was, waiting at the stoop in stiff attention as Schiff came up the damp and steaming pavement: a rare sight in this man's Army or Navy: an American Negro, looking sharp in his short-sleeved starched whites. No hat. No sunglasses.

Schiff saluted: "—*Chief.*"

Mr. Abraham saluted: "—*Captain.*"

Down came the clipboard: "If I could have you initial here, sir, acknowledging the time of entry, and your signature *here*, warranting you'll leave all items within the premises intact . . ."

Normally Schiff would announce that he knew how to read a fucking contract but he signed the paper blind just to get on with it and then the Chief unlocked the door and they both stepped into a time capsule.

The air inside was the same air as the morning of Pearl Harbor, Schiff couldn't help thinking. There was a mail slot in the door but no accumulated mail inside on the floor and *mail* was the one thing he was looking for to identify the relatives of Suzy's so he had to ask, How come there isn't any mail?

"All mail's delivered to the base. Post boxes, sir. Even for the MOQs."

"Uh-*huh*," Schiff said, calibrating all the shit he'd have to plow through (Federal, Navy) just to get permission to look at *that* . . .

"What are we looking for in here, exactly, sir?"

Personalities, Schiff answered: Missing People—especially the kids and wife. He filled the Chief in on what he knew; what he was hoping to discover (evidence of Suzy's Stateside family, her aunt's address in California: anything that pointed to her history and who she was), but as soon as the Chief opened the blinds in the front window and the island's grey light filtered in to illuminate the scene it became clear to both of them that this was *Stryker*'s house and—with the exception of a crib in the corner of the living room—everybody else who'd lived here was pretty much invisible.

Two surfboards leaned against the wall inside the door and on the mantel over the fake fireplace there was a cheap framed reproduction poster for the John Wayne movie *Stagecoach*. There were two upholstered chairs dressed in mismatched Hawaiian chintz and a davenport which had seen better days.

"Do these MOQs come furnished, Chief?"

"No . . . but officers get reassigned and no one wants to have to pay to ship a sofa from Hawaii so a lot gets left behind."

Behind the davenport a little writing desk doubled as an *intime* dining table and tucked up with the salt and pepper shakers there was a napkin tray into which was propped a single opened letter whose envelope bore Sunny's familiar handwriting and the purple ink Schiff had come to know so well.

"—you all right, sir? Do you need to take a look at that?"

Schiff shook his head, and they went into the kitchen: no dishes in the sink but two cups and saucers stacked on the drying rack.

"Very tidy," the Chief observed.

They had had their morning coffee and someone (most likely Suzy) had washed the cups, but the coffeepot (with coffee still inside) was on a front burner on the stove:

"She left the coffee," Schiff pointed out: "She thought he was coming back . . ."

They went down the shotgun hall past the bathroom—nothing of note—to the bedroom where there was another chintz-upholstered chair, a bureau, a double bed, two nightstands, two lamps, a sliding-door closet and two bassinets along one wall. The bed was made and at its foot was a large open gift box from Gump's in San Francisco with a discarded price tag among the tissue paper inside and a card which read, "To keep you warm until I get there, S."

"He bought her a coat," Schiff concluded, "to go Stateside."

Chief lifted the price tag and let out a whistle:

"—some *coat*," he said.

"—he has money.—*had* . . ."

On the upholstered chair in the corner was an open suitcase, packed, with a handwritten note on top, DON'T FORGET CAMERA—PACK SHOES! and a little heart drawn underneath.

"Chief, did we see a camera?"

"Maybe he had it with him . . . for the airport."

It was clear Stryker had not returned, having gone from seeing his family off to the fated poker game on the *Arizona*. There was nothing telling in the bureau drawers nor in the closet—no documents, no pictures, no correspondence—but in the nightstand on the side of the bed nearest to the bassinets Schiff found an empty medicine bottle issued to SUZY KOMOKO from a Honolulu doctor whose name he copied down.

"*Benzo-thi-aze-pine*," he read.

"—that's a vasodilator: 'CHD' . . . congenital heart disease," Chief told him. Schiff looked at him:

"—my momma takes it. Heart disease and diabetes: two biggest killers among the American Negro. Unless, of course, you count the white man."

Schiff let him smile without participation.

In Stryker's night table he found another bottle, one of Suzy's scrubbed clean of its label. He unscrewed the top and shook some of the contents out onto his open palm, looked at it and smelled it.

"What is it?" Chief asked.

Schiff rolled his finger over it, trying to define it:

"I think it's . . . *dirt*," he finally said.

Chief laughed: "—no . . . old sailor's trick . . ." He slipped the clipboard beneath his arm and drew his billfold from his pocket. Inside he found one of those little paper envelopes they use in church to put your coins in, for the offering, and held it up for Schiff to see before he knocked some of its contents—bright red clay—into his hand.

"*Alabama*, right here—Tallapoosa County, where I'm from . . . Sailor su-perstition is you take a little of your *earth* with you when you ship out—a little of your land—it gets you back to shore again."

The night Stryker had left—that night of the elephant when Cas had spir-ited Hace and him away—Sunny told Schiff that Stryker had stood in the driveway of Three Chairs facing her under all of Rocky's anger, speechless, not knowing what to say, and she'd leaned down and scraped some soil and gravel up and dumped it in the pocket of his cowboy shirt and how the gesture had seemed hokey at the time, just something to do to ease the tension . . . not the last thing she'd offer to him in their life.

"Where'd you say your boy was from again?"

"California."

"—well that's *California* you got right there in your hand."

Schiff took another look at it:

—granite miniatures, mineral extracts, clay, basalt dust, sand, schist, sili-cates, salt, quartz pebbles, plant particulates . . .

"What happens to this stuff, Chief? This personal property. If no one comes to claim it?"

"This particular place? . . . probably stay as it is for the time being. No demand for MOQs, everyone's deployed. Eventually I guess someone will come in and pack it up."

Schiff returned his handful of California to the bottle and secured the lid.

"Think you could let me sign off on this one item?"

Chief smiled.

"I think we could let that go," he said. "Is that 'home' for you, too, Captain?"

"No," Schiff had to say. "Home" was the Loop the El the red streetcars the erratic arctic wind banging at you off Lake Michigan, the Drake, Marshall Field's, crossing Wabash, State Street, Lincoln Park, the briny tang of salted herring and the static on the radio's Saturday morning Yiddish program. His mother ironing in the kitchen with rosewater spritzes. "Not 'home,'" he ad-mitted to the Chief: "Not where I'm from but maybe where I'm going." Not where I'm from but where I want to be.

"—oh that's the *promise* land," Chief laughed.

Schiff wasn't certain Chief had made him for a Jew—people in the Army always did—but he would bet he had, and the moment that had arisen to this American Jew from this American Negro on this tropical island in the middle of a war from a reference to the Old Testament made Schiff laugh right along with him.

Just come back, Sunny had countered all his marriage proposals: Don't make any *promises* don't promise you won't die just *show up* at the end of this get out alive and then come back to me and Three Chairs and back to California:

Promise land.

the ninth property
of thirst
is
submersion

IF HE HAD TO THINK ABOUT IT—which he didn't want to do; *what was the point?*—he'd guess he'd first become aware of them the way you notice stuff that's always there, the things that *are*, the resident smells that follow you around the place you live, the dogs, turned milk, coal dust, wet boots, tar paper walls, earth floor, old skin and liquor. Like all the other things that he had got used to, "they" had been a part of every day as long as he remembered, kept in a place of honor over the fireplace and on another rack beside the door *always* where you saw them first thing every morning when you came in, always where a stranger with the wrong idea could be made to feel their stopping power: *Guns.* Taken down and polished and refigured and admired, always *loaded* even as they rested snug against the wall while everyone inside the house was sleeping. *Reason* they could sleep so *tight.* Every man who was a man had one, didn't go outside without one, and came calling with his shouldered or at least poised at the ready on the buckboard or the sidepack on his pony or, later, racked behind him on the seat inside his car or truck. Goodboy shooters. Every man's best friend; and trustier than dogs because whereas a dog will die on you a gun will last until you're dead. You didn't think about them, really, like the way you didn't think about your sister being something special or your parents being anything but ordinary: these were your facts of life, the rifles and your family, and you woke up every morning to the plain reality of what they were and what they can do and just got on with it.

He didn't know when he had touched his first one he assumed it was early as a child just as he assumed it must have been his father's but he remembers being on the floor next to where his Daddy sat while he wiped it down, the way it smelled, the gun oil and tobacco and the coal soot and the kitchen. First domestic lesson: *Clean It*: keep it clean, bore the sucker out and keep 'er cherry else she'll stove up onya. Treat 'er right she'll be your serving bitch forever. Treat her wrong she'll choke, *mis*-fire. Or worse. Humiliate you while you're standing before Nature. Right in front of God.

It was their domesticated faith—a religion, really—all the cleaning of the guns. Manly thing to do. Daddy let him clean the gun before he'd let him shoot it, sitting there at evening while the women stitched, all of them wrapped up in each one's task, the best part being that while the women clicked their stitches he and Daddy had held weapons in their laps which meant that what was on their minds while they were sitting there was what they'd shoot next, what they'd kill.

Snow was slow, the teacher told them so, she'd held him back a grade then had to hold him back a second year so he was bigger than the other boys he shared his lessons with and he'd seen Daddy watching him for telltale signs of his stupidity. There were things that Snow could do (he could clean the gun) and things he couldn't do (read), so it had come as overdue when Daddy finally let him shoulder up and then to everyone's surprise (including his) he'd let fly the head off a rabid fox at fifty feet.

Too sweet.

To this day life's fondest recollection: that one shocked moment he and Daddy had stared dumbstruck when they'd seen what happened.

Boy can shoot.

Boy could shoot a rat's ass on the moon—

Boy was *money.*

So when he'd stood guard watching the surveyors, when those first Water boys he worked with from Los Angeles had let him take a gander through their lenses, on their sextants, got to telling him about triangulation and degrees of arc, *he got it*, by instinct—got the whole idea of it how the ground is curved and how the air will curve the bullet, too, in its trajectory—(he had learned by then he wasn't *stupid*, just merely kinda "blind")—he got that the majority of sharpshooters made split-second calculations with their eyes based on a kind of science or on math but that a small percentage of sharpshooters like himself had an unscientific gift, a *feel* for it—call it "natural" or "animal" if that's what suits your politics—where the whole set of possibilities presents itself not as a calculation or an exercise in plane geometry but as a future picture, *a thing that hasn't happened yet* but is gonna happen, as a certainty: the whole picture presenting everything at once, including death, before it comes.

Snow was that freak of nature—the trick shooter—(the word "trick" here standing in for Death). *Kill* shooters they're called, their value counted out in kills.

80 ducks an hour (more than one a minute).

1000 in an afternoon.

It made sense to get himself out into the field where he could make the money, drop from school. He could write his name and he could recognize a couple words so what he needed was not more schooling but a gun that he could call his own and soon after he had proved to Daddy he could shoot, Daddy up and got him a Smith & Wesson, a "Yellow Boy," so called for the brass inlay on its stock and butt.

How he loved that gun. That Yellow Boy.

He was tall so he was shooting full-size from the start and most grain growers who hired him to kill out the migrating birds thought he was teenaged while he was only ten, living on his own, sleeping in duck-blinds, sending money home.

It was seasonal, the work—most people called it that—but really it was three or four weeks twice a year, once in fall when the birds were heading north and then once again in spring when they were flocking south. He was paid per piece and not by day, so when the kill was on, when the birds were coming in he had to have four rifles going with two loaders by his side and sometimes, when it got heavy and the birds put out a panic in themselves, you couldn't hear for all the noise, for the terror and the shrieking sounds they made and from the bullets, from the guns, igniting in the air.

He was making so much money, then, in those two months, he could afford to pay the local boys (sometimes boys five years older than himself) as runners and as skinners, to go out, under fire, and retrieve the birds and pile them up and skin them for the feathers and the meat.

He was paid not only by the grain growers but also by the poultrymen, the duck and geese provenders. There were growers, too, who hired him to shoot at crows and at the hungry small grey birds who targeted the rice and wheat and millet every harvest season, but the money made from crows was chicken scratch compared to money made from ducks and geese. What sane person ever thinks of eating crow or stuffing her bed pillow with sharp black feathers? No one.

He had earned enough with Yellow Boy before he hit fourteen to put his money into land so Daddy could work a place that they could call their own, and he had earned enough to help them build a proper house with a real roof and proper floors that weren't just dirt.

Daddy's old man moved in with them the summer that the house was built—he had his own room 'side the kitchen at the back—owing to the fact that his eyes had given up and he couldn't even see to drive a mule or swing his scythe. Snow had always liked his Gramp—felt more comfortable with him than with Daddy. Gramp had had an indoor self, a habit of telling stories out loud to the family in the evenings that was more forgiving to the children than Daddy's palpable frustration with being pent-up indoors with the woman and the kids at night. Before he'd come to live with them—when he'd only used to visit—Gramp would read his weeklies to them and read aloud from what he called his tales of inspiration the lives of Jesus and the Prophets but when the blindness set in for good, after he'd moved in with them and Snow had been at home, not shooting, he'd asked Snow to read to him and that was when the truth came out: Daddy told Gramp Snow was slow, so stupid he had never learned to read and then Daddy started in with reading nightly to his father without joy in that flat non-informing voice he had.

You're not stupid, son, Gramp had told Snow: Look what you done, whole family's in your owe.

What Snow had never told was that he, too, was in an owe, big one.

What he had never told was how he got the thing to come to him, how he "called" it into his sights, how he could "see" the thing before it came into the crosshairs, "see" it when it wasn't there, "see" where it *could* be at the instant when he knew he *knew* to stroke the trigger.

He had no interest in shooting stable things the cans and bottles on the fence, all the targets at the fairs and rodeos stacked there in imitation of what nature offers up—the easy targets, "sitting" ducks—took no talent nor no luck to shoot. You couldn't call those targets to you—they were just sitting there—you didn't have to organize the blind thing in your mind to take a shot at them, to take out an empty can or reduce Daddy's likker bottle down to smithereens, those things were already *dead* so what's the point of shooting just for shooting just to prove how sharp you are. Unless there's extra money in it.

So he'd done those rodeos and fairs, the ones where locals pay good money to see freaks of nature and *trick* shootings and he'd accepted challenges from rousters in the crowd, nearly always drunk and always stupid who wanted him to shoot a cigarette from someone's mouth or shoot the artificial flowers off their fat wife's hat or shoot at something with a length of cloth tied 'round his eyes, blind; blindfolded.

There was money in it so he did it, working in the off months when he wasn't killing birds for the grain ranchers but the exercise of it always left him empty, left him feeling like plain dirt and he was glad whenever time allowed him to get back home, to set with Gramp in the back room and not have to aim at anything that couldn't move.

Snow wasn't sure which year it happened—maybe winter '16; maybe '17— but Gramp had got the Braille Lady from the State with her Braille books, and she had started coming by the house to see to Gramp, but whichever winter that had been Snow had gone back home and Gramp had had those playing cards, the ones with the raised pips on them in all four corners.

Up 'til then Snow had never told no one about the Shadow mainly 'cause he'd figured Shadow wasn't his to tell.

Shadow was his Visitation, plain and simple, act of privacy and faith. The way God visited those saints and people in the Bible when they least expected. What they called a Vision.

Visionaries they were called and when Snow first saw the Shadow back when he was five or six he had known from all the Bible stories that what was happening to him, the thing that was occurring in his field of sight, had to be a private message sent from God.

Old boys on the road and at the fairs had been adept at cards and Snow had always sat them out, those late-night games, owing to his trouble with the numbers, with the reading, but when Gramp had pressed a game on him and explained the system of the raised dots in the corners of the cards and showed him a whole page of those raised pips, a whole *book* of them, and guided Snow's slow mind over a line, a light went on and he could see—see through his fingertips—if not exactly what you'd call "a letter" then at least *a sound*.

Double-you. Gramp had told him that he'd most likely seen this letter from the alphabet written out on signs (<u>w</u>ARNING!) it had that shape the mountains have (down-*up*, down-*up*) and makes a sound like blowing out between your lips like blowing out a candle.

Ay: First letter in the ordinary alphabet shaped sort of like an arrow, sounds like "ah" the same as *ah*-row, makes it easy to remember.

Tee. Shaped like The Cross. Sound you make at the end of spi*t*.

W   A   T   —   —

Next two "letters" were an "*ee*," and an "*are*," and he remembered Gramp saying sound them out and his fingers making singular sounds inside his mind and then, the miracle, combining them, like liquid, like something sung in time, like music, into a single understandable communicated thought, a *word*:

450

W A T E R

Three things had proved the wellsprings in his life so far:

:·: Knowing that the Shadow in his field of vision was his Gift from God.

:·: Knowing that without even looking he could draw his Target to him.

:··: Knowing (finally) that he wasn't stupid. (He could *read*.)

It was at the Sacramento Fair, the Farm Show, where he was turning gun tricks that this smart fella came up to him and handed him a little card he couldn't read

BOBBY KAYE
entrepreneur
Hollywood

and Snow could tell the guy was from a city, somewhere "urban" (another word for "Hebrew," one of those "Jew" types), guy says You shoot that thing like you were born to do it. How'd you like to be in pictures?

Snow thought immediately the guy was just another hustler and he'd seen his share of them.

You can't take a picture of a shooting bullet, Snow had told him. Cuz it moves too fast.

"Ever hear of *moving* pictures?—what people call the *move*-ees?"

Who hasn't? Snow had said (though he'd never seen one).

That Bobby Kaye, that guy in a flashy suit and those expensive shoes with all the cow-and-bullshit crusted on them had told Snow he was making cowboy pictures—*Ever hear of Hollywood?*—and that Snow's way with a gun was worth a reel or two (Snow had figured "reel" must mean some kind of money) and he'd pay Snow's fare, plus something extra, for Snow to do his stuff in front of cameras.

"In Hollywood?"

(Snow had heard of Hollywood.)

"*Near* Hollywood—*outside* of it. In the real Wild West. Real rocks, real sky. The desert. Ever been to *Lone Pine, California?*"

Ten dollars a day plus room and board and transportation: Snow thought he'd died and landed in hog heaven. Not since he'd picked up his first gun and called the Target to him had he been so happy, and so sure. The Shadow then, as now, was still an element of calculation in his vision and he'd adjusted to it by that slight turning of his head which no one seemed to notice. But once he'd got to Lone Pine and submitted to the "cowboy" costume and had heard from Bobby Kaye what he was supposed to do, another kind of unexpected problem raised its devil head:

In the movie they were making they'd expected him to aim at people.

I don't shoot at people, Snow told them.

Bobby Kaye, who'd christened him Gun Boy, had had to get up from his chair with the umbrella over it and stop the shoot and weigh in on the problem.

"What's the problem, Gun Boy?"

Gun Boy told him he had never aimed at people.

"Since when?"

Since forever. "I won't aim at people, no, sir," Snow had told them. "Not 'less they've got something on them I can shoot."

"Like what?"

"A hat. A cigarette. Buttons."

"But the people here—they're not 'people,' Gun Boy: they are actors. Actors playing Indians and stage robbers. Are you telling me that if your life depended on it you couldn't shoot an Indian out there, maybe threatening your wife, you couldn't draw a bead to stop a robbery?"

"Well it's like you said, sir: they're just actors. They're no threat to me. They're not real."

"Neither are the bullets."

"—but my *aim* is, sir."

That was the nature of his Gift from God, his surefire aim, that when he closed his eyes and held his breath and held the gun a certain way the Gift would *call* the Target to him, call it into range, summon it, the way God summons souls to Heaven, the way God summons souls to peace. He could be lying there, in blinds, waiting for the flocks to come and he would close his eyes and summon them. To shooting. He could halt up in the woods behind a tree and close his eyes and deer, silent as the light, would suddenly appear. This was the nature of God's Gift to him, as holy as God's contract with the world and he had known it from the start that it would be a bad bad thing for him to ever aim his Yellow Boy at humans.

So Bobby Kaye had fired him.

Right there on the spot, beneath the towering Sierras, standing in the dry heat of the Alabama Hills: out of a job. Far from home and unemployed. Friendless. 'Cept for Yellow Boy.

All things being equal, he had always fallen short and the gun had been his equalizer. Like they said—

GOD MADE ALL MEN BUT SAM COLT MADE THEM EQUAL

—that was the Samuel Colt Patent Fire Arms Manufacturing Company's slogan and no truer words in Snow's estimation had ever been downwrit (except the Bible).

So it was back to shooting dimes at 90 feet for him. Shooting buttons off shirt collars. Targets of diminishing sizes—iceberg lettuce, oranges, lemons, radishes then marbles—ending in his trademark trick SHOOTING AN ASPIRIN which left a little white puff in the air where it was shot, like dandelion fluff.

Buffalo Bill, Annie Oakley, A. H. Bogardus—all these shooters had the tent-pole personalities for exhibition, the exhibitionism needed to do circuses or movies: all Snow had going for him was his patience and his faith in God's gift. And some *luck*, apparently. As he was packing up his bindle in the Alabama Hills he was approached by one of the "private" men assigned to guard the cameras, horses, saddles, what-all on the set—anything of value that could be stolen—one of the famous "Pinkertons," the men in tweed suits and felt homburgs, toting .22s.

"We could use a man like you," he was propositioned. "There's folks down in Los Angeles got their eyes on land up here and they're looking to employ protection."

He'd handed Snow another of those business cards Snow couldn't read. Aside from the writing he couldn't decipher—

PINKERTONS EMPLOYMENT

STRONG

SAFE

SECURE

"WE NEVER SLEEP"

—there had been an eye printed on the card—an open eye, like on our U.S. money, and he'd liked that. That had been a lucky sign. It spoke to him. He liked that a lot.

"What would I have to do?" Snow asked. "—cuz I won't shoot at people never have and never will."

Some called them a private army but nationally the Pinks were the most feared, most reliable policemen-for-hire you could get. Their presence—and you could *tell* them, you were *supposed* to make them on sight, by their tweeds and bowlers—in Owens Valley in the hire of Los Angeles had been greeted first by cautious skepticism as to what the hey it was they thought they were up to in the rural backwater and then, starting with the night patrols they ran, the around-the-clock patrolling of the Los Angeles–owned property as if they were patrolling a foreign border in their onerous black coupes, the noses of their .22s just visible inside the open windows, people lost their skepticism and started to steer clear of them, back off, not so much in fear as in distrust.

They charged him for the bowler hat and for the suit (plus extra pants) against future wages but the money was topline and he liked the company, the type of men attracted to the work, a higher kind of smarts than what he saw in rodeos. CORPORATE AMERICA'S COPS—well that was something—he liked the sound of "corporate" it sounded upclass and important. True, the Pinks had once been hired to safeguard President Lincoln (and look how *that* had turned out) but these days they were most likely working for U.S. Steel or the big rails or Misters Otis and Mulholland from Los Angeles. Big-money men. Important. (Not that President Lincoln hadn't been important.) *Western* men with *Western* interests in expansion, minerals, water, gold.

They wanted him to take an eye test and he shot an aspirin out of the sky. *There's my eye test* he had told them.

Construction in the Owens Valley on the viaducts and such, the sluices and slurries and the tailbacks, the runbacks and the weirs, had gotten under way and there were miles to cover, as well as a hundred, two hundred workers to protect from nosy neighbors, from the grain and cattle boys who'd kept their land and now were worried where "their" water would be going, and from a couple loudmouth ranchers—one in particular right here north of Lone Pine who started mouthing off to folks and writing letters to the paper and organizing meetings and speaking out at churches and messing into places where he shouldn't go. *Rhodes.* Big guy, *tall*; Easterner who walked and talked like he was native.

THE GREATER GOOD—that's what the signs said, a buddy read for him— the signs the Water boys plastered around town in answer to the ranchers' protests. Most of these folks was Christians like himself, *nice* people, peaceable, God-fearing, but there had been exceptions—and the Pinks had been made to feel notwelcome in the businesses in town: they quartered at the Dow, but they ate sequestered, took their chow like cowboys at their own field mess and stayed away from the sole saloon and pool hall after dark. *After dark* was when the main patrols went out, anyway: Rumor had it that Rhodes had been the money and the brains behind the opposition taking the out-of-town concern all the way to the Supreme Court in an attempt to rule Los Angeles off-limits, out-of-bounds up here, illegal. As a stall the whole thing worked, kept everybody sitting on their hands for months until the Big Bull Moose, Teddy Roosevelt, himself (another Easterner) overruled it from the White House with an "executive" order giving the L.A. boys the nod to start up work again on the grounds that "the needs of the many outweigh the needs of the few," the "many," here, meaning the City to the south and the "few" meaning Owens Valley ranchers. The Greater Good.

This led to a heat-up in the local temperaments, the Valley people pushed into doing what the Pinks called "civil disobedience" and, in the extreme, "unrest" and "socialism."

What the Valley people "said" they were going to do—what attracted the press—was "occupy" the main spillway at the Alabama Gates, sit down, camp out, *reside* in the canal itself, stopping water flowing south.

—but what they *really* planned to do, the Pinks had paid good money to find out—was to blow the whole thing sky-high to kingdom come.

Blow up the Alabama Gates spillway.

Blow up the aqueduct.

Blow up the canals, the intakes, the outlets, pipes, the tunnels, tailraces one-by-one DEWATER Los Angeles and turn it back into the property of thirst God had intended when He first created it.

They got the movie folks involved who were up here making Westerns—they got Tom Mix the silent Western star to ride up on his horse in costume—they got Church Ladies coming out with icebox cakes and casseroles they got the flash photographers and Eastern newsprint people, gawkers, sympathizers: whole thing was a carnival, another rodeo, until the Pinks rode in and tore it up.

Re-occupied the site.

Patrolled it.

Snow didn't mind the all-night shifts—he volunteered. Most of the boys would stand up top, pace around the concrete levees, let themselves be seen and known to any interloper. Made themselves easy targets. What Snow did was the same thing that he knew large animals to do—mule deer, big bucks and such—and that was to lay up in a blind, bed high with a natural cover behind you, in this case the concrete walls that kept the water in. He banked himself against the wall, against an ambush like a predator against a thicket, so he could watch, and prey. In his pocket he kept one of the pamphlets Gramps had sent him—Braille "Proverbs of the Country Man," which he ran his fingers over, reading in the dark: memorizing.

IF YOU'RE BORN TO BE HANGED THEN YOU'LL NEVER BE DROWNED

WHAT THE EYE DOESN'T SEE, THE HEART DOESN'T GRIEVE OVER

HE WHO LAUGHS LAST LAUGHS LONGEST

3,000 men up here, 40 work camps, building 230 miles of water transport—the municipalization of water—at a cost of $50 to $75 a foot. For the first time in his life Snow felt he was part of something "greater" than himself, his family of the little local church back home—part of a Greater Good—and he gave himself to these all-night shifts like a nun or a pilgrim, sitting stone still except his one hand worrying the Braille inside his pocket—sitting stone still like one of the select few, like one of the first twelve disciples at the foot of Christ, until one night out there—under a fingernail of moon—the darkness bled, a shape of movement formed and Snow shifted the focus of his mind from the finger of his left hand on the Braille to the finger of his right hand on the trigger.

He lost his ice—that's what his Daddy always said of the dang fool who lost his nerve, stove up, choked the trigger, could-or-would not shoot.

Snow was not about to lose his ice.

Some dang fool no more than twenty yards from him had struck a match—Snow could see him in the shadows, *tall* man, dressed all in black to match the night. He struck a match and lit a stick of dynamite that he was holding, intended to ignite the pack that he had planted at the foot of the spillway where Snow was sitting.

Put that down: I've got a bead on you, Snow had said: I'm not gonna shoot you but I'll shoot that stick right off your hand if you don't put it down. You're trespassin'.

Go ahead, the tall man said—it was *Rhodes*, Snow would bet his life on it—*Shoot*, the tall man said: You'll blow both of us and this damn aqueduct to Hell.

"I'm a Pinkerton," Snow recited the way he'd been taught, "and under authority from the County of Los Angeles I hereby place you under—"

Fully loaded, chambers full, not a single bullet discharged, Snow had the evidence the living *proof*, after it was over, that he hadn't fired that the stick of dynamite had *gone up* by itself just exploded in the tall man's hand blowing Snow, even at twenty yards, back against the concrete wall where he had struck his head and blowing the tall man's hand Godknows halfway to smithereens, guy's blood was everywhere along the ramparts when Snow got back up on his feet, the Pink dogs alerted, searchlights on, Pinks running like bats outta hell lanterns held up high but the tall man had slipped through their dragnet, one more elusive shadow in the desert as if he, himself, understood the Valley's magic, was part of the desert's ancient disappearing act.

Part of Rhodes's hand—or at least part of a finger bone—had been blasted against Snow's chest, stuck against his tweed lapel in thick blood, like a citation, bone fragment and goo dangling on him like a medal, and at its center a gold *ring* like the rings in a bullseye, marking Snow, as if he were a target.

It was the tall man's wedding band—intact—blown off his finger and after he had given chase with all the others, after they had lost the Criminal Trespass, Snow had washed the ring in the very water that the Trespass had tried to liberate and, running his finger around the inside could feel that there was "writing" there, etched in, in the symbols, in the written "language" that the greater world—not him—employed.

No damage done, nobody injured ('cept the Trespass, Snow knew) and for service rendered, the Pinkerton Company awarded him a FLAG PIN—a lapel pin of the Stars and Stripes in color—which to the general population looked like he was an avid patriot but which, when he met another Pinkerton, broadcast his bravery.

He told no one else about the ring but a few weeks later took it to Assay Bob, a fella on the crew who assayed samples that the boys knocked loose digging tunnels through the granite and the shale and gneiss that they thought might be gold.

It's *gold* all right: one hunnert percent. Where'd you get a thing like this? Assay Bob had asked.

It . . . It came to me. Can you see what's on the inside?

—well: letters clear around no end no start: UISIANALO? Injun? No . . . here we go: LOUISIANA. That's a state.

"I know it is a state," Snow bragged.

"Well. Some people don't know their states."

"Well I'm not one of um."

Always jumpy—still was—about how people judged his learnin'.

Why he'd kept the ring—instead of giving it over to his commander as evidence to implicate the Trespass—he didn't know. He hadn't thought it was "withholding" evidence he just had a sense that *it had come to him* and it could prove important in the future and that whatever the importance might turn out to be, it was *his* and it was solely in his power to determine it.

The Trespass didn't try again. The aqueduct got built, the thing got up and running and it was hailed, deservedly, as the greatest engineering feat in all man's history. And he'd been part of it. The Greater Good.

Once the thing was up-and-running the Pinkertons' job in Owens Valley was done and the Company started re-assigning agents back to San Francisco and Los Angeles to "police," as regular, the corporate trouble spots—union shops and union organizers; personal "security" on families of the country's executives—and Snow had thought he'd have to leave the business—the business of protection—owing to the fact he didn't trust the cities, didn't want to live there, didn't want to be that far removed from where he felt most comfortable (in *country*) until he heard Los Angeles was hiring, the Water fellas were, recruiting Pinkertons at the same pay to stay in Owens Valley and police the water system working for L.A.

A way to stay in country among decent simple people, still get paid.

So he'd volunteered.

Couple of the other Pinkertons went over, too, and he'd partnered up with this one fella came from Stockton so they had the same background same way of speaking same make-sense on life.

McCloud.

He and Snow had patrolled together—McCloud driving; Snow on shotgun—roomed together at the Dow and when McCloud went up to Stockton to his wife and son on furlough, he always asked if Snow would like to come along.

They'd been out on the valley floor one day—what they had to do was drive around make sure no one was tampering, make sure there were no animals inside the weirs, nothing bunging up the flow of water—and once a week they took water samples, Snow's least favorite part of what they had to do—water samples for the science boys which meant getting down beside the ditches with your jacket off, your sleeve rolled up and dipping in with glass jars and they took turns at this, McCloud and Snow, neither one the keener owing to the fact they had to crouch down on all fours to do it.

They'd been out there and it had been Snow's turn to take the water sample and he'd slipped the empty jar along the surface when a mother raccoon, alarmed at his intrusion on her litter of kits, rose out of the brush and, without warning, attacked his arm—scratching at it with her paws and latching to him with her tiny teeth and articulated jaw, she must have weighed fifteen, twenty pounds—these things are *huge*—the force of her attack knocking him onto his back—

Kill it! he'd cried out to McCloud, "for Godsake *shoot!*" but McCloud couldn't get a sure bead on the coon as the two rassled until Snow held up his free hand and McCloud tossed the rifle to him and Snow whipped it 'round and stuck the end of the barrel close-range to the coon's broadside and pulled the trigger. Killed it.

Nothing left but flyin' fur and splattered guts and blood and half the raccoon's jaw embedded in Snow's arm.

McCloud had the presence of mind *thank God* to wrap his handkerchief above the wound and haul Snow to the car where he had a flask beneath the seat—Snow never drank—which he emptied on Snow's mangled flesh while he sped across the hardpan.

I'm not gonna make it, Snow remembers thinking, not that the wound would kill him but because he didn't think he could withstand the pain. Thirteen miles to Lone Pine, to Doc Bridges and who's to say he'd be there when they arrived, that some Shoshone squaw on the reservation wasn't halfway through her labor or that Doc hadn't been called down to Olancha at a death-bed. Snow had been chivvying himself to stay alert when, in less than a couple of minutes, McCloud plowed the Water Department coupe into a yard of chickens and Shoshone women weaving baskets behind a large white adobe structure, hit the horn and jumped out to wrangle Snow onto his feet.

"Where are we?" Snow remembers asking.

"At the *clinica*."

'—*where?*"

"Three Chairs."

Two squaws came running and picked Snow's legs up and with McCloud carried him through a wooden gate into a courtyard and then inside a cool low-roofed building into what appeared to be a "doctor's office" where they sat him on a raised padded table and a small dark-haired woman in a white coat appeared and very gently touched his arm.

McCloud had done the talking, told her what had happened and, when she'd asked him, told her Snow's name.

She'd talked with a funny accent, hard to understand.

She'd tried to touch Snow's arm again and, despite the pain, he pulled back.

Are you a doctor? he remembered asking.

She'd smiled at him:

I *am*.

She had a pretty smile.

"—there's my certificate to practice, and my diploma . . ."

She pointed toward two framed pieces of paper on the wall neither one of which he was capable of reading. One had a circle of gold foil on it, the other had a ribbon and for all Snow knew each one could just as well have said PRIZE BULL.

She'd got in close and started picking at his wound with tweezers and cotton gauze and while she'd worked she'd asked him to describe the animal that attacked him.

Coon, Snow had repeated.

"Well, Mr. Snow"—every word she uttered, even though straight English, sounded *really* foreign—"have you taken any medications in the past? Have you had any problems with them?"

She'd asked him to show her his tongue.

Then she'd lifted his eyelid and shined a tiny light into his eye.

She stepped back and asked him, "Do you have any trouble seeing, Mr. Snow?"

No.

She'd stared at him the way he'd seen his mother stare at men when she knew that they were lying.

"Eyesight's perfect," he'd declared, looking over at McCloud more than straight at her.

She'd stared at him until he reckoned she had got his gist and then she'd gone on working, talking about a cream that was going to make his arm numb and about sewing him all back together again and then about the rabies. "I'm going to start you on a rabies series . . . first one's a little painful, it will make your muscles sore . . . you'll have to come back for another every week for four weeks . . . or you can go see Doctor Bridges if you want. In town. He'll charge you a dollar for each one."

How much are *you* gonna charge me?

Nothing. This is a free clinic. But you can buy a basket from one of the Shoshone women on your way out. Or you can make a donation . . .

The cream had started to make his arm go numb and she started sewing his skin back together and he'd turned his head away just in time to see a giant of a man outfitted for a bronco bust, leather gloves and Stetson hat and chaps, standing in the doorway like he'd been warned before never to step in.

What the hell's a goddamn L.A. Water coupe doing outside here in my backyard?

The man turned to McCloud and demanded of him, Is it *yours?* but before McCloud could answer the doctor lady started talking to him in that foreign language without turning around, using pleasant laughter to make like the story she was telling was a piece of entertainment or a fairy tale. Went on for like a stitch or two.

Well it goddamn better be a case of Life or Death, the tall man said. Pulled his gloves off and Snow saw the hand.

The doctor lady went on talking in her lingo, never turning 'round, and

Snow remembered in the middle of her strange words he thought he'd heard her say "raccoon" and then the tall man—*Rhodes*—answered her in English, Oh hell yes you have, we saw them in Yosemite, the animals with *masks* the ones you said had tiny hands.

The doc lady had laughed at that and asked something else in her foreign lingo to which Rhodes had answered English, Christ *yes* they're rabid. Rabid as the day is long! Then he'd looked Snow straight in the face—never recognized him!—and said I hope you appreciate this woman here has saved your life.

When he'd left, she looked at Snow from where she was working on his arm and had smiled, again, at him and said, "—*my husband*," as if that would explain it.

And he *had* appreciated what she'd done—he *had*—it was just the two things that bothered him that kept him from going back, the first being that she was a woman and he didn't like a woman touching him (and looking at his eyes) and the second was that by that time he'd started to erect a real resentment, *nurse* it, toward the Criminal Trespass.

Sometime around the next month he'd been walking up Main Street in Lone Pine one morning for his coffee and he'd heard his name and she'd come running from the bank across the street, saying Mister Snow Mister Snow how are you, Mister Snow, grabbing at his arm and pulling up his sleeve to have a look in front of the whole town.

Oh my, she'd said.

—and she'd run her finger on the scar like she was reading it in Braille.

"This is healing nicely . . . Who took the stitches out?"

Doc Bridges, he'd explained.

She'd been nice about it. Hadn't given him a hard time.

"And the rabies inoculations?"

"Yes, ma'am."

"That's very good, Mr. Snow. I'm glad you're in good health."

"Doc said he'd never seen such fancy stitching. Like a work of art, he said."

She'd laughed:

"Well inside every Frenchwoman there's a seamstress."

"—'French'?" he'd said.

"That's me! From *France*! But now I am American as you, American as apple cake—! You come and see me if you ever want to have those eyes of yours examined . . ."

She'd started to walk away but Snow had called to her, Hold up.

He'd reached for the billfold in his back pocket and she'd said, "Why that's very kind of you, Mr. Snow," thinking he was going to donate money and then he was embarrassed and gave up a dollar but really what he'd gone for was the ring which for some reason he'd kept there for safe-keeping since the Trespass incident almost, then, two years ago.

When he'd handed it to her she'd seemed taken by surprise.

"I found out 'Louisiana' is your name," he'd said.

A change had happened on her like a change in weather.

"Where did you get this, Mr. Snow?"

"It came to me."

He could see the friendly going out of her.

"I'm tempted to inquire why you kept something that you knew had special value to someone—why you kept it for so long—but my better instinct is to rejoice and thank you—thank you, Mister Snow, for its safe return."

That had been the last time she'd spoken to him.

He'd seen her around town, from a distance—never making eye contact—and once maybe a year after that one time on Main Street, he'd seen her from the diner window passing by outside all pregnant and he'd had to look away, his cheeks all hot.

Sometimes he'd see the Trespass, see him on his horse out on his land, see him riding fences with his dogs or loading goods into his truck in town and he made it his business to be special alert along the water ditches bordering Three Chairs, along the boundaries where Water property sat right up against the Trespass land.

Must have been a year or so went by, maybe three, and he joined McCloud like usual for breakfast one morning and McCloud had bought *The Inyo Register* and it was folded right there on the table and on the front page, face up, there had been a picture of doc lady in what looked to be her wedding dress inside a thick black border.

McCloud by that time knew about Snow's reading. He knew a little, too, about what Snow could and couldn't see.

She *died*, McCloud had said.

That's not the way God works, Snow remembers having thought right then:

If God was going to punish someone then God would punish Trespass.

Or maybe that's what God had done.

Polio, McCloud had said. Picked it up out by the Shoshones, that's what folks in town are saying. Goddamn injuns. Hookworm, ringworm, gonorrhea, pinworm, *polio*. Can't trust a people who wear *blankets* where they go to church.

Maybe he had shed a tear—truth was, he could not remember—there'd been no funeral to attend, as such, the Trespass keeping folks away.

After a while another woman had come to be associated with him—*giant* woman, giant as the Trespass himself and uglier than sin—and Snow would see her toting the doc lady's two children around—twins, neither of whom had her dark hair nor her smile.

What happens when the pay is good and the job permits you riding all around the country in a car—and lately in a *truck*: you stay with it, send good money back home to the folks, don't get lazy, necessarily, don't get *fat*, but, still, you doze off in your mind, ambition does, you sorta start to forget what took you out of where you'd started from in the first place, sorta start to think the fight for that Greater Good had moved its combat elsewhere, someplace where the livin' weren't so easy.

He'd see the lady doc's kids in town, the son especially, always broad and loud and showing off and then one night he and McCloud had been assigned an unexpected patrol (they had both gotten, it had to be said, pretty *old* among the new boys on the job) and they'd been coming down along the ditch from Independence right there north of Lone Pine when they'd seen the elephant.

They'd heard there were some elephants in town—Bobby Kaye had brought them in, the same Bobby Kaye who'd hired him a decade—no, *two*—ago, to make another movie, not a Western this time, something about Romans, Snow hadn't been too sure. Kaye had got these elephants up here by train in time for the Fourth of July Parade on Main Street where the whole town could see 'um and then he'd hired that Mex kid from the apple orchard there in Manzanar to roust them. Kept the elephants at the foot of the Alabama Hills out on the Whitney Portal road.

McCloud and he had been driving south along the ditch from Independence where it goes right up against the service road to Lone Pine and at like three, four in the morning, still dark, before the dawn, they'd come up on this elephant.

And Eddy's Cadillac.

And the two boys.

What the hell these boys thought they were doing at that time of night with the elephant and Cadillac and all, to this day Snow didn't know.

But the one thing that he does know is that the boys had been there—despite what everybody testified. He'd bet his Yellow Boy on it.

The boys had been there—Snow had seen them, he had seen them with his very *eyes*, the Mex kid with the elephant the Rhodes kid with the Cadillac all brash and loud and *drunk* and dancin' in front of them like what McCloud and him were doin' what their *job* was somethin' bootless and disputable in the kid's opinion like he and McCloud were Trespassers, themselves, on this kid's birthright, on this kid's land.

The whole thing looked suspicious and McCloud had told him—which he'd *never* told him—"Get your gun out, Snow."

Start of summer, couple months before, their trucks had been outfitted with these new lights on top, high-watt tungsten lamps like on tugboats in New York Harbor and San Francisco Bay and the joke McCloud had made when he first tested them was that the Man in the Moon must hafta blink each time a driver turned them on. They were new and they were *blinding* but they lit up everything in the foreseeable and they gave the dark a depth of field Snow needed if he was gonna meet the challenge with his gun.

Lights, he remembers saying to McCloud as he got out.

After that, the things that he remembers don't break down in parts but swim around inside his memory like an evaporating liquid. Like an ice cube melting.

Soon as the lights went on the elephant went vertical, rose up on its hind feet to twice, three times its height and let out that banshee scream you only hear in jungle movies, *Tarzan* and *King Kong*.

Mex had had a little harness on him, a thin rope which tore right off and Snow was looking straight up into the belly of the beast its forelegs like the swinging claw of a steam shovel pawing in the air and *shoot!* his mind was telling him just *kill* the thing so he let go the first one, aimed and shot and caught it, he thought, right where its beasty heart should have been between the front legs high up in the torso maybe *too* high because the thing went on a rampage after that like it had just been woken up from dead by its adrenaline and it was all that Snow could do to stay on his feet keep pounding bullets at it pounding ammunition, 'til it dropped.

Two broken ribs, four cracked ones, a perforated lung.

They said if he'd been out there longer he'd have died, plain suffocation.

You don't ever want an elephant to land on you.

Nothing to remember of the trip to Los Angeles down to the hospital the Water bosses used. He'd cracked a jaw, too, so that had been braced up. When he'd finally got awake he couldn't talk so they told him he could *write* but that was no use whatsoever. You don't think when you're a boy out shooting crows an elephant will land on you but that's what had happened to him sure as shootin' out of nowhere, middle of life.

When they'd handed him a slate and the piece of chalk he'd drawn the dots to spell MCCLOUD and they'd had to find someone who could translate Braille to sound it out, and then the men in suits had come to ask him questions and they told him that his friend—McCloud—"had not survived the elephant."

That's what they'd said: had not survived the elephant.

The elephant was dead, too.

Six bullets.

Through his clamped jaw Snow had been able to communicate *What about the Mex?*

What "Mex"?

What about the Rhodes kid?

A man was dead—a good man with a wife and son in Stockton; a son who'd now grow up without a father—and Snow needed to be told that justice would be done. Instead different men in suits had come to take his testimony, "*de*-pose" him, they'd said, because the owner of the elephant (Bobby Kaye had rented it and Bobby Kaye had not purchased the insurance that he'd said he had) was suing Bobby Kaye and Bobby Kaye was suing the Department of Water, Snow specifically, for killing the elephant.

But we're behind you, they had said: Picking up the cost on this—lawsuit and the hospital—and we're holding your old job for you should you still want it.

The Greater Good.

McCloud was dead—and had been for five weeks—and Snow had not been able to attend his funeral nor say a word about him, not that he would have stood up in front of people but he would have spoken to the boy and spoken to the missus about the kind of man his friend had been and all this paper and *de*-posing for an *elephant* just wasn't right. Snow had not been the one who'd set the night's events in motion: it had been the Rhodes kid and the Mex kid and Ron Eddy's Cadillac.

Problem was: the evidence.

There had been no evidence that there had been anyone or anything else there except Snow, McCloud, their truck and the rampaging elephant.

The Rhodes boy hadn't even been in town the night it happened—when they'd questioned his father at Snow's insistence, the Trespass had confided that his son had left for New York that same day and then on to England where he still was.

And the Mex boy had gone back to Mexico to see where he'd come from.

And Ron Eddy's Cadillac was in Ron Eddy's widow's garage where it had always been.

Liars.

And on top of all of that the other problem was macular *de*-something. Macular degenerates.

Before they'd let him go, once the ribs were healing enough to let him breathe and once he got some breath back in the perforated lung, this one doctor had come to check him out and told him he was going blind. Seventy percent, he'd said. Snow was seeing "seventy percent" inside his "visual field." And it will only get worse, he'd said.

What did *he* know:

It hasn't gotten any worse in twenty years, Snow had told him.

"Well I can't let you get behind a wheel or operate machinery," the doc told him.

That was fine: he didn't operate machinery anyway and he had a driver who could drive. New partner named Coop who was nice enough but no McCloud. Two years on the job, formerly along the Colorado side, the other aqueduct. Bit stand-offish 'til Snow shot six aspirin in quick succession just to show him, shot six aspirin outta the sky, *de*-materialized the suckers in plain sight right before Coop's eyes where they'd been standing by the road in Lone Pine first day back on the job.

Still had it.

He'd been thankful to the Company for place-keeping his spot—he didn't need it; he was set up pretty good with what he'd put aside—he was grateful for their loyalty to him but the reason he had come back on the job, the real reason to return to Owens Valley was to sort this out, do justice.

He couldn't rest couldn't sleep some nights and he'd started to see *they*'d had enough, too, the other boys on his and Cooper's crew, see they'd had enough of him going on and on about the Mex and the Rhodes kid and the Cadillac like a mongrel in his lonesome corner working at a thorn in his paw. They'd pull back—not physically but in their manner—whenever he was in their midst like that time with the lady doc there on the street in Lone Pine before she died. Not Coop so much, Coop could tolerate him but the rest thought he was a little *loco* that he'd gone clear off his head.

Some nights—they were few—but *some* nights even *he*'d begun to think that maybe he was bats that the whole thing was what the docs explained was an "aberration" in his brain from the time he'd been lying beneath the elephant with his "reduced intake of oxygen." All about the *oxygen*, he'd learned. It's "oxygen" that fires up the brain.

He still got winded.

As a result.

They'd told him that he'd find his breathing harder at high altitudes the higher that he went the harder on his lung so for a bit there at the beginning of his "recovery" he'd started asking Coop to take him up the Whitney Portal road, drive them higher so Snow could sit up there awhile, put pressure on his lung, and then after the pain of the first few times he'd started to feel—inside—he'd started to feel his old self returning started to feel the lung like a patched bellows filling up with fresh air and blowing vigor back into the world.

Then of course the war and all.

That had changed a lot of what was going on in Owens Valley when all the Japs had been shipped in.

Stories on the radio about the way people were dying over there, people worried about boys they knew, their sons and cousins, nephews, called up to do the thing expected of them, for the Greater Good, the world, this world, had just—he had to admit it—got away from his understanding and all these things they wear on you, the widows and injustices, they take a toll.

So he'd put in his notice.

For twenty years he had tithed himself, keeping 10% of every payday for himself and sending the rest back home. And he could still drive a tractor, couldn't he? Despite the macular degenerate. Across some land he owned, across familiar ground.

Rice and millet, flatland. Maybe put in some alfalfa.

Coop had helped him set it up, the road trip home, passing Snow along among the Water boys they knew—there were Water boys on every inch of California—passing Snow along one town to the next like a packet on the Pony Express one good ol' boy to another 'til he made it all the way back home.

But first he had in mind to say so long to the Sierras.

McCloud had once told him that the snowcap—sitting there on top of all those mountains—the snowmelt off all that provided a full third of the water in the state of California—drinking water, laundry water, bathing water, irrigation: *one-third*. Just sittin' there. As snow.

Where he'd come up was flatland all around you could kinda see Mount Shasta in the distance but everything was flat and he was going back to where a mountain and its harder-to-breathe air would be lost things to him so he had got this idea in his head to finish with a couple nights up there, alone, and he packed a light tuck and some minimal grub and ammunition and got Coop to drive him up to where the road ran out at nearly seven thousand feet.

"You gonna be okay up here for three nights, buddy?"

Snow had told him, Sure.

"'Cause I'll come lookin' forya—"

"I know you would."

"And don't get up above the tree line there's no water up there. And watch out for bear."

He'd passed Snow a map which was a useless thing to do but Snow had taken it from him because he'd understood that if he didn't Coop's feelings would be hurt.

First night had been a little rough he hadn't counted on the clouds, the darkness, and the sounds the mountains made but he could feel the *oxygen* at work. He liked it. Second night he'd trekked too far and got himself above the tree line where he couldn't feel his fingertips—blind-sided in that unexpected way from too much altitude—and he'd spent the whole night waiting for the dawn against this one lone pine which dropped its cones one or two an hour all night long keeping him awake, still he felt *great* at grey light, *great* to greet the dawn—*oxygen*-ated—full of newfound pep.

He'd started down as soon as there was light and within an hour he could see a blue lake not too distant—there were lakes up here hidden in the bowls between the peaks brimming with that icy clean snowmelt water—and he got Coop's map out, puzzled over it and finally figured it must be the one they called Lone Pine Lake over to the north above the town and he made for it.

Got below the tree line in another half an hour, got among the white-barked trees and scattered skree and knee-high brush and yellow flowers. He could see a cabin on the northern shore, there was white smoke on the lake itself but a rope of blue smoke from a fire was snaking below, and he could see a dog running up and down the shoreline scaring up some birds.

A man came out on the porch and threw something toward the dog then went down the cabin steps toward where a small boat had been pulled ashore.

Binoculars were useless to Snow's eyes—*large* intervening shadows—but he could manage with one eye on a single *de*-tached rifle scope and he went down a little farther, careful not to show himself, and hid along the ground behind a rock and had a look.

The man had on some kinda hat—straw, it looked; *sun*hat—and he was wearing a blue shirt and a fishing vest, regular-type pants and some kind of lightweight shoes—not boots—and he was rigging out the boat with rods and a lure box, some nets . . . the dog was prancing beside the boat—handsome dog, Snow made her out as a pointer—but the man waved her off and signaled her to Stay and he pushed the boat out and started up the motor.

Snow could barely hear the faint *put put* but then, as it headed through the sifting mist into the center of the lake the stippled rhythm of the motor rose into the air and came to him.

He gave his eye a rest. The boat, still far away, was near enough to make out through the thinning fog upon the water, maybe he should make himself known, call out to the man and spend the morning fishing have himself some fried-up bacon and a cup of coffee which, in his hunger, he thought he smelled—

Must be flies out there the man had taken off his hat to swat the air.

And show his face.

Snow could not believe his eyes.

—he trusted them but this was too good to be true he needed the scope to verify which, indeed, before the man, the *tall* man with the white ponytail, put his hat back on, the scope did. Verify.

Well wasn't this the gas.

Pure oxygen.

The Trespass and him, alone, out here in the middle of God's whole creation.

Him and Rhodes.

And Yellow Boy.

Wouldn't it just be the cat's *peejays* to shoot the dang hat off his head in
the middle of the lake!
Outta nowhere!
—wouldn't have a clue!
It was a trick Snow had performed a thousand times.
He'd have to get closer, and it would still be at the far end of the range that
Yellow Boy could handle, but it would be worth it.
For the Greater Good if not for the sheer oxygenated fun of it.
What a send-off.
What a thing to brag about to Coop and all the boys.
What a thing to put his mind to rest at least, at last: to even up the score.
Careful not to move too quick and not to make a sound, he got himself
farther down more toward the lake but still above it, waiting for the mist to
lift, to clear.
Rhodes had cut the motor and set up two lines.
Snow waited.

What he'd always done, what he'd counted on, his magic gift, was he'd line the
Target up and stare at it until it pressed itself into his mind and he could close
his eyes and see it, he could close his eyes and it would be there like a picture
like the thing itself and then he'd take a breath and let it out real slow and then
when his lungs were empty and he felt the need real bad to take a breath he'd
spring his eyes back open as he touched the trigger and the thing would fall.
The trick with shooting hats off is you have to get right under where the
brim ends, at the side of it or at the edge in front—not *at* it you don't aim *at*

the brim you want the bullet to whiz by not *touch*, exactly, but sort of race along beneath the brim like a skipping stone on water: *skimming*, knocking the hat up and backwards in its wake.

Aim *beneath* the brim, in this case along the outer left, send the hat careening right, shooting from behind.

The sun was up now, full-on—mist gone—so Snow shouldered his gun.

And stared.

Target absolutely set and still inside his mind.

He closed his eyes, inhaled the sharp clean air and exhaled all at once, snapping his eyes open to the world to see the Target had stood up.

No no no no no, he thought.

But he had already stroked the trigger.

Filling up the granite bowl the lake was in there was a loud report like a tree branch cracked by lightning like a tree cracked down its middle, there must have been a splash Snow couldn't hear and then the dog began to bark and barked and barked and kept on barking.

the tenth property
of thirst
is
the taste of the inevitable

THE CATHOLIC CHURCH ON THE SOUTH SIDE OF THE HOTEL had been razed and a large parking lot constructed in its stead along with a "motor annex," an L-shaped wing built on the motel model where guests could drive up to their rooms and park out front, a design, the aesthetic of which escaped Schiff, newly returned from Japan to what felt more and more like a foreign country—because the view from every room of the new annex was the parking lot. And cars.

The old lobby had been reconfigured with the recessed reception desk positioned by the door so people arriving in their cars didn't have to walk the extra distance or succumb to the sensation that they were actually in a building, with a history.

This, he supposed, was postwar prosperity.

Or something like it.

Schiff had driven to Lone Pine down from San Francisco in a new 1947 Plymouth coupe that he had purchased with his mustering-out bonus. He had seen it through, Japan's Constitution, working under MacArthur's unrelenting eye. Four years of polishing language into something he could be proud of, something important. Manzanar, as it had been, was gone—except in his memory. Nothing left on the land but the stone gatehouse like a sentinel protecting a territory of ghosts. A yellow cloud from the dry lakebed hung over the landscape like steam from a locomotive. Across the road, Three Chairs was sequestered behind a locked gate and an electrified fence along its perimeter. Schiff parked on the road and walked the edge of it, looking for an opening but the fence appeared to be unbroken; on the other side, the landscape was as empty as the camp. He stood and looked in at it, trying to imagine his way back in time. He felt lost here, but that had always been the case—lost and far from shore. This was Sunny's territory, and he was only now understanding that he had expected to find her here, waiting for him. But it had been more than four years since he'd last heard from her, a telegram sent to him in the Pacific, yellow envelope from Western Union, which had raised his CO's ire.

The message had featured a headline of run-on letters, ciphers—transmission codes—an entire prologue of them, then, halfway down the page:

DARLING,

Schiff had felt the CO's gaze.

DARLING,

ROCKY GONE.

COME HOME.

NEED YOU.

SUNNY

"Do you know the wait-time between General MacArthur sending me a telex from PAC-HQ and it landing on my desk here, Major?" the CO had asked him.

"No, sir."

"Standard: one to three days. Urgent: eighteen to twenty-four hours."

WASP eyes, the remoteness of which Schiff had never learned to translate.

"And if my wife in Pasadena needs to contact me by telegram—God knows why she ever would—do you think she would be able to?"

Schiff was betting no but he could never tell what was up with WASP rhetoricals. Should he answer? With Jews—you ask to God? you answer your own question. God may be listening but God is busy. God has other things to do.

Ceiling fan, above them, was the only noise.

"You, nevertheless; *you* . . ."

When was the last time Schiff had heard "nevertheless" in spoken conversation.

Oh, yeah. He remembered:

Law school.

"—you, on the other hand, in the middle of the war, in the middle of the Pacific, can get a telex through channels inaccessible to *me*. How is that? How did you *do* that? Who the hell are *you*?"

Ceiling fan, again.

'Round and 'round.

The WASP rhetorical.

"So I pulled your service record—not enlightening. Easy duty. Combat, none. No clues there. Desk-jockey. So what I have to ask you, Major, is: who the hell is *she*?"

Who the hell indeed? He couldn't answer. He wasn't sure that he had ever known.

"Please tell me 'Rocky' isn't someone's *dog*."

"*No, sir.*"

The CO continued:

"Your service record tells me you're not married."

"No, sir."

"So who's this 'Sunny'?"

It was easier to lie:

"Fiancée, sir. Rocky is her father."

The CO drilled his eyes into Schiff:

"Here's what I suggest you do." He looked at his watch. "I suggest you step outside to my adjutant's office and write this girl an answer. I'll have to read it, the censors will have to give it their OK, but if you get it done in the next ten minutes I'll put it on tonight's plane, Stateside, with the confidential mail. She'll have it in two days."

"Thank you, sir."

In lieu of shaking hands the two of them saluted.

And Schiff was left staring at the clock and a blank page.

He took the telex and re-read it, not the words in CAPITALS, those words had seared themselves into his memory, but the coded stuff up top, a cipher trail identifying where the message had originated, what it had gone through, where it had been. From all the coded gobbledygook he could at least decipher WASH-DC and SECY WAR—a sign that no less a force than Aunt Cas had engineered this. Her fingerprints were there, except on the actual message itself. It—to the point, succinct—was Sunny's.

COME HOME.

She must have known it was impossible.

NEED YOU.

She must have known this was a final plea.

Because Sunny had never admitted to needing anyone.

Eight minutes.

DARLING

He had never called her "darling." "Darling" was hers, an affectation influenced by Cas, or class, or reading English novels. Depending on his mood or on his state of mind, or state of playfulness, he usually began his letters My heart's own or My heart's desire or (proving he'd read Kipling) Best Beloved. Dearest, he now wrote, stopping himself from Dearest Sunny because it sounded somber. Dearest . . .

Your letter   Your message   I am   Your shocking words   news leaves me   shocked   and grief-stricken

Something about wanting more than anything to be beside her in her time of greatest need

Something about the war

Inconsolable,

Signing it, as always,

Schiff.

He handed the unsealed envelope to the CO's adjutant who made him sign a form authorizing a deduction for the transmission of the message from his pay.

He looked at the clock.

He'd written it in under two minutes.

He stared at the thin envelope on the adjutant's desk, on which his handwriting seemed too confident, too cheerful

> SUNNY RHODES
> THREE CHAIRS
> LONE PINE, CALIFORNIA
> U.S.A.

As they say about the end of things in Army talk: *That's all she wrote.*

He'd fucked up. He knew he had. He hadn't found the right tone, right words; he hadn't even said he loved her.

Praise the lord and pass the bullets: this goose is cooked.

The fire's out.

She's *done.*

The wire perimeter surrounding Three Chairs brought to mind his mother's prohibition *Don't Touch, Don't Touch* and her fear of Life. A landscape of restricted areas. A Los Angeles Department of Water and Power truck pulled off the road, the driver looked familiar, but it was only when he got out of the vehicle that Schiff remembered who he was: Coop. He didn't look well, gait unsteady, eyes bloodshot and bleary. At first, he didn't seem to recognize Schiff, but as the other man drew closer, Coop's lips curled into a tight and sullen grin.

"This is owned by the Department now," he said, by way of greeting. "You're trespassing on Los Angeles land."

Coop coughed and spat onto the dry earth of the roadside, a clot of mucus laced with blood. He pressed his chest and coughed again, more blood this time, a thin and slimy trail.

"Are you okay?" Schiff asked but Coop waved him off.

"It's nothing," he said. "Just something going 'round."

Coop glanced up at the sky—the air was thick and yellow—then lowered his gaze to Schiff again. "Your girlfriend don't live here no more. She left after the old man died, had to sell the place."

"To the Department?" Schiff asked.

"The old man didn't get a say. He went a little off his rocker at the end there, giving all his money to the Japs, before he killed himself."

"Killed himself?"

"Yeah. Didn't you know?" Coop barked out a short, sharp laugh. "Guess you and her weren't so close as you thought."

For a moment, Schiff said nothing. Then: "Do you know where she went?"

Which was how he ended up at the Dow, after Coop suggested that he'd have to ask in town. Schiff walked back to the Plymouth without another word, feeling the other man's eyes on him, until he drove away.

At the hotel, Schiff was greeted by a callow-seeming youth.

No Phyllis, as before.

No discernable judgmental attitude.

Just a young man dripping Hospitality.

Hello there! what can we do for you this afternoon?

I'd like a roo—

A phone rang in the office behind the desk and the young man raised a finger and went to answer it.

When he came back, he cocked his head as if to prompt Schiff's purpose:

"Looking for a room tonight," Schiff said.

"Are you with them?"

"—who?"

"The movie people."

"Movie people?"

"—maybe with the Water people?"

"No."

"—because I've got those people doubled-up three and four a room: we're full. Honestly I haven't got a vacancy for weeks. Maybe try in Independence. It's only fifteen minutes, glad to give the hotel up there a call—"

"—no. Thank you. I— Is there a public phone somewhere—?"

"—left out the door, can't miss it in the parking lot." The young man hauled up an unofficial-looking cash box from beneath the counter and told Schiff, "I can change a bill for you," and Schiff pulled a single from his wallet and asked What's the movie's name? while the kid was counting out the dimes.

Schiff clutched the coins in his left fist and stepped inside the booth and dialed the Operator and asked her for Long Distance and then asked to be connected to any number in Santa Barbara County, California, for a Lyndon Finn or a Caswell Finn or the Finn Ranch and then the Operator told him Hang up and stay put and that she'd ring him right back with the connection.

While he was waiting he surveyed the lot—four trucks with the Department of Water and Power shield printed on them, two limousines and several late-model streamlined coupes. A Chevy with its top down pulled in while he was waiting—a brand-new '47 burgundy white-walled Fleetmaster drop top with the camel interior—and he knew he recognized the driver, if not her car, he'd seen her before, probably in town, but what with her sunglasses and the scarf over her hair he couldn't make an absolute ID—he *knew* her—so he smiled and gave a friendly wave. She smiled back and sent a sharp salute in his direction which disconcerted him because even when he was still in uniform he never thought his manner signaled Army. She got out of the car—she was dressed in fluid slacks and a kind of man's shirt—and leaned into the back seat for an overnight bag and a small valise. Schiff called, "I'll handle that," but just as he stepped forward the telephone inside the booth began to ring and he gave her an apologetic shrug and she let out a distinctive laugh and said, "So much for American chivalry," and her voice sounded just like Katharine Hepburn's and then it hit him that this *was* Katharine Hep—

"I have that call for you now . . . if you'll deposit forty cents . . ."

The coins seemed to take forever to drop and their clatter into the little money vault was amplified both by the echo chamber of the booth and by the receiver and then there was a hollow silence in his ear as if he'd stuck his head into a well, a silence at the end of which he swore he could hear water.

"—hel-*lo?*" he said.

Another watery silence and then that unmistakable alto saying "Attorney Schiff! Well knock me over with a feather—!"

"Caswell Rhodes . . . or do I call you Caswell *Finn* these days?"

"'Aunt Cas' has always served us, my dear boy—and anyway we're living in sin, both too propertied to marry, the sole advantages would all go to the government—from where are you calling?"

"Lone Pine."

"*Lone* Pine—what the hell are you doing *there?*"

"Looking for Sunny."

"—what in godsname are you thinking, Sunny hasn't lived there since she sold Three Chairs, they've been up in Point Reyes Station for my god, two years—"

This time it was Cas who heard the silence.

"—you know she adopted that boy from camp . . . one of the orphans . . ."

"Cas . . . Sunny hasn't . . . I haven't had a letter back from Sunny since Rocky died."

"—Oh for godsake. Well you get up there and imprint some of your good sense on her, she has a restaurant going, the whole town is no larger than Lone Pine, it's about an hour north of San Francisco on the coast, you'll see it on the map."

There was a pause before Cas added, "That is some beautiful Constitution you wrote. Lyndon followed it in all the papers, recognized your fingerprints all over it—universal suffrage, 'lawfully prohibiting in perpetuity' a standing army in Japan—marvelous stuff!—. . . You served us well, Attorney Schiff: your nation thanks you . . ."

Another gap, and then: "Now, tell me all the tawdry news from Lone Pine . . ."

"Manzanar is gone. The camp."

"—knew that."

"—I mean, there's nothing there."

"Salted Carthage. What else?"

"There's another movie being made in town, and the Department of Water and Power is everywhere."

—laugh? The woman had a thunder no Norse god could emulate.

"Well," she told him, "that's as good a reason to get out of town as I can think of. You've got a drive ahead of you to get to Point Reyes Station. Remember, as my West Texas late-in-life shacker-upper is wont to say:

'Some love don't want for rain.' "

Schiff heard her disconnect and was left, like a survivor, standing in the corner of the claustrophobic booth listening to the hollow silence.

He drove all night, Lone Pine to Independence to Big Pine, Bishop to Mammoth Lakes. He crossed the Sierras north of June Lake, the Plymouth straining at the heights. Up there the air was thin and hard to breathe.

Maybe all mountains look the same from far enough away: at Manzanar some Japanese had whispered that Mount Whitney resembled "Fuji-san" because they needed that anchor for their imagination. To Schiff, arriving in Tokyo on Mount Fuji's plain beside the devastated city, the mountain had looked like an exotic *isolato* cut from the Sierras: the shape was clearly that of a volcano, Euclidian in its trigonometric precision like a theorized function unlike the smash and mass of the Sierras: the shape of God's temper tantrum, His warning to the world of what He could do with granite (forget volcanoes) when He got angry with real stone. The view from Tokyo of Fuji-san had reminded him of the time he had spent with the Sierras as his touchstone, as his daily view: Because he had needed something in that strange land to remind him of the life he had already lived, to connect him to the strangeness of the present so that he, too, like the devil mountain in the distance, did not become exotic in his own life, an *isolato* in his own landscape.

For his last approach to Tokyo, he'd come by sea and he had finally had the chance to be on the Pacific, see it face-to-face and witness its expanse. He'd been hoping this would make him feel heroic and historic. Instead, it made him feel puny and forlorn; alone and *lost at sea* and not a little terrified of its violent relentless maw. There were only other distant ships to interrupt its terrible monotony, and christ knew what horrors lay beneath. At night the thing was one enormous blackness and by day it posed an overwhelming threat to all his senses and it hadn't taken long for him to know beyond a shadow of a doubt that he didn't trust the ocean and that like other brainy Jews before him he was only comfy face-to-face with water when the waters parted. If there was Someone there to part them.

Maybe every ocean, like every mountain, is the same as every other, every ocean looks the same from far enough away:

Schiff thought this was probably the truth.

—really, when he thought about it, how is the Pacific, at its shores, that distinguishable a water from its twin a continent away: who the hell in his right mind standing on Bermuda or Tahiti can tell the hell the difference if he wasn't an ethnographer or a marine biologist? A sea by any other name is still a . . .

And maybe every *woman* is the same as every other, too, he thought:

If one is far enough away.

Distance reveals the shape of things.

He'd gone to the Tōhoku region outside the reach of the Bs' bombardment a few weeks before to prepare himself for Stateside, to reacquaint himself with a world outside a war zone, which he imagined California still was. He had wanted the mountains to be a peaceful landscape. But instead, the terrain there had looked like the Sierras to him and Sunny's memory haunted him. He had found himself at a *ryokan* in Ōkura village, where to his surprise he had met another round-eye, a boy named Rafi, maybe six years old. The boy was taller than the other children in the village, thinner, too, and his hair was thick and brown. Rafi hadn't appeared to be an orphaned street urchin; his clothes had been clean and he had seemed reasonably well-fed. He had never seen a "GI" before—Ōkura was so remote, there was no train service—but Schiff had been in the country long enough to recognize him as a mix-breed, half *gaijin*. Schiff had learned to speak some Japanese—enough to ask for directions or to order a meal or to navigate certain ceremonial boundaries—but with Rafi there were many gaps. Even so, the boy had kept coming around. Schiff had seen how he was ridiculed by the other villagers—not just by the children but also by the women and the men.

Once, walking through town with Rafi at his heels, Schiff had felt the surface of the earth lurch like it was trying to sit up and he'd watched as the boy had scrambled into the middle of the street toward the center of the danger and the ground had slid sideways in liquid paroxysms for five seconds before it had stopped.

Earthquake.

He'd stood in the middle of Ōkura and collected himself. People had come out of the low buildings of the village, chattering in tones that had sounded like relief.

Rafi had been laughing.

A tremor had run through Owens Valley one morning at Manzanar, as well, and Schiff had thought it was The End. The Californians, the internees, had stood laughing, same as Rafi, 'til it had been over, oddly giddy, having just survived the roller coaster.

Schiff laughed at the cosmic irony of what it would be like to survive the war and then die in a natural disaster. *Deus ex machina*—Mother Nature writing her own Jewish joke. What he remembered most was Rafi's palpable joy at surviving. As if the earthquake had been his own personal carnival ride. And how he'd undulated his arms like rolling waves, swaying his skinny hips 'round and 'round in celebration.

Schiff slept in the car stretched across the back seat, legs folded underneath him. The seat was hard and the air was cold; memory crowded around him like the blanket he wished he had.

Both Rocky and Cas had written sustaining letters to him in Hawaii, the bold flourishes of their handwriting vitalized by their individual florid inks. Cas had written to him about politics and social issues and sent him book reviews, while Rocky had written about the goddamn news in Lone Pine: hunters poaching elk in the Sierras to supplement the beef ration, the sudden rise of Sunkist-imported Mexican *braceros* in California as seasonal fruit pickers to replace the imprisoned Japanese-Americans, the fall of interest in the California courts to try his water case against Los Angeles, all of which he blamed entirely on the war. Rocky's letters, tight-knit with info, always ran beyond the wartime limit for airmail and came written on the kind of fiber-content paper rivaling the Declaration. His last letter told Schiff Dr. Arakawa from Manzanar had finally assembled the data to point to an increase in pulmonary distresses in the internees, induced by airborne particulates from Owens Lake—things were looking up for a renewed case against L.A. Water. He was going fishing up in the Sierras for a while. So don't worry when a letter doesn't come.

In the middle of the night, in a fitful dream, he'd had the sensation that a woman was touching him—her hand on his back, tenderly at first, but then slowly more insistent and forceful, as if he were being shoved. "Stop," he'd said, or had meant to say. "Sunny, stop," her spoken name was the sound that had cut him loose from sleep.

Light, a blade, teased a corner of the horizon. He lit a cigarette. The smoke tasted like oats, or maybe that was wishful thinking. He was hungry. Only thing to do was come down from the mountains past Half Dome and west through Stockton and Modesto, find a diner before heading to the coast. He ate when he stopped for gas, real eggs and fresh-brewed coffee. He barely noticed as the landscape changed—mountains to softly crumpled hills. He got to Point

Reyes mid-afternoon, a town so insignificant it hardly appeared a town at all, and parked along Main Street: a saloon, a dry goods store, a garage. At three in the afternoon the streets were as empty as Ōkura's had ever been.

He sat for a moment listening as the engine ticked down. What if Sunny didn't want to see him? What if she didn't want to have anything to do with him? What if . . . he remembered something she had said as they'd slept under the stars in the Sierras, his mind still occupied with war: "*Do not suffer future pain.*"

He had learned in law school that one day you are going to be called upon to make a speech. One day, too, at the death of a friend or of a parent, at the birth of your child, on first falling in love or defending your life—you are going to need to find the words to describe what you are feeling, to communicate the fullness of what feels like the Indescribable inside of you, a vortex or a fire or a fog, or, quite simply, the shape of your own soul. Stand and deliver. And at these moments, you don't want to get it wrong. You don't want to reach inside yourself and come up: wordless. You want, because you owe it to yourself, to shape something from nothing, to be able to drag meaning from the silence, being from non-being. Language should light the wick of image in the mind, strike the match that lights the candle, kindle action, thought. Language should be brought to testify before the courtship ends; it should raise the roof, swear to the proof, profess its credibility. He had lost his voice with Sunny in his telegram, and their conversation had ended, the written word proving deadlier than the spoken. And he'd be damned if he'd ever let that happen to him again and that was why he'd carved his words into the Japanese Constitution, and that was why he was here, back in this state, a state he never thought he'd see again:

California.

Do not suffer future pain.

He unfolded himself from the driver's seat and stepped out. A light wind was blowing off the Pacific. He caught a glimpse of himself in a store window, hair uncombed, jacket rumpled, pants that looked like he had slept in them. He wished there was a place for him to clean up. At the end of Main Street he saw a restaurant in a ramshackle Victorian—tall plate-glass windows, stairways leading to balconies, a structure built by committee. As he approached, he noticed three rocking chairs on the porch by the front door. He mounted the steps and tried the doorknob; it was locked. Through the window, he could see a dining room with a dozen tables and a fireplace, a bar curved along the back wall—Lou's had looked like this, snug and welcoming. He stepped back. Then he noticed the chairs again. Three chairs. The force of them almost brought him to his knees when he looked more closely and saw across the top of one of the chairs, his own name, like a placeholder, in Rocky's elaborate Gothic script.

He went around the side of the building where there was a yard in the back and a locked entry to the kitchen. Suspended in the kitchen window was a clear glass sphere full of water, a beam of multi-colored light refracting through it onto the wall. Sunny's kitchen. In the next room, he could see a long table covered with books.

The past is carried to us on simple things—a written page, a spoon, a glove, a bowl of water: carried by the souls who touched them, those plain relics emanate a language freed of time, a language without cadence—mute and eerie as the sound a granite planet makes giving birth to mountains, coursing its way through space.

Outside, around the front, a school bus stopped and discharged some children. They were shouting back and forth, kids cut loose, their voices crisp in the coastal air. Then one turned and started toward the porch with the three rockers and in that moment Schiff could not remember where he was. The kid was about six and a dead ringer for Rafi, hair thick and tousled, eyes wide and brown. Without thinking, Schiff greeted him in Japanese: *Konnichiwa*. Good day.

The boy seemed startled, but replied in kind.

"*Rafi?*" Schiff said, knowing that it couldn't be. Time had imploded on itself and he felt he was in two places in two *times* at once. The boy drew closer, and Schiff saw that he was taller than Rafi. He had stronger teeth. And American clothes.

"My name is Emerson," the boy said in English, intonation flat and drawn out in that California way. "But my mother says I'm not supposed to talk to strangers."

"Your mother's right," Schiff told him.

"So I guess I shouldn't talk to you. At least not until my mother gets home."

"Yes," Schiff agreed. "Or you could get to know me. Then I wouldn't be a stranger anymore."

He could see thoughts spinning in the kid's dark eyes.

"We'll just sit out here until your mother comes. In the meantime, you can ask me anything you want to know."

Emerson edged onto the porch and sat in the rocker closest to the steps. Schiff followed and sat in the chair next to him.

"That's my mom's chair," the kid said. "No one sits in it but her."

"Well then," Schiff replied. "We better keep it free for when she comes." He sidled along the porch to the last rocker, the one with his name on it and sat down. "How's this?" he asked: "Good thing you have three chairs."

"I don't know why," Emerson answered, "since there's only two of us. What should we talk about?"

"Well, what do you want to know?"

For a moment, the boy remained silent. Then, a smile began to flicker across his lips. "Okay," he said, "I have three questions. They're my Vox Tops. I ask everyone."

Vox Tops? Schiff wondered. Don't you mean *Vox pop*? But he let it go. No need to distract the kid. Better to play along.

"Everyone?" he asked. "I bet you don't get too many 'everyones' around here."

"Too many 'everyones'?" The boy laughed. Then his face grew serious.

"Okay," he said. "Here we go: Who's your favorite character in Shakespeare?"

Schiff's heart stopped. He could see himself back in the hall at Three Chairs, disarmed by the question. "Cordelia," he whispered, as if in the act of naming her, he had turned back time and could feel Rocky joining them on the porch.

"Man-in-the-Moon or Rabbit?" the boy asked next, and Schiff again felt the pull of *déjà vu*. He had the sense that he was under a spell here, and he did not want to break it, did not want to dissipate whatever was going on.

"Rabbit," he said, and smiled as Emerson asked the final question.

What's your idea of the Perfect Food?

Avocados, Schiff wanted to say, like Sunny had told him all those years ago. But before he could answer, he spotted a woman walking down the road in the near distance, a dog trailing behind her. She had short hair and wore a yellow dress and green galoshes, pulling a red wagon full of farm vegetables.

"Mom!" Emerson shouted and rushed down the steps to meet her.

Silence overtook Schiff. Language *lives*, and it is as old as water, he *knew* that, yet seeing Sunny now approaching him, he lost all words.

Unconditional surrender is what love is, not the treaty terms of defeat.

She knelt and talked to the boy as the dog ran loops around them. She stood again and fixed her eyes on Schiff.

"Sunny," he said, but his voice was just a mumble. She had turned to him in grief, with love, and he had not been brilliant. COME HOME, she'd requested, as if the war had been some big diversion that he could just walk away from when she needed him.

"*Sunny*," he whispered again.

She shook her head once, then looked behind her for the boy and the dog.

"Emerson," she said: "Why don't you and Esco go around the back?"

"Esco?" Schiff asked. This was not how he wanted to begin.

"The dog's name is 'Escoffier.'"

She pulled the wagon around the back, following Emerson and the dog. The boy was throwing sticks for Esco in the side yard when Schiff caught up. Sunny opened the kitchen door and scooped up an armful of carrots and carried them inside.

When she came back outside he still hadn't moved. She reached down for butter lettuce, cloves of garlic, corn on the cob, spinach.

"Ya' know," Schiff said, "this might be easier if . . ." But the way she looked back at him made him wish he'd held his tongue.

"Easier if what?" she asked. "How could I make your life more comfortable?"

He grabbed the remaining items from the wagon and followed her into the kitchen. On the stove, there was a ten-gallon pot of water. She struck a match and lit the burner to raise the water to a boil. The kitchen smelled of cooked meat and the earthy tincture of freshly-harvested produce.

"Staff doesn't show up 'til five," she said. "Less than two hours from now. First seating is six-thirty. So if you thought you might want to help me out, Mr. Schiff—"

"Why, yes, Miss Rhodes," he said, sarcastically. "What is it that you'd like me to do?"

Sunny backed away from the question and leaned into the refrigerator, shifting trays.

"Give me a hand with this." Her voice was so low he wasn't sure she'd spoken. She was gesturing at the stockpot, so he helped her wrestle it from the refrigerator onto the stovetop. The broth in it was translucent, like chicken stock, but smelled like the sea. Bits of seaweed floated in the pot.

"Turn the front burner up to simmer," she told him. When he didn't move or answer, she continued. "Come on, you can do that much."

"Is this—?" he asked.

"*Dashi,*" she murmured. "I learned to make it with the women. You remember. They came to Three Chairs."

At her direction, he made a few trips back and forth to the cold cellar under the house. At the back of the yard stood a small smokehouse, where he found salmon and goose breast she served as *carpaccio*. They worked together in silence. She avoided eye contact with him or any conversation.

Around four o'clock, she called in Emerson; they had a quick conversation and he went out again. Schiff watched as she glazed a tray of *poulets* with *dashi* and slid them in the oven. She pulled out tofu from the refrigerator and started cutting it into cubes. He watched her make a *dashi* sauce and set the tofu in small bowls, two pieces each, sprinkled with cut scallions.

She looked up and caught him staring.

"*What?*" she said, and when he did not respond, she went back to what she was doing.

Emerson returned, alone.

"Where's Char?" Sunny asked. "I told you to go get her."

"She's sick," the boy said.

"She can't be sick. I need her. Pie can't do it alone."

Pie, Schiff remembered. "She say, 'Come.'" The first time he had done what Sunny told him, come when she had called.

"Maybe I can help," he volunteered.

"It's the hired girl," Sunny told him. "Charlotte. Local kid. Helps with the bussing and the dishes. Apparently, she's taken ill."

"Well, *I'm* here," Schiff told her.

Sunny glared at him.

"*Now* you are," she said. "Fine, you want to help?" She gestured at the pans in the double sink. "As I recall, you know how to wash dishes. You can get started with these."

Service was as service always is: a complex and familiar dance. Mostly, they stayed out of one another's way, pirouetting in and out of the kitchen and into the dining room.

By nine-thirty, the last dinner plates had been cleared and the customers were gone. Schiff moved through the dining room collecting coffee cups and dessert plates. His shoulders ached, his apron was streaked with food. Sunny had hardly spoken to him all night, just told him what to do and when to do it, and he had followed through on everything she'd asked: washing, drying, plating, serving. It was as if both knew their steps, their movements, the way one part of the process yields to another. Pie had gone home after the tables had been cleared; she had not acknowledged him other than by a curt nod when she'd arrived for her shift. Emerson had come in to say goodnight around eight o'clock. Once he left, they were alone.

"Can you untie me?" Sunny asked. She turned her back to him and waited. He hesitated before going toward her. All night long she had given no indication that she wanted to engage with him, although they both knew she needed his help. She could have untied her own apron with little trouble, he thought; she couldn't be that tired, or that sore. He drew the white straps of the apron into his fingers and pulled on one of the loose ends, unraveling the bow. The cloth appeared to bloom, like a sail or a bird's wing.

"Thanks," she said, and shrugged the apron off.

Schiff untied his own apron, hanging it next to the sink.

"Thank you for your help tonight," Sunny told him, her voice softening for the first time. She neither looked at him nor looked away, but gazed off into the middle distance, as if she were remembering something from their past. She cracked her shoulder, finally fixing her eyes on him as if a decision had been reached. "Would you like some wine?" she asked.

Schiff assented without speaking, and she gathered a bottle and two glasses, waving him from the kitchen to the room with the long table. In the room, she occupied one of a pair of overstuffed wing chairs and gestured at him to take the other. She poured the wine, then untied her shoes and removed them. A silence settled.

Esco snuck in, trailing his canine motive behind him and insinuated his head onto Sunny's lap. She began to stroke behind his ears, making circular patterns in his fur until he relaxed beside her chair. She looked up at Schiff: "I didn't think you were coming back. I wish you hadn't taken so long." She took a drink and ran a hand across her eyes.

"I needed you. You let me down."

There it was, as much as she could say.

"I did the best I could. I went to Stryker's apartment." She didn't look up, but neither did she caution him to stop. "The Navy had to send someone to let me in. We walked through all the rooms, looking for—I don't know, for clues. We didn't find anything, or nothing that told us what had happened. I *did* find the jar of dirt you gave him from Three Chairs."

"Yes, I gave him that dirt," she said, remembering, "the night of the elephant."

She stood and looked at their empty glasses.

"I have a jar of it, too," she said, gesturing to a jar on the shelf above the bar. "I took it the day I left Three Chairs. All I have of the place now. I don't think I'll be going back."

"There's nothing there," Schiff said.

"My father's there," Sunny said. "Even though we never found him."

Schiff got to his feet and moved toward her but came up against a wall of silence, so turned to the table instead. There he saw piles of books in many languages—German, Spanish, Swedish, Italian, Latin, Greek, Leonardo da Vinci's *Notes on Cookery and Table Etiquette* . . . and then a line of French leather notebooks, still wrapped in tissue paper except for the used ones, labeled, in purple ink, MA CUISINE, Volumes 1, 2 and 3:

The cookbook Lou had been writing when she died:

The legacy Sunny had carried with her from Lone Pine.

Save this, he told himself.

"*Impart to the platter a silent prayer; then serve*," she'd told him climbing into bed with him the first time.

Her kitchen aphorisms.

"*Never try to boil a cooked egg twice.*"

Sunny was rubbing her feet and he pulled his chair closer. "Here," he said, "let me help you." She leaned back and closed her eyes. "Your boy, Emerson," he said as he began to massage her muscles, "he asked me what I thought the perfect food was. Just like the old days."

"I missed you," she finally admitted, her eyes swimming with unexpected tears, and then her face closed, as if she had revealed too much. Her words took him by surprise and he looked back to the notebooks.

"Are those your mother's recipes?"

"Mine now," Sunny said. "Ours. Mine and hers." She focused on the ceiling to gain control of her emotions. "Twenty-five years after tasting it for the first time people could remember the *mole* my mother made, redolent of *piñon*, *ancho*, chocolate. They remembered her *menudo*. Her grits with walnut honey. Her venison with cream. Charcoal-roasted quail. Her chocolate cake with moonshine icing. The recipes were not in any order—so I transcribed them onto cards." Sunny stood and began shuffling through the pile of cards. "Some have ingredients, but no measurements, no description of the finished dish. Some read like shopping lists—potatoes, onion, two leeks, carrot, s + p, loin of lamb. Some have instructions, but no mention of ingredients. Some sound like an old-fashioned almanac,

MOON, Waning
Plant root vegetables.
Do NOT make jam, Wait For Waxing Moon
Sugar dissolves best in Waning."

"Will you show me? I want to see," he said and stepped toward her, picking up one of the cards. The words were English, faded purple ink on yellowed paper.

Of all the impromptu chance meetings on Earth this is the greatest miracle:

RECIPE FOR LOVE
Human + Human (H_2)+O   O, the circle of Life
Know yourself   Find another   Add water
Dissolve in starlight
Bring to a boil   Let simmer

Aspire
Let rise.

THE FIRST TIME SHE LEFT EARTH was to find her father's body.

Stryker had flown:

—he'd gone up at a moment in his life when flying was the most exhilarating thing he'd ever done . . . before all the other things he'd live to risk, before the alcohol and cigarettes and sex, before the brilliant final realization he was dying.

When the Forest Ranger arrived with the rabidly crazed Scarlett O'Hara in a leather mask, penned up in a cage rendered filthy, rancid with her feces and her fear, the first thing Sunny did was to draw water for the dog. She had been alone at Three Chairs and was pathologically incapable of piecing together any of the words the man was saying to her—any of his gestures, the almost clown-like extreme expressions of his eyebrows—into a pattern that could approach explaining why her father's dog was in such a state of excruciating psychic disarray. *What's happened to her? Where did you find her? Why is she caged up?* Sunny kept repeating as she tried to coax the dog to drink, until the Forest Ranger, clearly agonized as well, drove away only to return half an hour later with Dr. Arakawa from across the road.

The facts were these:

The Ranger, on horseback, had been patrolling up around the Rhodes camp when he'd heard a distant shot and then a dog's barking that wouldn't stop. He'd found Scarlett outside the cabin racing back and forth on the shore and Rocky's boat out in the center of the lake. With his binoculars he had seen two fishing lines set, but no sign of their owner. Two mules and a horse penned in. Place was open; four guns racked and locked inside.

"Did he go up to hunt?" the Ranger seemed to need to know.

"He doesn't hunt. The guns are there in case of bears."

He was still giving off the mixed clues of a cosmic alien, and she offered him a cup of coffee to relax him. Finally Dr. Arakawa touched her arm and told her plainly, "Sunny, the evidence suggests that something might have happened to your father."

"That's impossible."

"The Rangers want to portage up a rubber raft to try to get out to your father's boat and see what they can find."

"Well I'll go with them—they don't have to take a raft we've got a rubber raft up there already in the cabin . . ."

"Let's . . . let's get your aunt's advice . . ."

She was aware that he was speaking very slowly:

"Where is the elder Miss Rhodes?"

"Bakersfield, with Lyndon. Inspecting the properties of internees." And, as the only lucky thing to happen for many days, still at their hotel when Sunny rang.

From Bakersfield Lyndon had a prop plane on the field at Manzanar in under three hours to take them up into the mountains to the lake. The pilot was a woman who introduced herself as Gloria, and Sunny sat beside her pointing the way, reading the reduced landmarks on the ground, as if they'd been notations on a map she was holding: roofs of Lone Pine giving way to tiny roads and tiny paths and singularly unrealistic identical toy trees. What routinely hazarded her on the ground had taken twenty minutes to traverse by air and before she had accommodated her perspective to the humbling height, they were already over the blue water and Rocky's boat looked like another toy beneath them. Gloria made several passes, getting closer every time until Rocky's sunhat took on a human size and Sunny could see the separate square compartments in his tackle box.

It was clear that Rocky had been in the boat—his *hat* was there; and, as the Ranger had said, two drop lines had been set—but there was nowhere to land, no purchase on the narrow shore so, breaking the silent speculation that had occupied them since takeoff, Sunny yielded to Lyndon's sane reasoning and they returned to Lone Pine to regroup. (Sunny had wanted to jump from the plane into the lake next to her father's boat to find him.) They'd gone back up with sensible intent and clothing at dawn the next day, when Gloria landed them soundly in a meadow a couple miles away, and then they'd trekked in, the two of them—Sunny and Lyndon—to be joined by two Rangers on horseback from their station down in Lone Pine later the same day.

No Rocky.

No sign of him.

They rowed the raft out to the boat and motored back to shore after setting a buoy (the outboard had started on first pull) but found no clues other than the hat and a spray of blood inside the bow—a random misting, like a nebula, which could have come as factually from fishing as from any other source of violence. Sunny insisted on circumnavigating the lake on foot to see if anything had washed up. One of the Rangers tried to dissuade her, pointing out (at length) that although the lake had tides (all standing Earth water is captive to the moon's gravitational influence, he'd said, even water underground, in artesian wells . . .) the tidal work was not as *profound* in lakes as it was in oceans and that it was highly doubtful anything would "wash up" from the bottom . . . on and on he'd gone until Lyndon told the man to goddamn please *shut up*. He and Sunny set out on foot around the lake (it took four hours) and then Sunny had gone alone, again, on horseback. Not a footprint; not even a bear track. Just the bobbing buoy—hideous pink—in the middle of the lake, a false and brazen satellite to remind her where her father had last been.

After three days, they stopped searching.

Doc Lake had wanted to put Scarlett down but Cas—not an "animal" person in any sense of the word—was set against it ("No more death!") and had taken charge of the dog who, let off her restraints, would bolt for the lake, where her master had last been. Doc tranquilized her and once they were all together at Three Chairs Lyndon had calmed and nursed her as he'd watched his friend Kai-san do with their Wagyu cattle. The four of them—plus the intermittent other dogs—had taken up residence in the Great Room, never sleeping. Cas was ever vigilant that Sunny would lapse to that state of inactive despair that had beset her following Hace's betrayal—and Sunny was ever vigilant toward a previously unseen vulnerability in her intrepid aunt: Rocky had been her *twin* goddammit she had known him all her life how dare he up and wander off like this . . . Each was afraid of saying anything that might upset the other; which, perversely, kept them strong—and Finn, empathetic Finn, was the perfect sounding board for the tuning of their grief. *I suppose we should go through his papers*, someone—Cas—had finally said. Still, they put it off because to go into Rocky's rooms would be admitting that he wasn't coming back.

The ghost rooms, Stryker called their father's part of the household—which was unfair, there was nothing "ghostly" about them—but Sunny felt they were haunted by a separate past and different life—her parents' *marital* life—that neither she nor Stryker could remember. The last time Sunny had been in there was when her mother was alive; and the last time Cas had gone in there was in the weeks just after Lou had died.

When Rocky had first dreamed his dream for the house these rooms had been its heart: a marital suite just off the Great Room; a library/study (converted, after Stryker and Sunny were born, to a nursery) down three stairs into the bedroom (*en suite* bath) whose French doors in the south wall led to a walled bedroom garden with a locking gate that gave directly onto the larger kitchen garden. Lou could wake, walk from the bedroom through the gardens and into the kitchen without passing along hallways or through other rooms. It made perfect sense—she and the babies could spend entire days in Edenic seclusion—*ex*clusion—of the larger world. The *portales* had been an afterthought (even though it had been the first wing to be built, to house the workers), Rocky never having intended to press it into domestic service until Sunny and Stryker were old enough for rooms of their own. But with Cas and Sunny and Stryker moving there (before Stryker moved to the *casita*) the *portales* had gained in importance—not only by population but owing to its direct ingress to the kitchen. These days everyone proceeded down the hall past the dining room to the *portales* and into the kitchen. That there was even a way from the kitchen garden into her parents' bedroom garden had been lost on Sunny because the gate had been locked for so long from the other side she had forgotten it led anywhere. The various Tias (Lupe et alia) went in to dust and polish but Rocky had always been, since his days on horseback, a systematically clean man, organized in his composure and *toilette* and demanding little, if any, lint-collecting from the women of the household. Pie, in fact, had reported to Cas six months earlier that Rocky had stopped sleeping in the bed, preferring, from the evidence she could gather, to spend nights—even cold ones—suspended in the hammock in the bedroom garden wrapped in a serape under bright stars.

Moi, j'y marche, Cas finally said, standing. To Sunny: "—*avec, toi?*"

Such a strange experience: living in a house so large there are rooms one never visits *for a lifetime*, rooms outside one's memory.

At the threshold Sunny held back—they used to play here, on the floor, she and Stryker, she had vague memories of the room's dimensions, its light, its earthy potpourri . . .

There were two facing leather davenports—smaller than the ones in the Great Room—with a low table between them that Rocky had transformed into a sort of war-room campaign desk where his briefs against Los Angeles Water were all spread out . . . Navajo rugs, the patterns of which Sunny remembered with a jolt . . . floor-to-ceiling shelves of books and, on a side table beneath a rawhide-shaded lamp, the donated stack of Schiff's law books Rocky had no doubt intended to peruse.

The bedroom, which the study overlooked, was not so much feminine as feminine-by-comparison; the bed—as *all* the beds at Three Chairs and even Sunny's in her room above the restaurant—was out-sized, built for *Talls*, special-ordered way back when by Rocky (a half dozen of them) from a mattress company whose sole products were, literally, Royalty-sized hotel beds. Lou's French damask linen still draped its contours and her European-sized square pillows graced the headboard. There were floor-to-ceiling bookshelves, too, on both sides of the bed, behind the reading lamps on the night tables. It was, for Sunny, the most "private" place in the whole house. Only Scarlett descended there, climbing on the bed and turning 'round and 'round and 'round in a vain effort to put the vortex of her emptiness to rest, then nosing out one of Rocky's felt slippers from beneath the bed, and settling.

Lyndon—another tidy and methodical man—collected Rocky's papers in neat piles and transferred everything to the Great Room. His Will—*a* Will—was not in question—Sunny wasn't going to argue that half of everything must go to Stryker's wife and children—she never once referred to Three Chairs as being anything other than in the trust of heirs, always plural. What *was* in question, and what she was starting to feel as an emerging force she couldn't control, was what to do with all *this*, all the things that were Rocky, his arguments with the world, his imprint on it, the *size* of his dreams, of his ambitions . . . *his* attraction to the West had held their attraction to it in its power; everything at Three Chairs had spun 'round Rocky at its center and now, she was starting to feel, the center couldn't hold except by an exertion of her will. And you can't save what you don't love.

"I count . . . ten, eleven, *twelve* different lawsuits here . . ." Lyndon finally said: "in three different courts. Four different law firms. All with Rocky as the individual Plaintiff. All against Los Angeles . . ."

"I don't know what to do," Sunny said.

"What happens in a lawsuit when the Plaintiff is . . . deceased?" Cas asked.

"You could pick it up, as heir," Lyndon told Sunny. "Any of us could pick it up . . . but I think most of these are specific to the property, to Three Chairs . . ."

"Could we win any of them?"

This was Sunny.

Lyndon shrugged. "I'm not a lawyer."

"I need Schiff."

Among the other papers was a file marked STRYKER that contained Rocky's correspondence with Administrators of the Relocation Camps about locating Suzy and/or her aunt and the two boys; the most recent exchanges confirmed at least seven women with the family name Komoko in three different camps (though none with the given name of Suzy; and no one with the surname Rhodes).

All three of them were thinking it so Sunny asked aloud, "How is it possible that she hasn't been in touch with us about her share, what's owed to her?"

Because she's been deported to Japan, was the only answer.

Or because she's dead.

"—Sunny!"

"I'm sorry, Cas . . ."

"We're in a morbid state of mind, I understand . . . But I won't hear it."

"Maybe he never told her about . . . all this," Lyndon attempted to explain.

"But he was trying to send her here," Cas said. "That was the reason for the trip to California . . ."

She seemed, sitting next to Lyndon in this massive room, smaller and more frail than Sunny had ever measured her. They all did—even the dogs—diminished in their bodies by Rocky's absence.

Sunny got up and said goodnight to Cas and Finn and told them she loved them. She took a bath and washed her hair and crawled between the sheets in her pyjamas and lay there with the light on. Had a cry. Silent one, but deep. Not exactly the same feeling, this despair, as sitting in the boat when Stryker and her father had both disappeared into the water right in front of her—she was older now and she could swim—but the feeling that she was, nevertheless, in deep water came over her . . . and that was all right, strangely, there was a kind of peace to that, that she would have to figure out the way to save herself. She had said the honest things to both her brother and her father that she had needed to say . . . but was now deprived of saying them enough. And her mother—that was the most unfinished part of her whole life . . .

She turned the light out but still lay awake.

If this were a normal night, she couldn't stop herself from thinking, I could turn the light back on and read a cookbook before sleeping.

She jack-knifed up.

Lyndon got to his feet and Cas looked alarmed as Sunny barreled past them in the Great Room, insisting, "—I'm okay, don't worry," as she opened the door to her parents' suite and walked in through the study, down the stairs, and straight into the bedroom. *If I read cookbooks in my bed at night then maybe she did, too:*

And there they were.

She gathered up her mother's notebooks. She was not sure what she planned to do with such a harvest, only that she was unwilling to let their legacy go.

You can't save what you do not love.

the last property
of thirst
is
evaporation

GUNMETAL LIGHT ON THE HEIGHTS. This time of year, the sun rose late over the Sierras and set early behind the Wilderness Range. Light ricocheted between the mountain walls like a sunbeam in a hall of mirrors, harried, like a live thing trapped inside a box. Rocky peered out from the boat into the surrounding cover to see if the light would flash again.

He glanced down at the knife and the stick in his hands. When had he started whittling? On the road, out here scouting for his father, overcome by longing and by solitude. Nothing to do while he sat by firelight. Nothing to do, under the stars. Pick up a stick. Pick up a nothing and make a something. Like his father picking up a railroad. Carving out a name, a fortune—or, in Rocky's case: just carving.

He remembered where he'd bought the knife: in a pawn shop in New York City when he was twelve on one of the many occasions he was planning to run away from home. An alley knife, the pawnbroker had called it, longer than Rocky's hand, and the shopkeeper had refused to take it from the case until Rocky had slammed a twenty-dollar bill down and said, in his cracking adolescent tenor, "Deposit. Visiting fee. You can keep it if I walk away."

Not for nothing had he listened every night to the way Punch negotiated, the language he used when he talked business.

"What does a boy like you want with an alley knife?"

Company, he'd known, even then:

Something to keep him busy.

You're an idiot, Cas had shamed him: find a girlfriend, find a job. Join a choir. Don't get a knife.

The pawnbroker had been wrong, it was not an *alley* knife. Scrimshaw inlay in the handle into which had been carved the mariner's name: STRYKER. His son's name sounded for a moment in the water.

In the distance, he could see dark blue shadows etched across the snow into the rising granite of Mount Whitney, and then, in one graphic instant, the sky opened and he could see the whole—alpenglow against the topside of a continent. The colors dripping off its peak were all pastel colors—not the colors one applied to land unless one's name was Monet, Degas, Cézanne. Lou would have called them sorbet colors—cherry, rose, watermelon, *framboise*—melting sorbets dripping down the mountain's inverted cone.

"Margarita light," she also called it—something that took the shape of recognition when laughter, soundless, finds its soul within the eyes. The entire landscape is a place for dreaming, she'd say. And now he saw that it was true: the surface of the world up here was very near the sky. You got effects you didn't get at lower elevations: ball lightning. Snow blindness and the walk-through cloud. You got to live through different time, or live through time differently, time that didn't tick to Valley rhythm, time that spreads and drops you into darkness, or delivers you to light. Once, he'd watched a cloud come on like a black sheep, late afternoon, and the next thing sparks were crackling off his hair.

He hefted the knife. Beneath him the boat stirred, leaf-like.

Stryker had made the mistake of believing that the point of fishing was to catch fish, when the whole idea was to catch *time*: time as water, time as light, time as a fluid substance, sluicing forward and back.

Lately Rocky had begun doing something he had never done before—catching and releasing. Not because the stocks were thinning out—they weren't—not because the lake was overfished (it wasn't). Not even because, after he lost his fingers, he couldn't tie his own lures. No. Because he had started to commune with something in the eye of every fish, to imagine something there in the light behind the eye, beneath the flesh, he had started to intuit something *shared*. No one ever tells you what you'll feel the first time—and every time—you gut a fish. Surprise, for one thing. It's a color field. Plus you never know what's in there, what the fish had had for breakfast (smaller fish) how intensely fertile some dams are, their red roe, pink roe, golden roe, like dripping fruit, engorged and ready as raw sex.

No one ever tells you how the heat escapes the living how the temperature inside the fish escapes in death into the air, a steam, streaming its genetic history into a little cloud that rushes off and rises sometimes every way at once and sometimes sideways, into nothing.

They smell of iodine, freshwater fish, of something cold and elemental, almost metal.

They smell like water.

Like water running underneath or within every life. Lou had called him Romantic, but that wasn't true, he was not Romantic about the water but saw it as a necessity. To see ourselves reflected in nature (the Romantic view) is to make Nature our servant, and Rocky knew better than that. So had Thoreau.

There were things he was less-than-Romantic about, things, as a realist, that he recognized as the counterfeits they were, things, even, that rendered him cynical: the Water boys and the long tentacles of *that* city.

But there was a Lyric in his blood, as well: *LOU.*

If he slowed his breath, he could still hear the bellows sound as it breathed for her, he could still see the light caress of Stryker's feet on the underside of her iron lung, but he couldn't see her outline anymore.

He used to see her in his dreams but the truth was he hadn't dreamed for twenty years. First from grief at losing her and then from fear of finding her in dreams and losing her again, on waking.

And then from the habit of keeping one eye open through the night for any mischief Stryker might be up to. At Three Chairs it had not been such a worry—because where was his son to go? But here at camp and on their journeys, Rocky had stayed awake to safeguard both their lives.

You can't save what you don't love.

But what if love does not save *you*?

He had loved Lou, and she had left him. He had loved the land and had watched it parch and buckle, water tapped and stolen by . . . he didn't even like to think the name. Los Angeles.

You can't save what you don't love—and even when you build a fortress around the ones you love, life will come at you and them in ways you never thought, all your faith can't save the people and the places closest to you. He knew that, he had learned that, living in this Valley, living in California, its first test of survival being aimed not at your stomach but at your thirst, at your soul.

The Easterner had come with Eastern expectations—residual cell memory—that rain would fall with regularity, that rain, as promised Biblically, was a natural function of the sky, and out here the sky is everywhere, the sky's the goddamn air you breathe, the ground you walk on, the clouds you confront each day. Then more people had come, he among them, thinking that the water underground . . . all you had to do was sink a well, stand back, and pump. Nothing out here but space and time. Existence became the space between you and rain.

How do you hold an immense landscape inside cognition? How do you be Einstein? When Rocky looked at things he saw their surface; when Einstein looked at things, he saw their frequencies.

He was never going to be Albert Einstein—who could?—but he was going to try to move toward joy commensurate to Einstein's joy, commensurate to waking up each morning saying *thank you, thank you* for this problem, this display, this universe *this* roll of the dice, *this* chance to be alive.

One night they were looking at the moon and Rocky had asked him: if he could go there and return to Earth what would he bring back?

There's nothing to bring back, Einstein had said: a rock.

The more important question is—If I could go there and I had to stay, what would I take *with* me?

Wasser. Water.

Here he could hear the water, he could see the water, the ghost of the water, the shadow of the water: ice on the mountains, vapor in the clouds.

Like a mountain, truth rises from resistance. The honesty of anything is at its boundary of resistance.

He wouldn't mind going down as the sonofabitch who fought the goddamn city of Los Angeles, on principle. If a man has got to go down being known for something, being known for standing up for a principle ain't that bad, even though he'd rather go down for having loved one woman most his life.

This was where they used to come, filling their lungs with the lake vapors, as if the lake were breathing, as if they and it were sharing a single breath. So much history on this water: a liquid page on which their story had been written. You can't save what you don't love, but lakes are born to disappear. You can't save what you don't love, but sometimes—*most* times—you can't save what you *love*, regardless.

You are either for this land or against this land, but you are never not a part of it. It is never not a part of you. When you come out to these colossal mountains from the flat land of your birth (Manhattan) you have to learn to re-size the known world and teach yourself improvisation when it comes to measuring the things in Nature, measuring the natural world against yourself to find out who you are, as opposed to measuring your ascent in a man-made elevator to a skyscraper's roof terrace to measure what you've earned, how high you've come, and where you (artificially) are. The point was—*the point was*—to keep some wildness in your life. Bad lands make good dreamers the way New England farmers make good fences from their rock-strewn soils. Know your country first before horsing in, scope it out, that long horizon ever in your steely gaze. Watch the shadows flicker 'round your campfire. Love a woman, hold her like you hold pure water in your fingers. Love her 'til the day you die.

What he remembered now was being here with Stryker, steam rising off his son's bare back. Stryker's body heat evaporating into cooler air like the light around a saint's head elapsing into sky. What he remembered was Stryker standing and leaping over the side of the boat—*this* boat—in one fluid movement, even though he had not yet learned to swim.

Stryker's look: a depth of many fathoms. But then, the boy had always been inscrutable. Willing, even as a boy, to breach any, every gulf between himself and the unknown, himself and the invisible, himself and the divine.

Rocky had distanced himself from the God of his childhood long before Lou's death, but whatever faith he held—in the land, in memory, in the principle of place, in the wildness that he felt both *around* him and *inside* him—had calcified once she was gone. He knew men who had histories locked within them—he had met them on the trail, in bars, in camps, and when you tried to speak to them they clammed up. He had become the same, he thought now, his history locked inside him.

He was becoming a curmudgeon,

—no:

He was becoming a recalcitrant Thoreau refusing to accept the forward step of time, refusing to admit defeat, refusing to abandon ship (*kin*ship of solitude) and sinking, stubborn captain, into unfathomed but embracing depths. From husband/father/brother he'd become the widower/survivor. The Man Whose Family Dies. The man who carries love inside him, unexpressed.

Counting up the minutes of his life, the sum he'd spent in silence far outstretched the time he'd spent talking to another, time in conversation: maybe tenfold, maybe fifty or a hundred, if he added in the hours lost in sleeping, hours working with his hands in solitude, nights alone and days on horseback, before meeting Lou. Hours spent composing letters to her that first year—was that another form of "silence"? For that matter, was it "prayer" and was prayer "silence" and—for another matter—what are hours spent in reading, even if someone else is in the room?

Serenity, he thought—that was what it was. He and Cas had circled it late at night in their conversations (*calv*/gin-fueled): never calling it "happiness" (a debased word, in their opinion). *Serenity*—a smooth spiritual state across which the mind could glide as if on glassy water, like the surface of this lake.

Perfect subject for the painter on the shore, this (now old) codger sitting in his boat, year in year out, not moving. Watching the driftline at that silver point where it disappears into the water like a star, only to burst to life again the instant the bait is taken and death starts. If he had a dollar for every time he'd sat alone and silent in a boat out here on this lake he'd be (had to crack a smile at this:) a wealthy man.

The thought brought to mind that dreadful solipsistic final line of Keats: Here lies one whose name was writ in water. He'd always thought it was *on* water until Lou had corrected him.

She had loved the California desert, she'd said when she'd come out here, because it was the first place that she'd ever been, outside a hospital, *alive with death*.

And when he realized—that's what it had been, a *realization*—when he'd *realized* that he'd fallen headlong in love with her he'd had to give up hunting, pack the guns away, to think of them as things he'd only ever use to *save* a life and not to take one, he'd had to stop the killing, not because, christ knows, love had changed him overnight into a troubadour but because love had made him overnight, the way love does, sensitive to loss.

He had always felt that moral recoil, bagging an elk, a deer—even facing off a bear—but it had never stopped him at the trigger until, after he'd met Lou, he'd been out on horseback early one morning all alone when a four-point buck, his doe, and a scattering of fawns had come out from the grassy understory into sunlight downhill. His first impulse had been to take the big buck dead-to-rights, until his finger stalled and his eyes had filled with tears.

He couldn't remember when the incidence of tears had started to be frequent like a physical complaint, like an ache that starts while you're walking—barely noticed—like that small tug in your shoulder you are sure will go away which stays through dinner then through morning. You don't notice it at first. You don't notice that you're tearing up at things that never made you cry before—ordinary things; common, unspectacular. Like someone singing. Dust motes in a shaft of sun, just hanging there: sawdust from the plane, the fine sandpaper, sawdust lifting off the wood like the soul of Nature from a forest suspended in sunlight for the few—the blessed—to see. Christ, he'd seen some men get sappy in old age and he'd be damned if he was going to be *another* one. Still, the weeps had pretty much moved in on him and if his prayers for water had been answered after all this time as tears, then he'd have to re-think his opinion of theology because a godless universe, as he perceived it, couldn't be so funny.

The first time he ever slept on water was in a neighbor's skiff off Newport, the summer he had learned to swim in '86 when he was six years old. The man who owned the boat was tall—much taller than Rocky's father—and muscular, and acted, Rocky thought, as if the ocean were his private playground. Sailing was not up Punch's alley—the Rhode Island social summer scene, Punch believed, had been contracted solely for what it could render to him, profit-wise, and he was rarely on the lawns, in white, or on the decks, in different whites, without an abacus.

That first night, Rocky had been too scared to close his eyes. He must have slept because all these seasons later, he remembered having wakened in the twilight of pre-dawn, panicked that he was going down. The constant shifts, the oscillations, all that rolling: you can't be on water without learning solid truths about the nature of Earth's movements. We are all afloat in space and either you find this exhilarating or, as Rocky had all night, you find the nearest solid thing and clutch on to it for dear life.

The older boys, the sons of the tall man, had shed their shirts and shoes and skittered on the polished deck like insects but Rocky's instincts had alerted him to the depths. It was the loss of shore that frightened him: the fact of ocean: that it was massive: its neutrality: that "it" did not care if he survived or was extinguished: whether he rode it freely or was drowned.

"Salt is the memory of water," Lou had told him.

Once her body had succumbed to polio, she was only ever comfortable afloat, freed of earth's gravity. In water her limbs could animate her spirit, like fins or wings, instead of anchoring her down.

Every adult human being, she had long insisted, should know how to

—swim

—cook

—make something from some other thing

—save a life

He remembered Stryker's body slipping through the water like a knife, one moment he was in the boat, and the next, he was—nowhere, as if he had erased himself. A whaler had once described to him the water after a whale breaches: an oily look to it, the molecules disturbed in the shape of the whale but when Stryker had disappeared, there was no mark, no disturbance, nothing but stillness, collapsing on his image into water, as if the boy were a pebble dropped into a well. Rocky hadn't had to think about it, he'd flung himself into the depths, reaching for his son's body as it had made its descent. Afterward, in the boat, Stryker had not been able to stop laughing but Rocky's heart had been full of fear. Swim, cook, save a life:

Yes, he thought: He would have a swim.

His knees had stiffened, sitting there so long in stillness. He unwound to shake them out. But stretching caused the boat to rock a bit and him to lose his balance. He reached out with both hands to the gunwales to steady himself. On the shore, the dog noticed and began barking, bounding back and forth. The one Cas had named Miss Scarlett from the Margaret Mitchell novel for the pup's high-strung beauty, the haughtiness with which she had her way. Can't say how or when this little lady dog had become his favorite—everybody knew it—slept at his feet and knew his sounds, went everywhere with him. But jesus christ she could no longer bird-dog, you couldn't take her anywhere, now, where *stealth* might be required and couldn't—could not—ever put her on a boat.

Now Scarlett was dashing along the shoreline, yapping as if in warning. Or maybe at the shine of light across the water, its ghostly glimmering. There is such a thing as invisible light: dogs see it, an ambience, the spectra of which exist over-and-above the human eye's capacity to see.

Chalky light this a.m.:

—but then what had begun as chalky light down in the Valley developed to a stalking blight obscuring sky and sun, its mass blooming like a yeast on air, like something live and thriving, siphoning the purest elements of human breath into its caulked and hulking maw: *the cloud.*

Particulates rising off the dead surface of Owens Lake—its distant corpse left to rot on top of the ground by the Water boys—deadly particulates rising off the lake. Worst he'd ever seen it this morning, as if every poisonous element left to haunt posterity by water's theft had jettisoned its ghost into the sky:

Those fuckers:

First they're going to make me die of thirst:

Then they're going to take away my air.

History will always find you. He knew that.

Every veteran of every war would tell you, every survivor of an oppressive regime, every victim of poverty, every martyr to religion, any gull of economic promise, every dupe of political idealism, any woman on the street with nothing left to lose but the clothes on her back:

History will find you.

—on the dust-ravaged Plains in 1932; in France or Germany, Belgium, Italy or Japan; in California in its rainshadow, on your wedding day or when your kid is born, when your boat sails or when your loved one disappears: history will find you. Your own history will come for you when you are sleeping in your bed or starting breakfast, staring out a window. What we do with these unbidden moments may define how we choose—or do not choose—to live. For most people the range of choices comes in tiny increments: Dare I look another in the eye? Dare I ask for help? Whelped by chance, none of us can claim to outrun fate's chicanery, that History finds us where we live. History has borne us to a time when all the gaps on all the maps have been filled in, when the *known* world means the *whole* world, where the prospect of a fixed point to the plot's beginning is as distant as a faded star in a fabled far-off galaxy.

Where do I begin?—not to tell a story, that's the easy part, a story starts with some first words, or with a datable event—

> *I was born*
> *We went to war*
> *She died*

— but where do *I*—and you—or anyone—*begin*? The past is much more mesmerizing than the future: the future will reveal itself, regardless, but the past is made to disappear . . .

Laugh a little for godsake, Cas had told him. Find something to laugh about. It had been so long since anything had made him feel lighthearted, feel like laughing. In those rooms, the ones he had shared with Lou, he drifted like a mist, running his fingers across the spines of her books, not wanting to disturb them. *No more displacement*, he had thought to himself: he had had enough.

He saw something in the water, light striking it, a shadow or another ghost.

"*Lou?*" he breathed, and for a moment he could see her outline, a hole in the water the shape of love. Then he was pushing himself upright, the boat rocking wildly, his body out of balance.

There was an echoing crack through the air, the sound of metal ringing against itself like the bell in his tower, and Rocky was falling, falling out of this life, through the surface of the water,

toward Eternity.

Weightless
wordless

watermark of love on memory.

Massive stroke.

That's what the cardiologist on the phone was trying to explain to me. I could hear Marianne's voice in my head, "Oh, give me a break. *Massive.* Really? Why not *gargantuan, super-sized* or better yet, something more cosmic like *galactic . . . seismic . . .* why not call it a *seismic stroke*?? *That* seems more operatic." I remember thinking, why is this doctor's voice shaking so much? "In all my years practicing stent procedures I've never had a patient stroke on my table—at first I thought she was having a seizure . . ." The distraught doctor was clearly over-sharing, still processing the trauma he'd just witnessed. *Helicopter. Searching now for a hospital in Los Angeles County with the appropriate facility to perform the thrombectomy.*

As he rambled on and my grief began its stranglehold, all I managed to do was mutter on a mantric loop: "Please save my mother's brain . . . she's brilliant . . . she's writing her novel . . . she's brilliant . . . she's a professor . . . she was nominated for a Pulitzer . . . her novel is almost finished . . . her novel is beautiful . . . please save her brain . . . she was nominated for . . ."

Maybe all children would run a list of their parents' achievements in an attempt to resuscitate life into the unresponsive body lying on the hospital bed . . . maybe not . . . *I* did. And once I started I never stopped. Marianne was in five hospitals for four months and we met over sixty health-care professionals in various positions and I told each one that Marianne was working on a novel—only a few chapters left to go!—and in response, each would stare at me, most of them dismissively, asking only her weight and age. Isn't that on her chart? Why don't medical charts have a section for the patient's accomplishments? Hobbies. Places they've traveled. The people they love.

The doctor who removed the clots from Marianne's brain told me she would "probably" be blind, "most definitely" never read and write due to quadruple vision (which sounded worse than double vision)—because one clot was in her occipital lobe. One? How many clots had he extracted? Three. She would "most certainly" still have all her language but it was "highly doubtful" she would ever walk again. She might have a permanently paralyzed left arm, at best suffering neuropathy on her left side. She had had a right brain stroke but she might never open her right eye. Her stent was never put in so she might soon suffer a heart attack . . .

The first days in the ICU were spent translating the "mights" and "maybes," "probablys" and "definitelys." I was waiting to discover the scope of her untethered reality and trying not to implode from my exasperation with our waking-nightmare, soul-destroying health insurance system.

A daughter's denial can be very powerful. Mine kept me going. That, mixed with an injection of magical realism—it was a few hours after holding Marianne's limp hand the first night in the ICU when I saw it: the maker's mark of the medical bed Mom was lying in, the manufacturer's name STRYKER.

Properties of Thirst was there in the hospital room with us.

That piece of magical realism got me through to the next: Day Three in the ICU Marianne was still unresponsive but I watched her lift her right arm and begin a swirling pattern in the air. She always writes longhand and I convinced myself she was writing the final chapters in her dreams. Physical disabilities, I told myself, are not disabilities of spirit. Or talent.

And talent she has. Marianne is a force of nature, a behemoth of knowledge, lightning in a bottle, a woman who, with one roasted and spicy insight and a well-crafted phrase, can make you laugh riotously in the same moment that she puts your hidden weaknesses on public display. She can eviscerate with an adverb, inspire with an adjective.

She never went to college but was hired as a tenured professor at USC. She taught an autobiography class and called it "Just because it happened to you, doesn't make it interesting." She was known on campus as a professor with a big heart for anyone attempting to be an artist (she gave an A for a good Attempt)—but if you were her student and she liked your writing but not your ego, or worse, she didn't like your writing *or* your ego, she would let you know it in a verbal surgical procedure in full view of the entire class.

She was—and still is—a gorgeous woman.

Since my childhood, I've witnessed men fall in love with her at a glance and then wince from pain from one upper cut adjective to their simian ids. The woman is a prizefighter with words.

A male stranger once asked her if she was a model and she replied, "No, I'm full-size."

No daughter age forty-nine dreams of having her mother move in with her, and it is doubtful you'd find an independent mother age sixty-nine volunteering to live with her independent daughter, but we are now roommates and I am now her caregiver. And her new medical care is 24/7.

Both our lives have changed dramatically these last five years.

What can I tell you that has changed in Marianne since her stroke? So much.

I'd rather tell you what hasn't: her feistiness and wit.

Her ceaseless curiosity still propels her days forward.

My mother is a dreamer. All novelists dream for a living. She would tell you, "I lie for a living," but I'd rather call her a dreamer than a liar.

Sure, the stroke altered her timeline, smashed her compass, shifted her sense of physical balance, and she can no longer cross the room unattended, but she can still murder the *New York Times* crossword *in ink* in record time. And now her treasure chest vocabulary has even more descriptive post-stroke words and terms: *hemiplegia, dysphagia, homonymous hemianopia, left neglect, CAD in native artery, diplopia, nystagmus, facial weakness* . . . and these are just for her physical struggles. Her cognitive struggles have their own set:

perseveration, impulsivity, emotional lability, cognitive fatigue, short-term memory loss (the last being perhaps the saddest).

Marianne lost a significant part of her memory in a single blow, most critically, her recent past—wiped out in a single stroke. It took a colossal amount of repetition to reacquaint her with Rocky, Sunny, Cas and Schiff—thankfully, they were there on the page, waiting to greet her.

Marianne's right brain stroke may have eradicated her logic for quotidian sequencing (first the toothpaste, *then* the brushing) but she can quote Márquez, Borges and Shakespeare and she knows the lyrics to *every* song even if heard only once—because words are her lifeblood. When she was rendered speechless by her stroke and lying in the ICU bed, I read to her around-the-clock, fueled by my adrenaline of grief, to help drone out the incessant metronomic beeping of the medical machines.

I was told by the doctors that the first ninety days for stroke survivors are the most significant for brain healing, so I latched on to that as a rescue line and read to her words words words words. By the time we were moved to the fifth and final hospital I had asked a friend to bring the unfinished manuscript of *Properties of Thirst* to the room. And I read it to Marianne on a constant loop. I must've read it to her ten times. Twenty-five times. Convincing myself all along that her own words could-and-would heal her brain, somehow creating a parallel existence: her shadow self living a shadow life reading her former self's words. Her past words resonating to heal her present narrative. A fogged vintage mirror for her to view her own reflection in once again.

The level of language Marianne lives with separates her from small talk. She abhors it. She much prefers to pass her time patching together the crazy quilt of a colorful sentence. With that level of language comes a certain loneliness but from *Marianne's* loneliness, an extremely rich interior life was born. Her characters became her closest friends. At age three she had an imaginary husband named Jake and by age five was writing her first character-driven prose. The first time I remember being reprimanded by Marianne was when I was seven and had carried only two dinner plates to the table—Marianne sharply informed me we needed another three for the three characters she was writing a short story about.

Life with my mom the last fifty-four years has been complicated, shifting like peripatetic wildfire, always dramatic, often beautiful, and our relationship was more times than not, in a word, painful. But being raised within Marianne's writer's weather patterns of silence and thunder charted my own artistic path. Marianne's lifelong commitment to putting her art before everything—and *everyone*—the very decision that was difficult for a young daughter to understand, is now the mandate which guides *my* decisions as a working photographer. Picking up Marianne's film camera at a young age to archive our many house pets opened a window onto the world of artistic magic for me. And my desire for Marianne's approval as the first viewer of my imagery was most assuredly my master's degree in seeking beauty. I fell in love with, and found my voice with, the medium of black-and-white film photography and it is still my passion.

When I saw STRYKER written on Marianne's ICU hospital bed, the very bed in which she lifted her writing hand into the air in a comatose state to "write" her dreams with, I decided not only as a daughter, but also as a fellow artist, to do everything in my power to help the unfinished book I love and the *novelist* I love. And during many exasperating mother/daughter-patient/caregiver exchanges over these past five years, it was our artist-to-artist bond that got me through. *You can't save what you don't love.* Helping Marianne to regain her balance within the terrain of her art form—a landscape which isn't mine—was a vertigo-inducing expedition and it will remain the journey I am most proud of having walked.

Marianne and I both believe that the sum total of the individual is the number of people who have touched one's life, even those who do so briefly. The Acknowledgments page may give the impression that *Properties of Thirst* took a village to help with verbs, paragraphs and plot points. It didn't. But it did take the daily kindnesses (small and large) and the shared conviction of others that Marianne's brain could heal and that she could regain her sense of artistic self.

Most of the names are of the people who helped sustain Marianne's life, and therefore her creativity, since her stroke in 2016. One person we don't even know how to contact was a social worker who swept into an awful situation in hospital Number One at the exact right moment and advised me to do an insurance appeal (uncharted waters that I would, in turn, only advise family members with pocketsful of Dramamine to navigate). We won the appeal allowing the course of Marianne's health care to shift toward the better, and without her decision to help our small family of two this book never would have been resurrected.

Roads to recovery are paved with small generosities and Marianne's road map was drafted by many compassionate, selfless people. Every nurse, therapist, doctor, technician and caregiver Marianne saw deserves special mention on the Acknowledgments page. One life-changing doctor, for example, who asked in Year Two, "Marianne, are you writing?" and when she replied, "No," was quick to respond, "Oh, you must. Marianne, do not let this crisis go to waste." A motto every artist should have tacked on his, her and their walls.

Joseph Boone, who spearheaded the hiring of Marianne at USC, believed in Marianne's teaching abilities before she had discovered them in herself and has been an enthusiast for this novel before and after her stroke. The ever-backpack-clad Joe (JoBeau) Bohlinger, Marianne's former student, turned up at our doorstep countless times to read passages of his favorite novels, short stories and poems to a healing Marianne in the winter of 2016, always calling her "Professor," always bringing his good cheer—I firmly believe those shared days of teacher-student readings healed Marianne's soul. It quickly became clear that Joe was the perfect person to help Marianne reunite with her own words. In 2017, after Marianne had received multiple eye surgeries and could maneuver a ruler line-by-line down the page to keep her focus steady, the three of us started reading *Properties of Thirst* aloud, this time with Marianne's voice taking the lead: an extremely slow process which never seemed arduous thanks to the beauty of the prose and the excitement and incredulous outbursts from Marianne: "This is so well written!" "Lara, this is fantastic!" and each time reminding her, "Momma, you wrote it," we'd hear the exact response with Scooby Doo–like inflection: "I di-*id*?!?!?"

And then that megawatt smile.

We read the manuscript aloud multiple times over the course of 2017 and 2018. Eventually Marianne and I began discussing Rocky, Cas, Schiff, Snow and Sunny as if they were relatives—gossiping about their daily shenanigans and potential adventures, anything to bring them back into the fabric of Mom's memory. I would place them into different scenarios and ask Marianne how they would react, attempting to bring them back to the forefront of her brain. Each time we reached Rocky's death she'd gasp: "Oh, no! He's DEAD?!?!" "Yes, Momma." "WHY?!?!?" She'd cry at the thought of losing him and then we'd have the same experience the following month. Thankfully, with time, the trenches for her new neural pathways were dug deep enough and *Properties of Thirst* was back in her memory and she began dreaming her novel again.

Henry Dunow has been at the helm of Marianne's career as her stalwart agent for decades and in the winter of 2018, with the help of the solicitous Ira Silverberg at Simon & Schuster, David Ulin was brought on as editor. David had written a glowing piece for the *Los Angeles Times* about Marianne when she had first moved to California, and Marianne and he ended up teaching at the same university: their paths had crossed, but they didn't know each other well. David's blind leap of faith jumping into our lives during our season of catastrophic change was nothing less than an epic gesture of kindness. Only a special type of human could take on the resuscitation of a creative force such as *Properties of Thirst*. Neither of us knew exactly how to tackle the enormity of helping Marianne, so we decided to simply meet weekly to read the pages aloud and discuss. Three newly acquainted friends with the same goal of finishing the novel always discussing art, often sharing stories of interactions with other artists (aka gossiping about artists), dishing dirt on the politics of our nation and sometimes creating good ideas for dialogue and a possible ending. Many pistachios and cheeses were consumed sitting around Marianne's small writing desk as Marianne, David and I read, massaged and discussed passages and, in time, completed the novel.

At night I would try to read Mom's chicken scratch handwriting in her pre-stroke notebooks, searching for directions to The End. At the time of her stroke, she was working on a book involving Gertrude Stein and Alice B. Toklas, a play about Queen Lear, a memoir titled *How to Write a Novel,* multiple short story ideas and even some lines of poetry. I chiseled my favorite passages out, "nuggets" I called them, and made a lengthy patchwork document for me and David to stitch together—a navigational map to an unseen destination which eventually led the way to The End.

At some point during those months the powerful alchemy of Art happened: the process of finishing the novel shifted from being an impossible burden to being the very life-affirming thing that helped us to heal.

And that's how we did it. Wisely, and slowly. Word by word.

Not insurmountable.

I recently found this scribbled in one of Marianne's old notebooks:

"A NOVEL'S NINE LIVES:
1. It visits you. Inspiration.
2. It takes shape in your mind.
3. It assumes characters.
4. It won't leave you alone.
5. You fail it.
6. You fail it better.
7. It's a curse.
8. It's a blessing.
9. It goes and lives in strangers."

And *now*, dear stranger, it's yours.
Thank you for keeping this novel alive.

Lara Porzak
July 2021
Venice, California

GRATITUDE LIST

Thank you each for caring for my heart:

Thank you for bestowing hope for the impossible.

Without the input, care and love from each one of you, the completion of this novel would have been insurmountable:

Henry Abrams, J. J. Abrams, Lashanda Anakwah, Glenda Asuncion, Jane Berman, Joe Bohlinger, Jenny & Fredrik Bond, Joseph Boone, Anthony Bourdain, Jesse Brooks, Gia Canali, Sarah Caplan, the staff at Casa Colina, Joanna Ceppi, Dr. Grace Chen, Henry Dunow, Noureddine El-Warari, Alexis Eskenazi, Becky Farfan, Lisa Vincent Farnell, Lucy Fisher, Jonathan Gold, Matt Gross, Carina Guiterman, Jenn Hall, Deli & Dave Haynes, Dr. James Hoff, Krystyna & Dan Houser, Cynthia Iselin, Kamilla Jaberek, Zack Knoll, Geri Knorr, the Guardian of the novel Michelle Kydd, Amy Lafayette, Carolina Lara, Carter Lee, Diane & Jon Levin, Carly Loman, Clare MacKenzie, Michelle McCaslin, my Dedicatee Katie McGrath, Herleen McLees, John McPhee, Beatrice Masi, Becky Moore, Lisa Negrele, the Champion of the novel Deb Newmyer, the Godmother of the novel Ginger Newmyer, James Newmyer, Sofi Newmyer, Teddy Newmyer, Becky & Ted Nicolaou, Evan Paley, Lana Parrilla, Darvesa Perry, Byrdie Lifson Pompan, Ali Porzak, Grey Rembert, Rebecca Ressler, Dr. Lucas Restrepo-Jimenez, Mahindra Rock, Scott Rubenstein, David St. John, Ben Schultz, Ira Silverberg, Wendy Smith, Snowy, Carrie Solomon, Lisa Sutton, Christie Tomashek, David Ulin, Julia Wick, Arnetta Williams.